MW01674036

# Nautical Dictionary

SALZWASSER
VERLAG

**Arthur Young**

# Nautical Dictionary

Reprint of the original, first published in 1863.

1st Edition 2022 | ISBN: 978-3-37500-132-2

Verlag (Publisher): Salzwasser Verlag GmbH, Zeilweg 44, 60439 Frankfurt, Deutschland
Vertretungsberechtigt (Authorized to represent): E. Roepke, Zeilweg 44, 60439 Frankfurt, Deutschland
Druck (Print): Books on Demand GmbH, In de Tarpen 42, 22848 Norderstedt, Deutschland

# NAUTICAL DICTIONARY.

# NAUTICAL DICTIONARY.

DEFINING

THE TECHNICAL LANGUAGE
RELATIVE TO THE BUILDING AND EQUIPMENT OF
SAILING VESSELS AND STEAMERS, SEAMANSHIP, NAVIGATION,
NAUTICAL ASTRONOMY, NAVAL GUNNERY, MARITIME LAW AND COMMERCE,
GENERAL AND PARTICULAR AVERAGE AND MARINE
INSURANCE, AND OTHER TERMS RELATING
TO MARITIME AFFAIRS.

WITH AN APPENDIX CONTAINING THE INTERNATIONAL REGULATIONS FOR PREVENTING
COLLISIONS AT SEA, AND A VOCABULARY OF FRENCH TERMS.

BY

ARTHUR YOUNG.

ASSISTED IN THE NAUTICAL DEPARTMENT BY JAMES BRISBANE.

*SECOND EDITION,*

*ILLUSTRATED WITH PLATES AND NUMEROUS WOODCUTS.*

LONDON:

1863.

# PREFACE.

In this great maritime country, with the exception of the present work, the first edition of which has been for a number of years out of print, there is no modern Dictionary of maritime terms.

The latest work of the kind is Dr. Burney's edition of Falconer's Dictionary of the Marine, published at a time when the learned editor thought that steam vessels, which had been 'invented and introduced by a native of Scotland,' and successfully navigated on some of the American rivers at six knots an hour, 'might be of use in our navigable rivers and canals and on the Scotch and Irish lakes,' and that, 'even in a military point of view, advantage might be obtained from this invention.'

Now, the ocean in every quarter of the globe is traversed by merchant steamers, and almost every ship of war is provided with steam machinery as a moving power. The recent progress of improvement in the building and equipment of ships, and many other causes, have likewise wrought material and most extensive change in the language of seafaring men.

This Dictionary has been framed chiefly for the compiler's own use in performing the duties of a practical and consulting average adjuster.

In the first edition, published in 1846, the nautical language was therefore defined with especial reference to merchant shipping.

Prior to the year 1854 that edition was rendered more extensively applicable to ships of war. Numerous additional terms, including obsolete words, were also defined, and the information regarding legislative enactments, and the treatises on shipping and marine insurance law and average, along with other matter of a peculiarly fluctuating character, were withdrawn. Care, however, has been taken to give necessary effect to statutory regulations and legal decisions, as well as to the usages of shipowners, merchants, and underwriters, in defining the relative terms.

The additional manuscript prepared at that time has now been subjected to a thorough revision, and every effort made to adapt the book to the present condition of nautical science. It is confined mainly to the purpose of definition, but some interesting and instructive general information will be found scattered through its pages.

The original matter relating to shipbuilding and seamanship has been mostly derived from the extensive knowledge of Mr. Brisbane, who was a thoroughly experienced shipwright and seaman, several years in command of coasting steamers, and afterwards accustomed to prepare specifications of repairs to sailing vessels and steam ships, and who latterly became surveyor for the New York Board of Underwriters and for the American Lloyd's in the port of Liverpool.

The compiler has the grief of intimating Mr. Brisbane's death, which took place shortly after he had revised the manuscript of the present edition. He was a most friendly, able, and intelligent adviser in everything relating to nautical affairs.

In the first edition, the most cordial thanks were tendered generally to those who had freely given much valuable aid in the compilation, as well as to those who had accorded permission to make extracts from published works.

In particular, either in the preparation of the first edition or during past years in its extension and correction, many contributions and suggestions were obtained, in matters relating to the Royal Navy, from Vice-Admiral W. H. Smyth, Vice-Admiral W. J. Mingaye, Rear-Admiral H. T. Austin, C.B., Captain Robert D. Aldrich, R.N., and Mr. John Bathie, Gunner, R.N.; and on other subjects from Mr. George Bayley, Surveyor of Shipping in London, an experienced shipbuilder; Mr. R. Bruce Bell, Glasgow; Mr. Wm. Clark, Teacher of Navigation; Mr. David Dickie, Shipwright, and Captain Luckie of the Merchant Service, Dundee.

Acknowledgement of useful assistance formerly rendered is likewise due to Mr. Brown, late of the firm of Messrs. James Watt & Co., Engineers, London; Mr. David Crighton, Surveyor of Shipping, Dundee; Captain George Duncan of Dundee, now Ship and Insurance Broker, London; Mr. Mather, Engineer, Dundee; Mr. James Maxwell, Gunner, R.N.; Captain James Neish, late of Bombay; Messrs. Ritherdon & Carr, London; Captain Reid, and Captain Sturrock, of the Davis' Straits Whale Fishing, Dundee; Mrs. Janet Taylor, of London; and to many others.

It might appear ungrateful to omit special notice also of the constant attention and facilities afforded at the Navigation Warehouse and Naval Academy of Mr. Charles Wilson (late J. W. Norie & Wilson), Leadenhall Street.

In defining the language of seamen, it is often more convenient and clear, if indeed not absolutely necessary, to make use of technical expressions.

To simplify the definitions, therefore, and to impart a greater interest to the general reader, they are now, to a large extent, illustrated by woodcuts, chiefly from sketches by an eminent artist.

The Screw Propeller, in several of its leading varieties of form, the Armstrong Gun, some of the Admiralty models of ships of war, and various nautical inventions, are likewise similarly illustrated; and at the end of the book there are engraved plates of a steam ship, with the side lever condensing engine, formerly in general use for marine purposes, and not yet wholly superseded, and of several kinds of merchant vessels, along with sectional sketches of their frame.

Each of the engraved plates has an index prefixed to it. That prefixed to the plate of the steam ship forms also an index to the description of the marine engine, given under the title *Steam Engine.*

The introduction of French words in the Dictionary, and of a French vocabulary, by way of supplement, is intended to give, to a certain extent, a more accurate groundwork for the study of the French nautical language than the ordinary French and English dictionaries afford. Those who wish more extensive information should refer to the able and comprehensive *Naval and Military Dictionary of the French Language*, by Lieut.-Colonel Burn.

The accuracy of the vocabulary has been tested by a careful examination of the definitions in the *Dictionnaire de Marine à voiles, par MM. Le Baron de Bonnefoux et Paris,* published at Paris in 1848, 'under the auspices of M. Le Vice-Amiral Baron de Mackau, Ministre de la Marine et des Colonies.'

Other information of an interesting and useful character has been also derived from that work.

The regulations for preventing collisions at sea, issued simultaneously by the authorities in England and France, and which it is expected will be adopted by other nations in general, as already to a great extent has taken place, are, by the permission of the Board of Trade, added as an Appendix.

They constitute a comparative example of the use of the French and English languages on an important nautical subject, and they contain information immediately required by every able seaman and officer in the Merchant Service and Royal Navy.

London: 1863.

THE "MORNING STAR" APPROACHING HONOLULU.

# LIST OF ILLUSTRATIONS.

## PLATES.



## WOODCUTS.

# NAUTICAL DICTIONARY.

ABACÁ (*Fr.* Abaca). A kind of banana tree, abounding chiefly in the Philippine Islands, with the fibres whereof they make cordage. This cordage, like coir, has the property of floating in water; and it does not require to be tarred, as it is not subject to rot in water.

ABACK. The position of the sails of a vessel when their surfaces are pressed aft by the force of the wind. *All aback* implies that all the sails are aback. The sails are *laid aback* (*Fr.* coiffé) when they are intentionally adjusted in the above manner, either to stop the ship, to deaden her way, or to make her move astern. They are *taken aback* (*Fr.* coiffé) when suddenly thrown aback by a change of wind, or through the negligence of the helmsman. See *Brace aback* and *Full.*

When the action of a marine engine is reversed, so as to urge the steam-vessel astern, the machinery is said to *work aback.*

ABAFT. Behind; nearer or towards the stern of a vessel. This term is not used with reference to things out of the ship.

ABAFT THE BEAM. See *Bearing.*

ABANDONMENT (*Fr.* Abandonnement), in Marine Insurance, implies the yielding up to the insurer all that may be saved of the property insured, when some misfortune, for the consequences of which he is responsible, has taken place, and the circumstances are such as to entitle the assured to recover as for a total loss.

ABEAM *of any vessel*: the same as *On her beam.* See the article *Bearing.* Guns are said to be *pointed abeam* when they are pointed in a line at right angles to the ship's keel.

ABLE SEAMAN. See the article *Seaman.*

ABOARD, or ON BOARD. Within or on the deck of a vessel. It also means into the ship. See also *Keep the Land Aboard*, and *Tack*.

FALL ABOARD OF (*Fr.* Aborder). To run foul of; to strike or drive against another ship.

ABOUT SHIP! The order to tack, or 'go about' (*Fr.* Revirer). See *Tack*.

READY ABOUT! An order to the crew that all hands be at their stations, ready for tacking, or 'putting the ship about.'

ABREAST *of any place*, means off or opposite to it. One vessel is said to be *abreast* of another when directly upon the 'line of her beam,' that is, of her midship beam. In this sense it is the same as *abeam*; but the term *Abreast* is more peculiarly applicable when the sides of the vessels are parallel to each other and one ship on the line of the other's beam.

A-BURTON. Casks are said to be stowed *a-burton* when placed athwartships in the hold.

ABUT. The same as to *Butt*.

ACCOMMODATION-LADDER. See *Ladder*.

A-COCK-BILL. *The anchor is a-cock-bill* when it hangs down by its ring from the cathead. *To cock-bill the anchor* is to

bring it into this position previously to dropping the anchor.

*Yards* are said to be *a-cock-bill* when they are topped up at an angle with the deck.

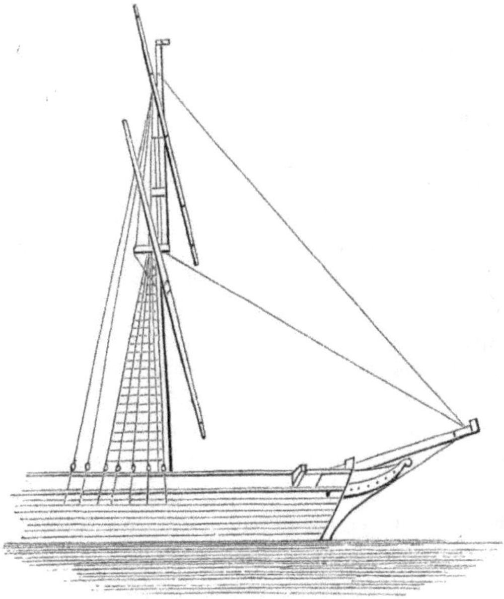

ACTION (*Fr.* Action), in a naval sense, an engagement, a fight between ships or fleets.

ADJUSTMENT, in Marine Insurance, the final arrangement of claims for loss or damage, to be settled by the underwriters.

An Adjuster of Averages, or Average Stater, is an individual employed to adjust, that is, to make out, statements or 'adjustments' of such claims, whether of average or of salvage loss. He commonly acts also as an arbitrator in cases of dispute.

The adjustment of a ship's compasses is noticed under the title *Compass.*

ADMIRAL (*Fr.* Amiral), in the Royal Navy, an officer of the highest rank in a fleet, distinguished by a square flag, which is carried above the main-mast. Next to him is the Vice-Admiral, whose flag is carried above the fore-mast. Next, the Rear-Admiral, whose flag is carried above the mizen-mast.

The Admirals, Vice-Admirals, and Rear-Admirals of Her Majesty's Navy are classed into three squadrons, named after the colours of their respective flags, viz., the *red,* the *white,* and the *blue.* These have precedence in the order here noted.

The ADMIRAL OF THE FLEET is the officer of highest rank in

the naval service. The Union flag is worn by him, as his proper flag, at the main top-gallant-masthead.

ADMIRALTY (*Fr.* Amirauté). The office and jurisdiction of the Lord High Admiral, or rather of the Lords Commissioners appointed for executing the duties of his office (which is now extinct), in taking the general management of maritime affairs, and of all matters relating to the Royal Navy, with the government of it in its various departments.

THE HIGH COURT OF ADMIRALTY is a supreme tribunal wherein cognisance is taken by the Judge of the Admiralty of maritime cases, whether civil or criminal. He has jurisdiction 'to decide questions as to the title or ownership of any vessel, or the proceeds thereof, remaining in the registry of the said Court, arising in any cause of possession, salvage, damage, wages, or bottomry, instituted in that court — to take cognisance of all claims for salvage or towage, and for necessaries supplied to foreign vessels—and of all claims and causes of action in respect to any mortgages of vessels arrested by process issuing from the court, and questions relating to booty of war which Her Majesty may refer to its judgment'—and so on.

From the judgments of the High Court of Admiralty an appeal may be made to the Judicial Committee of the Privy Council.

VICE ADMIRALTY COURTS are, for the like purposes, instituted in several of our Colonies. There is also a High Court of Admiralty of Ireland. The Admiralty Court of Scotland was abolished by the Act 1 Will. IV., c. 69, and the cases of which it took cognisance are now prosecuted in the Court of Session, or Sheriff's Courts if civil causes; and 'if of a criminal nature, in the Court of Justiciary or the inferior Courts of Judicature, instituted for the trial of the less important offences.'

DROITS OF THE ADMIRALTY. Vessels improperly captured before a declaration of hostilities are considered *Droits of the Admiralty,* implying 'that they are not given as lawful prize to the captors, but claimed and applied as *droits* (rights) of the Sovereign.' Goods found derelict, or under the denomination of *flotsam, jetsam,* or *lagan,* if not claimed within twelve months, are also deemed to be Droits of the Admiralty.

RECEIVERS OF DROITS OF ADMIRALTY, now called *Receivers of Wreck.* Persons appointed under special regulations of the legislature to take the custody of wrecked property, and to interpose in matters of wreck or salvage for the benefit of the shipping interests. The office of the Receiver-General, who took the general superintendence of such matters, is now abolished, and his duties are now merged in the Board of Trade.

ADRIFT. A ship or boat, or anything on board of a ship, is said to be Adrift, when broken loose from her anchors or moorings, or from its lashings.

ADVANCE NOTE. An Advance Note is an order to pay a seaman, or to his order, a sum of money in part of his wages, (an advance, *Fr.* Avance), within a certain number of days after the sailing of the ship for which he is hired, provided he sail by the vessel. This bill is endorsed by the seaman and may be discounted for him by any person, who will then be entitled to recover it, in a summary manner, from the shipowner or his agent.

ADZE (*Fr.* Herminette). A species of hatchet, having a thin arching blade with its edge at right angles to the handle. It is used in shipbuilding where the axe or ordinary hatchet cannot be conveniently applied.

AFFREIGHTMENT. See *Charter-Party, Freight.*

AFLOAT (*Fr.* À flot). Borne up by the water.

AFORE. Before: towards or nearer the bow of a vessel, spoken of things in the ship. *Abaft* is the opposite term.

AFT. Behind or nearer the stern of a vessel, spoken only of things in the ship. Also, towards the stern (*Fr.* à l'arrière).

*To haul aft a sheet* means to pull it more towards the stern. This phrase implies the trimming of a sail so as to come nearer to the wind. *To ease off the sheet* is the reverse. See *Fore and aft.*

AFTER. A term applied relatively as an adjective, to signify next to or nearer the stern. The reverse of *Fore.*

The AFTER-END of a vessel (*Fr.* Arrière) is her stern.

AFTER-PEAK. The aftermost part of the hold of a vessel. See *Fore-Peak.*

The AFTER-SAILS comprehend all those sails which are abaft the centre of the vessel; those upon the fore-mast and bowsprit being termed the *head-sails.*

AGENT. A person employed to transact business with another; the person so employing him is termed the *principal.* See *Factor* and *Brokers.*

NAVY AGENT. An agent employed for behoof of officers or

seamen in the Royal Navy, to receive their pay, &c., and to apply it as they may direct.

AGROUND. The situation of a vessel when her bottom rests upon the ground.

AHEAD (*Fr.* Avant). Before a vessel's head; farther in advance of her. Astern is the opposite term. The terms are used with reference to the relative position or motion of other objects, and to the movement of the ship herself. See *Bearing* and *Reckoning*.

AIR-CONE. See description of *Steam Engine*, Sect. 19.

AIR-PUMP (*Fr.* la pompe à l'air), with its appendages. See description of *Steam Engine*, Sects. 14 to 19.

A-LEE (*Fr.* Envoyez! Put the helm a-lee). The position of the helm when the tiller is put down to a vessel's lee-side, which makes her head come up in the direction of the wind. *A-weather* is its position when the tiller is put up in the direction whence the wind blows, which makes the ship's head move to leeward. See *Helm*.

ALLOTMENT NOTES, or MONTHLY ALLOTMENT NOTES, often termed simply *Monthly Notes*, are orders on a ship-owner, by the master or other authorised officer of a ship, to pay any portion of the monthly wages of a seaman, until further advice, to such person as the seaman may direct.

ALLOWANCES. The quantum of provisions, &c., served out to seamen on board of a vessel. Also, a term for refreshments given to shipwrights, labourers, or other workmen. See also Chaps. 29 and 30 of *The Queen's Regulations as to Allowances for Clothing, Instruments, &c.*, and Passage Allowances, that is, allowances made for passengers carried at the public expense in ships of war.

ALMADY (*Fr.* Almadie). A name given to a kind of large Indian canoe in some parts of Africa. On the coast of Malabar the Almady was a very sharp-bottomed vessel, pointed at both ends. (*Dict. de Marine à Voiles.*)

ALMANACK (NAUTICAL). See *Nautical Almanack and Astronomical Ephemeris.*

ALOFT. Anywhere up in the rigging, or about the masts or yards of a vessel, particularly above the lower masts.

ALONG-SIDE. Side by side.

ALTITUDE (*Fr.* Altitude) *of a celestial object*: an arc of a vertical circle, contained between the centre of the object and the horizon, in other words its elevation above the horizon. When an object is on the meridian its altitude is called *Meridian Altitude.* By observations of these, the latitude of any place may be ascertained.

Altitudes of the sun or moon, taken at sea, require four corrections in order to obtain the true altitude of their centre. These are for semidiameter of the body, dip, refraction, and parallax. The altitude of the sun, or moon, or of a planet, can be observed only at the edge of its disc, not at the centre, hence the necessity for taking the semidiameter into account. But the fixed stars, being at such an infinite distance, appear to us but as luminous points; their semidiameter, therefore, does not require to enter into the calculation in finding the latitude at sea.

AMIDSHIPS. In the middle of a vessel or boat, with reference to her length; as, *the enemy boarded us amidships*; or, with reference to her breadth, as, *put the helm amidships*, that is, put it in a line with the keel.

AMMUNITION. A general name for all kinds of warlike stores, more especially powder and shot.

AMPLITUDE *of any celestial object*: an arc of the horizon contained between the east or west point of the horizon and the centre of the object at the time of its rising or setting. It is termed eastern or western amplitude according as it relates to the rising or setting of the object. When the observation is made with a compass, the result obtained is termed *magnetic amplitude*, and this will be affected by the variation of the needle. The difference between this observed amplitude and the true amplitude ascertained by calculation thus shews the variation of the compass. See *Astronomy* (13) and *Azimuth Compass.*

ANCHOR (*Fr.* Ancre). A well-known instrument, by which, when it is dropped to the bottom of the water, with a cable attached, a vessel is held fast. In this situation she is said to be *at anchor*.

To ANCHOR, or to CAST ANCHOR (*Fr.* Ancrer, mouiller), is to drop or 'let go' an anchor, that the ship may ride thereby.

1. The anchor consists of two hooked *arms*, for penetrating and fixing themselves into the soil, attached to one extremity of a long bar, the *shank*, having a ring at its other end, to which the cable is made fast, and the *stock*, which is attached at right angles to this end of the shank. When the anchor is dropped, the stock serves to direct one of the points of the arms downwards into the soil; the weight of the anchor then causes the point to penetrate

more or less, according to the softness or hardness of the bottom; and the action of the vessel on the cable has a tendency to fix it deeper. When the stock is made of wood, it consists of two pieces clamped together by strong *hoops*, binding them to the shank, and the end of the shank is made square to receive and hold it steadily in its place without turning. To keep the stock from shifting along the shank, there are raised on the latter, from the solid iron, or welded on it, two square tenon-like projections, called *nuts*. That end of the shank which is next the stock is called the *small round*; the point where the arms and shank unite, *the crown*; and the rounded angle at its junction with each of the arms, *the throat.* A distance equal to that between the throat of one arm and its bill, marked on the shank from the place where it joins the arms, is called *the trend.* The *arms* are made either round or polygonal for about half their length; the remainder of each arm consisting of three parts — the blade, the palm, and the bill. The *blade*, or *wrist*, is merely the continuation of the arm in a square or rounded form towards the *palm* or *fluke*, which is a broad, flat, triangular plate of iron, fixed on the inside of the blade, the use whereof is, by exposing a broad surface, to take the greater hold of the ground. The *bill*, or *pea*, is the very extremity of the arm, where it is tapered nearly to a point, for the purpose of penetrating readily into the soil. (*Encyclopædia Britannica.*)

2. There are statutory regulations requiring the manufacturer of bower, stream, or kedge anchors, to place his name or initials, together with a progressive number and also the weight of the anchor, in legible characters, on the crown, and also on the shank, under the stock of each anchor manufactured by him.

3. Lieut. Rodger, R.N., has made great improvements in the construction of anchors, giving them increased strength and holding power; he says 'that the inefficiency of the large palm is owing to its loosening the ground in front of it, and to its liability to get "shod," and consequent tendency to rise out of the ground; and when this takes place, no dependence can be had on its again taking hold, and therefore another anchor must be let go, when it would otherwise have been desirable to ride by one.

'The small palm, however, does not disturb the ground, which, on the contrary, passes freely over it, and this is to be attributed to its making a more favourable angle with the resisting medium, which gives the anchors thus constructed a natural tendency to penetrate deeper, and without the least liability to get "shod." This being the case, a ship will never run away with an anchor with small palms, of the form represented by the accompanying drawing, which, if dragged by riding too short, will again hold on with a sufficient scope of cable; for it has no tendency whatsoever to rise out of the ground.'

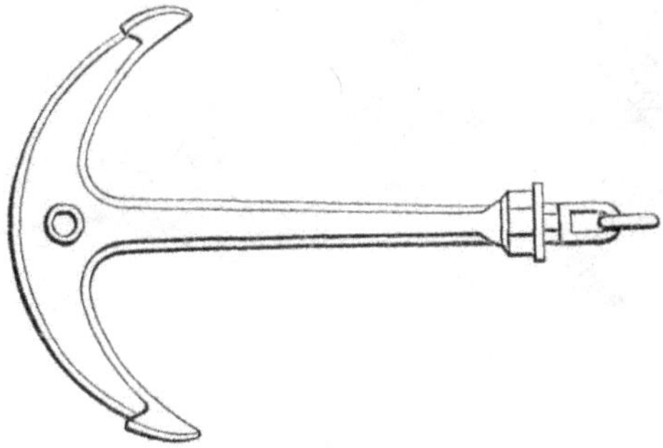

He has also made important improvements in the construction of the arms and stock. The advantages of his Pickaxe Kedge Anchor are that 'it holds much better than the kedges of the usual construction, and having no palms, there is no danger of tearing out the gunwale, or capsizing the boat in throwing it.'

4. In PORTER'S PATENT ANCHOR, the arms are formed by a bar extending from pea to pea without any crossing or welding, joined to the shank by a bolt forming a pivot, whereon they have free motion towards the shank on either side; near the extremity of each arm there is attached outwardly a spur, horn, or toggle, one of which spurs strikes the ground first when the anchor is dropped, and acts as a fulcrum in bringing the bill also upon the ground; the continued strain of the cable then causes the upper arm to descend and close upon the shank, above which it forms an arch. This kind of anchor is not subject to get foul by the cable when slack, entangling itself about the upper fluke of the anchor, and it is said to bite quickly, and to bear a greater strain, as well as to be less liable to be broken by sudden jerks, than anchors of the ordinary construction, combining simplicity, strength, and security in an eminent degree. It is said by Captain Boyd, late of the Royal Navy, not to bite readily, and is therefore 'not a favourite' when necessary to bring up short. (*United*

*Service Magazine. Practical Mechanic and Engineer's Magazine. Boyd's Naval Cadet's Manual,* 236.)

TROTMAN'S ANCHOR is an improvement on Porter's Anchor; it is, as the French term it, a Porter's Anchor brought to perfection.

The following is a sketch of Trotman's Anchor shown at the moment when the strain on the cable is acting on the anchor when it is on the ground.

MARTIN'S ANCHOR is a further modification of the same principle, making the stock to be stopped by the projecting sector B,

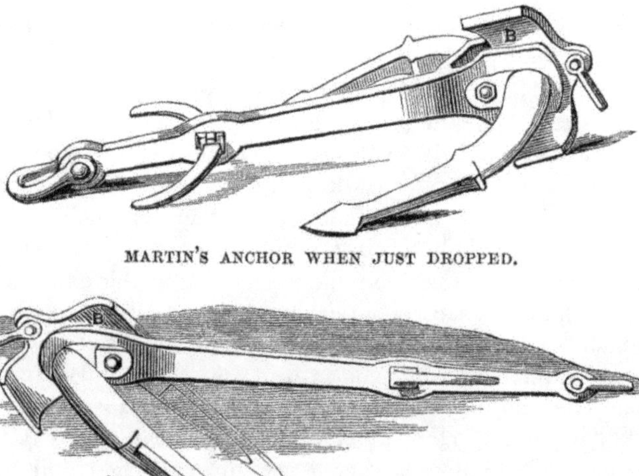


MARTIN'S ANCHOR WHEN JUST DROPPED.

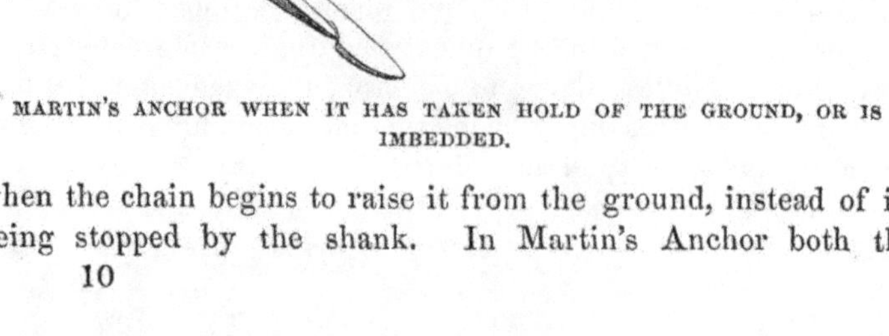


MARTIN'S ANCHOR WHEN IT HAS TAKEN HOLD OF THE GROUND, OR IS IMBEDDED.

when the chain begins to raise it from the ground, instead of its being stopped by the shank. In Martin's Anchor both the flukes take hold of the ground, instead of only one as in all other anchors.

This anchor has very great holding power. It is an improvement on Piper's Anchor, patented in 1822. Sketches of the ADMIRALTY ANCHOR are given by Captain Boyd, in his *Naval Cadet's Manual.*

Further information on this subject may be obtained in the *Treatise on Ships' Anchors*, by Mr. George Cotsell.

The anchors carried in ships of war and merchant vessels are distinguished (without reference to their construction) by the following names:—

5. The SHEET ANCHOR, the largest of all the anchors; it is a *spare anchor* kept in reserve for cases of great emergency. Vessels under 200 tons burden are not furnished with a sheet anchor.

6. The BOWER ANCHOR, viz. *the best Bower Anchor*, the second in point of size, seldom used on board of merchantmen but when the working anchor is not thought sufficient, or does not hold, or when some accident befals it; and *the small Bower Anchor*, which in ordinary weather is generally used alone as the working anchor; its cable is usually kept bent and rove through one of the hawse-holes to be in readiness, except in long voyages. All vessels of 200 tons and upwards should be provided with at least *three* bower anchors. The *spare anchor* is an additional bower anchor carried in large vessels or in ships of war; in the latter it is called the *Waist Anchor.*

7. The KEDGE, a small anchor which is put out by means of a boat, for various purposes; as, to haul by during calm weather in a river, (an operation which is termed *Warping* or *Kedging*); or to keep a vessel clear of her anchor, &c. A small vessel has generally two or more kedges; a ship of great burden carries four kedges or upwards.

8. The STREAM ANCHOR, which is of a size between the small bower anchor and the kedge. It is also used for warping and like purposes, and sometimes as a lighter anchor to moor by with a hawser.

9. See *Floating Anchor*, *Grapnel, Ice Anchor*, and also the articles *A-cock-bill, A-peek, A-stay, A-trip, A-wash, A-weigh, Jury Anchor*, and *Under foot.*

10. BACK AN ANCHOR. To carry out an anchor beyond the one by which a vessel is riding, in order to take off some of the strain, and so prevent it from being dragged.

11. CAST ANCHOR. The same as to *Anchor.*

12. CAT THE ANCHOR. See *Cathead.*

13. COCK-BILL THE ANCHOR. See *A-cock-bill.*

14. COME HOME. An anchor is said to come home, when it is dislodged through the violence of the wind, &c., straining the cable so as to tear up the anchor from the bed into which it had sunk, and is dragged along; this is especially liable to take place if the ground be soft and oozy, or rocky. In such a case *the ship is said to drag her anchor.*

15. COME TO AN ANCHOR. To anchor a vessel.

16. DRAG THE ANCHOR. See above explanation of *Come Home.*

17. FISH THE ANCHOR. See *Fish.*

18. FOUL ANCHOR. The anchor is said *to be foul,* or *to be fouled,* when it hooks some other object under the surface of the water, or when, by the wind suddenly shifting, or the tide turning, the vessel slackens her strain, and *swinging* round the bed of the anchor, entangles her slack cable above the upper fluke of it. To prevent the latter occurrence, which might have the effect of dislodging the anchor from its bed, it is usual, in light winds, as she approaches the anchor, to draw the slack of the cable into the ship as fast as possible. In ships of war, so great a scope of cable is veered out, except when there is a lee tide, that the anchor will not foul in this way.

19. RIDE AT ANCHOR. See *Ride.*

20. SHEER THE SHIP TO HER ANCHOR. To steer her towards the anchor while weighing it, so as to keep the wind or current ahead and thus lessen the friction on the hawse-pipe.

21. SHOE OF THE ANCHOR. See *Shoe.*

The anchor is said to be *Shod,* when, in breaking out of the ground a quantity of firm soil adheres to it between the fluke and shank, so as to prevent it from again taking hold. In order to avoid this, the flukes may be greased before letting the anchor go.

22. SWEEP FOR AN ANCHOR. See the article *Sweep.*

23. TRIP THE ANCHOR. See *Atrip.*

24. WEIGH THE ANCHOR. To heave it up from the ground by the cable, in order to prepare for sailing. See *Capstan* and *Windlass.*

*To weigh the anchor by the long boat* is performed by hauling on the buoy-rope with a tackle over the boat's davit. To weigh it by *under-running* is done by placing the cable over the boat's davit head, and under-running the cable till the anchor is nearly apeek, when it is tripped by means of the *buoy-rope*; this is adopted only when the ship cannot get near her anchor for want of water.

25. The following is a Table of the proportional dimensions and weights of anchors and chains for merchant vessels. Compare with those given in Lloyd's Register of British and Foreign Shipping. For those of ships of war reference is made to *Boyd's Naval Cadet's Manual*, 246, 248.

| Average Lengths of Chain required | Diameter of Chain | Weight of Chain per fathom in lbs. | Diameter of Rope | Proof Tons | Weight of Anchor | | Tonnage of Ship |
|---|---|---|---|---|---|---|---|
| | | | | | wood stocked | iron stocked | |
| fathoms | inches | | inches | | | | tons |
| | 5/16 | 5½ to 6 | 2½ | ¾ | | | |
| | ⅜ | 8 ,, 9 | 3¾ | 1½ | | | 5 |
| | 7/16 | 10 ,, 12 | 4 | 2½ | | | 10 |
| 45 | ½ | 14 ,, 15 | 4¾ | 3½ | 1½ to | 2 cwt. | 20 |
| | 9/16 | 18 ,, 19 | 5½ | 4½ | 1½ ,, | 2½ ,, | 30 |
| | ⅝ | 24 ,, 26 | 6¼ | 6 | | 2½ ,, | 40 |
| 60 | 11/16 | 28 ,, 30 | 7 | 7½ | | 3 ,, | 50 |
| | ¾ | 32 ,, 34 | 7¾ | 9 | 3½ ,, | 4 ,, | 60 |
| 75 | 13/16 | 38 ,, 40 | 8½ | 11 | | 4½ ,, | 75 |
| | ⅞ | 44 ,, 46 | 9¼ | 13 | 5½ ,, | 6 ,, | 95 |
| | 15/16 | 50 ,, 53 | 10 | 15 | 6½ ,, | 7 ,, | 120 |
| 90 | 1 | 56 ,, 58 | 10¾ | 17 | 8 ,, | 8½ ,, | 150 |
| | 1 1/16 | 62 ,, 65 | 11¼ | 19 | 9½ ,, | 10½ ,, | 180 |
| | 1⅛ | 70 ,, 73 | 12 | 21½ | 11 ,, | 12 ,, | 210 |
| | 1 3/16 | 78 ,, 80 | 12¾ | 24 | 12½ ,, | 13 ,, | 240 |
| | 1¼ | 86 ,, 88 | 13½ | 27 | 14 ,, | 15½ ,, | 280 |
| 110 | 1 5/16 | 96 | 14¼ | 30 | 15½ ,, | 16½ ,, | 320 |
| | 1⅜ | 105 to 106 | 15 | 33 | 17 ,, | 19½ ,, | 360 |
| | 1 7/16 | 115 | 15½ | 36 | 18½ ,, | 20½ ,, | 400 |
| 120 | 1½ | 125 | 16 | 40 | | 22½ ,, | 450 |
| | 1⅝ | 145 | 17¼ | 48 | | 25 ,, | 550 |
| | 1¾ | 170 | 18½ | 56 | | 30 ,, | 700 |
| 150 | 1⅞ | 195 | 20 | 64 | | 37 ,, | 850 |
| | 2 | 230 | 22 | 72 | | 45 ,, | 1000 |

The above Table was originally framed from the tables of Anchors and Chains, issued by Messrs. Pow and Fawens, North Shields; and Mr. J. Gunn, Leith. It has been thought needful now to make only a few alterations in the columns of weights.

ANCHOR-DAVIT. See *Davits*, 1.

ANCHOR-HOOPS. See *Anchor*, 1.

ANCHOR-LINING. The same as *Bill-boards.*

ANCHOR-RING (*Fr.* Cigale, Organeau). See description of *Anchor.*

ANCHOR-STOCK. See description of *Anchor.*

ANCHOR-STOCK, in Shipbuilding, the term applied to a mode of working planks by fashioning them in a tapering form from the middle so as to resemble the stocks of anchors, and placing them so that the broad or middle part of one plank shall be immediately above or below the butt of two others. *Top and Butt* implies a method similar to this.

ANCHOR-STOCK-TACKLE. The same as *Fish-Tackle.*

ANCHOR-WATCH. See *Watch* (*Anchor*).

ANCHORAGE, or ANCHORING-GROUND. A bottom suitable, from its depth and the nature of the ground, for casting anchor upon. Clay is considered to be of the best holding nature. ANCHORAGE also implies a duty charged against ships for the use of a roadstead or harbour.

ANEMOMETER (*Fr.* Anemomètre). An instrument for registering the varying forces and directions of the wind. These are marked by means of a pencil guided by mechanism over a cylinder covered with paper.

AN-END. To strike any piece of wood *an-end* is to drive it in the direction of its length.

A spar is *an-end*, when it is perpendicular to the plane of a vessel's deck.

ANEROID BAROMETER. See *Barometer.*

ANGLE-IRON (*Fr.* Cornière). See *Iron.*

ANTARCTIC. See *Zone* (*Frigid*).

A-PEAK, or A-PEEK. *An anchor is a-peak*, when the cable has been drawn in till the ship is almost directly over it, and the *vessel* is then said to be *hove a-peak.* See *A-stay.* A *yard* or *gaff* is *a-peak*, when it hangs obliquely to the mast.

APHELION. That point of the earth's or any planet's orbit, which is at the greatest distance from the sun. That point which is nearest the sun is called the *Perihelion.*

APOGEE. That point of the moon's orbit which is furthest from the earth. The point at which she is nearest to the earth is called the *Perigee.* The moon is said to be *in Apogee* or *in Perigee* when at one or other of these points. The terms *Apogee* and *Perigee* are also applied to the like points of the sun's apparent orbit.

A-PORT. The helm is *a-port*, when the tiller is put to the ship's port side: *a-starboard*, when put to the starboard side.

APPARENT denotes things as they appear to us, in contradistinction from their true situation or description. Thus we speak of the *apparent distance, motion*, or *magnitude* of a heavenly body. See also the article *Mean Time*.

To find the true distance — that is, to clear the observed distance (or in other words, the apparent distance ascertained by observation) from the effects of refraction and parallax, is a very intricate calculation in navigation.

APPRENTICES TO THE SEA (*Fr.* Elèves, Novices). Youths who are bound, by a writing called an *Indenture*, to serve under the master of a vessel for a certain period.

APRON, or STOMACH PIECE. A piece of curved timber which is bolted on the inside of a vessel's main-stem to strengthen it and to give shifts to its scarphs. The lower end of the apron is scarphed to the fore deadwood-knee. The fore-ends of the bow planking are bolted to the apron. Plate IV. 13.

*Apron* also signifies a square piece of metal used as a cover for the vent and lock or the detonating hammer of a gun, in order to keep it dry.

The *Apron of a dock* is 'that portion of the structure under and in front of the gates, upon which the *sill* (the piece of wood against which the gates shut) is fastened down.'

ARCH-BOARD. A plank across a vessel's stern immediately under the knuckles of the stern-timbers; on this, or more commonly on a board called the *name-board*, fitted above it, the ship's name is painted. (Plate II. fig. 5.)

ARCHIMEDEAN SCREW. See *Screw Propeller*.

ARCHIPELAGO (*Fr.* Archipel). A considerable number of islands grouped together.

ARCTIC. See *Zone (Frigid)*.

ARCTIC POLE. The North Pole of the world. See *Zone (Frigid)*.

*The Arctic Expeditions* to discover a north-west passage, impracticable for all useful purposes of navigation, through the frozen waters of the Arctic Seas, have now terminated. To use the words of Sir Charles Wood, the objects to be attained by such an expedition to the Arctic Regions cannot justify the Government in exposing the lives of officers and men to the risk inseparable from it.

The fatal expedition of Sir John Franklin and his companions, the melancholy traces of which were successively found by Captain Ommanney, R.N., Captain Penney, and Dr. Rae, and finally reduced to certainty by Captain M'Clintock, R.N., has accomplished the discovery of one north-west passage. Another passage through these icy regions has been discovered by Captain M'Clure, R.N. It may be hoped that, with the humane efforts of our own country and of the United States of America in prosecuting the search for Sir John Franklin's ships, all voyages of this description cease.

The screw steam yacht 'Fox' in which Captain M'Clintoch prosecuted his adventurous and successful search, was, according to his own account, 'externally sheathed with stout planking and internally fortified by strong cross beams, longitudinal beams, iron stanchions and diagonal fastenings, fitted with a massive iron screw propeller, and the sharp stem cased in iron until it resembled a ponderous chisel set up edgeways.' The expenses of the expedition exceeded 10,000*l.*

ARDENCY. A term used to denote the tendency of a vessel to gripe. If the ship have this tendency, she is accordingly said to be *ardent.* (*Fr.* Ardent.)

ARM. The extremity of a yard, beam, or bracket. See also description of *Anchor.*

ARM *of the Sea.* A portion of the sea running into the land, or dividing an island from the main land adjacent. An estuary.

ARMADILLA. A small squadron of Spanish ships which was stationed at different points off the coast of Peru and Chili, before these provinces were declared independent states. (*Dict. de Marine à voiles.*)

ARMAMENT OF A SHIP OF WAR. The number and weight of all the guns which she carries. The disposition of the armament on the different decks is explained in *Peake's Rudimentary Treatise on the Practice of Shipbuilding,* p. 99.

ARMED SHIP. A merchant vessel taken into the service of Government at any time during war, and fitted out as a ship of war.

ARMOUR PLATED, ARMOUR CLAD, IRON CLAD, or IRON CASED, SHIPS, are ships of war fitted with iron plates on the outside to make them shot proof. The casing of iron is called Armour plating. See *Cupola Ships, Shield Ship,* and Ericsson's *Floating Battery.*

ARMOURER OF A SHIP OF WAR. A petty officer, whose duty is to repair and clean the small arms, namely muskets, pistols, tomahawks, and boarding pikes. He used to do all kinds of smith work on board, but men of war now carry a blacksmith for this purpose.

ARMSTRONG GUN. See *Gun.*

ARSENAL (NAVAL). A magazine or place of deposit for ammunition and other naval stores. The principal Arsenals in this country are Woolwich Arsenal and the Gun Wharfs at Portsmouth and Plymouth.

ARSENIC. This poisonous mineral substance is mixed with coal tar, or both coal and vegetable tar and sulphur, thinned with naphtha to reduce it to a proper consistency, for paying the bottoms of vessels, as a temporary protection to the plank from worms.

ARTICLES OF WAR. Certain regulations for the better government and discipline of the Royal Navy. They are established by Act of Parliament.

ARTILLERY (ROYAL MARINE). See *Marines.*

ASCENSION. *The right ascension* of a celestial body is an arc of the equinoctial contained between the first point of Aries (viz. the point where the equinoctial and ecliptic intersect each other at the vernal equinox) and that point of the equinoctial which is cut by a meridian passing through the body. See the articles *Astronomy,* 9, and *Declination*; and the *Nautical Almanack,* p. 516.

*The Ascensional Difference* is an arc of the equinoctial intercepted between the sun, fixed star or planet's meridian, and that point of the equinoctial which rises with the object.

*The Oblique Ascension or Descension* is the sum or difference of the right ascension and ascensional difference. (*Norie's Epitome.*)

ASHORE. On the shore or land. Aground.

ASLEEP. *The canvass is said to be asleep* when there is just as much wind as to fill the vessel's sails and keep them from shaking.

ASSURANCE. See *Insurance.*

A-STARBOARD. See *A-port.*

A-STAY. *The anchor is a-stay* when, in heaving it, the cable forms an acute angle with the water's edge. This is called a *long stay-peak* or a *short stay-peak* according as the anchor is further from or nearer to the ship. When almost up and down it is said to be *apeak.*

ASTERN. Behind a vessel's stern; further in that direction. See *Ahead* and *Bearing*.

*To Drop astern*, or *to Fall astern*, is to lessen a ship's way, so as to allow another to get ahead of her, whether intentionally or otherwise.

ASTRONOMY (NAUTICAL) (*Fr.* Astronomie Nautique). The science which treats of the heavenly bodies so far as relates to the purposes of navigation. See the articles *Navigation* and *Nautical Almanack*.

The following diagram of the celestial sphere, contributed by Mr. William Clark, Teacher of Navigation in Dundee, illustrates the definitions of many astronomical terms throughout this dictionary.

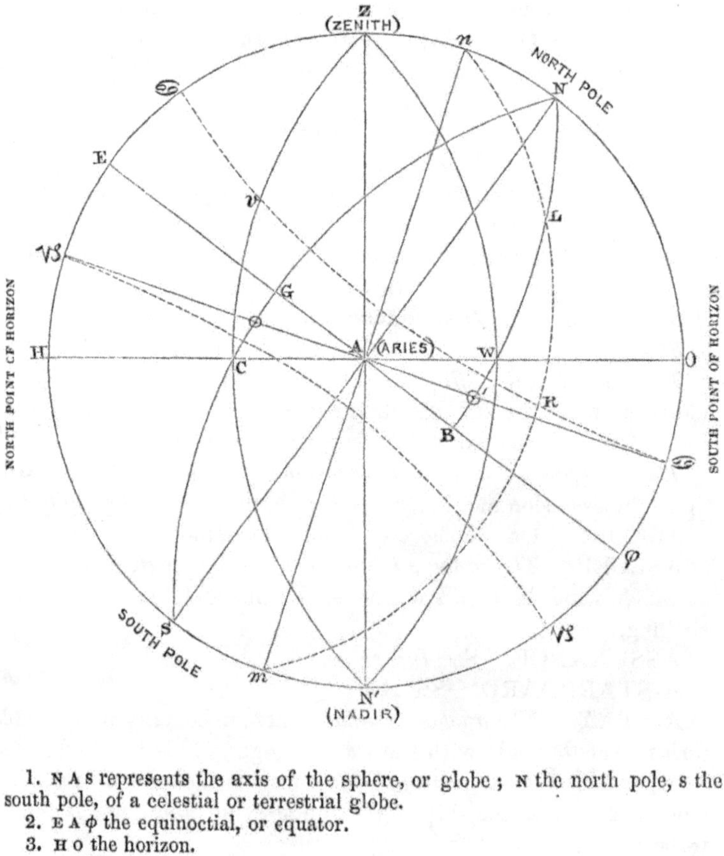


1. N A S represents the axis of the sphere, or globe; N the north pole, S the south pole, of a celestial or terrestrial globe.
2. E A φ the equinoctial, or equator.
3. H O the horizon.

4. *vs* ♋ the ecliptic; *n* its north pole, *m* its south pole.

5. ♋ ♋ the tropic of Cancer (parallel to the equator), the sun's greatest north declination.

6. *vs vs*, the tropic of Capricorn (parallel to the equator), the sun's greatest south declination.

7. Z *v* C N (or Z W N′), an azimuth circle, or vertical circle [Z A N′ the prime vertical].

8. A ☉, the sun's longitude, an arc of the ecliptic measured from Aries. (Note. In this and following cases the sun is supposed to be in some part of the horary circle N G O S.)

9. A G (or A B, if the sun were in the horary circle N L W B), the sun's right ascension an arc of the equinoctial.

10. G ☉, sun's south declination, an arc of a meridian (the sun being supposed at ☉).

11. B O′, the sun's north declination (the sun being supposed at ☉′).

12. G A ☉ (or B A ☉′), the obliquity of the ecliptic, or the angle formed by the equinoctial and the ecliptic (expressed also by the arcs E *vs* and ♋ $\phi$).

13. A C (or A W), an amplitude.

14. C O (or H C), an azimuth.

15. L R, the latitude of a star, its distance north from the ecliptic (the star being supposed at L).

Notice may here be taken of a publication by Mrs. Janet Taylor, London, which appears to be a very useful one: namely, *A Planisphere of the Stars* on a black ground: exhibiting a view of the heavens in three maps, with the distances, magnitudes, and relative positions of the fixed stars; accompanied by a book of directions to assist the student in acquiring a knowledge of them, containing various problems, and a short sketch of the planetary system, &c.

For the use of seamen there is published a set of Celestial maps by Mr. J. W. Norie in one volume, with a book of explanations for acquiring a knowledge of and finding the principal fixed stars in the heavens. It is peculiarly adapted to the purpose of finding the stars proper for ascertaining the latitude and apparent time at sea, the longitude by lunar observations, &c.

On this subject generally the leading work in the catalogue of nautical publications is *A Cycle of Celestial Objects, for the use of Naval Officers and private Astronomers, observed, reduced, and discussed* by Captain (now Vice Admiral) W. H. Smyth, R.N.

A-TAUNT, or A-TAUNTO. See *Taunt*.

ATHWART-HAWSE expresses the transverse position of a vessel when driven across the fore-part of another, whether they come into collision or not; it is most commonly applied to the case of a vessel under sail coming across another which is lying at anchor. The sailing vessel is said to come athwart-hawse of the other.

ATHWART-SHIPS. Across the ship. The reverse of *Fore-and-Aft.*

ATHWART THE FOREFOOT is a phrase applied to a shot being fired across a vessel's way, a little a-head of her, as a warning to bring to, or to drop astern.

ATMOSPHERIC, or SINGLE ACTION, ENGINE. A condensing steam engine (*Fr.* Machine à Vapeur Atmosphérique) in which 'the downward stroke of the piston is performed by the pressure of the atmosphere acting against a vacuum.' (*Murray's Treatise on Marine Engines,* 16.) See *Double Acting Engine.*

A-TRIP. *The position of an anchor* when it is raised clear of the ground. *A-weigh* has the same meaning. The operation itself is called *tripping the anchor.*

The *topsails* are said to be a-trip, when they are just started from the cap in hoisting. In like manner, an *upper mast* is said to be a-trip, when by means of the tripping-line it is started, preparatory to being sent down.

AUGER. A tool, consisting of a long iron shank having at one end a cross socket into which a wooden handle is fitted, and at the other end a grooved piece of steel somewhat resembling a bit, welded to the shank. It is used for boring large round holes.

AUGMENTATION OF THE MOON. The increase of her apparent diameter occasioned by an increase of altitude.

AUTOMATIC BLOW OFF APPARATUS. See *Steam Engine,* Sect. 45.

AUXILIARY AND RESERVE RUDDER (Mulley's). See *Rudder.*

AVAST. Enough; stop; cease.

AVERAGE (*Fr.* Avarie). There are three kinds of average, viz. *General Average, Particular Average,* and *Petty Average.* The term, however, is mostly used with reference to the two former, and in its original acceptation it denoted only general average.

When a ship has put into a port in distress, she is said to have arrived 'under average.'

*Petty Average* is now obsolete; it is what is referred to in the printed part of a bill of lading, by the words 'average as customary;' but this clause is superseded by the agreement that the stipulated freight shall be in lieu of port charges and other expenses, which are the things originally denominated 'Petty

Average.' Any charges of an ordinary nature, such as port dues, &c., incurred incidentally and not through sea perils in the course of a voyage, are denominated *petty average*.

General Average arises in consequence of any sacrifice being voluntarily made under circumstances of danger, or extraordinary expenses incurred, in the course of a sea adventure, for the joint preservation or benefit of ship and cargo; and it implies an assessment or contribution levied on all the parties interested in the ship, freight, and cargo, to make good the loss which has thus fallen upon one or more of them.

Particular Average is a term used to signify damage or partial loss unavoidably happening to any of the individual interests, whether ship, cargo or freight, by one of the perils covered by a policy of marine insurance.

*Particular Average on Ship.* Under this head are included damage sustained from being driven ashore, or from coming into collision with another vessel—by lightning or accidental fire-plunder or damage in consequence of capture by pirates or an enemy—damage to the ship's upper works, &c., by shipping heavy seas—and similar losses.

*Particular Average on Goods.* This term, according to its ordinary acceptation among merchants and underwriters, denotes loss by depreciation in the value of the goods sustained by their being sea-damaged, calculated upon the amount insured. It has also been virtually and properly applied in practice to charges incurred for the purpose of staying the progress of sea-damage. A more extended meaning has been lately applied to the expression by two of our courts of law, but without proof being had of the commonly accepted interpretation of it, the case not having been brought forward as a trial by jury, but in the form of a question for the opinion of the judges.

*Particular Average on Freight*, says Mr. Stevens, can arise only from a total loss of part of the cargo, and it is therefore correctly termed a partial loss on freight. This may arise either from the article of which the freight is insured being washed out of the package which contained it, or from its being lost in bulk by one of the perils insured against. (*Stevens' Essay on Average*, p. 174.)

AVERAGE ADJUSTER (*Fr.* Dispacheur), Average Stater, or Adjuster of Averages. An individual engaged in the business of making up statements to show the proper application of loss, damage, or expenses incurred in consequence of perils or accidents in the course of a sea adventure, whether as between the shipowner and merchant, or between either of them and his insurers. It is necessary that he should have an extensive knowledge of maritime law, of the practice and usages of marine insurance, and general and particular average, and of the phraseology used by shipwrights and seamen. He ought not to be a shipowner, merchant, underwriter, or marine insurance broker. He usually acts as an arbitrator in cases of dispute under the order of any court of law or otherwise when required.

AVERAGE AGREEMENT. A written agreement signed by the consignees of a cargo, binding themselves to pay any proportion of general average that may justly arise against them in consequence of some accident with which the ship has met. It is not drawn up in the form of a bond, and ought not to contain an arbitration clause.

AVERAGE STATER. See *Average Adjuster.*

A-WASH. At the surface of the water. *Heave and a-wash* is an encouraging call given during the act of heaving, when the anchor-ring is just out of the water, and the stock is seen to stir the surface.

A-WEATHER. See *A-lee.*

A-WEIGH. The same as *A-trip* when applied to an anchor.

AWNING (*Fr.* Tente). A canopy or covering of canvass over a ship's deck, or over a boat, as a protection from the sun, rain, or night dews. In a ship, the edges of the awning are supported by iron stanchions fixed in the rail, and it is suspended from the middle by a *crowfoot*, which is formed by a number of small lines rove through a circular piece of wood with holes in it, called the *euphroe*, hung by a whip from the masthead. Side awnings are termed *curtains.*

In East India ships, the awning also signifies part of the poop deck which is continued forward beyond the bulkhead of the cuddy. (*Norie's Epitome.*)

AXIS OF THE EARTH. In Astronomy, an imaginary line passing through the centre of the earth, round which axis it revolves once in twenty-four hours; the extremities of this line are termed the poles, the one the North, or 'Arctic' Pole, and the other the South or 'Antarctic' Pole.

Around this line, extended both ways to the sphere of the fixed stars, the heavenly bodies appear, by the motion of the earth on its axis, to perform their diurnal revolutions: it likewise determines two fixed points in the celestial sphere, the ***north celestial pole***, and the ***south celestial pole***. The star nearest to the north celestial pole is called the ***pole-star***.

Of the two poles of the earth, that which is above the horizon of an observer is relatively termed the ***elevated*** pole; and the other, the ***depressed*** pole. See *Astronomy*, 1.

AZIMUTH (*Fr.* Azimut) OF A CELESTIAL BODY. An arc of the horizon contained between the azimuth circle or vertical circle passing through the centre of the body and the north or south point of the horizon; in other words, the angle formed at the zenith by this vertical circle and the meridian of the place of an observer. See *Astronomy*, 14.

The most favourable moment for the observation of the azimuth of a celestial body is in general that which approaches nearest to its rising or setting. But the body must have sufficient altitude, at least six degrees, above the horizon, to enable the refraction to be estimated exactly, and the corrected altitude of the object observed, at the same moment, to be deduced with precision.

If the azimuth be ascertained by means of an azimuth compass, this will be affected by the variation of the magnetic needle, and it is termed the ***observed*** or ***magnetic*** azimuth. By comparing it with the ***true*** azimuth, the variation of the compass, therefore, is obtained.

AZIMUTH CIRCLES, called also *Azimuths*, or *Vertical Circles*, are great circles of the celestial sphere passing through the Zenith and Nadir, and consequently intersecting the horizon at right angles. That vertical circle which passes through the east and west points of the horizon is termed the *prime vertical*. See *Astronomy*, 7.

THE AZIMUTH COMPASS (*Fr.* Compas Azimutal) is an instrument similar to the steering compass, but of superior construction. It is adapted to observe the ***magnetic*** azimuths or amplitudes of the sun in order to ascertain the variation of the compass, and is fitted with vertical sight vanes for the purpose of observing objects elevated above the horizon. (*Norie's Epitome*, and *Raper's Practice of Navigation and Nautical Astronomy*, &c.)

AZIMUTH DIAL (Captain Toovey's). A modification of the dumb-card, showing, when determining the error of the compass, 'both the amount of error and its direction, i. e. the course by ship's head and the true course on the same card. The instrument consists of a double disc of metal, swinging freely on a tripod, and is of sufficient weight to be always horizontal, whatever may be the list of the ship. The outer rim of the disc is graduated to the points (or degrees) of the compass, and turning on the same centre is a second disc similarly graduated. There

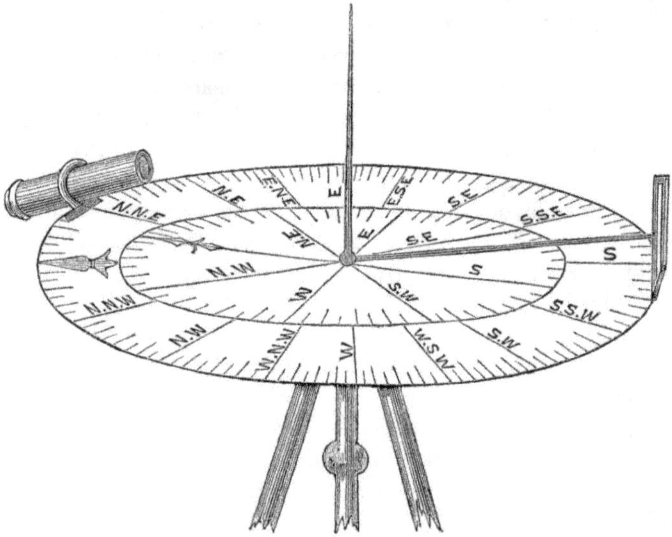


is a small pointer for indicating the direction of the ship's head; and it is also fitted with a style for obtaining the sun's shadow, but this can be removed, and the ordinary telescope and sight vane applied in the usual mode of taking an azimuth of an object.' (*Practical Mechanic and Engineer's Magazine.*)

AZOGA. A name given to the Spanish vessels which carried into America the quicksilver to be used in working the gold mines. (*Dictionnaire de Marine à voiles.*)

BACK AN ANCHOR. See *Anchor*, 10.

BACK ASTERN, in rowing, means to reverse the action of the oars (or, as it is called, to *back the oars*) so that the boat may move astern. The oars may be backed also on one side only, in order to assist in bringing the boat's head speedily round in this direction. A *sailing vessel* is backed by means of the sails; a *steamer*, by reversing the paddles or screw propeller, or in other words by *backing the engine.* See *Steam Ship* and description of *Steam Engine*, Sect. 36.

BACK AND FILL. Alternately to back and fill a vessel's sails. This is practised when driving in a narrow tideway, in order to keep the ship in the channel without the operation of tacking, the vessel being thus forced alternately ahead and astern by the trimming of the sails.

BACK THE SAILS (*Fr.* Coiffer les voiles). To throw them aback.

BACK OF A PIECE OF KNEE TIMBER. See *Belly.*

BACK-ROPES. See *Martingale.*

BACKSTAYS (*Fr.* Galhaubans). Ropes extended from the topmast, topgallantmast, and royal mast heads to the after part of each channel for the support of these masts. They are distinguished by the name of *Standing-Backstays.* (Plates III and IV.)

*Breast-Backstays* are those set up with a tackle, and extending from the head of an upper mast, through an outrigger bolted on the side of the top, down to the channels before the standing backstays: they are used chiefly for topgallant and royal masts; and in large ships for the topmasts also.

BACKSTAY-STOOLS. See *Stools* (*Backstay*).

BAGGALA. A large Arabian ship remarkable by the elevation of its stern, which is ornamented with carved work like the ancient ships of Europe. It has a very high poop. The bows are low and have a great rake. This vessel carries guns on the upper deck, and sometimes on two decks. (*Dict. de Marine à voiles.*)

BALANCELLE. The French name for a boat used in the Mediterranean, especially at Naples. It is generally sharp at both ends, somewhat like a French fishing boat. It is rigged with a lateen sail, and navigated also with oars. (*Dictionnaire de Marine à voiles.*)

BALANCE-FRAMES. See *Frames*, 2.

BALANCE-REEF. See *Reef.*

BALCONY. See *Gallery.*

BALE A BOAT. To throw water out of her.

BALISTIC PENDULUM, in Gunnery, an instrument for finding the force and velocity of a cannon ball. The gun from which the ball is fired is suspended in a gun pendulum for measuring its recoil, opposite to the balistic pendulum, which is 'an iron cylinder suspended so as to spring back easily; it is filled with sand and has in front a cover of lead which the bullet strikes and passes through it. The cylinder swings back, and by means of a small catch indicates how far it has moved, and so measures the force and velocity of the shot.'

BALK. See *Baulk.*

BALLAST (*Fr.*Lest). Heavy materials, such as stones, pig-iron, sand, &c., placed in the bottom of a vessel's hold to lower the centre of gravity, and thereby to increase her stability, so that she may not be liable to cant over too much, or to be overturned by the impulse of the wind and waves, as well as to present a greater lateral surface to the resistance of the water when sailing on a wind and thereby check her from falling to leeward.

When a vessel has no cargo on board, but only stores for the use of the ship's company, and ballast, she is said to be *in ballast.* To *ballast a ship*, or *a boat* (*Fr.* Lester), is to put the needful quantity of ballast on board of her.

Unless stones, metal, or other such material, cannot be obtained, it is not considered proper, nor perhaps warrantable, to take sand ballast, which is apt to get to the pumps and choke them, even when every precaution is used by clearing the limbers, by protection with matting and otherwise. (*Lorimer's Letters to a Young Master Mariner.*)

The impropriety of taking sand ballast is the greater when the ship has a perishable cargo on board.

The advantages of water ballast are treated of in *Grantham on Iron Shipbuilding*, p. 83. See *Water Ballast Platform.*

In ships of war, pig-iron alone is used for ballast. See *Kentledge* and *Limber-Kentledge.*

BALLASTAGE. A rate levied for supplying ships with ballast. In the river Thames ballast is put on board of ships by means of *ballast lighters* fitted for the purpose ; this is subject to special regulations of the port, under the superintending control of *the Ballast Master.*

BALLAST MARK. See *Water Lines.*

BALLAST PORTS. Ports cut in the sides of a vessel for taking in and unloading ballast, &c. See *Port.*

BALLAST SHOVEL. An iron shovel generally formed with a square spoon, used in heaving ballast.

BALSAS, and BALZA. A sailing canoe of Ceylon. A name given to certain kinds of boats, or rather rafts used as boats on the West Coast of South America.

BANDS. Strips of canvass sewed across a sail to strengthen

it; such as *reef-bands*, which are put on in the way of the reef-points. See also *Rudder-Bands.*

BANIAN DAYS. The name which was given to those three days of the week on which, according to former custom on board of ships, the sailors had no flesh meat served out to them. So called after Banians in India.

BANK (*Fr.* Danger). An accumulation of sand or other soil, either elevated somewhat above the surface of the sea, or over which there is shoal water. On charts, banks are indicated by *dots* and reefs by *crosses.* See DOUBLE BANK and FOG BANK.

BANKA. A canoe of Manila. It is made of a single piece.

BANKER. See *Banking.*

BANKING. A term applied to fishing on the banks of Newfoundland. A vessel so employed is called A BANKER (*Fr.* Banquier, Terreneuvier).

BAR. A bank or shoal at the entrance of a river or harbour. See also *Capstan-* and *Hatch-Bars.*

BAR SHALLOW. A term sometimes applied to a portion of a bar with less water on it than on other parts of the bar.

BARCA-LONGA. A Spanish gun-boat, having many sweeps for impelling her.

BARE POLES. A ship at sea is said to be under *bare poles* when she has no sail set; as in scudding during a severe storm.

BARGE (*Fr.* Acon, gabare). A general name for boats of state or pleasure. A large double-banked boat used by an Admiral or Captain in the Royal Navy. See *Boat,* 1.

Also a flat-bottomed vessel of burden, used in loading or unloading ships, &c. In vessels of this description (*Fr.* gabares), when employed for the carriage of goods on a river, or through a canal, the mast, if needful, is made to work upon a hinge, so that it may be lowered in passing under bridges, and hoisted again by means of a tackle made fast to the stem or by the fore-stay. See *Lee-Board.*

CRANE-BARGE. A low-built barge having a flat bottom, and either square or rounded extremities. It is decked, and is made of great breadth, in order to give stability sufficient to counteract the strain upon the crane with which it is fitted for the purpose of lifting the stones, piles, &c., carried on its deck, to be used in the building of sea walls, timber or stone jetties, and similar erections.

BARK. A popular name for any small vessel. See also *Barque.*

BARNACLE, or BARNICLE (*Fr.* Bernacle). A species of small shell-fish often found adhering to the surface of a vessel's bottom. These are not injurious to the plank, but tend to deaden the ship's way. They are found occasionally even on coppered vessels, particularly if the copper has been paid over with coarse oil, which on drying leaves a rough surface; or if the vessel has lain long in still water in a hot climate.

BAROMETER (*Fr.* Baromètre). A well-known philosophical instrument for measuring, by means of a column of mercury in a glass tube, the comparative weight or pressure of the atmosphere. This is called the *Mercurial Barometer.* The *Aneroid Barometer,* invented by M. Vidi, measures the variation of the atmosphere by the pressure of the atmosphere upon a metallic box hermetically sealed. It is described by Mr. Belville in his *Manual of the Mercurial and Aneroid Barometer* 1858. Marine barometers are constructed in such a manner as to check the oscillations and vibrations of the mercury, which might be occasioned by the motion of the ship. With a view to that important object, they ought always to be hung by the arm which is prepared for this purpose, and not by the upper ring only.

The barometer is subject to slight daily variations, particularly towards noon and midnight; but if at any time the mercury fall *considerably* from its usual height, some material change may be expected to take place, and when it falls very low, for instance in our climate to 29 inches or below that mark, a gale is sure to follow.

This instrument is peculiarly useful in *high* latitudes, and even near the tropics. But within 9 or 10 degrees of the Equator, though storms of long duration are almost invariably prognosticated by the barometer, yet whirlwinds and squalls of a few hours' continuance are said to be sometimes experienced without any fall of the mercury.

In the evidence given some years ago by Captain (now Rear Admiral) Fitzroy before the Committee of the House of Commons on Shipwrecks, he attributed the loss of many vessels to the neglect of the use of this instrument, whereby they have either closed the land when at sea, or put to sea at improper times, and so been overtaken by bad weather coming on suddenly. Every vessel, he observed, ought to have either a barometer or a *sympiesometer*, which is an efficient substitute for it.

Important information on this subject is contained in the Introduction to Horsburgh's *India Directory* (from which some of the above particulars are extracted), in Lieut. Jenning's *Hints on Sea Risks*, and in Mrs. Taylor's *Diurnal Register for the Barometer, Sympiesometer, and Thermometer.*

The Barometer Manual published in 1861 by Rear Admiral Fitzroy, Chief of the Meteorological Department at the Board of Trade, contains an explanation of his *Storm Warning Signals* in use at different stations in the British Islands, and of the Weather Tables now published daily in the *Times*, &c. The Weather Book since published by Admiral Fitzroy is a Manual of Practical Meteorology, explaining the use of meteorological instruments, such as weather glasses on land as well as at sea, and giving full details of the present system of 'Meteorologic Telegraphy.'

BARQUE, or BARK (*Fr.* Barque). A three-masted vessel having her fore and main masts rigged like those of a ship, but her mizen mast rigged like a schooner's main mast. (Plate III.)

BARRATRY (*Fr.* Baratérie). Any fraudulent or illegal act on the part of the master or mariners, or criminal conduct in breach of the trust reposed in them, to the prejudice of the owners of a vessel, and without the consent or privity of the latter. A master who is part owner can commit barratry against his co-owners, or against the freighters.

BARREL-BULK, in Shipping, a measure of capacity for freight, equal to five cubic feet. Eight barrel bulk are equal to one ton measurement. (*Waterston's Cyclopædia of Commerce.*)

BARRICADE. A wooden fence at any part of a vessel formed by rails and stanchions.

BARTON, or properly BURTON. 'A small tackle is usually called a jigger: a larger one a *Barton.*' (*Boyd's Naval Cadet's Manual.*) See *Burton.*

BASIN (*Fr.* Bassin). The same as a *Wet Dock.* The term basin is also applied to a portion of a tide-harbour, having a narrow entrance, and forming an inner harbour sheltered and commodious for shipping.

BATTENS. Long narrow slips of wood nailed to the coamings of a vessel's hatches in order to secure the tarpaulins which are placed over the hatches when required. This is called battening down the hatches. Bands of iron are sometimes used for the purpose instead of wooden battens, especially in coasters.

Battens (sometimes called in cant phrase *Scotchmen*, but properly CHAFING-BOARDS) are also seized upon rigging to prevent its being chafed. Battens are likewise nailed for this purpose on the after side of the yards.

In Shipbuilding, battens are used for applying on the side of the vessel in order to determine the sheer, as well as to fair the ship; and for drawing lines by in the moulding loft. See *Deals*.

HAMMOCK-BATTENS. See *Hammock-Racks*.

BATTERIES (FLOATING). Vessels fitted for harbour defence. See also *Floating Battery*.

BAULK, or BALK. In Shipbuilding, a piece of plank nailed across each of the frames to keep them at their proper breadth till the vessel is planked outside. They also get the name of *Cross-Spales* or *Cross-Pawls*. See *Bilgeways* and *Spaling*.

The name of Balks is also given to short pieces of timber, from five to twelve inches square, imported from certain places abroad.

BAY (*Fr.* Baie). A kind of small gulf not running very deep into the land.

SICK BAY. See that title.

BAYS, in a ship of war. The starboard and port sides between decks before the bitts. (*Darcy Lever.*)

BAYDAR. A bark or canoe of the north coast of Siberia, Kamtschatka, and the north-west coast of America. It is made of the skins of seals joined together by flat seams sewed with the sinews of these animals, and is kept at its proper stretch by a frame of wood work. (*Dict. de Marine à voiles.*)

BAY-ICE. See *Iceberg*, 3.

BAZARAS. A large flat-bottomed pleasure-boat in use on the Ganges; navigated with sails and oars. (*Dict. de Marine à voiles.*)

BEACH. The sea-shore, the strand. See *Careen*.

TO BEACH (*Fr.* Ensabler) is a term used to denote the act of intentionally running a vessel ashore in order to preserve her from sinking after having sprung a leak, or when she is otherwise placed in circumstances of inevitable danger. See *Stranding*. It is also applied to the act of running a vessel up on the beach for the purpose of loading her, &c., at a place where there is no other accommodation.

BEACHMEN. A term applied to boatmen, &c., who land

people on a beach, especially in places where there is a heavy surf. See *Catamaran.*

BEACON (*Fr.* Balise). Any mark or sign erected on the coast, or over rocks or shoals, for the safe guidance of vessels.

BEACONAGE. A payment levied for the use and maintaining of beacons.

BEAMS (*Fr.* Baux). In Shipbuilding, strong pieces of timber resting on the clamps or shelf-pieces, and extending from the timbers on one side to those on the other side of the vessel; they are secured to the timbers by means of knees, and bind the ship together, besides acting as the support of her decks. (Plate II. fig. 6.)

1. A vessel is said to be *on her beam ends*, when heeled over so that her beams are vertical or nearly so.

*On the Beam, or A-beam.* See *Bearing.*

2. BREAK BEAMS. Beams introduced at the break of a deck.

3. BREAST BEAMS. Those beams at the fore part of the quarter-deck, and after part of the forecastle, in a vessel which has a poop and a top-gallant forecastle.

4. HALF BEAMS, or FORK BEAMS. Short beams introduced to support the deck where there is no framing, as in those parts where the beams are kept asunder by hatchways. When these do not exceed one half the dimensions of the beams, and are not fastened at their ends by knees or T plates, they get the name of *ledges*, or in some places, *cross-carlings.*

5. HOLD BEAMS. The lowest range of beams in a merchant vessel. When there is an orlop-deck, as in the case in large ships of war, these beams support that deck, and hence get the name of the ORLOP BEAMS. (Plate II. fig. 6.) There is in the between decks of a merchant vessel space used as a hold for cargo, &c.; the hold beams are often termed the *lower hold beams*, in contradistinction from the orlop beams, and the deck beams, that is the beams in the between decks.

PADDLE BEAMS. See *Paddle Wheels.*

BEAM ENDS. See *Beams*, 1.

BEAM FILLINGS. See *Filling.*

BEAN-COD. A Portuguese boat.

BEAR. A name given to a large holystone with ropes attached to drag it along the decks for the purpose of scrubbing or cleaning them; and also to a coir mat filled with sand used in some ships for the same purpose.

An object *bears* so and so when it is in such a direction from the person looking. With reference to the wind it is said to bear N. or N.E. &c. according to the quarter whence it blows. See *Bearing*.

BEAR A HAND. To make haste.

BEAR AWAY, or BEAR UP (*Fr.* Arriver, larguer). To make a vessel's head recede from the wind when she is sailing close-hauled, or with a side wind: in either case, this is done by putting the helm up, that is, by putting the tiller up in the direction whence the wind is blowing.

BEAR DOWN UPON A VESSEL. To approach her from windward.

BEAR IN WITH and OFF FROM the land, imply respectively to steer a vessel *towards* and *from* the land.

BEAR OFF. To keep anything, in the act of being hoisted or lowered, from chafing against the ship's side. To thrust off.

BEAR UP, or BEAR UP THE HELM. The same as to *Bear away.*

BEARDING, in Shipbuilding, diminishing the edge or surface of a piece of timber or plank, &c., from a given line.' (*Shipwright's Vade Mecum.*)

BEARDING LINE. A curved line made by bearding or reducing the dead-wood to the form of the ship's body. The lower points of the timbers come down to this line, which is often called the *stepping-line.*

BEARING. The situation of one object from another with reference to the points of the compass.

Also, the situation or direction of any object, or of the wind,

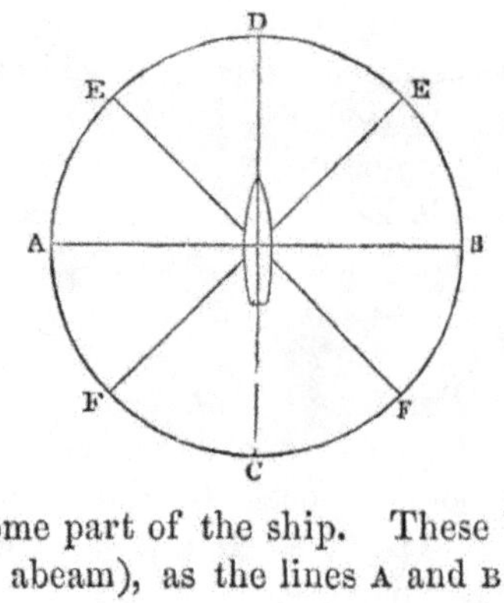


estimated from some part of the ship. These bearings are either *On the beam* (or abeam), as the lines A and B: *Before the beam,* as the arcs A D and D B: *Abaft the beam,* as the arcs A C and C B: *On the lee or weather bow,* as the lines E E: *On the lee or weather quarter,* as the lines F F: Ahead, as the line D: or *Astern,* as the line C. (*Seamanship both in Theory and Practice.*)

BEARINGS OF A VESSEL. The widest part of her below the planksheer; that part of her which is on the water-line when she sits upright with a full cargo on board.

BEAT TO WINDWARD (*Fr.* Louvoyer). To sail against the direction of the wind by means of alternate tacks.

*Working to windward* and *Turning to windward* are terms synonymous therewith.

BECALM (*Fr.* Abrier, Cacher, Déventer). A vessel is becalmed when there is not a breath of wind to fill her sails. Any object becalms a vessel, or one sail becalms another, when it prevents the wind from reaching it.

BECKET. A piece of rope, sometimes with a knot at one end and an eye in the other, sometimes with its two ends spliced together, used for confining pump gear, oars, or spars together, and for other purposes.

A piece of wood in the form of a cleat seized on a vessel's fore or main rigging for the sheets and tacks to lie in (while they are not required) in order to avoid chafing.

A ring of rope or iron fixed to the bottom of a block for the standing end of the fall to be made fast to.

BED. A flat thick piece of wood, two of which are lodged under the quarters of any cask that is stowed in a vessel's hold, in order to keep it *bilge-free.* Casks are steadied upon the beds by means of wedges called *Quoins.* See *Bilge of a cask.*

*Beds for Guns* are pieces of wood for the breech of the gun to rest on. *Beds for Mortars,* or *Bomb-Beds,* are solid frames of timber whereon the mortars in a bomb-vessel are supported.

BEES (*Fr.* Violons). Pieces of hard wood bolted to the outer end of a vessel's bowsprit to reeve the fore-topmast stays through.

BEETLE. A wooden maul hooped with iron used for driving reeming irons and treenails. See *Maul* and *Reeming.*

BEFORE THE BEAM. See *Bearing.*

BELAY (*Fr.* Amarrer). To make fast any running rope by turns round a pin or coil without hitching or seizing: chiefly applicable to running rigging.

BELAYING PINS are wooden or iron pins, fixed in different parts of a vessel for belaying ropes to. They are illustrated

under the titles *Rack*, *Spider-hoop*, No. 2, and *Topsail sheet bitts*, No. 3.

BELFRY. An ornamental frame fixed on the top of the pawl-bitt or elsewhere, in which the ship's bell is hung.

BELL-BUOY. A kind of large can-buoy (or cone-shaped pontoon) placed in a lofty erection of wicker work containing a bell with several tongues to sound by means of the heaving of the sea. See *Buoy*, 4.

BELLS. See *Watch*.

BELLY OF A SAIL, when inflated by the wind or *of a curved timber*, is the inside of its curve. The outside of a curved piece of timber is called the *back*.

BEND. To make fast. To fasten two ropes together.

*To Bend the Cable* (*Fr.* Etalinguer), means to make it fast to the anchor ring; a *chain* cable is secured to the ring by means of a shackle. See *Cable Bends*.

*To Bend the Sails* (*Fr.* Enverguer), is to extend and fasten them to their proper yards or stays.

BEND. A species of knot by which a rope is made fast to any thing or one rope to another.

CARRICK BEND.

HAWSER BEND.

SHEET BEND.

The key to the above sketches, and to most of the sketches of *hitches* given under that title, is contained in Darcy Lever's old but standard work, *The Young Sea Officer's Sheet Anchor.*

BENDS, or WALES (Préceintes), in Shipbuilding, the thickest strakes of plank put round the outside of a vessel between the black-strakes. See *Wales.*

BENTICK-BOOM. See *Boom* (Plate IV. 68).

BERMUDA SCHOONER-RIGGED BOAT, and BERMUDA SAILS. See *Schooner-rigged Boat.*

BERTH. The place which a vessel occupies alongside of a quay or elsewhere.

*To berth a vessel* means to fix upon and put her into the place she is to occupy. See also *Hawse,* 2.

BERTH (*Fr.* Cabane) also means a small room in a vessel set apart for the use of any officer, seaman, or passenger. Their beds, or the places where hammocks are slung, are likewise called *berths.*

To BERTH A SHIP'S COMPANY means to give each man the allotted space in which to sling his hammock.

To GIVE THE LAND (or any object) A WIDE BERTH is to keep at a due distance from it.

BERTH AND SPACE. See *Timber* and *Room.*

BERTHING. 'The term now frequently, perhaps most generally, used by seamen to denote the bulwark of a merchant ship. In naval architecture, it denotes the planking outside above the sheer-strake, and is called the berthing of *the quarter-deck, of the poop, or of the forecastle,* as the case may be. It is also applied to denote the close boarding between the head-rails, in which case it is called the *berthing* of the head ; this is frequently termed by seamen the '*head boards*.'

BETWEEN-DECKS, or 'TWIXT-DECKS (*Fr.* Entrepont). The space between any two decks of a vessel.

BEVELLED. Not square : formed with an acute or obtuse angle. The term is derived from an instrument called a *bevel*, by which such angles are taken.

Hence, *the bevelling* of a timber implies the angle contained between two of its adjacent sides : if an acute angle, it is termed an *under bevelling* (or *bevel*), and if an obtuse angle, a *standing bevel*. We also speak of a timber having a *square bevel*, that is, having its adjacent sides at right angles to each other, but this is an incorrect application of the term.

BIGHT. A bend in the shore forming a small bay or inlet.

BIGHT OF A ROPE. Its middle part, or some fold of it between the two ends. When any such parts of a vessel's rigging, as of the braces of yards, are slack, the braces are said to *hang in bights*.

BILANDER (*Fr.* Bélandre). 'A name almost indiscriminately applied to small coasters.' It formerly denoted a two-masted vessel with a peculiar form of mainsail 'bent to the whole length of a yard hanging fore and aft,' with an upward inclination of 'about 45 degrees :' a mode of rigging which came to be confined mostly to Dutch vessels.

BILBOES. Iron shackles to secure the feet of prisoners or offenders.

BILGE OF A CASK. Its middle part, which has the greatest diameter. See *Chime*. A cask when stowed in a ship is said to be BILGE FREE, if properly set upon beds so as to prevent its bilge, which is the weakest part, from resting on anything.

A *ship is said to be bilged*, when any part of her bottom or bilge is driven in by violence. When such an injury occurs to the upper portion of her hull, she is said *to be stove*.

BILGE, in Shipbuilding, that part of a vessel's bottom which begins to round upwards, at the point where the floors and second futtocks unite, and whereon the ship would rest if laid aground. It is strengthened outside and inside by thick planks, termed the bilge planks, a security which along with extra bolting is the more required, as the shiftings of the timbers at this part are generally shorter than elsewhere.

BILGE COAD. See *Bilge Keels* and *Launching Ways.*

BILGE KEELS, also called *Bilge Pieces* or *Bilge Coads*, are pieces of timber fayed on the bottom of a vessel edgeways, which, by their resistance to the water, serve to prevent the ship from rolling heavily, as well as from drifting to leeward. They should be wrought on parallel to the main keel, and in such a position that when the ship is sailing close-hauled, the one on the lee-side may be nearly vertical. In *iron vessels*, angle iron plates are in like manner used for the same purpose.

In a sharp-bottomed vessel such pieces are sometimes put upon the bilge for her to rest upon when aground, in order to prevent her taking too great a list.

BILGE KEELSONS. See *Keelson.*

BILGE PLANKS. Thick planks which run round a vessel's bilge in a fore and aft direction, both inside and outside. (Plate II. fig. 6.) See the article *Ceiling.*

BILGE PUMPS (*Fr.* Pompes d'épuisement de cale). See *Pump.*

BILGE TREES. A name given in some places to *Bilge Coads.*

BILGE WATER. Water which, by reason of the flatness of a vessel's bottom, lies on her floor and cannot go to the well of the pumps. Not being drawn off, it acquires an offensive smell. This is most apt to accumulate in very tight vessels. When the ship is listed over, it may be removed by means of the bilge pumps. In some vessels a pipe is inserted through the side with a cock, which gets the name of a *sweetening cock*, fitted to its inner end, for admitting water to mix with the bilge water.

BILGE WAYS. See *Launching Ways.*

BILL, or PEA. The extremity of the arm of an anchor, where it is tapered nearly to a point.

BILL BOARDS, or ANCHOR LINING. Pieces of board or plank fixed between the projecting planks of the bow (sometimes having iron plates called *Bill-board Plates* nailed to them) — and likewise pieces attached to the bulwarks — to guide the bill of the anchor past these projecting planks.

BILL OF HEALTH. A document obtained from the consul or other proper authority, certifying the state of health in the place she sails from and of the ship's company at the time of her departure from it. See *Quarantine.*

BILL OF LADING (*Fr.* Connaissement). A document whereby the master of a vessel acknowledges the receipt of goods shipped on board of it, and binds himself ('dangers and accidents of the seas, fire, enemies, &c. excepted') to deliver them in like good order and condition to the party to whom they are addressed, upon payment of the stipulated freight. The holder of a bill of lading may transfer it by indorsement, and it is a negotiable instrument.

BILL OF SALE. An instrument in writing, by which the property of a vessel, or shares thereof, are transferred to a purchaser.

BILL OF SIGHT, or BILL OF VIEW. A form of entry at the Custom House, by the best description that can be given of goods, which, upon importation, cannot be correctly described by the importer or his agent; whereupon a warrant is granted for their being provisionally landed and examined by him in presence of the proper officers.

BILL OF STORE. A Custom House document which may be issued by the searcher, permitting goods which had been shipped for foreign ports, but not sold there, to be re-imported duty free, at any time within six years after they were exported, upon a declaration being signed by the proprietor that at the time of re-importation he still continues to hold the property in such goods, and that since their entry for exportation they had not been sold or disposed of to any other person.

BILL (VICTUALLING). See *Victualling Bill.*

BILLET-HEAD, or BOLLARD. A round piece of wood, fixed in the bow or stern of a whale fishing boat, about which the line is veered when a whale sets off at full speed after being harpooned. See also *Head.*

BILLY BOAT. 'A kind of half decked river boat.'

BILLY BOY. 'A flat-bottomed vessel built for the navigation of the Humber and its tributaries. Those which go to sea are generally clincher built and sloop rigged. Many of them have still a square topsail which was formerly considered as an indispensable portion of the complete equipment of a sea-going billy boy. Some of them are schooner rigged and carvel built. They all draw very little water in proportion to their burthen; and to enable them to hold a good wind, those employed on short coasting voyages are fitted with lee boards which are unshipped when they have to proceed inland to Leeds or Wakefield: the masts of these are fitted into a strong trunk on the deck called a *tabernacle*, which forms a kind of hinge to enable them to lower the mast when going under bridges.'

BINDINGS, in Shipbuilding, a general term for the beams, knees, clamps, shelf-pieces, keelson, water-ways, breast-hooks, transoms, wales, and other principal connecting parts of a vessel.

BINDING-STRAKES. The principal strakes of plank in a vessel, especially the sheer-strake and wales, which are bolted to the knees and shelf-pieces.

BINNACLE (*Fr.* Habitacle). A turret-shaped case or box on the deck of a vessel near the helm, containing the compasses, by the aid of which she is steered. It is commonly fitted with two compasses, having a light placed between them for night service, but it is thought better to have only a single compass in it. Some compasses are more sensitive, quicker in their action than others, and one of this nature is suitable to be used during calm weather: in a heavy seaway, it may be replaced with one of a slower action. Reflectors fitted on each side of the binnacle, at a proper angle to throw the light upon the cards, assist greatly in keeping the compasses well illumined, even when the ship labours. This plan is said to have been adopted and found advantageous, by Captain Cox, of H. M. revenue cutter 'Lapwing.' There is a new kind of *binnacle lamp*, invented by Mrs. Janet Taylor, 104 Minories, London, having a parabolical reflector placed above it, which throws the light brilliantly over the compass card; this lamp is said to burn with a steady light, and to save about two-thirds of the oil usually consumed.

We understand that there are compasses made of amber for night service.

BINS. A sort of large chests, or erections, 'generally made of rabbeted deal, with lids on the top' for containing a vessel's stores.

BITE. An anchor, when dropped, is said to *bite* if it take hold of the ground.

BITTACLE. Properly *Binnacle*.

BITTS. Strong upright pieces of timber let down through a vessel's deck and bolted securely to the beams: as the WINDLASS BITTS and WINCH BITTS, which respectively support the windlass and winch near their ends, and the RIDING BITTS, to which, when at anchor, the cable is made fast in a vessel that weighs its anchor by a capstan. See *Cross-Piece* and *Topsail-Sheet-Bitts.*

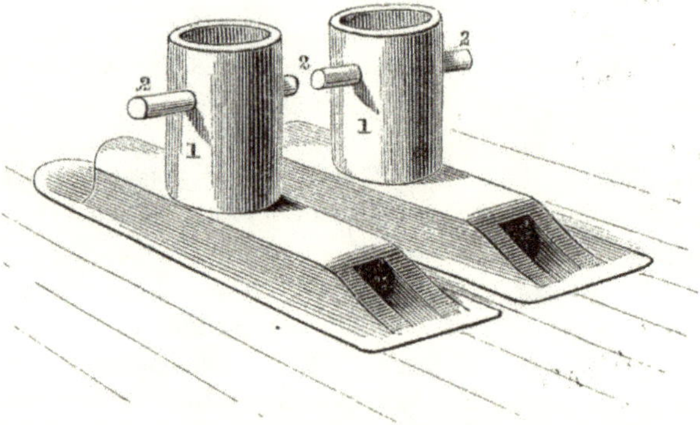


RIDING BITTS OF A SHIP OF WAR.

To Bitt (*Fr.* Bitter) is to place the bight of a cable or any rope over the bitts.

Bowsprit-Bitts. See *Partners.*

Gallows-Bitts. See *Gallows.*

Pawl-Bitt. A strong piece of timber placed vertically at the back of the windlass for its security, and on which the pawl-plate of the windlass is fitted. Its lower end rests on the keelson or on the keelson-rider.

Topsail-Sheet-Bitts. See that title.

BITTER END *of a cable or warp when run out from a vessel,* means the extreme end of it within board. Hence the chain or rope is said to be paid out *to the bitter end* when you can let no more go.

BLACKENED. A local term, having the same meaning as *sewed.*

BLACKING DOWN, or BLACKING. A term commonly applied to the tarring of rigging, or to the operation of blacking a ship's bends or bottom with tar, &c.

BLACK-STRAKES. The strakes of plank in a ship's side one or more immediately above and below the wales. See *Strake,* and Plate IV. 32, 34.

BLACKWALL HITCH. See *Hitch.*

BLADE. See descriptions of *Anchor, Oar,* and *Screw Propeller.*

BLAIR. A mixture of hair and Archangel tar, made into a kind of paste, used for tightening the seams of boats.

BLAST ENGINE. Schiele's Blast Engine or Ventilator is a machine to draw off the foul air from the cabin or hold of a ship and induce a current of fresh air into it. The inventor describes the machine as suited 'for ventilating the holds and cabins of passenger and cattle steamers, transports, &c., for cooling firing rooms and urging deficient draughts, especially in hot climates, for exhausting explosive gases in coal vessels, and noxious vapours arising from cargo, for blowing the furnaces in gun boats, &c., and to avoid the necessity of funnels.'

BLOCK (*Fr.* Poulie). A piece of wood with one or more *sheaves* or wheels in it, through which a rope may be rove to obtain a convenient or increased purchase. There are blocks made of iron for reefing chains through. Blocks are termed *single*, *double* or *treble*, &c., according to the number of sheaves which they contain. Wooden blocks are either *built* or *morticed*. A Built Block consists of four parts: the *shell*, or outer case wherein the sheave traverses; the *sheave*, on which the rope runs; the *pin*, (*Fr.* Essieu) on which, as an axle, the sheave revolves; and the *strop* (or strap) either of rope or iron which encircles the whole. (See the article *Strop.*) The space in the shell where the sheave revolves is termed the *jaw*. The sheave is generally strengthened by letting in at the centre a circular piece of iron or brass, called a bush. A Morticed Block is formed of a single piece of wood 'morticed' out to contain one or more sheaves. The illustrations of blocks given below are drawn partly after Lieut. Nares and partly after Darcy Lever. For a variety of information on this subject reference may be made to *Nares on Seamanship*, pages 26, 47.

1. Cant Blocks. A name given to large purchase blocks, used in ships at the Davis' Straits' fishing, for canting the whales during the process of flensing.

2. Cat Block. See *Cathead.*

3. Clump Blocks. A name given to any blocks that are made thicker or stronger than ordinary blocks.

4. Fiddle Blocks, or Long Tackle Blocks, have two sheaves of different sizes placed one above the other. These are used chiefly for the runner-and-tackles of sloops.

5. Fly Block. Any block which, forming part of a tackle, shifts its position when hauled upon.

6. Jewel Blocks are small blocks suspended from the extremities of any yard-arm to lead the studding-sail-halyards through.

7. Leading Blocks. A general name for those blocks which are used for guiding the direction of any purchase; they may be distinguished into three kinds:—

8. *Hook Blocks,* which are leading blocks iron-stropped, with a hook at one end.

9. *Sister Blocks.* Two single blocks or bull's eyes formed in one piece of wood. In the Merchant Service they are used

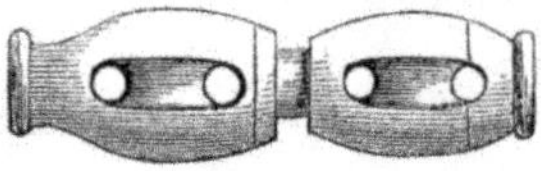

mostly for the buntlines and leachlines of the courses in large ships; in ships of war they are seized between the two foremost shrouds of the topmast rigging for the reef tackles and topsail lifts to lead through. (See *Lieut. Nares on Seamanship,* page 47.)

10. *Snatch Blocks* (or *Notch Blocks*), which are single blocks with a notch cut in one cheek, to receive the bight of a rope or fall, so as to save the trouble of reeving and unreeving the whole.

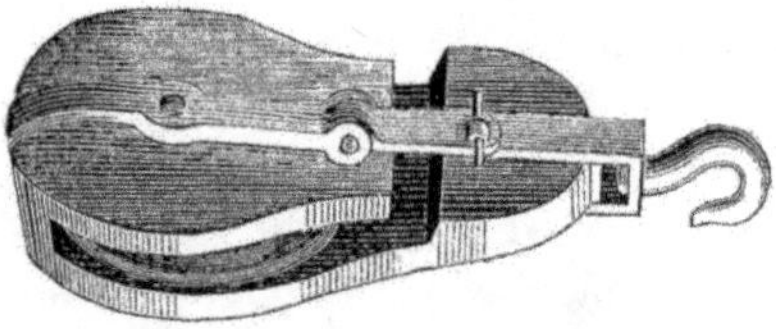

These are used sometimes for leading a rope fair to the winch or windlass, and for various similar purposes.

11. *Tail Blocks* are single blocks, rope stropped, having an end or 'tail' of the rope left by which they may be lashed to the rigging, or made fast at any other part where they happen to be required.

12. Purchase Blocks. See *Purchase.*

13. Shoulder Blocks are 'made with a projection left on one side of the top of the shell to prevent the falls from being jammed.'

14. Top Block. See *Mast Rope.*

15. *Bowline Blocks, Brace, Brace-pendant, Brail, Bunt-line, Clue garnet, Clue-line, Fore-sheet, Girt-line, Halyard, Jear, Leech-line, Lift, Main-sheet, Main-tack, Peak-halyard, Reef-tackle, Stay-tackle, Throat-halyard, Topping Lift, Topsail-sheet, Tye,* and *Yard-tackle blocks, &c.,* are all named respectively after the ropes or chains which are rove through them.

See *Bull's-eye*, *Clamp*, *Dead-eye*, and *Plumber-blocks*.

BLOCKS, termed *keel-blocks*, also signify short ends of logs of timber, piled upon each other, to lay the keel of a vessel upon while building, or to place her upon for repairs.

SLIDING BILGE BLOCKS are those made to slide under the bilge of the ship in order to support her.

BLOCK AND BLOCK. The situation of a tackle when the blocks are hauled close together. See *Chock-a-block*.

BLOCKADE. *To blockade a seaport* is to station cruisers before it, in order to prevent any communication therewith by sea. *To raise a blockade* is to put an end to it.

According to the rules of international law, a port cannot be said to be blockaded unless there be ships stationed to keep up the blockade, in such force as to cut off all access of neutral ships, to render it imminently dangerous to attempt to enter or quit the port.

BLOCKMAKER (*Fr.* Poulieur). A manufacturer of blocks.

BLOW OFF APPARATUS (AUTOMATIC). See *Salinometer*.

BLOW OFF PIPE (*and cocks*) and BLOWING OFF. See description of *Steam Engine*, Sect. 45.

BLOW THROUGH VALVE (*Fr.* Soupape à purger l'air). See description of *Steam Engine*, Sect. 12.

BLUE PETER. A flag having a blue ground with a white square in the middle. When hoisted at the fore-topmast head, it is the signal for sailing.

BLUFF. Broad and full. Thus a ship is *bluff-bowed* when her bows are made very full and flat. *Lean* is the reverse term. The reverse of *full* is *sharp*: applied to the build of ships or boats.

BLUFF. A high abrupt projecting point of land.

BOARD (*Fr.* Bordée). The stretch which a vessel makes on each tack in beating to windward. The ship is said *to make a good board*, when on either tack she sails well up to the line of her desired course — *a long board*, when she stands long on one tack — *a short board*, when she is put about soon — *a stern board*, when, on either tack, she fetches sternway instead of gaining ground.

*To* BOARD *or to* HAUL ABOARD *the fore and main tacks*, means to haul them forward, and down to the chestrees on the weather side of a vessel, when sailing on a wind. See *Tack*.

*To* BOARD *a ship* (*Fr.* Aborder). To enter an enemy's or pirate's vessel in order forcibly to take possession of her. The men appointed either to make or repel such an attack are called *boarders*; in the former case, they carry each a cutlass, a tomahawk, and two pistols; in the latter they are armed with *boarding-pikes.* It also means simply to go on board of any vessel. To board customs officers on a vessel means to put them on board of her. See *By the Board* and *Out-Board.*

BOARD OF TRADE. 'The Committee of Her Majesty's Privy Council appointed for the consideration of matters relating to trade and foreign plantations.'

BOARDERS. See *Board a ship.*

BOARDING-NETTINGS. See *Nettings.*

BOARDING-PIKE. A weapon used in defending a ship against being boarded.

BOAT (*Fr.* Bateau, Canot, Chaloupe, Embarcation). A small open vessel adapted either for rowing or sailing. See *Oar*, *Stern-Sheets*, *Thwart*, &c.

1. The boats taken to sea in a *ship of war* are as follows:—(1) The *launch*, or *long-boat*, which is the largest on board, and is built full, flat, and high, so as to carry a great weight. (2) The *barge*, next in size, of a slighter frame, rowed with ten or twelve oars, and intended for carrying commanding officers to and from the ship. (3) The *pinnace*, of a similar form, but somewhat smaller than the barge, pulling six or eight oars; it is for the accommodation of the lieutenants and subordinate officers, &c., or is used instead of the barge for the smaller classes of ships. (4) The *yawl*, a boat of the same description as the pinnace, but somewhat smaller. The above mentioned boats used to be all carvel built. Captain Boyd, in his *Naval Cadet's Manual* (284), mentions that in the Navy, launches, barges, pinnaces, and paddle-box boats (for steamers), are now diagonally built and mostly made of mahogany. (5) *Cutters*, which are clinker built, and are shorter and broader in proportion to their length than the long-boat; they are used for the conveyance of stores, &c. (6) The *jolly-boat*, similar to that of a merchant vessel. (7) The *gig*, a long narrow boat, also clinker built, adapted for rowing expeditiously, and also for sailing; it usually belongs to the captain.

2. The boats belonging to a *merchant vessel* are:—(1) The *launch* or *long-boat*, already described. (2) The *skiff*, next in

size: used for towing, running out a kedge, &c. (3) The *jolly-boat* or *yawl*, the third in size: kept for shore purposes, and other light work. It is very commonly called the *stern-boat*, if hung to davits over the ship's stern. (4) The *quarter-boat*, which is so called from being hung to davits over the ship's quarter; it is longer than the jolly-boat. Some vessels are provided with only one quarter-boat; others have a boat over each quarter. (5) The *captain's gig* frequently forms one of the quarter boats. Reference may here be made to the following heads: *Barge*, *Coble*, *Fly-boat*, *Life-boat*, *Paddle-box boat*, under the title *Paddle-wheels*, *Punt*, *Skiff*, *Whale Fisheries*, *Wherry*, and *Yawl*.

*The Sailing Boat*, by H. C. Folkard, is a treatise on the boats of every nation, describing their different forms and varieties, with practical directions for their management.

Mr. Nathan Thompson, of New York, has recently introduced into this country his system of *boat building* by machinery worked by a steam engine.

BOAT BUOY, for giving increased buoyancy to any kind of boat. See *Life-Boat*, 3.

BOAT'S CHOCKS (*Fr.* Chantiers d'embarcation). Clamps of wood for a boat resting upon when stowed on a vessel's deck.

BOAT HIRE. The charge for the use of a boat.

BOAT HOOK. A well known instrument, consisting of a pole with its end fitted into an iron socket, which has two prongs formed upon it, the one straight, and the other hooked. This is used in a boat, or in the rafting of timber, for pushing off from and holding on by anything.

BOAT'S GRIPES. Bars of iron with lanyards, rings, and hooks, whereby a boat is lashed to the ring-bolts in a vessel's deck. See *Gripes*.

BOAT LOWERING APPARATUS. Among the many inventions for lowering a ship's boat into the water the first and most successful is Clifford's Boat Lowering Apparatus.

'By this one of the crew in the boat can, by one act, instantly and safely, unlash from the ship's side, lower evenly, and entirely disengage a boat when laden with any number of persons, and when the ship is moving rapidly through the water. The principal other inventions of the kind have been by Messrs. Lacon, Russell, Jefferys, Cornish, Gladstone, Webb, Clarke, Watson, Taylor, Kynaston, and Wood and Rogers. The first three of these lower the boat with pendants by machinery in the ship, and when it is near the water detach both ends of the boat simultaneously, whilst all the others lower the boat by the falls as heretofore and detach it in like manner though with differently designed apparatus, on the principle of the ordinary slip hooks or stoppers, and provide no means for preventing the descent of one end of the boat before the other; and all require two or more men in the ship for lowering, and one or more men in the boat for disengaging it; but in Clifford's to unlash the boat, to lower it down evenly end by end, so that it cannot cant, and to disengage it entirely from the ship, are the simple act of one man in the boat.'

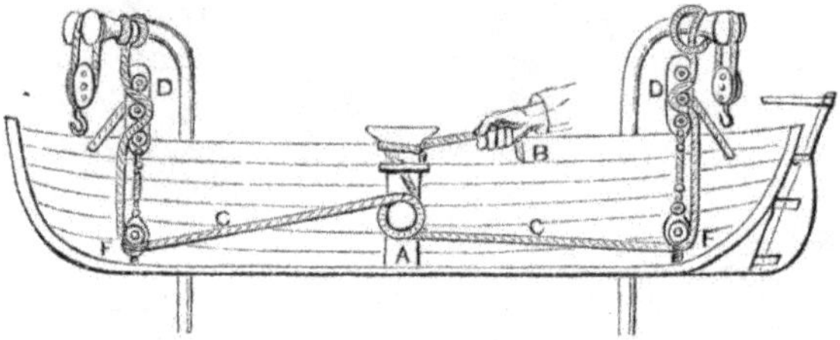


SIDE VIEW.

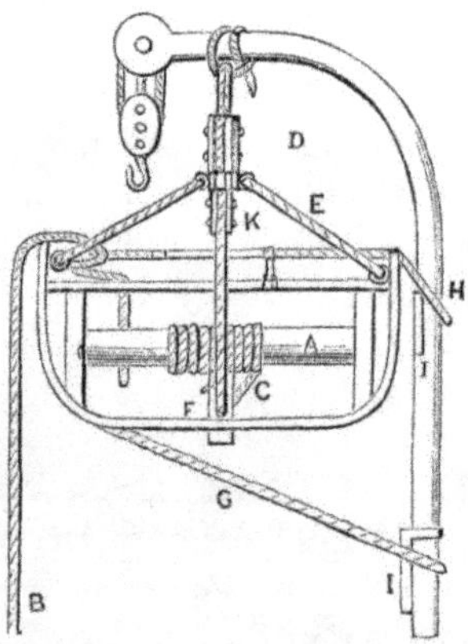


CROSS VIEW.

On slacking off the lowering line B, the roller A revolves, and the pendants CC are unwound evenly as the boat descends into the water, when the pendants being tapered at the ends, overhaul themselves, and the boat is perfectly free. The controlling power is obtained by the blocks DD, which act like a sailor's 'turn and a half' in the boat on each pendant: the *nip* of the blocks exists only when they sustain the weight of the boat, and ceases when it reaches the water. This power in the block to decrease the weight of the boat, and thus enabling the man attending the lowering line

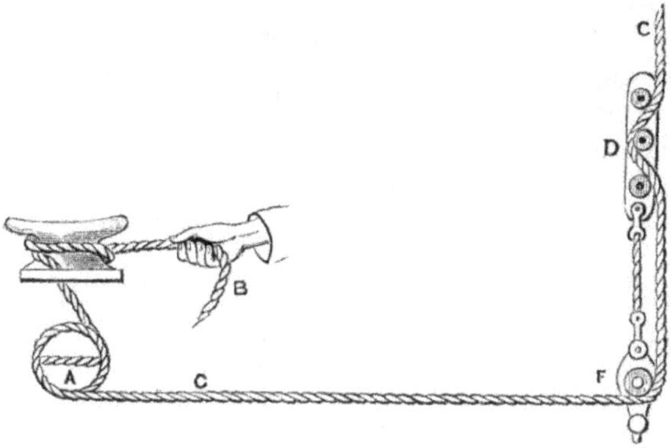


DESCRIPTION OF THE PLATES.

A, Roller on which pendants are wound.
B, Lowering line, which is slacked off when lowering.
C, Pendants.
D, Three-sheave block, the *nip* giving controlling power.
E, Steadying lines, to prevent the boat from canting.
F, Single block on keel, taking the weight of the boat.
G, Boat's gripes in two parts.
H, Thimbles at each end of gripes, which pass down prongs.
I, Prongs down which the thimbles pass as the boat is lowered.
K, Lanyard for setting up gripes.

to control the descent, whatever the weight may be, but yet allowing all to run free the moment the lowering line is let go, is its chief feature, and that which befits it for the purpose to which it is here applied, and for which it was specially designed.

INSTRUCTIONS FOR LOWERING. One of the boat's crew takes charge of the lowering line B, and with one round turn on the cleet, slackens it off slowly. The lashings release themselves by the thimbles passing down the prongs H. When the boat reaches the water, the lowering line is let go, the pendants overhaul themselves, and the boat is perfectly free.

Thus by this one simple act of the one man, the boat is unlashed, lowered, and released from the ship.

BOATMAN. A sailor having charge of a boat.

BOAT-SKIDS. See *Skids*.

BOAT-SLINGS. See *Slings*.

BOATILA. A flat-bottomed boat of the Gulf of Manar. The stern is very sharp, the stem curved.

BOATSWAIN. An officer who has charge of a ship's cordage, rigging, anchors, &c., and calls or 'pipes' the crew to their different duties,

BOBSTAY (*Fr.* Sous-barbe). A chain (formerly a rope) used to confine a vessel's bowsprit down upon or towards the stem or cutwater, counteracting the upward strain of the stays. The upper end of the bobstay is attached to the bowsprit by a hoop or 'collar' of iron, and the lower end to the stem by means of iron plates termed the ***bobstay plates.*** Most vessels of war, however, still use rope bobstays, (those of chain having been found to spring the bowsprits of large ships on the upper part) the upper end of the bobstay and the iron collar having each a heart or dead eye attached to it, with a lanyard rove through them for setting up the bobstay. (Plates III., IV., and V.)

BODY-PLAN and BODIES. See *Shipbuilding*, 5.

BODY POST. An additional stern post introduced at the fore part of an aperture cut in the dead wood in a ship fitted with a screw propeller. (*Fincham's Outlines of Naval Architecture.*)

BOILER OF A MARINE ENGINE. See description of *Steam Engine*, Sect. 37, &c.

BOLD. A bold *shore* is one which rises abruptly from the margin of the water. It generally indicates that the shore is 'steep-to.'

BOLLARDS, or BOLLARD-HEADS. A name given to stancheons, the heads of which project above the rail of the ship

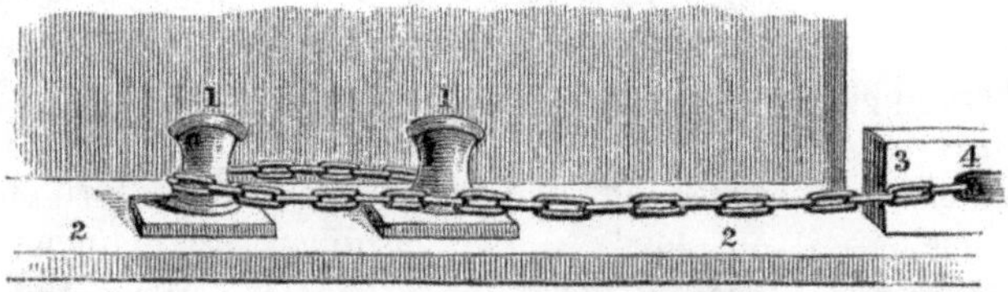


BOLLARD HEADS IN A SHIP OF WAR.

so much as to allow ropes to be made fast to them. See also *Billet-Head.*

BOLSTERS. Pieces of soft wood clothed with tarred canvass, placed on the trestle-trees for the eyes of the shrouds and back-stays to rest upon. See also *Hawse bolsters.*

BOLT. To fasten any parts of a vessel together by means of bolts. See *Copper-fastened.*

BOLTS (*Fr.* Chevilles, Boulons). Cylindrical bars of iron or copper, which are used to fasten pieces of timber, &c., together: *square* bolts also are often used in Shipbuilding to fasten the frames together for their better security, while being laid on the keel. See *Mastre.*

1. Workmen have sometimes a custom of dipping the ends of bolts into tar to make them drive more freely. As tar is injurious to the bolts, oil should rather be used for this purpose.

2. All BUTT-BOLTS, that is, bolts driven into the butt-ends of the planking, 'ought to be cut and properly headed in the smithy. A safe and substantial head cannot be formed in driving the bolt.' This remark is not applicable to through copper bolts.

3. BARB-BOLTS. The same as *Rag-pointed Bolts.*

4. CHANNEL-BOLTS or CHAIN-BOLTS. See *Chain Plates.*

5. CLINCH-BOLT. A bolt that is clinched by means of a ring, or an iron plate, at its point.

6. COPPER-BOLTS. See *Copper-fastened.*

7. DRIFT-BOLTS are commonly made of steel; they are used for driving out other bolts.

8. DUMP-BOLT. A short bolt driven into the plank and timber, as a partial security, previous to the through fastenings being put in. The *butt-ends* of the outside planking should have at least one through bolt in each.

9. EYE-BOLTS are bolts which have an *eye* or opening in one end. They are fixed in various parts of a vessel's hull for hooking tackles and fastening ropes to.

10. RAG-POINTED BOLTS, RAG-BOLTS, or BARB-BOLTS, are such as have their points jagged or barbed, to make them hold the more securely: these are used chiefly where common bolts could not be clinched. Dump-Bolts are sometimes rag-pointed.

11. RING-BOLTS have an iron ring of about three, four, or five inches in diameter, passing through an eye or opening in one end of the bolt. In Shipbuilding, they are used with the wrain-staff in the ring, for setting to the planks. A few ring-bolts are fixed in the ship's deck for lashing the boats, &c.; in ships of war, span-shackle bolts are used for this purpose.

12. SAUCER-HEAD-BOLTS are bolts with very flat heads.

SPAN-SHACKLE-BOLTS. See *Span Shackle.*

THROAT-BOLTS. See *Throat.*

THROUGH-BOLTS. See *Through.*

BOLT-ROPES. Ropes sewed round the edges of a sail. The bolt-rope along each of its sides is called the *leach-rope*; that on the upper edge, the *head-rope*; and that on the lower edge, the *foot-rope.*

BOLT-STRAKE, in Shipbuilding, a name sometimes given to certain strakes of plank which the beam fastenings pass through.

BOMB, or BOMB-SHELL, now called simply *Shell* (*Fr.* Bombe). A hollow iron ball or shell filled with gunpowder, having a vent or fuze-hole into which a fuzee is fitted to set the powder on fire after the shell is thrown out of a mortar. This destructive missile is intended to do injury both by its force in falling, and by bursting after it falls.

BOMB-BEDS. See *Bed.*

BOMB-SHELL. See *Bomb.*

BOMB-VESSEL (now called *Mortar-Vessel*). A ship of war fitted for firing shells from mortars. It is strongly fortified to withstand the shocks of the mortars when throwing shells. In our navy steam-ships are now sometimes employed in this way as being peculiarly suitable for the purpose.

BOMBARD (*Fr.* Bombarder). To attack a town or fortress, whether from land or sea, by firing bombs into it. This mode of attack is termed BOMBARDMENT.

BONNET. An additional piece of canvass made to lace on to the foot of a sail. An additional piece of canvass laced to the bonnet gets the name of a *Drabler.*

BOOANGA. A Malay vessel, having sometimes as many as three banks of oars besides those pulled by the men, who are seated on a kind of raft on each side, forming part of the double outrigger with which the vessel is fitted. (*Dict. de Marine à voiles.*)

BOOBY HATCH. See *Hatch.*

BOOM (*Fr.* Bome). A spar used to extend the foot of a fore-and-aft sail, or of a studding sail. See *Swinging-boom.* The *Bentick-boom* is that which stretches the foot of the foresail in colliers and many small square-rigged Merchant vessels. Other booms, such as the *Driver-boom* (or *Spanker-boom*), the *Jib-boom*, *Studding-sail-booms*, &c., are named respectively after the sails for which they are used. The *Main-boom* is that which stretches the foot of the mainsail in a fore-and-aft rigged vessel. (Plates III., IV., and V).

Boom is also the name for a strong beam stretched across the mouth of a river, or the entrance of a harbour, in order to secure it against the approach of an enemy. A cable is sometimes used for this purpose. See also *Fire-booms* and *Guess-warp-boom.*

BOOM-IRONS. Iron rings on a vessel's yards, through which the studding-sail booms traverse.

BOOM-MAINSAIL. The mainsail of a fore-and-aft rigged vessel, so called from being spread by the main boom. See *Main.*

BOOMS. A space in a vessel's waist, set apart for the boats and spare spars.

BOOPAA. A small canoe with a single outrigger, of the neighbourhood of Tongatabou. (*Dict. de Marine à voiles.*)

BOOT-TOPPING. A term formerly used to denote the scraping a ship's bottom, or that part of it near the surface of the water, and paying it over with a mixture of tallow, sulphur, rosin, &c., as a temporary protection to the plank from worms.

The term is now used to signify the sheathing a vessel's outside planking with wood from the termination of the copper fastenings of the bottom, or beginning of the iron fastenings to a height sufficient to protect the iron fastenings of the wales. By means of boot-topping which is put on over felt, the metal sheathing may be carried to any required height.

BORE. A great rush of water in a river or tideway.

BORE, in Gunnery. See *Gun.*

BORROW. When a vessel is sailing through a channel, she is said to 'borrow' if she diverges a certain distance towards either side in order to save tacking, or for some other purpose. A vessel may get ashore by *borrowing* too much. The term is sometimes also applied to sailing very close to the wind.

BOTH SHEETS AFT, expressed of a square-rigged vessel, implies that the yards are squared, and the ship is running before the wind.

BOTTOM (*Fr.* Fond). The ground under the water.

BOTTOM *of a ship.* That part which is below the wales. (Plate II. fig. 6.) Hence the term *bottom* is applied to denote the ship itself; thus, we speak of goods imported or exported in foreign bottoms, that is, in foreign ships.

In like manner, the *bottom of a boat* is that part of her which is below water.

BOTTOM-PLANK. See *Strake.*

BOTTOMRY (*Fr.* Bomerie, Contrat à la Grosse). The contract of bottomry, which is always in writing, commonly in the form of a bond, is one whereby a ship is pledged in security of money advanced for the purposes of her voyage; a high rate of interest, termed *Maritime Interest*, or *Bottomry Premium*, being charged, under the stipulation that if the ship be lost, the lender shall lose his whole money, including this premium, but that, if she reach her intended port in safety, the ship, or the ship, freight, and cargo, as well as the person of the borrower, shall be liable for the money lent, and for the maritime interest thereon. Where the master of the ship is the borrower, the owner is not personally liable to the lender. It is only in cases of necessity, where the master cannot communicate with the owners, and has no means of obtaining funds on their personal credit to enable a ship to complete her voyage, that the master has power to borrow money on bottomry.

BOUND. Destined. *Outward Bound* is expressed of a vessel destined for a foreign port. *Homeward Bound*, of one returning to the country to which she belongs. A vessel leaving any port is *outward bound* in contradistinction from those coming to it, which are *inward bound*. See also *Ice Bound*, and *Wind Bound*.

BOW (*Fr.* Devant). The fore end of a ship or of a boat. We speak of the starboard and larboard bows, the weather and lee bows.

ON THE BOW. See *Bearing*.

BOW-BY. When a vessel is in stays, the helm being a-lee and it has not sufficient power to bring her round, so that the ship's head falls away back again off the wind, she is said to be bow-by, or to fall bow-by.

BOW-CHASERS. See *Chase*.

BOW-FAST. See *Fast*.

BOW-GRACE. 'A frame of old rope or junk laid round the bows, stern, and sides of a vessel, as a fender to prevent her being injured by ice.'

BOW-LOG TIMBERS. A local name given, in Ireland, to the hawse-wood.

BOW-MAN. (See *Oar*.)

BOW-TIMBERS. See *Timbers*.

BOWER. An abbreviation for Bower Anchor. See *Anchor*, 6.

BOWLINE (*Fr.* Bouline). A rope fastened by a cringle to the bowline-bridles near the middle of the leach of a square sail, and rove through a block fixed at some convenient part before the sail; it is used to hold the leach well out and steady, when sailing close hauled, in order to enable the ship to keep near the wind. Hence, she is said to *stand on a bowline*, or *on a taut bowline*, when close-hauled.

BOWLINE-BRIDLES. Spans of rope attached to the leach of a square sail; to which, as already explained, the bowline is made fast.

BOWLINE-KNOT (*Fr.* Nœud de bouline), and BOWLINE ON A BIGHT. See *Knot.*

BOWSE (pronounced *bowce*). To pull upon a tackle.

BOWSPRIT (*Fr.* Beaupré). A large and strong spar which runs out from a vessel's bow: to this all the stays of the fore-mast are secured, except in sloops and schooners whose fore-stay is secured to the stem-head. (See *Partners.*) It also supports, by means of the *Bowsprit-Cap* and *Bowsprit-Heart*, the jibboom which runs out over its top. (Plates III., IV., and V.)

*A standing bowsprit* is one that is fixed permanently in its place; *a running bowsprit* (used for sloops and smacks) is one that can be eased in like a jibboom.

BOWSPRIT-BITTS. See *Partners.*

BOWSPRIT-CAP. See *Crance.*

BOWSPRIT-HEART. See *Heart.*

BOWSPRIT-HORSES. Ridge-Ropes.

BOWSPRIT-NETTING. See *Netting.*

BOWSPRIT-RACK, or BOWSPRIT-RAIL. 'The pin-rail, or -rack, over the bowsprit, for belaying the running gear about the bowsprit.'

BOWSPRIT-SHROUDS. Strong ropes leading from nearly the outer end of the bowsprit to the luff of the bow, to support and strengthen the bowsprit. We may here notice that the ropes used in a similar way for the jibboom are termed *Jib-guys*, (Plates III., IV., and V.)

BOX THE COMPASS. To repeat the 32 points of the compass in their order.

BOX-HAULING, or BOXING A VESSEL OFF, is performed by bracing to the head-yards, that is, hauling in their weather braces, until the head sails are brought aback and by their operation pay the ship's head off to leeward when she would not otherwise answer the weather-helm. It is further explained in *Seamanship by Lieut. Nares*, page 157.

BOXING. See preceding article, and *Dowells.*

'THE BOXING OF THE STEM is the part where the stem is joined to the fore end of the keel by a side scarph of a peculiar form.' The stem is said to be *boxed* into the keel when so united with it. It is said to be *stepped* upon or into the keel when it is connected with the top of the keel by a tenon or dowell.

BRACES, or RIDERS, in Shipbuilding, strops of iron which are used to bind a vessel efficiently; such as those which are bolted to the ship's sides over the ceiling, and reach from the heads of the floors to the clamps of the lower deck between the hold-beams, or else are connected with the hanging knees of these beams. Of the various methods of placing iron knees or braces in a ship's hold in order to obtain the greatest binding and security, Mr. Brisbane recommends the following: that they should be put on vertically along the whole range of the floor in midships, with their tails running down so as to get at least one bolt into the floor timber and diagonally only on a few of the foremost and aftermost beams, with their tails running forward and aft respectively, the effects of the pitching motion being most felt in these places, as the rolling motion is most felt along the middle of the ship. See also *Trussing (Diagonal)* and *Rudder Bands.*

Braces also denote ropes by which yards are turned about to trim the sails to the wind. They are fastened to, or rove through blocks at, the yard-arms. (Plates III., IV., and V.)

*To brace a yard* (*Fr.* Brasser). To turn it about horizontally by means of the braces.

*To counter-brace the yards,* means to brace a vessel's head yards one way and the after yards another.

BRACE-ABACK. To brace the yards so as to lay the sails aback.

BRACE-ABOUT. To brace the yards round in any direction, either for the purpose of tacking, or in consequence of a change of wind.

BRACE-BY. To brace the yards in contrary directions to each other on the different masts, which has the effect of stopping the vessel.

BRACE-PENDANTS. See *Pendants.*

BRACE-ROUND. The same as *Brace-About.*

BRACE-SHARP. The same as *Brace-Up.*

BRACE-TO. To brace the head yards a little aback by easing off the lee braces and hauling in the weather ones, in order to assist the motion of the ship's head in tacking.

BRACE-UP, or *Brace sharp up*. To lay the yards more fore and aft, by easing off the weather braces and hauling up the lee braces; which makes the ship sail closer to the wind.

BRACKETS. Short triangular pieces of wood or metal fixed under anything as supports. They are sometimes plain, sometimes ornamented with scrolls.

BRAGOZO. An open fishing-boat of the Adriatic, carrying two masts with lug sails.

BRAILS (*Fr.* Cargues). Ropes made fast to the outer leach of a fore and aft sail, and passing through leading blocks on the mast or gaff down to the deck, to assist in taking in the sail.

The stowing of a *jib* at sea is frequently attended with much danger; and brails (for spilling it during this process) have been introduced into some vessels; they are made fast to the head of the jib and are led down through a lizard sewed about the middle of each side of the sail and through blocks fixed to the jibboom. These deserve to be strongly recommended for general adoption. See *Traveller (Jib)*.

*To brail up a sail*, means to haul it in by means of the brails.

THROAT-BRAILS. See *Throat.*

BRAKE. See *Pump.*

BRANCH PILOT. See *Pilot.*

BREACH. The sea is said to *make a breach* over a vessel when a wave breaks over her.

BREAD-ROOM. A place parted off below-deck for containing bread or biscuit. It should be lined with tin or some similar metal in order to exclude vermin. In a ship of war, the bread room is in the lowest and aftermost part of the ship.

BREADTH (*Fr.* Largeur). See *Shipbuilding* 6, and *Straight of Breadth.*

BREAK, in Shipbuilding, any sudden termination and rise of a deck, such as the termination of the main deck, in some merchant vessels, where the quarter deck commences.

BREAK-BEAMS. See *Beams*, 2.

BREAK-BULK (*Fr.* Désarrimer). To begin to unload a vessel. See *Bulk.*

BREAK-GROUND. To weigh anchor in order to quit any place.

BREAK-SHEER (*Fr.* Embarder). To swerve from the proper direction in which a vessel should be when at anchor. (*Darcy Lever.*) Thus 'when a ship is riding at anchor with the tide setting to windward, the wind blowing on one of the quarters, and the vessel being sheered by the helm either to windward or leeward of her anchor — in such a case she is said to *break sheer* if any change in the strength of the wind or tide should have the effect of bringing the ship round with the wind on the other quarter, and forcing her to the opposite side of her anchor; which is frequently the means of fouling it.'

BREAKAGE, in speaking of the stowage of a vessel, implies the leaving of empty spaces.

In Marine Insurance, the term *Breakage* alludes to damage occurring to goods by breaking.

BREAKWATER. Some erection or object sunk at the entrance of a harbour, or any projection from the land into the sea — as a mole, pier, or jetty — so placed at the entrance, that it may break the force of the waves as they roll inwards. Reference may here be made to the *Parliamentary Report on Floating Breakwaters.*

BREAKER (SHIP). See *Ship-Breaker.*

BREAKERS (*Fr.* Brisants). Billows that break in foam over rocks or sand-banks rising nearly to the surface of the sea.

BREAKERS. Small casks used for bringing water aboard in boats. They are often made of an oval shape in order to stow snugly in a boat. GANG-CASKS are of a larger size, and are used for the like purposes.

BREAM. To clean a vessel's bottom by burning off the filth, &c., and sweeping it with a broom.

BREAST-BEAMS. See *Beams*, 3.

BREAST-FAST. See *Fast.*

BREAST-HOOKS (*Fr.* Guirlandes). Large crooked pieces of timber bolted horizontally athwart a vessel's bow inside, connecting the stem and the timbers and planks of the bow, and thus binding the sides of the ship together forward, as the transoms secure them abaft. In very sharp vessels, where wood cannot be made available, the breast-hooks are wholly of iron. The breast-hook whereon the ends of the upper deck rest is called the *Deck-Hook*; and that which crosses the hawse-timber above this deck gets the name of a *Dowsing-Chock*, or *Hawse-Hook.* (Plate IV. 12.)

BREAST-RAIL. See *Breast-work.*

BREAST-ROPE. A rope put round a man in the chains while sounding.

BREAST-WORK, or BREAST-RAIL A railing in front of the quarter-deck, or at the after part of the forecastle-deck. The term is but seldom used in the merchant service.

BREECH (*Fr.* Culasse). The angular part *of knee timber.* The solid part *of a gun* behind the bore. See *Gun.*

BREECHING. A rope used to check the recoil of a gun in time of action; and also to lash it when housed during the course of a voyage.

BREECH-LOADING GUN. A gun which is loaded at the breech instead of at the muzzle. See *Gun* (*Armstrong*).

BREEZE (*Fr.* Brise) commonly denotes a gentle wind : but this term is more specially applied to a kind of alternating winds generally experienced in settled weather upon coasts or islands situated between the tropics, occasioned by the action of the sun raising the temperature of the land above that of the sea. *The land breeze* is a current of air which draws off the land during the night; while it lasts, it is very dangerous to sleep in the open air in these hot climates. *The sea breeze* is one which during the day sets from the sea towards the shore. They prevail during the fair season with remarkable regularity on the Malabar coast. Breezes of this description, particularly *sea breezes,* occur also in the temporate zones during summer. (*Horsburgh's India Directory.*)

See *Fanning Breeze* and *Fresh Breeze.*

BRIDGE, or BRIDGE-BOARD. See *Gangway.*

BRIDGE (FLOATING). See *Floating Bridge.*

BRIDLES. See *Bowline-Bridles,* and *Towing-Bridle.*

The bridle *of moorings* is the chain or cable connecting the two mooring anchors, having a swivel in its middle to which the chain is made fast. *Mooring-Brdle* also denotes the two parts of the mooring chain or rope taken on board through the hawse-holes or on each bow, having usually a swivel at its bight where it is connected with the ring of the buoy or moorings by which the vessel is secured.

BRIDLE-PORT. See *Ports.*

BRIG (*Fr.* Brig). A square-rigged vessel with two masts. (Plate IV.)

¶. *A Brig* bends her fore and aft mainsail (or, as it is called, her *trysail* or *boom mainsail*) to the mainmast, while a *Snow* bends it to a trysail mast: in other respects these two vessels are alike.

2. A *Brigantine* properly signifies a brig without her square mainsail. The term *Brigantine* is now applied to what have been hitherto called *square-rigged schooners*, or *hermaphrodite brigs* (*Fr.* Brigs goëlettes), having the foremast rigged as a brig's, and the mainmast rigged as a schooner's. See *Cutter*.

BRIGANTINE. See *Brig*, 2.

BRINE GAUGE. An instrument for indicating the density of brine in the boilers of marine steam engines. See *Salinometer* and *Steam Engine*, Sect. 45.

BRINE PUMPS (*Fr.* Pompes de saumure). See description of *Steam Engine*, Sect. 45.

BRING BY THE LEE (*Fr.* Empanner). The following distinct explanation of this phrase is given in *Seamanship both in Theory and Practice*:—'Suppose a ship under great sail to be steering south, having the wind NNW.; then, west is the weather side; east, the lee side. Now if by any accident her head be turned round to the westward, so that her sails are all taken aback on the weather side, she is said to *Broach-to*, but if, on the contrary, her head decline so far eastward as to lay her sails aback on that side which was the lee side, it is termed *Bringing by the Lee*.'

BRING TO, or HEAVE TO. To adjust a vessel's sails so as to counteract each other, and thus stop her progress. See *Round to*.

BRING UP, or *To bring a vessel up*, is the same as to cast anchor.

BRISBANE'S BOAT BUOYING, or LIFE BOAT APPARATUS. See *Life-Boat*, 3.

BROACH-TO. See *Bring by the Lee*.

BROAD PENDANT. See *Pendant*.

BROAD-SIDE. The whole side of a vessel. In reference to a naval engagement it signifies a simultaneous discharge of all the guns on one side of a ship of war. See also *End on*.

BROKEN-BACKED. The same as HOGGED. The former term, however, seems more properly applicable to the case of a vessel which not only droops at each end, but whose keel and keelson are consequently broken.

BROKERS (*Fr.* Courtiers. Courtiers maritimes). SHIP BROKERS are persons who undertake the management of business matters between shipowners and merchants, in the way of procuring cargoes and charters for vessels, entering and clearing them at the custom house, collecting freights, &c. Ship brokers very generally act also as INSURANCE BROKERS, in which capacity they get policies of marine insurance effected for their employers, and attend to the recovery of claims under these policies. The merchants or shipowners for whom such insurances or charters are negociated, 'look to the broker for the regularity of the contract, and for a proper selection of responsible underwriters: to him, also, the underwriters look for a fair and candid disclosure of all material circumstances affecting the risk, and for payment of the premiums of insurance.' (*Marshall on Insurance.*)

BROWS. See *Stages.*

BRUSH ICE. See *Iceberg*, 4.

BUCCANEERS (*Fr.* Boucanniers). A name originally given to the piratical adventurers who united together against the Spaniards in America; it has also been applied to denote 'sea rovers' or pirates.

BUCKETS are used on board of ships for washing the decks and for other purposes. They get the name of *wash-deck buckets.*

FIRE-BUCKETS are buckets used on board of ships of war in case of fire, and in time of action for holding the fighting lanterns, and for carrying powder.

BUCKET VALVE *of Air Pump.* See description of *Steam Engine*, Sect. 16.

BUCKLERS. 'Pieces of wood fitted inside a ship's bows in the way of the hawse-holes, to prevent water from rushing in. They are of two kinds: the one termed *Riding Bucklers*, used when the cable is bent, are in two pieces, which, when placed in contact, have an aperture of sufficient size to fit as closely as possible to the chain or rope cable: the other kind, termed *Blind Bucklers*, which have no aperture, are usually fitted in the form of strong shutters attached to the inside of the bows under the hawse-holes, so that, when turned up, they may completely close the hawse-holes, and are secured inside by a strong bar of wood or iron, to prevent the sea forcing them open.

'Bucklers are used instead of hawse-plugs in ships of war and large merchantmen.'

BUGLA. A particular kind of merchant vessel trading between Bombay and the Persian Gulf.

BUILT is compounded with other terms to imply the distinguishing form or construction of a vessel, as *Frigate-built*, *Carvel-built*, &c.

*A built* (or *made*) mast, or block, means one which is composed of several pieces. The lower masts of large ships are *built*, but small vessels have their lower as well as their upper masts formed of whole spars.

BULGE. Bilge.

BULK. The whole of a vessel's cargo when stowed.

Goods are said to be *stowed in bulk*, when they are stowed loose instead of being packed in casks, bags, or the like.

Break Bulk (*Fr.* Désarrimer). To begin to unload a vessel. If after the arrival of any ship within a certain distance of the coast of the United Kingdom, any alteration be made in the stowage of the cargo so as to facilitate the unloading of any portion of it, or if any part of it be staved, destroyed or thrown overboard, (except, it would seem proper to add, in the case of jettison,) or if any package of the cargo be opened, such ship is considered as having *broken bulk*. This is prohibited under heavy penalties until the vessel be duly reported and entry of the goods made at the Custom-house.

BULKER. A person employed to measure the capacity of goods, in order to ascertain the amount of freight or port dues chargeable against them.

BULKHEAD, or BULKSHEAD (*Fr.* Cloison). A partition; in particular, the boarding which separates one part or cabin of a vessel from another. In a merchant vessel, the *fore bulkhead* separates the forecastle, the *after bulkhead* separates the cabin, from the hold.

Some vessels, especially those which are built of iron, are divided into compartments by athwart ship water-tight bulkheads, so that a leak sprung in any compartment may not communicate with the rest of the ship. These bulkheads, in order to resist the pressure of the water, should increase in strength in proportion to their depth below the surface of the water. They tend to strengthen the vessel, and of late years are deservedly coming into more general use. There have been special statutory regulations now enacted as to steamers being provided with water-tight bulkheads, which are also required by the rules of Lloyd's Register of British and Foreign Shipping.

The mode of fitting bulkheads in iron ships is explained and illustrated in *Grantham on Iron Shipbuilding*, page 48.

Mr. Grantham states that 'water-tight bulkheads have been for ages in use in China.'

Bulkheads are also temporarily used to prevent any cargo, such as grain in bulk, from shifting in a vessel's hold.

See also *Screen-Bulkheads.*

BULL'S EYE. A species of block formed of a piece of stout wood having a hole in the centre, without any sheave, for a small stay or rope to reeve through; it has a groove round it for the strop, which is sometimes of iron.

Also, a round piece of thick glass convex on one side, inserted into the decks, ports, scuttle hatches, or skylight covers of a vessel for the purpose of admitting light. Instead of bull's eyes, patent glasses of a rectangular form are now in common use.

BULWARKS, or BERTHING (*Fr.* Pavois). A fencing of boards nailed round a vessel on the outside of the stanchions and timber heads above the level of the decks. See *Quarter-boards, Rail,* and *Waist-boards* (Plate IV. 24, 35.)

BULWARK-NETTING. See *Netting.*

BUM-BOATS. Boats of provision dealers, &c., which come alongside of ships in port, not moored at a quay or other landing place.

BUMPKIN. A short boom of wood or iron projecting from each side of the bow of a square-rigged vessel, used to extend the clue of the foresail to windward, or (in nautical phrase) to board the fore tack to. There are, in like manner, bumpkins projecting over the quarters with blocks at their outer ends to reeve the main braces through.

BUNT. The middle of a square sail, more particularly when furled to the yard.

*To bunt a sail,* means to haul it up to the yard and stow the middle part of it

BUNT-GASKET. See *Gasket.*

BUNTINE, or BUNTING. A kind of thin woollen cloth whereof a ship's colours and signals are usually made.

BUNTLINES. Ropes fastened to the foot ropes of square sails to draw them up to the middle of the yards, for facility in furling.

*In Darcy Lever's Young Sea Officer's Sheet Anchor,* the following judicious observation occurs, 'As many coasting vessels have no buntlines to their top-gallant sails, it would be well if the necessity of carrying them were strongly enforced: because, when it blows fresh, these sails (generally left to the management of boys) are very heavy to hand; and if there be no buntlines to spill them, the result may be fatal to those on the yard arm by the sails blowing over to leeward.'

BUNTLINE CLOTH. A piece of cloth sewed upon a sail to keep the buntlines from chafing the sail. See *Lining*.

BUOY (*Fr.* Bouée). A floating cask, or block of wood, attached by a rope called the BUOY-ROPE to an anchor, in order to show its position after being cast. The buoy-rope is made fast to the anchor by a small chain called the BUOY-CHAIN, which prevents the rope from being chafed by friction on the anchor. The rope should be of sufficient strength to weigh the anchor in case of need. See *Strop*.

1. When it is found necessary to slip a cable, a buoy and buoy-rope are, if possible, bent to the chain outside the hawse-hole, before slipping.

2. Buoys are also floated over dangerous banks, shallows, or other obstructions to navigation, in order to warn vessels off.

3. *To stream a buoy* means to let it drop into the water previously to casting anchor. *A buoy is said to watch* so long as it appears on the surface of the water.

4. BELL-BUOY. A kind of large can-buoy (or a kind of pontoon almost level with the water and having its bottom in the form of a cone), whereon is placed a lofty erection of iron wicker work, containing a bell which has several tongues to sound it by means of the heaving of the sea. The tongues are suspended outside of the bell from two beams fitted above it, at right angles to each other. Not only is this contrivance valuable as a signal, during foggy weather, to warn vessels from off the bank or other obstruction over or in the way of which the buoy is placed, but in some of these machines, above the bell there is a large chamber formed also of iron wicker-work, which can be entered by means of ladders within the receptacle for the bell, and is intended as a temporary place of safety for shipwrecked mariners.

5. BOAT-BUOYS. For giving increased buoyancy to any kind of boat. See *Life-Boat*.

6. CAN-BUOYS, or more properly, *Cone-buoys*, from their being shaped like a cone, are generally of a very large size; they are used chiefly for being placed over banks, or any other object which obstructs the navigation.

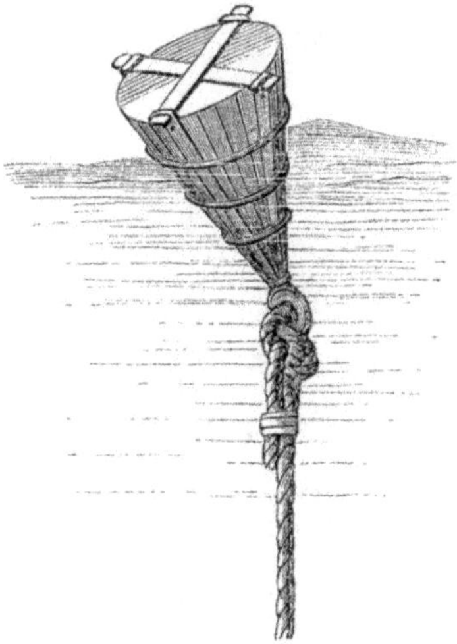

CAN-BUOY.

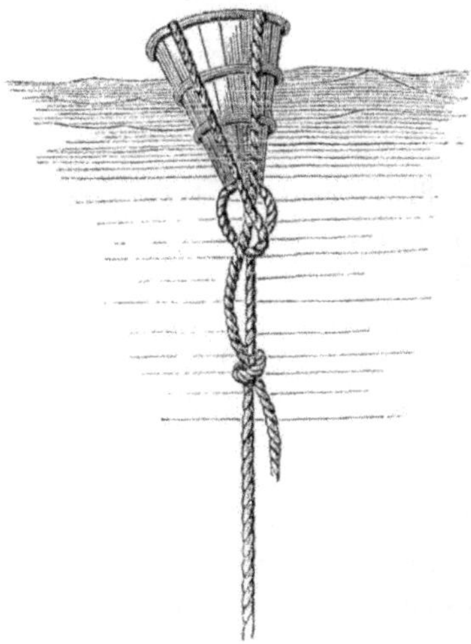

CAN-BUOY WITH ROPE STROPS.

7. NUN-BUOYS are somewhat in the form of casks, being large in the middle and tapering towards each end.

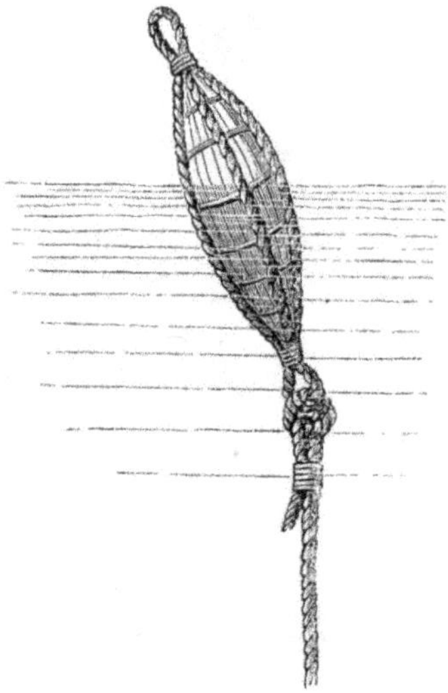

NUN-BUOY.

8. LIFE-BUOYS, which are of various descriptions, are used to throw overboard for a person who has fallen into the water to lay hold of, and for similar purposes.

CARTE'S LIFE-BUOYS, which have long been in general use, are made of solid cork in a circular form.

There are also life-buoys made of gutta percha. Mr. Gladstone, Surveyor to the Board of Trade, has contrived an ingenious improvement on life-buoys, to enable them to be more easily seen after being thrown into the water, consisting simply of a bar of wood pivoting at right angles to the periphery of the buoy, and having a small weight at one end to bring the other end uppermost with a piece of buntine attached to this end, which is thus seen floating above the surface of the water.

9. WOODEN BUOYS are blocks of wood, of various shapes, generally having a bolt through them, with a ring at each extremity. They are sometimes called *Dolphins*.

BUOY-ROPE. See description of *Buoy*.

BURDEN, or BURTHEN (*Fr.* Capacité). The weight which a vessel will carry when loaded to a proper sea trim; it is generally stated in tons. The registered tonnage of a vessel is ascertained by certain fixed rules of measurement, which are noticed under the head *Tonnage*; and we may observe that the number of tons register is usually much less than the ship's burden, except in very sharp vessels.

*A vessel of burden* is a name given generally to any vessel built for the purpose of carrying cargo.

The burden of vessels in the coal trade is very frequently stated in *Keels*.

BURGOO, or LOBLOLLY. A name given by sailors to gruel made of oatmeal, or groats, seasoned with a little salt, butter, and sugar.

BURNETISING. A term applied to the impregnating timber, canvass, or cordage, with the solution of chloride of zinc, as noticed under the title *Dry Rot*.

BURTON. A small tackle formed by several blocks till the rope becomes three or four fold, and acquires additional power in proportion. It is used for many purposes; especially to set up topmast shrouds, whence it has been called a *top-burton-tackle*.

*A single Spanish burton* has three single blocks, or two

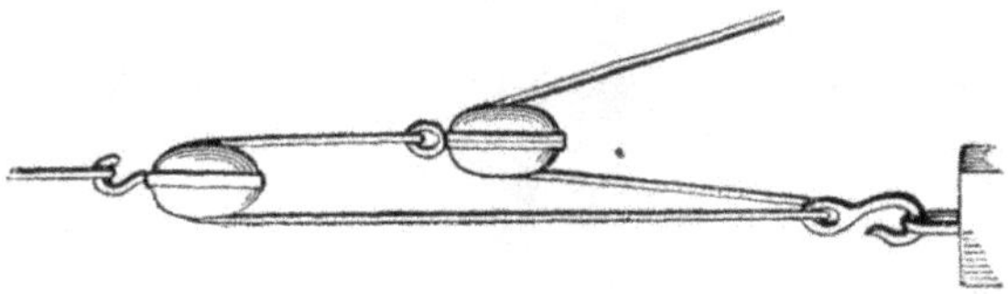

single blocks and a hook fixed to one of the bights of the standing part of the tackle. *A double Spanish burton*, has one double and two single blocks.

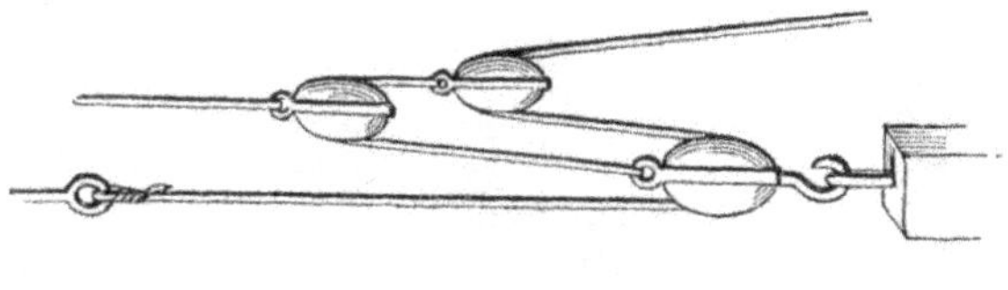

BUSH. A circular piece of metal let into the sheave of a block. The operation of letting it in is called *bushing* or *coaking*.

The bushes in which the crank-shaft, side levers, &c., of a marine engine work, are commonly made of brass, in order to have little friction.

The term BUSHING is also applied to the operation of dove-tailing a piece of metal into the vent of a gun, particularly of a brass one, when the vent has got too large; such a repair is very insufficient.

BUSS. A stout built vessel with two masts, employed in the herring fisheries.

BUTT. The joining of two timbers or planks which unite endways. See *Hook-Scarph.*

When a plank has been loosened at one end, by a vessel's weakness, by labouring, or otherwise, she is said to have *started a butt.*

Planks or pieces of timber which unite endways, are said to *butt* or *abut* against each other; and in like manner, the planks on a vessel's side which run to the stem or to the sternpost, are said to butt against the stem or sternpost respectively.

*Butt* also means the larger end of a tapering piece of timber. Hence the phrase *top and butt.* See *Scuttled Butt.*

BUTT-BOLTS. See *Bolts,* 2, 8.

BUTTOCK. The rounding part of a vessel's after body, under the counter.

BUTTOCK-LINES. Longitudinal curves at the buttock and bow representing the ship's body cut in vertical section.

BUTTON. See *Gun,* 20.

BUXIS. A gratuity (a term used in India).

BUYSE. A fishing vessel of Holland, whereof the bows are very full; it has three short masts, capable of being lowered abaft, rigged with square sails. These vessels are employed chiefly in the herring and mackerel fishing.

BY THE BOARD. A mast falling is said *to go by the board,* when it has given way at or near deck.

BY THE HEAD. If a vessel draws more water forward than aft, she is BY THE HEAD. If her stern be lower in the water than her head, she is BY THE STERN.

BY THE WIND, or FULL AND BY. The same as close-hauled, expressing the situation of a vessel when she keeps as close to the wind as can be done without shaking the sails.

CABIN (*Fr.* Chambre). An apartment for the accommodation of the officers, crew, or passengers, on board of a vessel. This term is sometimes applied to the berths in which they sleep.

Bed-rooms detached from the main cabin or saloon, get the name of *state-rooms.*

CABIN-BOY. A boy employed to serve in the cabin.

CABLE (*Fr.* Cable). A large strong rope, or chain, to hold a vessel when at anchor. Most vessels of this country are now supplied with chain cables: the rope cable being almost entirely out of use except in some foreign vessels. Chains have the advantage of not being liable to chafe by friction; in riding by them, also, the weight of the chain causes it to form a bight or curve which makes it rise and fall easily with the action of the sea upon the ship, and serves to prevent any sudden jerk upon the anchor. See *Chain* and *Hawse.*

*The Stream Cable,* is a hawser or rope used for warping a vessel, or to moor her by means of the stream anchor after coming to anchor in a river or haven. It is the largest of the water-laid ropes of a vessel.

BEND THE CABLE. See *Bend.*

BITT THE CABLE. See *Bitts.*

HEAVE IN THE CABLE, to draw it into the ship by winding about the capstan or windlass.

See *Heave short, Pay out, Range of Cable* and *Slip.*

CABLE BENDS. Two small ropes for lashing the ends of a rope cable to its own part, in order to secure the knot (or *clinch*) by which it is fastened to the anchor-ring.

CABLE-BITTS, or RIDING-BITTS. See *Bitts.*

CABLE-LAID ROPE. A rope formed by three ropes of three strand yarn laid up into one. See *Rope.*

CABLE'S-LENGTH (*Fr.* Encablure). A measure of 120 fathoms — the usual length of a hempen cable.

CABLET. A small rope cable.

CABONIGRO. A species of palm tree, producing a kind of thick fibre used in the Philippine Islands to make cordage somewhat resembling Abaca cordage. (*Dict. de Marine à voiles.*)

CABOOSE. A cast-iron cooking apparatus used on board of vessels. It is also called a *Fire Hearth.* See *Cook-house.*

CADETS (NAVAL). 'The designation of young officers when they first enter the service of the royal navy, and before they become midshipmen.' They are educated in 'training ships' in harbour or at sea. The rules of the Admiralty in regard to naval cadets are contained in Chapter VIII. of the *Queen's Regulations.*

CAIQUE. A small narrow flat-bottomed rowing boat used at Constantinople and neighbouring places. Also, a small vessel of the Levant.

CAISSON, or CAISSOON (*Fr.* Forme flottante). A kind of floating dock made of wood or iron, which is sunk to the required depth by letting water into it. It contains an air receptacle, which allows it to sink only to a certain depth, whereupon it is hauled under the ship's bottom, the entrance is closed, the water pumped out, and the ship, after being steadied upon it by shores or sliding bilge blocks, is by this means completely raised out of the water without leaving her moorings. See *Dock* (*Floating*).

A machine for the above purpose, called a *Screw-dock*, is met with in the United States of America. This apparatus consists of a platform, which is sunk below the water to a sufficient depth, suspended by iron screws from a strong wooden framework; the vessel to be raised is floated over the platform, and, being steadied upon it by means of shores, is lifted high and dry between the frames by the combined power of the lever, wheel and pinion, and screw. There is also a similar machine in use there, called the *Hydraulic-dock*, the platform whereof is suspended by chains which pass through cast-iron pulleys on the top of the framework, and are connected with a hydraulic engine. (*Stevenson's Civil Engineering of North America.*)

*Caisson* also denotes a vessel used instead of gates for a dry dock. It is usually in the form of a ship divided longitudinally, and is fitted with valves or sluices to admit or eject water as may be required, for sinking it in its place to close the entrance, or floating it to open the dock. This gets the name also of a *floating dam.*

CALIBRE *of a Gun.* The diameter of its bore.

CALK. See *Caulk.*

CALL. A pipe or whistle used by the boatswain in a ship to call or 'pipe' the hands to their different duties.

CALLIPERS, used for Shipbuilding purposes, a kind of compasses with bowed legs; at that part of the legs next the joint, where they are straight, there is generally a sword in the form of a quadrant fixed to one and running through the other leg, and it is fitted with a screw to fasten it at any stretch. This instrument is used chiefly in mast making to measure the sizes of different logs or of different parts of the same log. 'Also, an instrument for gauging the diameter of work in the lathe, &c. Engineers' Callipers are of thin steel; they are used for not only ascertaining the external diameter of cylindrical objects, but likewise the internal diameter of holes, &c.

CALM (*Fr.* Calme). *A calm* is a state of stillness in the atmosphere. It is a *dead calm* (*calme plat*) when there is not a breath of wind to inflate a vessel's sails. The wind is said to *fall calm* (*mollir*) when it ceases to blow. The sea is *calm* when its surface is unruffled.

CALM LATITUDES. That tract of the ocean which is situated near the Equator and subject to calms of long continuance. See *Trade Winds.*

CAMBER. In Shipbuilding, a slight arching upwards.

A vessel whose floor is higher at the middle than towards the stem and stern is said to be *cambered.*

*Camber* is also a name given to a small dock in any of the royal dockyards, used for boats and for loading and discharging timber. There is a *Camber dock* at Portsmouth.

CAMBOOSE. See *Caboose.*

CAMEL. A machine which has been used for raising ships in the water in order to enable them to pass over a bar on which there is not so much water as the ship draws. It is made in two separate parts which fit and are made fast to the hull of the ship on each side; in the chambers of the camel there are plugs which, after the vessel has been towed to the bar, are taken out till sufficient water is admitted to sink the ship to the ground. The water is then pumped out, and the camel raises the ship sufficiently in the water. Such is the general description of this machine given by some nautical writers. It seems more probable that the plugs would be taken out in order to admit water into the two parts of the camel and sink them beneath the bilges of the ship, so that, the machine being then made fast to the ship and enclosing it on each side, and the water being pumped out, the camel might act with a force like that of empty casks in raising the ship above the ordinary depth of water which she draws.

The Floating Graving Docks which have to a certain extent been long in use in Scotland, and recently carried out on a more extensive scale in England, are constructed on this principle.

CAMFERING. See *Chamfering.*

CAN-BUOY. A large cone-shaped buoy. See *Buoy*, 6.

CAN-HOOKS, or CAN-HOOK SLINGS. Slings commonly made of rope or chain with flat iron hooks at each end. They are

used for hoisting light casks, the hooks being placed on the chimes of the cask, and the tackle hooked to the centre of the slings.

CANISTER SHOT, or CASE-SHOT. Small balls in a cylindrical case or canister. See *Shot.*

CANNON. See *Gun.*

CANNONADE. In marine affairs *to cannonade* means to keep up a continual discharge of the guns of one or more ships of war against some object intended to be taken or destroyed, and this continued discharge of the guns is termed *a cannonade.*

CANOE. A peculiar kind of boat used by the natives of America and other parts. It is sometimes formed of the trunk of a tree hollowed, and sometimes of one or more pieces of bark, skin, or the like, fastened together.

Some canoes are made to carry sail, but they are commonly rowed with paddles.

CANT. To turn anything over. See also *Flensing.*

CANT-BLOCKS. A name given to large purchase blocks used in ships at the Davis' Straits' Fishing. See *Block,* 1.

CANT-TIMBERS (*Fr.* Coltis). The timbers at the bow and stern of a vessel which stand obliquely to the line of the keel.

CANVASS, or SAIL-CLOTH (*Fr.* Toile). The cloth of which sails are made.

It is generally made 24 inches, sometimes 30 inches, wide, in pieces called *bolts,* varying from 36 to 42, but most commonly 38 to 40, yards in length. A bolt of Navy canvass, which is always of the best quality, is about 40 yards in length. To distinguish the different qualities of canvass, each bolt is numbered, and a bolt 39 yards long and 24 inches in breadth ought to weigh as follows: — No. 1, 46 lbs; No. 2, 43; No. 3, 40; No. 4, 36; No. 5, 33; No. 6, 30; No. 7, 27; No. 8, 25; No. 9, 23; and No. 10, 21 lbs. The two last numbers are not common.

The term *canvass* is used also to denote the sails themselves. Thus, a vessel is said either to have all her sails or all her canvass set. Again, a vessel in motion by means of her sails is said to be *under canvass.*

CAP (*Fr.* Chouquet). A strong thick block of wood with two holes through it, the one square and the other round, used to confine together the head of one mast and the lower end of the mast next above it. When made of iron it is called a *crance* (Plates III. IV. and V.).

*Caps* also denote square pieces of wood laid upon the upper blocks on which a vessel is built to receive the keel.

The term *cap* is also applied to any covering, such as lead, put over the heads of iron bolts, to prevent their being corroded by exposure to the action of water or copper.

BOWSPRIT CAP. See *Crance.*

CAP-SQUARES. Crooked clamps of iron forelocked one on each of the trunnions of a gun, to keep it steady in its carriage at sea.

CAPE. The extremity towards the sea of a high or mountainous promontory. See *Promontory.*

CAPSIZE (*Fr.* Chavirer). To overset.

CAPSTAN, or CAPSTERN (*Fr.* Cabestan). A machine

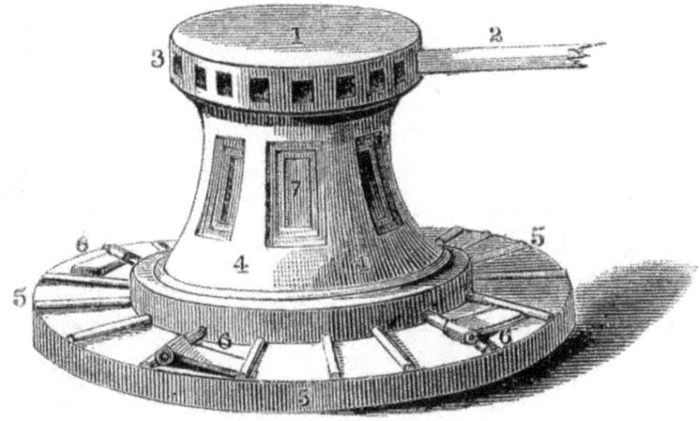


CAPSTAN OF THE 'NORTHUMBERLAND' STEAM SHIP OF WAR, NOW BUILDING (DRAWN FROM MODEL).

1. Capstan head.
2. One of the capstan bars.
3. Holes.
4. Whelps.
5. Pawl rim.
6. Pawls.
7. Barrel of the capstan.

consisting of a cylinder or *barrel,* as it is called, which revolves round a vertical spindle fixed in the deck; the barrel having a broad cylindrical piece of wood, sometimes made of two semi-circular pieces, fixed upon its upper extremity, forming what is termed the *drumhead*, which is pierced with a number of holes to receive the bars or levers, called the *capstan bars*, whereby it is turned round. In many vessels these holes have ornamental plugs fitted into them, which can be unshipped when required. An iron pin is inserted through the drumhead and each of the bars, in order to prevent the latter from flying out during the revolution of the capstan. The spindle is fitted into a block of wood, called the *Step of the capstan*, which is fixed securely between two of the ship's beams.

This machine is used, like a windlass, for weighing the anchor, or generally for a strong purchase in heaving or hoisting. Men-of-war and some large merchant ships weigh their anchors by capstans; other vessels use a windlass. Ships of great burden have often two or more capstans, the *fore capstan*, and the *after* or *main capstan*, &c.

Several capstans of an improved construction are now in use; of these *Brown's Patent Capstan* is one of the best. A *double capstan* is one constructed to be worked both on an upper and lower deck on one shaft.

The following invention, described in the *Dictionnaire de Marine à voiles et à vapeur, par MM. Bonnefoux et Paris*, appears to have been adopted in the French navy. The lower rim of the capstan is furnished with a very strong cast-iron hoop (called after the inventor the *Barbotin* or *Couronne-Barbotin*) having the demi-impressions of the alternate links of a chain-cable indented round its whole periphery, to serve as catches for the chain, which is thereby retained while heaving it in by means of the capstan; the weight of the chain descending into its 'well' being brought to bear so as to keep it close to the capstan rim. The necessity of using a messenger is thereby avoided, and a good deal of time saved in weighing the anchor. But, as in the case of Rendall's Chain Ferry Boat, it will probably be found that in the course of use the links of the chain gradually become unsuited in their length to the impressions or indentations on the cast-iron hoop.* See *Drumhead*, *Messenger*, *Pawls*, and *Swift*.

* The above remark was suggested upwards of ten years past; the writer is not aware what has since been the experience of the French in respect of this invention.

COME UP THE CAPSTAN. To slack off the rope or cable on which they had been heaving.

HEAVE THE CAPSTAN. To move it round by means of the bars, in order to create the required purchase upon the chain or rope that is wound around its barrel.

RIG THE CAPSTAN. To fix the bars in the capstan holes in order to prepare for heaving.

SURGE THE CAPSTAN. To slacken the rope which is round the barrel while heaving, in order to let it fly up towards the smaller end, and so prevent its parts from riding or getting foul.

CAPTAIN (*Fr.* Capitaine). The commander of a vessel. In merchant ships, he is commonly called the MASTER. In the Royal Navy, the title of Captain is properly given only to *post captains,* i.e. to those who have been posted to the rank of Captain, which is next above that of a Commander, R.N. The term *post captain,* however, is now in disuse.

In the Royal Navy, *captain* is also a designation given to the principal seamen of particular gangs of men, as *captain of the forecastle,* of the *hold,* of the *main, fore,* or *mizen top,* &c.

CAPTAIN OF THE FLEET. 'A temporary appointment given through the Lords Commissioners of the Admiralty to a captain. All the orders of the Commander-in-Chief are issued, and all returns made, through the Captain of the Fleet.' (See the *Queen's Regulations,* p. 35.)

CAPTURE (*Fr.* Prendre), as applied to maritime affairs, is the taking forcible possession of ships or goods belonging to the subjects of one nation by those of a hostile nation. The ship which captures is called the *captor* (*Fr.* capteur), and the captured ship (preneur) is called a *prize.*

CARAMOUSAL. A Turkish vessel of commerce having two masts (the after one a small mast) and a very elevated stern.

CARAVEL. In Turkey, this name is given to large ships. In Portugal, it is a small vessel carrying lateen sails. The three vessels which composed the expedition of Columbus on the occasion of his discovering America were caravels, but there is said to be no authentic account of their form, size, or rig. (*Dict. de Marine à voiles.*)

CARCASS. An iron frame or hollow shot perforated with three holes and filled with a composition of highly inflammable combustibles, fired like shell from a mortar. (See *Boyd's Naval Cadet's Manual,* 276.)

CARDINAL POINTS, *of the compass*, the general name by which the *North*, *South*, *East*, and *West* points are distinguished. See *Compass*.

CAREEN. *A vessel is said to careen*, when she lies over with a considerable list in the water. *To careen a ship*, is to heave her down upon her side in the water by purchases upon the masts, in order to repair or clean any part which is below the water-mark. And a beach prepared for laying vessels upon for the purpose of effecting such repair &c. is called a *Careening-beach*. The word *Carener* (to careen) in French is applied to the repairing of a ship when laid on a careening beach or hove down.

CAREENING BEACH. See preceding article.

CARGO (*Fr.* Cargaison). The lading or merchandise with which a vessel is freighted; the goods with which she is laden.

CARGO-BOOK. A book kept by the master of every coasting vessel, stating the name of the ship, of the master, of the port to which she belongs, and of the port to which she is bound on each voyage: in this book is entered, at the port of lading, an account of all goods taken on board, with the names of the respective shippers and consignees, so far as they are known to him, and at the port of discharge, the respective days on which such goods are delivered out of the ship; also the respective times of departure from the port of lading, and of arrival at any port of discharge.

CARLINGS. Fore-and-aft pieces of wood fitted in tiers between a vessel's beams, with the upper sides of which they are made flush. Between the carlings, and between the ship's sides and the carlings, there are athwartship pieces termed *ledges*, introduced in like manner. The whole of these form a framing for the deck to rest upon. *Mast Carlings, Hatchway Carlings, Pump well Carlings, Riding bitt Carlings, Bowsprit bitt Carlings, Topsail sheet bitt Carlings*, are so named from the parts with which they are respectively connected. The mast carlings are carlings fitted for the mast partners (of which they form a part) in large ships. See *Beams*, 4; and *Coamings*.

CARPENTER *of a vessel*. A person whose peculiar duty it is to keep in order the hull and spars, and the boats belonging to her. In merchant vessels, more especially in small ones, he has also to do the ordinary duties of a seaman. See also *Shipwright*.

CARRICK BEND. See *Bend*.

CARRICK-BITTS. The same as Windlass-bitts.

CARRONADE (*Fr.* Caronade). A kind of short gun, having (like a mortar) a chamber for the powder.

CARRY AWAY. To break a spar, &c., or to part a rope; it is used chiefly in the former sense.

CARTEL-SHIPS (*Fr.* Parlémentaires). Old ships of war employed for conveying and exchanging prisoners. See *Transports*.

CARTRIDGE (*Fr.* Cartouche, Gargousse). A case containing the charge of a fire-arm and made to fit its bore. Cartridges for heavy guns or mortars are made of flannel.

CARVEL-BUILT, implies that the planks of a ship or boat are all flush; that is to say, their edges being fayed to each other, and not overlapping as in *clinker work*. When the plates of an iron vessel are flush, they are said to be *Jump-jointed*.

CASCABLE. See *Gun*, 8.

CASCO. A boat or lighter of Manilla, somewhat resembling a large punt, used in the transport of goods.

CASE-SHOT, or CANISTER-SHOT. Small balls in a cylindrical case or canister. See *Shot*.

CASED. A mast is said to be cased when it has a casing built round it to prevent the necessity of discharging or shifting cargo in order to unstep and step the mast when required.

CASING, in Shipbuilding, a method of lining similar to veneering, commonly used for the beams and ceiling in cabins.

CASK. A barrel for liquor, provisions, or the like. See *Bilge of a Cask*, *Chimes*; and also *Bed*, *Aburton*, *Stowage*, and *Stow-wood*.

CAST (*Fr.* Abattre). To pay a ship's head off, in getting under weigh on the tack she is to sail upon. We say cast to *starboard*, or to *port*, according as her head is to be paid off to the right or to the left.

CAST *the lead*, is the same as to heave it. In the same sense we also say, 'take a cast of the lead.'

CAST AWAY. Shipwrecked.

CAST OFF. To loosen or to let go; as to cast off a vessel in tow.

CAST-KNEES. Those hanging knees which crook or arch over the corner of a gun port, rider, &c., in a ship of war. (*Shipwright's Vade Mecum.*)

CAT. A vessel of commerce of the Danes and other people of the North, built with flat floors and rounded extremities, and having pole masts rigged with square sails to lower on deck. (*Dict. de Marine à voiles.*)

CAT, or CAT-TACKLE. The tackle used to hoist an anchor up to the *Cat-head*. See this last term for explanation of *Catting the Anchor*.

CATALAN. A Spanish fishing boat, clean built and having little depth.

CATAMARÁN (*Fr.* Catimaron). A sort of raft or float formed by fastening a number of poles to each other sideways, and laying boards, planks, &c., on the top. The catamaráns used in the Brazils, and which are also common in the East Indies, consist of three logs of wood tapered at one end and lashed together. They are furnished with paddles, and are said to pull as fast as boats, the men being squatted in a kneeling position, and managing them with wonderful dexterity in passing the surf which beats on the shores. Those used in the Brazils also carry sail.

CAT-BLOCK. See *Cat-head* and *Cat-hook.*

CAT-FALL. The rope by which an anchor is catted. See *Cat-head.*

CATHARPINS, or CATHARPIN-LEGS (*Fr.* Trelingage). Ropes or irons used to confine the standing rigging to the mast at the lower extremity of the futtock-shrouds. These are out of use, as the futtock-shrouds now come down to the mast itself, to which they are bound by a hoop of iron.

CAT-HEAD. A strong piece of oak projecting over the bow

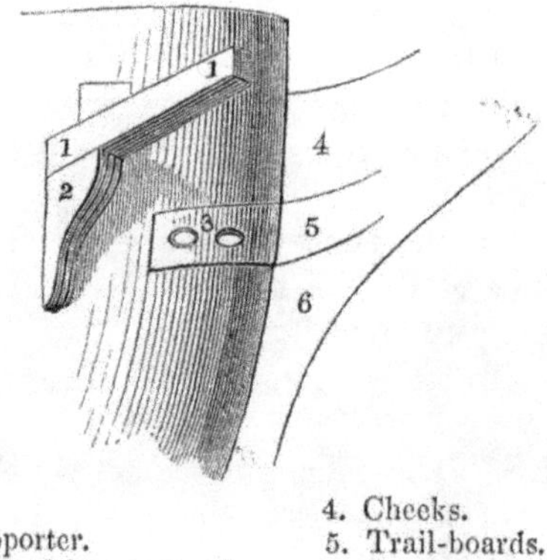


1. Cat-head.
2. Cat-head-supporter.
3. Hawse-holes, and hawse-wood.
4. Cheeks.
5. Trail-boards.
6. Cutwater, or head knee.

of a vessel at each side; it has at its outer end generally three sheaves, through which and a large block called the *Cat-block* (having the same number of sheaves) the cat-fall is rove; with this the sailors *cat the anchor*, that is to say, hook the cat-block to the ring of the anchor and haul it up from the hawse-hole to the cat-head. The cat-stopper is then rove through the ring and belayed in-board, for the purpose of hanging the anchor, after which the cat-block is unhooked. See *Fish the Anchor*.

(Plate IV. 21.) A further explanation may be found in *Seamanship*, by Lieutenant Nares, p. 139.

CAT-HEAD-STOPPER, or CAT-STOPPER. A piece of chain rove through the ring of an anchor for hanging it by when catted, or previously to bending the cable. The ordinary kind of Cat-stopper goes through the cat-head and is suspended from it by a toggle attached to the end of the stopper; its other end is rove through the ring of the anchor, brought round an iron cleat on the side of the cat-head, and belayed in-board. This end has thus to be let go, when the anchor is to be dropped. There is a *patent Cat-stopper*, the end of which, instead of having a toggle to suspend it from the cat-head, has a tapered piece of iron attached to it by means of an eye. This tapered piece of iron is nippered or jammed between two clamps of iron on the upper edge of the cat-head, the one fixed, the other pivoting on a bolt, and secured in its place by a pin, which can be driven out, so as to allow this end of the stopper to be unrove, when the anchor is to be dropped, leaving the other end in-board. See *Shank-painter*.

CAT-HOOK. A hook attached to the cat-block, for hooking the ring of the anchor.

CATSPAW, or CATSKIN. A partial current of air sweeping the surface of the water lightly, while all around is calm, and then passing away. *Catspaw* is also a name for a certain hitch made on a rope, thus:

CAULK (*Fr.* Calfater). To drive oakum into the seams between a vessel's planks in order to render them water-tight: when well performed, it serves as an additional binding to the vessel.

An iron instrument, called a *caulking iron*, resembling a chisel, is used with a mallet for this purpose; after which, another iron, called a *making iron*, which has a groove in it, is employed to finish off the seam. See also *Rasing-iron*, *Rave-hook*, and *Reeming*.

CAVILS. See *Kevels*.

CAVITY, in the science of Shipbuilding, signifies the hollow formed in the water by the bottom and sides of the vessel. See *Centre*.

CEILING (*Fr.* Vaigre). The inside planking of a vessel. It has also received the name of *footwaling*, but this term seems more applicable to the thicker planks, viz. those inside the bilge, which are termed bilge-planks, and the limber-strake or futtock-plank. (Plate II. fig. 6.)

CEMENT (*Roman*). A manufactured mineral of great tenacity; it is mixed with a little water when used, and, from the rapidity with which it hardens, is peculiarly adapted for any mason work under water, as for building docks, &c. See also *Mastic*.

CENTRE OF DISPLACEMENT, or CENTRE OF CAVITY, in the science of Shipbuilding, is the mean centre of that part of the vessel which is immersed in the water. It is sometimes called the *centre of immersion*, or *centre of buoyancy*; and is also the centre of vertical pressure that the water exerts to support the ship.

See *Meta-Centre*.

CERTIFICATES *of competency*, and *of service*, granted to masters or mates in the merchant service—as SEA-GOING CERTIFICATES and RIVER CERTIFICATES;—are certificates of being competent to act, or of having served for a certain period in one or other of these capacities on board of sea-going merchant vessels or in river navigation respectively. The names of masters and mates who have passed the necessary examination and received certificates are published in the *Mercantile Navy List*.

CHAFING-BOARDS. Battens seized upon rigging to prevent its being chafed. See *Battens*.

CHAFING-GEAR. Mats or other stuff put upon a vessel's rigging and spars to prevent their being chafed.

CHAIN (*Fr.* Cable, Chaine). A vessel's *chain-cable* is familiarly called her *chain.* As already mentioned under the article 'Cable,' few vessels belonging to this country now carry rope cables, the former being considered preferable. A certificate of all new chains, having been tested (by a hydraulic or other chain-proving machine), and of the strain applied to them, must be produced before a ship is classed in Lloyd's Register of British and Foreign Shipping. For table of the proportionate dimensions of chain cables compared with the tonnage of ships &c. see the title 'Anchor,' 25.

1. *Chain-cables* are divided into parts of from fifteen to twenty-five fathoms in length, these parts being connected by shackles, any one of which may be cast off when it is found necessary to slip from the anchor.

2. *Stud-chain,* is chain made with a small piece of cast-iron called a *stud,* introduced into the middle of each link crossways,

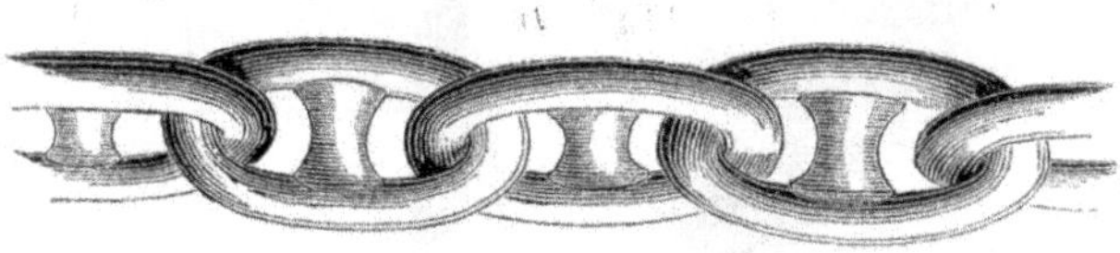

dividing the link into two equal parts, and answering the purpose of strengthening each so as to prevent its being collapsed by any heavy strain or sudden jerk, and at the same time of keeping the links endways to each other. *Short-link chain* has no studs, and the links, are, therefore, made shorter than those of stud-chain. *Chain-cables* should always be of stud-chain except in the case of very small vessels.

In Sisco and Sinibaldi's patent chain cable the links are made of rolled hoop iron and oval in shape. The hoop iron is coiled when cold and brazed or galvanised. There is thus no welding, as in ordinary chain cables. The links are 'made of sixteen layers of iron, and every layer has a skin, so that the chain has immense strength and will not snap. If one skin is broken fifteen remain.' In Corfield's chain four links are combined in one, the inner links serving the purpose of studs or stays.

3. THE CHAIN WELL, or CHAIN LOCKER, is a receptacle below deck for containing the chain cable, which is passed through an iron pipe called a *deck pipe.* Steam vessels have frequently also

a box on deck for this purpose, which is mounted on wheels, so that it may be easily moved about in order to trim the ship.

4. Chain is now often used for mooring vessels alongside of a quay or other landing place. And part of the running rigging of sailing vessels, the funnel stays of most steamers, &c., are made of small chain.

CHAIN-BOLTS, or CHANNEL-BOLTS. Bolts by which the channel plates are fastened to a vessel's sides.

CHAIN CABLE. See *Chain.*

CHAIN-CABLE CONTROLLER. Kendall and Rogers's Chain Cable Controller and Double Norman is a contrivance to

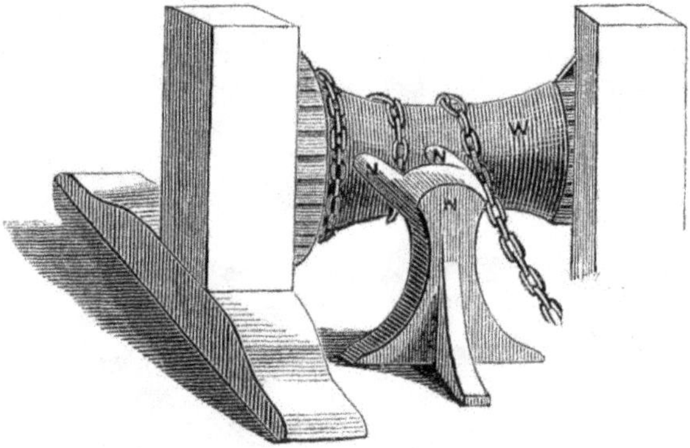


prevent one part of the chain from riding on another while revolving round a windlass. The machine is bolted to the deck before the windlass. The Normans (N) are projections abutting on the windlass (W) to control the chain.

CHAIN FERRY BOAT, or STEAM FLOATING BRIDGE. A kind of oblong punt, open on deck at both ends, with chains passing through hawse-holes at the bow and stern, and laid from shore to shore over two pitch wheels, driven in the punt by one or two steam engines. See *Ferry Boat* (*Chain*).

CHAIN PIPE. An aperture or pipe through which a chain cable passes up from the chain locker to the deck above.

CHAIN-HOOK. An iron rod formed with a large eye in one end, and a hook at the other end for hauling along chain-cables, pigs of iron, &c.

CHAIN-PLATES, or CHANNEL PLATES. Iron plates fastened to a vessel's sides for the purpose of securing the shrouds of the lower rigging. The bolts by which they are fastened get the name of CHAIN-BOLTS or CHANNEL-BOLTS. See *Dead-eyes* and *Channels.* (Plate IV. 35.)

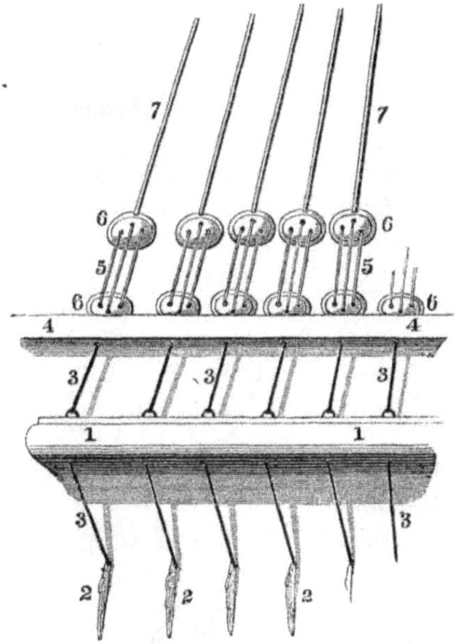


CHAIN-PLATES AND CHANNELS OF THE 'NORTHUMBERLAND' STEAM SHIP OF WAR, NOW BUILDING (DRAWN FROM MODEL).

1. Channel, or guard-board.
2. Preventer plates.
3. Chain plates.
4. Main-rail.
5. Lanyards.
6. Dead-eyes.
7. Shrouds.

CHAIN PUMP (*Fr.* Pompe à Chapelet). A pump worked by means of an endless chain passing over a roller or sprocket wheel on deck. See *Boyd's Naval Cadet's Manual,* 59.

CHAIN-SLINGS. Chains attached to the sling-hoop and mast-head, by which a lower yard is hung. (Plate IV.)

CHAIN-STOPPERS. See *Stopper.*

CHAIN-WELL. A receptacle below deck for containing the chain cable. See *Chain,* 3.

CHAINS, *Main, Fore,* or *Mizen.* A name given to the channels and chain-plates, to which the lower rigging of a vessel's main, fore, or mizen mast is secured.

CHALDERS, or CHALDER IRONS. See *Rudder-Bands.*

CHAMBERS, in vessels which have floor and futtock riders, are the clear spaces between the riders. See also descriptions of *Carronade, Mortar* and *Pump.*

CHAMFERING, or CAMFERING. Cutting the sharp angles off the edge of a plank or piece of timber.

CHANNEL (*Fr.* Chenal, Manche). The navigable track of a river, or the like; in this sense it is the same as *fairway.* The term *channel* is also applied to an arm of the sea separating an island from the main land, or two islands from each other.

CHANNELS, *Main, Fore,* and *Mizen* (*Fr.* Porte-haubans). Thick pieces of plank fayed and bolted edgeways to a vessel's sides, nearly abreast of each respective mast: through notches on their outer edge the chain-plates are carried, in order to give greater spread to the shrouds of the lower rigging, and keep them clear of the rail. They also get the name of *Guard-boards* or *Channel-boards.* See *Dead-eyes.*

CHANNEL-BOLTS, CHANNEL-PLATES. Iron bolts and plates for securing the shrouds of the lower rigging to a vessel's sides. See *Chain-plates.*

CHANNEL-WALES, in a ship of war, the outside plank which receives the bolts of the chain-plates.

CHAPLAIN. A clergyman appointed to religious service on board of a ship of war. See Chapter LI. of the *Queen's Regulations.*

CHART, or SEA CHART (*Fr.* Carte Marine). A representation or *hydrographical map* of the terraqueous globe, or of any portion of it that is composed principally of water wherein are laid down with great precision and minuteness the objects on the sea coast, such as beacons, lighthouses, &c., the rocks, shoals and soundings, the directions of the winds where they are peculiarly prevalent, together with the variations of the magnetic needle and other particulars for the guidance of mariners.

The charts principally in use among seamen are the Plane and Mercator's charts. A *plane chart* is constructed on the supposition that the earth is an extended plane; ' and when on such charts it is attempted to exhibit the latitudes and longitudes of places, the meridians are drawn parallel to each other, the degrees of the parallels of latitude and those of the meridians being represented as equal to the degrees of the equator: hence the relative positions of places are so erroneously laid down as to be of scarcely any practical utility, except when, from the small surface intended to be represented, neither latitude nor longitude require to be considered.' Plane charts are accordingly seldom used in any but coasting vessels. *Mercator's chart* (*Fr.* Carte Reduite), so called from Gerard Mercator, who first brought it into use about the year 1556*) has all the meridians made parallel to each other, and the degrees of longitude all equal; the degrees of latitude on this chart increase towards the poles in the same proportion as the degrees of longitude on the globe are diminished. Mercator's chart is most commonly used in navigation, 'because on it alone the track of a ship, always steering the same course, appears a straight line, and thus all calculations respecting the latitude and longitude of a ship steering a course which cuts all the meridians at the same angle are reduced to the utmost simplicity.' (*Mrs. Taylor's Epitome of Navigation; Raper's Practice of Navigation.*)

*Halley's Chart*, commonly called the *Variation Chart*, is a Mercator's chart, whereon are drawn a number of curve lines showing the variation of the compass in the places through which they pass. (*Baharie's Marine Board Examination.*)

*Bottle Charts*, are charts 'exhibiting the direction and strength of currents so nearly as can be ascertained from data obtained by papers found in bottles sent adrift for that purpose on the ocean.' See *Nautical Magazine*, vol. xii., wherein a bottle chart of the Atlantic is presented, along with a variety of general information on the subject.

CHARTER (*Fr.* Fréter). *To charter a vessel*, is to take her to freight under a charter-party.

CHARTER-PARTY, or CHARTER (*Fr.* Charte-Partie). A deed or written contract for the letting to freight the whole or part of a vessel for one or more voyages. This agreement is termed a *contract of affreightment*, and the ship is said to be chartered for the voyage. It is now an agreement not under seal, and is technically called a *Memorandum of Charter*. The merchant so hiring or *chartering* a ship is the *Charterer*.

The parties to a charter may be either the principals themselves, or their agents: that is to say, either the shipowner or ship's husband and the merchant; or the master and the factor

* In an article of the *Penny Cyclopædia* bearing reference to works of high authority, and also in the *Dictionnaire de Marine à voiles*, it is stated that 'the credit of first investigating the principles of Mercator's projection and applying it to the purposes of navigation, appears to be due to Edward Wright.'

or mercantile agent. It is not correct, however, to make out a charter in name of the *master*, except at a foreign port, or when he is a part-owner of the ship.

A penalty is often attached for non-performance of the agreement.

CHARTERER. See *Charter-party.*

CHASE, in Shipbuilding, a long sloping mortice. See also *Gun.*

CHASE, or GIVE CHASE, means to pursue a ship or fleet. *Chase* denotes also the act of pursuit.

A vessel pursued is called a *chase*, that pursuing is termed the *chaser.*

The guns pointed from the bows and the stern of a ship of war get the name of *bow-chasers* and *stern-chasers* respectively ; they are generally long, in order to carry to a great distance.

CHASE-PORTS. The gun ports at the bows and the stern of a ship of war.

CHASER. See *Chase.*

CHECK. *To check a brace*, implies to slack off a little upon it, and belay it again. *To check a yard*, is to lay it a little more square, by slacking the brace in like manner, when braced sharp. This is done when the wind becomes more favourable, or when the ship has to sail more free.

CHEEKS. See *Gaff* and *Hounds.*

CHEERLY. Quickly, heartily, with a will.

CHEQUE (*Clerk of the*). An officer who keeps the muster rolls of a dock-yard. See *Clerk of the Cheque.*

CHESTREES, or CHESS-TREES. Pieces of wood bolted one on each side of a square rigged vessel with a large hole through which the main tack is boarded, that is to say, hauled down. Instead of wood, iron plates, with thimble eyes, are now in common use, the tacks themselves being frequently of chain in place of rope.

CHIMES. The ends of the staves of a cask, where they project beyond the head of the cask.

The parts between these and the bilge are called the *quarters.*

CHIME, or CHINE, in Shipbuilding, that part of the water-ways which projects above the deck plank, and is notched or hollowed in front to form a water-course. *Chimed*, implies notched or hollowed out in the above manner.

CHINSE. To caulk lightly.

CHISELS (COLD), are short stout chisels made of steel, used for cutting iron bolts, and for like purposes.

CHOCK, in Shipbuilding, a piece of wood used for filling up any want or defect. In the building of merchant vessels there are chocks for fillings to the timbers. (See Plate II. fig. 6; and *Peake's Rudimentary Treatise on the Practice of Ship-building*, p. 26.) In ships of war there are *chocks* brought under the ends of the beams, or under the shelf immediately beneath the beams, to support them and to receive the bolts of the knees which connect their ends with the ship's sides.

*Anchor Chocks*, are pieces indented into a wooden anchor stock where it is defective in the way of the shank.

*Boat's-Chocks*, are clamps of wood for a boat resting upon when stowed on a vessel's deck.

CHOCK (TRANSPORTING). The following is a sketch of a *transporting chock*, fitted on the waterways of a ship for taking

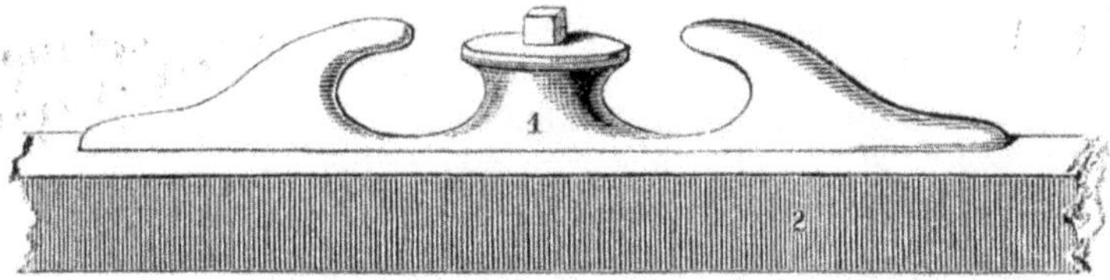


the turn of a hawser round to haul upon in transporting the ship from place to place in port, &c. See *Rudder Chocks*, and *Stow Wood.*

CHOCK-A-BLOCK, or BLOCK AND BLOCK, is the situation of a tackle when the blocks are hauled close together, and the effect of the tackle is thereby inoperative until it be fleeted. The same as hauled *two-blocks.*

CHOCK-AFT, CHOCK-HOME, and CHOCK-OUT, &c., imply as far aft, home, &c., as possible.

CHOKE THE LUFF. To place the leading part or fall of a tackle into the jaw of the block to prevent the tackle from rendering.

CHOP ABOUT. The wind is said to *chop about* when it changes suddenly. When it changes frequently during a short space of time, we say the wind is *flying about.*

CHRONOMETER (*Fr.* Montre Marine). A particular kind of watch or time-keeper with a 'compensation adjustment' calculated to prevent the expansion and contraction of the metal by the action of heat or cold from affecting its movements, which enables it (and that with great accuracy and minuteness) to measure time equally in all climates or temperatures. It is used at sea to determine the longitude. Marine chronometers are generally hung by a species of gimbals in square boxes. Ships going distant voyages ought to be furnished with several chronometers, for the purpose of correction, and in case of accident to any single one.

The *rate* of a chronometer is that number of seconds which it loses or gains on the twenty-four hours of a mean day: this is called *plus* when there are more, *minus* when there are less, than twenty-four hours indicated by it in that space of time.

By making allowance for the rate, the actual time at Greenwich (from which our longitudes are calculated) is obtained, and the difference between this and the time ascertained by observations of the altitude, at the place where the ship may be — calculating fifteen degrees for every hour of this difference — gives the longitude of the place. The reason of this is obvious, the earth's revolution being performed in twenty-four hours, and fifteen being the twenty-fourth part of 360 degrees.

*To rate a chronometer* means to correct its rate.

See *Horary Angle.*

Some important directions as to the use of this instrument are given in the Introduction to *Horsburgh's India Directory.* On this subject we would also specially refer to *Riddle's Epitome of Navigation and Nautical Astronomy; Seamanship, by Lieut. Alston, R.N.*, p. 252; and to *Notes on the Management of the Chronometer and the Measurement of Meridian Distance, by Captain Shadwell, R.N.*

CILLS. See *Sills.*

CINQUE PORTS, or FIVE PORTS. A term applied to the ports of Sandwich, Dover, Hythe, Romney, and Hastings, which, for political purposes, were invested by William I. with certain privileges and immunities, and placed under the charge of the Constable of Dover Castle, with the title of Lord Warden of the Cinque Ports: to these are to be added Winchelsea and Rye, 'two ancient towns which were originally only members.' 'The organisation of the Cinque Ports,' says Mr. Waterston in his *Cyclopædia of Commerce*, 'was almost entirely broken up by the Parliamentary and Municipal Reform Acts, but the Warden still possesses an Admiralty jurisdiction with the execution of writs and custody of debtors. He also 'appoints three or more commissioners at each of the Cinque Ports, who are authorised to decide upon all claims for services rendered to vessels and their cargoes, or for saving and recovering anchors, &c., and goods wrecked or cast away.' The Lord Warden and his Lieutenant have power to license pilots within certain limits.

CIRCLES. The circles supposed to be described on the celestial sphere, in order to point out the positions of the bodies, are distinguished as *great* or *less*.

A GREAT CIRCLE, is one whose plane passes through the centre of the sphere; A LESS CIRCLE, is one whose plane does not pass through the centre of the sphere. 'All great circles upon a sphere, therefore, divide it equally, and all less circles divide it unequally. Those two points on the surface of a sphere which are equidistant from every part of the circumference of one of its *great circles* are called the *poles* of that great circle.' (*Norie's Epitome of Navigation.*)

AZIMUTH CIRCLES, or VERTICAL CIRCLES. Great circles of the celestial sphere passing through the Zenith and Nadir. See *Azimuth*, and *Sailing (Great Circle)*.

CIRCLES OF LONGITUDE. Great circles passing through the poles of the Ecliptic. See *Longitude.*

CIRCUMNAVIGATION. The act of performing a voyage round—that is, *circumnavigating* the world.

CLAMP. Any plate of iron made to turn or open and shut, so as to confine a spar or boom; as a studding-sail boom or a boat's mast.

CLAMP is also the name of a species of block, either wood or iron, with only one cheek, the mast or boom, &c., to which it is nailed forming the other cheek.

CLAMPS, also called *Seacrafts* (*Fr.* Bauquières), in Shipbuilding, the uppermost strake of ceiling, which, like the bilge plank, is thicker than the rest of the ceiling. This is considered to be one of the principal binding strakes. (Plate II. fig. 6.) The clamps are scarphed together, and should be securely bolted to the ship's sides: the ends of the beams, as well as the fore and aft knees, rest upon their upper edge. Immediately under the clamps of the lower deck a second range of clamps is often introduced, which (if due attention be paid to have them bolted to the proper timbers) affords a substantial binding in the pitching, and also in the rolling motion of the vessel.

CLAMP NAILS. Short stout nails with large heads for fastening iron clamps or plates.

CLAP ON. An order to men who are standing by in readiness to lay hold of a rope or tackle in order to haul upon it; to man the windlass or capstan; to apply a stopper, or tackle, &c., where it may happen to be required.

CLAPPER. A name for the valve of a pump-box.

CLASSIFICATION of SHIPS. See *Lloyd's Register*, and *Navy*.

CLAW-OFF. A term sometimes used to denote the act of beating to windward in order to get off a lee shore.

CLEAN signifies that a vessel is sharp, in opposition to full. See *Lean*.

CLEAN *a ship's bottom.* To burn and scrape off the seaweed, barnacles, or other substances which have adhered to the bottom, tending to impede the ship's progress through the water, and afterwards to lay on a coat of tar, paint, or varnish.

CLEAR. The opposite term to foul. See *Foul.*

*To clear* (*Fr.* dégager) *a rope*, or *a chain*, &c., means to free it from obstruction. *To clear a point of land*, or any other object at sea, is to weather it. See also the articles *Clearance* and *Hawse.*

CLEARANCE. The act of *clearing a vessel* and her *cargo*, which consists in entering at the Custom House all particulars relating to her so far as these may be required upon arrival at, or previously to departing from, any port, as well as in the payment by the parties concerned of such duties as may be exigible upon her cargo, &c.

CLEATS (*Fr.* Taquets), in Shipbuilding, pieces of hard wood

A BELAYING CLEAT.

A THUMB CLEAT.

with notches in them, used for setting shores against. There are also cleats made of wood or iron of various forms, used for belaying ropes to, and for other purposes.

CLENCH. See *Clinch.*

CLENCHER BUILT. The same as *Clincher Built.*

CLERK OF THE CHEQUE, or CHECK. 'The officer who keeps the muster-rolls of a dockyard, and musters the ship's companies of vessels in the port to check false entries.'

CLEW. See *Clue.*

CLINCH, or CLENCH (*Fr.* Étalingure). A half hitch stopped

to its own part. By this species of running knot secured by the cable-bends, a rope cable is made fast to the anchor-ring.

To CLINCH A BOLT, is to fasten it by hammering down its point upon a ring or piece of plate-iron.

CLINCHER-BUILT (pronounced Clinker), CLENCHER-BUILT, or CLINKER-BUILT, implies that the planks of a ship or boat overlap each other and form projections on her bottom. This disposition of the planks is called *Clinker work,* as opposed to *Carvel work.*

When the plates of an iron vessel are disposed in the above manner, they are said to be *Lap-jointed.*

CLIP HOOK. A hook employed for the ends of topsail sheets, topgallant sheets, jib halyards, &c.

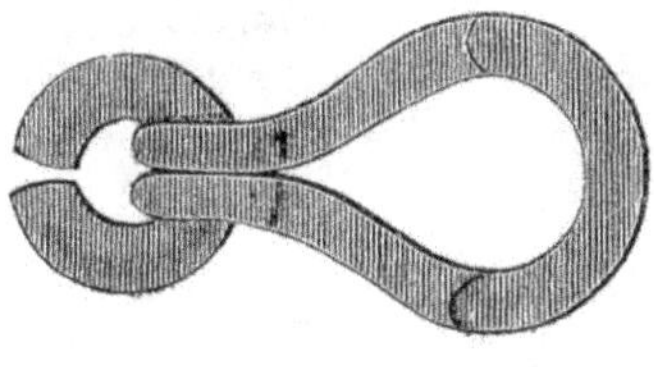

CLIPPER (*Fr.* Klipper). A term applied to a sharp built vessel whereof the stem and stern-post, especially the former, have a great rake, the planking of the bow or 'fore hoods' being carried forward to step in a rabbet in the cut-water. This kind of bow is termed a CLIPPER BOW, and a vessel so built a CLIPPER, or a clipper-built vessel. The fine lines of this vessel in conjunction with a large quantity of canvass carried upon her, whether rigged as a ship, barque, or schooner, are suited to command speed in sailing. Annexed is a sketch of a *clipper schooner.*

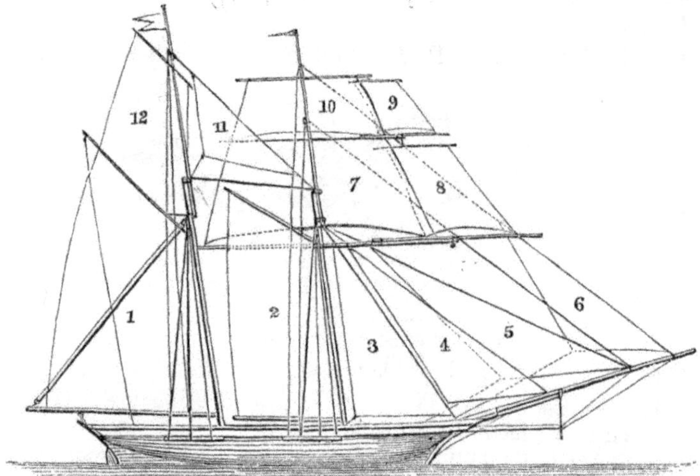


1. Mainsail.
2. Boom foresail.
3. Fore staysail.
4. Standing jib.
5. Jib.
6. Flying jib.
7. Foretopsail.
8. Fore topmast studding-sail.
9. Fore topgallant studding-sail.
10. Fore topgallant sail.
11. Main topmast staysail.
12. Gaff topsail.

CLOSE THE LAND. An expression sometimes used to imply coming near to it.

CLOSE. A vessel sails *close to the wind,* when her head is just so near the wind as to fill the sails without shaking them. She is then said to sail *on a wind,* or to be *close-hauled.* See *Near.*

CLOSE-HAULED. A term implying that a square rigged vessel is sailing with her yards braced up, so as to lie with her head close to the wind, and thereby get as much as possible to windward. The same as *On a taut bow-line,* or *Full and by.*

The terms *Close-hauled, By the wind,* and *Full and by,* are in like manner applicable to fore and aft rigged vessels sailing close to the wind.

In general, a vessel sailing close-hauled is reckoned to have her head not more than six points off the direction of the wind; if somewhat more she is sailing *free.*

CLOVE-HITCH. See *Hitch*, fig. 2.

CLOVE-HOOK. An iron clasp in two parts moving upon a pivot, and overlapping one another. It is used for bending chain-sheets to the clues of sails.

CLUB-HAUL. A particular method of getting a vessel on another tack, in order to clear the land when she is close upon it, and it blows so hard with a head-swell that she will not stay; while the effect of standing on, or of wearing, would be to run the ship ashore. It is done by putting the helm alee, and when the ship's headway is stopped, letting go the lee anchor, which brings her head up to the wind, then casting on the other tack by means of the sails, after slipping the cable.

Club-hauling may sometimes be resorted to with advantage, in the case of steamers, when a vessel is in a narrow river, or when she is caught with a violent wind on a lee shore, and owing to her great length she cannot be otherwise brought round; in such a case, also, if due care be taken, the anchor may be hove up again, so soon as she swings to it, by keeping the ship (by means of the steam-power) moving slowly in that direction.

CLUBBING. Drifting down a current with an anchor out.

CLUE or CLEW. Either of the lower corners of a square sail: the after lower corner of a fore and aft sail. See also *Hammock.*

CLUE-GARNET. See the following explanation of *Clue-line.*

CLUE-LINE. A rope leading through a block on the yard down to the deck, for hauling, or, as it is termed, *clueing* up the lower corner of a square sail. The clue-lines used for the courses are rove through blocks made fast to the clues of the sails, and they get the name of *clue-garnets.* (Plates III. IV. and V.)

CLUE-ROPE. An eye or loop generally formed by the bolt-rope at the lower end of a square sail, and to which the sheets are made fast.

CLUMP-BLOCKS. A name given to any blocks that are made thicker and stronger than ordinary blocks.

CLUTCHES. See *Crutches.*

COACH. A name which was given to a sort of apartment beneath the poop-deck near the stern of a large ship of war; generally occupied by the Captain.

COAKS or COGGS. Cylindrical pieces of wood three inches in diameter and the same in length, used chiefly as an additional security in scarphing two pieces of timber. See *Dowells.*

The term *Coaking* is also used in the same sense as *bushing.*

COALED. A steam ship is said to be *coaled* when she has received on board the necessary fuel for any voyage. She is said to call at a port for the purpose of *coaling* when she touches at it for a supply of coals.

COAL-TRIMMERS. Persons employed to stow and trim the fuel used for the furnaces in marine steam engines. See *Stoker.*

COAMINGS, COMBINGS, or COMINGS. Pieces of plank, generally fayed on carlings, and raised higher than the flat of the deck, forming the fore and aft boundaries to openings in it, such as the hatchways or skylights, in order to prevent water running down into the vessel off the deck. The athwartship boundaries of such openings, when not formed by the ship's beams, are called *ledges.* A sketch representing the main hatch of the Northumberland steam ship of war now building, with its coamings and ledges (drawn from model), is given under the title *Hatch.*

COAST, or SEA-COAST (*Fr.* Côte). That portion of any country which is bounded by the sea.

COAST-GUARD. Officers and boat's crews employed for the prevention of smuggling in the United Kingdom. See *Preventive Service.*

COAST-WAITERS. Landing waiters employed in superintending the landing and shipping of goods coastways. See *Customs.*

COASTING. Sailing along a coast.

COASTING-VESSEL, or COASTER (*Fr.* Caboteur, Cabotier). A vessel employed in the coasting trade.

THE COASTING TRADE (*Fr.* Cabotage) of the United Kingdom embraces all trade by sea from any part of the United Kingdom and Isle of Man to another part thereof. Vessels engaged in it are termed *Coasters* or *Coasting Vessels*; and the goods on board of them are said to be carried *coastwise.*

COAT. A piece of stout canvass painted or tarred, nailed

round a mast at the hole where it enters the deck to make it water-tight. This is called a *mast-coat.*

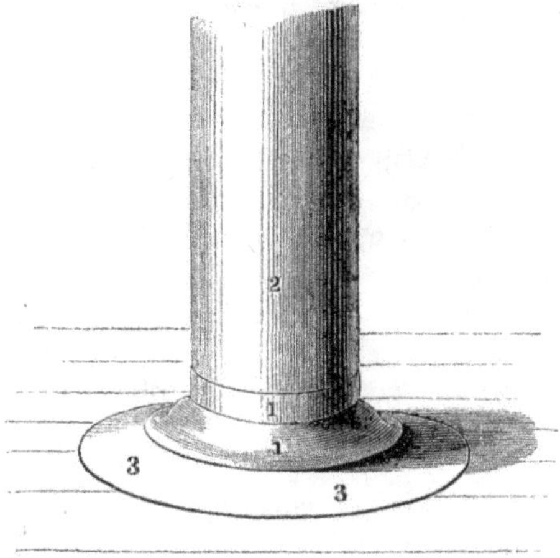


1. Mast-coat. 2. Mast. 3. Coaming (of wood).

A similar piece of canvass attached to the pumps is called a *pump-coat.*

In some ships, particularly in any sharp deep-waisted vessel not having a patent rudder, there is a *coat for the rudder* nailed round it on the bottom of the rudder-case, to prevent the admission of water in the event of the ship fetching sternway.

*A coat,* as is well known, is also applicable to every single layer of the materials with which a ship is painted, or her sides and bottom payed, as a 'coat of tar,' or the like.

COBLE. A low flat boat, with a square stern, principally used by salmon fishers.

COCKBILL THE ANCHOR. To hang it down by the ring from the cat-head. See *A-cock-bill.*

COCK-PIT. An apartment beneath the lower deck of a vessel of war, used by the surgeon and his assistants during an action. In large vessels, there is a fore and an after cockpit, the latter containing the medicine chest, &c. Frigates and line-of-battle ships have dispensaries fitted up to contain the medicines, the medicine chest being returned on shore. In frigates, and ships of a higher rate, the gunner's, boatswain's, and carpenter's store rooms are in the fore cockpit; in smaller vessels, again, there are bins nearly amidships of the mess deck for containing these officers' stores.

COCKET. A document given to a person exporting goods certifying under the hands of the Collector or Comptroller of Customs that the goods have been duly entered and the duties paid thereon.

COCKSWAIN or COXSWAIN. The individual who steers a boat, and has the charge of her.

CODE OF SIGNALS (COMMERCIAL). See *Signals.*

COGGS or COAKS. See *Dowells.*

COIL. To lay a rope up in the form of a ring with one turn or fake over another.

A COIL is a quantity of rope laid up in this manner. *A Flemish coil* is made by coiling the rope in a circular or elliptical form, with each fake outside of the other, beginning in the middle.

COIN. See *Quoin.*

COIR ROPE. A kind of cordage made in Ceylon and other places from the fibrous covering of the cocoa nut. It is inferior in quality and value to European rope ; but having no tar in its composition, it is more durable in hot climates; and it has also the advantage of floating in water. Captain Boyd in his *Naval Cadet's Manual* states that it decays rapidly when stowed away wet.

COLD CHISELS. Short stout chisels made of steel for cutting iron bolts, &c.

COLLAR (*Fr.* Collet). An eye in the end or bight of a shroud or stay to go over the mast head. The strops which attach the heart of the forestay and the bobstay to the bowsprit, and other similar strops, also receive the name of *collars.*

COLLECTOR OF CUSTOMS. An officer who takes the general superintendence of the customs at any port.

COLLIER (*Fr.* Charbonnier). A vessel employed exclusively in the coal trade.

SCREW COLLIERS, are long iron steam vessels propelled by the screw, which are now used in that trade. At page 110 of *Kipping's Elementary Treatise on Sails and Sailmaking* this kind of vessel is fully described.

COLLISION (*Fr.* Abordage) implies the act of one vessel by accident or negligence driving against or running foul of another either when one or both are in motion. The ships are said to come into collision with each other. The law of this subject is treated in Serjeant Shee's edition of *Lord Tenterden's Treatise,* in

*Maclachlan on the Law of Merchant Shipping*, and in *Pritchard's Admiralty Digest.* A digested index to Dr. Lushington's decisions on the subject is appended to the *Series of Reports of Maritime Law Cases*, issued at the *Law Times* office. See *Rules of the Sea.*

COLOURS. The distinguishing flags of any nation.

COLOUR SERGEANT. 'A non-commissioned officer of the marines having slight additional rank and pay above the other sergeants.'

COLURES. Great circles which pass through the equinoctial and solstitial points and the poles of the earth. See *Ecliptic.*

COMBINGS. See *Coamings.*

COME HOME. An anchor is said to *come home* when it is torn up from its bed by the violence of the wind and is dragged along. See *Anchor*, 14.

COME UP *a rope or tackle.* To slack it off. See *Capstan.*

COMING TO, or COMING UP, denotes the approach of the ship's head towards the direction of the wind. See *Falling-off.*

COMINGS. See *Coamings.*

COMMANDER (*Fr.* Capitaine). The master of a merchant vessel. In the Royal Navy it is a title given to officers (next in rank above lieutenants) appointed to the command of ships, previously to their being posted as captains; vessels commanded by them receive the name of *Sloops of war.* Fifty senior commanders on the Navy List have the option of receiving the retired rank of Captain with the lowest rate of half-pay allowed to a Captain.

COMMERCIAL CODE OF SIGNALS. See *Signals.*

COMMISSION. An allowance generally stated at so much per cent. given to agents or factors for transacting the business of others. COMMISSION ON ADVANCE, is a per centage charged on sums of money advanced by them for behoof of their employers.

COMMISSION also signifies the warrant of office granted by the Lords Commissioners of the Admiralty to second masters or any other officer of higher rank in the Royal Navy. Hence they are styled *Commissioned Officers.* When a captain and officers are appointed to a ship of war, the vessel is said to be IN COMMISSION as soon as the pendant is hoisted. See *Warrant Officers.*

COMMISSIONERS OF CUSTOMS. A board of Commissioners by whom the Customs Department of the public revenue is conducted in London. See *Customs.*

COMMODORE (*Fr.* Commodore). A flag officer next in rank and command below a Rear-Admiral. A captain when authorised to hoist a broad pendant in his ship has the temporary rank and title of Commodore. A commodore of the first class has a captain of the same ship under him, and hoists a plain red broad pendant, or a white broad pendant with a red cross in it. A commodore of the second class has not a captain under him in his ship; he carries a blue broad pendant.

COMPANION. A raised hatch, or cover, to the cabin stair of a merchant vessel.

COMPANION-WAY, or COMPANION-LADDER. The staircase to a vessel's cabin.

COMPANY (SHIP'S). The whole officers, men, and boys, employed on board a vessel.

COMPASS, or MARINER'S COMPASS (*Fr.* Compas, Bous-

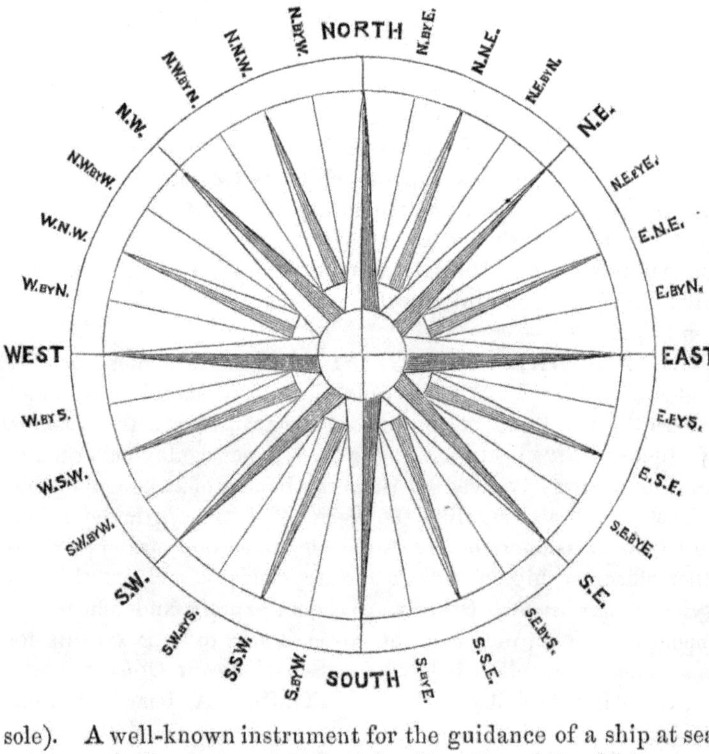


sole). A well-known instrument for the guidance of a ship at sea, serving to indicate at any moment the direction of the ship's course with reference to the points of the horizon, whence it is called the STEERING COMPASS. It consists of a circular *case* either of brass or wood, suspended within a square wooden box by two concentric rings called *gimbals*, forming universal joints, so as to allow the case to remain horizontal in any position of the ship; within the case there is a circular *card*, called the *fly*, supported at its centre on a pin whereon it turns freely; and to the under side of the card there is attached a steel bar which gets the name of the *needle*, and which, from being magnetised, has the property of pointing one of its ends towards the North Pole.

1. The compass card or *fly* is divided by lines called *rhumb-lines*, radiating from the centre, into thirty-two equal parts, called *points* or *rhumbs*, representing the divisions of the horizon, as in the diagram (p. 96); the *North*, *South*, *East*, and *West* points are distinguished by the name of the *cardinal points*. The circumference is also divided into 360°. Each point or rhumb is thus equal to 11° 15′.

2. On the inside of the case is drawn a dark vertical line, called *Lubber's-point*. This line and the pin on which the card turns are in the same plane with the keel of the ship, and hence the rhumb opposite to lubber's-point shows the course of the ship at any time—that is to say, the angle which the line of her course makes with the magnetic meridian. 'But as lubber's-point deviates a little from its proper position when the ship is heeled over, seamen do not implicitly depend upon it, as indeed its name implies.'

3. The needle almost everywhere is subject to a certain *variation* either east or west from the true north point. 'This variation' (says Mr. Horsburgh in the Introduction to his *India Directory*, where valuable information on this subject is presented) 'is in a state of continued change in most places of the globe, and there is also a *diurnal* and *annual* variation of the *variation*.' The variation is in practice ascertained by comparing the sun's true and magnetic *amplitudes* or *azimuths*. In some parts of the world, a difference, which is called an *aberration* or a *deviation*, is often found between the bearings taken when the ship's head is pointed in different directions. Owing to the influence of iron upon the needle, a compass will alter when taken from one ship to another, or when shifted to a different situation in the same ship. (*Norie's Epitome of Navigation; Encyclopædia Britannica; Raper's Practice of Navigation.*)

4. There is a *local attraction* caused by iron articles on board of a ship, but peculiarly in iron ships causing a deviation of the magnetic needle.

Professor Airey's directions for correcting or *adjusting* the compass by means of magnets in iron-built ships are quoted in the *United Service Journal*, and the subject amply discussed in *Grantham's Treatise on Iron Shipbuilding.*

On this subject the following valuable observations were supplied a number of years since, along with other valuable information for this Dictionary, by Mr. George Bayley, the well-known surveyor of Shipping in London. 'So far,' he observed, 'as any experience has gone, I am not disposed to rely upon any other correction than that of the compass to be actually used. In the Peninsular and Oriental Steam Navigation Company, the practice has been to swing the ship to every point of the compass, and accurately observe and record the variation or error upon each point, and make a card to these observed points for every steering compass. This in practical navigation was found a safe plan, inasmuch as it was free from the liability to errors in adding to or deducting from the apparent course by compass. It was frequently found that, after the lapse of six months, the local attraction had altered, perhaps from some portion of the ship becoming more or less magnetised; but whatever variation of this kind was found, it was always a gradual one. I do not remember any instance of one of the iron ship's compasses being affected by lightning, although several instances occurred of their discharging tremendous volumes of electric fluid.'

There are special statutory regulations regarding the adjustment of the compasses in passenger ships.

5. AZIMUTH-COMPASS. An instrument adapted to observe the *magnetic* azimuths or amplitudes of the sun in order to ascertain the variation of the compass. See *Azimuth.*

6. HANGING-COMPASS. A compass so constructed as to hang with its face downwards. This is found convenient when it is intended to be used in the cabin of a vessel. It is sometimes called a *Tell-tale.*

7. THE FLUID COMPASS is a compass in which the card revolves in its bowl alcohol or some other suitable fluid which prevents the needle from having undue vibration from any violent motion of the ship. *Dent's Patent Fluid Compass, with Annular Fountain Reservoir*, is so contrived as to avoid the air bubble in

the fluid, which caused a great impediment to the use of fluid compasses. Another subsequent invention of this kind is *The Self-Compensating Liquid Compass* patented by J. G. West and Co. It is said to be 'particularly adapted for iron ships.'

COMPASS-TIMBER. Curved or crooked timber. When very crooked it is termed *Knee-timber.*

COMPASSING. A name for *Compass-timber.*

COMPENSATOR (MAGNETIC). See *Magnetic Compensator.*

COMPLEMENT. In Navigation, the *complement of the course* is what it wants of 90° or 8 points; the *complement of latitude* (or, as it is termed by way of abbreviation, the *co-latitude*) is what the latitude of a place wants of 90°. See the article *Supplement.*

*A vessel's complement,* signifies the proper number of the ship's company.

COMPOSITION, used in shipbuilding for various purposes, is a species of brass composed of a mixture of copper, zinc, and other substances. See *Nails* (*Composition*).

COMPRESSOR-STOPPERS, COMPRESSORS, or COMPRESSOR CHAIN-CABLE STOPPERS, are made of various forms on the principle of holding the chain by compression to stop it from running. See *Stopper.*

COMPTROLLER (or CONTROLLER) OF CUSTOMS. See *Customs.*

CONDEMNATION. A vessel is said to be *condemned* when declared by the sentence of the Court of Admiralty or other competent court, in the event of being captured, to be lawful prize,—to be forfeited to the state for smuggling, or any other offence,—or declared by surveyors to be incapable through the effects of damage or decay of being recovered and repaired to the advantage of the owners thereof.

CONDENSER. See description of *Steam Engine,* Sect. 11.

CONDUCTOR (MARINE). A metal wire or chain or strip of copper reaching from the head of each of a vessel's highest masts downwards into the water in order to defend the ship from lightning, by conveying the electric fluid into the sea. Wire rope is said to form an excellent lightning conductor.

CONJUNCTION. Celestial bodies are *in conjunction,* when in a line together as seen from the centre of the earth; or in other words, when they have the same degree of longitude: they are *in opposition*, when 180° from each other. (*Raper's Practice of Navigation ; Squire's Grammar of Astronomy.*)

CONN. See *Conning*.

CONNECTING-ROD. See description of *Steam Engine*, Sect. 27.

CONNING. The operation of directing the steerage of a vessel. The person so occupied is said to be *at the conn.*

CONSIGN. To consign goods, is to send them to the care of an agent or factor for the purpose of being sold or disposed of. The party to whom they are sent is called the *Consignee* (*Fr.* Consignataire), and the goods themselves are termed a *Consignment* (*Fr.* Consignation).

To CONSIGN A SHIP, is to address her to the charge of an agent for the purpose of transacting the ship's business at the port to which she is to carry, or where she is to receive her cargo. The agent or broker so entrusted is called the *Ship's consignee.*

CONSORT. A vessel sailing in company with another.

CONSTELLATIONS. Clusters of fixed stars into which astronomers have subdivided the starry firmament. The different constellations are illustrated in a publication called *The Stars,* issued by the Society of Useful Knowledge. Mention may also here be made of *Norie's Zodiacal Stars,* a work intended especially to enable the astronomical student to acquire a knowledge of the stars near the ecliptic.

CONSTRUCTION. The method of ascertaining a ship's way by means of trigonometrical problems and diagrams. See *Inspection.*

CONSTRUCTIVE TOTAL LOSS. In Insurance Law, when the repairs of damage sustained by perils of the sea would cost more than the ship would be worth after being repaired—that is, a constructive total loss of the ship. There may be likewise a constructive total loss of a cargo. A right to recover for a constructive total loss is secured by notice of abandonment being given by the owners to the insurers.

CONSUL (*Fr.* Consul). An officer appointed by a Government to reside in some foreign country for the purpose, in particular, of facilitating and protecting the commerce of the subjects of such Government.

A British Consul is also empowered to act in the capacity of a Notary Public.

CONTENT. A document delivered to the searcher by the

master of a ship clearing outwards, describing her destination and detailing the goods shipped, with other particulars.

CONTINENT. A vast tract of land containing several empires, kingdoms, or countries, not separated from each other by the sea.

CONTRABAND GOODS—that is to say, goods which are intended to be exported or imported without paying customs duties, or otherwise contrary to the laws of this country—ought not to be taken on board by the master of any vessel, as this may subject the cargo and ship to forfeiture, and the freight of such goods cannot be legally recovered.

Those articles which neutrals are prohibited from carrying to belligerent powers are termed *Contraband of War*; under which denomination are arms, ammunition, and other stores (in some cases even money and provisions), tending probably to aid the hostilities of either of the contending powers. Such articles, along with the ship in which they are carried, are liable to seizure by the other contending power.

CONTRABAND OF WAR. See *Contraband Goods.*

CONTRACT TICKET. A printed form of agreement with every passenger on board of a 'passenger ship,' prescribed by the Legislature.

CONTRARY. The wind is contrary when opposed to a vessel's intended course.

CONTROLLER OF THE CUSTOMS. See *Comptroller.* See *Chain Cable Controller.*

CONVERTING TIMBER. Selecting proper pieces of timber to suit the different purposes of shipbuilding with the least possible waste. The person who has charge of this at a dockyard is called the *Timber Converter.*

CONVOY (*Fr.* Convoi, Escorte). An escort of ships of war appointed to accompany merchant ships proceeding to certain ports or places, whether for their protection against an enemy or pirates. The term is sometimes incorrectly applied to the fleet of merchantmen so escorted.

COOK. The man employed to cook the victuals on board a merchant vessel is generally an able seaman.

COOK-HOUSE (*Fr.* Cuisine). An erection on the deck of a vessel for containing the 'caboose' or *cooking apparatus.* It is often called the *galley.* See that article.

COPING, in Shipbuilding, implies turning the ends of iron

lodging-knees, so that they may hook into the beams, which serves to ease the strain off the necks of the bolts in the rolling motion of the vessel. For the like purpose, dowelling may be applied to wooden knees in large ships.

COPPER (*Fr.* Cuivre) rolled into sheets, or, as it is called, *Sheet copper*, is in extensive use for the *sheathing* of ships.

It is distinguished, according to its thickness, into 18 oz.—20 oz.—copper, and so on; indicating the number of ounces contained in one square foot, which varies from 18 to 32 ounces.

That part of the hull of the ship which is in the water is covered with sheet copper, nailed on the planks with composition nails (very generally termed *copper nails*), sometimes over paper or coarse linen cloth, but generally over felt, which is more suitable for the purpose. This covering preserves the wood from the attacks of the worm, to which it is particularly exposed in warm climates; it also gives the ship the advantage of passing more rapidly through the water, as the copper bottom remains always smooth; for, owing to the galvanic effect produced by the action of the sea-water upon it, sea-weed and shells will not adhere to copper as they do to the bare planks. This action produces a rapid decay of copper, which lasts in some cases five years, in others not more than two or three years, according to the thickness of the sheets and quality of the copper and the trade in which the vessel may be employed. See *Draft.*

Copper sheathing has of late years been much adulterated, and a composition metal, known by the name of *Muntz's Patent Yellow Metal*, or '*Patent Metal Ship Sheathing*,' is now generally used in its stead for merchant vessels. Regarding its application to ships of war, see *Peake's Rudimentary Treatise on the Practice of Shipbuilding*, p. 171.

COPPER-FASTENED. A term implying that a vessel has her keel, keelson, breast-hooks, transoms, butt-ends, and other parts (below the wales), securely bound by copper or patent metal bolts, the dove-tail plates for the keel and the stem-foot being also of the same material. In any contract for the building of a copper-fastened ship, it is well, in order to avoid dispute, specially to notice whether the rudder-bands shall be of iron or of composition metal.

COPPER NAILS are used for boat-building and for other purposes in preference to iron nails. See *Nails* (*Composition* and *Copper*).

COPPERS, or SHIP'S COPPERS. A general name for the cast-iron apparatus used on board a vessel for cooking.

CORAL REEFS, or CORAL SHOALS. Chains of coral rocks, which (Captain Horsburgh mentions) abound chiefly within the tropics, particularly in the Indian and Pacific Oceans, and round New Holland; many of the islands being surrounded by these reefs, or standing upon a coral base. They are produced by what are called zoophytes, a species of animal partaking of the nature of plants; these take root at the bottom of the sea in deep water, whence the stems gradually branch upwards, and become transformed into solid rock. When these concretions of coral reach near the surface of the sea, they become dangerous obstructions to navigation; after they appear above it, they form into islands of various dimensions, according to the extent of their original basis. (*Horsburgh's India Directory.*)

Malte Brun, in his *System of Geography*, mentions that 'the calcareous secretion of the zoophytes is rock or stone the very moment the animal dies.'

Some mariners assert that by digging into any coral reef to a depth below the surface of the sea, fresh water may be obtained. Without vouching for the truth of the allegation, it seems advisable to notice it.

The probability of the circumstance here noticed appears to be confirmed by the following remarks in Malte Brun's *System of Geography.* Quoting certain historical facts in support of his theory, he presumes that 'the phenomena of capillary tubes may obtain in the interior of the earth. The sea-waters, deprived of their salt and bitter elements, may ascend through the imperceptible pores of several rocks, from which, being disengaged by heat, they will form those subterraneous vapours to which many springs owe their origin. The change effected in the saline nature of salt water is satisfactorily proved by the diminution of saltness in the springs which evidently result from such filtrations. The fresh as well as the salt springs in Bermuda rise and fall with the flow and ebb of the tide.'

CORDAGE (*Fr.* Cordage). A general term for rope of any size. Cordage for ships is commonly tarred; when not so, it is called *white rope* (*Fr.* blanc cordage).

COROCORA. A general name for the Malay coasting vessels, which are distinguished by a great breadth of beam amidships, a flat bottom, clean and symmetrical in the run and entrance, and a short keel forming a continuation of the curve of the stem and stern-post, which have great rake. The very remarkable construction of this kind of vessel, and of the Booanga, may throw some light on that of the vessels with several banks of oars peculiar to the maritime states of the Mediterranean in ancient times. (*Dict. de Marine à voiles.*)

CORPORAL *of a Ship of War*. A petty officer, whose duty, among other things, is to assist the master-at-arms in detecting offenders, and watching the safety of lights on board.

CORPOSANT. 'A name given to the luminous appearance often beheld in a dark tempestuous night about the decks and rigging of a ship,' especially about the mast-heads, yard-arms, &c., caused by the electric fluid passing upwards and downwards 'by means of the humidity on the masts and rigging,' and 'most frequent in heavy rain accompanied with lightning.'

CORRECTIONS OF ALTITUDE are noticed under the title *Altitude.*

CORSAIR. A pirate. A piratical cruiser.

CORVETTE. A particular kind of vessel of war; it is rigged like a ship, and carries one tier of guns on a flush deck.

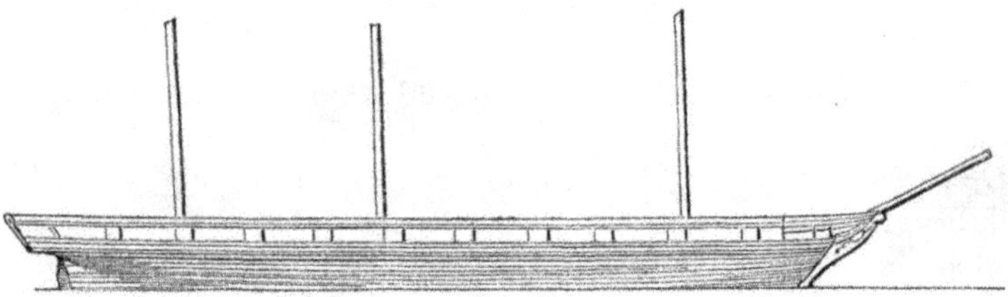

COT, or COTT. A square bed frame slung from a vessel's beams. Cots are used for the accommodation of commanding officers, and sometimes of lieutenants in ships of war: they are specially supplied for the use of the sick or wounded.

COUNCIL OF WAR. In the Royal Navy, an assembly of the commanding officers in a fleet, sometimes called by the Commander-in-Chief, on any emergent occasion of doubt, to concert measures, whether of attack or retreat, proper to be taken under the circumstances.

COUNTER (*Fr.* Voûte). That part of a vessel's stern between the wing transom and the archboard. (Plate II. fig. 5.)

COUNTER BALANCE WEIGHT, and LEVER. See description of *Steam Engine*, Sect. 5.

COUNTER-BRACE THE YARDS, means to brace a vessel's head yards one way and the after yards another.

COUNTER-RAILS. Ornamented rails, or rather a sort of ornamental moulding across a square stern, at the lower part of the vessel's counter; into these the counter and the ends of the bottom plank finish.

COUNTER-SUNK, implies a hollow cut round the edge of a hole by means of a small triangular tool with two cutting edges, called a *counter-sunk-bit.* Its most common application is for the purpose of allowing the head of a nail to be sunk so as to be even with the surface into which it is driven.

COUNTER-TIMBERS. The timbers wrought into a vessel's counter. See *Timbers.*

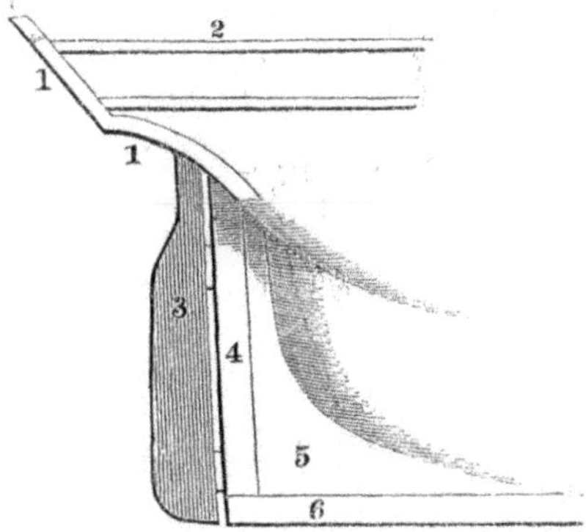


1. Side counter timbers.
2. Mainrail.
3. Rudder.
4. Sternpost.
5. Deadwood.
6. Keel

COURSE (*Fr.* Route), in Navigation, the angle which a vessel's track or path makes with the meridian from which she takes her departure: it is expressed in points of the compass.

Also, the direction in which a vessel is intended to go. In this sense we speak of *shaping a course.*

A vessel is said to *lay her course* when the wind is 'shy,' so as barely to allow the vessel to sail directly for her point of destination; and to *steer her course* when going with the wind free.

COURSES. The common term for the sails which, in a square-rigged vessel, hang from the lower yards. The foresail is called the *forecourse*; the mainsail, the *maincourse*.

COURT-MARTIAL. In the Royal Navy, a tribunal assembled for the investigation of any offence or offences against the Articles of War under the Naval Discipline Act. It is composed of Flag Officers, Captains, and Commanders, assisted by a judicial officer, or deputy judge advocate.

COVE (*Fr.* Crique). A creek or small bay forming a natural harbour.

COVERS for sails, &c., are made generally of coarse canvass, tarred or painted, and are used to protect them from the effects of the weather when stowed. 'In men of war, the only sails which have coverings are jibs, trysails, and spanker; they are made of No. 6 half-worn canvass, and are never tarred or painted.' Of these two opposite practices (if the latter still continues) the preferable one seems obvious.

COVERING-BOARD. The same as *Planksheer*. (Plate IV. 29.)

COXSWAIN. The same as *Cockswain*.

CRAB. A portable machine, the frame of which is made either of wood or cast-iron, fitted with wheels and pinions similar to those of a winch. It is used chiefly in loading and discharging vessels employed in the timber trade.

CRADLE (*Fr.* Berçeau). In Shipbuilding, a frame placed under the bottom of a vessel in order to conduct her steadily in the ways when she is launched. See also *Slip (Patent)*.

CRADLE is also a name given to a boat's chocks.

CRAFT. A general name for river traders, lighters, or any boats or vessels employed in shipping and discharging goods. Also a cant term applied by seamen to any vessel whatever.

CRAMP. A machine for screwing two pieces of timber together. It is much used in boat-building.

CRANAGE. The liberty of using, or the money paid for the use of a crane, which is a well-known machine employed for raising and lowering great weights.

CRANCE. A kind of iron cap on the outer end of the bowsprit, through which the jibboom traverses. This is termed the *Bowsprit Cap*, which in merchant vessels used to be made of wood. CRANCE is also a name sometimes given to any boom-iron. See *Cap*.

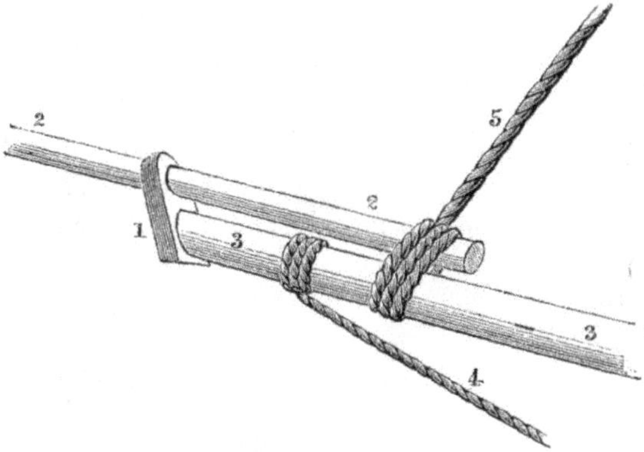


BOWSPRIT CAP OF A SHIP OF WAR.

1. Bowsprit cap.
2. Jibboom
3. Bowsprit.
4. Bobstay.
5. Forestay.

CRANE (STEAM), TAYLOR AND CO.'S PATENT. A particular kind of crane, of which several may be worked at the same time by means of a small steam engine.

'When these cranes are fitted with turning apparatus,' Messrs. Taylor and Co. observe, 'they are peculiarly adapted for delivering or taking a cargo over the ship's side. The number of hands employed in working them is very small compared to the work they perform—viz. one man attending the boiler, which supplies steam for two or more cranes, and one man at each crane, who stops and starts the engines, throws into gear the turning apparatus by means of a clutch, and regulates the lowering of the weight by a break lever.'

'These cranes are capable of lifting two tons (the average lift of a general cargo not exceeding one ton), with which weight as many as forty lifts are made per hour; but lighter weights can be arranged to be lifted much quicker. The number of lifts is limited by the difficulty, at present, of bringing goods to or removing them from the hatchway.'

'The arrangement of levers for working the cranes is so simple that ordinary labourers or seamen can work them, the man attending the boiler keeping the cranes in order.'

Messrs. Taylor and Co. have invented a portable *steam-hoist* used in working pumps and in shipbuilding purposes, &c., which being mounted on wheels are easily moved from one place to another, and are provided with a water tank placed below the fire, which serves as a protection to the decks when used on board ship for discharging cargo.

CRANK (*Fr.* Faible, Jaloux). A term applied to a vessel which will not stand up to her canvass, or, in other words, is too apt to heel over by the pressure of her sails. This may be owing to her stowage, or to her construction, particularly from being built too deep in proportion to her breadth, or from being overmasted. *Stiff* is the opposite term.

CRANKS *of a Steam Engine*, CRANK-PIN, AND CRANK-SHAFT. See description of *Steam Engine*, Sect. 29.

CRANK-HATCHES. Hatches raised on coamings to a proper height on a steam vessel's deck in order to form coverings for the cranks of the engines.

CREEK (*Fr.* Abri, Crique). A small inlet of a river or of the sea.

CREEPER. An iron instrument with several hooked claws, used for dragging the bottom of the water for anything lost.

CREW. The whole persons employed on board of a ship or boat; it is more particularly applied to all who are under the master of the ship.

In a ship of war, the men employed respectively under the boatswain, gunner, and carpenter, are called their *crews*.

CRIMPS. A dishonest class of men who before the establishment of shipping offices and sailors' homes speculated in the shipping of seamen and in drawing their pay; often, also, keeping lodging-houses for them.

CRINGLE. A kind of eye or loop, formed by a short piece of rope with each end spliced into the bolt-rope of a sail; commonly confining an iron ring or thimble. There are likewise small cringles in the eyelet-holes, to prevent the points from tearing the canvass when in the act of reefing the sail.

BOWLINE, BUNTLINE, REEF-PENDANT, and REEF-TACKLE-PENDANT CRINGLES, are so named after the ropes to which they are respectively attached. EARING-CRINGLES are for lashing the extremities of a sail to the yard when bending or reefing. Those at the upper corners of the sail are termed *Head* or *Head-earing cringles.* Those further down the edge of the sail are termed *Reef-cringles.* See *Earings.*

CROSS-HEAD (*Fr.* Travesse, Tête Croissée). See description of *Steam Engine*, Sects. 22 and 24.

CROSS-JACK-YARD (pronounced by sailors crojek). The lower yard on a mizen mast. Also a yard that is hoisted upon a sloop's mast, or upon the foremast of a fore-and-aft schooner, to set the square sail upon when going before the wind. This yard in a sloop or schooner also gets the name of the *square sail yard.*

CROSS-PIECE, or CROSS-BITT. A piece of timber bolted athwart two bitts for belaying ropes to. The cross-pieces of the cable-bitts and topsail-sheet-bitts are cased with iron. Also a rack with belaying pins through it, extending from the carrick-bitts over the windlass. See *Timbers.*

CROSS SPALES, CROSS PAWLS, or BAULKS. Pieces of plank nailed across each of the frames to keep them at their proper breadth till the vessel is planked outside.

CROSS-STAFF, or FORE-STAFF. An instrument used in ancient times, as the quadrant now is, for observing altitudes at sea; for a description of which see *Fore-staff.*

CROSS-TIMBERS, or CROSS-PIECES. Short timbers laid across the keel of a heavy ship of war and scarphed to the lower ends of the first futtocks. See *Timbers* (*Cross*).

CROSS-TREES. Athwartship pieces of timber resting upon the trestle-trees or on a cap at that part of a mast where it is connected with the mast immediately above; used for spreading the rigging of the upper mast. In a vessel with tops they form part of the framing of each top. (Plates III. IV. and V.)

JACK-CROSS-TREES. Iron cross-trees at the head of any long topgallant mast.

CROTCHES. See *Crutches.*

CROW. A bar of iron slightly bent at one end with a claw for drawing nails. A CROW-BAR is also bent at one end, but has no claw; it is used as a lever for moving heavy bodies. A SHACKLE-CROW is a similar bar of iron with a shackle instead of a claw at the bent end; it is used for drawing bolts.

CROWFOOT (*Fr.* Araignée). A particular kind of iron stand attached to the end of a table, in a ship of war, and hooked to one of the beams above; on this the mess-kids, &c., are hung.

See also description of *Awning.*

CROW'S-NEST. A name given to a sort of sentry box or watch tower (invented by the late Captain Scoresby), which is placed on the main topmast-cross-trees, or main topgallant cross-trees of a whale fishing vessel, for the shelter of the look-out and when employed on the fishing ground at Davis's Strait.

CROWN *of an anchor* (*Fr.* Collet d'une ancre), that part where the arms are joined to the shank.

CROWN *a knot,* to pass the strands of the rope over and under each other above the knot, by way of finish. See *Knot.*

CRUISE. To sail about in quest of an enemy. An expedition of this kind is called a *Cruise* (*Fr.* Croisière) and the vessel so employed a *Cruiser.* See *Cutter* (*Revenue*).

CRUTCHES. Iron knees or pieces of knee-timber placed horizontally athwartships in the after peak of a vessel, to secure the heels of the cant timbers abaft and to connect them with the stern frame. This binding is rendered the more substantial when the tails of the crutches extend forward sufficiently far to be connected to the after floor heads. Every ship above 150 tons burden should have at least one crutch.

Also, stanchions of wood or iron whose upper parts are forked to receive rails, spars, masts, yards, &c., they are fixed along the ship's sides and gangways and elsewhere.

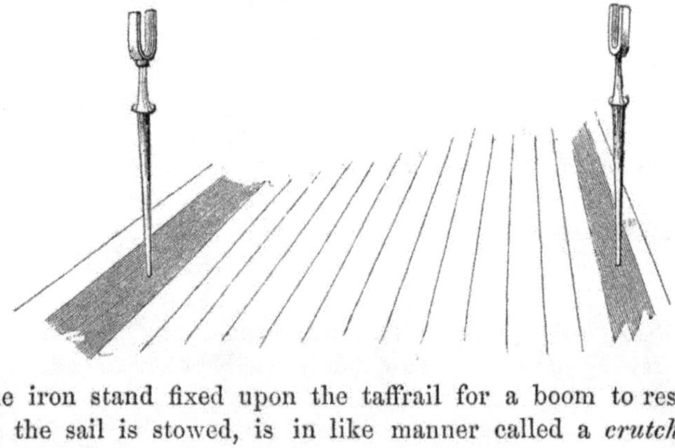

The iron stand fixed upon the taffrail for a boom to rest on when the sail is stowed, is in like manner called a *crutch* or *crutch-iron.*

CUCKOLD'S NECK. A knot by which a rope is secured to a spar, the two parts of the rope crossing each other and being seized together.

CUDDY, in East India ships, a name for the cabin under the poop in which the captain, &c., and passengers mess.

A small cabin such as that in a pleasure boat sometimes gets the name of a *cuddy.*

CULMINATION, in Astronomy, the transit or passing of a star over the meridian. A star is said to *culminate*, when it passes the meridian.

CULVERTAILED. A term applied to the fastening or letting one timber into another so as not to slip out: for instance, the carlings into the beams of a vessel.

CUPOLA SHIP. A vessel of war or a floating battery, iron plated over the deck and sides, and having one or more shields or cupolas built above the deck with a grating over it, open at the top, constructed of iron plates, and made to revolve by steam-power when occasion requires to turn the guns to any point.

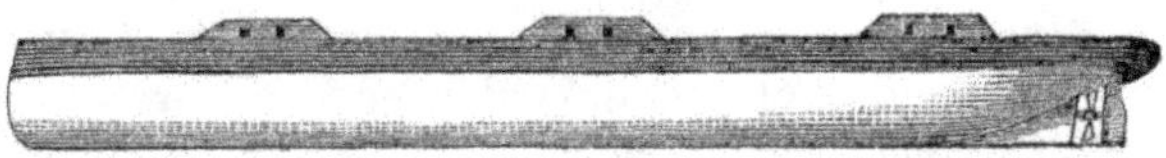

THE 'PRINCE ALBERT' IRON-CASED CUPOLA SHIP, 12 GUNS, 2,529 TONS, 500 HORSE-POWER, BUILT IN 1862 (DRAWN BY PERMISSION FROM ADMIRALTY MODEL).

It is fitted with one or more guns of the heaviest class. These shields give unlimited means of working such guns.

By this arrangement the weight of the guns is disposed about the middle of the vessel instead of on each side as hitherto, and a much less surface is presented by the ship's side as a mark for shot.

In a paper contributed by Captain Coles to the *Illustrated Times* of April 19, 1862, he described his proposed sea-going cupola ships as having iron pole masts fitted with Cunningham's self-reefing topsails, and mentioned that it was 'his study to give the greatest amount of canvass with the least area of masts and yards when steaming head to wind.' See *Shield Ship* and *Floating Battery* (*Ericsson's*).

CURRENTS (*Fr.* Courants) *of the Sea.* Its progressive motions at different places.

1. The *drift* of a current means the rate at which it flows. The *set* of a current is its direction: and in that direction it is said *to set.* The direction of a current, is generally named from the point of the compass towards which it is running; the direction of the wind or waves from that point whence they come. Thus, a *northerly current* is one setting northwards; a *north wind,* as is well known, means one blowing from the north.

2. The currents of the ocean appear to be produced and regulated by various causes; as, the rotation of the earth, the oscillation of tides, the action of the sun, and the prevailing winds. They are modified in their force and direction by many local causes. And by the meeting of currents with other currents, and with islands, rocks, and similar obstructions, whirlpools and counter currents are produced. The melting of the polar ice is said to contribute materially to form the currents which set from either pole towards the equator.

3. The study of these currents is of very great importance to the mariner, on account of their effects on the way of a ship, which for the purpose of safe navigation require to enter into all the reckonings of her courses. At one time they increase the dangers of navigation; at another they may be made use of to assist it. The motion of a ship is affected by a current either in its direction or velocity, or in both, and is thus compounded of its velocity and the setting of the current. See *Sailing* (*Current*).

4. The following general view of the principal currents of the ocean is abridged from *Malte Brun's System of Geography*. Between the tropics, and as far as 30° of north and of south latitude, there is a continual westerly current in a direction similar to that of the trade-winds. The Pacific Ocean retreats from the coasts of America, and flows with a very powerful motion from east to west. 'Ships are carried with rapidity from the port of Acapulco in Mexico to the Philippine Islands; but, in order to return, they are obliged to go to the north of the tropics to seek the polar currents and the variable winds.' This great ocean is impeded in its westerly progress by an immense extent of islands, &c., which gives rise to other currents in various directions.

5. In the Indian Ocean, the pressure of the south polar current, that is to say, the current which sets from the south pole to the equator, upon the large opening presented by that ocean to the south, occasions a constant northerly current, tending to incline more and more towards the north-west, which runs along New Holland and the island of Sumatra as far as the bottom of the Gulf of Bengal. Towards Ceylon and the Maldive Islands, the great body of this current, affected by the general westerly movement, or *equatorial current* of the sea, sets to the west, and is then, by chains of islands and other natural obstacles,

turned towards the south-west, till it reaches the point where the coast of Africa bends to the westwards.

6. Of the currents of the Atlantic Ocean, the most important are—1, that which sets along the coast of Brazil and through the Straits of Magellan into the Pacific Ocean; and, 2, the current known by the name of the *Gulf Stream*, which begins to be felt to the south-west of the Azores, is directed towards the Bay of Honduras, traverses the Gulf of Mexico, flows impetuously out by the Straits of Bahama (after which it receives the name of the *Florida Current*), then pursues its course with great rapidity towards the north, or rather the north-east, till it arrives at the bank of Newfoundland, and thence returns to the African Coast, completing a circuit of 3,800 leagues in about the space of three years. The temperature of this current in the fortieth and forty-first degrees of north latitude, and in the parallel of Charleston, is higher than that of the waters of the sea out of the current. From the forty-fifth to the fiftieth degree of latitude, it has a north-easterly branch setting towards the coasts of Europe.

The most valuable repertory of information on this subject generally is *Lieut. Maury's Investigations of the Winds and Currents of the Sea*, together with his *Wind and Current Charts*, published by authority of the Bureau of Ordnance and Hydrography at Washington, U.S.

CURRENT-SAILING. The method of resolving those problems in sailing in which the effect of the current or of the heave of the sea or of both is to be taken into consideration. See *Sailing* (*Current*).

CUSTOMS. Duties levied upon goods exported or imported.

1. The term *Custom-house* is applied in a general manner to the establishment by which the Customs revenue is collected and its regulations enforced: and in a more limited sense, to the building in which, at any port, the business is carried on. The Customs department of the public revenue is conducted in London by a board of commissioners.

2. Collector of Customs. An officer who takes the general superintendence of the Customs at any port; the Comptroller acts as a check upon him.

3. The Landing Surveyor appoints and superintends the *Landing-waiters*.

4. THE LANDING-WAITERS keep an account of goods discharged from vessels arriving from foreign ports, and act likewise as *Coast-waiters* in superintending the landing and shipping of goods coastways. The JERQUER's duty is to examine and check the Landing-waiters' books.

5. THE SEARCHERS are employed in taking an account of goods to be exported to foreign parts.

6. THE TIDE-SURVEYOR superintends the tide-waiters, &c., and boards them on vessels arriving from foreign parts; he is also employed in admeasuring vessels for registry. The duty of *jerquing* vessels is performed by him.

7. THE TIDE-WAITERS, as already noticed, are boarded by the tide-surveyors on ships arriving from foreign parts, for the purpose of preventing any fraud on the revenue from being committed. They keep an account of goods as landed from vessels. An extensive repertory of information regarding the Customs, &c., is the *Mercantile and Maritime Guide*, by Graham Willmore and Edwin Beedell, a work which has taken the place of *Steel's Shipmaster's Assistant.*

CUSTOM-HOUSE AGENT. A person who attends to the duty of passing the Customs entries of goods on their importation and exportation, and transacting the relative business at the Custom-house, andalso of passing the entries required for the clearance of ships.

CUSTOM-HOUSE OFFICERS. A general name for the officials employed in the Customs department.

CUTLASS. 'A sword with a slight curve in the blade. But the term is now applied generally to the swords furnished to ships of war.'

CUTTER (*Fr.* Cotre, Cutter). A sharp-built vessel, of considerable breadth in proportion to its length, and having one mast, rigged like that of a smack (fig. p. 115). See also *Boat*, 1.

PILOT CUTTERS, are vessels of the above description used by pilots in pursuing their important vocations.

REVENUE-CUTTERS, or REVENUE-CRUISERS, are armed vessels of this description employed for the prevention of smuggling.

There are also vessels rigged as brigs and schooners employed in this service.

CUTTING-DOWN LINE, in Shipbuilding, a curve in the

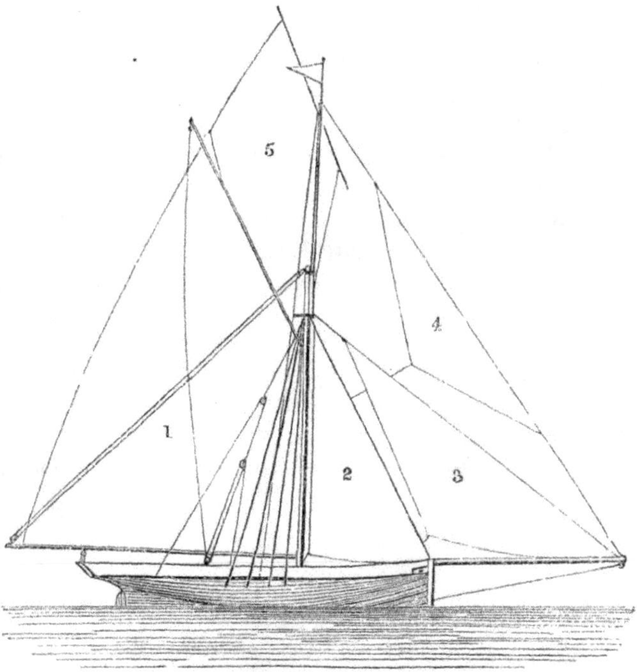


SKETCH OF A CUTTER.

1. Mainsail.
2. Foresail.
3. Jib.
4. Jib topsail.
5. Gaff topsail.

sheer-draught corresponding to the upper surface of the throats of the floors amidships and to the under side of the keelson.

CUTWATER, or FALSE STEM (*Fr.* Guibre). A piece of hard wood fayed to the fore part of a vessel's main stem, its tail covering in the fore end of the keel. Its upper end supports the ornament called the figure-head placed under the bowsprit; it is also called the ***knee of the head.*** (Plate IV. 15.)

CYCLE (*Fr.* Cycle). The period of the revolution of a celestial body. (***Dict. de Marine à voiles.***)

CYLINDER (STEAM) (*Fr.* Cylindre), with appendages. See description of *Steam Engine*, Sects. 1, 22, and 23.

CYLINDER ESCAPE-VALVES. See description of *Steam Engine*, Sect. 6.

DAGGER. A term applied to anything placed obliquely in a

vessel. It is now very generally superseded by the term *Diagonal.*

DAGGER-PIECE. See *Poppets.*

DAK. A kind of boat used at the mouths of the Ganges in carrying despatches. It is decked and copper-sheathed; has two masts carrying lug sails, and is also navigated with oars which work on the top of a forked standard.

DAMELOPRA. An ancient Dutch vessel with a flat bottom; constructed for inland navigation, and suited to carry a heavy lading with little draught of water. (*Dict. de Marine à voiles.*)

DAMMER. A resinous substance, much used in the East Indies for paying the bottoms and seams of vessels. For this purpose in a hot climate it is preferable to pitch. Dammer is also employed in making small hand torches to be used in examining or repairing ships at night.

DANDY. A vessel rigged as a sloop, and having also a jigger

(AFTER BIDDLECOMBE.)

1. Jib.
2. Foresail.
3. Mainsail.
4. Jigger, or Mizen.
5. Gaff topsail.

mast. The mode of rigging the jigger or mizen is explained in *Biddlecombe's Art of Rigging*, p. 112. See *Jigger.*

DAVITS (*Fr.* Bossoires d'embarcation). Pieces of iron or timber, with sheaves or blocks at their outer ends projecting over a vessel's quarters or stern to hoist boats up to. Those projecting from the stern are termed STERN-DAVITS (Plate IV. 39); those from the quarters are termed QUARTER-DAVITS; the latter bend outwards at their upper ends over the rail, and they are made to traverse on their axis in order to bring the boats in-board when required.

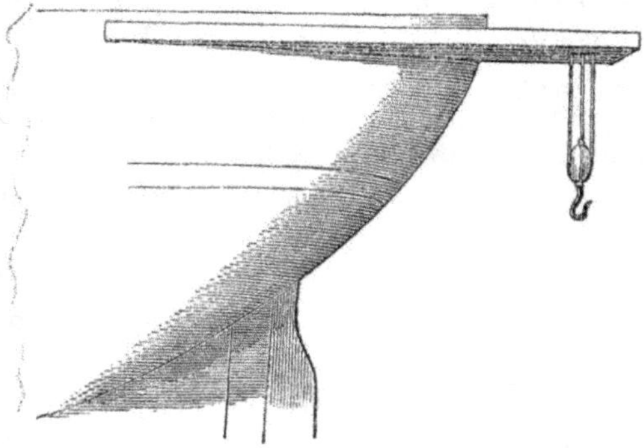

STERN-DAVITS.

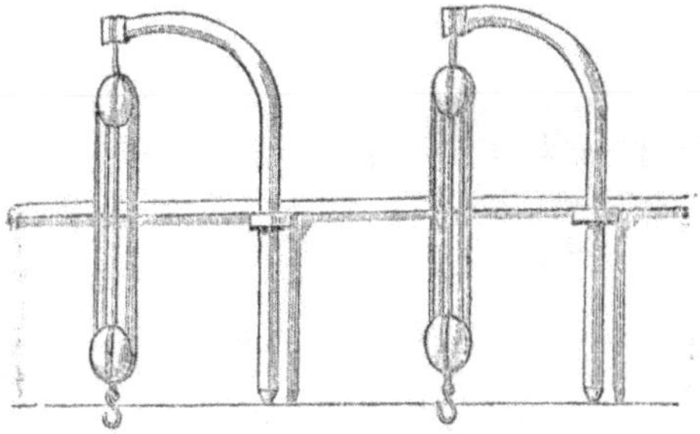

QUARTER-DAVITS OF A STEAM-SHIP OF 50 GUNS.

ANCHOR-DAVIT, or FISH-DAVIT. A spar with a roller or sheave at its outer end. It steps into and traverses in a shoe-piece on the deck or gunwale of a vessel, and is confined to the rail by means of a clamp, and bends outward over the rail. It is furnished with guys to steady it in the required direction. This is used in large vessels for the purpose of fishing an anchor with the aid of a *davit-topping lift*, in order to lay the anchor with its arm resting on the rail, or to bring it in-board if desired; and vice versâ. It is sometimes called a HALF-DAVIT.

BOAT'S DAVIT. A curved piece of oak with a sheave at its outer end: to its inner end it has a cross piece attached, shipping into a cleat on each side of the bottom of the boat, in which cleats it is made to traverse. The davit when shipped projects over the boat's stern, and is used for weighing anchors by means of the buoy-rope with a tackle bent to it inside the sheave.

DAVIT-TOPPING LIFT. See *Topping-Lift.*

DAY. *The astronomical day* is reckoned from noon to noon continuously through the twenty-four hours, and commences twelve hours after the civil day, that is, the day as it is generally reckoned among mankind from midnight to midnight; thus 9 o'clock in the morning of July 3 is by astronomers called July 2 at twenty-one hours. The interval between the departure and return of a meridian to the sun is called a *solar day*: in the case of the moon the interval is termed a *lunar day*, and in that of a star a *sidereal day*.

*The Nautical* (or *Sea*) *day* commences at noon, twelve hours before the civil day, and ends at noon of the day following. Like the civil day, it is divided into parts of twelve hours each, the first twelve hours being likewise marked A.M., denoting *ante meridiem* or before noon, the remaining twelve hours marked P.M., that is, *post meridiem*, or after noon. This mode of reckoning arises from the custom of seamen dating their 'day's work' for the preceding twenty-four hours the same as the civil day; so that occurrences which happen, for instance, on Monday (21st) afternoon, are entered in the log under the date Tuesday (22nd).

Hence it appears that noon of the civil day, the beginning of the astronomical day, and the end of the nautical day, take place at the same time. (*Norie's Epitome of Navigation; Baharie's Marine Board Examination; Nautical Almanack,* p. 513.) See the articles *Mean Time* and *Lay Days*.

DAY'S WORK, in Navigation, the reckoning of a vessel's course or courses during the twenty-four hours of a nautical day, and thence ascertaining her latitude and longitude.

DEAD, is used with some terms to mark the superlative degree, or for the purpose of emphasis. Thus, a wind blowing directly towards the shore is said to blow dead in upon the land. See also *Calm* and *Dead-on-end.*

DEADEN A SHIP'S WAY. To diminish her speed.

DEAD-EYES (*Fr.* Caps de mouton). Circular blocks of wood, through every two of which the lanyards of a vessel's lower rigging are rove. They have three holes in them, without sheaves, and have a groove round them. The under dead-eyes are fixed to the chain-plates by an iron strop going over the groove, and the upper ones are attached to the shrouds of the rigging. Formerly they were so attached to the chain-plates and shrouds on each side of the ship at the channels; but in merchant ships the channels are

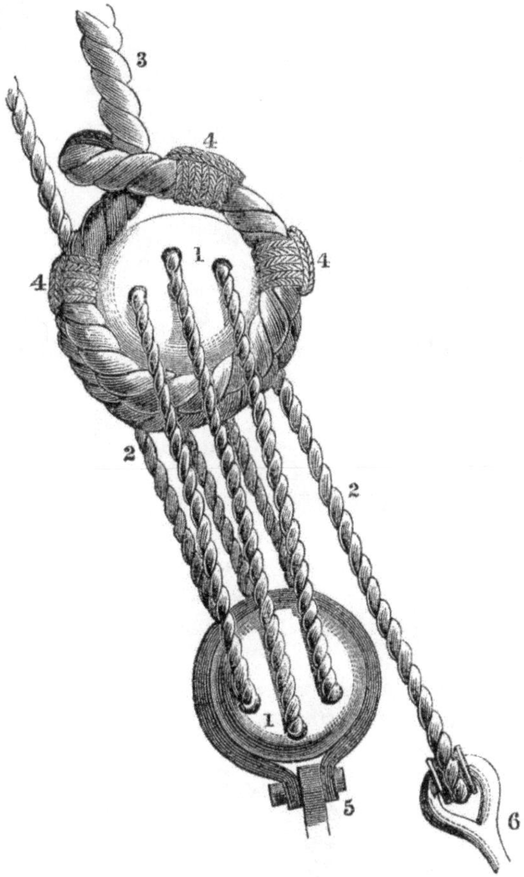


DEAD-EYES WITH LANYARDS (DRAWN AFTER LIEUT. NARES, R.N.)
See his work on 'Seamanship,' p. 33.

1. Dead-eyes.
2. Lanyards.
3. Shroud.
4. Seizing.
5. Shroud-plate.
6. Eyebolt.

now for the most part laid aside, and the chain-plates extend from their original connecting point on the vessel's side to the *top of the rail*, where they are connected with the dead-eyes. Under this new plan the channels are sometimes still retained, but of a smaller size than formerly, and the chain-plates are carried over or through them to the connecting point on the top of the rail. There are likewise dead-eyes for the topmast rigging, the lower ones fixed to the upper ends of the futtock-plates, and the upper dead-eyes attached to the topmast rigging; these are in like manner set up by lanyards. (Plate IV. 36.)

Mr. Chapman's patent invention of *Shroud-blocks* is intended as a substitute for dead-eyes. Each shroud-block is fitted with an endless screw worked by a key.

There is also a kind of dead-eyes called *hearts,* used for stays.

DEAD-FLAT, in Shipbuilding, a term for the midship-frame, or (as Mr. Creuze describes it) the widest transverse section; it is always distinguished by this mark ⊕.

DEAD-LIGHTS. Ports or shutters for the stern and gallery lights, to prevent the water from rushing into the ship in a high sea.

DEAD-ON-END. *The wind is said to be dead-on-end* when blowing directly contrary to a vessel's intended course.

DEAD RECKONING (*Fr.* Estime). The estimation of a vessel's position by the courses steered and distance run, made merely by means of the log and compass. See *Reckoning.*

DEAD-RISING, in Shipbuilding, the rising of the midship floor timber from the horizontal, which is described by the rising-line.

DEAD-WATER (*Fr.* Eau morte). The eddying water which closes in with a vessel's stern and counter when she is under weigh.

DEAD-WEIGHT. A term applied to a vessel's lading when it consists of heavy goods, particularly such as pay freight according to their weight—for example, iron, lead, copper ore, coals, sugar, saltpetre, rice, &c. Those which usually pay freight according to their bulk, those of which a ship could in general float with more than she is capable of containing, are termed *Stowage Goods.*

DEAD-WOOD, in Shipbuilding, pieces of timber fitted together lengthways on the fore and after ends of a vessel's keel, in order to form a rising basis for the frame at these parts; they also afford a stepping for the heels of the cant timbers, and several of the floor timbers forward and aft rest upon them. (Plate IV. 2.)

The upper foremost and upper aftermost pieces of dead-wood

are called *Deadwood-knees,* being crooked pieces of timber, the bolting of which connects the keel with the stem and stern-post. They are termed respectively *Stem-knees* and *Heel-knees.* (Plate IV. 3.)

DEAD-WORKS. A name formerly given to a ship's upper works.

DEALS. The name given to the timber of the pine or fir when sawn into planks. STANDARD DEALS are such as exceed seven inches in width and six feet in length; when under seven inches in width they are termed *battens,* and when under six feet in length, *deal-ends.* (*Waterston's Cyclopædia of Commerce.*) See also *Plank.*

DEBENTURE. A certificate given at the Custom-house to the exporter of goods on which a bounty or drawback is allowed, bearing that he has complied with the statutory regulations, or paid the duties on these goods, and is entitled to such allowance. (*Waterston's Cyclopædia of Commerce.*)

DECKS (*Fr.* Ponts, Tillacs). The flats or floors which are formed by laying the beams of a vessel with plank running in a fore and aft direction.

In merchant ships, the *Quarter-deck* is the aftermost deck, which is raised higher than the *Upper-deck* to give head-room to the cabins; if the vessel be flush-decked, it is the aftermost part of the upper-deck; if she have a poop, the upper-deck is continued, as in the latter case, aft to the stern, and the deck which covers in the poop is called either the *Poop-deck,* or *Quarter-deck.* 'Large ships often have both a *poop-deck* and a *quarter-deck*; the former, not coming much before the mizen-mast, leaves the quarter-deck clear to the gangway.' *The Forecastle-deck* is the foremost part of the upper-deck, under which (if the deck be flush) the sailors generally have their berths; if there be a raised deck above it, this is called the *Topgallant forecastle-deck.* That part of the upper-deck which is between the forecastle and poop, that is to say, in the *waist,* is termed the *Main-deck.* The decks which form the floors of the cabin and forecastle are called respectively the cabin and forecastle *Soles.* If the sole be continued forward to the cabin bulkhead, or aft from the forecastle, this portion of it gets the name of the *Half-deck.* See *Orlop-deck,* and *Steerage.*

In a merchant vessel of two decks they receive the name of the upper and lower deck; in a vessel of three decks, they are called successively the upper, middle, and lower or orlop decks.

In a first-rate ship of war, the decks below the *Main* or *Upper deck* are successively called the *Middle-deck, Lower-deck,* or *Gun-deck* and *Orlop-deck*; guns are not carried on the orlop-deck. The *Quarter-deck,* which is distinct from the *Poop-deck,* extends from the poop to the mainmast; the *Main-deck,* from the mainmast to the foremast; and the *Forecastle-deck* from the foremast to the bow. The gun-deck is sometimes termed the *lower gun-deck,* and the middle-deck is then the *gun-deck.* In *Peake's Rudimentary Treatise on the Practice of Shipbuilding,* the decks from the hold upwards are successively said to be named—1, the orlop; 2, the lower, or gun-deck; 3, the main or upper-deck (also called the middle-deck); 4, the quarter-deck, waist and forecastle.

Mr. Grantham in his treatise on *Iron Shipbuilding* (p. 31) says that decks formed entirely of iron are found to be objectionable.

DECKED. A vessel having a deck or decks is said to be *decked.* A boat or other vessel without decks is said to be *open*; if only partially covered by a deck, she is *half-decked.*

DECKER. This term is applied to a ship of war with reference to the number of decks on which she carries guns. Thus a ship carrying 121 or 110 guns on three decks besides the upper-deck

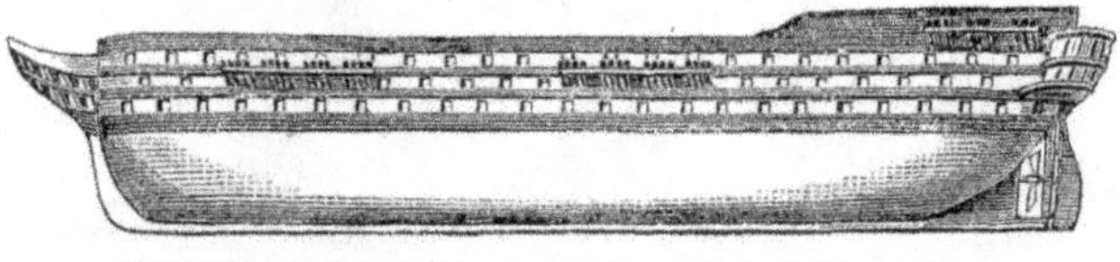

DRAWN BY PERMISSION FROM ADMIRALTY MODEL.

(that is, the quarter-deck, waist and forecastle) is termed a *three-decker.* A ship carrying 101 or 80 guns on two decks besides

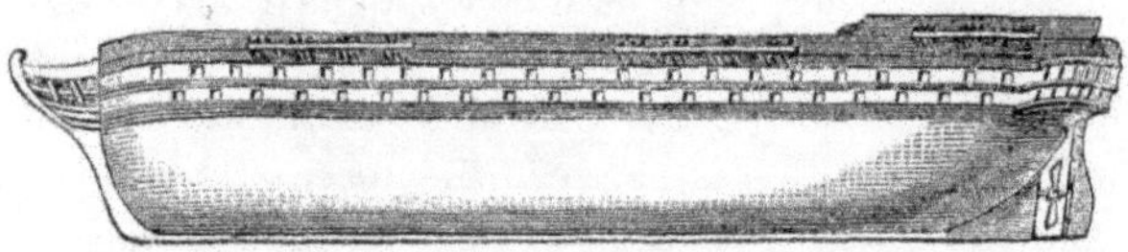

DRAWN BY PERMISSION FROM ADMIRALTY MODEL.

the upper-deck, is a *two-decker.* See *Decks.* Razees and frigates have guns only on one deck, besides those on the upper-deck.

DECK-CARGO, or DECK-LOAD. Goods carried on a vessel's deck.

The usage of any particular trade by sea or special agreement with the merchant or shipper alone can sanction the stowage of goods on deck.

DECK-HOUSE. A kind of round house in some steamers forming a cabin above the deck from the stern to the topgallant forecastle, built in the middle of the vessel, leaving a few planks of deck on each side of it.

DECK-NAILS, are a kind of spike nails or spikes with large heads made in a diamond form. See *Nails* (*Spike*).

DECK-PIPE. An iron pipe for passing the chain cable into the chain well. See *Chain*, 3.

DECK-PUMPS *of a steam vessel.* See description of *Steam Engine*, Sect. 39.

DECLINATION (*Fr.* Declinaison) *of a celestial object.* Its distance from the equinoctial, that is, an arc of a meridian contained between the equinoctial and the centre of the object. It is reckoned from the celestial equator toward the pole, and is called *north* or *south* declination, according as the object is on the north or south side of the equinoctial. The *Polar distance* of a star or other celestial body being in like manner its angular distance from the elevated pole of the observer's horizon, it follows that, according as the star is in the same hemisphere with the observer, or in the opposite hemisphere, its polar distance is equal to 90° *minus* its declination, or to 90° *plus* its declination; in other words, its polar distance is the complement or supplement of its declination. The one or the other enters as an element into the most of astronomical calculations; and the declination of those stars which can best be observed is calculated in advance in the *Nautical Almanack.* Now the declination of an object or the angular distance of its centre from the equinoctial being known, the determination of its position in the heavens is completed by ascertaining its right ascension, which is an arc of the equinoctial contained between the vernal equinoctial point and that point where the arc measuring the declination of the object intersects the equinoctial. It is in a manner precisely similar that the geographical position of any place on the terrestrial globe is determined by ascertaining its latitude and longitude. (*Dict. de Marine à voiles et à vapeur, par Bonnefoux et Paris,* 1848.) See *Astronomy*, 10, 11.

DECOY. Any stratagem used to mislead an enemy's ship or ships into an incautious pursuit; or to misguide them for the purpose of eluding the chase of a superior force.

DEEPS. Any place on a coast where there are deep pools in which soundings can hardly be taken; as *Boston Deeps,* off the river *Humber.*

DEEP-SEA LEAD. A lead of a large size, used for sounding at great depths. See *Lead.*

DEEP-WAISTED (*Fr.* Haut). When the quarter-deck and forecastle are elevated considerably above the upper-deck, the ship is said to be *deep-waisted.*

DEGREE (*Fr.* Degré). A division of a circle equal to $\frac{1}{360}$th part of its circumference. Each degree is divided into 60 equal parts called minutes, and each minute into 60 seconds; marked thus, for example, 26° 59′ 6.″

DELIVER *a cargo.* To discharge it from a vessel into the custody of its proprietor or consignee.

DEMURRAGE. The compensation due to the shipowner from the freighter under a charter-party, or from the individual who claims and receives goods under a bill of lading, on account of undue delay in the loading or unloading of them, or on account of this not being done within the time specified in the charter-party, or in the bill of lading; in such a case the vessel is said to be *on demurrage.*

The rate per day at which this charge for extra time is to be made, is usually and should always be stipulated in the agreement.

DENNET'S ROCKETS. See *Rockets.*

DEPARTURE (*Fr.* Départ, Partance). The east or west distance which a vessel has made from the meridian of the place she departed from; it is reckoned on a parallel of latitude. Also, the bearing of an object on the coast where a vessel commences her dead reckoning; the ascertaining of its bearing, and of the distance of the object from the ship, is termed *taking the departure.* (*Norie; Dana.*)

DEPRESSED POLE. The relative term applied to that pole of the earth which is below the horizon of an observer according as he is in the northern or the southern hemisphere. See *Axis of the Earth.*

DEPRESSION (or DIP) *of the horizon.* The angle contained between the sensible and apparent horizons. See *Horizon.*

DERELICT. A ship or anything cast away or abandoned at sea. When such derelict property has not been thrown ashore, it is distinguished in legal phraseology by the following uncouth and perhaps obsolete names: *flotsam*, implying articles that continue floating at sea; *jetsam*, those which are sunk in the water; *lagam*, those which are sunk, but with a buoy attached, in order that they may be found again.

DERRICK. A single spar set up on a vessel's deck, supported by 'stays' or 'guys,' and having a tackle attached to its upper end; it is used chiefly in shipping and discharging goods by the hatchway. Annexed is a sketch of a derrick set up on deck for lifting the bowsprit.

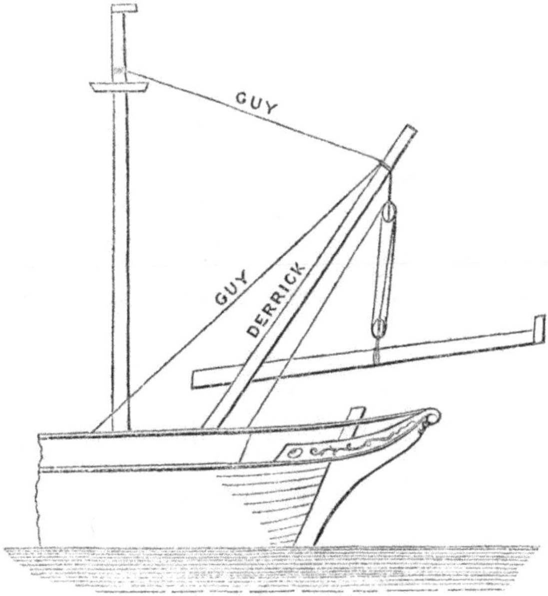


A FLOATING DERRICK, used for raising sunken vessels, is composed of iron tanks fitted together, which can be filled with water or emptied at pleasure to counterbalance the weight to be lifted; the tanks on the side opposite the vessel to be lifted are filled while those next to it are empty. This floating machine is fitted with a crane post, strong iron pillar, or species of derrick, from which project two arms, with a number of purchase tackles to raise the sunken vessel.

DESCENSION. See *Ascension*.

DETACHMENT *of a fleet*, &c. A certain number of ships selected from the rest of a fleet to execute some particular service.

DEVIATION (*Fr.* Déviation). A voluntary departure, without any necessity or justifiable cause, from the usual course of a ship's intended voyage.

DHONEY. The principal kind of vessel used by the natives of Ceylon for the purposes of trade.

DIAGONAL BRACES, KNEES, &c., are such as cross a vessel's timbers obliquely.

According to a regulation of Lloyd's Register of Foreign and British Shipping any vessel to be classed in it, if its length from the fore part of the stem to the after part of the stern-post, on the range of the upper-deck, exceeds five times its extreme breadth, is required to have diagonal iron plates closely inserted inside or outside the frame. Mr. Grantham in his *Treatise on Iron Shipbuilding* (p. 38) says that diagonal ties have been used advantageously in iron ships in a horizontal position as a brace to the upper part of the ship.

DIAGONAL TRUSSING, in Shipbuilding, a particular method of binding and strengthening a vessel internally. See *Trussing*.

A diagonally built boat is 'not timbered, but the planking is double, rising in opposite directions from the keel at an angle of about 45°.' (*Boyd's Naval Cadet Officer's Manual*, p. 284.)

DIAMOND KNOT. See *Knot*.

DIFFERENCE OF LATITUDE between any two places, is an arc of a meridian contained between their parallels of latitude. See *Latitude*.

THE DIFFERENCE OF LONGITUDE, is an arc of the equator contained between their meridians showing how far one of them is to the eastward or westward of the other. See *Longitude*.

DIMINISHING STUFF, or DIMINISHING PLANK, in Shipbuilding, a term for the planking wrought under the wales; it is so called because it diminishes progressively till it comes to the thickness of the bottom plank.

DINGY (*Fr.* Dingui). A name given in the East Indies to small boats hired to attend ships in port.

DIP (*Fr.* Dépression) *of the horizon*. See *Horizon*.

DIP *of the magnetic needle*. See *Dipping-Needle*.

DIPPING. An object, or any part of it, is said to be *dipping* when visible just above the horizon.

DIPPING-NEEDLE (*Fr.* Boussole d'Inclinaison). An instrument used for ascertaining the amount of inclination towards the earth or 'dip' assumed by the magnetic needle. This tendency to incline below the horizontal level increases the nearer we approach the north or south pole. The action or power of the dipping-needle is considerably greater than that of the horizontal needle.

By this instrument the latitude or longitude may be found; but it is too delicate to be used with accuracy at sea.

DIRECT ACTING ENGINE (*Fr.* Machine à action directe). A steam engine in which the connecting rod is led at once from the head of the piston to the crank to communicate the rotatory movement without the intervention of side levers. (*Murray's Treatise*, 6.)

DISC, or DISK, in Astronomy, the circular face which the sun or any other celestial body presents to the eye of a spectator.

DISCHARGE (*Fr.* Décharger). *To discharge a ship*, or to *discharge the cargo*, or *the ship's stores* or *ammunition*, is to take them out of her—in other words, to unlade the ship. The operation is termed the discharge of the ship or cargo, or of the stores or ammunition respectively.

DISCHARGE-VALVE of *Air-Pump*. See description of *Steam Engine*, Sect. 17.

DISCOVERY SHIP. A ship employed in discovering any part of the globe previously unknown—in other words, employed in *a voyage of discovery*.

.DISEMBARK (*Fr.* Débarquer). The reverse of *Embark*.

DISMANTLE *a vessel*. To unrig her; that is, to send down the rigging, yards, and upper masts.

DISMASTED (*Fr.* Dématé). A vessel is said to be *dismasted* when her masts are carried away in a storm or by any accident, or when they are intentionally taken out of her.

DISPART *a gun*. To adjust its elevation so as to bring the line of sight and line of metal or axis of the bore to be parallel. This is done by means of *sights* fixed on the gun; it may be noticed that in the Royal Navy *Miller's sights* are now commonly used instead of those which were invented by Colonel Congreve. The projection on a gun thus used in directing its bore to an object is called the dispart. See *Boyd's Naval Cadet's Manual*, pp. 268, 269.

DISPLACEMENT (*Fr.* Déplacement). The weight of the quantity of water which a vessel displaces when she is floating at rest; it is the same as the weight of the ship.

DISTANCE (*Fr.* Distance). In Navigation, the *east* or *west distance* which a ship has made implies the amount of her progress eastwards or westwards reckoned in a parallel of latitude. So her distance northwards or southwards is reckoned on a meridian. The distance run, also implies the amount of direct progress which the ship has made in any particular direction. See *Departure* and *Sailing* (*Traverse*).

There is a useful publication entitled *Distance Tables for ascertaining a Ship's distance from the summit of High Land, together with Short Distance Tables*, by Jas. M. Share, R.N.

DISTILLING APPARATUS for converting sea-water into pure fresh water. Steam ships in the Royal Navy are fitted with such an apparatus to provide a sufficient supply of fresh water. See *Boyd's Naval Cadet's Manual*, p. 495.

DISTRESS (*Fr.* Détresse). A ship is said to be in *distress* when standing in need of assistance, or requiring to put into a port, in consequence of damages received at sea, or from being otherwise placed in circumstances of danger. A SIGNAL OF DISTRESS is made by hoisting the national flag upside down or by firing guns, &c.

DIVE. To descend voluntarily under water. A person skilled in the art of so descending and remaining below water a certain time for any purpose is called a *Diver*.

A DIVING BELL, is a machine so contrived that persons may descend in it below water, and remain so for a considerable time: an invention of much service in the construction of piers and breakwaters, and otherwise.

There are also water-tight india rubber *diving dresses* invented for this purpose, the head-piece fitted with strong glass eyes, and a pipe being attached for keeping up a supply of air.

DOCK. An artificial receptacle for shipping, constructed so that its entrance may be closed when required. There are two kinds: 1st, *Wet Docks*, in which a uniform level of water is maintained, sufficient to keep ships afloat (an object of great importance), and where the business of discharging and loading may proceed with convenience and safety. The entrance of a wet dock is generally provided with two double gates, having a *lock* between them (similar to that of a canal), which allows the ingress and egress of vessels for some time before and after high water, without much diminishing the supply of water in the dock. 2nd, *Dry Docks*, or *Graving Docks*, used for inspecting or repairing vessels; these are so contrived that, after the ship is floated in, the water may run out with the fall of the tide, or be pumped out, the shutting of the gates preventing its return. See *Harbour.*

The charges for the use of these are termed ***Dock dues*** and ***Graving dock dues.***

*To Dock a vessel*, is to place her on blocks in a graving dock, steadying her in an upright position by means of shores or sliding blocks.

FLOATING DOCK (*Fr.* Forme flottante). A capacious wooden or iron structure, somewhat in the form of a ship's hull, to serve the purpose of a graving dock. It is very flat-bottomed, and calculated to bear a great weight without being much depressed in the water. It is fitted with keel-blocks and sliding bilge-blocks, for steadying a ship upon. The stern of the floating dock is open, and when the machine is sunk till aground, the ship to be repaired is hauled into it. In its bottom there are scuttle-holes, by which the water is allowed to run off, when the tide recedes, and the machine is then made water-tight, so that it may float with its burden upon the making of the tide. See *Caisson.*

Messrs. Rennie and Sons' floating graving dock, patented since the above description was written, is fitted with an engine and pumps placed on the upper part of the side walls, to pump the water out of the chambers of the base or lower compartment till the ship in the dock is raised out of the water. The upper parts of the sides are used as buoyant air-chambers to prevent the dock sinking altogether through negligence at any time. Graving docks of this description, capable of lifting ships of from 5,000 to 6,000 tons dead weight, have been constructed.

HYDRAULIC DOCK. A machine, the platform whereof is suspended by chains and cast-iron pulleys on the top of the framework, connected with a hydraulic engine. See *Caisson.*

SCREW DOCK, consists of a platform suspended by iron screws from a strong wooden framework. See *Caisson.*

DOCKYARDS (ROYAL) (*Fr.* Arsenaux). Places where shipbuilding stores for the Royal Navy are deposited, and which have the appurtenances of slips, docks, &c., for the building, repairing, and fitting out ships of war. The royal dockyards in England are at Deptford, Woolwich, Chatham, Sheerness, Deal, Portsmouth, Devonport, and Pembroke; those established abroad are at the Cape of Good Hope, Gibraltar, Malta, Bermuda, Halifax, Jamaica, Antigua, Trincomalee, and Hong Kong.

THE VICTUALLING YARDS for the Royal Navy, where provisions and similar stores are deposited, are at Deptford, Gosport, Plymouth, and Cork; and abroad, at Malta, Gibraltar, the Cape of Good Hope, Halifax, Jamaica, Trincomalee, and Hong Kong.

DOG. An iron implement having a fang at each end, to be driven into two pieces of wood, for supporting one of them while hewing, &c. Dogs used for masts and yards are of the same

SHIPWRIGHT'S DOG.

form, but smaller; they are driven in at the side of any sheave-hole, to prevent the rope or chain which is rove through it from cutting the spar. Another sort has a fang at one end, and in the other an eye, in which a rope may be made fast, in order to haul anything along. Two of this latter kind fastened together through the eyes by a rope, or by a strand of good rope yarns woolded with canvass to prevent chafing, are called *Sling-dogs.* If connected by rings going through the eyes, they are called

TIMBER DOG.

*Ring-dogs.* Both of the last-mentioned kinds of dogs are used for lifting timber.

DOG-SHORES are shores used to prevent a vessel from starting while the keel blocks are in the act of being taken out preparatory to launching.

DOG-VANE. A small vane made of feathers, or of buntine, placed in a position to show the direction of the wind. See *Vane.*

DOG-WATCHES. Two half watches of two hours each, dividing the time from 4 to 8 P.M. See *Watch.*

DOGGER. A vessel similar in form to the galliot, used by the Dutch in their fishings; some doggers have but one mast, others two. (*Waterston's Cyclopædia of Commerce.*)

DOLPHIN. A spar or buoy secured to an anchor, and generally having a ring in it for vessels to ride by. See also *Buoy,* 9; and *Gun.*

DOLPHIN-STRIKER. See *Martingale.*

DONKEY-ENGINE (*Fr.* Machine Alimentaire). An auxiliary steam engine for feeding the boilers of the principal steam engines when they are stopped.

DOUBLE (*Fr.* Doubler). A ship is said to *double a projecting point of land* when she sails round it. See also the article *Doubling.*

DOUBLE-ACTING ENGINE (*Fr.* Machine à double action). A steam engine in which the steam acts upon the piston against a vacuum both in the upward and downward movement. See *Atmospheric Engine.*

DOUBLE-BANK *an oar,* to have it pulled by two men. *A boat is double-banked* when there are two men on every thwart, each pulling a short oar. The term is derived from 'Bank of oars,' that is, a bench of rowers in a galley—a kind of vessel which has been common in the Mediterranean.

DOUBLE-BANKERS. Frigates which carry guns on two decks, having no elevation at the quarter-deck or forecastle. See *Frigate.*

DOUBLE CAPSTAN is so constructed as to be worked both on an upper and lower deck on one shaft. See *Drumhead.*

DOUBLING (*Fr.* Doublage), in Shipbuilding, signifies planking a ship's bottom twice; this is done in order to strengthen a vessel, when, through age, in consequence of bad shiftings, or otherwise, she has become loosened. The usual mode of fastening off doubling is to have at least every third bolt to go through and clinch inside the ceiling, the rest being short or 'dump' bolts. The term *doubling* is applied to plank not less than two inches thick used for this purpose: if below this in thickness, it gets the name of *Wood sheathing.*

Whale-fishing ships, for the Greenland and Davis' Straits fisheries, require to be *doubled*, and round the bows of such vessels *trebling* is often resorted to, in order the more effectually to withstand the pressure and tear of the ice. For the bows of such vessels African teak is found more suitable than any other kind of timber, being very hard, tenacious, and durable.

DOUELLS. See *Dowells.*

DOUSE. To lower or haul down suddenly.

DOVE-TAIL, in Shipbuilding, a particular kind of mortise, consisting of a score at the end of a piece of wood, resembling the end of a dove's tail, into which a corresponding piece is fitted. It is cut larger within than without, in order that the two pieces may be held together the more firmly. (*Shipwright's Vade Mecum.*) The operation is called *Dove-tailing*.

DOVE-TAIL PLATES. Metal plates, formed like dove-tails, let into the heel of the sternpost and the keel of a vessel, in order to bind them together. Similar plates are used for connecting the stern foot with the fore end of the keel. Rings are sometimes employed which connect the cutwater, stem and keel; but the dove-tail plates are preferable, for, if connected by a ring, and the ship strike the ground with her fore-foot, the lower end of the stem runs a great risk of being shivered : if a ring be used for this purpose, it should be kept clear of the cutwater.

DOWELLS, COAKS, or COGGS (*Fr.* Adents). Cylindrical pieces of dry hard wood, about three inches in diameter, and the same in length, used chiefly as an additional security in scarphing two pieces of timber, for which purpose half of the dowell is let into each of the two pieces. In the modern plan of building ships for the Royal Navy, dowells are used in like manner to connect the butts of the frame timbers when their ends are square, and no cross chocks are therefore required. The operation is called *Dowelling.*

*Boxing* or *Tabling*, is a similar operation, done with square pieces of hard wood.

DOWN WITH THE HELM, is an order to put the helm *a-lee.*

DOWN-HAUL, or DOWN-HAULER. A rope by which any fore and aft sail is hauled down.

PEAK-DOWN-HAULER. A rope rove through a block at the 'peak' or outer end of a gaff to haul it down by.

DOWNS. Barriers of sand along the sea shore, gathered by the force of the wind or waves. Also the name given to the well-known roads for shipping in the English Channel, along the eastern coast of Kent.

DOWSING-CHOCK. The breast hook which crosses the hawse-timber above the upper deck of a vessel.

DRABLER. An additional piece of canvass laced to the bonnet. See *Bonnet.*

DRAFT *of men.* A certain number of men appointed to serve in one or more ships of war; they are said to be *drafted* to the particular ships.

DRAFT, also means a small allowance for waste on goods sold by weight. The draft usually allowed on copper sheathing stripped off a vessel's bottom is about 5 lbs. to the cwt.

DRAG, or DRAG-NET. A frame with a bag-net attached, for *dragging* on the bottom of the water for flat fish, or for anything lost. It also gets the name of a *Trawl-net*; and the operation of fishing with this net is called *Trawling.* A similar frame, with a bag formed of leather thongs (called a *Dredge*) is used in oyster-fishing. See *Sweep,* and *Floating Anchor.*

DRAGGING THE ANCHOR. *A ship is said to drag her anchor* when from the violence of the wind the anchor is torn up from its bed and dragged along. See *Anchor,* 14.

DRAKKAR. A kind of large boat in which the Norman pirates used to ascend the Seine about the ninth century in order to commit their depredations. (*Dict. de Marine à voiles.*)

DRAUGHT (*Fr.* Plan), in Shipbuilding, the drawing or plan of a vessel upon paper, describing the different parts, and from which when extended to a full scale on the floor of the moulding-loft the ship is to be built. See the article *Shipbuilding.*

DRAUGHT OF WATER (*Fr.* Tirant d'eau). The depth of water which a vessel displaces when she is afloat. If she be fully laden it is termed the *load water draught*; if unloaded, the *light water draught.* The number of feet which a vessel draws is indicated by figures on the stem and stern post.

An *easy* draught of water implies the same as a light draught of water.

DRAW. *A sail draws* when it is filled by the wind. *Let draw!* is the order to let the wind take the after leaches of the head sails over to the lee-side, when the ship has come sufficiently round in the act of tacking.

DRAW-BELLOWS. A name given in some parts of Scotland to the limber-holes. See *Limbers.*

DRAW-SPRING, for ships' cables and towing lines. (Thew's patent.) An apparatus consisting of a cylinder, having a piston rod with india rubber bands fitted to it, and a chain to which the tow-rope of a boat or cable of a ship at anchor is made fast. Its object is to take off the recoil or shock in case of the tow-rope or cable breaking.

DREDGE. See *Drag*, and *Dredging vessel.*

DREDGING VESSEL, or DREDGING MACHINE. A kind of large lighter or flat-bottomed vessel, fitted with a steam engine and machinery, for removing the mud and other deposited matter from the bottom of a river, harbour, or basin, by means of iron buckets in an endless chain, that raise the mud, and throw it into large punts, called '*Mud-lighters*,' which are brought alongside the dredging machine for this purpose: the operation is termed *Dredging.*

DRIFT, in Navigation, the leeway which a vessel makes when she is lying-to during a gale. See also *Current*, 1; and *Drive.*

DRIFTS, in Shipbuilding, those parts where the sheer is raised according to the height of the decks or gangways, and where the rails are cut off and ended by scroles, which are formed by solid pieces of wood fitted at these parts, called *Drift-pieces.* (*Shipwright's Vade Mecum.*)

DRIFT-BOLTS, are commonly made of steel; they are used for driving out other bolts.

DRIFT-ICE, consists of pieces less than floes, of various shapes and magnitudes.

DRIFT-PIECES. See *Drifts.*

DRILL SHIPS for the Royal Naval Reserve. Ships in which the volunteers composing the Royal Naval Reserve are drilled in the practice of managing sails, guns, &c.

DRIP-STONE. A familiar name given by seamen to a filtering stone.

DRIVE, or DRIFT (*Fr.* Dérader). To be carried at random by the force of the wind or tide, particularly in the case of a vessel's anchor losing its hold of the ground. We also speak of a vessel driving or drifting in a tide way when she is purposely allowed to be carried along by the influence of the tide.

DRIVER (*Fr.* Brigantine). The aftermost sail of a ship or barque. See *Spanker*, and *Trysail.*

DROITS *of the Admiralty.* Vessels improperly captured before a declaration of hostilities. See *Admiralty.*

DROMON. A vessel navigated with oars, employed as late as the sixteenth century in military expeditions as well as in commercial adventures. (*Dict. de Marine à voiles.*)

DROP (*Fr.* Chûte). A name given to the depth of lower square sails.

DROPS, in Shipbuilding, small foliages of carved work in the stern munions, &c.

DRUM-HEAD. A broad cylindrical piece of wood fixed upon the upper extremity of the capstan. We may here notice that in the case of a *double capstan*, which is so constructed as to be worked both on an upper and lower deck on one shaft, the drum-head of the lower capstan is called a *Trundle-head.* See *Capstan.*

DRUXY. The condition of timber which has decayed streaks or spots in it of a whitish colour.

DRY DOCK, used for inspecting or repairing vessels. See *Dock.*

DRY-ROT (*Fr.* Carie, Pourriture Sèche). A disease, caused by the vegetation of fungi, sometimes affecting timber, especially the oak, employed in shipbuilding. It tends to spread rapidly, and is very destructive, the decomposed wood becoming 'a dry friable mass, without fibrous tenacity.' Dryness, cleanliness, and free ventilation appear to be the best preservatives against, or checks to, this vegetable decomposition, while damp accumulations and a vitiated atmosphere rapidly induce it. Timber ought never to be used for shipbuilding purposes unless properly seasoned and dry, while all decayed portions and the whole of the sap or imperfect wood should be carefully removed. The boiling of planks in salt water is recommended as a good preservative against dry-rot, long practised by Mr. Bayley of Ipswich. Various preventive solutions with which to saturate timber have been proposed. A plan introduced by Mr. Kyan is to soak timber in a solution of corrosive sublimate (see *Creuze's Treatise on Naval Architecture*, p. 67). This solution preserves timber from dry-rot and other causes of decay, and it is applied also to the preservation of canvass and cordage. It appears to be extensively used in this country, and is stated to have been adopted by the Dutch Government for their navy. Sir William Burnet has substituted for this process saturation with the chloride of zinc, one pound of which dissolved in ten gallons of water is sufficient to prepare and preserve half a load of timber.

It is also applied to the preservation of canvass and cordage. A stronger solution of the chloride of zinc renders wood, canvass, cordage, &c., incombustible: and ships of war have now their magazines fitted with wood and felt prepared in this way.

Whale oil is found to be so good a preservative of timber that no whale fishing vessel is ever touched with dry-rot. The best time for laying it (by means of a tar brush) on a vessel's timbers during the process of building, is after the outside planking is put on, and when the timbers have been thoroughly seasoned, and their inside is properly faired for the ceiling; the upper ends of the top timbers, the beam ends, and the keelson in many places should also be bored with an augre, and the holes filled with oil. See *Kiln.*

DUBBING. The act of dressing plank or timber with an adze.

*To dubb a vessel bright* is to remove the outer surface of the plank completely with an adze. See *Boottopping.*

DUCK. A fine description of canvass, used principally for skysails and other light sails.

DUMB-CHALDER. A sort of cleat (of iron or composition) bolted to the back of the stern-post for one of the gudgeons to rest upon. See *Rudder-bands.*

DUMB-CRAFT. A general term applied to lighters, barges, &c., not having sails. Also a local name for the screws used in lifting a vessel clear of the ground on a slip, or in a graving dock, or when ashore.

DUMP-BOLTS, or SHORT-BOLTS. Bolts driven into the plank and timber previous to the through fastenings being put in. See *Bolts*, 8, 10.

DUNGIYAH. A heavily built flat-bottomed coasting vessel of Arabia, which navigates from the Persian Gulf to the Coast of Malabar. It has great breadth of beam, and is very sharp at the stem and stern. The larger dungiyahs have two masts, of which, as in the Baggala, the after one is the larger of the two: they carry a species of lug-sail. (*Dict. de Marine à voiles.*)

DUNNAGE (*Fr.* Fardage). Loose wood, shingle, or other materials laid in the bottom of a vessel in order to elevate the stowage, either with a view to raise the heavy goods which might make her too stiff, or in order to keep the cargo sufficiently above the bottom (at the least nine inches from the skin in the bottom, and six in the bilges) that it may sustain no damage by water should the vessel prove leaky; when the ship has a perishable cargo on board dunnage is sometimes required on the sides of the vessel.

In evidence before the Court of Exchequer on 8th July, 1840, upon a question of unseaworthiness (*Castles* v. *Irving*), it was stated by one of the surveyors to Lloyd's that sugar requires three beds of dunnage.

Dunnage is also used to keep goods from being injured on a damp floor when deposited in a warehouse.

DUNNAGE GRATINGS, are gratings placed on a steamer's deck to place cargo upon, which is stowed on deck so as to serve the purpose of dunnage in keeping the goods clear of any water flowing over the deck.

DWANG-STAFF. A local name given to the 'wrain-staff' or 'wrung-staff.'

DYNANOMETER (*Fr.* Dynamomètre). 'An instrument for indicating the thrust of a screw propeller,' that is, the force it exerts in propelling the ship. (*Murray's Treatise on Marine Engines*, 101.)

EARINGS. Ropes attached to the earing-cringles of a sail, by which the upper corners and the leaches of the sail are secured to the yard when it is bent or reefed. They are called *head* or *reef* earings, according to the particular cringles for which they are used. See *Cringles* (*Earing*).

EASE AWAY, or EASE OFF. To slacken out a rope or tackle.

EASE OFF *a sheet.* The reverse of haul aft a sheet. See *Aft.*

EASE THE HELM. To let it come more amidships when it has been put hard up or down.

EASE THE SHIP. When a vessel is sailing close-hauled, *to ease her* implies to let her head fall off a little so as to meet a coming wave with less resistance: this is done by giving the helm more freedom.

See also the article *Steam-ship.*

EASTING. The distance sailed eastwards. See *Northing.*

EBB (*Fr.* Baisse, Èbe, Jusant). The falling of the waters of the sea, which takes place generally twice in the course of a lunar day. See *Tide,* 1.

ECCENTRIC (*Fr.* Eccentrique) and ECCENTRIC-ROD. See description of *Steam Engine.* Sects. 31, 32, 36.

ECLIPSE (*Fr.* Eclipse). The temporary obscuration of the light of the sun, or of the moon, &c., by the interposition of another heavenly body. Thus the eclipses of the sun are caused by the interposition of the moon between this luminous body and the earth: they are *total* when the disc is entirely hidden; *annular,* when the moon, being at a greater distance from the earth, allows the periphery of the sun's disc to appear, its rays forming a brilliant circle around the moon; and *partial,* when only a portion of the sun's disc is obscured by the moon. An eclipse of the moon is caused by the earth coming between the sun and moon, and preventing the sun's rays from illuminating her.

ECLIPTIC (*Fr.* Ecliptique). In Astronomy, that great circle in the heavens which, by the motion of the earth in its orbit, the sun appears to describe in the course of a year. It is inclined to the equinoctial at an angle of nearly 23° 28′, called the *obliquity of the ecliptic,* and cuts it in two points diametrically opposite to each other, called the *equinoctial points.* The time when the sun enters each of these points (which occurs about the 20th of March and 23rd of September respectively) is termed the *equinox*—day and night being then equal; at these periods, especially about the time of the vernal equinox, storms, called the *equinoctial gales,* are prevalent in many parts of the globe. Those two points of the ecliptic which are each 90° distant from the equinoctial points are called the *solstitial points.* The time when the sun is in one or other of these points is termed the *solstice*; the sun being then at his greatest distance north or south of the equator. That great circle which passes through the equinoctial points and the poles of the earth is called the *equinoctial colure*; and that which passes through the solstitial points and the poles of the earth the *solstitial colure.* See *Zodiac.* (*Norie's Epitome of Navigation and Nautical Astronomy.*) See *Astronomy,* 4, 12.

EDGE AWAY. To sail a little larger when running free.

EDGE DOWN *on any object,* is to approach it in an oblique direction.

ELASTIC PROPELLER (MACINTOSH'S). See *Screw Propeller.*

ELBOW IN THE HAWSE. See *Hawse.*

ELEVATED POLE. The relative term applied to that pole of the earth which is above the horizon of an observer. See *Axis of the Earth.*

ELEVATION, or SHEER DRAUGHT. A vertical and longitudinal view representing the outboard works of a ship with sectional view of the centres of the frames. See *Shipbuilding*, 1.

EMBARGO (*Fr.* Embargo). A temporary injunction by the Government of a country to prohibit the sailing of ships from any port or ports.

EMBARK (*Fr.* Embarquer). To go on board, or to put on board of a vessel. EMBARKATION, is a term more particularly applied to the shipping of troops and naval stores.

EMBAYED (*Fr.* Encapé). A vessel is said to be embayed when the wind is blowing right into a bay, and she is so far within it as to be unable to weather either of its points.

EMIGRATION. Under recent provisions of the legislature, there are Government Emigration *commissioners*, *officers*, and *surveyors* appointed with a view to securing attention to the health, comfort, and proper treatment of emigrants on board of passenger ships, &c.

END FOR END. A term applied to a rope or to any article, such as a log of timber, a spar, a cask, &c., being reversed or turned about so that the one end occupies the place which the other did before.

END ON. A vessel is *end on* to the shore, or to any object, when her head or her stern is pointing directly towards it: in contradistinction to *broadside on.*

Figuratively, a vessel is said to be going end on to a reef of rocks, &c., when driving towards it without any apparent possibility of preventing her.

ENGINE (MARINE). See *Steam Engine.*

ENGINE-BEARERS (*Fr.* Poutres de fondement). The same as *Sleepers.*

ENGINE-ROOM TELEGRAPH. A contrivance invented by Mr. Hornsey of Southampton consisting of a dial on deck, as in the sketch (p. 140), moved by the hand, and communicating its movement to a similar dial in the engine-room of a steam ship to enable the officer in charge of her to convey to the engineer, with certainty and quickness, the necessary orders for working the engines.

ENGINEERS, in the Royal Steam Navy, that is to say, the

officers who superintend and work the steam-engines on board of the ships of war, &c., are distributed into three classes—Engineers, and first and second class assistant engineers.

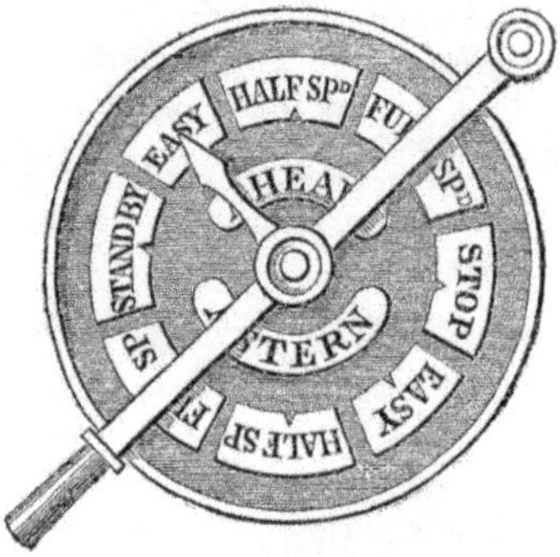


DIAL ON DECK.

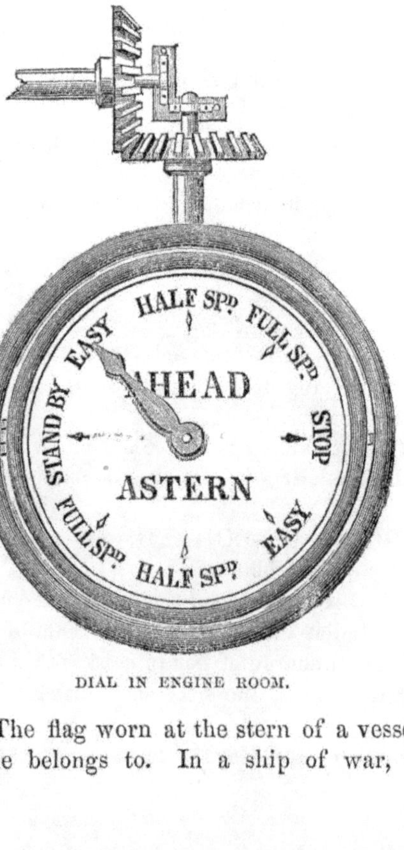


DIAL IN ENGINE ROOM.

ENSIGN. The flag worn at the stern of a vessel, to denote what nation she belongs to. In a ship of war, the British

Ensign is hoisted at the peak, or on a staff called the Ensign-Staff, shipped on the taffrail, and inclining over the stern. Every Admiral's ship, and all ships attached to his squadron or division, wear the ensign of the same colour as his flag, red, white, or blue. See the *Queen's Regulations,* Chap. III. Sect. 11.

ENTERING AT CUSTOM-HOUSE. The act of clearing a vessel outwards or inwards and paying the duties upon her cargo, &c. See *Clearance,* and *Outwards.*

ENTRANCE. The lower part of a vessel's bottom next the stem.

EPHEMERIS (ASTRONOMICAL), and NAUTICAL ALMANACK. An annual publication containing accounts of astronomical phenomena, the declination, &c., of the heavenly bodies and other particulars to assist the mariner in observing the latitude and longitude at sea. See *Nautical Almanack.*

EQUATION OF TIME. The acceleration or retardation of the sun's return to the meridian. See *Mean Time.*

EQUATOR (*Fr.* Equateur). A great circle of the terrestrial globe (sometimes also called the *Equinoctial Line,* or simply the *Line*), equally distant from the poles, its plane being at right angles to that of the earth's axis: it divides the globe into two equal parts, the *Northern Hemisphere* and the *Southern Hemisphere.* The plane of the terrestrial equator extended to the heavens forms a circle called the *Celestial Equator* or the *Equinoctial,* which in like manner divides the heavens into two equal parts, the Northern and Southern Hemispheres. See *Astronomy,* 2.

EQUINOCTIAL. See *Equator.*

EQUINOCTIAL POINTS. Two opposite points at which the equinoctial is cut by the ecliptic. See *Ecliptic.*

EQUINOX. The time when the sun enters each of the equinoctial points. See *Ecliptic.*

EQUIP. To fit out a ship, whether for a voyage or for war.

ERICSSON'S FLOATING BATTERY. See *Floating Battery* (*Ericsson's*).

ERICSSON'S PROPELLER. See *Screw Propeller.*

ESCAPE-VALVES, or PRIMING-VALVES (*Fr.* Soupapes d'échappement). See description of *Steam Engine,* Sect. 6.

ESTUARY. 'An arm of the sea, or the mouth of a lake or river in which the tide reciprocates.'

EUPHROE, UPHROE, or UVRON. Small lines rove through

a circular piece of wood with holes in it forming a *Crowfoot*, by which an awning is suspended. See *Awning*.

EVEN KEEL. When a vessel's draught of water is the same at the bow as at the stern, she is said to be *on an even keel.*

EXAMINATION of masters and mates in the merchant service as to their fitness for undertaking their respective duties is now provided for by the legislature, with regulations as to granting certificates of competency or of 'service.'

EXCHANGE. A term employed by merchants to designate both the bills or negotiable instruments by which remittances are made from one country to another without the transmission of money: and the varying price or 'course' of such instruments in the market.

*Waterston's Manual of Commerce* contains, along with other matter, useful and conveniently arranged information as to exchanges, as well as in regard to the weights and measures of foreign countries.

A comprehensive work on Exchanges, such as the *German Contorist*, is much wanted.

*Reid's Tables of Exchange* of sterling money, dollars, and North American Currency reduced into each other is an exceedingly useful book, enabling the results of the calculations of such exchanges at every rate of premium to be ascertained and their accuracy checked with great expedition. There are, in like manner, Tables by J. H. Roberts, for converting *rupees*, and also Tables by James Laurie for converting *francs* into sterling money, and vice versâ.

EXPANSION-VALVE. See description of *Steam Engine*, Sect. 20.

EXPORT. To send commodities out of a country for the purposes of traffic. To *import* is the reverse. The goods thus sent are respectively called *exports* or *imports*; the person who sends them is called the *exporter* or *importer*; and the act of sending them *exportation* or *importation.*

EYELET-HOLES. Holes made in a sail for the robands or points to go through, in order to bend it to its yard or boom, or to reef it.

EYE-SPLICE. See *Eyes of the Rigging.*

EYES OF THE RIGGING. The circular parts of the

shrouds which are formed like a collar to go over the mast. The eyes of *stays* are termed *collars.*

FLEMISH EYE, or MADE EYE. An eye formed by unlaying one strand of a rope's end, and laying it up round the eye formed by the other portion of the rope's end.

FLEMISH EYE (AFTER DARCY LEVER).

LASHING EYE. A spliced eye made on the end or ends of any rope for a lashing, being rove through in order to set it tight.

MADE EYE. The same as *Flemish Eye.*

SPLICED EYE, or EYE SPLICE. An eye formed by turning the end of a rope back, opening the strands, and splicing it by putting them through the strands of the standing part.

FACING, in Shipbuilding, implies letting one piece of timber on to another to give it additional strength or finish.

FACTOR. A commercial agent residing at a distance from his principal, of some part of whose trade he has the superintendence. He is paid by a percentage (termed *Factorage* or commission) on the price of the goods which he sells or buys.

FAG. A rope is *fagged* when the end is untwisted.

FAG-END. The extreme end of a rope, more particularly when it has become untwisted.

FAIR, in Shipbuilding, denotes the evenness or regularity of a curve or line. Applied to the wind, it signifies favourable as opposed to *foul*: but in a more particular sense a fair wind implies a wind blowing from abaft the ship's beam, being rather applicable when the ship is sailing 'large' than when sailing 'free.' A rope is said to *lead fair* when it moves freely through a block or the like.

*To fair a ship* means to chip the timbers fair.

FAIRLEADER. A strip of board or plank with holes in it, or a thimble, seized where required, for running rigging or any rope to lead through in order to keep it clear. The term is also generally applied to anything used for this purpose. See *Rack*, *Rack-block*, *Shroud-trucks*, *Span*.

FAIRWAY (*Fr* Chénal). The navigable track of a river or the like. See *Channel*, and *Narrows*.

PILOT'S FAIRWAY. A passage or channel wherein, according to usage or special regulation, a pilot must be employed. See *Pilot*.

FAKE. A single coil of rope.

FRENCH FAKE. If a rope be laid in this manner, it is termed

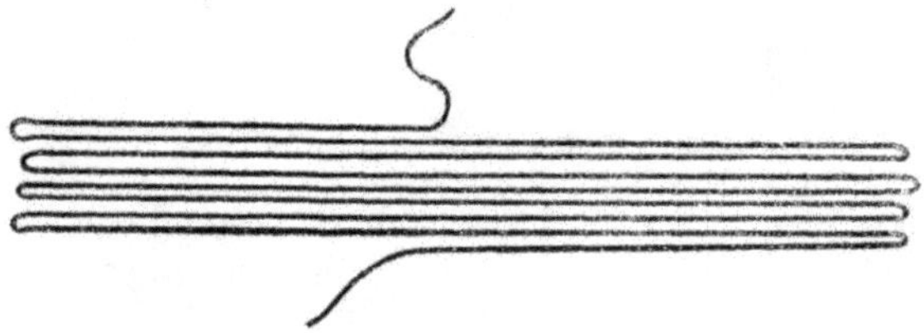

a *French Fake*, which method, when the rope has to be let go suddenly, is adopted, in order to allow it to run freely, without the parts getting foul of each other. A chain-cable is so ranged before letting go the anchor.

FALL (*Fr.* Garant). That part of a tackle which is hauled upon is termed the *fall*. See *Tackle*.

CAT-FALL. The rope by which an anchor is catted. See *Cathead*.

FALL ABOARD OF. To strike or encounter another vessel.

FALL ASTERN. To lessen a ship's way, so as to allow another to get ahead of her. See *Astern*.

FALL CALM (*Fr.* Calmer, Mollir). The wind *falls calm* when it ceases to blow. See *Calm*.

FALLING HOME. The same as *Tumbling Home*.

FALLING OFF. When, in sailing by the wind, the vessel's head falls away to leeward. This is the opposite of *Coming up to the wind*, or *Griping*.

FALSE KEEL. A second keel fastened in a slight manner under the main keel for its preservation. See *Keel*.

FALSE RAIL. A thin piece of plank fayed to the inside of the head-rail. See *Head-rails*.

FALSE STEM. The same as *Cutwater*.

FALSE STERN-POST, is a piece tabled on to the after edge of the main stern-post for improving the steering. See *Stern-post.*

FANCY-LINE. A line used for overhauling the lee topping-lift of the main or spanker boom. It is often called a *Tripping-line.*

Also cord laid up neatly (braided or otherwise) for sash windows, &c. See *Tracing-line.*

FANG. When the pump boxes are dry, and the pump will in consequence not draw, it is said to have *lost its fang.* See *Fetch the pump.*

FANNING BREEZE. 'A wind just sufficient to cause the light sails of a vessel to swell and collapse under the double influence of the air and the motion of the hull.'

FASHION PIECES, or FASHION TIMBERS. Two timbers in the run of a vessel. They are united one to each end of the transoms to terminate the breadth and form the shape of the stern frame. (Plate II. fig. 5.)

FAST. A rope or chain by which a vessel is secured to a wharf or quay. They are called *bow, head, quarter,* and *stern* fasts, according to the part of the vessel to which they are respectively attached. A *breast fast* is one which of itself confines the ship's broadside to the wharf.

MAKE FAST (*Fr.* Amarrer). The same as to fasten; it is most frequently expressed of tying or securing *ropes.*

FATHOM (*Fr.* Brasse). A measure of six feet, used to show the length of chain, cordage, &c., and also the depth of water.

FAY, in Shipbuilding, to join two pieces of wood closely together; as a vessel's planking to the timbers.

FEATHER AN OAR, in Rowing, is to turn the blade horizontally when lifted out of the water, so that its upper edge may point aft. See *Oar.*

FEATHER-EDGED, expresses that a plank has one edge thicker than the other.

FEATHERING SCREW (MAUDSLEY'S). See *Screw Propeller.*

FEED-PUMP. See description of *Steam Engine,* Sects. 19, 25, and 39.

FELT (*Fr.* Feutre). Stuff made of wool or hair, or of both, and tarred over: it is used to lay inside of doubling, or of copper or wood sheathing, on a vessel's bottom. In the case of old ships, this kind of felt is, from its flexibility, peculiarly serviceable by seeking into and filling up crevices, should the vessel be strained. There is also a kind of felt called the *Patent Asphalted Felt* (manufactured by Messrs. F. M'Neill and Co. of London), which is of a stronger, closer, and more fibrous texture than the former. Owing to this firmness of texture, and its evenness of surface, it is well suited to prevent puckering in the nailing on of copper. There is another description of a thicker quality, adapted for use under wood sheathing; but for this purpose hair felt is preferable.

Felt has the property of resisting the worm, and it prevents the heat of the sun, in tropical climates, from opening or rending the planks under the copper sheathing.

Messrs. M'Neill and Co.'s *Dry Hair Felt* is used for covering the boilers, pipes, and cylinders of steam engines, and from its non-conducting property effects a considerable saving of fuel. It is also employed for lining the bulkheads of steamers and other vessels, in order to intercept heat or deaden sound.

Reference may here be made to the 7th paragraph of the article *Shipbuilding.*

FELUCCA (*Fr.* Felouque). A small vessel with sweeps and lateen sails, common in the Mediterranean.

FEND OFF (*Fr.* Défendre). To push or press off, in order to avoid contact or collision.

FENDERS (*Fr.* Défenses). Pieces of wood, rope, or other material, hung over the side or over the bow or stern of a ship or boat, to protect it from being chafed.

FERRY-BOAT (CHAIN). Mr. Rendell's *Chain Ferry-boat* or *Steam Floating Bridge* consists of a kind of oblong-decked punt, open on deck at both ends, and having hawse-holes at the bow and stern through which two chains laid from shore to shore pass over two pitch wheels, or wheels with the impressions of the links of a chain indented in their periphery, driven in the punt by one or two steam engines. There are also similar chain ferry-boats on a small scale, with a pitch wheel on either side driven simply by a crank handle, to work the boat over from shore to shore.

FETCH. To reach; as to *fetch the harbour*, or to *fetch to windward of a point.*

*To fetch headway* or *sternway*, is expressed of a vessel acquiring motion ahead or astern.

When any object in a vessel gets loose from its lashings, it is said to *fetch way.*

The whole *fetch* of a gulf means the whole stretch or extent from the entrance to the top of it.

FETCH THE PUMP (*Fr.* Allumer, Charger la pompe). To pour water above the pump-boxes (when they are dry, and the pump will in consequence not draw, or, as it is termed, *has lost its fang*), and work the upper box up and down by means of the brake, till the air ascending through the water is expelled from beneath, and the water in the well, following it to supply the vacuum, rises through the valves of the pump-boxes, and so enables the pump to work.

FID, or FIDD. A piece of wood or iron made to go through the heel of an upper mast, and resting on the trestle-trees, to keep the mast in its place. *The Patent Screw Fid* (by Messrs. Pearce and Gardiner, Liverpool) is recommended, as allowing the tension of the rigging to be adjusted without taking in sail, and the upper masts to be struck and replaced without casting off or slacking any part of the rigging: it is an iron fid with screws through each end, which work in a plate (having steel sockets) fastened to the upper edge of the trestle-trees.

A fid is also a tapered wooden pin used to open the strands in splicing large ropes, to open the eyes of ropes, and for like purposes; this gets the name of a *Splicing-fid.*

FIDDLE-BLOCKS have two sheaves of different sizes placed one above the other. See *Block,* 4.

FIDDLE-HEAD. A carved ornament at the bow of a vessel over the cutwater in the form of a scrole, bent inwards like the handle of a violin. See *Head.*

FIFE-RAIL. A curved rail fixed on the head of stanchions, encircling a vessel's mainmast and pumps. Tackspins are inserted into it for belaying running rigging.

FIGALE. A small boat of the East Indies in former times, having a single mast and a poop. It had little elevation above the water, and was navigated by sails as well as by oars. (*Dict. de Marine à voiles.*)

FIGURE, or FIGURE-HEAD (*Fr.* Figure). A carved figure at the bow of a vessel over the cutwater. See *Cutwater,* and *Head.*

FILL. To adjust a vessel's sails so that the wind may force her ahead. The reverse of this is *Backing.* See *Back and fill.*

FILLETS. See *Gun.*

FILLING, in Shipbuilding, a piece of wood fitted on a timber or elsewhere to make up a want or defect, particularly to supply the deficiency of the timber in the moulding way. The timber should not have fillings when it can be avoided, especially on the outside. The name of fillings is sometimes given to *chocks,* which see.

BEAM-FILLINGS, for timber-laden ships, are short lengths of wood cut to go between the beams, in order to fill up the stowage, and reaching a little above them, so as to prevent the weight of the cargo between decks from resting upon the beams.

FILLING A SHIP'S BOTTOM. The act of driving nails with broad heads into the outside planking—an operation formerly adopted in order to form a protection to the plank similar to that which is obtained by copper or patent metal sheathing.

FILLING-ROOM. A small place in the magazine of a ship of war, wherein the spare powder used to be started loosely in order to fill cartridges.

In bomb vessels there is a similar place for preparing the shells and cutting the fuses.

FILLING-TIMBERS, or FILLING-IN TIMBERS, are those timbers which are introduced, in some vessels, between the frames, for the purpose of making a solid framing. See *Frames,* 1.

FILTER (*Fr.* Filtre). A strainer for passing (or, as it is termed, *filtering*) water or any other fluid through, to free it of its impurities. These machines are very useful at sea, particularly in long voyages, should the water get foul.

The self-acting filters, which may be introduced into a vessel's scuttled-butt, or into the service tanks of passenger ships, and are so constructed that the water runs freely through them, are especially suitable for use at sea.

FILTERING-STONE. A soft white stone hollowed out to receive water which is filtered through its pores. Among seamen it also gets the name of a *Drip-stone.*

FIRE. The risk of fire in a ship is one with reference to which it is necessary to use every precaution that prudence can suggest against the occurrence of such a catastrophe. And especial care should be taken to avoid receiving on board, except in as dry a condition as possible, any articles which are subject to ignite spontaneously.

FIRE-BOOMS. Long booms, each of them fitted with a

gooseneck, to ship into a bolt in the lower part of a vessel's wales, their ends reaching down nearly to the water's edge, and formed with open prongs, through which a rope is rove and carried round the vessel in order to prevent the boats of an enemy from getting alongside at night.

FIRE-BUCKETS, are buckets used on board ships of war in case of fire, and in time of action for holding the fighting lanterns, and for carrying powder.

FIRE-HEARTH. A cast-iron cooking apparatus used on board of vessels. See *Caboose.*

FIREMAN (*Fr.* Chauffeur). See *Stoker.*

FIRE-SHIP (*Fr.* Brûlot). A vessel filled with combustible matter to be set on fire in order to destroy an enemy's vessels. FIRE-RAFTS are used by the Chinese in their rivers for the same purpose.

FIRE-SWAB. See *Tompion.*

FIRTH. The same as *Frith.*

FISH (*Fr.* Jumelle). A piece of hard wood fastened with bolts and hoops to any spar for the purpose of strengthening or securing it. This operation is called *fishing* the spar.

FISH THE ANCHOR (*Fr.* Traverser l'ancre). To hoist the flukes of the anchor up to the gunwale after it has been catted. The tackle used for this purpose is called the *fish tackle*, to which there is attached a pendant, having a large iron hook, termed the *fish-hook*, made fast to its end.

FISH-DAVIT, or ANCHOR-DAVIT. A spar with a roller

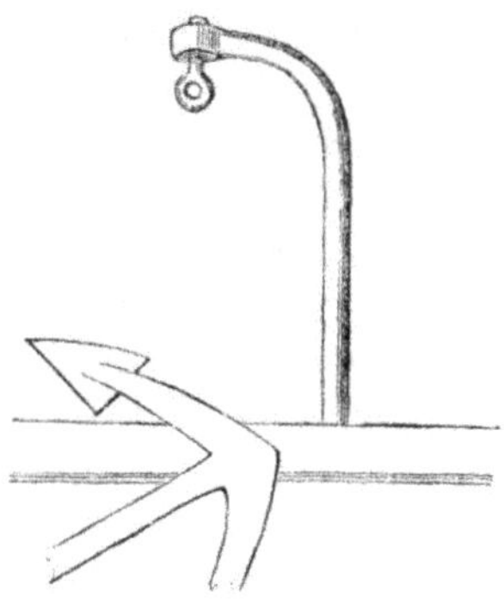

or sheave at its outer end. It traverses in a shoe-piece on the deck or gunwale of a vessel, and bends outward over the rail.

This is used in large vessels for the purpose of fishing an anchor. See *Davits.*

FISH GIG. The name which was given to an instrument, consisting of a staff with three or more barbed prongs of steel; used, like 'grains,' for striking dolphins and other fish.

FISH-HOOK. See *Fish the Anchor.*

FISH-ROOM. In a ship of war, the space between the after-hold and the spirit room. It is now used chiefly for storing lumber.

FISH-TACKLE. See *Fish the Anchor.*

FISHING-SMACK. A sloop constructed to be used as a fishing vessel, having in its hold a well, wherein to preserve the fish alive. The well renders this vessel very easy in a seaway. They are clean-built vessels, generally in cutter fashion, and smack-rigged; hence their peculiar capabilities for encountering stormy weather and so often rendering important salvage services. Some fishing-smacks have no well.

FISHING STORES. See *Tackle.*

FISHING VESSELS. See *Fishing-Smack,* and *Whale Fisheries.*

FIT OUT A SHIP (*Fr.* Equiper). To provide her complement of men, and supply everything necessary to put her in a proper condition for proceeding to sea. See *Outfit.*

FIT RIGGING. To fit the standing and running rigging to a vessel's masts, &c.

FIT-ROD. A small iron rod with a hook on the end used for being inserted into the holes made in a vessel's sides, in order to ascertain the required length of the bolts or treenails which are to be driven in. When the rod is pushed through a hole and drawn back, the hook catches the farther side of the hole, and thus enables its length to be ascertained.

FLAG (*Fr.* Pavillon). A general name for the distinguishing colours of any nation. The different flags used in the Royal Navy are described and illustrated in *Boyd's Naval Officer's Manual,* 501. See the *Queen's Regulations,* Chap. IV. Sect. 9. The statute 8 & 9 Vict. c. 87 prohibits any of Her Majesty's subjects from hoisting in their vessels and boats the Union Jack or any pendants, &c., usually worn by ships in the Royal Navy, or any flag, jack, pendant, or colours whatever resembling those of Her Majesty, or any pendant, ensigns, or colours whatever other than those prescribed by proclamation January 1, 1801, under a penalty not exceeding 500*l.* See *Admiral.*

There are also small flags used for signals or telegraphs.

FLAG-OFFICER. A general distinguishing title for any Admiral, Vice-Admiral, or Rear-Admiral, or Commodore of the first class. Their vessels are called *Flag-ships,* distinguished by the respective flags which they carry.

FLAKE. A platform made of hurdles, used at the fishing harbours of Newfoundland for drying cod-fish. Also a name formerly given to shifting stages.

FLANCHING, or FLANCHING OUT, in Shipbuilding, the same as *flaring*—that is to say, bellying out.

FLANGE. A projecting rim formed on the end of *each* of two pipes for the purpose of uniting them. The rims formed on the ends of a steam cylinder for bolting it to the engine bottom and to the cylinder cover are also called *Flanges.* There are likewise flanges made on the truck wheels of the cradle of a patent slip, in order to keep the cradle from running off its iron railway.

PORT FLANGE, in Shipbuilding, a piece of wood fixed on the ship's side over a port, to prevent water or dirt from going into the port when open.

FLARING, FLARING OFF, or FLARING OUT. The reverse of *tumbling home.*

FLAT, in Shipbuilding, a straight part in a curve. *To* FLAT IN or *to* FLATTEN *a sail,* is to haul its clue or sheet aft.

FLATS. A name given to certain banks having shoal water over them. Also a term applied to a kind of lighters employed in river navigation. Those used in the Mersey are rigged sloop fashion. They are flat in the bottom and very flat built.

FLAT-BOTTOMED. A term implying that a vessel's bottom does not rise, or has little upward inclination.

FLATTEN, or FLAT IN. See *Flat.*

FLAW. A term applied to a gust of wind.

FLEET (*Fr.* Flotte, Force Navale, Armée Navale). A general name given to the Royal Navy, or to any part of it employed in a particular service or expedition.

Also a number of merchant vessels sailing in company.

TO FLEET. To 'come up,' that is, to slack off a tackle, and draw the blocks apart for another pull, after they have been hauled chock-a-block—in other words, after the blocks forming the purchase have been hauled close together.

Also, 'to shift the position of a block or fall, &c., so as to haul to more advantage.'

*To fleet the messenger* is to cast off the lashing, and shift the messenger for another pull.

FLEMISH COIL. See *Coil.*

FLEMISH EYE. See *Eye* (*Flemish*).

FLEMISH HORSE. A small foot-rope at a topsail yard-arm. See *Horse.*

FLENSING. The operation of clearing a whale of its blubber and bone. In the northern whale fisheries, the man who directs the cutting operations is called the *specksioneer*: the *speck-falls,* whereof there are two, for hoisting the blubber and bone off the whale, are ropes rove through two blocks made fast to the *blubber-guy,* which is a large rope stretched from the main to the fore mast head.

*The Cant* (or *Kent*) *purchase* is formed by a block suspended from the mainmast head, and another block which is made fast to a circle called the *Cant,* cut in the whale between the neck and fins: it is used to cant the fish round during the above operation.

The blubber, on being hoisted on board the vessel, is cut into square pieces and stowed in the hold; afterwards these are again taken on deck, skinned, cleared of any *kreng* (that is, any useless part of the carcass) which adheres to them, and cut into smaller pieces to be stowed away in casks: this latter process is termed *Making-off.*

For more minute details on this subject, and in regard to the mode of flensing adopted in the southern whale fisheries, reference may be made to Captain Scoresby's valuable *Account of the Arctic Regions and Northern Whale Fishery,* and the Appendix thereto.

FLOAT (*Fr.* Flotter). To rise to, or remain on, the surface of the water.

*To float a ship* (*Fr.* Déchouer), is to raise her to the surface of the water when sunk or to bring her afloat when aground. See also the article *Swim.*

FLOAT. A raft. See also *Paddle-wheels.*

FLOAT-BOARDS. The same as *Floats* of a paddle-wheel.

FLOATING ANCHOR (*Fr.* Ancre de cape). A machine contrived to prevent a vessel from driving rapidly where there is no anchoring ground. This might be peculiarly serviceable in the case of her being disabled about the masts, and thereby rendered unable to keep off a lee shore.

The following description of it is partly adjusted from *Seamanship both in Theory and Practice*, wherein a plate of the machine is given. It consists of two flat bars of iron, each in length about half the breadth of the midship frame of the vessel for which it is used: these bars are connected together in the middle by means of a bolt. When intended to be used, the bars are swivelled at right angles to each other, and kept so by a swifter of rope or small chain passed through a hole in the end of each bar, which swifter must be hove tight, or four spars are cut to about half the breadth and lashed together so as to form a square. To this there is marled a double fold of No. 1 canvass, laid on that side

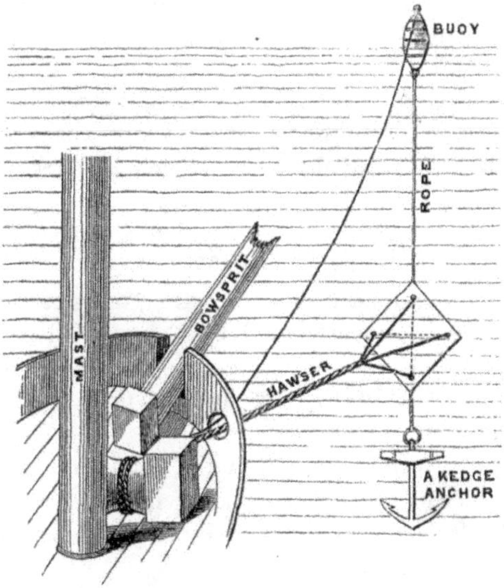


FLOATING ANCHOR (SHOWN IN PERSPECTIVE).

which is next the ship when the machine is used. By ropes made fast near each corner a crowfoot is formed, having an eye for a large hawser to bend to; a kedge anchor is then applied as a balance is to the tail of a kite, and to prevent its going too deep in the water the whole is suspended by a buoy or small cask. When it is thrown overboard, the hawser and a rope made fast to the head of the buoy are veered away sufficiently to ride the vessel. To get it on board, haul on the buoy-rope, which will bring it to the water's surface, so as to be easily drawn to the ship. It can only be used with propriety in plenty of sea room.

Occasionally vessels put out a spar or other thing suitable, with the end of a warp attached to it as a *drag*, to serve the like purpose as the floating anchor.

FLOATING BATTERY. An old vessel fitted for harbour defence.

The following is an account of the kind of Floating Battery used by the Federal States of America. It is a flat-bottomed wooden vessel of war, very wide in the middle and narrowing towards the ends, 'forming a kind of elongated oval, over which is laid a thick flat iron cover with sides dipping into the water. In battle these sides show a surface of only 12 to 20 inches above the water, and the funnel is let down after the telescope fashion till its covered top alone is seen on deck.' 'On the centre of the vessel rises a vast circular pillar or *cupola* (or turret), built of several thicknesses of inch iron, fastened by screws inside, and the joinings so arranged that no two can any where be struck by the same shot.' This cupola or turret contains two heavy guns, and is moved round with them at pleasure by steam power. Such is a description of Ericsson's floating battery the 'Monitor,' extracted from the *Illustrated London News* of April 5, 1862. Many years before a floating battery of this kind, or 'steam shield raft' (as it is also called), was designed by Captain Coles, R. N. See *Cupola Ships*.

FLOATING BRIDGE. A bridge formed by boats or pontoons &c.

STEAM FLOATING BRIDGE. A kind of oblong-decked punt open at both ends, having two chains passed from shore to shore over two pitch wheels driven in the punt by one or two steam engines. See *Ferry Boat* (*Chain*).

FLOATING DAM. See *Caisson*.

FLOATING DERRICK. See *Derrick*.

FLOATING DOCK (*Fr.* Forme flottante). See *Caisson*, and *Dock* (*Floating*).

FLOE. 'A piece of ice, similar to a field, but the extent of which can be distinguished.' See *Iceberg*, 5 and 11.

FLOOD and FLOOD TIDE (*Fr.* Flot). The rising of the waters of the sea, which generally takes place twice in a lunar day. See *Tides*, 1.

FLOOD MARK. The line made by the tide upon the shore when at its greatest height. See *Tides*, 3.

FLOOR. The bottom of a vessel on each side of the keelson. In the midship body, the flattest part of the floor is at the flat frame, called the midship frame.

The *floor-timbers* are by way of abbreviation called the *floors*. In this sense, the RISING-FLOORS imply those floor-timbers which rise gradually from the plane of the midship floor, so as to sharpen the form of the vessel towards the bow and the stern. See *Peake's Rudimentary Treatise on the Practice of Shipbuilding*, p. 15.

FLOOR-GUIDE, in Shipbuilding, is a ribband which is placed between the floor-ribband and the keel. See *Ribbands*.

FLOOR-HEADS. The upper extremities of a vessel's floor-timbers.

FLOOR-PLAN, or HALF-BREADTH PLAN, in Shipbuilding, is a section upon a longitudinal plane whereon is represented the water-lines and the ribband-lines.

FLOOR-RIBBAND. See *Ribbands*.

FLOOR-TIMBERS, or FLOORS (*Fr.* Varangues). Large and strong pieces of timber placed across a vessel's keel at right angles to it, forming the lower structure of the frame. (Plate II. fig. 6.) See the articles *Floor*, *Frame*, and *Keelson*.

FLORY-BOATS. A local term applied to boats employed in carrying passengers to and from steamers which cannot come alongside of a landing-place at low water.

FLOTILLA (*Fr.* Flotille). A fleet of small vessels, more especially of gun-boats.

FLOTSAM, JETSAM, and LAGAN. Legal terms (out of ordinary use) applied respectively to articles that continue floating at sea, those which are sunk in the water, and those which are sunk but with a buoy attached to them. See *Derelict*.

FLOW. The rising of the tide. See *Tide*, 1.

FLOWING-SHEET. When a vessel has the wind free or large, and the lee clues eased off, she is said *to sail with a flowing sheet*.

FLUES (BOILER). See description of *Steam Engine*, Sect. 37.

FLUID COMPASS. See *Compass*, 7.

FLUKE. A broad flat triangular plate of iron, fixed on the

inside of the blade of an anchor to take the greater hold of the ground. See *Anchor*, 1.

FLURRY. A name which has been given to a light breeze, shifting about and slightly ruffling here and there the surface of the sea.

FLUSH. With a continuous even surface; thus a *flush deck* is one which stretches fore and aft upon one line without any falls or intervals.

FLY. The length of a flag from the staff to the outer edge. If a union flag, it is that part which extends from the union to the extreme end.

The opposite of this, or rather the breadth of a flag next the staff, is called its *hoist*.

FLY *of the Compass* (*Fr.* Rose des vents). A card supported by a pin and divided by *rhumb lines* into thirty-two equal parts representing the divisions of the horizon. See *Compass*.

FLY-BLOCK. Any block which, forming part of a tackle, shifts its position when hauled upon.

FLY-BOAT. A name sometimes given to a swift canal passage boat.

FLY-BY-NIGHT. A name given in some places to a square sail, like a studding-sail, used in sloops when running before the wind. It is set on the topmast, having its foot stretched to the cross-jack-yard.

FLY-UP, in Shipbuilding, a term similar to *flight*, implying a sudden deviation upwards from a sheer line: as that of the after ends of the wales in a square-sterned vessel.

FLYING ABOUT. The frequent changing of the wind during a short space of time. See *Chop About*.

FLYING JIB (*Fr.* Clin Foc). A sail set outside of the jib upon a boom, called a flying jib-boom. See *Jib*.

FOG-BANK. A dense mass of fog, presenting the appearance of a thick cloud resting upon the horizon.

FOG-HORN. A horn used on board of a vessel to sound as a warning signal in foggy weather. Bells and gongs, &c., in sailing ships, and the steam whistle in steamers, are likewise employed as *fog signals*.

FOOT-HOOKS. See *Futtocks*.

FOOT-ROPES. Ropes stretching from the middle of a yard to each of its extremities, for men to stand on when reefing, furling, &c.: they were formerly termed *Horses*. In order to keep them more nearly parallel with the yard, they are suspended from it at convenient distances by short pieces of rope called *Stirrups*, each of these having a thimble spliced into its lower end, through which the foot-rope is rove. There is likewise a foot-rope beneath the jib-boom. See the articles *Boltrope* and *Horse.* (Plate IV. 121.)

FOOT-VALVE (*Fr.* Clapet de fond). See description of *Steam Engine*, Sect. 15.

FOOTWALING. See *Ceiling.*

FORE (*Fr.* Avant, Petit—the latter term applied to masts, &c.). A term used to distinguish that part of a vessel at or near her bow, or things at that part in opposition to *after.*

FORE-AND-AFT. Lengthways of the vessel, as opposed to athwartships. A fore-and-aft rigged vessel, called also by way of abbreviation a *Fore-and-after,* is a vessel rigged with fore-and-aft sails. See the article *Sails.*

FORE-BODY, in Shipbuilding, is that part before the midship frame as seen from ahead. See *Shipbuilding*, 5.

FORECASTLE, or FORECASTLE DECK. The fore part of the upper deck at a vessel's bows. In a merchantman, the forecastle more properly implies the fore part of the vessel under the deck, wherein are the sailors' berths.

If there be a sort of cabin formed by a short deck raised above the forecastle-deck, it gets the name of a *Topgallant Forecastle.*

FOREFOOT. The lower part of the cutwater, and fore end of a vessel's keel which is covered in by it.

FORE-GANGER, or FORE-GOER. A short piece of rope which is grafted to the shank of a harpoon, and to which the line is bent. See *Harpoon.*

FORE-GRIPE. The lower ends of a véssel's stem and cutwater connected with the keel.

FORE-HOODS. The foremost of the outside and inside planks of a vessel.

FORE-HOOKS. The same as *Breast-hooks.*

FORE-LOCK (*Fr.* Goupille). A flat piece of iron which is driven through a hole in the end of a bolt to prevent it from drawing. A bolt when secured in this way is said to be *fore-locked.*

*Spring Fore-locks*, or (as they are sometimes termed) *Split Fore-locks,* are split at their points, thereby forming springs to prevent their coming out.

FORE-MAST (*Fr.* Mât de Misaine). The lower mast placed in the fore part of a vessel. See *Mast.*

FORE-MAST MEN, or MEN BEFORE THE MAST. A name given to the common sailors, distinguishing them from the officers on board of any vessel.

FORE-PEAK. The *fore peak* and *after peak* are the extreme forward and aftermost spaces or parts of the hold of a vessel formed by the contracted points of the bow and stern.

FORE-REACH, or HEAD-REACH. To shoot ahead when sailing on a wind. Thus one vessel is said to fore-reach on another when she is sailing faster on a wind. Again, if it, in lying to a vessel's head, tends to come up in the wind, it is necessary to adjust the sail or sails, so as to make her 'fore-reach,' that is, to gain a little additional headway, and thereby increase the power of the helm.

FORESAIL (*Fr.* Misaine). The principal sail set on the foremast.

FORE-SHEET HORSE. An iron rod or piece of wood fastened at its ends athwart the deck of a single-masted vessel before the mast, for the fore-sheet to travel upon.

FORE-STAFF, or CROSS-STAFF. 'An instrument which in ancient times was, as the quadrant now is, used for observing altitudes at sea. It consisted of a wooden staff, having a scale of degrees and parts of degrees marked upon it, and cross pieces fitted to glide along it at their middle parts. The smallest cross pieces were used for observing the least altitudes. And the observation of the sun's altitude appears to have been made by means of the shadow which the extremity of the cross-piece cast on the staff when the instrument was adjusted.'

FORGE AHEAD. To shoot ahead when at anchor.

*To Forge a vessel over a bank,* or *bar,* is forcibly by press of sail to make her careen or lie over, by which means she gradually forces or 'forges' herself over the bar.

FORK-BEAMS. Short beams introduced to support the deck where there is no framing. See *Beams,* 4.

FORMER, in Gunnery, a round flat piece of wood with a hole in its centre, of the same size with the bore of the gun; used for making wads. There are likewise cylindrical pieces of wood called *Formers,* used for rolling cartridges upon, to fit the piece for which the cartridges are intended.

FORTIFYING. The operation of strengthening a ship's

stem and bows by the application of double planks, as well as strong chocks or knees of wood, bolted securely to the stem, and to the bow plank and timbers, outside, and cased over with thick iron plates, the inside being also strongly secured by additional breast-hooks, and additional beams (called *ice-beams*) connected with a number of cross-riders, pointers, and stanchions; the whole of these properly fitted and bolted firmly together render the bow almost impregnable. This system is adopted for all ships employed in the northern whale fishery, to enable them to withstand the concussion and pressure of ice. See *Doubling*.

FORWARD. Towards or in the fore part of a vessel.

FOTHER. To draw a sail, with tarred oakum spread and sewed over one side of it, beneath a vessel's bottom, in order to stop a leak. Instead of the oakum being sewed over it, the sail may be thrummed, and the strands of yarn then teased out into oakum.

FOUL. *A rope is said to be foul* when it is entangled or obstructed. *The bottom of the water is foul* when it abounds with rocks or shoals. In these senses, *clear* is the opposite term. See also *Anchor*, 18; and *Fair*.

FOUNDER (*Fr.* Sancir). A vessel *founders* when she sinks at sea by filling with water.

FOX. A seizing made by twisting together two or more short lengths of rope-yarn with the hand.

'*A Spanish fox*, is made by untwisting a single yarn, and laying it up the contrary way.' (*Dana's Seaman's Manual.*)

FOXEY, implies 'a defect in timber of a reddish cast or hue, arising from over-age and other causes.' (*Shipwright's Vade Mecum.*)

FOY. A term in some places applied to the charge made for the use of a boat.

FRAME *of Marine Engine* (*Fr.* Châssis, Cadre). See description of *Steam Engine*, Sect. 34.

A ship in the course of building is said to be *in frame* when the hull is completed with the exception of the ceiling and outside planking being put on.

FRAMES, or FRAME-TIMBERS (*Fr.* Couples, Membrures), in Shipbuilding, the floor-timbers, futtocks, and top timbers, the whole of which, after being moulded, fitted, and bolted together, compose what is termed the *Frame*. These are placed upon the keel at right angles to it, and form the bottom and sides of the ship. The floor-timbers are securely bolted down to the keel The frames of an iron ship are designated simply as side frames and flooring.

1. FILLING-IN-TIMBERS, are those timbers which are introduced, in some vessels, between the frames, for the purpose of making a solid framing. In steamers, the framing is made quite compact, sometimes as high as the light water mark, and is caulked outside and inside, so as to bind it firmly, and make it water-tight independent of the planking; the whole being secured by fore-and-aft bolting, affords, along with the main keelson and additional keelsons, a substantial basis for the engines and boilers, at the same time presenting an efficient resistance to the strain and vibration of the machinery.

2. BALANCE-FRAMES. Those frames of an equal capacity or area which are equally distant from the ship's centre of gravity.

3. MIDSHIP-FRAME. The frame which forms the extreme breadth of a vessel. See *Midship Frame*.

4. SQUARE FRAMES. Those frames which are square with the line of the keel, having no bevelling upon them.

*The Frames of an iron ship* are explained and illustrated in *Grantham on Iron Shipbuilding*, p. 24.

FRAMING and WARPING the TIMBERS, in Shipbuilding, implies putting in the beams, knees, coamings, &c., and dividing the spaces between the beams into equal parts (perhaps three or four) from side to side of the vessel, by fitting fore-and-aft pieces, termed *carlings*, between the beams.

FRAP. To pass ropes round a sail, in order to prevent it from blowing loose. To pass ropes or chains round the hull of a vessel which is weakened, in order to keep her together. To secure the ropes of a tackle together, by means of spun-yarn, rope-yarn, or any lashing wound around them. The bowsprit gammoning is likewise frapped in order to tighten all its parts.

FREE. *A vessel is sailing free*, or has the *wind free*, when she is not close-hauled, but sailing with her head somewhat farther off the wind; if the wind be abaft the beam, she is *sailing large*, or has a *fair wind*.

*A vessel is said to be free*, when the water is pumped out of her; and pumping *frees* (*Fr.* affranchit) *the ship* when it discharges more water than what leaks into her.

FREIGHT (*Fr.* Fret). The sum agreed on between a ship-owner and merchant to be paid for the use of a vessel in conveying goods. The term freight is sometimes used to imply the lading itself.

*To freight a vessel* (*Fr.* Affréter, Fréter, Noliser), means to employ her for the carriage of goods, or of goods and passengers.

FREIGHTER (*Fr.* Affréteur). The person who hires a vessel or part of a vessel for the carriage of goods.

*The Freighter's Guide and Commission Merchant's Assistant*, by George Harrison, is a work which contains tables of first and second class goods on a decimal scale, of which wheat is the standard, with rules, examples, and demonstrations, and a new set of tables of *proportionate rates of freight* by inspection. The same gentleman has also published a *Ready Reckoner for the Coal Trade*, to be used in computing the amounts of cargoes of coals shipped and delivered, and the amount of freight.

FRENCH FAKE. See *Fake*.

FRESH. *A fresh breeze*, implies a wind in which a vessel may safely carry all her canvass; *a stiff breeze*, implies one somewhat stronger than this, but not so violent as a gale.

*A vessel is said to have fresh way* when she moves with speed, or with increased speed, through the water.

FRESHEN (*Fr.* Rafraîchir). To relieve a rope by altering the position of that part which had been exposed to friction: thus, *to freshen the nip of a stay*, or *of a rope cable*, is to shift it in order to prevent its being chafed through; *to freshen the hawse*, means to veer out or heave in a little of the cable of a vessel at anchor, so as to let another part of it bear the stress at the hawse-hole. A memorandum issued by the Lords Commissioners of the Admiralty on 17th June 1846, enforces upon the commanding officers of Her Majesty's ships the necessity of paying attention to freshen the hawse when riding hard in order to prevent the prolonged action upon the same links at the hawse-holes, &c.

*When the wind increases*, it is said to freshen.

FRICTION-ROLLER. A cylinder of hard wood, or metal,

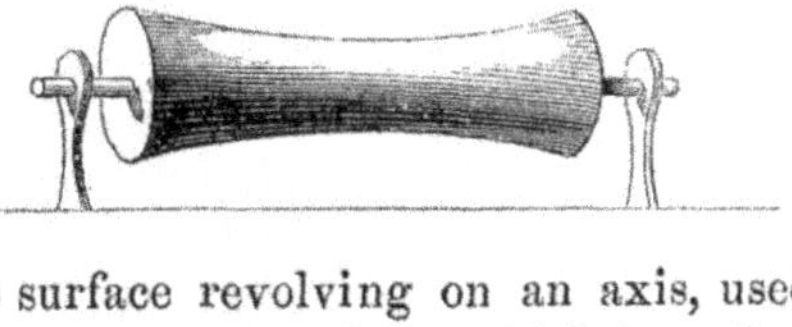

with a concave surface revolving on an axis, used to lessen the friction of a rope or any other thing which is made to pass over it.

FRIGATE (*Fr.* Frégate). A particular kind of ship of war constructed with a special view to swiftness of sailing, and therefore well adapted for cruising. These vessels mount from thirty-two to fifty guns, which are carried on the main-deck, quarter-deck, and forecastle.

*Double-banked Frigates*, or *Double-bankers*, are such as carry guns on two decks, having no elevation at the quarter-deck, or forecastle, but the tier of guns on the upper-deck being uninterrupted except generally at the gangways. Seventy-four gunships have been sometimes razeed and converted into double-banked frigates.

*Steam Frigates* are large armed steam ships, with a battery on a flush upper-deck, including four or more heavy pivot-guns, adapted to throw both shot and shells to a great distance: like a frigate, they have also a tier of guns on their lower or main deck, and are generally commanded by a captain of the Royal Navy.

The following are sketches of a *Steam Frigate* (a frigate propelled at will by steam power) and of an *Iron-cased Frigate*

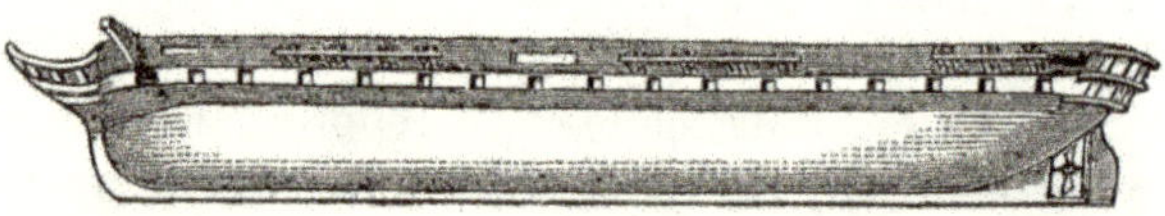

A STEAM FRIGATE (DRAWN, BY PERMISSION, FROM ADMIRALTY MODEL).

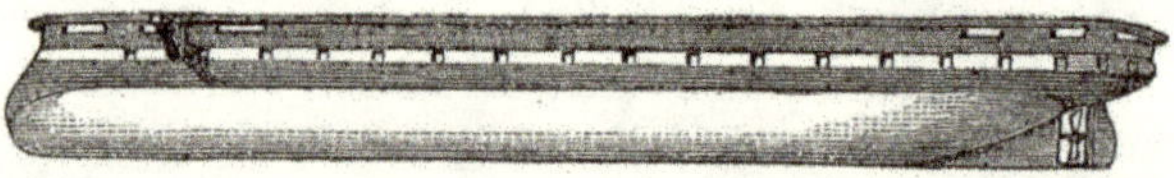

AN IRON-CASED OR ARMOUR-PLATED STEAM FRIGATE (DRAWN, BY PERMISSION, FROM ADMIRALTY MODEL).

(or armour-plated steam frigate), both of them fitted with screw engines.

FRIGATE-BUILT. A term applied to a merchant vessel whose decks are ranged similarly to those of a frigate.

FRITH, or FIRTH. An arm of the sea into which a river flows; such as the Solway Frith, or the Firth of Forth.

FULL. The state of a vessel's sails when they are filled with the wind so as to carry her ahead: if full a-back, that is, filled so as to carry her astern, they are said to be *flat a-back.* See also *Lean.*

FULL AND BY, or BY THE WIND. The same as *close-*

*hauled*, that is, sailing with a vessel's head close to the wind in order to get to windward.

FUMIGATION-LAMP. A kind of lamp (described in *Dr. Burney's edition of Falconer's Marine Dictionary*) invented for the purpose of purifying the air of close or infected places, and which is peculiarly serviceable in hospital ships.

FUNNEL. An iron tube used as a chimney for carrying off the smoke from a vessel's cook-house. Also the cylindrical stalk for the furnaces of a steam ship: this is secured by chains or ropes called the *funnel stays*, leading from eye-plates near the top of the funnel to the ship's sides. See description of *Steam Engine*, Sect. 38.

FUNNEL-STAYS. See *Funnel.*

FURL (*Fr.* Ferler, Serrer). To roll up and bind a sail upon its yard or boom.

FURNITURE. See *Tackle.*

FURRENS, in Shipbuilding, a term sometimes used to imply the same as *fillings* ; that is to say, pieces supplying the deficiency of timber in the moulding way.

FUSE, or FUZE. A conical wooden pipe or hollow plug filled with a combustible composition, and wedged into a hole, called the *fuse-hole*, in a shell to explode the shell at a certain period after it leaves the mortar or howitzer whence it is fired.

*Bickford's Fuse*, is a tube of powder sewn round with tarred twine and the outside covered with pitch. It is inextinguishable by water. (*Boyd's Naval Cadet's Manual.*)

FUTTOCKS, or FUTTOCK-TIMBERS (*Fr.* Allonges). As explained under the title *Floor-Timbers*, a vessel's floor-timbers are laid across the keel: the frame-timbers fitted on the ends of these are called *second futtocks* (Plate II. fig. 6), and between the floor-timbers there are timbers, called *first futtocks*, which come down almost to the keel on each side; the timber above each of the first futtocks is called a *top-timber*, or *long top-timber*, and that above each of the second futtocks, a *short top-timber*, or *lengthening-piece.*

In large ships there may be *a third* and *a fifth* futtock introduced between the first futtock and long top-timber; and *a fourth* and *a sixth* futtock between the second futtock and lengthening-piece.

The whole of these timbers ought to be properly shifted, and they compose what is termed the *Frame* of the ship.

FUTTOCK-HOLES. See *Futtock-Shrouds.*

FUTTOCK-PLANK. A name sometimes given to the first

plank of the ceiling next the keelson, wrought over the lower ends of the first futtocks. See *Limber-strake.*

FUTTOCK-PLATES. Iron plates crossing the sides of the top rim perpendicularly at the outer end of a vessel's cross-trees. The dead-eyes of the topmast rigging are fitted to their upper ends, and the *futtock-shrouds* to their lower ends.

FUTTOCK-RIDERS. See *Riders.*

FUTTOCK-SHROUDS (*Fr.* Gambes). Short shrouds leading from the lower ends of the futtock-plates to a hoop of iron round the lower mast, a little below the top. To this hoop shackles are attached which secure the futtock-shrouds at their lower ends; while the upper ends go through the top rim, and have dead-eyes fixed to them, with lanyards for setting up the topmast rigging. In some merchant vessels the futtock-shrouds are formed by a continuation of the topmast rigging coming down through holes in the top, called *futtock-holes.* The present mode of fitting the futtock-shrouds is illustrated in p. 13 of *Kipping's Rudimentary Treatise on Masting.* See *Catharpins.*

FUTTOCK-STAFF (*Fr.* Bastet). A short piece of wood or an iron rod, seized across the upper part of a vessel's rigging, to keep the rigging fair aloft: it was formerly used to secure the catharpins.

FUTTOCK-TIMBERS. The same as *Futtocks.*

FUZE, or FUZEE, and FUZE-HOLE. See *Fuse.*

GAB, and GAB-LEVER. See description of *Steam Engine,* Sect. 32.

GABART. A long narrow flat vessel, or lighter, with a hatchway extending almost the length of her decks, sometimes fitted with one or two masts, which are made so that they may be lowered in passing under bridges. Gabarts are used chiefly in canals and in rivers. *Gabart* is a local term for a *derrick,* and it is also applied to a kind of sheers with three legs set up to assist in weighing goods at discharging or loading.

GAFF (*Fr.* Corne). A spar to which the head of a fore-and-aft sail, such as a boom-mainsail, spanker, spencer, or trysail is bent. (Plates III. and IV.) There is a main gaff and a fore gaff in a schooner.

The gaff embraces the mast by two projections at its end, called *cheeks,* and it is secured by means of a rope called the *jaw-rope,* taken round the mast from cheek to cheek. The gaff for a fore or main spencer goes with a swivel eye into the truss hoop of the fore or main mast.

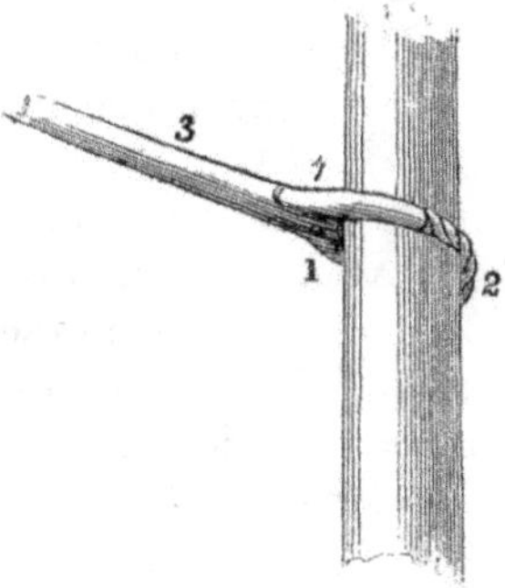


JAWS OF TRYSAIL GAFF.

1. Cheeks. 2. Jaw-ropes. 3. Trysail gaff.

There is an ingenious contrivance, in some places called a *tumbler*, to avoid the necessity of having copper nailed on the mast to prevent a gaff from chafing it. This consists of a piece of wood about 18 inches long and 6 inches broad, hollowed out in its fore part to fit the mast betwixt the cheeks of the gaff. It works on a bolt going through it, and through both cheeks of the gaff. And in the middle of the after part there is a round projection to fit into the hollow of the gaff.

GAFF-TOPSAIL (*Fr.* Flèche-en-cul). A light sail set on the topmast over a gaff, its foot being spread by the gaff. (Plates III. and IV.)

GAGE. See *Gauge.*

GALE. 'A wind not tempestuous, but stronger than a breeze.' (*Johnson.*)

*Gales*, or *Gales of wind*, are more particularly understood by mariners to be those storms which, chiefly during winter in high latitudes, blow sometimes from one direction for several days together. These, Mr. Horsburgh notices in his *India Directory*, prevail mostly from the westward, and are not so liable to shift suddenly as the gales met with near the tropics, which are generally of short duration. It may be remarked, however, that in the Atlantic Ocean, when the wind has been blowing heavily from the southward, it is very common for it to veer round suddenly to the westward.

EQUINOCTIAL GALES. Storms which are prevalent at those

periods of the year when the sun enters the equinoctial points, especially about the time of the vernal equinox. See *Ecliptic.*

GALEASS (*Fr.* Galéasse). A large vessel, in form resembling the galley, navigated with sails and oars. Of these vessels the Venetians have long made use. (*Dict. de Marine à voiles.*)

GALLEON. A term at first denoting a ship of war with three or four decks. Afterwards it was applied to the large merchant ships sent by the Spaniards in the trade to America.

GALLERY (*Fr.* Galerie). A projecting balcony on each of the quarters, and sometimes on the stern, of a large ship. They are often decorated with ornamental devices. Some small vessels have imitation galleries on their quarters. The stern gallery of a large ship gets the name of the *balcony.*

GALLEY (*Fr.* Galère). The cook-house; or more properly the cook-room, or apartment built either on deck or below in which the cooking is carried on. See *Cook-House.*

Also, a low flat-built vessel, worked with sails and oars, which has long been common in the Mediterranean. A person condemned to work at an oar in one of these vessels is called a *galley-slave.*

GALLIOT (*Fr.* Galiote). A flat-bottomed vessel, whose bow and stern are similar, being round and bluff. It is commonly fitted with lee boards, and has two masts; the fore mast, which is the tallest, is rigged like a sloop's mast, while the after mast carries a sail which, like the foresail, is also set upon a boom and gaff. This kind of vessel, drawing little water, is especially common in Holland, the coasts of which abound in banks and shoals.

GALLOWS. A strong frame erected on the deck of a small vessel to support spare spars, &c., in port. It consists of two 'gallows-bitts,' or 'gallows-stanchions,' and the 'gallows-top,' which is a cross piece of timber tenoned on to the top of these bitts. The bitts are supported by knees on deck at their fore-and-after parts. There are usually two of these frames in a vessel, one abaft the fore mast, and another before the main mast. The double winch works on the after gallows, the axle of the winch revolving in bushes on the two bitts, and the handles being at each side of the frame.

Large vessels are fitted with cross beams elevated to the height of the poop deck. They go from side to side, secured by stanchions. Large merchant ships carry their boats on these beams, which sometimes get the name of *Skid beams.*

GAMMONING. The rope or chain lashing used to secure a vessel's bowsprit down to the stem-head. It is generally made fast to a triangular ring, called the *Gammon-shackle,* formed on the end of the *Gammon-plate,* which is an iron plate bolted to the stem; or, in vessels of war, to a wooden knee called the *Gammon-knee,* which is fayed and bolted to the stem a little beneath the bowsprit. The gammoning is frapped round to tighten all its parts. In very large ships of war there are usually two gammonings at a little distance from each other.

In some ships, instead of using a gammoning, the bowsprit is secured down to the stem-head only by a chock of hard wood driven between the knight-heads, into which the chock is dove-tailed, and fastened with screw bolts through them.

SCREW-GAMMONING. A chain or plate for the above purpose, fastened by means of a screw. This is used in some coasters that have occasion to go through canals, for convenience in tracing up the bowsprit when required.

GAMMON-KNEE. See *Gammoning.*

GANG. A certain number of a ship's company selected for a particular work or duty.

GANG-BOARD. A broad thick plank used for the convenience of getting into or out of a vessel when she is alongside of a quay or elsewhere.

GANG-CASKS. Large casks used for bringing water aboard in boats. See *Breakers.*

GANGWAY (*Fr.* Passe-avant). That part of a vessel's side opposite to the main hatchway, where people pass into and out of the ship: the bulwark and rail at that part is sometimes made to ship and unship when required, to facilitate the shipping, and discharging goods, &c., by the hatchway.

A platform temporarily laid as a communication between a vessel and the shore is also called a *Gangway.*

The name of *Gangway* is likewise given to a range of plank fenced with rails, laid between the quarter-deck or poop and forecastle, on each side of a deep-waisted vessel, as well as to that which forms a communication between the paddle-boxes of a steam ship; this latter (which is more generally called the *Bridge* or *Bridge-board*), being bolted and fastened with knees to the paddle-boxes, serves to lessen their vibration. In many steamers, two bridges cross the ship, one at each of the foremost and aftermost extremities of the paddle-boxes, with a fore-and-aft 'bridge' or 'gangway' in-board of each of the paddle-boxes to connect them.

GANTLINE. A name sometimes given to *Girtline.*

GARBOARD-STRAKE. The first outside strake of planking next the keel. See *Strake.*

GARLAND. An ornament decked with ribbons hoisted up between the masts of a North Sea whaler on the 1st of May, &c., or in a vessel of war on the occasion of a marriage.

Also, 'a name for a large strop or grommet lashed to a spar when hoisting it on board of a vessel.'

GARNET. A purchase made fast to a vessel's mainstay for hoisting cargo.

See also *Clue-garnets,* under explanation of *Clue-lines.*

GAROO-KUH. A coasting vessel, or large fishing boat of the Persian Gulf.

GASKET (*Fr.* Garcette). A plated cord made with two or three yarn foxes, or with spun yarn, used to secure a sail to its yard or boom when furled. They are called *bunt, quarter,* or *yard-arm* gaskets, according to their position on the yard.

GATHER AFT A SHEET. To haul in the slack of it.

GAUB-LINE. See *Gob-line.*

GAUGE, or GAGE. When one vessel is to windward of another, she is said to have the *weather gauge* of such ship; if to leeward, the *lee gauge.*

The depth of water that a vessel draws is sometimes termed her gauge.

There are instruments called gauges contrived for measuring the depth of the sea, the height of tides, the force of the wind, &c., named respectively a *Sea-gauge, Tide-gauge, Wind-gauge,* and so on, according to the purposes to which they are applied. There is an instrument invented by M. Clement, called a *Sillometre,* or *Marine speed-gauge,* which measures the speed of a vessel through the water, and (for convenient observation) is connected with a dial on deck. See also *Salinometer* (a *Brine-gauge*).

*A shot-gauge,* is a ring of iron, with a handle attached to it, for measuring the size of shot; it is numbered according to the calibre of the gun for which the shot is intended.

GAUGE-COCKS (*Fr.* Robinets d'épreuve), and MERCURIAL

GAUGE (*Fr.* Manomètre de verre mercurial). See description of *Steam Engine*, Sects. 42 and 43.

GAY-DIANG. A coasting vessel of Cochin China, sharp at each end, rigged with three triangular sails.

GAY-YOU. A fishing boat of Touranne on the coast of Cochin China, of singular build and rig.

GEAR. A term used to denote the ropes and blocks, &c., belonging to any particular sail or spar, as the *topsail-gear*, the *bowsprit-gear*. The *running gear* denotes all the running rigging. We also speak of the *pump-gear*, which implies everything belonging to the pumps.

GEARING. A complication of wheels and pinions, or of shafts and pulleys, &c.

GENERAL SHIP. A vessel engaged to convey to a certain port or ports of destination the goods of various merchants unconnected with each other.

GIG (*Fr.* Guigue). A long narrow boat, chiefly adapted for rowing expeditiously, and also furnished with sails. See *Boat*, 1, 2.

GIMBALS, or JIMBALS. ~~Two concentric~~ rings used for suspending the case of the compass within a square wooden box. See description of *Compass*.

GIN. A small iron frame with a wheel working in it, and having a chain, called a *Gin-chain*, over the wheel to serve as a pulley in discharging cargo, &c. The frame has a swivel hook at its upper end for hooking on to a gaff or derrick or elsewhere for the purpose required.

GIN-CHAIN. See *Gin*.

GIRT. A vessel is said to be *girt*, when, in riding with two anchors out, a change of wind or tide causes her to swing round, and, owing to the cables being too taut, she is interrupted by one of them, which therefore requires to be slacked down in order to allow her to move over it. This is not liable to happen with chain-cables, unless one of them have very little scope. When riding with a single anchor and chain out, and moored with the stream-cable, the vessel may become girt by the latter.

GIRTLINE. A rope rove through a single block aloft, making what is called a whip purchase, commonly used to hoist rigging by in fitting it, or to steady the head of a mast while swaying it up. It sometimes gets the name of a *gantline*, which perhaps would be more properly rendered *cantline*.

GIVE WAY! An order to men in a boat to pull with greater force, or to commence pulling. The same as *Lay out on your oars.*

GLASS. A familiar name given by seamen to a telescope or 'spy glass,' and also to a barometer.

GLUE (MARINE) (*Fr.* Glu marin, Colle marine). An adhesive composition, composed of gum-lac, caoutchouc, and naphtha or mineral oil, invented by Mr. Alfred Jeffery of Limehouse, possessing properties most useful and important for shipbuilding and other purposes. From a series of experiments publicly made, it has been shown to possess the peculiar properties required in a substance to be used for joining a vessel's timbers together: it is insoluble in water, and impervious thereto; elastic, so as to contract and expand according to the strain on the timber; sufficiently solid to fill up the joint and give strength; and it has great power of adhesion.

To render the marine glue more available in its application, various degrees of hardness and elasticity are made, viz. No. 1, the hardest and most adhesive; No. 5, the softest, consequently the most elastic.

'No. 1 is used for paying decks of steamers over and about the boilers, and for decks and top-sides of ships engaged in hot climates, for sealing bottles, jars, &c., intended for shipment to tropical climates, and for various other purposes, where it is exposed to excessive heat.

'No. 2, for paying decks and top-sides of vessels engaged in all climates. If the seams are very narrow on deck or round the stanchions use No. 3.

'No. 3, for paying the seams of the decks, sides, and bottoms of ships; for uniting large timbers in general, as masts, yards, spars, beams, &c.

'No. 4, for coating the inside of tanks, cisterns, waterbutts, &c.; for covering surfaces to prevent the admission of water; for leather bands for machinery; and various purposes, where not exposed to great heat.

'No. 5 is used for filling up shakes in timber, and for filling between the planks and timbers to prevent leakage, and protect them from rot and decay.'

The following are instructions and observations issued by the patentees.

PROPERTIES OF THE MARINE GLUE. *The marine glue* possesses *four* essential properties, viz.: —

1st. *As to its power of adhesion.* It resists a strain of several hundred pounds per square inch; a less strain than this will tear asunder the fibres of the wood.

2nd. *As to its elasticity.* It contracts and expands according to the strain on the timber, still adhering to the edges of the planks.

3rd. *As to its insolubility in water.* Each of its component parts is insoluble in water; therefore it is impervious to water, and a security against leakage and damps.

4th. *As to its power of resisting atmospheric changes.* The hottest climate will neither dissolve it nor make it sticky, and the coldest neither cracks it nor makes it brittle, like pitch. It also resists acids in general, and is a perfect non-conductor of electricity.

UTILITY OF THE MARINE GLUE. The attention of the patentees has been principally given to the application of the *Marine Glue* to Naval architecture in Her Majesty's dockyards; but a composition of this nature is equally valuable for merchant ships. The patentees, in order to render the *Marine Glue* more available in its application, make it of various degrees of hardness and elasticity. The following numbers have been most successfully applied in Her Majesty's dockyards.

No. 3. For paying the seams of decks, and top-sides, and seams in the floors of warehouses, hospitals, flat roofs, and balconies. For joining made main masts, spars, bowsprits, yards, jib-booms, scarfings, keels, keelsons, beams, and large timbers in general; and for fixing deck lights.

No. 4. It also is used for the last-named purposes, and for lighter timbers, and is found in testing to be sufficiently adhesive to break almost every description of wood. This number is easier to melt, and will bear boiling longer than No. 3. It is also more convenient in its application, and is probably the more generally useful in timber constructions—such as dock and lock gates, piers, aqueducts, bridges, and floating breakwaters.

No. 5. For filling up the fine shakes or rends of timber. For coating the inside of water-tanks, and various purposes. For coating iron pipes, or other works which are situated underground.

A liquid marine glue is also made; its application and uses will be found below.

General application of the Marine Glue to nautical purposes.

Melting. *Strict attention required.* Cut the glue into small pieces; melt in a pot over a moderate *coke* or *charcoal* fire, keeping it gently stirred all the time it is melting.

*Note.* When the glue is all melted, the heat is about 212° Fahr., but much too thick to run into the seams of decks or floors, and if used in this state will cause air bubbles in hot weather; therefore it requires boiling and stirring a few minutes longer, when the heat will rise to 300° Fahr.; it then becomes perfectly liquid, and should be used as quickly as possible. The safest way to melt small quantities is in the common glue kettle, using oil in the outer kettle instead of water, as oil produces a greater heat; common observation will soon enable the workman to see the proper heat at which the glue should be used. If a white steam be observed in the pot after the glue has been boiling a few minutes, it is evident that it will soon become *charred*; therefore remove the pot from the fire.

Safety from Fire. The marine glue never boils over into the fire like pitch, although it will occasionally ignite whilst being melted, and it would continue so to burn until the glue would be destroyed. When this takes place, gently remove the pot from the fire, and cover it over with a piece of sacking or any air-tight substance; this will immediately extinguish the flame without the least injury having been done to the glue.

Laying and Caulking Decks. In laying decks, the planks to be slightly bevelled in the ordinary manner. The situation of the nail-head to be countersunk with a $\frac{7}{8}$ inch *centre-bit* to the depth of an inch, previous to the nail being driven. Afterwards the nail to be completely covered with a small quantity of the glue, and the plug dipped in the glue to be driven down upon it. Iron nails (which have the greatest holding power) may be used instead of copper or metal nails, as by the use of the glue they are protected from oxidation. The oakum to be laid well down in the seam, *hard*, leaving the seam *one inch deep and a quarter of an inch wide after caulking* for the glue in the seam, and, as usual, to be payed immediately.

Coal naphtha or coal oil to be used in dipping the *caulking irons*, as linseed oil or grease prevents the glue from adhering to the edge of the plank.

Paying Decks. In paying decks, the glue should be poured from the ladle into the seams, holding the nose of the ladle one inch from the deck.

*Note.* If the ladle is drawn on the seams, which is frequently done when pitch is used, a quantity of atmosphere is enveloped, and has not time to escape before the glue becomes set; this also will cause air bubbles in hot weather, and leave the seams hollow and unsound. When the decks have been payed with pitch or rosin, the old materials to be broken out, and a *race knife* used to clear the seams, in order that the glue may adhere to the edge of the plank; the seams may be afterwards caulked or hardened down, as may be required, to the depth before described, viz. one inch, if the thickness of the timber will allow of it.

Cleaning off. The deck to be cleaned off on the following day, if the ship be required for immediate service; otherwise it is best to *clean off* when she goes to sea.

Paying Top-sides. The seams of the sides to be payed with a *thrum mop*, precisely in the same manner as with pitch, leaving the seam slightly hollow; taking care to cover well the oakum.

Shakes. Expel the dirt and moisture from them, and then run them full with the glue, as in the case of deck seams.

Application of the Glue to Masts, Yards, Beams, and other large Timbers. When the glue has been melted, as described in its application to decks, spread over the surface of each timber a uniform thickness of glue, using for the purpose a stiff brush, and if the surfaces are of great length and width, and be found *slightly hollow* in the middle, as is sometimes the case in mast work, make some allowance, and give rather more glue in the middle of such timbers. The thickness of each coat of glue on the surface, it is difficult here to describe, further than to say, that a section of the joint when viewed should appear like a line, thus ━━━━━━. *Too* much glue of course is an evil, as it would prevent the work *faying*; too little glue, or *wood* to *wood*, as with animal glue, is also an evil: a portion of glue like the above line should be given.

Method of Joining Timbers. The operation of spreading the glue over each surface being finished, the glue will be found *set*, and non-adhesive to the fingers when pressed upon it. To unite the surfaces of the glue as one body, a solution is used, called *Joint Solution*; this solution may be washed over each surface with a sponge, or hair brush, leaving a small portion of the solution on the surface; in about a quarter of an hour, more or less, the solution will be found to have acted on the surfaces and made them *tacky*, and when they are in this *tacky* state, the timbers may be *canted*, the coags properly entered, and the sets and wedges applied, until the joint comes down; a good joint may be known by the glue *oozing* out, which it will continue to do for a time, even after the hoops are driven, until the whole mass becomes consolidated. The sets should be continued until the hoops or other usual fastenings are applied, and the glue must be viewed in all cases as an *additional power gained in their construction*, rendering the spar as a solid spar, although it be composed of twenty pieces.

PARTICULAR NOTICE. The marine glue is more or less elastic; therefore it will be found necessary in all cases in joining timbers to use fastenings, in order to take off their gravity and *prevent* sliding.

The glue being insoluble in water has no affinity for it; therefore a *perfect contact* cannot be formed with wet or damp surfaces. Dryness of the surface is best to obtain a perfect adhesion.

Oil, grease, dust, and dirt must be avoided.

Excess of boiling and repeated melting injures the glue; therefore melt no more than is required for immediate use. Should any remain in the pot, pour it out on a wet stone or sheet iron, and mix it with fresh glue when required.

APPLICATION OF THE LIQUID MARINE GLUE. This may be applied at nearly boiling point, with a stiff brush, putting on a thin coat each time; two or three thin coats being preferable to one or two thick ones. Sufficient time must be allowed for each coat to dry. Metal surfaces should be heated, when it can be conveniently done, before applying the first coat of the liquid glue. It is adapted for coating the top-sides of vessels, for buoys and tanks, for guns and their carriages, mortars, shot, leather pipes for fire engines, machinery, and iron work exposed to wet, and for iron ships. Iron bolts, nails, or other iron work, made excessively hot and dipped in the glue liquid, will be effectually preserved from oxidation.'

GLUT. A piece of wood inserted as a fulcrum to get a better

lever power on anything, or inserted beneath the thing prized in order to prevent its recoil when freshening the nip of the lever.

Mr. Dana, in his *Seaman's Manual*, defines *glut* as a piece of canvass sewed into the centre of a sail, near the head, having an eyelet-hole in its middle for the bunt jigger or becket to go through.

GO ABOUT. The same as to *tack*.

GOB-LINES, or GAUB-LINES. A name for the martingale back-ropes.

GÓNDOLA (*Fr.* Gondole). A very beautiful kind of light barge common at Venice, used as a pleasure-boat and a passage-boat. It is flat-bottomed, about thirty feet long, and breadth of beam about six feet, and draws three inches water. It is rowed by a single man, who is called a *gondolier* (*Fr.* Gondolier). The

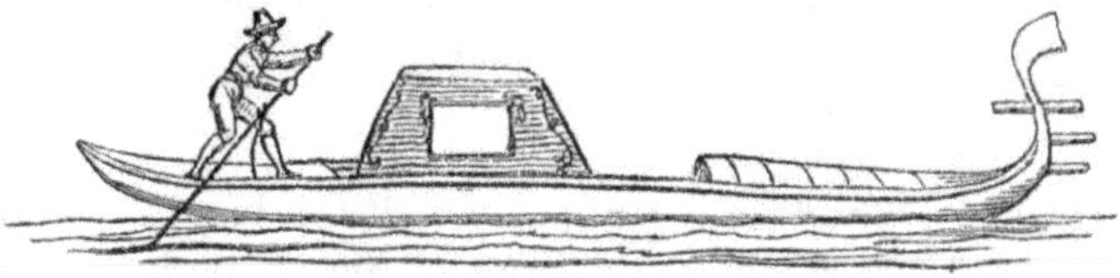

gondola has a small cabin amidships most luxuriously furnished, and there is a little deck at the fore, and one at the after end, on which the gondolier runs and stands. A London waterman cannot be compared in dexterity to a gondolier. Gondolas are all black, with gilt and brass mountings, and the prow is armed with

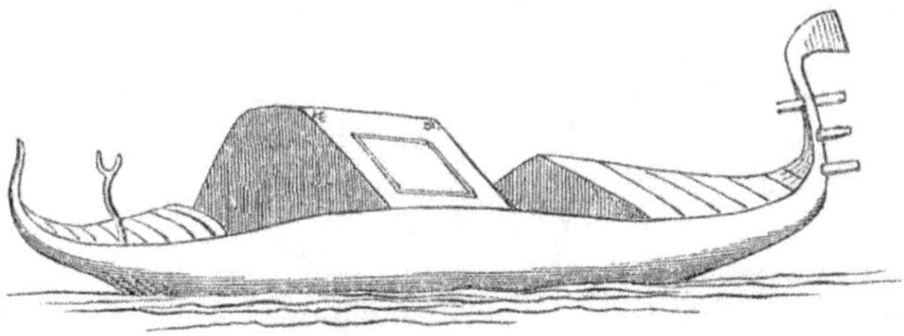

a knife or axe of antique form, having three cross bars of burnished iron. Such is the account of these interesting boats given by an eye-witness, an artist of eminence, by whom the annexed rough sketches or views of them, with many other of the illustrations throughout this dictionary, have been contributed.

GONG. A species of cymbal, of Chinese origin. On account of its peculiarity and great power of tone, this instrument is well adapted for the use of steam vessels as a signal during foggy weather. Gongs are now used on board of many floating-light-vessels instead of bells.

GOODS, or MERCHANDISE. See *Average, Cargo.*

GOOSENECK. An iron hook fitted to the end of a boom for various purposes.

GOOSE-WINGS. When the middle part of a square main-sail or foresail is bound up by a lashing to the yard, and the clues alone left loose, they form what are called *Goose-wings.* This is resorted to in scudding, if the gale be too severe to allow the ship to carry greater sail.

GORES. Angular pieces of plank inserted to fill up a vessel's planking at any part either inside or outside.

GORES, or GORING-CLOTHS. Angular pieces of canvass put in to increase the breadth of a sail.

GOUGINGS. See *Gudgeons.*

GOURABE. A merchant vessel or boat of India, rigged almost like a ketch. The stern is massive and elevated; the bows long and sharp. (*Dict. de Marine à voiles.*) See *Sala-Sala.*

GOVERNOR (*Fr.* Regulateur), in a marine or other steam engine, contrivance for shutting off the steam by the centrifugal force of two balls increasing their divergence when the velocity increases.

GRAFTING. A mode of forming a neat species of splice, partly covered over by knittles wove or plaited with rope-yarns.

GRAINS. An iron instrument with four or more barbed points, and a line attached to it: used for striking dolphins and other fish.

GRAPE-SHOT (*Fr.* Anges), consists of a number of balls marled strongly over with canvass, and placed in the form of a bunch of grapes round an upright piece of iron. See *Shot.*

GRAPNEL, or GRAPLING (*Fr.* Grappin). A species of small anchor, consisting of a piece of iron having a ring at one end, and at the other end four hooks or claws formed at right angles to each other. Some grapnels have a greater number of hooks.

GRAPPLING-IRONS. Crooked irons used to seize and hold fast an enemy's vessel.

GRATINGS. Open lattice work of wood, used chiefly to cover the hatches of a vessel in good weather. There are also gratings made of iron for protecting skylights, &c.

GRAVE. To clean a vessel's bottom, and pay it over with tar or any other substance.

GRAVING-DOCK. A dry dock used for inspecting or repairing vessels. See *Dock*.

GRAVING-PIECES, in Shipbuilding, 'small pieces put in to supply defects in a plank. If used to make good where part of a plank is removed, they should be called *through pieces*. But in common parlance the term graving-pieces is now applied to all, whether through or not.'

GREAT CIRCLE SAILING. See *Sailing*, and *Circle*.

GREENWICH HOSPITAL. An hospital established at Greenwich for the reception and support of seamen and marines who by old age, wounds, or infirmities, have become incapable of further active service in the Royal Navy.

GRIDIRON. A frame formed of cross beams of wood, for laying a vessel upon in order to inspect or repair her at low water.

GRIPE. The lower ends of a vessel's stem and cutwater which are connected with the keel. It is also called the *Fore-gripe*.

A vessel is said *to gripe*, if her head tends to come up in the wind while sailing close-hauled. See also *Gripes*.

GRIPES. Bars of iron with lanyards, rings, and hooks, whereby a large boat is lashed to the ring-bolts in a vessel's deck. Boat's gripes are also sometimes made of rope; sometimes of chain parcelled and served, and with large thimbles in the end; and sometimes of chain, with clamps to fix on the gunwale. Those for a quarter-boat or stern-boat are made of long strips of mat going round it and set taut by a lanyard.

When a boat is secured in this manner, it is said to be *griped*.

GROMMET, or GRUMMET. A ring formed of a rope by

(After Darcy Lever.)

laying round a single strand, or sometimes by splicing together the ends of a short piece of rope or line.

A SHOT-GROMMET, is a similar piece of rope made to contain shot for use in time of action.

GROUND (*Fr.* Échouer). A vessel is said to ground when she gets ashore. She is then *aground.*

GROUNDAGE. A local duty charged against vessels coming to anchor. It is more properly termed *Anchorage.*

GROUND-STRAKE, or SAND-STRAKE. A name sometimes given to the *Garboard-strake.*

GROUND-SWELL. The heavy rolling of the sea, occasioned along the shore by a distant storm.

GROUND-TACKLE. A general name for the anchors, cables, warps, &c., used for anchoring, kedging, or mooring vessels.

GROUND-TIER. The tier of anything (as of casks or timber) which is stowed lowest in a vessel's hold. See *Stowage*, 6.

GROUNDWAYS, in Shipbuilding, a substantial foundation of wood or stone for the blocks whereon a vessel is built.

GRUMMET. See *Grommet.*

GUARD-BOARDS. A name for the *Channels* or *Channel-boards.*

GUARD-BOAT. A boat appointed to row the rounds at night among the ships of war in any harbour, &c., in order to see that a good look-out is kept by the vessels. On coming alongside, she must be hailed by each ship with the watchword of the night. During the day, the guard-boat carries despatches or orders for casual duties through the fleet when required.

*Guard-boat* also denotes a boat used by the health-guard in attending to the enforcement of quarantine regulations at a port.

GUARD-IRONS. Curved or arched bars of iron fixed over the carved work of yachts, &c., particularly over the head ornament and quarter pieces, to prevent their being damaged. (*Shipwright's Vade Mecum.*)

GUARD-SHIP (*Fr.* Arrière-garde). The ship of war from which all orders of the commander-in-chief at a port are made to emanate, being dated as on board of that vessel.

GUDGEONS, or GOUGINGS. A name for the hook part of the hinges *of a rudder*, that is to say, those parts of the rudder bands which are attached to the stern-post; the eye part into which the rudder gudgeon goes down is termed the *brace* or *chalder*. In some places the gudgeons are termed *pintles.*

The *Gudgeons of a windlass* consist of a stout bar of iron in each extremity of the body or centre piece of the windlass, and in each of the windlass ends, its middle part forming a journal for the windlass revolving on the metal bushes in the carrick-bitts.

GUESS-WARP, or GUESS-ROPE. A rope which, for the purpose of being fastened to a distant object, in order to warp a vessel towards it, is taken out in a boat, one end made fast to the object, and the other end brought back to the ship to haul by: this is done when it is thought that the boat's crew cannot make headway against a tide or current in carrying out an end of the warp from the ship. A kedge is often run out in the same way.

GUESS-WARP BOOM. A spar rigged out from each of a vessel's sides, having a rope (also called a *Guess-rope*) rove through a thimble near its outer end for boats to ride by when the ship is at her moorings. In merchant vessels, the lower studding sail booms are often used for this purpose.

GUIDE-RODS (Air-pump). See description of *Steam Engine*, Sect. 24.

GULF. A portion of the sea or ocean surrounded by land except at the part where it communicates with the main.

GUN (*Fr.* Canon). The common name given to the cannon or pieces of ordnance, whether of iron or brass, used on board of ships. Those formed of iron are better than brass guns for continued and heavy firing, but the latter have the advantage of being lighter and more durable, and they are not liable, like iron guns, to burst and fly in pieces when overcharged or overheated.

Guns are distinguished from the weight of balls which they are used to discharge; thus, a piece which is fitted for discharging a ball of the weight of twenty-four pounds is called a *twenty-four pounder*, and so on.

The following is a sketch of a BRASS SERVICE GUN. It is a *muzzle-loading gun.*

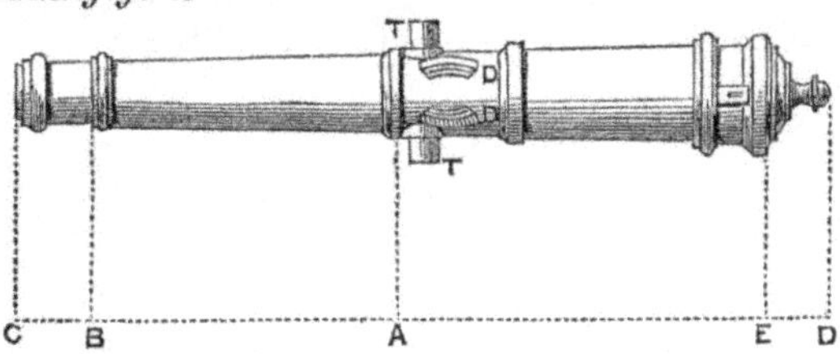


A—B. The chase. E—D. The cascable. D and D. The dolphins or handles.
B—C. The muzzle. T and T. The trunnions.

The diameter of the bore, that is, of the interior cylinder into which the charge is rammed, is termed the calibre of the gun.

More copious and authentic information on this subject is given in *Knight's Penny Cyclopædia.*

ARMSTRONG GUN. A well-known *breech-loading gun,* the invention of Sir William Armstrong. In the annexed drawing of a 100-pounder Armstrong gun, 1, 2, 3, 4, 5 and 6 are the wrought iron coils of which the gun is composed. The coils formerly used were plain rings of iron, but in the Armstrong gun they are formed of bars of iron twisted in a spiral form. In the manufacture of the gun each of the coils is shrunk on to the smaller

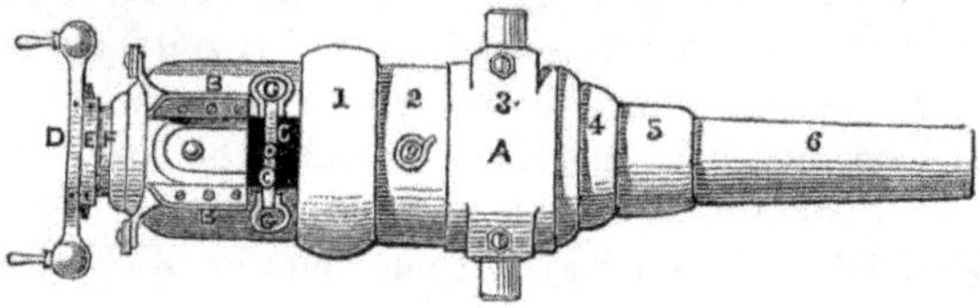


(By permission of the Lords Commissioners of the Admiralty.)

one next to it. For this purpose the larger coil or barrel is let down into a cast iron tank sunk in the ground, and is brought to a red heat in order to expand it sufficiently for the reception of the smaller one, which is then let down into it to the proper distance, and kept cool by means of water till the outer coil, becoming cool, contracts and bites hard upon the smaller coil, the two being thus inseparably united together. The gun is rifled with 76 grooves.

A is termed the *trunnion coil*; B is a brass (or, to speak more correctly, a 'gun metal') saddle fixed on the breech of the gun to receive the vent piece C, which is drawn up and laid back upon it while the gun is being loaded; D the lever, E the lappet, both fixed on the breech screw F to turn it by in order to slacken the vent piece before loading the gun, and to tighten it when dropped into its place after loading.

The bore of the gun goes right through from end to end, and is thus quite open when the vent piece is taken up; the gun is then loaded at the after end or breech instead of at the muzzle.

THE WHITWORTH GUN (the invention of Mr. Whitworth) is similar in construction to the Armstrong gun, but much heavier. It is rifled hexagonally, a mode which seems to be thought preferable to that adopted in the Armstrong gun. It has been hitherto supposed that shells are of no effect against armour plating, but very recent experiments with the Whitworth gun and the Whitworth shells have proved the contrary. Experiments made with the HORSFALL GUN are said to have proved that the smooth-bored gun is more destructive on armour plating than the rifled gun at short ranges.

PIVOT-GUN. A gun set upon a frame carriage, which can be turned about so as to point the piece in any direction. Heavy pivot-guns of great length are used for war steamers.

GUN-BOAT (*Fr.* Canonnière). A vessel of about fifty tons, of a very light draught of water, carrying a heavy piece of ordnance; it is fitted with a mast which lowers down, and is provided with a number of sweeps or oars. The fleet of *gun-boats* recently built for the Royal Navy is composed of 'screw ships of 200 feet in length, carrying several heavy guns. They are fitted with screw engines, and manned by a crew of from 36 to 100 men each, according to the class of boat.' See *Kipping's Elementary Treatise on Sails and Sailmaking*, p. 108. These are termed *Screw Steam Gun-boats*, and vary in burden from 209 to 270 tons.

GUN-BRIG. A ship of war rigged as a brig.

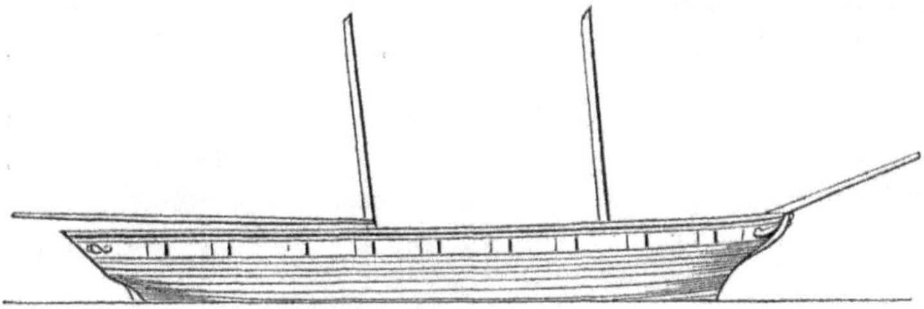

GUN-DECK. See *Deck.*

GUNNEL. See *Gunwale.*

GUNNER (*Fr.* Canonnier) of a ship of war. A warrant officer, who has the general charge and superintendence of the ordnance and ammunition, and of the practice of gunnery, on board of her. The men serving under the gunners and their mates are termed seamen gunners. See *Gunnery, Mate,* and *Quarter-Gunner.*

GUNNERY (*Fr.* Canonnage). The art of charging, pointing, and firing guns and mortars. The best modern treatises on the subject are those by Sir Howard Douglas and by Mr. Greene. A system of training men in the practice of gunnery for the Royal Navy has been established on board H.M.S. 'Excellent' at Portsmouth.

*Seamen Gunners*, are seamen so trained at Portsmouth to the practice of gunnery, a certain number of whom are appointed to every ship and commissioned to instruct the crew in this art.

GUNNING PUNT. A name frequently given to a flat-bottomed boat used in wild fowl shooting. See *Punt.*

GUN-PENDULUM. See *Balistic Pendulum.*

GUN-PORTS (*Fr.* Sabords), or PORT-HOLES. The ports through which a ship's guns are fired. See *Ports.*

GUN-ROOM. The after division or room on the lower gun-deck of a ship of war, having ports through the counter, which are hence called gun-room ports. In line-of-battle ships, the mates and midshipmen mess in the gun-room, and it is partly occupied by the gunner; in small vessels, it is used as a mess-room for the lieutenants and other officers. See *Ward-room.*

GUN-SEARCHER. An iron instrument with several sharp pointed prongs, used to discover if a gun be honeycombed. See *Searcher.*

GUN-TACKLE PURCHASE. A tackle formed by a rope rove through two single blocks, the standing part being made fast to the strop of the fixed block. See *Tackle.*

GUNWALE, or GUNNEL. The same as *Plank-sheer.* (Plate IV. 29.)

The gunwale *of a boat*, is a square piece of wood going round the upper edge of the sheer strake, either inside or outside, in order to form a proper binding for the top of the boat.

GUN-WHARF. A place prepared for landing and shipping ordnance for naval and military service.

GUY. A rope attached to anything in order to steady it and bear it either way in hoisting or lowering. Also, a rope extended from the head of sheers, and made fast at a distance on each side to keep them steady.

In like manner, ropes used to steady boats' davits are called *Davit-guys.*

A Guy is also a large rope stretched between a vessel's main and fore mast heads, with tackles made fast to its bight, to assist in loading and discharging. In whale-fishing vessels these are called *Blubber-guys*, from being used (among other purposes) in hoisting blubber on board.

See *Gybe*, *Jib-guys*, and *Windsail.*

GYBE (pronounced JIBE). To shift over the boom of a fore-and-aft sail from one side of the vessel to the other while sailing before the wind. The sail may gybe by the effort of the wind shifting suddenly, by bad steering, &c.: as this would run a great risk of breaking the boom and doing other damage, it should be carefully provided against by using a guy. This guy gets the name of a *lazy guy*.

HAIL. To call out to another vessel, or to men in a different part of the ship. A ship also is said to *hail* from the port where she is registered.

HALF-BEAMS. Short beams introduced to support the deck where there is no framing. See *Beams*, 4.

HALF-BREADTH PLANS, or FLOOR-PLANS, in Ship-building, are sections upon a longitudinal plane, whereon are represented the water-lines and the ribband-lines.

HALF-DECK. That portion of the sole continued forward from the cabin bulkhead, or aft from the forecastle. See *Deck*.

HALF-TIDE ROCK. A rock seen above water at half ebb.

HALF-WATCH TACKLE. A luff-tackle purchase with a hook in the end of the single block and a tail to the upper end of the double block. See *Tackle*.

HALYARDS, or HALLIARDS. Ropes or tackles used for hoisting and lowering yards and gaffs. The halyards for hoisting and lowering any upper yard, respectively termed the topsail halyards, topgallant halyards, and royal halyards (main, fore, and mizen), are rove through the fly block at the extremity of the tye, and through a block hooked to an eyebolt inside of a stanchion abreast of the backstays, or through a block attached to the backstay-stool. The halyards attached to the outer end (or *peak*) of a gaff, are called *peak halyards*: those attached to the inner end, *throat halyards*. See *Jeers*. (Plates III. IV. and V.)

HAMBRO' LINE, or HAMBERLINE. Small line used for any occasional purpose, such as seizings or lashings on board of a ship. The topmast rigging of some small vessels is rattled down with it.

HAMMOCK (*Fr.* Hamac, Branle). A piece of canvass slung from both ends, for a seaman to sleep in. The cords by which it is slung are called knittles or nettles, forming the *head-clue* and *foot-clue* of the hammock.

HAMMOCK-BATTENS. See *Hammock-Racks*.

HAMMOCK-CLOTHS. Covers of painted canvass for the hammocks while stowed in the hammock nettings.

HAMMOCK-NETTINGS. Frames of netting (or boards), for stowing the seamen's hammocks in. See *Nettings* (*Hammock*).

HAMMOCK-RACKS, or HAMMOCK-BATTENS. Cleats or battens nailed to a vessel's beams, from which to suspend the hammocks.

HAND. *To hand a sail* is to furl it. See also *Bear a hand*, and *Lend a hand.*

HAND-LEAD, is that used for sounding in rivers, harbours, or shoal water. See *Lead.*

HAND OVER HAND, applies to the act of hauling on a rope, or of ascending it, by passing one hand before or above the other alternately.

HAND-TIGHT. A term to imply that a rope is hauled as tight merely as it can be done by the hand.

HANDLES OF GUN. See *Gun.*

HANDSOMELY. Gradually and carefully.

HANDSPIKE. A wooden lever, chiefly used for heaving at a windlass.

In a ship of war, several handspikes are supplied to each gun: some of these have claws like those of a 'crow.' There are also handspikes, resembling crow-bars, used in shipbuilding yards for moving logs.

HANG. *To hang on a rope*, or *on a tackle fall*, is to hold on without making it fast; also, to give all your weight in pulling upon it. See the article *Sny.*

HANKS. Rings or hoops of rope, wood, or iron, put round a stay, and seized to the luff of a fore-and-aft sail in order to confine it to the stay.

HANSE TOWNS. A name given to certain towns situated in the north of Europe, which in the thirteenth century formed an association called the *Hanseatic League*, having for its object the protection of mercantile property. The name of Hanse Towns is now confined to Lubeck, Hamburgh, and Bremen, whose mercantile consuls are occupied with the individual concerns of their own respective constituents. (*Waterston's Cyclopædia of Commerce.*)

HARBOUR, HAVEN, or PORT. A general name for any place constructed to admit shipping, and wherein vessels may discharge and load cargoes in shelter and security. The term *harbour* is also applied to any natural inlet of the sea in which vessels may find secure anchorage. See *Dock* and *Port*.

BAR-HARBOUR. A harbour which, from having a bar or bank at its entrance, cannot admit ships of heavy burden, or can do so only at high water.

TIDE-HARBOUR, or TIDAL-HARBOUR. A harbour wherein the tide ebbs and flows; in contradistinction from a wet dock.

HARBOUR-DUES, or PORT-CHARGES, are charges exigible on vessels resorting to a port.

HARBOUR-MASTER. A person appointed to attend to the mooring of vessels in a harbour, and to see that the regulations of the port are properly attended to by the ships frequenting it.

HARBOUR-REACH. That reach or stretch of a winding river which leads direct to any harbour.

HARD. The wind is said to *blow hard* when it is strong and steady. It may be remarked generally that in a stiff breeze a ship's royals would be furled; when it blows hard, the topgallant sails would be furled and the topsails reefed. When it blows a gale, her sail would be still further reduced.

HARD A-LEE, HARD A-WEATHER, or HARD UP, HARD A-PORT, and HARD A-STARBOARD, are phrases respectively expressed of the tiller being put *close* to the lee, weather, port, and starboard sides of a vessel.

HARPINGS, or HARPINS, in Shipbuilding, pieces of oak similar to ribbands, but trimmed and bevelled to the shape of the body of the ship, used to hold the fore- and the after cant bodies together, at the height of the wales, until she is planked. The term is especially applicable to those at the bow: hence we speak of a vessel having 'full' or 'clean harpins,' according as the ship is at this part more or less acute. (*Shipwright's Vade Mecum.*)

HARPOON. A sort of spear, with a barbed iron point, and having a line attached to it; used for striking whales. The line is bent to a short piece of rope, called a *foreganger*, which is grafted to the shank of the harpoon. A portion (called the *stray-line*), consisting of about five or six fathoms of the line put into the boat, is left uncovered by the remainder of the line, and is coiled by itself at the stern of the boat; it is furnished with an eye, for the facility of connecting it with the lines of any other boat. The GUN-HARPOON, which is fired from a gun of a peculiar description, is made wholly of iron, and has a chain, or long shackle, to which the whale line is made fast. To HARPOON a whale, is to strike it with a harpoon.

The man who throws or fires harpoons from a whale fishing boat is called a *Harpooner.* He also guides the lines, and has lances for the purpose of killing any entangled whale. When in pursuit he pulls the bow oar. The boat is commanded by him.

In the Davis's Straits fishing, when a whale has plunged into the waves after being struck, it remains under water for about half an hour, more or less, and the boats meanwhile separate in various directions, in order that one, at least, may be within *a start*— that is, about 200 yards from the point of its rising, at which distance they may reach and pierce the whale with one or more harpoons before it again descends, as it usually does for a few minutes.

A full account of these and other interesting particulars is given in *Captain Scoresby's Description of the Northern Whale Fishery*, already referred to under the title *Flensing.*

HARPOONER.<br>HARPOON-GUN. } See *Harpoon.*

HASLAR HOSPITAL. An hospital established at Haslar, near Gosport, for the reception and cure of sick and wounded seamen and marines of the Royal Navy.

HASP *for a Bowsprit.* A semicircular clamp, turning in an eyebolt fixed in the stem head of a sloop or boat, and fastened by a forelock, in order to secure the bowsprit down to the bows.

HAT-MONEY. See *Primage.*

HATCH, or HATCHWAY. An opening in a vessel's deck to afford an entrance into the hold, or from one deck to another.

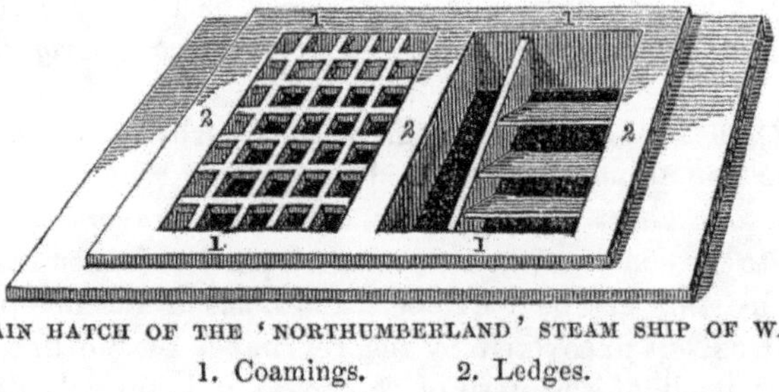


MAIN HATCH OF THE 'NORTHUMBERLAND' STEAM SHIP OF WAR.

1. Coamings. 2. Ledges.

*The fore hatch* is near the bow; *the main hatch*, in or about the middle of the ship; and the *after hatch*, or *quarter hatch*, abaft the main mast.

The coverings over such an opening are also called *hatches. A booby-hatch* is a covering for the hatchway, which lifts off in a whole piece. See also *Crank-hatches* and *Coamings.*

HATCH-BARS. Iron bars going across hatches to keep them down over the hatchway.

HATCH-BOAT. A boat having a deck composed almost entirely of hatches.

HATCHWAY-NETTINGS, are nettings sometimes placed over the hatchways for security, and to allow a free circulation of air below. See *Nettings.*

HATCHWAY-SCREENS. Pieces of thick woollen cloth put round the hatchways of a ship of war in time of an engagement.

HAUL OFF. To sail closer to the wind in order to get farther off from any object. *To haul in with the object,* implies to sail close to the wind in order to approach it more nearly.

These expressions have their derivation from the phrase, *haul your wind,* or *haul to the wind,* which means to bring the ship's head nearer the wind when she has been going free.

*Mainsail haul!* is the order given to haul the after-yards round when the ship is head to wind in tacking. If the mainsail be not set, *topsail haul!* is the order given. *Let go and haul!* is the order to haul the head yards round when the ship is cast on the other tack.

The wind is said to *haul round* to the north, or to any other point of the compass, when it shifts gradually to that direction.

HAVEN. See *Harbour.*

HAWSE. That part of a vessel's bow where holes, called the *Hawse-holes,* are cut for her cables going through.

1. Hence we speak of a *foul hawse,* which implies that, when a vessel is riding with two anchors out, the cables are crossed or twisted. The hawse may be foul by having a *cross,* an *elbow,* or a *round turn. A cross in the hawse* is when, by the ship swinging round and her stern passing over the cables, the one cable is made to lie upon the other. If she continue to move round till her head is directed the same way as at first, this produces what is called *an elbow*; and *a round turn* is produced by the ship performing another half revolution. If, after this, she comes round till her head is directed the same way as at first, this makes *a round turn and elbow.* The reverse of a foul hawse is a *clear* or

*open hawse. To clear the hawse*, is to take the turns out of the cables when they have so got foul of each other.

2. A vessel is said to be anchored *in the hawse* of another vessel at anchor, when brought to anchor right ahead of her; and this is termed giving a *foul berth* to the one previously anchored.

3. *To cross a vessel's hawse* is to sail across the line of the ship's course, a little ahead of her. See *Athwart-hawse*, and *Freshen.*

HAWSE-BLOCKS. See *Hawse-Plugs.*

HAWSE-BOLSTERS. Pieces of canvass, stuffed with oakum and roped round, used at sea for plugging the hawse-holes, when the cables are bent.

HAWSE-BOX, or HAWSE-PIECES, called also *Naval Hoods.* Pieces of plank bolted outside round each of the hawse-holes to support the projecting part of the hawse-pipe.

HAWSE-BUCKLERS, are described under the title *Bucklers.* See also *Hawse-Plugs.*

HAWSE-HOLE. The hole on either side of a vessel's bows, through which the cable is run out. In large ships there are two hawse-holes on each side. (Plate IV. 18.)

HAWSE-HOOKS. Breast-hooks which cross the hawse-timber above the upper deck. See *Breast-hooks.*

HAWSE-PIECES. See *Hawse-Box.*

HAWSE-PIPE. A cast-iron pipe, fitted into a hawse-hole to prevent the chain cable from cutting the wood. In vessels which have rope cables a leaden pipe is used.

HAWSE-PLUGS (*Fr.* Tampons), or HAWSE-BLOCKS. Blocks of wood made to fit into the hawse-pipes, and put in from the outside, when at sea. They are, of course, used only when the cables are not bent. See *Bucklers.*

HAWSE-TIMBERS. The upright timbers in the bow, bolted on each side of the stem, and in which the hawse-holes are cut. (Plate II. fig. 7; Plate IV. 19.)

HAWSE-WOOD. A general name for the hawse-timbers.

HAWSER. A kind of small cable used on various occasions; as for mooring, &c.

HAWSER-BEND. See *Bend.*

HAWSER-LAID ROPE, is formed of three small ropes laid up into one, and is used for hawsers, &c. See *Rope.*

HEAD. A term applied generally to the fore part of a vessel.

Hence we say, 'head sails,' 'head yards,' &c., in opposition to 'after sails,' &c. See *By the Head.*

It is employed to signify the upper end of anything; as *a mast head, a timber head, the stem head,* and so on.

Also, an ornament at the bow of a vessel over the cutwater. If it be a carved figure, this is called a *figure-head*; if simple carved work, in the form of a volute or scrole turning outwards, it is called a *billet-head* or *scrole-head* (Plate III.); and if the scrole bend inwards, like the handle of a violin, it gets the name of a *fiddle-head.*

HEAD-BOARDS, or BERTHING. Boards put in between the head-rails, whereon the ship's name is sometimes painted.

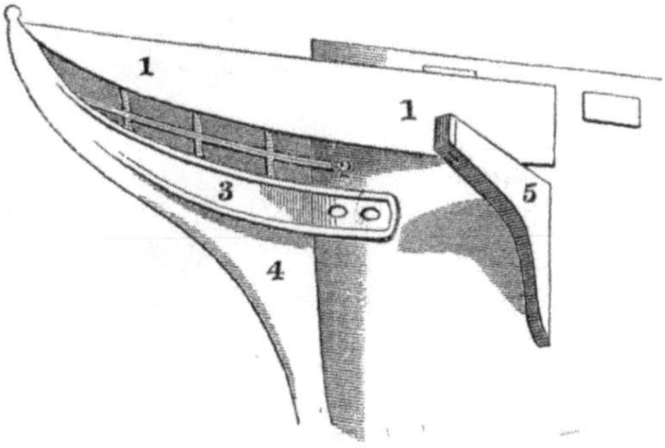


1. Head-boards.
2. Head-timbers.
3. Arch-board.
4. Knee of the head, or cutwater.
5. Cathead.

HEAD CRINGLES. Earing cringles at the upper corners of a sail. See *Cringles.*

HEAD-EARINGS. See *Earings.*

HEAD-FAST. A rope or chain by which the head of a vessel is secured to a wharf or quay.

HEAD-MONEY. An allowance made by government, at so much per head, for prisoners taken in war, or pirates captured or destroyed, &c.

HEAD-NETTING. See *Head-Rails.*

HEAD-PUMP. A small pump fixed at the vessel's bow. See *Pump.*

HEAD-RAILS. Short pieces of timber put in between the luff of the bow and the back of the figure on a vessel's head. There are two on each side, one straight and the other curved: a thin piece of plank fayed to the inside of the latter, in order to strengthen it, is called the *false-rail*; and the boards or netting fixed between the head-rails are called the ***head-boards***, or ***head-netting***. See the article *Berthing*, and Plate IV. 16.

The head-rails assist in securing the upper end of the cutwater, on which the figure is placed, and at the same time they make an ornamental finish to the whole.

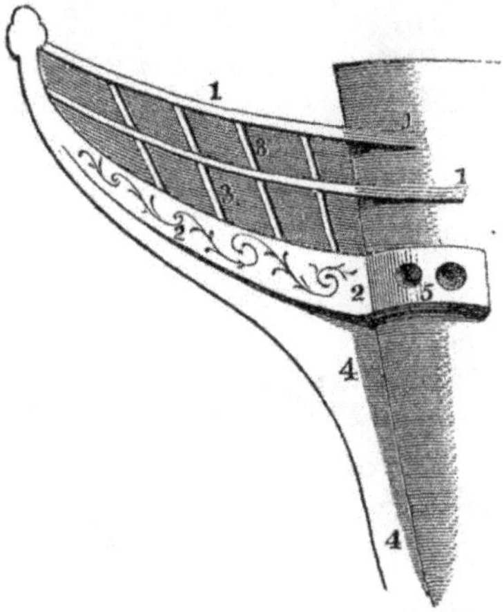


HEAD-RAILS OF A SHIP-OF-WAR BUILT IN 1859.

1. Head-rails.
2. Trail-board.
3. Head-timbers.
4. Knee of the head, or cutwater.
5. Hawse-holes.

Beneath them, at the heel of the figure, there are corresponding pieces of moulded knee-timber, called *head-knees* or *cheek-knees*, fayed edgeways to the cutwater and stem, for steadying the cutwater; and there are upright pieces of timber, which get the name of the *head timbers*, inserted between the upper knee and the curved rail, to support the frame of the head-rails.

*The Trail-boards*, are ornamented boards between the cheek-knees. (Plate IV. 7.)

HEAD-REACH. The same as *Fore-Reach.*

HEAD-ROPE. The bolt-rope on the upper edge of a sail. See *Bolt-Ropes.*

HEAD-SEA. When the waves meet the head of a vessel under way, they are called a *head-sea.*

HEAD-WAY. A vessel has *head-way* when she is moving ahead; *stern-way*, when moving astern.

HEAD-TO-WIND. A vessel is said to be *head-to-wind,* when her head points directly to windward, particularly in the act of tacking, or while lying at anchor.

HEAD-WIND. A wind blowing from a direction opposite, or very nearly opposite, to that of a ship's intended course.

HEADING. A vessel is said to be heading in a particular direction when advancing in that direction, whether by means of sails or steam power. It is properly applied to a sailing vessel on a wind.

HEALTH-GUARD. Officers appointed to attend to the due observance of quarantine regulations at a port.

HEART. A block of wood, or kind of dead-eye (in shape sometimes resembling a heart), used to secure the lower ends of stays. That for the fore-stay is called the *Bowsprit-heart,* through which the inner end of the jib-boom is inserted.

HEAVE *of the Sea.* The power which the swell of the sea exerts upon a vessel, in driving her out of or faster on in her course. For this allowance has to be made in the day's work.

HEAVE. To throw; as to *heave the lead,* or to *heave the log.*

The term HEAVE is also applied by seamen to the act of turning round the capstan, windlass, or any machine of a similar kind, by means of bars, handspikes, or otherwise; this is called *heaving* at the capstan, &c.; and when a rope or chain is by such means drawn tight, it is said to be *hove taut. Heave and away!* is an encouraging order given to the men to lend greater force in heaving up the anchor, in order to make it quit its hold of the ground. *Heave and rally!* a similar order to heave briskly. See *Cable,* and *A-wash.*

HEAVE ABOUT *a vessel.* To put her on the other tack.

HEAVE AHEAD. To advance the ship by heaving on a cable or rope fastened to an anchor or other object ahead of her. *To heave astern* is the reverse.

HEAVE DOWN (*Fr.* Abattre en carène, Éventer). To bring a ship down upon one of her sides in the water, by means of purchases upon the masts, in order to repair any part which is below her water-mark.

In proceeding to heave down a ship, care must be taken, in the first place, to close every aperture on the side which is to be submerged, and thoroughly caulk all the butts and seams by which the water might penetrate. Notwithstanding every such precaution, water will force its way, in greater or less quantity, into the ship when hove down, and it is therefore necessary to have several pumps ready to free the ship.

The masts on which the strain is to be hove are supported on either side by sheer-shores, the upper ends of which may be bevelled to fit the better against the surface of the masts, to which they are secured by strong cross lashings and seizings. From the upper extremities descend purchase tackles, which are made fast to the gunwale of a 'pontoon' or decked punt, loaded with ballast and firmly moored alongside. The falls of these tackles are led to capstans fitted on the deck of the pontoon. If there be no such punt at hand, a raft may be made for the purpose, or, when the ship can approach near enough to the shore, she may be hove down by means of guns, rings, or other objects forming points of resistance, firmly fixed in the ground.

An outrigger, projecting horizontally from the ship's side abreast of each of the masts, is also required, in order to afford additional lever power in heaving down; which outriggers are stayed by guys connecting their ends with each of the mast-heads, and thereby giving additional security to the masts.

To use the descriptive language of the *Dictionnaire de Marine à voiles*—when the motive powers are brought into action, they draw the heads of the masts downwards, and force these levers to incline. The ship, yielding to the effort, revolves on her longitudinal axis and lays herself down upon her side, thereby bringing up the other side above the surface of the water; soon the keel makes its appearance at the water's edge, and the process of heaving down is completed.

This operation is attended with risk. The sudden righting of such a mass—that is to say, the resuming of its vertical position—would produce serious consequences. Every precaution of security, therefore, is adopted which prudence and experience may point out. This righting is not to be dreaded after the ship rises beyond a certain inclination. Its force, which results from the upward pressure of the water, attains its maximum when the fullest part of the ship's hull is just plunged in the water. This is the moment when the tackles and other apparatus are subjected to the greatest tension. Beyond this limit the tension necessarily diminishes, for the tendency of the ship to right herself—in other words, her stiffness—decreases progressively.

With a view to prevent any accident, from the heads of the

masts of the pontoon there descend purchase-tackles, the running-blocks whereof are lashed to the ship's side. These tackles, called *righting tackles*, serve either to bear up the ship, if she tend of herself to heel over too much, or to bring her back, when required, into the position in which she can righten by virtue of her own stiffness.

It may be observed that the effort of the strain brought to bear on the heads of the ship's masts is distributed generally over the ropes and shores which sustain these levers. Hence the necessity, previously to heaving down, of shoring up the deck beneath the heels of the sheer-shores, which endure so great a portion of the strain.

Another previous precaution not less important consists in placing some tons of ballast in the forehold, in order to compensate the difference of fullness which exists between the form of the bow and that of the stern. This weight, suitably disposed, is intended to make the keel emerge horizontally, without the necessity of acting with greater intensity upon the tackles of the mainmast than upon those of the foremast. The ballast is secured in the hold by means of bulkheads, which prevent its movement in any way.

It is needful, of course, to make fast every moveable thing which remains on board, or, as a more prudent step, entirely to unlade the ship. If the ship be difficult to heave down, the topmasts may be swayed up more or less in order to assist her inclination.

Such is the process adopted for the purpose of effecting repairs to the bottom of a ship when she is afloat. Independently, however, of the difficulties of execution, heaving down is detrimental to the compactness of her framing, and it is resorted to only at ports or places where there is no graving-dock or other accommodation for effecting such repairs to ships without laying them down on their side in the water.

HEAVE IN STAYS. See *Stay*.

HEAVER. A small piece of wood used in the same way as a lever, chiefly for the purpose of giving additional purchase on a rope.

HEAVE SHORT. To heave in on the cable till the ship is sufficiently near her anchor to allow the sails to be set before the anchor is tripped.

HEAVE TO, or BRING TO. To adjust a vessel's sails so as to counteract each other and so stop her progress. She is then *hove to.* The term *heave to* is often (perhaps improperly) applied to the act of laying a vessel to. See *Lying to.*

HEAVY ICE. That which has a considerable depth in the water. See *Iceberg*, 6.

HEEL. The lower end of anything, as of a *timber, mast,* or *bowsprit.*

*The heel of a ship* is the after end of the keel and lower end of the stern-post.

*A ship is said to heel* when she cants or inclines over from the vertical position.

HEEL-KNEE. The knee which connects the keel of a boat with the stern-post. See also *Dead-wood.*

HEEL-ROPE. A rope applied through the heel of anything, particularly that which is rove through a sheave at the heel of the jib-boom, or of the bowsprit, for the purpose of hauling it out. The ropes which are used at the heels of topmasts and topgallant masts are termed *mast-ropes.*

HEIGHT OF BREADTH. See *Shipbuilding.*

HELM. The machine by which a vessel is steered. It consists of the *Rudder*, the *Tiller*, and the *Wheel.* See these articles; and also *A-lee, Amidships, Hard a-lee,* and *Weather-helm.*

The following rule given by Darcy Lever is useful to be borne in mind. *In going ahead the tiller must be put the contrary way to that in which the bow is intended to move, and in going astern the same way that the head is to be turned.*

DOWN WITH THE HELM! is an order to put the helm a-lee. UP WITH THE HELM! to put it a-weather. EASE THE HELM! to let it come more amidships when it has been put hard up or down. To RIGHT THE HELM, to put it amidships, that is, in a line with the keel. PORT THE HELM! to put the tiller to the port side. STARBOARD THE HELM! to put it to the starboard side of the ship. SHIFT THE HELM! to put it from starboard to port, or the reverse.

HELM-PORT. The hole in a vessel's counter going up through the deck, and into which the rudder-case is inserted.

HELMSMAN. The person who steers a vessel is called the *Helmsman* or *Steersman.*

HEMISPHERES. Two equal parts into which the globe is divided by the *equator.*

HEN-COOP (*Fr.* Cage à poules). A kind of large box or

cage, having an open framing of laths in front of it; used for carrying live fowl during a voyage.

HERMAPHRODITE BRIG. A square-rigged schooner, having the foremast rigged as a brig's, and the mainmast as a schooner's. See *Brig*, 2.

HIGH AND DRY. The situation of a vessel when the receding tide leaves her dry upon the strand.

HIGH WATER. The rising of the waters of the sea. See *Tide*, 1.

HIGH-WATER MARK. The line made by the tide upon the shore when at its greatest height. See *Tide*, 3.

HITCH. A name applied to various kinds of knots used for

BLACKWALL HITCH.

CLOVE HITCH.

HALF HITCH.

TWO HALF HITCHES (after Biddlecombe in his 'Art of Rigging.' Another form of this hitch is illustrated in Captain Boyd's 'Manual,' p. 225).

making fast a rope to anything, or for connecting two ropes together. The annexed are illustrations of different kinds of

MAGNUS HITCH.

MARLINSPIKE HITCH.

hitches, the key to nearly all of which is found in the drawings in Darcy Lever's old but standard work, *The Young Sea Officer's*

HARNESS HITCH (according to Captain Boyd). See his 'Naval Cadet's Manual,' p. 233, where another hitch, termed a 'prolong,' of a somewhat similar character, is shown.

MIDSHIPMAN'S HITCH.

*Sheet Anchor*, where the mode of making them is clearly explained and illustrated. Farther information on the subject may also be found in *Dana's Seaman's Manual, Boyd's Naval Cadet's Manual*, and *Nares on Seamanship.*

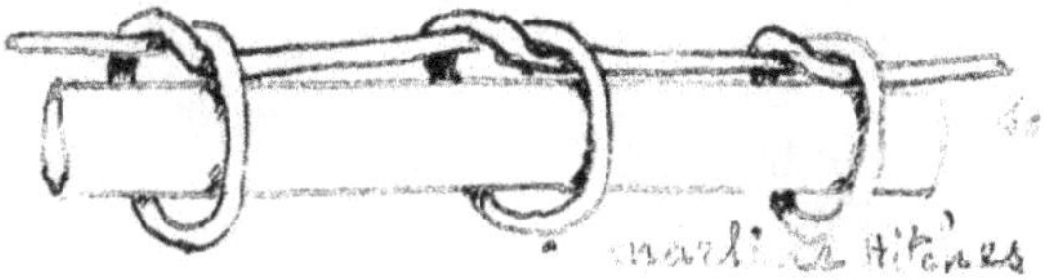

ROLLING HITCH.

TIMBER HITCH.

HOBBLERS. A name given to a class of men on the coast of Kent, &c., half smugglers, and half pilots without license, ready for either occupation, but qualified only for the first, who go out in their boats when the barometer indicates a storm, and hobble off and on to pick up a job.

HOG. A name for 'a flat rough broom used for scrubbing the bottom of a vessel.'

HOGGING. A vessel is said *to hog*, or *to be hogged*, when the middle part of her is so strained as to curve or arch upwards. When the strain causes her middle part to arch downwards she is said *to sag*.

'A weak vessel may become hogged, by the great upward

pressure of water on the broad part of the bottom when the cargo is unequally distributed towards the head and the stern. On the other hand, ships deeply laden, with their cargoes nearly amidships, may sag downwards, in proportion as the weight of the goods exceeds the upward pressure of the water.'

HOIST. To raise anything: particularly when done by means of a tackle. The term *hoist* is also used with reference to the height of any sail which is hoisted by a yard or boom: in this sense we say *give the sail more hoist,* that is, make it extend farther upwards. See *Fly.*

DOUBLE CYLINDER PORTABLE STEAM HOIST (TAYLOR'S PATENT). A machine employed in dockyards or at wharves in working pumps and hand crabs, in driving piles, stacking timber, in shipbuilding purposes, and in a variety of other work. Being mounted on wheels, these steam hoists are easily moved from one place to another; they are provided with a water tank, placed below the fire, which serves as a protection to the decks when used on board ship for discharging cargo.

HOLD. The space between the lowest deck and the ship's bottom, wherein the ballast and stores of a ship of war, and the cargo and ballast in a merchant vessel, are stowed. In a merchant vessel of two decks this space is called the *lower hold,* in contradistinction from the *between decks,* which serves also the purpose of a hold for cargo, there being hatchways on both decks one directly above the other.

HOLD *a good wind.* To present so great a lateral resistance to the water when sailing close-hauled as to make very little lee way. See *Weatherly.*

HOLD-BEAMS. The lowest range of beams in a vessel. See *Beams,* 5.

HOLDFAST, in Shipbuilding, a bolt going down through the rough tree rail and the fore or after part of each stanchion, its lower end being flattened and nailed to the stanchion. Instead of this, in some places, a bolt is driven diagonally down through the rail and stanchion, which is found to be very efficient.

HOLD *her own.* A vessel is said to *hold her own,* when she makes no progress but yet does not lose ground: also, when she advances as fast as another ship with which she is in company.

*Keep a good hold of the land,* or *keep the land aboard,* it being a weather shore, is to keep as near to it as can be done with safety.

HOLD *water*. To check the progress of a boat by holding the oars in the water so as to meet its resistance. This may be done only on one side of the boat to aid in turning her round in a particular direction.

HOLD-STANCHIONS (*Fr.* Épontilles de la câle). See *Stanchions*.

HOLIDAY. If in laying on a coat of tar, paint, or the like, or in paying the seams of a vessel, some part be neglected or passed over, it gets the name of a *holiday* among seamen.

HOLYSTONE. A soft sand stone used for scrubbing a vessel's decks.

HOME. A term implying the proper situation of any object. *The sheets of a square sail are said to be home*, when the clues are hauled chock out to the sheave-holes in the yard.

*The wind is said to blow home*, when it blows continuously over the sea and land with equal velocity: it is said *not to blow home*, when it is blowing from the sea right upon a mountainous tract of country, and the high land has the effect of rejecting the wind, and keeping it calm along shore. When the swell of the sea rolls into the shore it is termed *the home*.

COME HOME. An anchor is said to *come home* when it is dislodged from its bed by the violence of the wind and is dragged along. See *Anchor*, 14.

RAMMED HOME. The charge of a gun is said to be rammed home when rammed into the innermost part of the bore.

TUMBLE HOME. The inward curve on a vessel's top-sides. See *Tumble Home*.

HOME TRADE SHIPS. A general name for vessels employed in the coasting trade.

HONEYCOMBED. A term implying that in the bore of a gun, a steam cylinder, condenser, or any other casting, there are small internal cavities on the surface of the metal.

HOOD. A covering for a companion hatch, for a mortar, &c., a piece of tarred canvass put on the ends of standing rigging to prevent water from rotting them.

The upper part of a funnel which is bent and made to turn with the wind, so that the smoke from the cook-house may be carried to leeward, is called its *hood*.

HOODING-ENDS, HOOD-ENDS, or WOODS-ENDS. See *Hoods*.

HOODS. A name given to all the foremost and all the aftermost planks of a vessel's bottom both inside and outside. Hence the ends of these planks, which are next the stem or stern post, are termed *Hooding-ends.*

HOODS (NAVAL). The same as *Hawse-pieces.*

HOOK AND BUTT. See *Hook-Scarph.*

HOOK-BLOCK. An iron-stropped block with a Hook at one end. See *Block*, 8.

HOOKS. This term is, in sea affairs, applied not only to crooked pieces of iron for hooking on to anything, but also to the crooked or 'knee' pieces of timber bolted athwart a vessel's stem inside. See *Breast-hooks.*

BOAT-HOOK. A pole with its end fitted into an iron socket, which has two prongs; used in a boat for pushing off from and holding on by any thing.

CAN-HOOKS. Slings of rope or chain with flat iron hooks at each end, used for hoisting light casks. See the title *Can-hooks.*

CAT-HOOK. A hook attached to the cat-block for hooking the ring of the anchor.

CHAIN-HOOK. An iron rod with a large eye in one end and a hook at the other end for hauling along chain cables, &c.

CLOVE-HOOK. An iron clasp in two parts, moving upon a pivot and overlapping each other; used for bending chain-sheets to the clues of sails.

FISH-HOOK. See *Fish the Anchor.*

FOOT-HOOKS. The same as *Futtocks.*

PUMP-HOOK. A rod of iron with an eye and a hook used for drawing out and replacing the lower pump-boxes when required.

RAVE-HOOK. An iron instrument used by caulkers to get the oakum out of a vessel's seams when a rasing iron would not penetrate deep enough.

HOOK-SCARPH. Where two pieces of wood are scarphed together in this fashion it is called a *Hook-scarph.* In like

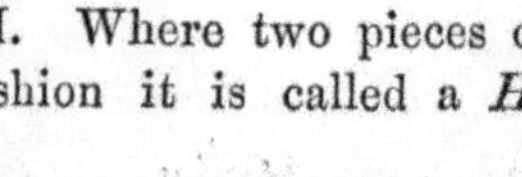

manner, the butt, or part where they join, is called a *Hook-butt*: and this method of connecting them together gets the name of *Hook and Butt*; the two pieces are said to be *scarphed hook and butt.*

HOOPS. Of the different kinds of hoops used for shipbuilding purposes we may notice the following:—

CLASP-HOOPS, *Slot-hoops*, or *Truss-hoops*, for masts or spars, are open hoops of iron made so that their ends, being let into each other, may be fastened by means of forelocks. They are used particularly for a mast when it is formed of several pieces or when it is fished.

MAST-HOOPS are wooden hoops which encircle a mast, and to which the fore leach of a fore-and-aft sail is bent.

SLING-HOOP. See *Slings of a Yard.*

SLOT-HOOP. The same as *Clasp-hoop.*

SPIDER-HOOP. The hoop going round a mast to secure the shackles to which the futtock-shrouds are attached. See the title *Spider-hoop.*

TRUSS-HOOP. The same as *Clasp-hoop.*

HOPPER PUNT, or MUD LIGHTER. A punt or lighter for carrying soil or mud with a HOPPER, that is, a receptacle in its centre to contain the lading. See *Punt* (*Hopper*).

HORARY ANGLE. The angle formed at the pole by the meridian of the place of an observer and the circle of declination passing through the centre of the sun. By reckoning the interval of time corresponding to the arc of the equator which measures this angle, allowing fifteen degrees for each hour, we obtain the precise hour of the place at the moment of the observation of the altitude of the sun, which is one of the trigonometrical elements necessary for the calculation of the horary angle. And if we compare this hour with the Greenwich time at the same moment, in the manner noticed under the title *Chronometer*, the difference between them gives the longitude of the place.

HORARY TABLES, are 'tables of logarithms intended to facilitate the computation of time deduced from the altitude of a celestial object.' See *Lunar Tables.*

HORIZON. *The apparent* or *visible horizon* is that circle which bounds the view of a spectator at sea, or on an open plain, the eye being supposed in the centre of the horizon; this circle is divided into thirty-two parts called *points*, or *rhumbs*, as to which see the article *Compass.* A circle whose plane passes through the eye of an observer, perpendicular to a plumb-line, is called the *sensible horizon*; and a circle parallel to this, passing through the centre of the earth, is *the rational horizon.* The rational or true horizon thus divides the terrestrial and celestial spheres into two equal parts or hemispheres. Its poles are the Zenith and Nadir. See *Astronomy*, 3.

*The depression* (or, as it is generally termed, *the dip*) *of the horizon*, is the angle contained between the sensible and apparent horizons, the angular point (E in subjoined sketch) being the eye of the observer; allowance requires to be made for this in any

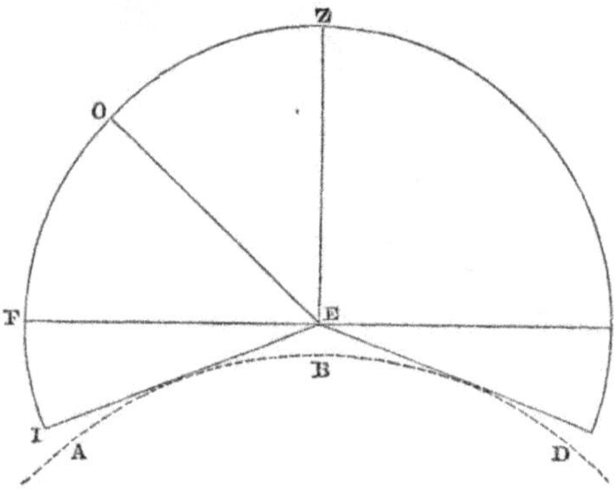


observation of altitude. Thus, let A B D be a section of the earth, B E the height of the observer's eye above the earth's surface; F E I will be the depression or dip of the apparent horizon below the sensible horizon. 'Let O be any object, the altitude whereof is to be observed; the angle O E I is the observed altitude, which is greater than the angle O E F, the altitude unaffected by dip, by the angle F E I.'

HORIZON, ARTIFICIAL (MARINE). An instrument contrived for the purpose of supplying the mariner with a horizon by artificial means, in order to enable him to obtain altitudes when the horizon of the sea is obscured by fog, or concealed by intervening land. A description of Captain Becher's *Pendulum Marine Artificial Horizon*, which is an instrument of this kind to be attached to the sextant, is given, along with directions for its use, in the *Nautical Magazine* for the year 1845. Reference may also be made to *Mrs. Taylor's Epitome*.

HORN CARD. 'A transparent card to use with reference to variable winds for the purpose of ascertaining approximately the centre of the circular path of the wind.'

HORNING, in Shipbuilding, implies placing or proving any of the timbers, particularly the floor-timbers and frames, to stand square from the middle line of the ship, by setting off equal distances on it from the middle line on each side by means of a batten or staff.

HORNS. The outer ends of a vessel's cross-trees. See also *Jaws* and *Rudder-pendants*.

HORSES, or YARD-HORSES. Ropes attached to a vessel's yards, for the men to stand on while reefing or furling; now known by the name of *foot-ropes*. See that article. They are used not only for the yards, but also for the bowsprit, jib-boom, and flying jib-boom.

'A *Horse* is also usually understood to be any rope or chain, on which another rope or a sail or yard traverses.'

FLEMISH-HORSE. A small foot-rope at a topsail yard-arm.

FORE-SHEET HORSE. An iron rod or piece of wood fastened at its ends athwart the deck of a single-masted vessel, before the mast, for the foresail sheet to travel upon.

MAIN-SHEET HORSE. This is generally a kind of iron dog fixed at the middle of a wooden beam which stretches across a vessel's stern from one quarter stanchion to the other. On it the main-sheet block travels. The beam itself often gets the name of the main-sheet horse.

TRAVERSE-HORSE. A name formerly given to jack-stays, sometimes used instead of hoops for fore-and-aft sails to traverse upon. See *Jack-stays*.

TRYSAIL-SHEET HORSE. A piece of rope or iron going across the stern, used in some vessels for the storm trysail sheet-block traversing upon. See *Trysail*.

HORSEFALL GUN. See *Gun*.

HORSE-IRON, or HORSING-IRON. An iron fixed in a handle, used with a beetle by caulkers to *horse up*, that is, to *harden in* the oakum in a vessel's seams.

HOSPITAL SHIP (*Fr.* Vaisseau Hôpital). A ship used as an hospital for the reception of sick or wounded men.

HOT WELL (*Fr.* Reservoir à eau chaude, Citerne). See description of *Steam Engine*, Sect. 19.

HOUNDS. Pieces of oak, one of which is bolted on each side of a lower mast to support the trestle-trees and the higher masts. They also get the name of *cheeks*.

HOUSE (pronounced HOWZE). *To house a gun* means to run it in clear of the port and secure it.

HOUSED IN. See *Tumbling Home*.

HOUSE-LINE (*Fr.* Lusin), or HOUSING. A small cord used to seize the clues of sails, and for other purposes.

HOUSING *of a lower mast.* That portion which is beneath the upper deck; *of a bowsprit,* that portion which is within the knight-heads.

HOWITZER. A kind of light mortar 'which can be employed on most occasions either as a cannon or mortar.'

It has been of late thought advisable that brass howitzers should be substituted instead of iron carronades in the boats of vessels in the Naval service.

HOWKER. A name for pilot and fishing-boats, common on the coast of Ireland.

HOWKER is also the name for a vessel with flat floors, bluff, and the stern boldly rounded, having two pole-masts, the one amidships, the other in the after part. These vessels, much used in Holland as vessels of transport, are generally so bad, that the name is applied to any ship slightingly on account of its bad sailing qualities or other defects. (*Dict. de Marine à voiles.*)

HOY. A name given to a sort of lighter, generally sloop-rigged. Such vessels are used at gun wharfs and victualling yards.

HUG THE WIND (*Fr.* Pincer). To sail as close to it as possible.

HULK. An old worn-out ship laid up to be used as an hospital or a prison ship, or to receive a ship's company when the ship is in dock or under repair. Such vessels when fitted with sheers, for lifting and putting in the lower masts of ships belonging to the Royal Navy, get the name of *sheer-hulks.* See *Sprit.*

HULL. The body of a vessel independent of her spars, rigging, and other furniture.

A vessel is said to be HULL-DOWN when she is so far off that, owing to the convexity of the globe, no part of her is visible but the masts and sails.

HUMMOCK. A term used by navigators to express 'circular and elevated mounts appearing at a distance,' or conical eminences on the sea coast. See also *Iceberg,* 12.

HURRICANE-HOUSE. A name occasionally given to the round-house on a vessel's deck.

HURRICANES. Dreadful tempests, in which the wind sometimes shifts suddenly from one direction to that opposite, raising the sea in pyramids. They occur among the West Indian Islands, occasionally from about the beginning of August till the month of January. They are also liable to happen near the islands of Mauritius and Bourbon from the beginning of November to the end of March and April respectively, and the effect of these sometimes extends nearly to the coast of New Holland. Hurricanes likewise happen near the coasts of India, particularly in the Bay of Bengal, at the changing of the monsoons. Those which are met with in the Chinese seas are called *Typhoons*. (*Horsburgh's India Directory.*) When a gale comes on to blow with extreme violence it is said to increase to a hurricane.

HUSBAND (SHIP'S). An agent for the owners of a vessel, employed to take a general management thereof, in purchasing stores, &c., seeing that the ship is properly repaired and equipped, attending to the ship's papers, entering into contracts of affreightment, receiving payment of freights, recovering losses and averages, settling with the master for wages and disbursements, and rendering an account of the whole to his employers. He may be either a part-owner of the ship or a stranger; if not a part-owner his appointment is usually made in writing. He cannot delegate his authority. (*Bell's Principles*, p. 449; *Waterston's Cyclopædia of Commerce.*)

In the treatise on Naval Book-keeping, which forms the subject of Chapter VIII. of *Steel's Shipmaster's Assistant*, a system of keeping and transacting ship's husband's accounts, and those of ship's consignees or agents, is given.

HYDRAULIC-DOCK. See *Caisson*.

HYDRAULIC-PURCHASE. See *Slip* (*Patent*).

HYDROGRAPHY. The art of surveying and describing the watery part of the terraqueous globe with everything which is of importance to the mariner, whether out at sea, along the coast, or in gulfs, bays, channels, or rivers. A person skilled in this art is called a *Hydrographer*.

The best modern treatise on *marine* or *nautical surveying* is that by Captain Sir Edward Belcher, R.N. There is also a brief treatise on this subject in *Lieut. Alston's Seamanship and its Associated Duties in the Royal Navy.*

HYGROMETER. An instrument for ascertaining the quantity of moisture in the atmosphere. Mrs. Taylor in the introduction to her *Lunar and Horary Tables,* notices that this forms a cheap and useful appendage to the marine barometer.

ICE-ANCHOR. An anchor resembling a pickaxe with one arm: it is used for securing whalers to floes of ice, &c.

ICE-BEAMS. See *Fortifying*.

ICEBERG, or ICE-MOUNTAIN, is the name not only for 'a glacier occupying a ravine or valley in an arctic country,' but also for 'a large insulated peak of floating ice.' These floating icebergs occur in many places in the arctic and antarctic regions, some of them of astonishing magnitude: the most abundant source of them known in the arctic regions (Captain Scoresby remarks) is Baffin's Bay, whence they make their way toward the south, down Davis's Strait, and are scattered abroad in the Atlantic to an amazing extent.

1. Icebergs have often the appearance of 'cliffs of chalk or of white or grey marble:' sometimes their surfaces glisten with the reflection of the sun's rays. 'Different shades of colour occur in the precipitous parts, accordingly as the ice is more or less solid, and accordingly as it contains strata of earth, gravel, or sand, or is free from any impurity. In the fresh fracture, greenish grey, approaching to emerald green, is the prevailing colour. In the night, icebergs are readily distinguished by their natural effulgence; and in foggy weather by a peculiar blackness in the atmosphere, whereby the danger to the navigator is diminished. As, however, they occur far from land, and often in unexpected situations, navigators crossing the Atlantic, in the gloom of night, between the parallels 50° and 60° of latitude, or even farther to the south, require to be always on the watch for them. In some places near Cape Farewell, or towards the mouth of Davis's Strait, they are occasionally met with in extensive chains; in which case fatal accidents have occurred by vessels getting involved among them in the night during storms.*

2. The situation of an iceberg is so little affected by the wind, owing to the great resistance it presents to the water in moving through it, that it often affords a stable mooring to a ship in strong adverse winds or on any other necessary occasions. But mooring to *lofty* icebergs is attended with considerable danger, as, from being sometimes finely balanced, they are apt to be overturned. When ships moor to icebergs, they should be as remote from them as their ropes will allow; yet even when riding at the distance of a hundred yards from the ice, accidents may happen by pieces, termed *calves*, becoming detached from beneath and rising with great velocity and force.

* According to Malte Brun, floating pieces of ice are in like manner frequently met with in the southern hemisphere between 50° and 60° of latitude.

Under this head it is deemed advisable to notice the following explanations of terms used in the icy seas, given in *Mr. Scoresby's Account of the Arctic Regions*, from which the above particulars are extracted.

3. 'BAY-ICE is that which is newly formed on the sea.

4. 'BRUSH-ICE is smaller than drift ice; it may be considered as the wreck of other kinds of ice, consisting of roundish nodules and fragments of ice broken off by the attrition of one piece against another.

5. 'DRIFT-ICE, consists of pieces less than floes, of various shapes and magnitudes.

6. 'HEAVY-ICE, is that which has a considerable depth in the water; *light-ice*, that which has very little depth: the former is dangerous to shipping, but the latter not.

7. 'LAND-ICE, consists of drift-ice attached to the shore, or which, by being covered with mud or gravel, appears to have been recently in contact with the shore, or the flat ice, resting on the land, not having the appearance or elevation of icebergs.

8. 'OPEN-ICE, or SAILING-ICE, a number of pieces sufficiently separate to admit of a ship sailing conveniently among them.

9. 'A CALF, is a portion of ice which has been depressed and is kept down by some larger mass, from beneath which it shows itself on one side. There is danger in sailing over a calf, as it may rise with violence to the surface of the water.

10. 'A FIELD, is a sheet of ice so extensive that its limits cannot be discerned from a ship's mast-head.' 'The whale-fishers at all times require unremitting vigilance to secure their safety, but scarcely in any situation so much as when navigating amidst those fields; in foggy weather they are particularly dangerous, as their motions cannot then be distinctly observed.'

11. 'A FLOE, is a piece of ice similar to a field, but the extent of which can be distinguished. This term is seldom applied to pieces of ice of less diameter than half a mile or a mile.

12. 'A HUMMOCK, is a protuberance raised by some pressure or force upon any plane of ice.

13. 'A LANE, or VEIN, is a narrow channel of water in packs or other large collections of ice.

14. 'A PACK, is a body of drift-ice of such magnitude that its extent is not discernible. A pack is said to be *open* when the pieces of ice, though very near each other, do not generally touch; and *close*, when the pieces are in complete contact.

15. 'A PATCH, is a collection of drift or bay-ice, of a circular or polygonal form. In point of magnitude, a pack corresponds with a field, and a patch with a floe.

16. 'SLUDGE, consists of a stratum of detached ice crystals, or of snow, or of the smaller fragments of brush-ice floating on the surface of the sea. This generally forms the rudiments of ice when the sea is in agitation.

17. 'A STREAM, is an oblong collection of drift or bay-ice, the pieces of which are continuous. It is called a *sea-stream* when it is exposed on one side to the ocean, and affords shelter from the sea to whatever is within it.

18. 'A TONGUE, is a point of ice projecting nearly horizontally from a part that is under water. Ships have sometimes run aground upon tongues of ice.'

ICE-BLINK. 'A stratum of a lucid whiteness which appears over ice in that part of the atmosphere adjoining the horizon; this phenomenon is seen wherever the horizon is tolerably free from clouds, and in some cases even under a thick sky.' The ice-blink, when occurring under very favourable circumstances, shows by reflection the figure of the ice, perhaps twenty or thirty miles beyond the limit of direct vision: it also 'enables the experienced observer to judge whether the ice thus pictured be field or packed ice; if the latter, whether it be compact or open, bay or heavy ice. Field ice affords the most lucid blink, accompanied with a tinge of yellow; that of packs is more purely white; and of bay-ice, greyish. The land, on account of its snowy covering, likewise occasions a blink, which is more yellow than that produced by the ice of fields.'

In the arctic regions, when there has been a fall of thick snow, which has cleared away, and a gale is at hand, 'a luminousness on the horizon, resembling the *ice-blink*, sometimes points out its direction, and a noise in the upper regions of the air announces its immediate approach.' On the subject of these sudden storms, and the value of the barometer in giving warning of them, Captain Scoresby gives farther important information in his work already referred to.

ICE-BOUND. A term implying that a vessel is surrounded by ice, so as to be prevented from proceeding on her voyage. It may be stated as a general rule, that the expenses attendant on such detention, or charges for cutting the ship out in order to avoid the delay, fall upon the shipowner.

ICE-FENDERS. Fenders of any kind, used to protect a vessel from injury by ice.

IDLERS. A name given on board a ship to those who are not employed to keep any watch, but sleep at night and work during the day. They are, however, called up, in case of need, to assist the watch on duty in various evolutions, in order to prevent the watch below from having to turn out.

IMPORT. To bring commodities into a country for the purposes of traffic. See *Export*.

IMPRESSMENT. The system of *pressing* seamen, that is to say, compelling them in time of war to serve in the Royal Navy. On this subject, reference may be made to *M'Culloch's Dictionary of Commerce*.

A party of seamen employed on shore in pressing men gets the name of a *Press-Gang*.

IN AND OUT BOLTS. The same as *through* bolts, going right through the planks and timbers, or knees, which they fasten together.

IN-BOARD, in Shipbuilding, signifies inside of the ship. See *Out-board*.

INCREASING PITCH SCREW (Woodcroft's). See *Screw Propeller*.

INDIAMAN (EAST). A term specially applied to the very large ships which were used by the East India Company as regular traders between this country and the British settlements in the East Indies. It is now occasionally applied to any ship in the East India trade.

IN-HAULER. A rope used for hauling in the clue of a boom-sail. See *Out-hauler*.

INJECTION PIPE (and COCK). See description of *Steam Engine*, Sect. 11.

INNER-POST. A name often given to the inner stern-post, which is fayed to the fore edge of the main stern-post to strengthen it. See *Stern-post*.

INSPECTION, in Navigation, the method of ascertaining a ship's way by reference to nautical tables. *Construction* is the method of ascertaining it by means of trigonometrical problems and diagrams.

INSURANCE (MARINE). A contract of indemnity, whereby one party engages for a stipulated sum to protect another who has an interest in any vessel, or in property on board of it, against the perils to which it may be exposed in the course of a certain voyage, or during a specified period of time.

1. The person taking the risk is called the *Insurer* or *Underwriter*; the person obtaining the insurance is called the *Insured*; the sum charged by the insurer in consideration of the risk run, the *Premium*; and the document by which the underwriter binds himself, a *Policy of Insurance.*

2. These contracts are effected either with private individual underwriters, with public insurance companies, or with insurance clubs, which last are associations formed by shipowners for the purpose of dividing amongst themselves one another's losses, each entering his ship for such an amount as he pleases, subject to agreed-on regulations. The private individuals engaged in this branch of business in London are the underwriters at *Lloyd's,* to which article reference may here be made.

3. *An Open Policy* is one in which the value of the interest at risk is not stated: *a Valued Policy* is one wherein the interest is expressly valued.

4. RE-INSURANCE is a contract whereby a third party takes upon himself a risk, or part of a risk, which had been previously insured by another. With this contract the insured has no concern whatever.

The most recent books of authority on the subject of marine insurance, are *Hildyard's Edition of Park, Arnould's Treatise, Maude and Pollock's Compendium, Shee's Edition of Marshall,* and the valuable American treatises by Duer, Phillips, and Parsons. An index to marine insurance cases decided since the date of Mr. Hildyard's work is appended to the series of current *Maritime Law Cases,* now reprinted from the *Law Times Reports.*

INWARDS. See *Bound,* and *Outwards.*

IRON, as is well known, has now come into extensive use for nautical purposes, not only as regards its application to the manufacture of chain cables, rigging, &c., and iron masts and bowsprits, but also in the construction of iron vessels. The following have long been considered by Mr. Grantham and other advocates for its general adoption as the leading qualities which render it a material peculiarly suitable for shipbuilding: the rapidity with which the raw material can be wrought up, instead of requiring, like timber, a long period to season it; the great specific strength of iron as compared with that of wood; its freedom from the attacks of the worm and the evils of dry-rot; and the union of strength with toughness, which is a characteristic property of wrought iron; and, it may be added, the great facility which iron affords for precision of workmanship in forming the mould of a vessel. Since the above was written Mr. Grantham has produced a valuable treatise on Iron Shipbuilding, to which, especially where illustrated by plates, occasional references will be found throughout this dictionary. Floating-docks are now also often made of iron; and armour-plated or iron-cased ships have been introduced into the Royal Navy. In the leading article of the *Shipping and Mercantile Gazette* of March 11, 1846, among other interesting particulars on this subject, it is remarked that iron ships have the advantage over timber-built ships of being not only stronger in their build, but much lighter in proportion to their admeasurement, and that consequently they can carry more cargo.

In tropical climates iron vessels are found to get very foul in the bottom in a remarkably short space of time, and to avoid the evils to which this would give rise, frequent cleaning becomes necessary, which is attended with considerable expense. The different means of preserving iron from oxidation are discussed in *Grantham on Iron Shipbuilding*, p. 105. *Lloyd's Register Book of British and Foreign Shipping* contains tables of dimensions of the frames, plating, rivets, keels, keelsons, stems, stern-posts, floor-plates, beams, bulkheads, stringers, &c., of iron ships.

See *Horse-iron, Reeming-iron*, and *Caulk.*

ANGLE-IRON. A general term for longitudinal strips of iron of various sizes, having their edges turned up at an angle to each other. Angle-iron is used for the frames or 'ribs,' and the knees, &c., of iron vessels, and also in forming the corners of steam-boilers, water-tanks, &c.

IRON-BOUND COAST. A coast which abounds with dangerous rocks, or, to use the words of Captain Chamier, 'which presents nothing but abrupt hills or cliffs rising perpendicularly from the high-water mark.'

IRON-CASED or IRON-CLAD SHIPS. See *Armour plated Ships, Cupola Ship, Frigate, Shield Ship.*

IRON-SICK. The condition of a vessel when the iron-work becomes loose, or more particularly when the iron bolts or nails in her have become so much corroded as to allow the entrance of water.

IRONS. *A ship is said to be in irons,* when, through mismanagement, she will neither cast one way nor another.

ISLAND, or ISLE. A portion of land entirely surrounded by water.

ISTHMUS. A narrow neck of land uniting a peninsula with the adjoining land, or connecting two continents.

JACK, or UNION JACK. A small union flag formed by the intersection of the red and white crosses. In merchant ships it is bordered with white. See *Flag.*

JACK-CROSS-TREES. Iron cross-trees at the head of any long topgallant mast. See *Cross-trees.*

JACK-SCREW. A purchase consisting of wheels and pinions which work inside of a wooden frame, and act upon an iron bar called the *Spear*; used in stowing cotton, flax, and other goods.

JACK-STAFF. A staff set up on the outer end of a vessel's bowsprit, to hoist the union jack upon.

JACK-STAYS. Ropes stretched taut along a yard, or iron rods or strips of wood fixed to the yard, for bending the head of a square sail to. There are sometimes jack-stays used for fore-and-aft sails to traverse upon, instead of hoops sliding up and down the mast: these formerly received the name of *Traverse-horses.*

JAM, or JAMB. A term applied to the act of anything being confined, and also to the act of confining it, so that it is immovable, or cannot be moved without difficulty. It is especially applied to ropes.

JAWS (*Fr.* Manches). Pieces of wood fixed upon the inner ends of booms or gaffs, forming a semicircle so as to enclose the after-part of the mast. The points of the jaws are sometimes called *Horns.*

THE JAW-ROPE is a rope attached to the jaws to prevent a gaff from coming off the mast.

JEARS, or JEERS. Strong tackles for hoisting lower yards. The ropes employed to hoist upper yards and gaffs are called *Halyards.*

JEPAN. The French name for a kind of raft used particularly at Ceylon, and which is seen also on the coasts of the Gulf of Manar. (*Dict. de Marine à voiles.*)

JERQUING *a vessel.* A search performed by an officer of the customs after she is unloaded, to see if there be any unentered goods concealed.

JERQUER. An officer whose duty is to examine and check the landing-waiters' books. See *Customs.*

JETSAM. An old legal name for wrecked articles which are sunk in the water. See *Derelict.*

JETTISON. The act of throwing articles overboard for the safety of a vessel in peril; as, to lighten her at sea in a storm, or when a leak has been sprung, or when pursued by an enemy, or for the purpose of floating her when she accidentally gets aground. Articles thus thrown overboard are said to be *jettisoned.* Their loss is contributed for as general average by the ship, freight, and cargo, the value so made good also contributing its proportion.

JETTY. A projection of stone or wood (but generally formed by piles of wood driven into the ground), affording a convenient place for landing from, and discharging vessels or boats; or simply intended as a breakwater in forming an entrance to a harbour.

Such a projection, whether of wood or stone, extending from the outer end of a wharf, is called a *Jetty-head.*

JETTY-HEAD. See *Jetty.*

JEWEL-BLOCKS, are small blocks suspended from the extremities of any yard-arm to lead the studding-sail halyards through.

JIB. A large sail extended on the *jib-stay* to the extremity of a boom, called the *jib-boom,* which runs out from a vessel's bowsprit. It gets the name of the *standing-jib,* in contradistinction to the *flying-jib.* See *Brail, Traveller,* and *Sails.* (Plates III. IV. and V.; also *Clipper,* Nos. 4, 5, and 6 of woodcut.)

*The flying-jib* sets outside of the jib upon a boom, called the *flying jib-boom,* and the *jib o' jib* outside of that. The last is not in common use.

JIB-BOOM. See *Jib.* (Plates III. IV. and V.)

JIBE. See *Gybe.*

JIB-GUYS, or JIB-BOOM GUYS. Ropes attached to the jib-boom end, and leading in upon deck through the spritsail yard-arms, or the ends of the whiskers, in order to act as a support to the jib-boom. (Plate IV. 97.) They are called *standing-guys*: there are sometimes also guys attached to the jib-traveller, which get the name of *travelling guys*; in ships of war travelling guys are always fitted.

JIB-STAY. The stay on which the jib is set.

JIB-TOPSAIL. A light sail set on the topmast-stay of a fore-and-aft rigged vessel.

JIB-TRAVELLER. See *Traveller.*

JIGGER. A small square sail rigged out on a mast and boom from the stern of a boat. Such a sail is sometimes used in a fore-and-aft rigged vessel, especially in the event of splitting the main-sail, or breaking the main-boom.

A vessel rigged as a sloop, and having also a jigger-mast, gets the name of a *Dandy.*

JIGGER. A tackle used on that part of a cable which is within the windlass in the time of weighing the anchor, to haul back the slack of the cable from the windlass.

BOOM-JIGGER. A tackle used in some large ships for rousing out the topmast studding-sail booms.

BUNT-JIGGER. A gun-tackle purchase (that is to say, a tackle composed of a rope rove through two single blocks) with a hook attached to each block; used in large vessels to hook on to the eyelet-holes in the bunt of a sail, in order to bowse it up when furling.

JIMBALS. See *Gimbals.* See description of *Compass.*

JOGGLE, or JUGLE, in Shipbuilding, a notch in the edge of a plank to admit the narrow butt of another, as of the narrow end of a stealing-strake. There are also notches called *joggles* at the ends of paddle-beam iron knees outside, to act as a stop to the diagonal iron stay which is extended between the arms of each knee. See the title *Paddle-wheels.*

JOLLY-BOAT. See *Boat,* 1, 2.

JOURNAL. The same as *Log-book.* Also a name for the turning part of a shaft; that part of the shaft of a windlass, winch, or other machine, on which it revolves.

JUGLE. See *Joggle.*

JUMP-JOINTED. The term applied to the plates of an iron vessel when they are flush.

JUNK (*Fr.* Jonque). Remnants of an old rope cut up usually for the purpose of making points, mats, gaskets, sennit, oakum, or the like. Also a name for a large flat-bottomed vessel common among the Chinese. It has three masts, one or more of them rigged with lug-sails made of cane, mat, or bamboo: the hull rises high at the stem and stern.

JURY-MAST. A temporary mast rigged in place of one

which has been carried away by accident, or erected in a new vessel for the purpose of navigating her to the place where she is to be properly fitted out.

A description of a JURY-ANCHOR, that is to say, a contrivance for temporarily putting an anchor to use when its shank happens to be broken, is given by Commander A. Milne, in the seventh volume of the *Nautical Magazine*, and in *Boyd's Naval Cadet's Manual*, p. 238.

JURY-RUDDER. Of the various plans for supplying a vessel with a temporary rudder when an accident has befallen the original one, we may notice the following ingenious method which has been adopted in the United States of America, and very justly recommended by Captain Basil Hall:—'Let a spare topmast be cut to the required length of the rudder-stock, making the heel of the mast to answer for the rudder-head; use the remainder for the after-part of the rudder, and leave a space near the lower end of the stock, wherein to stow a quantity of shot, pig-iron, or the like, as ballast to assist in keeping the rudder end on. Plank it up on both sides with slabs or deals bolted or nailed to the main and after parts of the rudder, and let there be a strong shoe-piece bolted horizontally under all. Let the main piece (the topmast used for the rudder-stock) have two mortice holes cut in it, one near the lower rudder-iron, the other about two-thirds up, through each of which pass a chain with a round turn, and carry the ends of these chains forward along the ship's counter, so that their crossings may lie against or embrace the stern-post. Clap tackles on the ends of these chains, and bowse them taut forwards in order to bind the rudder firmly against the stern-post. For greater security, also, the rudder may be hung by a rope or small chain passed through the fid-hole of the topmast, and made fast round a bar laid across the rudder-hole on deck. Bolt two spars to the upper end of the broad part of the rudder, one on each side, and lash them together in order to form a tiller projecting out from the rudder at an angle of elevation: make fast the tiller-ropes to its outer end, and lead them to the steering wheel.'

In *Lieutenant E. Jenning's Hints on Sea-risks,* there is a description given of a jury-rudder for the Royal Navy, *per* Admiralty order of January 28, 1839. See also p. 58 of *Boyd's Naval Cadet's Manual.*

KALIA (*Fr.* Calie). A double canoe of Tongatabu used for warlike purposes. It is formed of two irregularly-constructed canoes joined together by a platform: on this there is a cabin or round-house, against which the mast rests. Its sail is triangular. (*Dict. de Marine à voiles.*)

KAYACK (*Fr.* Kayak). A fishing boat of Greenland, made of seal skins stretched round a wooden frame, and having a hole pierced in its middle, into which the fisher places himself, wrapped in a frock of seal skin, which is laced close round the hole to prevent the admission of water. (*Dict. de Marine à voiles.*)

KEÇKLING. Old rope wound round cables to keep them from chafing.

KEDGE. See *Anchor*, 2, 3, 7.

To KEDGE or TO WARP a vessel, is to move her along by means of a kedge and warp run out from the ship.

KEEL. A flat-bottomed vessel used on the Tyne to carry coals; it contains, on an average, 8 Newcastle chaldrons = 15½ London chaldrons = 21 tons 4 cwt. (*Waterston's Cyclopædia of Commerce.*) This is commonly adopted as a measure of burden for colliers.

KEEL (*Fr.* Quille). The main and lowest timber in a vessel, extending from the stem to the stern-post, and forming the basis of the whole structure. In a small vessel it may consist of one piece throughout, but in vessels of a larger size, the keel is formed of several pieces, which are scarphed together endways. See Plate II. fig. 6; Plate IV. 1. The keel and keelson should be fastened with copper or patent metal bolts.

A description of the *Safety-keel* invented by Mr. Oliver Lang, master-builder at Woolwich dockyard, is given in the first volume of the *Nautical Magazine*; its construction is such that the planks and outer keel may be torn away by the ship striking on rocks, without any water being consequently admitted into her.

In the construction of *iron vessels*, the keel is formed of one or more plates of iron, having a concave curve on the upper surface, to afford a channel, or, as it may be termed, a limber passage for water throughout the ship's length. See *Bilge-keels* and *Sliding-keels*; also *Even-keel.*

FALSE-KEEL. A second keel fastened in a slight manner under the main keel, which, in case of the ship striking the ground, it may be the means of preserving. If the ship be coppered, it protects the copper from being rubbed off the keel; the false keel itself should, in this case, likewise be sheathed with copper. A false keel has also the effect of making the ship hold a better wind.

SAFETY-KEEL. See *Keel.*

KEEL (HUMBER). See *Billy-boy.*

KEELAGE. A local term for a duty charged on a vessel coming into or using a port or harbour.

KEEL-BLOCKS. Short ends of logs of timber to lay the keel of a vessel upon while building, or to place her upon for repairs.

KEELSON, or KELSON. An internal keel placed immediately above a vessel's floor timbers, and bolted down through every other floor and the keel. Its use is to give additional strength to the ship fore and aft, as well as to afford shifts to the scarphs of the keel, and more securely to bind the frames down to the keel and deadwood, forming a centre of connection for the whole parts. (Plate II. fig. 6; Plate IV. 10.)

It is called the *Main keelson*, to distinguish it from the *Keelson-rider*, or *False keelson*, which is a piece of timber wrought longitudinally over the top of the former. (Plate II. fig. 6.)

SISTER-KEELSONS, or SIDE-KEELSONS, are additional keelsons laid on the floors, one on each side of the main keelson, to afford additional strength and stability, especially to prevent the ship sagging by the weight of the masts. See *Peake's Rudimentary Treatise on the Practice of Shipbuilding*, p. 31.

BILGE-KEELSONS, are keelsons fitted on the inside of the bilge, to afford greater strength and security in vessels which are in the practice of loading heavy cargoes; such as iron, copper-ore, &c.

These also get the name of *Sister-keelsons.* In iron vessels they are made of angle-iron, and get the name of bilge pieces or stringers. (*Grantham on Iron Shipbuilding*, 26.)

KEEP AWAY. To alter the ship's course to leeward by sailing farther off the wind.

KEEP THE LAND ABOARD, or KEEP A GOOD HOLD OF THE LAND, it being a weather shore, is to keep as near it as can be done with safety.

KEEP YOUR LUFF! An order to sail with the vessel's head close to the wind; or rather to keep her head from falling off when sailing close-hauled. *Keep your wind*, and *Keep her to*, are phrases implying the same.

KELSON. See *Keelson.*

KENTLEDGE. Permanent iron ballast, consisting generally of pigs of cast iron cast in a peculiar form. See *Limber-kentledge.*

KETCH. A vessel with two masts, rigged somewhat like a galliot.

BOMB-KETCH. A vessel of the above description fitted up as a mortar vessel.

KEVELS, or CAVILS, in Shipbuilding, pieces of oak plank shaped like timber-heads, going down through a notch or mortice in the rail: they answer the purpose of timber-heads for belaying ropes to.

KEY, in Shipbuilding, a piece of dry wood used to wedge the deck planks, the parts of the rudder-case, or any pieces of wood, tightly to each other.

KEY *of Rudder*. The same as *Woodlock.*

KEYS. A name given in some parts of the West Indies to certain flats, or rocks having shoal water over them.

KILN, STOVE, or STEAMER. A particular sort of long wooden box, connected by a metal pipe with a boiler; used for steaming planks in order to make them pliable to bend round any circular or curving part of a ship, so that they may be made to assume the forms suitable for the different purposes to which they are to be applied in shipbuilding. In the Royal dockyards, there are similar trunks of metal, open at the top, employed for *boiling* the plank.

In *Creuze's Treatise on Naval Architecture*, a method, proposed by Mr. Maconochie, is described, of saturating timber with oil during the process of steaming: it is done in a steam-tight chamber by alternately subjecting the timber to the action of the steam, and condensing it, until the whole of the air, gases, and natural sap are withdrawn from the wood, which is then plunged into oil. This is considered highly serviceable in preserving the timber. See the title *Dry-rot.*

KINK. A twist in a rope. *To kink* is to twist.

KIOSK (*Fr.* Kiosque). The name given to a Turkish pleasure boat. Also a kind of turret erected on the poop of a Turkish caravel. (*Dict. de Marine à voiles.*)

KNEES. Crooked pieces of timber, or of iron, with two

branches or 'tails,' used to bind the beams to a vessel's sides, &c., the one tail or arm of the knee being bolted to the framing and the other to the beam. Of these, such as have one of their arms fayed vertically to the ship's side are called *hanging-knees*; such as are fixed parallel to, or with the hang of the deck, are called *lodging-knees*, or *deck-beam knees*; and such as cross the timbers in a slanting direction, *diagonal hanging knees.* See the latter title; and also *Cast-knees, Paddle-wheels, Standard-knees,* and *Transom-knees.*

There are knees used for supporting *the windlass-bitts* and *winch-bitts.* See description of *Gammoning*, and *Head-rails.*

The term *Knee-timber*, is applied to any piece of timber that is very crooked, such as the pieces used for knees, rising-floors, and crutches.

KNEE OF THE HEAD. See *Cutwater.*

KNEES (CHEEK). Pieces of moulded timber fayed at the heel of the figure-head for steadying the cutwater. See *Head-rails.*

KNEE-TIMBER. See *Knees*, and *Compass-Timber.*

KNIGHT-HEADS, or BOLLARD-TIMBERS, in Ship-building, two pieces of timber bolted one on each side of a vessel's main stem; between these the bowsprit is fixed. See Plates II. fig. 7; and IV. 20.

KNITTLES, or NETTLES. The halves of two adjoining yarns in a rope, twisted up together for pointing or grafting.

Also a kind of small line made of marline or rope-yarn twisted as a rope or plaited as sennit, used for seizings or for hammock clues, or to bend the square sails to the jackstays in lieu of robands, or to reef a fore-and-aft sail by its foot.

KNOT. A division on the log line answering to a mile of distance, or rather bearing the same proportion to a mile as half a minute does to an hour. In nautical language, the words *mile* and *knot* are used synonymously, implying a *geographical mile*, or, as it is sometimes called, the *nautical mile.* 'In one degree of latitude there are sixty nautical miles, or knots, while there are sixty-nine English statute miles, and about a thirteenth part (strictly 140 yards) contained within the same limits.' See *Log-Line.*

Knot also signifies a large knob made on a rope by means of its strands, used as a stop to prevent the rope from slipping.

The following illustrations of different kinds of knots are

mostly suggested by the drawings in Darcy Lever's old but standard work on Seamanship, *The Young Sea Officer's Sheet Anchor*, wherein the mode of forming the knots is clearly explained and illustrated. Information on this subject, and in regard to bends and hitches, may also be found in *Dana's*

BOWLINE KNOT.

BOWLINE ON A BIGHT.

BUOY-ROPE KNOT.

DIAMOND KNOT (SINGLE).

*Seaman's Manual, Biddlecombe's Art of Rigging, Boyd's Naval Cadet's Manual,* and *Nares on Seamanship.*

DIAMOND KNOT (DOUBLE).

FIGURE OF EIGHT KNOT.

FRENCH SHROUD KNOT.

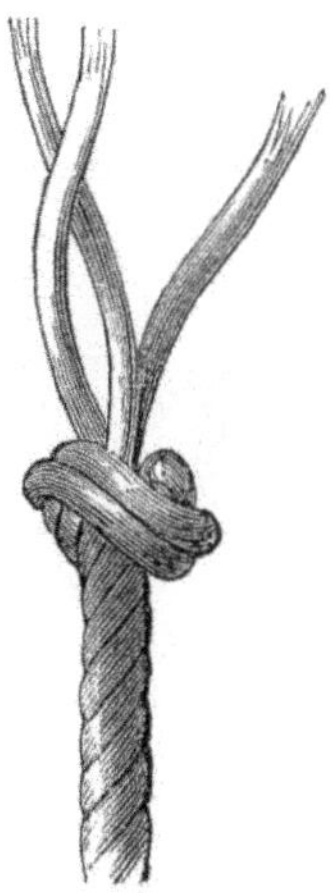

MATTHEW WALKER'S KNOT.

OVERHAND KNOT.

TURK'S HEAD KNOT.

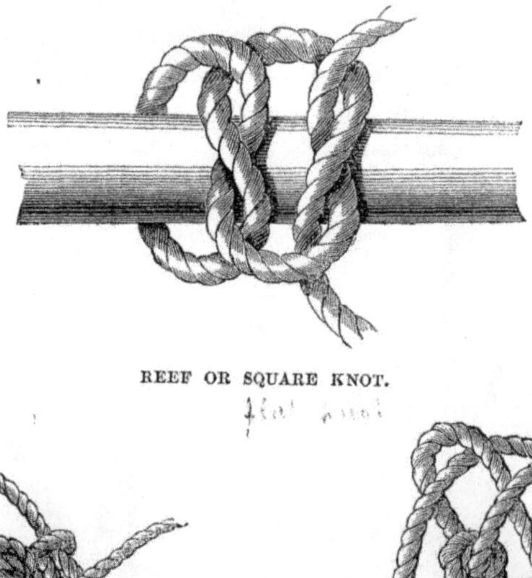

REEF OR SQUARE KNOT.

SINGLE WALL KNOT.

SINGLE WALL KNOT CROWNED (shown in process of being hauled taut).

SPRITSAIL SHEET KNOT.

KNUCKLE, or NIPPLE, in Shipbuilding, a sudden angle made on a timber, such as the knuckles of the long stern timbers at the archboard.

KOFF. A coasting vessel of Holland, having two masts rigged with spritsails and sometimes also a jigger-mast. (*Dict. de Marine à voiles.*)

KRENG. Any useless part of the carcass of a whale. See *Flensing*.

LABOURSOME. A ship is said to be *laboursome* at sea, when, either from some defect in her construction, or owing to improper stowage, she is subject to *labour*; that is, to pitch violently in a heavy sea, and roll to windward against both wind and sea, whereby she may be strained and injured. See *Rolling*.

LACING. Rope used to lash a sail to its yard or gaff, or a bonnet to a sail.

LADDER. A well-known frame with steps. There are various kinds of ladders used about a ship; such as the *Hold-ladders, Forecastle-ladders,* &c., for getting into or out of these parts of the ship.

ACCOMMODATION-LADDER. A light sort of staircase made of wood, having rails or man-ropes on each side of it; used in some vessels to be hung over the side for the convenience of people coming on board or going ashore.

SIDE-LADDER. A ladder made of rope with wooden steps, used for the side of a vessel. In large ships of war, there are steps bolted to the side for this purpose.

STERN-LADDERS are suspended from the sterns of large ships for convenience of getting into or out of the boats. They are usually made of rope, with occasional wooden steps to keep them at their proper stretch.

LADE *a ship.* To put goods on board of her. *To unlade* is the reverse.

LADEN. The opposite term to *Light.*

LADING. A vessel's cargo. See *Bill of Lading.*

LADLE *for a gun.* An instrument used for drawing any part of the charge of the gun that the worm may leave behind, and also for drawing shot.

LAGAN. An old legal term for articles which are sunk in the water, but with a buoy attached, so that they may be found again. See *Derelict.*

LAGOON is explained in *Brockhaus's Conversations Lexicon* to be 'the name given to that part of the coast of the Adriatic which the sea, by breaking through a dam formed by nature, has inundated and afterwards converted into many small lakes and islands. On sixty such islands Venice is built. The lakes, which especially bear the names of 'lagoons,' swell very much when the sea is high, but at other times become so shallow that their exhalations are dangerous to health.' The term seems, in like manner, applicable to any such lakes or inlets formed by accumulations of soil which has been carried down and deposited by a river or stream. Lagoons such as those above described, whether formed by encroachments of the sea or by a portion of it becoming confined with a bar or shoal at a river's mouth, and which are frequent in some parts of the coasts of America, bear the name of *marine lagoons,* in distinction from *fluvial lagoons,* formed by inundations on the borders of a river.

LAID TO. Often improperly rendered *Hove to.* See *Lay to,* and *Heave to.*

LAID UP. The situation of a vessel when partially or wholly dismantled, and moored in a harbour unemployed.

LAND-BREEZE. A current of air which draws off the land during the night. See *Breeze*.

LAND-FALL. The first sight of, or the making of land, after being out at sea. *A good land-fall* is when a vessel makes the land as intended or expected; *a bad land-fall* the reverse.

LAND-ICE. See *Iceberg*, 7.

LANDING-STRAKE, in a boat, the uppermost strake of plank but one; that is, the strake immediately below the sheer-strake.

LANDING-SURVEYORS and LANDING-WAITERS. See *Customs*, 3 and 4.

LAND-LOCKED. A harbour or roadstead is said to be *land-locked*, when it appears as if it were entirely surrounded by land.

LAND-MARK. Any object which serves to make the land known at sea, or as a guide in taking a harbour or a passage through any channel.

LANDSMAN. Any one not bred to the sea—not a seafaring person.

LANGRAGE. Old bolts, nails, pieces of iron, and the like, made fast together; used to increase the destructive effects of the fire of a gun.

LANGREL. See *Langrage*.

LANIARDS. See *Lanyards*.

LANTCHA. A Malay coasting vessel of European build, rigged like a lugger.

LANTEAS (*Fr.* Lantéas). A large boat used by European or American merchants at Canton and Macao. (*Dict. de Marine à voiles.*)

LANTERN. A well-known machine used as a case for light. *Poop-lanterns*, *top-lanterns*, &c., are so named after the places where they are carried in a ship. *Signal-lanterns*, or *signal-lights*, are those employed for the purpose of directing the course of other ships in a fleet or convoy, or of avoiding collision at night.

The lanterns which are used, one between each gun in a ship of war during action, are termed *fighting-lanterns*; they are kept in fire-buckets, which prevent any light being seen.

LANYARDS, or LANIARDS. Ropes rove between every two dead-eyes, forming a sort of tackle for setting up the shrouds of a vessel and keeping them at the proper stretch.

There are also short lanyards used for raising, lowering, or lashing in the ports, and for other purposes. The lanyards used for the ports of a ship of war are fitted as a tackle; and they get the name of *Port-tackle falls*.

LAP-JOINTED, signifies that the plates of an iron vessel overlap each other. See *Clincher-built.*

LAP-SIDED. A term expressive of the condition of a vessel when she will not swim upright, owing to her sides being unequally balanced.

LARBOARD, or LARBOARD-SIDE. The left side of a ship or boat when you stand with your face towards the bow. The term *Port* was many years ago ordered by the Lords Commissioners of the Admiralty to be used on all occasions throughout the Royal Navy instead of *Larboard,* which is an inconvenient term on account of its resemblance in sound to the term starboard; and this alteration is now very generally adopted in the merchant service.

LARBOWLINES. A cant name used by sailors for the men in the larboard or port watch.

LARGE. If the wind be abaft the beam, a vessel is said to be sailing *large,* or with a *fair wind.* See *Bearing.*

LASCARS. A name given to native East Indian sailors, particularly to those who serve on board our ships navigating the Indian seas or elsewhere.

LASH, in sea phrase, means to make fast anything with a rope. The rope so employed is called a *Lashing.*

LASTAGE (a term derived from the German *Last*), implies the lading of a vessel, or more particularly stowage-room for goods: thus, when a ship is laid on for a general cargo at any port in the Baltic or elsewhere, the shippers who may agree for a certain number of tons of lading are said to 'engage lastage.'

LATCHINGS. Loops on the head-rope of a bonnet, by which loops it is lashed to the foot of the sail.

LATEEN SAIL. A long triangular sail bent at its foremost

LATEEN RIG.

leach to a yard called a *lateen yard,* which hoists obliquely to the mast. The yard is attached to the mast by means of halyards, and, in working the boat or vessel, is shifted from side to side by means of a tack. Annexed is a sketch of the lateen rig.

LATITUDE *of any place on the globe.* Its distance from the equator, measured in degrees upon a meridian towards either pole; it is called north or south latitude, according as the place is in the northern or southern hemisphere, and never exceeds 90°, that being the distance of each pole from the equator. The latitude of any place is equal to the altitude of the pole above the horizon of that place; and the pole will of course rise above the horizon in the same proportion as the observer advances from the equator towards the pole. THE PARALLEL OF LATITUDE of any place is a circle passing through it parallel to the equator. These parallels diminish in circumference as they approach either pole. THE DIFFERENCE OF LATITUDE between any two places is an arc of a meridian contained between their parallels of latitude; in other words, the least distance between their parallels of latitude: it can never exceed 180°. See *Complement.*

The regions far removed from the equator are distinguished by the name of *high latitudes. Raper's Maritime Positions* is a table of latitudes and longitudes of different places for the use of mariners.

THE LATITUDE *of any object in the heavens* is an arc of a circle of longitude contained between the centre of that object and the ecliptic. It is called north or south latitude according as the object is north or south of the ecliptic. See *Astronomy,* 15; *Nautical Almanack,* 519, 520. See also *Signals.*

LAUNCH. To send a ship or boat off a building or repairing slip or off the shore into the water. The planks or logs laid on a building-slip for the bilge-coads to slide upon are termed *Bilge-ways* or *Launching-ways.* The launch of a ship is the act of launching her. The mode of launching ships is partially noticed under the title *Launching-ways.* It is fully explained and illustrated in *Peake's Rudimentary Treatise on the Practice of Shipbuilding,* p. 85. See also *Boat,* 1, 2.

LAUNCH-HO! High enough. The order to let an upper mast settle down on the fid after it has been swayed up.

LAUNCHING-WAYS, or LAUNCH, in Shipbuilding, consist first of tranverse blocks laid on the ground, or on the *groundways,* which are pieces of timber bedded in the ground to form a secure foundation on which to place these blocks; and on the blocks there are planks called *sliding planks* placed and firmly secured, their upper surface being planed smooth and coated with tallow, soft soap, and oil. The *bilgeways* consist of a square bed of timber placed under the vessel's bilge to support her while launching; they descend with the ship upon the sliding planks, and they form the basis or foundation for what is often termed the *cradle*, that is to say, the framework on which a large ship is supported while launching. The bilgeways are also called *Sliding Baulks* or *Bilge Coads.*

LAW OF NATIONS, &c. See *Maritime Law.*

LAY-DAYS. The number of days stipulated in a charter-party, or allowed by custom, for shipping or discharging a cargo.

LAY HER COURSE. A vessel is said to *lay her course,* when the wind is 'shy,' so as barely to allow the vessel to sail directly for her point of destination. See *Course.*

LAY IN *upon a yard.* To go nearer the middle of it.

*To lay out upon a yard,* is to go nearer the yard-arm.

LAYING OFF, or LAYING DOWN, in Shipbuilding, transferring the plans of the ship from the paper to the full size on the floor of the mould loft.

LAY *of a rope.* The direction in which its strands are twisted.

LAY OUT, or LAY OUT ON YOUR OARS. The same as *Give way.*

LAY TO. To lay a vessel to, means during a gale to bring and keep her weather-bow to the sea with one sail set and the helm lashed a-lee. The ship is then *laid to,* or *lying to.*

*To heave to* is often used by sailors in the same sense.

LAZARETTO. A name given to a hospital ship for the reception of the sick or of persons supposed to be infectious, and to those inclosed buildings in the Mediterranean ports, wherein ship's crews, passengers, and goods are lodged for the performance of quarantine.

It is also the name of a place parted off at the fore-part of the lower deck, in some large merchant ships, for the convenience of laying up the provisions and other stores necessary for the voyage.

(*Shipwright's Vade Mecum; Waterston's Cyclopædia of Commerce.*)

LAZY GUY. The name for a guy used to prevent the boom of a fore-and-aft sail from gybing.

LEACHES. The edges of a sail at its sides.

LEACH-LINE. A rope used for hauling up the leach of a course.

LEACH-LININGS. Pieces of cloth sewed upon a sail, which are used to keep the leach-lines from chafing the sail.

LEACH-ROPE. The bolt-rope along each of the sides of a sail.

LEAD. The name given to a conical piece of lead, with a line, called the *lead-line*, attached to its upper end. The *hand-lead*, is that used for sounding in rivers, harbours, or shoal water. The *deep-sea lead*, which is of a larger size, is used for sounding at great depths; in order to haul it in, the line is rove through a snatch-block hitched to the rigging by a tail-rope.

The *hand-lead* is hove by a single man. But the *deep-sea lead* is passed as far forward as possible, and attended by several men with slack line in their hands, stationed at certain distances from each other right aft to the quarter. When it is hove, each man successively calls out 'watch,' as soon as the lead has run out the portion of line in his hand. This operation is superintended by an officer.

The following account of the way in which the lines for the hand-lead and deep-sea lead are marked is given by Mr. Dana in his *Seaman's Manual*, along with general directions as to sounding. 'The proper way to mark a *hand-line* is black leather at 2 and 3 fathoms; white rag at 5; red rag at 7; wide strip of leather with a hole in it at 10; and 13, 15, and 17, marked like 3, 5, and 7; two knots at 20; three at 30; and 4 at 40; with single pieces of cord at 25 and 35. *The deep-sea line* has two knots at 20 fathoms, and an additional knot at every 10 fathoms, with single knots at each intermediate 5 fathoms; it sometimes has a strip of leather at ten fathoms, and from 3 to 10 is marked like the hand line.' There is often a blue rag at 13. See the title *Sound*. Also *Seamanship*, by Lieut. Nares, p. 14.

Many disastrous accidents to shipping arise from neglecting the use of the lead.

'The Bengal pilots have their own leadsman, who measures the lead-lines whenever he goes on board any ships, and marks them with coir and hemp rope-yarns at every fathom, and with a feather at about the ship's draught of water.'

LEADING-BLOCKS. A general name for those blocks which are used for guiding the direction of any purchase; they are generally portable. See *Block*, 7.

LEADING MARKS. Any objects serving for the guidance of mariners: whether *sea marks*, as buoys, light-houses, &c.; or *land marks*, such as spires on shore &c.

LEADING PART. See *Tackle.*

LEADING WIND. A wind upon or slightly *before the beam*, enabling a vessel with freedom to lay her course. See *Bearing.*

LEADSMAN. A man that heaves the lead.

LEAGUE, is understood by seamen to mean three *nautical* miles.

LEAGUER. A sort of large cask. Before the invention of water-tanks, leaguers composed the whole of the ground-tier of casks in ships of war, from frigates upwards.

LEAK. When the contents of a cask ooze out through any accidental chink, it is said to leak.

*A ship or boat leaks*, when water is *admitted* in this way; and when it commences to do so, she is said to *spring a leak.* Either of them is then said to be *leaky. To stop a leak* (*Fr.* Boucher), is to close or secure the leak so that the ship or boat may cease to make water.

In Vol. VII. of the *Nautical Magazine*, there is a description of an instrument called a *Well-gauge* and *Leak-alarm*, patented by Mr. J. H. Fiske, Portsmouth. This shows, by means of a scale, the increase or diminution of water in a ship's well, while to the back of the frame there is attached an 'alarm,' which is acted upon by a lever, and strikes a bell, to call the attention of those on duty to any particular increase of water in the well arising at any time from leakage.

LEAKAGE. The act of leaking. The loss of any liquid commodities, or of the quantity which runs out by leaking.

LEAKY. See *Leak.*

LEAN, or CLEAN, signifies that a vessel is sharp, in opposition to *full.* Thus she is said to be 'clean in the run,' or 'clean forward.'

LEDGE OF ROCKS. 'A long ridge of rocks near the surface of the sea.'

LEDGES. See *Carlings.*

LEE. That part towards which the wind is directed, and

which is said to be *to leeward*; the quarter whence it blows being called *to windward.*

If a vessel have the wind on her starboard side, this will be the *weather side*, and the larboard will be the *lee side.*

A *lee shore* means a shore lying to leeward. A *weather shore,* a shore lying to windward.

A current running to leeward is said to have a *leeward set*; the reverse is a *windward set.* So, a *lee tide* means a tide running to leeward; a *weather tide*, a tide running to windward.

*Under the lee of anything,* is when you have the object between you and the wind.

See *A-lee*, and *Bring by the lee.*

LEE-BOARD. A long flat piece of wood attached at one end to each side of a vessel by a bolt on which it traverses: when sailing on a wind, the one on the lee side is let down, and reaching below the keel, when the ship is listed over by the wind, it checks her from drifting fast to leeward. Lee-boards are used chiefly in Dutch vessels, which are built full and flat, and have keels of little depth; and also in barges, such as those which are common on the river Thames.

LEECH. See *Leach.*

LEE-GAUGE. When one vessel is to leeward of another, she is said to have the *lee-gauge* of such ship.

LEE-LURCHES. The sudden rolls which a vessel sometimes makes to *leeward* in a heavy sea.

LEE-SHORE. A shore against or towards which the wind is blowing.

LEE-SIDE, and LEE-TIDE. See *Lee.*

LEE-WAY. What a vessel loses by drifting to leeward in her course: *the angle of lee-way,* is the angle contained between the line of her apparent course and the line she really describes through the water.

LEEWARD. See *Lee.*

LEEWARDLY. The reverse of *Weatherly.*

LEND A HAND. Assist.

LENGTHENING-PIECE, or SHORT TOP-TIMBER, in Shipbuilding, the frame timber above each of the second futtocks.

LET DRAW! The order to let the wind take the after leaches of the head sails over to the lee-side while in the act of tacking. See *Draw.*

LET GO and HAUL! is the order to haul the head-yards round when the vessel is cast on the other tack.

LET IN. To fit any part of one piece of timber into a space made in order to receive it.

LETTER-BOARD, or NAME-BOARD. A board fitted above the arch-board on which the ship's name is commonly painted. See *Arch-board.*

LETTERS OF MARQUE. Commissions granted to private ships of war, empowering them to attack enemies without being liable to a charge of piracy. See *Privateer.*

LEVANTER. A name commonly given to an easterly wind in the Mediterranean.

LEVEL LINE. A horizontal line struck between the sur-marks of a floor-timber, upon which line a large square is placed with a plummet, in order to set the floor-timber to a proper level. See *Shipbuilding*, 3.

LEVER (or SPANNER) *of parallel motion.* See description of *Steam Engine*, Sect. 21.

LIE ALONG. A vessel is said to *lie along* when she leans over with a side wind. *To lie along the land* means to keep a course nearly parallel to it.

LIE TO. When a vessel's weather-bow is kept to the wind and sea, with one sail set, and the helm lashed a-lee, she is *lying to. To lay a ship to* is to bring her into this position.

LIEN. See *Maritime Lien.*

LIEUTENANT, in the Royal Navy, an officer next in rank to a commander. There are also sub-lieutenants, to which rank a midshipman is entitled to receive a commission so soon as he has passed. See *Master of Ship of War.*

LIFE-BELT. See *Life-buoy.*

LIFE-BOAT. A boat constructed so that it cannot sink or be swamped; used in saving the lives of shipwrecked persons.

1. The boat, whatever its form may be, is usually fitted with a deck made with open-work above the water-line, and with tubes of copper open at both ends, going through the bottom of the boat so that any water shipped flows down through them and falls to the level of the water outside.

2. The conclusions drawn by the Northumberland Life-Boat Committee are that 'the form best adapted for the general purposes of a life-boat is that usually given to a whale-boat, that is, both ends alike, but with more breadth of beam; fine lines to

enable the boat to pull well, but sufficient fullness forward to give buoyancy for launching through a surf; good sheer of gunwale, say an inch for each foot of length, but rounded off towards the extremes; a long flat floor; sides straight in the fore and aft direction; the gunwale strake in the midships to tumble home to protect the thole-pins, and the bow-strake to flare out to throw the sea off; as much curvature of keel as can be combined with steady steering and safe launching from a beach, in order that the boat may be turned quickly to meet a heavy roller when about to break on her side.' The most convenient length of such a boat is from twenty-five to thirty feet. The Report of the Committee from which the above is quoted is in some respects inaccurate, but it contains much valuable information.

The life-boat stations on the coasts of this country are shown in the *Wreck Chart of the British Isles* for 1860, in the *Mercantile Marine Magazine* for 1861, and additional life-boat stations are from time to time noticed in the *Journal of the National Life-Boat Institution.*

3. One of the most efficient and durable kind of fittings to give a ship's boat or any life-boat extra buoyancy, is that known by the name of *Brisbane's Boat-buoying* (or *Life boat*) *Apparatus.*

It is mentioned in the *Shipping and Mercantile Gazette* of October 15, 1853, that in the months of January and February 1851, when the subject of life-boats was under the consideration of the Northumberland Life-Boat Committee, a full description of this was given in letters to the Surveyor of the Navy and the Secretary of the Admiralty, describing it as consisting of several lengths of buoys placed along the sides of the boat beneath the thwarts, each length containing several short air-tubes of metal, gutta percha, or other suitable materials, surrounded, if of metal, with cork shavings or patent cork fibre, to protect them from contusion, by forming an elastic buoy, and the outer covering rendered watertight by a solution of gutta percha. That the Committee afterwards applied to Captain Patey, R.N., at that time Emigration Officer in Glasgow, where these buoying fittings had been used for a considerable time, for his opinion of the invention, and received from him a letter dated February 6, 1851, in which he stated that he considered it 'very superior to the usual manner of fitting life-boats.' That in a lecture given in the rooms of the Society of Arts, on March 3, 1852, Captain Washington observed that he 'considered cork, covered with gutta percha, to be the best mode of keeping boats afloat.' And in the instructions issued from the Colonial Land and Emigration Office in July 1851, it is set forth that 'the life-boat should be built whale-boat fashion, both ends alike, and the ends to a limited extent should be enclosed and made air-tight. She should have a sheer of about three-quarters of an inch to a foot, rising equally from the midships to the stem and stern, and be fitted along the sides and under the thwarts with strong metal or gutta percha air-tight tubes of about ten inches in diameter, and of convenient lengths, say about two or three feet each, properly cased in; between the tubes and the sides of the boat and the casings, cork shavings or some other appropriate article should be lightly stuffed, so as to prevent accidents from collision or friction.'

It may be thought that Mr. Brisbane's invention is preferable to either of the plans since suggested by Captain Washington and the Colonial Land and Emigration Office. On the one hand, solid cork is too heavy, and occupies too much space to be suitable for the purpose intended. On the other hand, it is evidently much better to have the air-tight tubes in several portable water-tight casings, or flexible buoys (each having several air-cells), which can be removed at pleasure and cared for, than to have them

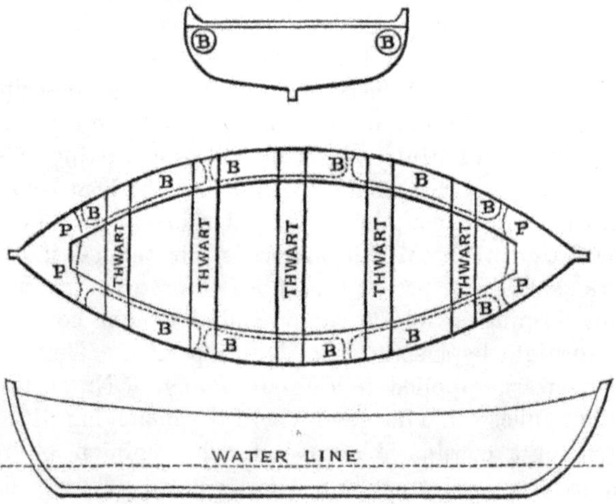


merely placed in the middle of cork shavings, cased in; for when the joints of the casing become leaky, by accident or otherwise, the cork shavings will be exposed to saturation with water. Since that time flexible buoys of this description have been supplied to the Margate Life-Boats, as an auxiliary to the air-cells, and on one occasion prevented one of them going to the bottom with her crew during a gale, when the air-cells, through neglect, had been left open.

The inventor of the buoying fittings above described is the late Mr. James Brisbane, Surveyor of Shipping in Liverpool, from whom the greater part of the original information throughout this dictionary in matters relating to shipbuilding and seamanship was obtained.

The annexed are sketches of the apparatus in a life-boat without any compartments, fitted in the same manner as they are when used for ordinary ship's boats.

B indicates by the dotted lines the tubular buoys in three lengths on each side of the boat beneath the thwarts; a fore-and-aft seat is represented in the sketch as run over the buoys from thwart to thwart. P are pad pieces for the bow and stern. Cork fitted round the upper part of a boat outside is much approved of by some competent judges of such matters, as a means of giving buoyancy to it as a life-boat.

LIFE-BUOYS, are of various descriptions, and are used to throw overboard for a person who has fallen into the water to lay hold of, and for similar purposes. There are also cork LIFE-BELTS to secure round the waist in order to buoy up a person in an upright position in the water. See *Buoy*, 8.

LIFE-HOOK. See *Slip-hook.*

LIFE-KITE. An effective and simple contrivance invented by Lieutenant Nares, R.N. (described and illustrated in his *Treatise on Seamanship*, p. 220), for saving the lives of shipwrecked persons by forming a communication between the wreck and a lee-shore. See *Loaded Shell*, and *Rockets.*

LIFE-LINES. Ropes stretched from each of the lifts to the tye on either side of an upper yard, a little above it, for the security of the men when reefing the sail or manning the yard.

Ropes stretched fore and aft and athwartships above the ship's decks, for the safety and convenience of men on duty when the ship is in violent motion, likewise also get the name of life-lines.

LIFTS. The ropes which come from the mast-heads to the ends of a yard to suspend it square and keep it steady when the sail is not set: those used for upper yards are termed *standing-lifts*; those for lower yards get the name of *running-lifts*, which are employed also to top up the yards. (Plates III. and IV.) See the article *Topping-lifts.*

LIGHT. A ship is said to be light, either when she is in ballast or has a light cargo on board. *Laden* is the opposite term.

To LIGHT *along a rope* or *sail,* means to lend assistance in hauling it along by lifting some part of it in the required direction.

LIGHTEN *a ship.* To render her lighter by throwing overboard, or discharging, the whole or any part of her ballast, stores, and cargo, &c.

LIGHTER. A large boat or vessel with heavy bearings generally used for loading and unloading vessels. See *Gabart* and *Lump.*

CARGO LIGHTER.

LIGHTER (MUD). See *Punt (Hopper).*

LIGHTERAGE. The charge made for the hire of a lighter. The act of conveying anything in a lighter.

LIGHTERMAN. A man who conveys goods to or from ships in a lighter for hire.

LIGHT-HANDED. A term implying that a vessel is short of her complement of men.

LIGHTHOUSE. An edifice on the sea coast, or on any island or rock whence lights are exhibited for the guidance of ships.

Mitchell's *Screw Pile Lighthouse* is built on screw piles, which are formed with a broad flange or screw at their lower ends, so that by turning the pile it draws into the ground as a screw or gimlet does into wood, and on the top of them the lighthouse is then erected.

We may notice two publications on this subject, namely, *Lighthouses, arranged by Captain the Hon. J. F. de Ros, R.N.*; and *Notices and Information to Mariners regarding the alteration and erection of Lighthouses, Beacons, Buoys, Sea-marks, &c., throughout the World,* by James Daniel; and *Lighthouses of the World,* by Alexander G. Findlay, supplements to which last-mentioned work are published periodically and delivered gratis to the purchasers of the book.

The most remarkable projected improvement in the mode of

illuminating lighthouses is the introduction by Professor Holmes of the magneto-electric light, produced by a number of magnets placed radially upon a wheel set in motion by a steam engine. An account of its application to lighthouses has been recently published by him.

LIGHTNING-CONDUCTOR. See *Conductor* (*Marine*).

LIGHT-ROOM, in a ship of war, an apartment lighted by sperm lamps, &c., separated from the magazine by a bulkhead, in which bull's-eyes are inserted to allow the light to strike upon reflectors fixed for that purpose at the opposite side of the magazine.

LIGHTS. Under this title reference is to be made to *Lantern*, *Lighthouse*, and *Signals*.

LIGHT-WATER LINE. See *Water-Line*.

LIMB *of the sun*, or *of the moon*, its edge at any part.

LIMBER-BOARDS, or LIMBER-PLATES. Short pieces of plank or plates placed over the limber-passage to keep out dirt and other obstructions. One edge of them is fitted to the limber-strake, and the other bevelled against the keelson. They are fitted in short pieces for the convenience of readily taking up one or more of them, in order to clear out the passage when required. (Plate II. fig. 6.) See *Peake's Rudimentary Treatise on the Practice of Shipbuilding*, p. 46.

LIMBER-CLEARER. A small chain, which in some vessels is rove fore and aft through the limber-passage, in order to clear it when necessary by hauling the chain backwards and forwards.

LIMBER-HOLES. See *Limbers*.

LIMBER-KENTLEDGE. Pigs of iron fitted to go down between the floor-timbers as ballast to lower the ship's centre of gravity; they also serve the purpose of limber-boards in preventing dirt from getting down into the limbers.

LIMBER-PASSAGE. See description of *Limbers*.

LIMBERS, or *Limber-holes*. Square holes beneath a vessel's floor-timbers on each side of the keel; forming with the open spaces between the ends of the first futtocks and each side of the keel a channel by which water may run towards the pumps throughout the length of the ship. The channel thus formed is sometimes called the *Limber-passage*, or simply the *Limbers*.

The limber-holes are in some parts of Scotland called *Draw-bellows*, and hence the feather-edged pieces of board, which in many cases are put on to form these holes (instead of cutting into the floor-timbers, which would tend to weaken them), are there termed *Drawbellows-boards.* Instead of using these feather-edged pieces, however, the water-course or limber-holes are more commonly formed by a groove cut out of the inside of the garboard-strake, or out of the chock, which is generally required (especially in sharp-bottomed vessels) to make good each floor-timber to its form at the angle next the keel.

LIMBER-STRAKE. The first plank of the ceiling next the keelson, wrought over the lower ends of the first futtocks, and for their security bolted over them to the floors. It is sometimes called the *futtock-plank* or *foot-waling.* See the article *Ceiling.* (Plate II. fig. 6.)

LINCH-PINS, in Gunnery, pins through the axle-tree of a gun-carriage, to prevent the wheel coming off.

LINE. The order of battle. *A ship of the line,* or *line-of-battle ship,* is one of sufficient force (viz. from 120 to 74 guns) to have a station in the line of battle. Small ropes get the name of *Lines.*

In Shipbuilding certain LINES are used in the plans for determining the shape of the vessel's body. These are enumerated under the title *Shipbuilding,* 3. See also *Equator.*

LINERS. A name given to packet-ships regularly trading to and from certain far-distant ports beyond seas. Also a name sometimes applied by seamen to ships of war and to their crews.

LINING. A piece of cloth sewed upon a sail, as the *bunt-line cloths, leach-linings,* or *top-linings,* which are used to keep the bunt-lines, leach-lines, or tops respectively from chafing the sail.

In shipbuilding it means thin dressed board, &c., nailed over any rough surface to give it a finish, and so on. See *Top-lining,* and *Windlass.*

LINSTOCK. A staff with a piece of iron at one end divided in two branches, formerly used for holding a lighted match in time of action. See *Match-tubs.*

LIST. A vessel is said *to have a list,* or *to list,* when she inclines or lies over to either side.

LISTING. A narrow strip cut out of the edge of a plank in order to expose the vessel's timbers for examination; or in order to put in a new piece instead of altogether replacing a defective or damaged plank.

LIZARD. A piece of rope with one or more thimbles or

blocks spliced into it. This is used in a vessel for sundry purposes.

LLOYD'S. The name formerly given to a subscription coffee house, now to a set of subscription-rooms in the Royal Exchange of London, wherein a society of individual underwriters transact business, their joint affairs being under the management of a committee. There is also a 'merchant's room' and a 'captain's room' for the transacting of general business, &c.

LLOYD'S AGENTS, or AGENTS TO LLOYD'S are persons appointed in various parts of the world, including the outports of the United Kingdom, by the association of underwriters at Lloyd's, for the purpose of forwarding to their constituents prompt and regular advices of the arrivals and departures of vessels, of losses or casualties occurring, or any other information that may be important in guiding the judgement of the individual underwriters upon the nature of the risks offered to them; and also for the purpose of assisting masters of merchant vessels in cases of misfortune. With regard to the last-mentioned branch of their duty, Mr. Lorimer, in his *Letters to a Young Master Mariner*, notices that on such occasions it is not absolutely necessary that their services should be called in, or their directions implicitly followed, whether right or wrong; but that, being *for the most part* intelligent and experienced men, it is generally prudent and advisable for the shipmaster to have their assistance. Their employment facilitates the settlement of loss or average with the underwriters. An agent to Lloyd's holds, and is bound to exhibit when required to act, a special appointment in writing from the Committee of Lloyd's, who are not, however, responsible for any business charges incurred to him. And according to the terms of their printed INSTRUCTIONS, he is not to be considered 'the representative of the underwriters on any particular policy, but is to attend to the interest of the subscribers to Lloyd's generally, and protect them from fraud and imposition in the mode of treating property in peril or under damage.'

LLOYD'S LIST, is a daily publication, containing (like the *Shipping and Mercantile Gazette*) full and early information as to the arrivals and departures of ships at and from foreign and home ports, and of casualties occurring to shipping.

LLOYD'S REGISTER OF BRITISH AND FOREIGN SHIPPING, which is published yearly, is an alphabetical list of vessels ranked in different classes according to their qualifications, upon report of *Surveyors* specially appointed for the purpose in London, and at most of the outports of the United Kingdom. The first description of the highest class of vessels is distinguished by the letter A, as being fit for conveyance of dry and perishable goods to all parts of the world. The second description, comprising vessels which after a stated number of years have not undergone the necessary repairs to entitle them to be continued in, or restored to, the first description, are designated by the diphthong Æ, as being fit for the conveyance of any kind of goods on shorter voyages; such of the latter as are found to be of a superior description have their character inserted (in red) thus *Æ. Second-class ships are designated by the letter E, and comprise all vessels which are fit for the carriage of such goods only as are not in their nature liable to sea-damage on any voyage; and third-class ships, designated by the letter I, are those which are found to be fit for the conveyance of such goods on shorter voyages. Their title to be on any class is determined by certain rules laid down in the register-book as to their construction, the nature of the materials, their state of repairs, &c., and a preference both in regard to employment and insurance is given to vessels according to the characters respectively assigned to them. The letters M C are used to denote that the boilers and machinery of a steam ship have been inspected and found to be in good order and safe working condition. This register includes both timber-built and iron vessels and steamers. There is a register of this description instituted in New York, termed *The American Lloyd's Register of Shipping*. There is also a register of shipping established in Paris, known by the name of *The French Veritas*.

LLOYD'S SURVEYORS. See *Lloyd's Register*.

LOAD-WATER LINE. See *Water-line*.

LOADED SHELL. A contrivance invented by Lieutenant Bell in 1792 for saving the lives of persons in imminent danger on board of a ship. It consists of a hollow shot or shell filled with lead, and having in it a staple, to which a small chain is attached, with a rope spliced into it. This shell, being thrown on shore from a small mortar, buries itself in the ground, and enables those on board to haul themselves on shore by means of the rope. The contrivances now chiefly used for this purpose, or rather for throwing a line from the shore over the ship, are *Manby's Mortars* and *Dennet's Rockets*. A contrivance for either of these purposes, or for throwing such a 'pass-rope' (*va-et-vient*) from one ship to another, invented by Mons. Delvigné, is described in the *Dict. de Marine à voiles.* It consists of a wooden cylinder (the *Porte-amarre*) serving to enclose a line wound on a long bobbin (*bobine*) or reel, and which is thrown out of a mortar or carronade. The bobbin when thrown winds itself round in its flight, and the cylinder thus carries out the line to form a means of communication with the desired point: the other end of the line being previously made fast to the carriage of the piece whence the cylinder is thrown. See remarks under the title *Rocket.* A valuable and simple contrivance for the same purpose by forming a communication between the wreck on a lee shore is the *Life-kite,* invented by Lieutenant Nares, R.N. It is described and illustrated in *Seamanship* by Lieutenant Nares, p. 220.

LOBLOLLY. See *Burgoo.*

LOBLOLLY-BOY, in a ship of war, the name formerly given to the *Sick-berth attendant.*

LOCAL ATTRACTION (*Fr.* Attraction locale). See *Compass,* 4.

LOCK, in gunnery, a well-known instrument for striking fire. The locks used instead of match for great guns on board of ships were screwed on the vent-field and had a lanyard attached to the trigger. In the Royal Navy these are superseded by the *detonating hammer,* which is made to descend (with the aid of a lanyard attached to it) forcibly upon a percussion cap, in order to fire the piece.

LOCK OF A WET DOCK. See *Dock.*

LOCKER. A chest, or box, or a small compartment built of

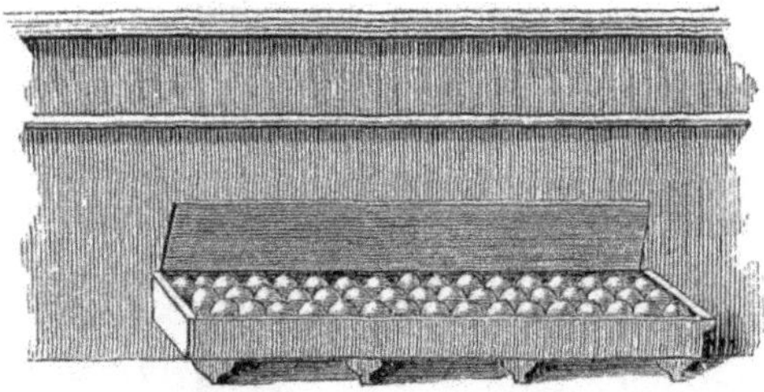

SHOT LOCKER, FOR HOLDING SHOT, AS ITS NAME IMPLIES.

deal, in the cabins or store-rooms of a vessel, for stowing anything in.

BOATSWAIN'S LOCKER. A locker in which tools and small stuff for working upon rigging are kept.

CHAIN LOCKER or CHAIN WELL. A receptacle below deck for containing the chain cable. See *Chain*, 3.

LODGING KNEES, or DECK-BEAM KNEES. Such knees as are fixed parallel to, or with the hang of the deck of, a vessel.

LOG, or LOG-BOOK (*Fr.* Journal, Livre de loch, Casernet). A journal kept by the chief mate or first officer in a merchant vessel, in which the situation of the ship from time to time, the winds, weather, courses, and distances, the misconduct or desertion of any of the crew, and everything of importance, are carefully noted down. That part of the log-book relating to transactions while the ship is in harbour is termed the *harbour-log*; and that part relating to whatever happens while the ship is at sea is termed the *sea-log*. In a ship of war the log-book is kept by the master, who every day at noon transcribes into it the particulars which have been noted on the log-board. Logs are also kept on board of ships of war at sea and in harbour.

The LOG-SHIP (*Fr.* Bateau de loch) with the log-line, &c., also get the general name of the LOG: thus we speak of heaving the log. See *Log-line.*

LOG-BOARD, or LOG-SLATE. A board made in two leaves on hinges, or a slate in two leaves in a casing of wood, divided into columns, in which are noted, in the first place, all the particulars that are desired to be registered: these are transferred from it to the log book.

LOG-BOOK. See *Log*.

LOG-GLASS. See *Log-Line*, 2.

LOG-LINE. A line about 70 or 80 fathoms long with a

piece of board called the *Log-Ship*, or *Log-Chip*, attached thereto; it is wound upon a *reel*, and used to ascertain the rate at which a vessel is sailing.

1. THE LOG-SHIP is in the form of a quadrant, the circumference of it being loaded with lead, to afford the greater resistance in order to prevent its coming home when it is 'hove' or thrown out from the ship's stern, and to make it sink perpendicularly in the water till the centre or angular point is just visible above the surface of the water. The log-ship has two holes in it near the corners of the circular part, and in order to present the flat surface of the board to the water while the reel is running out, the end of the line has two legs, one of which is made fast in the hole at one corner, and the other has a wooden peg attached to it, which is fitted into the hole at the opposite corner in such a manner, that when the line is checked, the peg is drawn out, by which means the flat face of the board instantly ceases to oppose itself to the water, one of its angles only is presented, and it is thus hauled in with the greater facility.

As long, however, as the peg remains in its place, the plane of the board offers so much resistance to the water, that as the vessel from which it is hove advances, the log-ship remains upright nearly in the same spot, and thus draws out the line off the reel, which is held up for the purpose.

Mr. Norie observes that 'in heaving the log, great care should be taken to veer out the line as fast as the log takes it, for if the log be left to turn the reel itself, it will come home and give an erroneous distance.'

2. In calculating the rate of sailing, a half minute sand-glass called the *log-glass* was commonly used. The line is marked off by pieces of knotted cord into equal parts, each representing a nautical mile or knot, the real distance between each mark being, however, $\frac{1}{120}$th of a mile, as a half minute is $\frac{1}{120}$th of an hour. At the end of the first portion of the line, one knot is made on the cord, at the second two knots, and so on. Now, each division of the line being the same portion of a mile as a half minute is of an hour, the number of them carried off while the glass is running out will show the rate a vessel goes in an hour. It is found better, however (particularly when the ship has little way), to use a glass made to run for twenty-eight seconds, which of course reduces the number of feet for a knot to forty-seven and six-tenths. 'But as the line is liable to stretch and the

glass to be affected by the weather, in order to avoid all danger of a vessel's overrunning her reckoning, and to be on the safe side, it is recommended (by Mr. Dana in his *Seaman's Manual*) to mark forty-five feet to a knot for a twenty-eight second glass.'

3. In order that the log-ship may get out of the eddy of the ship's wake, before the measuring begins, about ten fathoms of line (called *stray-line*) are left unmarked next the log-ship.

The end of the stray-line is marked by a white rag, and the first piece of knotted cord is 45 or 47 feet from the rag.

This mode of computing a vessel's course and distance, it may be added, is uncertain and precarious.

The most correct mode of thus measuring the distance run is by means of *Massey's Patent Log*, which is an instrument having a fan or rotator turned by the action of the water upon it, and communicating its motion by a connecting cord to a series of wheels called the index, to register the distance run. It is described and illustrated in *Seamanship* by Lieut. Nares, p. 17.

TYSSEN'S SHIP'S LOG, or SPEED INDICATOR, is a modification of this machine to serve the same purpose as the above without the necessity of hauling on board. It has an index or 'rotator' fitted on board the vessel.

WALKER'S SHIP LOG, also a modification of the same, has the rotator and the index combined in the instrument.

LOG-SLATE. See *Log-Board*.

LOGGERHEAD. A round ball of malleable iron with a handle, having a hook at the end of it; used for heating tar, &c.

LONG-BOAT (*Fr.* Chaloupe). See *Boat*, 1, 2.

LONG-TACKLE BLOCKS have two sheaves of different sizes placed one above the other. See *Block*, 4.

LONGITUDE (*Fr.* Longitude) *of any place on the globe*: an arc of the equator contained between the first meridian and that meridian which passes through the place. It is usual to reckon longitude from the first meridian, whether eastwards or westwards, until we reach the opposite meridian; therefore the longitude of a place in either hemisphere can never exceed 180 degrees.

THE DIFFERENCE OF LONGITUDE between two places is an arc of the equator contained between their meridians, showing how far one of them is to the eastward or westward of the other; it can never exceed 180 degrees. See *Chronometer*, *Lunar Distance*, and *Supplement*.

THE LONGITUDE OF A CELESTIAL BODY is an arc of the Ecliptic contained between the first point of the sign Aries (that is, the vernal equinoctial point), and a circle of longitude passing through the centre of the body. *Circles of Longitude* are great circles passing through the poles of the Ecliptic, and so cutting it at right angles. See *Astronomy*, 8. *Nautical Almanack*, 519, 520. (*Norie's Epitome.*) See also *Signals*.

LONGITUDINAL SECTION, in Shipbuilding, a representation or draught of a portion of the ship cut by a plane lengthways.

LOOF. See *Luff.*

LOOK OUT. To keep a good *look out* (*Fr.* Faire bonquart) means to keep a careful and efficient watch for any dangerous object in the track of the ship, &c. It is a self-explanatory term.

*A look-out man* (*Fr.* Vigie, Guetteur) is one employed on the look-out. Neglect to keep a proper look-out may subject the shipowner to liability in case of damage by collision.

LOOM OF AN OAR. That part which is within the row-lock.

LOOM, means to appear larger than nature, as in a fog.

LOOVERED BOARDS, or LOOVERED BATTENS. Boards or battens framed like Venetian blinds, used for admitting air into a vessel's ports.

LORCHA. A Chinese trading vessel, carrying guns.

LOW WATER. See *Tide*, 1.

LOWER HOLD. See *Hold.*

LOWER HOLD BEAMS. See *Beams*, 5.

LOWER MASTS, &c. See *Masts.*

LUBBER'S HOLE. A hole in a vessel's top intended for the men going up through, as an easier way than ascending by the futtock-shrouds.

LUBBER'S POINT. See *Compass*, 2.

LUFF. The fullest and broadest part *of a vessel's bow.* The weather part *of a fore-and-aft sail,* in other words, the side next the mast or stay to which it is attached.

LUFF (*Fr.* Lofer). To put the helm a-lee in order to bring a vessel's head up near the wind. *To spring the luff* is to bring her head closer to the wind. See *Keep your Luff.*

*To Luff round,* is to bring her head up to the wind in order to go about.

LUFF-TACKLE, or LUFF. A tackle variously used as

occasion requires, for setting up rigging or for similar purposes. It is usually composed of a single and a double block, the standing part of the rope being made fast to the strop of the single block. Sometimes it is composed of two double blocks.

Hence, *luff upon luff* means one luff-tackle hooked on to the fall of another in order to afford an increased purchase.

CHOKE THE LUFF. To place the leading part or fall of a tackle into the jaw of the block, so as to prevent the tackle from rendering.

LUG-SAIL (*Fr.* Bourcet). A quadrilateral or four-cornered sail, bent to a yard, the slings whereof are about one-third from its end; it is confined by means of a parrel to the mast, on which it traverses up and down. Lug-sails are very powerful, but they require to be lowered down and shifted on the mast at every tack. They are used chiefly in boats belonging to the Royal Navy and Preventive Service, and in fishing boats.

Vessels of burden carrying such sails (as in the annexed sketch) get the name of *luggers.* The rigging of this kind of vessel is described in page 106 of *Biddlecombe's Art of Rigging.*

LUGGER.—(After Biddlecombe. See his 'Art of Rigging.')

The fishing luggers which render so much valuable aid to ships when ashore on the Goodwin Sands, &c., or in distress in the vicinity of the Downs, have three masts, the main, fore, and mizen masts, each with one lug sail upon it; also a jib-boom, and an outrigger or boom guy projecting from the stern, through the end of which the sheet of the mizen is rove.

LUMP. A name for a kind of heavy lighter used at the

Royal Dockyards for carrying chain cables, tanks, or any other weighty stores to vessels, &c., and for weighing moorings.

LUMPERS. A name given to labourers employed in loading and unloading vessels: more particularly applicable to such as contract to do the work by the lump.

LUNAR DAY. The interval between the departure and return of a meridian to the moon. See *Day*.

LUNAR DISTANCE, in nautical astronomy, the distance of the moon from the sun or from a fixed star; the measurement of which is found to be of the greatest use in ascertaining longitudes. (*Squire's Grammar of Astronomy.*)

There are generally, or ought to be, four persons employed in taking the *lunar observations*, or (as they are called) *Lunars*: 'one to measure the lunar distance, another to take the altitude of the sun or a fixed star, the third to take the altitude of the moon, and a fourth to note the time per watch and to write down the different observations; the first observer, whenever his instrument brings the two bodies into apparent contact, calls out "stop," in order that the observations of the others may agree in time with his.'

LUNAR OBSERVATIONS. See *Lunar Distance*, and *Lunar Tables*.

LUNAR TABLES are 'logarithmic tables for correcting the apparent distance of the moon from the sun, or from a fixed star on account of refraction and parallax.' *Horary Tables*, are 'tables of logarithms intended to facilitate the computation of time deduced from the altitude of a celestial object.' There are several publications of this description: *Captain Shadwell's Tables for facilitating the reduction of Lunar Observations*; *Mr. David Thomson's Horary and Lunar Tables*; and those of Mrs. Taylor and Mr. Gordon.

LYING TO. When a vessel's weather-bow is kept to the wind and sea with one sail set and the helm lashed alee, she is lying to. *To lay a ship to* is to bring her into this position. *To heave to* is often (whether correctly or not) used in the same sense.

MADE. A made mast or block means one which is composed of several pieces. See *Built*.

MAGAZINE. A close apartment built in a ship's hold for containing powder. See *Light-room*.

MAGNETIC, or MAGNETICAL (*Fr.* Magnétique). In navigation, the magnetic amplitude, azimuth, or meridian, &c., implies the amplitude, azimuth, &c., *indicated by the compass*, the property of pointing towards the north pole being communicated to the needle by means of the magnet. In like manner the variation of the compass is termed the magnetical variation.

That extremity of a magnetic needle which directs itself towards the north is termed the *north pole*; and the other extremity its *south pole*. It is observed that of two different needles, the poles of the same denomination repel, and those of different denominations attract each other. Owing to the effects which the proximity of iron has on the magnetical needle, it is found necessary to correct the compasses in iron ships by magnets placed so as to neutralize these effects.

MAGNETIC COMPENSATOR (*Fr.* Compensateur magnétique). A plate of iron fixed on board of a ship near the compass to neutralize the effect of local attraction upon the needle. (*Dict. de Marine à voiles.*)

MAGNETIC NEEDLE. See *Needle.*

MAGNETIC TELEGRAPH. See *Telegraph* and *Submarine Telegraph.*

MAIN (*Fr.* Grand maître). Chief or principle. Thus we say mainmast, mainsail, mainyard, &c., to distinguish these from the fore and mizenmasts and the sails, yards, &c., which belong to them respectively; in like manner the main keel and main stem are distinguished from the false keel and false stem, and so on. See the articles *Mast, Keel, Deck, &c.*, and also *Rudder* and *Windlass.*

The mainsail of a square-rigged vessel is called a *square mainsail*: that of a fore-and-aft-rigged vessel, from being spread by the main boom, gets the name of a *boom mainsail.* The term *boom mainsail* is likewise used to distinguish a brig's trysail which sets on a boom, from her square mainsail which is bent to a yard.

The term MAIN is also used as a general name for the waters of the sea, the great body of the ocean.

MAINSAIL HAUL is the order given to haul the after yards round when the ship is head to wind in tacking.

MAKE. The tide is said to *make* when it is flowing.

MAKE FAST (*Fr.* Amarrer). To fasten a rope, &c.

MAKE HEADWAY. A ship makes headway when she advances through the water.

MAKE THE LAND. To come within sight of it when at sea.

MAKE LEEWAY (DERNIER). To drift to leeward in a vessel's course.

MAKE SAIL (*Fr.* Augmenter de voiles). To increase the sail already set on a vessel. It is sometimes used incorrectly in the same sense as to *set sail.*

MAKE-SHIFT RUDDER. The same as *Jury-rudder.*

MAKE STERNWAY. To move astern.

MAKE WATER. A vessel is said to make water when she leaks.

MAKING-IRON. An iron with a groove in it used to finish off the seam after caulking. See *Caulk.*

MAKING OFF. See *Flensing.*

MALL. See *Maul.*

MALLET (*Fr.* Maillet). A well-known kind of wooden hammer. Caulkers use it for driving oakum into the seams of a vessel with the caulking-iron or making-iron. See *Reeming.*

SERVING-MALLET. See *Mallet.*

MAN. This word, in such instances as the following, *a man of war, a merchantman, an East Indiaman, &c.*, is used to signify *ship.*

MAN. *To man a vessel* is to provide a number of competent hands for working her. *To man the Capstan,* or *the Windlass,* is to set a proper number of hands to heave at it. *To man the Yards* is to send a sufficient number of men upon them to reef or furl the sails; this last phrase also means to range men on the top of the yards, as a mark of respect to any person, or on some memorable occasion.

MAN-HOLE (*Fr.* Trou d'homme). See description of *Steam Engine,* Sect. 40.

MAN-ROPES. Ropes suspended from ornamental stanchions on each side of the gangway, to hold on by in going up or down a ship's side. See *Ladder* (*Accommodation*), and also *Ridge-ropes.*

MANBY'S MORTAR APPARATUS consists of a shell with a line and chain attached, which is coiled or faked in a box so as to allow it to run out without becoming entangled or broken, when the shell is fired from a mortar, in order to establish a communication between a shipwrecked vessel and the shore. See *Loaded Shell* and *Rockets.*

MANGER-BOARD. A strong athwartship bulkhead abaft the hawse-holes in a vessel of war. Alongside of it there is a *scupper* on each side of the ship to let off any water that may come in at the hawse-holes, and thus to keep the main deck from being flooded. The space before this board, chock forward to the bows, is called the *manger.*

MANIFEST, or SHIPPING MANIFEST. A document signed by the master of a vessel containing an account of his own name, of the name and tonnage of the ship, and the name of the place to which she belongs, with a particular description of all the goods, specifying the marks and numbers of each package, the names of the places where they have been laden and for which they are destined, and of the respective shippers and consignees, &c., so far as known to the master.

MANŒUVRING A SHIP. Working her by means of the helm and of the sails or steam power, according to the direction of the wind, &c. See *Lieutenant Nares on Seamanship*, p. 148.

MARINE (*Fr.* Marine). The Royal or the Mercantile Navy of any state. It also means *sea-affairs,* or (to use the explanation of Falconer) 'the whole economy of naval affairs,' whether civil or military. In these senses we speak of the mercantile marine with reference to merchant shipping. As an adjective, it has, in some instances, the same general signification as the term *maritime* ; but more properly implies *belonging to the sea.*

*The Royal Marines,* or *Royal Marine Forces,* are a body of troops employed in the service of the Royal Navy. There is also a body of Royal Marine Artillery employed in the naval service.

MARINE BOARDS (LOCAL) are appointed at different ports of the United Kingdom to carry into effect the provisions of the Merchant Shipping Act. The shipping offices are established, and examiners to grant certificates of competency to masters and mates are appointed by these local marine boards.

MARINE CONDUCTOR. See *Conductor.*

MARINE ENGINE. See *Steam Engine* (*Marine*).

MARINE GLUE (*Fr.* Glu Marin. Colle Marine). An adhesive substance composed of gum lac, caoutchouc, and naphtha or mineral oil, possessing properties most useful for shipbuilding and other purposes. See *Glue* (*Marine*).

MARINE INSURANCE. See *Insurance.*

MARINE INTEREST. See *Maritime Interest.*

MARINE RAILWAY. A name given by some to the patent slip for hauling vessels on for repairs.

MARINES (ROYAL), or ROYAL MARINE FORCES. Troops employed on board of Her Majesty's ships of war and in the naval service. They are composed of officers, non-commissioned officers, bombadiers, drummers, buglers, gunners, and privates.

'THE ROYAL MARINE ARTILLERY are required to be capable of shot, shell, and rocket firing, and of using all kinds of ordnance.'

There is an annual act of parliament for the regulation of the Royal Marine Forces while on shore.

MARINE STORES. Ropes, sails, provisions, and other outfit, with which a vessel is supplied. See *Stores.*

MARINER. A seaman or sailor; one skilled in the navigating of vessels. *A master mariner* is the same as the captain of a merchant vessel, or a shipmaster.

MARINER'S COMPASS. See *Compass.*

MARITIME (*Fr.* Maritime). Relating to the sea, or to sea affairs. Bounded by or bordering on the sea. *A maritime country* is a phrase applied not only to a country whose shores are washed by the sea, but also to any nation 'which makes a figure in maritime affairs.'

MARITIME INTEREST, or MARINE INTEREST. See *Bottomry.*

MARITIME LAW. The general maritime law is that branch of international law, or the law of nations, which consists of general principles chiefly derived from ancient codes of law and admitted by civilised nations as to commercial intercourse with enemies and neutrals in time of war, capture of ships, prize of war, transfer of property in ships, contracts of affreightment, bottomry, &c. The maritime law of this country is founded to a great extent on the general law maritime, and consists partly of statutory enactments, and partly of principles established by and mercantile usages ascertained before the judges in the various courts of law. It embraces both the law of shipping and marine insurance. The most recent works of authority on marine insurance are noticed under the title *Insurance.* Those on the law of shipping are *Serjeant Shee's Edition of Tenterden* and *Maclachlan on the Law of Merchant Shipping*, along with his edition of *The Merchant Shipping Amendment Act.* There are also editions of the *Merchant Shipping Acts* by Mr. O'Dowd and Mr. Greenhow.

A digested index to maritime law cases and salvage awards for upwards of twenty years past is appended to the series of current *Maritime Law Reports,* reprinted periodically from *The Law Times Reports.* It forms an index to the complete collection of Admiralty reports in the *Shipping Gazette,* and to the authoritative reports of maritime decisions during that time; and gives some occasional authentic information in notes as to the practice of marine insurance and average. The dates of the decisions are given. An index of this kind of the entire maritime law of this country, embracing all the cases in *Pritchard's Digest, Harrison's Digest,* and *Evans's Law Digest,* would be peculiarly useful, as we have not, like other nations, a code of maritime law.

MARITIME LIEN, as defined by Serjeant Shee in his edition of *Tenterden's or Abbot's Treatise on the Law of Shipping,* 'is a privileged claim in respect of service done to, or injury caused by, a ship, to be carried into effect by legal process.' A lien implies a right of retention, as that which the owner or captain of a ship has on the cargo for freight or general average, which a salvor has on a ship or other property which he has saved from shipwreck and loss, or which a shipwright has for the expense of repairs on a ship which continues in his possession.

MARK. Any object serving for the guidance of mariners, as sea-marks, land-marks, &c. See *Leading-mark.*

MARL. To wind or twist a small line or rope round another; or to lace the edge or clue of a sail to a rope instead of sewing it, when the rope has been served previously. *Roping* is the term for sewing the rope to the sail.

MARLINE (*Fr.* Merlin). Small two-stranded stuff, somewhat less than houseline; used like it for marling or seizing. Also a fine kind of spunyarn.

MARLING-SPIKE, or MARLINSPIKE. An iron pin tapering to a point; used to separate the strands of a rope in splicing or in marling.

MARLINSPIKE-HITCH. See *Hitch.*

MAROON. A name for a bright white light used for signals; common in the East Indies.

MARQUE (LETTERS OF). See *Privateer.*

MARRY. To join two ropes together by a worming over both.

MARTINGALE, or DOLPHIN-STRIKER. A short perpendicular piece of wood or iron, generally hooked to an eye-bolt, or otherwise secured under a vessel's bowsprit; to its lower end there are attached two ropes, or small chains, which get the name of the *Martingale Back-ropes,* one leading in to each bow, and one or more ropes or small chains, called the *Martingale-stays,* or *Guys,* stretched to the jib-boom end, for staying down this boom. (Plates III., IV., and V.) This is the sense in which these terms have been generally understood in the merchant service. In the Royal Navy the martingale seems now to receive the name of the dolphin-striker, and the stays or guys the name of the martingale. See *Biddlecombe's Edition of the Art of Rigging*; and *Seamanship,* by *Lieutenant Nares,* p. 45.

It would perhaps be more correct to distinguish the spar by the

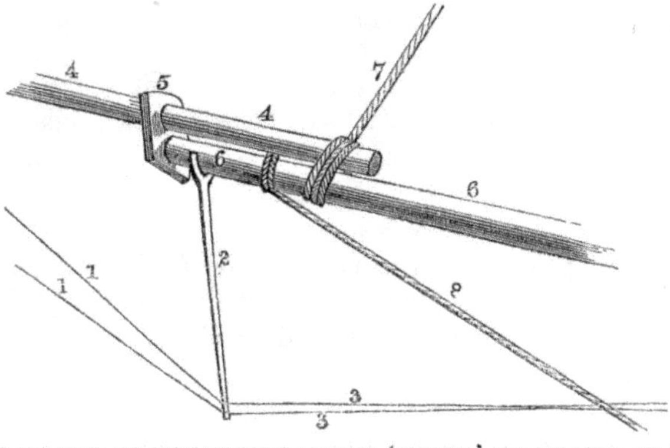


DOLPHIN STRIKER OR MARTINGALE OF THE 'QUEEN' STEAM-SHIP, OF 74 GUNS, DRAWN FROM MODEL.

1. Martingale stays or martingale.
2. Dolphin striker or martingale.
3. Martingale backropes.
4. Jibboom.
5. Bowsprit cap.
6. Bowsprit.
7. Forestay.
8. Bobstay.

name of the *dolphin striker,* the ropes by the name of *martingale stays* and *martingale backropes,* and the whole of these by the general name of the *martingale.*

MAST-CARLINGS. A name for the partners of a mast.

MAST-COAT. A piece of painted or tarred canvass nailed round a mast to make it water-tight. See *Coat,* and p. 254.

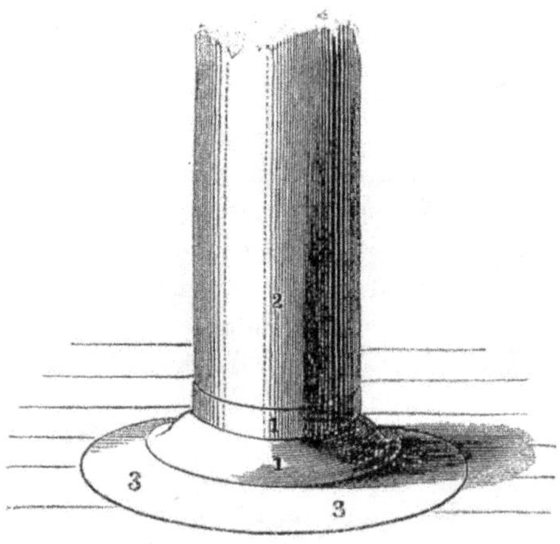


MAST COAT OF A SHIP OF WAR.

1. Mast coat. 2. Mast. 3. Coaming (of wood).

MASTS (*Fr.* Mâts). Upright spars to which the rigging and sails of a ship or boat are attached. That which is placed in the fore part of a ship, barque, or other three-masted vessel, is called the *Foremast*; that nearest the stern the *Mizenmast*; and the mast between these the *Mainmast*. In a vessel having two masts they are distinguished by the names of the *Fore* and *Main* masts. These masts receive the general name of the *lower masts*; and the term lower is in like manner applied generally to the yards and sails attached to them.

The spars erected above these lower masts are, in succession, called the *Topmasts*, *Top-gallant masts*, *Royal masts*, and the *Skysail masts* or *Poles of the Royal masts* (main, fore, or mizen respectively). The sails set on these masts are termed the topsails, top-gallant sails, royals, and skysails. (Plates III. IV. and V.) These and the yards and sails attached to them get the general name of *upper* masts, yards, and sails, respectively. See the articles *Built* and *Jury mast*.

To Mast (*Fr.* Mâter) a Vessel means to put her masts into their respective places. See *Sheers*. It is also applied to the supplying a vessel with suitable masts, and fixing them in proper stations. This subject is ably discussed in Mr. Henry Cleaver Chapman's *Rules for the Uniform Masting and Sparring of*

*Ships*, with *Suggestions on Ships and Shipbuilding*, by Mr. A. F. Jones (1862); in Mr. John Cock's *Treatise on Mast-making and the Masting of Vessels*; and in *Kipping's Rudimentary Treatise on Masting, Mast-making, and Rigging of Ships.* The advantages of iron masts are noticed in *Grantham on Iron Shipbuilding*, p. 51.

MAST-PARTNERS. Pieces of timber let in between two of the beams to form a framing for the support of a vessel's masts. See *Partners.*

MAST-RIM. A name given in some parts of England to the *Saddle.*

MAST-ROPE, or TOP-ROPE (*Fr.* Guinderesse). A rope used for sending a topmast or topgallant mast up and down. It is rove through a block called the *Top-block*, which is generally hooked to the lower part of the cap, or, as is now adopted in most merchant vessels, through a sheave-hole in the head of the lower mast, close beneath the cap. See also *Heel-rope.*

MAST-STEP. See *Step.* (Plate IV. 11.)

MASTER, SHIP-MASTER, or MASTER-MARINER. A common name for the captain or commander of a merchant vessel.

MASTER *of the Fleet.* 'A master on board the flag ship of the admiral commanding a fleet; having a general superintendence of the masters of the various vessels of the fleet.'

MASTER *of a ship of war.* An officer whose peculiar duty it is, under the control of the captain, to conduct the navigation of the ship. He has also a general superintendence of the outfit, and has charge of the charts and chronometers. Under him there is a SECOND MASTER (the lowest rank of commissioned officers) and MASTER'S ASSISTANTS.

Masters rank with lieutenants according to the dates of their commissions; but in all matters of command are subordinate to lieutenants without regard to seniority. Sub-lieutenants rank and command next after masters: and second masters after sub-lieutenants. See *Warrant Officers.*

MASTER ATTENDANT. The duties of a *Master Attendant* at one of the Royal Dockyards are to superintend the fitting or dismantling of ships, to attend to the mooring and transporting of ships, to see that all ships in ordinary are kept clean and in order, &c.

MASTIC. A particular kind of cement, now used in Shipbuilding, instead of putty, as a protection for the heads of bolts. A very good cement for that purpose is made of bright varnish and finely riddled lime. If the varnish is of good quality, this cement dries very fast.

MAT, or MATTING (*Fr.* Paillet, Sangle), made of strands of old rope or of spunyarn beaten flat and interwoven, is used to prevent chafing—such as the *Rigging-mats,* which are for this purpose seized upon a vessel's rigging and laniards. *A Paunch-mat* is a thick mat placed at the slings of a yard or elsewhere. *Sword-mats* are mats woven by means of a piece of wood resembling a sword. See *Thrum.*

Mats cause the rigging which is under them to rot, and instead of them, chafing boards of wood or of iron are now commonly used to keep the rigging from being chafed.

MATCH, for firing guns, is made of a kind of tow twisted up in two lays, and prepared with saltpetre and other inflammable ingredients: it is now used in vessels of war only when the gun-locks happen to get out of order. See *Lock.*

*To prime match* is to put a little wet bruised powder, made into a sort of paste, upon the end of it, with a piece of paper wrapped round; the object of this is to make the match ignite more easily.

MATCH-TUBS. Tubs widening towards the bottom, and having a cover perforated with holes to admit the lighted match inverted. Water is kept in them to extinguish any sparks that fall from the match. They are much safer and more convenient than the *linstock,* a staff having at one end of it a piece of iron divided into two branches, which was formerly used to be stuck upright in the deck for holding a lighted match in time of action.

MATE, or CHIEF MATE *of a merchant vessel.* The officer next to the master, and who, in the absence of the latter, acts as his deputy. In a coasting vessel there is seldom more than one mate: in other merchantmen there may be two or more, according to the size of the ship, denominated first, second, third, and fourth mates, &c.

In ships of war, the mates are such midshipmen as have passed the necessary examination qualifying them for appointment as lieutenants. And the *Boatswain, Gunner, Carpenter, &c.,* have each his 'mate' or assistant.

MATERIAL MEN. A legal term signifying persons who have furnished supplies to a ship.

MAUL, or MALL. A large iron hammer used for various purposes. The mauls employed for driving bolts or treenails, have a steel face at one end, and a point or pin drawn out at the other; they are hence called *Pin-mauls.* There are also wooden mauls called *beetles,* hooped with iron, used for driving treenails.

DOUBLE-HEADED MAULS, have a circular steel face at each end, of one size; they are used for driving large bolts, &c.

A TOP-MAUL, is a maul used for driving out and in the fid of any topmast, when required.

MEAN TIME, is that which is 'shown by good time-keepers properly regulated, which are conceived to have a uniform and regular motion.' *Apparent time,* is that which is ascertained by observations of the sun, or which is indicated by a sun-dial.

Owing to the unequal motion of the earth in its orbit, combined with the inclination of its axis to the plane of the ecliptic, the time of the sun's return to the meridian varies at different periods of the year, sometimes occurring sooner, sometimes later than at the hour of twelve, as indicated by an accurate watch. This acceleration or retardation, which sometimes amounts to more than sixteen minutes, is called the *Equation of Time*; it is set down in the *Nautical Almanack* in order to afford the ready means of reducing apparent to mean time, or mean to apparent time. (*Norie's Epitome of Navigation and Nautical Astronomy.*) See the *Nautical Almanack,* 527.

MEDICINE CHEST, in sea affairs, 'a portable chest containing all sorts of medicines necessary for a voyage, together with such instruments as are most necessary and useful for the purposes of surgery.' See *Cock-pit.*

MEDITERRANEAN PASS. An 'indenture of security' granted by the Lord Commissioners of the Admiralty to British merchant vessels to enable them, according to treaty with the Barbary States, to pass the seas unmolested by the cruisers of these states.

MERCANTILE MARINE. See *Marine.*

MERCANTILE MARINE FUND. A public fund accumulated by fees payable on account of merchant shipping to the Board of Trade, and applied to sundry purposes for the benefit of the merchant service under the Merchant Shipping Act.

MERCANTILE MARINE MAGAZINE. A periodical publication containing sailing directions, meteorological observations at sea, official reports, rewards and testimonials to merchant officers, notices of lights and buoys, &c.

MERCANTILE NAVY LIST. See *Navy List*, and *Signals* (*Commercial Code of*).

MERCATOR'S CHART. See *Chart.*

MERCATOR'S SAILING. See *Sailing.*

MERCHANTMAN. A name for a *merchant vessel*; that is a vessel employed for commercial purposes.

MERCURIAL GAUGE. See description of *Steam Engine*, Sect. 43.

MERIDIANS. Imaginary circles on the earth, passing through both poles, cutting the equator at right angles, and dividing the globe into equal parts, the eastern and western hemispheres; or rather, as understood by navigators, the meridian of a place is a semicircle passing through it and terminating at the north and south pole; the remaining semicircle being called the *opposite meridian.* Every place on the surface of the earth has its own meridian, and to it the sun is vertical at noon.

A meridian passing through some remarkable place is fixed upon by geographers as the *first meridian.* Thus, the British reckon that the first meridian passes through the Royal Observatory at Greenwich—the French, that it passes through the Royal Observatory at Paris — and so on.

*The meridian of a place on the celestial sphere*, is its terrestrial meridian extended to the heavens; in other words, that vertical circle which passes through the celestial poles, crosses the equinoctial at right angles, and intersects the horizon at the north and south points, dividing the heavens into two hemispheres, the eastern and western.

Twenty-four of these celestial meridians, or (as they are termed) *circles of right ascension*, dividing the equinoctial into parts of fifteen degrees each, are called *hour-circles.* (*Norie's Epitome of Navigation and Nautical Astronomy.*)

MESS. Any number of men belonging to a vessel who eat or lodge together: they are hence called *mess-mates*, and are said to mess with each other.

MESS-DECK. The deck on which a ship's crew mess.

MESS-KID. A kind of wooden bowl or platter for holding the men's victuals in when cooked.

MESS-MATES. See *Mess.*

MESSENGER. A rope or chain used for heaving in the cable of a vessel that weighs her anchor by a capstan: three or four turns of it are taken round the capstan; if of rope, it has an eye spliced at each end with a lashing to connect them, and if of chain the ends are connected by a shackle. It is made fast to the cable at several places by means of nippers. In a ship of war, the nippers are successively clapped on to the rope-messenger and cable near the hawse-hole, inside the ship, by fore-top-men, and taken off by main-top-men, as that part of the cable comes alongside the capstan in heaving; boys being employed to hold on the nippers when making fast, and to carry them back to the fore-top-men when taken off.

Instead of the above, a superior plan is now adopted, the messenger concisting of an endless pitch-chain (which has a double and single link alternately) working on iron spurs fastened to the periphery of the lowest collar of the capstan, and traversing round an iron block fixed near the hawse-hole: this avoids the trouble of shifting, or, as it is called, *fleeting* the messenger while heaving.

META-CENTRE, sometimes called the SHIFTING CENTRE, in Shipbuilding, that point below which the centre of gravity of the ship (that is to say, the point about which all the parts of the ship balance each other) must necessarily be placed in order that, when heeled over, she may be capable of recovering her upright position. See *Creuze's Treatise on Naval Architecture*, p. 33.

MIDDLE LATITUDE SAILING. See *Sailing.*

MIDDLE LINE, or CENTRE LINE, in Shipbuilding, a line run from the stem to the stern-post, dividing the ship into two equal parts. See Plate II. fig. 6.

MIDDLE WATCH. See *Watch.*

MIDSHIPS. The same as *amidships.*

MIDSHIP FLOOR. See *Floor.*

MIDSHIP-FRAME, or DEAD-FLAT. The frame which forms the extreme breadth of a vessel.

MIDSHIPMEN, in a ship of war, junior or petty officers under the lieutenants: 'they pass the word of command on board, attend parties of men sent on shore, &c., and in small vessels some of the older ones are intrusted with the watch,' in short, they are exercised in the various duties of their profession, to qualify them for becoming lieutenants. As soon as a midshipman has passed the necessary examination so qualifying him, he receives from the Admiralty an appointment as *Mate*.

Before a young man can be rated as a midshipman, he must have served as a 'Cadet' and attained the age of fourteen years.

MIRAGE. A remarkable optical illusion in nature; among other singular effects of which, the following are mentioned by *Malte-Brun* in his *System of Geography*: 'At sea, rocks and sands concealed under water appear as if they were raised above the surface,' and 'vessels sometimes present themselves to view as if they were upset, or as if sailing in the clouds.' 'At one time the English saw with terror the coasts of Calais and Boulogne apparently approaching the shores of their island.' 'The most celebrated example of the phenonomen is that which is frequently seen in the Straits of Messina; the spectator standing on the Italian coast perceives upon an inclined plane, formed by the waves driven toward the middle of the strait, images of palaces, embattled ramparts, houses and ships, at one time turned upside down, at another confusedly set up again, and presently the spectacle of towns and landscapes in the air.'

MISS STAYS. In tacking, if the head of a vessel will not come round she is said to *miss stays*.

MISTIC. A vessel rigged with lug sails and lateen sails; of the burden of about 80 tons: used in the Mediterranean, particularly on the coasts of Spain and the Levant. (*Dict. de Marine à voiles.*)

MITRED. Two pieces of wood are said to be *mitred*, when their ends are connected together so that the joint forms an angle, more especially when the pieces are perpendicular to each other, and the angle formed by the joint with each of their outer sides or edges is 45°.

MIZEN. A term used to distinguish the aftermost mast in any vessel which has three masts, and all the sails, spars and rigging connected therewith. See *Mast*.

The spanker, in a ship or barque, often gets the name of the *Mizen*.

MODEL. See *Shipbuilding*, 2.

MOLE. A massive work formed of large stones laid in the sea before a port or haven, to protect it from the violence of the waves; or to assist in defending it against hostile armaments.

MONKEY. A machine composed of a long pig of iron traversing in a groove; it is raised by a pulley and let fall on the heads of large bolts, for driving them in when the weight of mauls would be insufficient. When used for dead-wood bolts, or for the bolts in the cutwater, it has generally a frame with handles, with a groove on the under side, and slides upon a ridge of iron fixed in a bed, being drawn backwards and forcibly forwards by a rope on each side. (*Shipwright's Vade Mecum.*) It is also used for pile-driving.

MONSOONS. Periodical winds which blow during half of the year from one quarter, and the other half-year from the opposite direction. 'They blow more steadily in the East Indian Seas than in any other place, particularly to the northward of the equator, from the coast of Africa to the eastern side of the Bay of Bengal; also in the China Sea, but with somewhat less regularity in the northern part of it.'

The period of the north-east monsoon, which (according to *Horsburgh*) prevails from October to April in north latitude, is the dry season on the coasts of India, and that of the south-west monsoon the rainy season; 'for the wind blowing from the land brings fair weather, and the rainy season is produced by the wind blowing from the ocean towards the land, which is generally the case on both sides of the tropics.' To the southward of the equator, the period of the north-west monsoon is the rainy season, and that of the south-east monsoon is the dry season.

'Hurricanes are liable to happen near the coast of India, particularly in the Bay of Bengal at the changing of the monsoons,' which (according to Malte-Brun) usually takes place fifteen days or four weeks after the equinoxes; the change, he states, is announced by the decay of the existing monsoon, by calms and squalls in rapid succession, and by storms and hurricanes; and the beginnings of the subsequent monsoon are at first subject to variations, 'till finally it establishes an absolute dominion.'

'The monsoons constantly blow towards that hemisphere in which the sun is found.'

The south-west monsoon prevails from April to October between the equator and the tropic of Cancer, reaching from the east coast of Africa to the coasts of India, China, and the Philippine Islands; its influence extends sometimes to about longitude 145° east, and it reaches as far north as the Japan islands: 'in the same season a SSW. monsoon prevails to the southward of the equator in the Mozambique Channel.' The north-east monsoon prevails from October to May throughout nearly the same space over which the influence of the south-west monsoon extends.

The north-west monsoon prevails from October to April, and the south-east monsoon from April to October, between the north-east part of Madagascar and the west coast of New Holland. The north-west monsoon is generally confined between the equator and 10° or 11° of south latitude, but subject to irregularities; and the south-east monsoon, which may be considered as an extension of the south-east trade-wind following the sun, in some places reaches the equator, when that luminary is near the northern tropic, and on its return to the southern tropic recedes to latitude 10° or 12° south.

In the introduction to *Horsburgh's India Directory*, a work of the highest authority, from which the chief portion of the above particulars is obtained, it is observed that the monsoons meet with great obstructions from land, and in contracted places, such as the Malacca Strait, are changed into variable winds; and that their limits are not everywhere the same, nor do they always shift exactly at the same period. This subject is treated of in *Maury's Physical Geography of the Sea and its Meteorology.*

MOORING. The most common way of mooring a vessel in a river or tideway is by putting two anchors out ahead of her, connected by a chain; to the middle of this chain there is made fast a shackle or ring, having a swivel attached, to which the ship's cable is bent, and she has thereby freedom to swing round with the turn of the wind or tide without fouling her anchors. A vessel may be moored simply by putting out an anchor and chain from each bow; but in this case due care is required to avoid getting a foul hawse. Each anchor should have the same scope of cable out, equal to at least four or five times the depth of water. A vessel with only a single anchor out is said to be *moored* when there is a kedge run out abreast of it, the warp of which is hauled well taut so as to draw the ship's head a little towards the kedge, when required, to prevent the cable from getting foul of it.

When the ship has one anchor out from her bow, and another from her stern, with springs attached to each for steadying her, she is said to be moored *head and stern.*

The term *mooring* also implies the act of securing a ship or boat alongside of any landing-place.

MOORING CHOCKS. Large pieces of hard wood with a

hole in the centre, shod with iron collars, and fastened between two stanchions in large ships for the moorings to pass through.

MOORING-POSTS, or 'PALLS.' Strong upright posts of wood, stone, or cast iron, fixed securely into the ground, for mooring vessels by with chains or ropes alongside of a quay or other landing-place.

MOORING-RINGS are iron rings fixed on shore for securing vessels in like manner.

MOORING-POSTS are also strong pieces of oak inserted in the deck of a large ship for fastening the moorings when alongside of a quay.

MOORINGS. A vessel when moored, is said to be at her moorings. The term *moorings* also denotes anchors, &c., used in mooring vessels.

MORTAR. A kind of short gun with a very large bore, used on board of bomb-vessels, &c., for throwing shells. The inner end of its bore is of smaller diameter, forming what is called a *chamber* for the powder. See *Loaded Shell* and *Rockets.*

MORTAR VESSEL. The name now given to a *bomb-vessel.*

MORTGAGE *of a vessel.* A transfer of the whole or of any part of the interest or right of property in the ship, made by the owner thereof to another party in security of money advanced by the latter, with a condition of retransfer on payment of the debt. The party who grants the mortgage is termed the *mortgager*, the party obtaining such security the *mortgagee.*

MORTICE, or MORTICE-HOLE. A recess or notch made in one piece of timber to receive a tenon made on the end of another piece. See also *Dove-tail*, and description of *Block.*

MORTICED-BLOCK. See *Block.*

MORTISE (*Fr.* Mortaise). See *Mortice.*

MOULDS, in Shipbuilding, thin pieces of deal or board formed to the shape of the timbers: they are prepared in an apartment called the MOULD-LOFT, or MOULDING-LOFT, on the floor of which the draughts of the ship are laid down. Mr. Grantham in his *Treatise on Iron Shipbuilding*, p. 54, recommends that, instead of drawings on the floor of the mould-loft, drawings on paper to a large scale should be substituted in building iron ships. *Moulds for drawing plans of vessels* are thin pieces of wood of different forms, such as parts of circles, ellipses, and other figures. See *Ram-line.*

MOULDING-DIMENSION, and MOULDED. See *Siding-dimension.*

THE MOULDING EDGE of a timber, is that edge to which, in shaping it, the mould is applied.

MOULDING-LOFT, or MOULD-LOFT. See *Mould.*

MOUNT *a gun*; to put it in its carriage. A ship is said to mount so many guns, that is, to carry so many.

MOURNING. In this country vessels are painted with a strip of blue as a mark of mourning. When a square-rigged vessel appears in mourning in a harbour, the yards are topped alternately in opposite directions.

MOUSE, or MOUSING. A kind of ball or puddening made of yarns, sometimes wrought on the collars of stays. This is almost entirely out of use, the collar of a stay being now formed by laying back the end of the stay upon its own part, and splicing it in.

TO MOUSE, is to put turns of rope-yarn or spun-yarn round the point of a hook and its standing part, when hooked to anything, in order to prevent its slipping out.

MUD-HOLE (*Fr.* Orifice de nettoiement), in a marine engine, an orifice through which the deposit is removed from the boilers. It is fitted with doors which are steam-tight.

MUD-LIGHTERS. Large punts which are brought alongside of a dredging vessel for the purpose of receiving the mud removed from a river, &c. See *Dredging-machine.*

MUFFLE. Oars are muffled by putting mats or canvass round their looms in the rowlocks.

MUNIONS, or MUNTINS. Pieces of carved work placed between the lights in a vessel's stern and quarter galleries.

MUSTER ROLL. A document kept by the master of a vessel specifying his own name and the names of the whole ship's company, the place of each person's birth, the place and time of his entry to the ship, the place and time of his discharge from or leaving the same, and other particulars.

MUTINY. A kind of piratical revolt of seamen. See the title *Seaman.*

MUZZLE *of a gun*: the mouth, or outer end of its bore. See *Gun.*

MUZZLE-LOADING GUN. A gun which is loaded at the muzzle. Guns such as the Armstrong gun, which are loaded at the breech, are termed *breech-loading guns.* See *Gun.*

NADIR (*Fr.* Nadir), in astronomy, is that point in the heavens immediately under any place on the globe. See *Zenith.*

NAILS. Of the various descriptions of nails used for ship-building purposes, we may notice the following :—

Clamp-nails, are short stout nails with large heads for fastening iron clamps or plates.

Composition-nails, which are made of a mixed metal known by the name of *composition,* are used for various purposes, particularly for nailing on copper-sheathing, whence they often incorrectly get the name of *copper nails.* They are also sometimes made of a large size to be used for decks, or for the butt ends of small vessels ; for which latter purpose, however, bolts are preferable. Those used for wood-sheathing are of an intermediate size.

Copper-nails, are chiefly used in boatbuilding and for nailing in any splinters that may occur in a vessel's bottom-plank during the process of building ; also for nailing up the binnacle, for which purpose they are preferable to iron nails, because they have no effect on the magnetic needle. See *Composition nails.*

NAILS (DECK). See *Nails* (*Spike* and *Composition*).

Flat-nails, are small sharp-pointed nails, with flat thin heads, for nailing the scarphs of moulds, &c.

Ribband-nails, have large round heads, so that they may be the more easily drawn, &c. ; they are used chiefly for fastening ribbands, or for nailing any cleat which requires to be taken off again.

Rudder-nails, are similar to clamp-nails, but used mostly for fastening the pintles and braces of the rudder, which, however, are now more commonly fastened by copper or iron bolts : the most of these bolts should go right through and be clinched.

Scupper-nails, are short nails with very broad flat heads ; they are used for nailing down pieces of leather under the scuppers to carry off water while washing the decks, for nailing down tarpaulings, and for other purposes.

Sheathing-nails. Nails used for fastening copper, yellow-metal, or wood-sheathing, on a vessel's bottom, &c. Those used for wood-sheathing are either of iron or composition. For copper or yellow-metal sheathing, composition nails are employed.

Spike-nails, or Spikes. A name for nails of four inches and upwards in length.

Deck-nails, are a kind of spike, with larger heads, commonly made in a diamond form. Spikes are used for ceiling, &c. In some parts of the continent of Europe they are frequently made use of for fastening the bottom-planks of vessels, although, if iron be employed for this purpose, bolts (whereof the greater part ought to go through and be clinched inside) are greatly preferable. See *Composition-nails*, above.

NAME-BOARD, or LETTER-BOARD. A board on which the ship's name is commonly painted. See *Arch-board.*

NARROWS. Any contracted fairway; more particularly any narrow part of a navigable river where the stream is more rapid than at other parts.

NAUTICAL (*Fr.* Nautique). Pertaining to ships, seamen, or navigation.

NAUTICAL ALMANACK AND ASTRONOMICAL EPHEMERIS (*Fr.* Connaissance des temps). An annual publication, which, for the convenience of navigators going distant voyages, is issued several years in advance, containing accounts of astronomical phenomena, with the successive changes which take place in the course of a year, of all the heavenly bodies, to assist the mariner in obtaining by observation his latitude and longitude at sea. It comprehends information regarding the ephemeris of the moon and planets, eclipses, apogee and perigee of the moon, longitudes and latitudes, declination and right ascension of celestial bodies, apparent places of stars, aberration of the sun, tides, transits and sidereal time tables to find the latitude by the pole star, &c.

There is a useful publication entitled the *Companion to the Nautical Almanack, or Tables of Preparation by which the elements from that volume may be Corrected at Sight, and the Altitude Corrections of all the Heavenly Bodies used in Navigation, taken out in one term.* (1858.)

NAUTICAL ASSESSORS. Individuals possessed of nautical experience, appointed to assist the judge of the Admiralty Court, &c., when occasion requires, in deciding upon the merits of questions involving knowledge peculiar to them, or to assist the Board of Trade in enquiries regarding shipwrecks, &c.

NAUTICAL ASTRONOMY. See *Astronomy, Navigation,* and the preceding article.

NAUTICAL MAGAZINE AND NAVAL CHRONICLE. A periodical journal of papers on subjects connected with maritime affairs.

NAUTICAL MILE. See *Knot.*

NAVAL (*Fr.* Naval). Relating to ships. Consisting of ships. In a less extensive and now more commonly-adopted sense, it implies belonging or relating to the Royal Navy.

NAVAL ARCHITECTURE (*Fr.* Architecture Navale). The art or science of shipbuilding.

NAVAL ARMAMENT. A squadron of ships of war destined on a particular service.

NAVAL CADETS. See *Cadet (Naval).*

NAVAL HOODS. A name given to the *Hawse-pieces.* See *Hawse-box.*

NAVAL LINES. A name given to the lines which hold up the truss-pendants parallel to their parts round the centre of a lower yard, causing these pendants to render more easily.

NAVAL OFFICER (*Fr.* Officier de la Marine). An officer holding a commission in the Royal Navy.

NAVAL RESERVE (ROYAL). See *Royal Naval Reserve.*

NAVAL TACTICS (*Fr.* Tactique Navale). The warlike operations of fleets; or rather the art of arranging and conducting such operations. This nation has been indebted to John Clerk, Esq., of Eldin, for an ingenious system of naval tactics. The translation of *Pere Hoste,* by Captain Boswell, is a still more valuable work on this subject. Mr. George Biddlecombe, master in the Royal Navy, author of the new edition of the *Art of Rigging,* has recently also published a *Treatise of Naval Tactics,* illustrated with diagrams of the several evolutions.

NAVIGABLE. Capable of being passed through by ships or boats, more especially by vessels of burden.

NAVIGATE (*Fr.* Naviguer). To sail; to conduct the movements of a vessel at sea.

NAVIGATION (*Fr.* Navigation). The act of navigating vessels. That branch of a seaman's art which consists in ascertaining a ship's place on the globe, and shaping the courses to be steered. For explanations on this subject we have throughout the present work been mainly indebted to *Mr. J. W. Norie's Epitome of Navigation and Nautical Astronomy,* which has been long and still continues to be a standard work. We have also taken occasional advantage of the most scientific work of recent date, entitled *Raper's Practice of Navigation and Nautical Astronomy,* as well as of *Mrs. Taylor's Epitome,* which along with *Riddle's Treatise* on these branches of nautical science, is deserving of special notice. See *Sailing* and *Steam Ship*.

*Parlour's Tablets*, for facilitating and abbreviating the labour of working several problems in navigation, consist of 'a kind of slate whereon are engraven the common elements for the calculation of such problems as are in most frequent use; so that the operation in each instance is reduced to finding the remaining elements of the calculation in the ordinary tables, and placing them against the corresponding heads printed on the tablets, which when the figures so noted down are effaced by means of a wet sponge, remain uneffaced to serve for another computation.'

NAVIGATION LAWS. A term applied to those statutes, the object whereof was to promote the increase of native shipping, by securing a demand and employment for it. They have now been repealed.

NAVIGATOR (*Fr.* Navigateur). A person skilled in the art of navigating vessels; a seaman.

NAVY (*Fr.* Flotte). A fleet: also a general term for the ships belonging to any country, whether employed for the purposes of commerce or of war.

The most special application of this term, however, is to signify the ships of war in the service of the government of any nation.

The classes and general denominations of the ships of our Royal Navy are as follows:—

I. Rated Ships:

1st Rate.—All ships carrying 110 guns and upwards, or the complements of which consist of 1,000 men or more.

2nd Rate.—One of Her Majesty's yachts, and all ships carrying under 110 and more than 80 guns, or the complements of which consist of under 1,000 and not less than 800 men.

3rd Rate.—Her Majesty's other yachts, including such vessels as bear the flag or pendant of an Admiral Superintendent, or a Captain Superintendent of a dockyard, and all ships carrying 80 guns and not less than 60, or the complements of which consist of more than 600 and under 800 men.

4th Rate.—All frigate-built ships of which the complements are more than 410 men.

5th Rate.—Ships of which the complements are not more than 410 men, and not less than 300 men.

6th Rate.—All other ships commanded by a Captain.

II. Sloops of War, which comprise all vessels commanded by Commanders.

III. All other ships commanded by Lieutenants, or other officers inferior in rank to Commanders. (*Queen's Regulations*, p. 1.)

NAVY LIST (*Fr.* Annuaire de la Marine). An official account, published quarterly, of the flag-officers, captains, commanders, lieutenants, masters, chief engineers, &c., of the Royal Navy; also the medical officers, Royal Marine Forces, and Artillery, with their rates of pay, of the officers of the Royal Naval Reserve; and containing a variety of other information relating to the navy, with lists of all ships of war and other vessels employed in the naval service.

The *Mercantile Navy List* (by J. H. Brown, formerly Registrar-General of Seamen), published by authority of the Board of Trade, contains lists of British, American, and foreign ships, of masters and mates in our merchant service, with various relative information, and forms an annual appendage to the *Commercial Code of Signals for the use of all Nations.* It contains lists of British registered vessels, with their official numbers, signal letters, and ports of registry, &c., of the Local Marine Boards; and of masters and mates who have passed the necessary examination, and received certificates of competency, &c. See *Signals* (*Commercial Code of*).

NEAP TIDES (*Fr.* Marées de quadrature). See *Tide*, 4, 5.

NEAPED (*Fr.* Amorti). A vessel is said to be *neaped*, when she is left so far aground that she will not float at high water until the spring tides make.

NEAR. A term used with reference to the steering of a vessel, to imply close to the wind. Hence the order to the helmsman *no nearer*! or *no higher*! means not to let the ship's head come closer to the wind. *Off* is the opposite term; so *nothing off*! is an order not to let her fall off from the wind.

NECK. See *Gun*, 19.

NECKED. Tree-nails are said to be necked when they are found to be cracked, nipped, or bent at their necks between the outside skin and the timbers of a vessel, the effect of severe straining.

NEEDLE (MAGNETIC). See description of the *Compass* and *Dipping-needle*, and also *Magnetic*.

NESS. A term compounded with some proper name to distinguish a low point of land, as *Dungeness, Buchanness*, &c.

NETTING. Net-work of small rope, cord, or sennit. Nettings are used about several parts of vessels; we may notice the following:—

BOARDING-NETTINGS. A frame of stout nettings put round a ship to prevent her being boarded.

BOWSPRIT-NETTING, or *Staysail-netting.* The netting above a vessel's bowsprit, for stowing away the fore-topmast staysail. See *Ridge-rope.*

BULWARK-NETTING. An ornamental frame of netting answering the purpose of a bulwark. This is seldom used but for *Poop-bulwarks.*

HAMMOCK-NETTINGS. Frames of netting (or boards), supported by rails and stanchions erected over a vessel's bulwarks, upon the roughtree-rail, for stowing the seaman's hammocks in. They are termed *waist, poop, quarter,* or *forecastle-nettings,* according to their place in the ship.

HATCHWAY-NETTINGS, are nettings sometimes placed instead of gratings over the hatchways for security, and to allow at the same time a free circulation of air below. Some of them are made with an opening to let a windsail go through.

HEAD-NETTINGS. Boards or netting fixed between the head-rails. See *Head-rails.*

STAYSAIL-NETTING. The same as *Bowsprit-netting.*

NETTLES. The same as *Knittles.*

NEUTRAL (*Fr.* Neutre) SHIP. A vessel which in time of war does not take part with any of the contending powers.

• NIPPERING, means fastening two parts of a rope together in order to prevent it from rendering; this is often required to be done in setting up rigging. See also *Nippers.*

NIPPERS. A number of yarns marled together, used to secure the cable to the messenger in heaving up an anchor. The operation is termed *nippering the cable,* and the men employed to put them on and take them off are called *Nipper-men.* See *Messenger.*

NO HIGHER! or NO NEARER! See *Near.*

NORMAN. The name which was given to a wooden bar from three and a half to four feet long, with a head at one end, and made like a handspike at the other; stuck into the capstan or windlass to lash the cable to, or for taking a turn of a rope in order to lower or hoist anything through the hatchways. There were sometimes two of them put into the capstan-holes or through holes in the windlass, when at sea, to belay the fore braces to.

Also, a short wooden or iron tiller to ship into the rudder-head in order to steady the rudder in case of the tiller being carried away. This was used only in large ships.

See *Chain Cable Controller.*

NORTHING (*Fr.* Chemin au Nord). The distance sailed northwards. In like manner we speak of *southing*, *easting*, and *westing*. 'Northing and southing are measured in degrees of longitude on a meridian; easting and westing in degrees of latitude upon the Equator.'

NOSLES (or STEAM-PORTS) and NOSLE-FACES. See description of *Steam-Engine*, Sect. 2.

NOTARY, or NOTARY-PUBLIC. A person legally empowered to attest deeds or writings in order to give them the stamp of authenticity. A notary is employed, among other things, to note and to extend protests—that is, to enter a note of the particulars relating to the protest in a book (called a protocol book) kept by him for such purposes, and afterwards to write it out fully and execute the document in form upon stamped paper. British consuls and vice-consuls are empowered to act as notaries. When neither a notary nor a consul is on the spot, a justice of the peace may be employed in their stead; and in the absence of all these and of 'any person holding a public situation or office in some degree connected with the British government,' it would seem advisable generally to have the matter in question adjusted and arranged before two respectable merchants. See *Protest.*

NOTCH-BLOCKS. Single blocks with a notch cut in one cheek to receive the *bight* of a rope so as to save the trouble of reeving and unreeving the whole. See *Block*, 10.

NOTHING OFF! is the order not to let the ship's head fall off from the wind. See *Near.*

NUN-BUOYS, are somewhat in the form of casks, being large in the middle and tapering towards each end. See *Buoy.*

NUT. A small piece of iron with a screw hole cut through the middle of it; used for screwing on to the end of a bolt instead of clinching the bolt, and for similar purposes.

OAKUM (*Fr.* Étoupe). Old rope untwisted and loosened out to the original texture of hemp, in order to be used in caulking.

OAR (*Fr.* Aviron, Rame). A long piece of timber formed with a flat blade at one end; used for propelling boats, or small vessels of burden. The foremost oar is termed the *Bow-oar*; and the aftermost the *Stroke-oar.*

The men who pull the oars are called either *Oarsmen*, or *Rowers*: he that pulls the bow-oar is called *the Bow-man*; and he that pulls the stroke-oar, *the Strokesman*.

*To feather an oar*, in rowing, is to turn the blade horizontally when lifted out of the water, so that its upper edge may point aft: this is done in order to lessen the resistance of the air upon it.

*To ship the oars*, means to place them in the rowlocks, in readiness for pulling. *To unship the oars*, is to throw them out of the rowlocks, in order to lay them fore-and-aft inside the boat. See the articles *Back*, *Double-bank*, *Loom*, *Row*, *Scull*, *Sweeps*, and *Toss*.

OBLIQUE ASCENSION, or DESCENSION, is the 'sum or difference of the right ascension and ascensional difference.' (*Norie's Epitome.*)

OBLIQUE SAILING, consists in the application of oblique angled triangles to various cases, as in coasting, surveying, &c. See *Sailing*.

OBLIQUITY OF ECLIPTIC. See *Ecliptic*.

OBSERVATION (*Fr.* Observation), in nautical astronomy, denotes the act of observing with an instrument the altitude or relative position of any of the heavenly bodies, in order to estimate the latitude or longitude; which calculation is termed 'working an observation.'

OCCULTATION (*Fr.* Occultation). 'The obscuration of a fixed star or of a planet by the interposition of the moon. (*Squire's Grammar of Astronomy.*) See the *Nautical Almanack*, 536, 537.

OCEAN (*Fr.* Océan). A general name for the waters of the sea, the body of salt water on the terraqueous globe.

Also, a vast collection of its waters separating continents from each other, as the Atlantic and Pacific Oceans. A smaller part of the ocean confined by land within a narrower space, gets the name of a sea, as, the Mediterranean and Baltic Seas.

OFF. The opposite term to *Near*.

OFF AND ON. To stand off and on implies to stand alternately on different tacks from and towards the shore. See *Stand*.

OFFICER. This term is, both in the Royal Navy and merchant service, applied to any one of a ship's company who ranks above the foremast-men. See *Commission*; and *Warrant-Officers*.

OFFICER OF THE WATCH. The lieutenant, mate, or other officer who has the charge of a particular watch.

OFFING (*Fr.* Large). A situation at some distance from the shore; it is generally understood to imply beyond anchor ground.

*To keep a good offing*, means to keep well off from the land while under sail.

OFFWARD. On the side next or towards the offing, that is, off from the shore.

OGEE. See *Gun*, 12, 14, 15.

OIL, is subject to spontaneous combustion, especially in case of its leaking and coming into contact with certain kinds of dry goods. Due precaution, therefore, should be used when it is laden on board of any vessel. See *Dry Rot.*

ON THE BEAM, ON THE BOW, and ON THE QUARTER. See *Bearing.*

ON BOARD. The same as *Aboard.*

ON A WIND. A vessel is *on a wind*, or *sailing on a wind* when closehauled.

OPEN. *An open roadstead* means one which is not sheltered from the wind and sea. *An open hawse* is the reverse of a foul hawse. *Open ice*, a number of pieces of ice sufficiently separate to admit of a ship sailing conveniently among them. *An open policy* is one in which the value of the interest at risk is not stated.

OPENED OUT. The reverse of *Shut In.*

OPPOSITION. 'Celestial bodies are *in opposition*, when 180° from each other.'

ORBIT *of the earth*, or *of any planet*, the path which it describes in revolving round the sun.

ORDINARY. The establishment of such vessels of war as are out of commission, and laid up in harbour at the Royal dockyards. See also the article *Seaman.*

ORDNANCE (*Fr.* Artillerie de la Flotte), in naval affairs, a general name for cannon or great guns, carronades, mortars, and howitzers. See *Gun.*

ORLOP-DECK, or ORLOP. The lowest deck in a ship of war, or in any merchant vessel, which has three decks.

OSCILLATING ENGINES (*Fr.* Machine aux Cylindres oscillantes). A marine steam-engine 'in which the cylinders oscillate upon hollow axes, called trunnions, through which the steam enters the valve casing.' The rotatory motion is by this arrangement communicated from the head of the piston rod directly to the crank without the intervention of the parallel motion and connecting rod. (*Murray's Treatise on the Marine Engine.*)

OSCILLATING PUMP SPEARS. See *Pump.*

OUT OF WINDING. In Shipbuilding if the surface of a plank be quite fair, it is said to be *out of winding.*

OUT-BOARD, signifies on the outside of the ship: *in-board* is the reverse term. Thus in Shipbuilding, we speak of the *out-board* and *in-board works*, &c.

OUTFIT. The tackle, furniture, and provisions, and other stores, of every description, with which a vessel is fitted out for any voyage, forming part of the insurable interest in the ship. Outfit should always be included in the insurance on ship and not insured as a separate interest.

OUT-HAUL, or OUT-HAULER. A rope used for hauling out the clue of a boom-sail. A rope used for hauling it in is called an *In-hauler*, or a *Down-haul.*

OUT-PORT. A general name for any port in the United Kingdom out of London.

OUT-RIGGER. A spar rigged out from a vessel's top or crosstrees, to spread the top-gallant breast backstays.

Any boom rigged out from a vessel, to hang boats by, clear of the ship when at anchor, or for other purposes. See *Guess-Warp Boom.*

Also, a strong beam of wood stretched across a vessel, projecting from, and lashed to bolts on each side of the ship, tackles or guys connecting the end of it with a mast-head in order to secure the mast while the ship is hove down.

Outrigger also denotes a kind of frame rigged out from the sides of some very narrow boats and canoes in the Indian seas, for the purpose of forming a counterpoise to prevent the boat from being overset. If there be an outrigger on only one side of the boat, it is called a *single outrigger*, if one on each side they form what is called a *double outrigger*. The frame consists of two spars rigged out, one from each extremity of the canoe, with a block of wood connecting their ends, which block is often cut out in a form resembling the canoe that it serves to balance. If there is a single outrigger, the canoe always sails with the same side next the wind, making each of its extremities alternately the bow and stern. Some of these boats or canoes sail with the side to which the outrigger is attached, others with the opposite side, next the wind. See description of *Booanga.*

OUT-SAIL (*Fr.* Dépasser). One vessel is said to outsail another, when she performs any particular passage or voyage with greater despatch than the latter.

OUTWARDS. A vessel is said to be entered *outwards*, or *inwards*, according as she is entered at the Customhouse to depart for, or as having arrived from, foreign ports.

The pilotage or other charges incurred in entering any port are termed *inward* charges; and those incurred in departing from it *outward* charges. See the article *Bound.*

OVERBLOW (*Fr.* Surventer). The wind is said to *overblow*, when it blows so violently that it would be imprudent for a vessel to quit her moorings, or that a ship at sea could not carry sail with safety.

OVERBOARD. Off or out of a vessel: applied to any person or thing falling or thrown out of the ship, when afloat.

OVERFALL. 'A dangerous bank or shoal.'

OVERHAND KNOT. See *Knot.*

OVERHAUL. To overhaul *a ship*, or her *rigging*, &c., means to examine or inspect its condition. When we say that a vessel has got *a thorough overhaul*, this implies not only that she has been properly inspected, but that any defect has been made good.

*To overhaul a ship*, is a phrase also used to signify coming up with or gaining ground upon her. And in another sense, it implies to examine a vessel in search of contraband goods.

*To overhaul a tackle*, is to let go the fall and pull on the leading parts, so as to separate the blocks in order that the tackle may be placed again in a state of action.

*To overhaul a rope*, means to clear or disentangle it; or to pull a part of it through a block, so as to make it slack.

If a cable slip round the windlass when a vessel is at anchor, *the cable is said to overhaul.*

OVERLAUNCH, in Shipbuilding, to run the butts or scarphs of planks or pieces of timber to a certain distance beyond the butts or scarphs next above or beneath them, in order to make strong work. See *Shifting.*

OVERLOAD A SHIP, to lade her beyond what she is calculated to bear in a seaworthy condition. Such overloading is but too often attended with disastrous and even fatal results. It is the duty of a shipmaster to see that his vessel is laden for any voyage, to such an extent only as is suitable for the season of the year and the vicissitudes which may be encountered.

OVERMASTED, expresses that a vessel's masts are too long and heavy.

OVERRAKE. Heavy seas breaking over a vessel, when she is at anchor, head to the sea, are said *to overrake her*.

OWNER (*Fr.* Armateur). See *Shipowner*.

PACK. 'A body of drift-ice of such magnitude that its extent is not discernible.' See *Iceberg*, 14.

PACKET, or PACKET-SHIP (*Fr.* Paquebot). A term originally applied to any ship employed by government to carry the mails to and from places abroad. It is now also applied to any sea-going ship, whether a sailing vessel or steamer, trading regularly between two places with goods and passengers. A steam-vessel so employed is termed a *steam-packet.*

A *contract mail steam-vessel* is a private steam-ship employed under contract with government to carry the mails. *A government mail packet* is a sailing vessel or a steam-vessel in such service manned by officers and men belonging to the Royal Navy.

PAD-PIECE, or PAD, in Shipbuilding, a piece of timber placed on the top of a beam at its middle part, in order to make up the round of the deck. Pad-pieces are used more especially for paddle-beams. Fillings on the timbers also get the name of *Pads.*

PADDLE (*Fr.* Pagaie). A kind of short oar with a very broad blade; chiefly used for canoes.

PADDLE-BEAMS, PADDLE-BEAM KNEES, PADDLE-BOX, PADDLE-BOX-BOAT, PADDLE-SHAFT. See *Paddle-wheels.*

PADDLE-WHEELS, or PADDLES (*Fr.* Roues à aubes, Tambours). The wheels, one on each side of a steam-vessel, which are driven by means of machinery in order to impel her. The 'thwart boards forming the circumference of the paddle-wheel are termed *floats.*

The upper half of the wheel is encircled by a frame of wood called the *Paddle-box. The Paddle-box boat* invented by Captain George Smith, R.N., is a boat made to fit (with its bottom upwards) the top of the paddle-box rim, thus forming a covering or top to the paddle-box, while it can be conveniently turned up and put into immediate use on any emergency. These paddle-box boats are said, on account of their build and great buoyancy, to be very safe boats to venture out in when the surf is high, the more so as the rowers are able to turn and face either end of the boat in pulling. They have been long used in the paddle-steamers of the Royal Navy.

*The Paddle-beams* are two athwart-ship beams of large dimensions, projecting over the sides of the vessel; between these the paddle-wheels revolve: at their extreme ends on each side of the vessel there is a fore-and-aft beam, called a *Spring-beam,* connecting them together, and used to support the outer end of the *Paddle-shaft,* that is, the iron axis whereon the paddle-wheels revolve. The paddle beams are secured inside the ship by wooden and iron knees, and outside by iron knees: the latter have near the extremity of each tail, a 'joggle' or notch to act as a stop to an iron bar, called a *stay,* which is extended between the two tails of the knee as an additional support to the projecting ends of the beam. See the title *Screw-propeller,* and description of the *Steam-Engine,* Sect. 35. Also *Murray's Treatise on the Marine Engine,* 142.

PADDY-BOATS. Boats used at Ceylon, some as fishing boats with nets, some for the conveyance of 'paddy' and other goods, including timber, on the rivers and canals, &c.

PADOUAHAN, or PADOUACAN. A Malay vessel with two or three masts. Some of them have square sails, others lateen sails. And they carry several small guns (two bow and two stern chasers) for protection against pirates. (*Dict. de Marine à voiles.*)

PAINTER (*Fr.* Bosse d'embarcation). A rope used for securing a boat. See *Shank-Painter.*

PAINT-STRAKE, or SHEER-STRAKE. The uppermost strake of plank immediately below the gunwale. See *Strake.* (Plate IV. 30.)

PALLS. See *Mooring-Posts.*

PALM. A piece of leather made to fit over the hand, with an iron for the head of a needle to press against in sewing upon canvass. Also, the fluke of an *Anchor.*

PANSWAY. A kind of lighter used on the Ganges and Hooghly.

PARALLAX. The angular depression of a celestial body

caused by its being seen from the surface instead of from the centre of the earth. (*Raper.*)

'In deducing our conclusions from observations made upon the fixed stars which are at such an immense distance from the earth, the sensible and rational horizons may be considered as coinciding, and this will lead to no material error; but with respect to the sun, moon, and planets, the earth's semidiameter must be taken into account.

'The parallax of any object is measured by an arc of a vertical circle intercepted between a line extended from the centre of the earth, and a line extended from the eye of the observer, through the centre of the object. If the object be in the sensible horizon, this arc is called its ***horizontal parallax***; if above the horizon, its ***parallax in altitude***.

'It is evident that the altitude of an object seen from the earth's surface is less than it would be if seen from the centre:

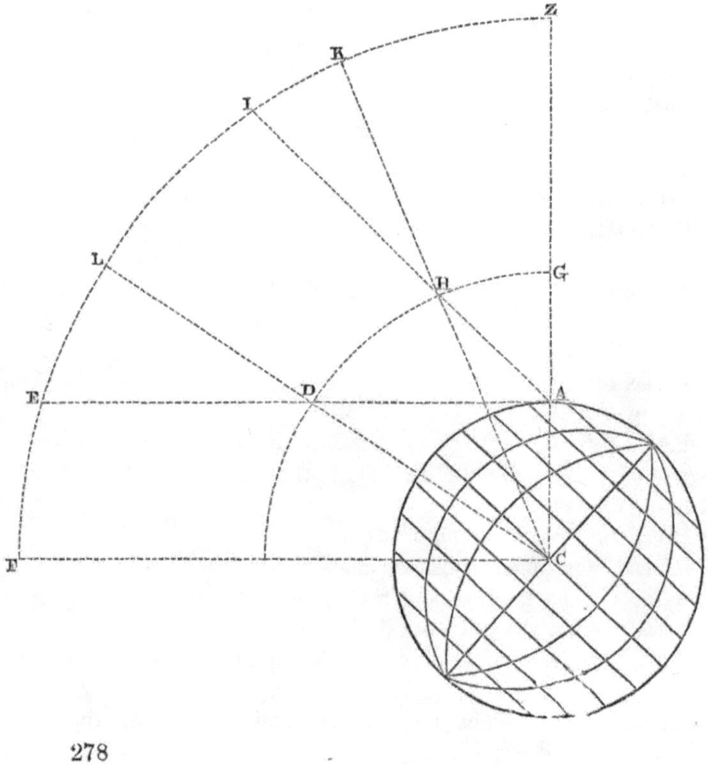

hence the parallax is to be added to the apparent altitude in order to obtain the true altitude.

'The nearer an object is to the earth, the greater is its parallax: the parallax, also, of any object is greatest at the horizon, and diminishes proportionally as it rises above the horizon till at the zenith where the parallax vanishes.' (*Norie's Epitome of Navigation and Nautical Astronomy.*)

The prefixed diagram and explanation by Mr. William Clark, teacher of navigation at Dundee, whose assistance has been of much service in treating of matters relating to navigation and nautical astronomy, throughout this Dictionary, will illustrate the definition of parallax. 'Let C represent the centre of the earth; A the place of an observer on its surface, whose sensible horizon is A E, rational or true horizon C F, and zenith Z. Also, let Z K E F be a great circle in the heavens; and G H D the apparent diurnal path of a planet arising from the rotation of the earth. Now, let the planet be in any point H of its diurnal path; then will I be its apparent place referred to in the heavens, and K its true place if seen from the centre of the earth. The difference between these, or the arc K I, is called the *parallax in altitude*, but if the planet be in the horizon at D, then the arc L E, which is the measure of the angle L D E=ADC, will be the *horizontal* parallax.' See the *Nautical Almanack*, 529.

PARALLEL OF LATITUDE (*Fr.* Parallèle de latitude) of any place, is a circle passing through it parallel to the equator. See *Latitude*.

PARALLEL BAR. See description of *Steam-Engine*, Sect. 21.

PARALLEL MOTION SHAFT. See description of *Steam-Engine*, Sect. 21.

PARALLEL SAILING, consists in finding the difference of longitude from the departure made good, that is to say, from the distance sailed due east or west. See *Sailing*.

PARAOS. A small vessel rigged like a junk, employed in the coasting trade of China and Cochin China. (*Dict. de Marine à voiles.*)

PARBUCKLE. A contrivance for shipping or discharging casks, by making fast the bight of a rope on board the ship, and passing the hauling parts of it round the quarters of the cask, so that the cask may be rolled up and down at pleasure; this is used also for bale goods, spars, &c., when the distance from the shore is too great for a crane or tackle conveniently to bear upon them. The operation is termed *parbuckling*.

PARCEL. To wind strips of tarred canvass (which in such cases gets the name of *parcelling*) round a rope previously to its being served, in order to secure it from being injured by water lodging between the parts of the service when worn.

PARREL (*Fr.* Racage). A rope or iron collar by which a

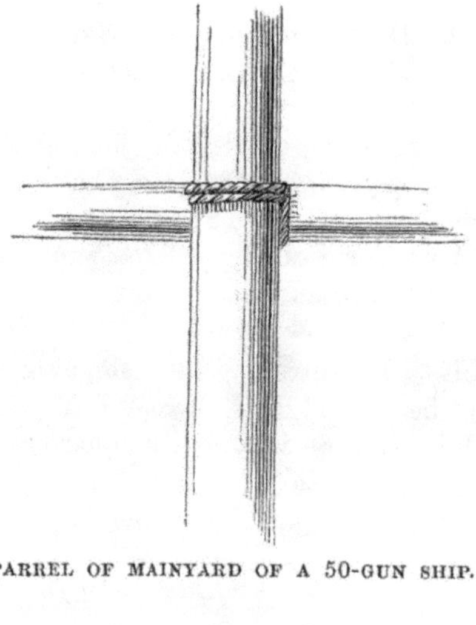

PARREL OF MAINYARD OF A 50-GUN SHIP.

yard is confined at its slings to a mast. Iron parrels are now commonly used.

The *lower* yards are generally confined to the masts by means of trusses.

TRUSS-PARREL. That part of a rope truss which goes round the yard.

PART. A vessel is said to *part from an anchor*, when she is driven from it in consequence of the cable breaking.

PARTICULAR AVERAGE, or PARTIAL LOSS. See *Average*.

PARTNERS (*Fr.* Étambrai). Pieces of timber let in between two of the beams to form a framing for the support of anything which passes through a vessel's deck: as of the masts, capstan, pumps, or pawl-bitt. In large ships the *bowsprit* generally steps on a frame-work called the *bowsprit partners*, bitts being let down, one on each side, termed the *bowsprit bitts*, which in some ships are used for belaying the topsail sheets to. The bowsprit of any small merchant vessel is commonly bolted to one of the deck beams.

PART-OWNER (*Fr.* Cobourgeois). The proprietor of a certain number of shares in a ship.

PASSAGE. This term is applied to the voyage which a vessel performs from one place to another; and also to the act of conveying a person thither in the vessel. Thus, a ship is said to have met with good or bad weather on her passage to any place; and a person pays so much for his passage to that place.

PASSAGE-BOAT. A name given to any steam or sailing vessel running short and frequent trips between different places in a river or frith, &c.

PASSAGE-BROKER. A person licensed to act in the sale or letting of passages by ships on any voyage.

PASSAGE-MONEY. The charge made for the conveyance of a passenger or of passengers in a merchant vessel.

PASSAREE. 'Any rope fastened round the cathead and foretack to keep tight the leach of the sail in light winds' when going large. It is not used in the merchant service.

PASSENGER SHIP. A vessel fitted for carrying passengers. Such ships are for the most part placed under certain statutory regulations.

PASSPORT (*Fr.* Passeport), in maritime affairs, a written permission granted by a ruling power to navigate a certain portion of the seas, or by a neutral state, in time of war, for a vessel to prosecute a certain voyage, without molestation.

PATAMAR (*Fr.* Patamar). A coasting vessel of the Malabar coast. Its keel has an upward curve amidships, and extends only about half the entire length of the vessel; the stem and stern, especially the former, have great rake; and the draught of water is much greater at the head than at the stern. Its mould resembles that of the Baggala. 'The Patamars are remarkable from bearing much analogy with the "djerms" of the Nile.' (*Dict. de Marine à voiles.*)

PATCH. 'A collection of drift or bay ice, of a circular or polygonal form.' See *Iceberg*, 15.

PATENT GLASSES. Glasses of a rectangular form, now in common use for admitting light through a vessel's decks, &c. See *Bull's-eye.*

PATENT METAL. A name given to the *yellow-metal* patented by Mr. Muntz, used for the sheathing of vessels. See *Copper.*

PATRON. A name which was formerly given to the commander of any small vessel or packet-boat, and to the coxswain of a boat.

PAUNCH-MAT, or PANCH. A thick mat placed at the slings of a yard or elsewhere. See *Mat.*

PAWLS (PAULS, or PALLS) *of a Capstan*, are short pieces of metal traversing on bolts fixed to the body of the lower part of the capstan, and falling into the notches of a cast-iron ring let into the ship's deck: *the pawls of a windlass*, in like manner, turn upon bolts going through a plate which is fixed upon the pawl-bitt, and they fall into the notches of a metal collar fitted round the middle of the windlass: *the pawls of a winch* traverse in the same way upon the winch-bitts. Their use is to prevent a recoil of these machines respectively, during the process of heaving. In the old form of the capstan, the pawls traverse on bolts fixed in the deck, and are made to fall into the sides of the whelps, when required, in order to prevent its recoil.

PAWL-BITT. A strong piece of timber placed vertically at the back of the windlass for its security. See *Bitts.*

PAY. To lay on a coat of tar or some other substance with a mop or brush, in order to preserve the surface of anything. The seams of a vessel, after being caulked, are paid with pitch, resin, or marine glue, to keep water from the oakum, &c.

PAY AWAY. The same as *Pay out.*

PAY OFF, in Seamanship, means to let a vessel's head fall off from the wind.

PAY OUT *a cable* or *rope*: to slacken it and shove it, or to let it run out at a hawse-hole or elsewhere. *To veer away the cable,* has the same meaning.

PAYMASTERS, are officers in a ship of war superintending the provisioning and paying of the ship's company, &c.

PEA *of an Anchor.* See description of *Anchor.*

*To peak a yard or gaff,* is to lay or raise it apeak. See the article *Apeak.* See also *A-stay* and *Forepeak.*

PEAK. The upper outer end of a gaff.

PEAK-DOWNHAULER. A rope rove through a block at the peak, or outer end of a gaff, to haul it down by.

PEAK-PURCHASE. A tackle on the peak-tye for hoisting it.

PEAK-TYE. A tye used in some ships for hoisting the peak of a heavy gaff.

PEDESTAL BLOCKS. The same as plummer blocks.

PELOTA. A kind of small skiff used at Buenos Ayres. It carries only one man seated; and a native of the country swims across any of the small rivers, &c., towing it after him by means of a short line which he holds between his teeth. (*Dict. de Marine à voiles.*)

PENDANT, or PENNANT (*Fr.* Pantoir). A long narrow piece of buntine carried at the mast-head of a ship of war.

*A broad pendant,* is a swallow-tailed piece carried in the same way in a commodore's vessel.

*Pendant* is also the name of a strop of rope fitted at one end to a mast-head or elsewhere, with a hook, thimble, or block at the other end, for a brace to reeve through or to attach a tackle to: for this purpose a short end of one of the shrouds on either side is often used. *A boom-brace pendant* is a rope attached to the extremity of a studding-sail, and leading down on deck; it is used for counteracting the pressure of the sail upon the boom. See *Reef-pendant* and *Rudder-pendant.*

PORT-PENDANTS are ropes spliced into rings on the outside of the port-lids, and rove through leaden pipes in the ship's side, to haul up or let down the port-lids with the aid of tackles.

PENINSULA. A piece of land almost encompassed by the sea, joined to the main land only by an isthmus or narrow neck.

PENNANT. See *Pendant.*

PEOTA. A Venetian boat, remarkable for its lightness, employed in the Adriatic in carrying despatches as well as in transporting passengers. (*Dict. de Marine à voiles.*)

PERIGEE. That point of the moon's orbit which is nearest to the earth. It is also applied to the like point of the sun's apparent orbit. See *Apogee.*

PERIHELION. That point of the earth's or any planet's orbit which is nearest to the sun. See *Aphelion.*

PETTY AVERAGE. See *Average.*

PHASES, in Astronomy, the varying appearances of the enlightened parts of the moon and of the planets Venus and Mercury. (*Squire's Grammar of Astronomy.*)

PIAHIAP (*Fr.* Piahiap). A large Malay boat employed in piratical expeditions. It is rigged somewhat like a French lugger, and carries one or two guns. (*Dict. de Marine à voiles.*)

PIER. A sort of quay, or a jetty, projecting into the water, serving as a landing-place, and at which vessels may be discharged and loaded.

PIER-HEAD. The outer extremity of a pier.

PIGS. An abbreviated name for pieces of pig-iron used as ballast.

PILASTERS, in Shipbuilding, flat columns placed as ornaments on the stern and quarter-galleries, or in the cabins, &c.

PILLARS, or STANCHIONS. Square or turned pieces of timber or round bars of iron, erected perpendicularly under the beams of a vessel for their support. See *Stanchions.*

PILOT (*Fr.* Pilote). A person whose business is to conduct vessels from or into roads, rivers, or harbours, over bars or shoals, or through intricate and dangerous channels. He ought to have a proper knowledge of the bearings of the sands, rocks, or other dangerous objects which obstruct the navigation, of the soundings at all times of the tide, of the marks or lights along the coast; in short, to possess every information which will enable him *to pilot* vessels in safety. *A Branch Pilot* is a pilot licensed for any particular localities.

PILOT BOAT (*Fr.* Pilote-bot). Any boat used by a pilot in pursuing his occupation.

PILOT CUTTERS. Sharp-built vessels used by pilots in pursuing their important avocations. See *Cutter.*

PILOT'S FAIRWAY. A passage or channel wherein, according to usage or special regulation, a pilot must be employed.

Any part of the sea, or of a river, where the assistance of a pilot is called for, gets the name of *Pilot's-water.*

PILOTAGE. The act of piloting vessels. The expense incurred for piloting any vessel. The statutory regulations in regard to pilotage may be seen in *The Shipmaster's Chart of Compulsory Pilotage on the Coasts and Seas of England and Wales,* by W. Holt, B.A., Oxon, Barrister at Law.

PINJADJAP (*Fr.* Pinjadjap). A coasting vessel of the Straits of Malacca. It has a kind of broad washboard or topgallant bulwark, the continuation of which projects beyond the stem and stern from each side of the vessel, and has spars across at intervals. It is navigated with sails and oars, and, like the ancient galleys, has two masts. The sails, which are made of Indian mats, are rectangular in shape, and have great drop. (*Dict. de Marine à voiles.*)

PINK (*Fr.* Pinque). A narrow-sterned vessel, chiefly of the Mediterranean, with an outrigger for hauling out the mizen.

PINK-STERNED. A term implying that a vessel has a round stern finished (by a continuation of the bulwarks aft) with a narrow square part above.

PINNACE (*Fr.* Pinasse, or Pinnace). A large boat, having generally three masts, and lateen sails. See also *Boat,* 1.

PINS. Short cylindrical pieces of wood or iron used for various purposes about a ship: as the pins which are inserted through the ends of the capstan-bars to prevent their unshipping.

BELAYING-PINS, or *Tacks-pins,* are pins inserted into holes in the fife rail and other parts of the vessel when required for belaying running-gear to.

PIPE. See *Call* and *Rudder-bands.*

PIRATE (*Fr.* Pirate, Forban). 'One who lives by pillage, and robbing on the sea.' A person occupied in seizing and plundering ships without the authority of any state. Such unlawful act or practice is termed *Piracy*; and the vessels so engaged are *piratical* vessels.

PISTON (STEAM), and PISTON-ROD. See description of *Steam-Engine,* Sects. 8 and 9.

PITCH (*Fr.* Brai, Guitran). A substance made by melting coarse hard resin with tar; the proportion of tar is generally one-half the quantity of resin, but it is regulated according to the consistency of the tar. (*Waterston's Cyclopædia of Commerce.*)

It is used chiefly for paying the seams of a ship or boat, after they have been caulked. It is melted in large cast-iron *pitch-pots*, from which it is carried in small *pitch-kettles* to the ship, and is laid on with *pitch-mops*.

PITCHING. The motion by which a vessel plunges (or 'pitches') her head and stern alternately into the trough of the sea. See *Laboursome*.

PITCH-KETTLES. See *Pitch*.

PITCH-MOPS. See *Pitch*.

PITCH-POTS. See *Pitch*.

PIVOT-GUN. A gun set upon a frame carriage which can be turned about so as to point the piece in any direction. See *Gun*.

PLANE SAILING. See *Sailing* (*Plane*).

PLANET. A celestial body revolving round the sun.

PLANK (*Fr.* Bordage). Wood sawn lengthways into pieces called *clefts*, less in thickness than in breadth. The term 'plank' is seldom applied to pieces exceeding six to eight inches in thickness: when under one and a half inches in thickness, they get the name of 'board' or 'deal.' See *Deals* and *Thickstuff*.

*To plank a ship*, is to cover her timbers with plank.

PLANK-SHEER, GUNWALE, or COVERING-BOARD, in Shipbuilding, a plank which is fitted round the ship, covering all the tops of the timbers, and encircling and securing the timber-heads. It has a moulding on its outer edge, projecting over the paint-strake, whereby the sheer of the vessel is distinctly marked out: hence the name of plank-sheer. (Plate II. fig. 6, and Plate IV. 29.)

PLANS used in Shipbuilding. See the article *Shipbuilding*, 1.

PLAT. A name formerly given to what seamen now call *foxes*.

PLUG. A piece of wood fitted into a hole in a ship or boat, in order to let in or keep out water as may be required. Ships of war are supplied with plugs made of oakum and tallow, to fill up shot holes made in time of action. See also *Hawse-Plug*, *Treenail-Plugs*, and *Vent-Plug*.

PLUMMER-BLOCKS, or PEDESTAL BLOCKS, in a marine steam-engine, pieces of metal, wherein are fixed the bushes in which the shafts traverse.

PLY. The same as to *beat to windward* (*Fr.* Louvoyer).

The term *plying* also denotes the act of a vessel running regularly between any two ports.

PLY *an oar*. To pull an oar; to row.

POINT. See *Promontory* and *Reef-Points*.

POINTING *a rope*. The operation of unlaying its end and tapering the inside yarns with a knife, then weaving a sort of mat with the ends of the outer yarns about it, in order that it may thrust more easily through any hole without untwisting, and generally to keep it from fagging.

POINT-BLANK (*Fr.* But-en-blanc). A gun is laid point-blank for an object, when the axis of its bore and the point aimed at are in one line. If a gun be spoken of as at point-blank, without reference to an object, it is understood that its axis is perfectly horizontal. The *point-blank range* implies the first graze, supposing the gun horizontal. For further information on this subject, we may refer to the first volume of the *United Service Magazine* for the year 1830, from which the above explanation is obtained, and to the article *Ordnance* in the *Penny Cyclopædia*.

POINTERS, SNAKE-PIECES, or BRACES. Pieces of timber fixed fore-and-aft and diagonally inside of a vessel's run or quarter, of a sufficient length properly to connect the stern-frame with the rest of her after-body. The bolts in these pieces ought to go right through and be clinched. Every merchant vessel exceeding 150 tons' burden should have 'one pair of pointers in addition to a knee at each end of the wing-transom.' (*Lloyd's Register.*)

The name *pointers* is also given to certain pieces of timber which connect the foremost hold beam of a whale-fishing ship with the riders, breast-hooks, and other fortification inside of her bows.

POLACRE (*Fr.* Polacre). A vessel peculiar to the Mediterranean, having pole masts, and therefore without tops or cross-trees.

POLAR CIRCLES. Lesser circles of the sphere parallel to the equator, as far removed from the poles of the earth (23° 28′), as the tropics are from the equator. That in the northern hemisphere is called the *arctic polar circle*, and that in the southern hemisphere the *antarctic polar circle*.

POLAR DISTANCE, of a star or other celestial body, its

angular distance from the elevated pole of an observer's horizon. See *Declination*.

POLARITY. The tendency of the magnetic needle to point towards the north pole.

POLE. The upper end of a vessel's highest mast (main, fore, or mizen) when it projects above the rigging; more particularly that of the royal mast. It is used merely to carry a vane, or for hoisting signals upon. (Plate III. and IV.) See also *Axis of the Earth*, *Circles*, and *Astronomy*, 1.

POLE-AXE. See *Tomahawk*.

POLE-MAST. A mast formed of one continuous piece, instead of having detached upper masts hoisted upon it.

POLICY OF INSURANCE. See *Insurance*.

PONTOON (*Fr.* Ponton). A kind of large decked punt, or stout flat-bottomed boat of rectangular form, used in heaving down ships, or serving to make temporary bridges for the passage of troops or the conveyance of munitions.

POOP. The highest and aftermost part of a vessel's hull, forming a cabin above the quarter deck. In ships of war, &c., it is called the 'round-house.' See the article *Deck*. In merchantmen, the quarter-deck, if elevated, is often called the poop.

A vessel is *pooped*, when the sea breaks over her stern. This is apt to occur, especially to a deeply laden ship, if she continue scudding too long in a heavy and increasing sea: caution should therefore be exercised in heaving her to in proper time.

POPPETS, in Shipbuilding, pieces of wood fixed perpendicularly between a vessel's bottom and the bilgeways at the foremost and aftermost parts of the ship, as shores to support her in launching. They are chiefly used, along with up-making for sharp vessels: if the ship be full built, the up-making, that is to say, a number of planks (some of which are wedge pieces) piled one above another, is alone used for supporting her when launching.

'A piece of timber or plank bolted on to the bottom of the ship over the heads of the foremost and aftermost poppets, in an oblique direction with the plane of the keel, is termed a *Dagger-piece*.'

PORT (*Fr.* Port) or *Seaport*. The same as harbour. A general name for any place where there are docks or other similar accommodation for vessels. It may be well to notice the legal interpretation of this term as laid down in the case of *Gavin against the Sea Insurance Company of Scotland* (*Bell's Dictionary of Decisions of the Court of Session*, p. 548), wherein 'it was decided, on appeal to the House of Lords, that "port" is not synonymous with "harbour," but is descriptive of any place where there is a constant resort of vessels for the purpose of loading and unloading, with provision made by the government of the country for enabling them to do so.' See also *Hildyard's edition of Park on Insurance*, pp. 76, 77.

A very useful book giving accounts of the PORT-CHARGES at most of the principal ports and harbours in this country, and also a similar book of *Foreign* port-charges, have been published by Mr. James Daniel of Aberdeen. Much authentic information on this subject is to be found in *Mc Culloch's Dictionary of Commerce.*

PORT, or PORT-SIDE (*Fr.* Bâbord). The left (or, as it has been called, the *larboard*) side of a vessel when you stand on board of her with your face to the bows.

By order of the Lords Commissioners of the Admiralty, the term *port* was many years ago directed to be used throughout the Royal Navy instead of *larboard*, in order to prevent mistakes which are so apt to arise at sea from the resemblance between the sounds of the words starboard and larboard; and the change has been very generally adopted in the merchant service.

PORT THE HELM. To put the tiller to the port side of the ship; in other words, to put the helm a-port.

PORTS (*Fr.* Sabords). Square holes cut in the sides, bow, or stern of a merchant ship, for taking in and discharging timber cargoes, and for similar purposes. Those in the sides are commonly used for ballast, and hence called *ballast-ports.* The others get the name of *raft-ports. Bridle-ports* are ports cut in a vessel's counter, for getting out hawsers either to moor by in harbour, or to clap springs upon. Ports intended merely for the admission of air, get the name of *air-ports*, or *air-scuttles.*

The *covers* for these are also called *ports*; they are each secured to a bar of wood inside by means of a rope called the *port-lashing.* See *Port-lifter.*

There are also long narrow openings termed *air-ports,* used for admitting air into the hold, &c., of a merchant vessel. Another method of ventilating ships consists in cutting holes through the gunwale at intervals to admit air between the timbers. These holes have each a brass bush with a cover which works in it by means of a screw to let it be made water-tight in bad weather. See also *Row-ports.*

PORT-HOLES, or GUN-PORTS. The ports through which a ship's guns are fired.

The ropes for hauling up and suspending the ports, or covers for these, are termed *port-ropes*, or *port-tackles.* See *Port-lifter.* When the covers are each made in two pieces, these pieces are called *half-ports. Port-sashes* are made of double plate-glass, fitting over the half-ports to admit light.

PORTS (STEAM). See description of *Steam Engine*, Sect. 2.

PORT-CILLS. See *Port-sills.*

PORT-FIRE. 'A composition rammed in a paper case to fire guns and mortars, which has been used occasionally instead of linstock and match.'

PORT-FLANGE, in Shipbuilding, a piece of wood fixed on the ship's side over a port, to prevent water or dirt from going into the port when open.

PORT-HOLES. See *Ports.*

PORT-LID, or PORT. The cover or shutter for a gun-port. See *Ports.*

PORT-LIFTER. A contrivance for raising and lowering any heavy port, invented by Mr. Carr, of the late firm of Messrs. Ritherdon and Carr, London. It consists of a screw fitted inside the ship between two metal standards: a nut is made to run along the screw by turning a crank handle; and to this nut are attached arms, which extend and are fixed to either side of the port.

PORT-PENDANTS. See *Pendant.*

PORT-SASHES. See *Ports.*

PORT-SILLS, or PORT-CILLS, in Shipbuilding, pieces of timber put in horizontally between the framing to form the top and bottom of a port.

PORT-TACKLE-FALLS. Lanyards fitted as a tackle for the ports of a ship of war.

PORTER'S ANCHOR. See *Anchor*, 4.

POUNDER. See *Gun.*

PRAAM (*Fr.* Prame). A sort of lighter, used chiefly in the Baltic, for bringing cargoes down the rivers, and also for loading and discharging ships.

There are also large and strong flat-bottomed vessels called *praams,* capable of carrying heavy artillery, used as floating batteries for the defence of coasts.

PRAHU. 'A boat or vessel used in the Indian Archipelago. There are various kinds of them. Some are remarkable for fast sailing, particularly those of the Ladrone islands. Some of them are very large, carrying a great number of men, and engaged in piracy.'

PRATIQUE (*Fr.* Pratique). A license or permission to hold intercourse with any place, after having performed quarantine, or upon production of a clean bill of health, that is to say, a certificate that the ship did not come from an infected place. (*Maunder's Scientific and Literary Treasury.*)

PREMIUM OF INSURANCE (*Fr.* Prime d'assurance). See *Insurance.*

PRESS, and PRESS-GANG. See *Impressment.*

PRESS SAIL, or CROWD SAIL (*Fr.* Forcer de voiles). To carry a press of sail, that is, a great quantity of sail upon a vessel.

PREVENTER. An additional rope employed occasionally to strengthen and support another rope, as *Preventer-backstays, Preventer-shrouds* (faux haubans), *Preventer-braces,* &c. *Preventer-plates,* in like manner, signify plates bolted as an additional security to the lower part of the channel plates on a vessel's sides.

PREVENTIVE SERVICE. The establishment of the 'coastguard' (consisting of officers, boats with their crews, patrols, &c.) at numerous stations on the shores of the United Kingdom, for the prevention of smuggling.

PRICK OFF *the Ship, or the Ship's place on a Chart,* or *Prick the Chart.* To mark the ship's place on the chart, after ascertaining her latitude and longitude, or the bearings of the land, &c.

PRICKER. A kind of small marlinspike used in sailmaking; it generally has a wooden handle.

PRIMAGE, or HAT-MONEY. A small allowance which used to be paid to the master of a vessel for his care and trouble in taking charge of the goods laden on board. It is now generally commuted for a certain per centage on the freight, and retained by the shipowner; the captain receiving also a stipulated gratuity from the freighter.

PRIME (*Fr.* Amorcer) *a gun.* To pierce or prick the cartridge with a piece of wire, called a *priming-wire*, inserted through the vent, and put a quill tube filled with a paste made of milled powder and spirits of wine into the vent, and a little powder in the pan, in order to fire the piece. See *Lock*.

PRIVATEERS (*Fr.* Corsaires) may be defined as private ships of war, or vessels having commissions (known by the name of *Letters of Marque*) granted to them, whereby they are empowered to attack enemies without being liable to a charge of piracy, and which secure to the owners and ship's companies a right to the prizes made by them. Privateering is now abolished among the civilized nations of Europe.

PRIZE (*Fr.* Prise). A vessel captured from an enemy.

PRIZING, or PUNCHING, implies the act of moving any heavy body by means of a lever.

PROA (*Fr.* Pros). A long narrow vessel used principally in the Malayan islands. Almost all the proas have two helms, one over each quarter, and steer by the lee one. They have great breadth of beam, and little depth, and are beautifully moulded.

BEDOUANG PROA. A canoe with a double outrigger, of the eastern coast of Java; narrow, deep, and having two triangular sails.

The FLYING PROA of the Ladrone islands is a canoe with a single outrigger.

MAYANG PROA. A Malay coaster of which the stem and stern post are curved, the bottom flat, but the extremities (the run and entrance) sharp and almost symmetrical. They have sometimes a cabin amidships, and are painted with brilliant colours, the bottom white, surmounted with a black stripe. The sails are of Indian mat. The sketch of a Mayang Proa, which is given in the *Dictionnaire de Marine à voiles,* resembles a Javanese coaster or fishing boat.

PROMONTORY. A portion of land projecting into the sea beyond the rest of the adjacent coast. When high or mountainous, the extremity of it towards the sea is called a *Cape*; when it has but little elevation, this is usually styled a *Point, Head,* or *Headland.* (*Norie's Epitome.*)

PROPORTIONATE RATES OF FREIGHT. See *Freighter.*

PROPPETS, in Shipbuilding, a name sometimes given to shores, especially when they stand nearly vertical.

PROTEST, in seafaring matters (*Ship's protest,* or *Sea protest*), a formal declaration made by the master, mate, and part of the crew of a merchant vessel before a notary-public, or if there be no notary at hand, before a consul, justice of the peace, or any other person empowered to perform notarial acts; this declaration is written out, or (as it is termed) *extended* on stamped paper, and should detail the material events of the voyage, and the particulars of the accident or accidents on account of which it is taken, being made up of faithful but amplified extracts from the log-book, which ought for this purpose to be laid before the notary, and the fact of his having seen it should be specially noticed, so that the protest may in case of accident supply the loss of that book. The tonnage of the vessel should always be mentioned in the protest. See the article *Notary.*

When any misfortune has happened, the master should cause a protest to be noted within forty-eight hours after the ship's arrival at her port of destination, or at an intermediate port, if any such port have been sought in distress, and to be afterwards extended. In trifling cases, the insurers and other parties concerned sometimes agree to settle claims upon production merely of an extract from the log-book, signed by the captain.

If there be no means whatever of noting a protest at the place where a vessel happens to be wrecked, Mr. Lorimer in his *Letters to a Young Master Mariner* very properly observes that the proper course of the master is to use every means in the first place to save the property, and then to take steps for protesting. There is no call for imprudent haste in leaving the ship to note a protest.

There are other kinds of marine *Protests*; for example, that which a master takes when a vessel comes on demurrage, and that which is taken by him when he finds himself justified (under a contract for a full cargo) in proceeding on the voyage with an incomplete lading.

PROVISIONS (*Fr.* Vivres), for the subsistence of seamen or passengers on board of merchant ships, are subject to statutory regulations. There is likewise a scale of victualling for ships of the Royal Navy set down in Chap. 25 of the *Queen's Regulations.*

PROVOST-MARTIAL. 'The officer appointed to secure criminals, and take charge of prisoners at a court-martial, and to retain them in custody till their sentence is executed.'

PROW (*Fr.* Proue). A name for a vessel's bow. *Prow* is

also 'a name given to the boats used by the Malay pirates in the eastern archipelago.'

PUDDENING. A quantity of yarns, mats, or oakum wrought round a rope, to make a stop upon it, or for other purposes. Puddening was also laid round rings of anchors, when rope cables were in use, to prevent chafing.

PULL AWAY! (*Fr.* Doublez!) The order to men to pull the oars in a boat with vigour to make her advance with speed through the water.

PUMP (*Fr.* Pompe). A well-known machine for drawing up water. The common working pump used in merchant vessels consists of a cylindrical tube or pipe, the upper part of which widens out to form a chamber for the *Pump-boxes*: the lower pump-box is fixed at the foot of this chamber, which it fits tightly; the upper or working box is moved like a steam-piston up and down in the chamber by means of a rod called the *Pump-spear*, the lever attached to which gets the name of the *Pump-brake.* Both of the pump-boxes have valves opening upwards, through which the water is made to rise in a manner similar to what is described of the air pump under section 18 of the article *Steam-Engine.* The pump-brake works on a bolt inserted through the head of a standard which is fixed to the upper edge of the pump. The pumps of a vessel are sometimes worked by means of a contrivance called the *vangee*, or *weegee*, or *wheejee*; this usually consists of a barrel of an octagonal form turning backwards and forwards on a pivot fixed in a frame between the pumps; the pump-spears are attached by arms to this barrel, and the pumps are worked by two brakes inserted into it at right angles to each other, with ropes attached to their ends for hauling upon. Another contrivance by which the pumps of a large vessel are generally worked consists of *oscillating pump spears* connected with a crank shaft and fly-wheel driven by handles in the same way as a winch. See *Well* and *Fetch the Pump.*

THE CHAIN-PUMP, used in ships of war, but very rarely in merchantmen, is composed of two long metal tubes let down through the decks somewhat apart from each other, but united together at their lower ends, in which many small holes are pierced to admit the water. Above the upper extremities of these tubes there is fixed a sproket-wheel worked by crank-handles: over this wheel, and passing through both tubes, is placed an endless chain having a number of bucket-valves or pistons fixed to it at certain distances, and turning round a friction-roller in the lower joint of the tubes. The tube by which the water ascends has a narrow chamber which the valves nearly fit, while the other parts of both tubes are wider so as to avoid any friction. The chain with its bucket valves being set in motion by means of the crank-handles, passes down through one tube, and up the other tube in which the valves raise the water very rapidly.

The various pumps connected with marine steam-engines are noticed in the alphabetical index at the end of the description of the *Steam-Engine*.

BILGE-PUMPS. Small pumps used for drawing off any water which may lodge about the bilges of the ship when she is lying so much to one side that the water does not reach the foot of the main pumps. See also description of *Steam-Engine*, Sect. 26.

CHAIN-PUMP. See above description of the *Pump*.

HEAD-PUMP. A small pump fixed at the vessel's bow; its lower end communicating with the sea, and protected by a rose: it is used for washing the decks.

MASSEY'S PUMP is 'a double action lift and forcing pump.' (*Boyd's Naval Cadet's Manual*, 60.)

PUMP A VESSEL. To remove water out of her by means of the pumps.

PUMP-BRAKE. See description of *Pump*.

PUMP-CISTERNS. Cisterns fixed over the heads of chain-pumps to receive the water; whence it is conveyed through the ship's sides by the pump-dales. (*Shipwright's Vade Mecum.*)

PUMP-DALE (*Fr.* Dalle de pompe). A wooden spout for leading water from the pumps over or through the ship's side without wetting the decks.

PUMP-HOOK. A rod of iron with an eye at one end, and at the other a hook, for the purpose of drawing out and replacing the lower pump-boxes when occasion requires.

PUMP-SPEAR (*Fr.* Verge d'une pompe). See description of *Pump*.

PUMP-TACKS. Small iron or copper tacks, used for nailing the leather on the pump-boxes.

PUMP-WELL (*Fr.* Archipompe). A compartment formed by bulkheads round a vessel's pumps to keep them clear of obstructions, to protect them from injury and give ready admittance for examining the condition of the pumps at any time. See *Well.*

PUNCH. An iron instrument used for starting bolts *in* a little, or for driving them out: the punch used for the latter purpose is called a *Teaming-punch*; the other a *Starting-punch.* See also *Prizing.*

PUNT. A species of boat, barge, or large square-built vessel without masts or sails, employed as a lighter for carrying goods. Such vessels are also used for receiving the mud, &c., from dredging-machines.

A sort of oblong flat-bottomed boat like a floating stage, used by shipwrights and caulkers for any work to be done to a vessel about the water's edge.

A small flat-bottomed boat.

Also a flat-bottomed boat rounded at one or both ends; from boats of this kind being used in wild fowl shooting, it frequently gets the name of a *gunning-punt.*

GUNNING-PUNT. See above description of *Punt.*

HOPPER-PUNT, or MUD-LIGHTER. A punt or lighter for carrying soil or mud with a *hopper*, that is, a square or an oblong receptacle fitted in the centre of the punt to contain the lading.

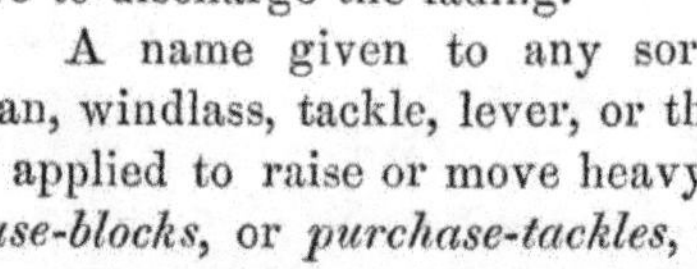

There is a trap-door at the bottom of the hopper which can be opened at pleasure to discharge the lading.

PURCHASE. A name given to any sort of mechanical power, as a capstan, windlass, tackle, lever, or the like which increases the force applied to raise or move heavy bodies. Hence the name *purchase-blocks*, or *purchase-tackles*, is given to such blocks or tackles as are used in moving very heavy weights. The term *purchase* is also applicable to the increase of force thus acquired. *To purchase* is to move anything by means of a purchase. See *Tackle.*

PURSER. An officer who has charge of the provisions and such like stores of a ship of war. This designation does not now appear in the Queen's regulations. See *Paymasters.*

*The Purser's Steward* is a kind of deputy purser, who delivers such stores and keeps an account of all that are expended or received.

PUT ABOUT. See *About.*

PUT TO SEA. To quit a port or roadstead and proceed on a voyage or cruise. *To put into a port* (relâcher) is to enter an intermediate port in the course of a voyage. *To put back* to the port of loading or departure is to return to it.

PUTTOCK-SHROUDS. A name which seems to be erroneously given by some to the *Futtock-shrouds.*

QUADRANT (*Fr.* Octant, Quart de nonant). An instrument used at sea to take the altitude of the sun, or moon, or of any star, in order to estimate the latitude of a place. It was invented by Captain Davis.

The following is a general description of Hadley's quadrant, abridged from *Nore's Epitome of Navigation.* The *Octant*, or frame of ebony or other hard wood, consists of an arc or limb divided into ninety degrees, firmly attached to two *radii*, or bars, to which it is bound by two braces to prevent it from warping. On the centre of the instrument there is a flat brass bar (*the index*) with a scale called a 'nonius scale,' fixed to an oblong opening near its lower end. To the index there is also fixed a plane speculum or mirror of glass quicksilvered, called the *index glass*, which moves along with it, and is designed to reflect the image of the sun or other object upon either of the horizon-glasses, whence it is reflected to the eye of the observer. *The horizon-glasses* are two small speculums on one of the *radii*; the one half of the fore horizon-glass is silvered, while the other half is transparent, in order that any object may be seen directly through it; the back horizon-glass is silvered at both ends, and in the middle there is a transparent slit through which the horizon may be seen. *The dark glasses* or *shades* are for preventing the bright rays of the object from hurting the eye of the observer. *The sight vanes* are pieces of brass standing perpendicularly to the plane of the instrument. That one which is opposite to the fore horizon-glass is called the *foresight-vane*, the other the *backsight-vane.*

QUADRATE *a gun*; 'to adjust it for firing by means of a quadrant, which is fitted to the gun carriage, and is subdivided into degrees to mark the different elevations.'

QUARANTINE LAWS, consist of certain regulations suspending intercourse, for a limited time, with vessels arriving from places affected by, or suspected to be visited with, contagious diseases, and subjecting the goods on board of such ships to a process of ventilation, and, in some cases, of fumigation. This performance of 'quarantine' varies in duration from five to forty days, from which last number (*quarante* in French) the term is derived. In some parts of the Mediterranean quarantine is performed in *Lazarettoes*, established for receiving persons and goods coming from infected places.

A Bill of Health is a document obtained from the consul or other proper authority at any port, certifying the state of health in the place, and that of the ship's company at the time of her departure therefrom. If *a clean bill* (which is a certificate that the ship did not come from an infected place), it generally exempts the ship from quarantine, but not so if a *suspected* or a *foul bill.*

QUARTER. That part of a vessel's side which is between the after part of the main chains and the stern. See *Bearing.* See also *Chimes* and *Yard.*

QUARTER-BILL. A list of the stations or quarters of the officers and crew of a ship of war in time of action.

QUARTER-BOARDS, or TOPGALLANT QUARTER-BOARDS. A thin bulwark boarding, forming an additional height to the bulwarks at the after part of a vessel. They also get the name of *Topgallant-bulwarks.*

QUARTER-BOAT. A boat so called from being hung to davits over the ship's quarter. See *Boat,* 2.

QUARTER-CLOTHS. Oil or painted cloths or canvass, fitted to the outside of the quarter-nettings to shelter the quarter-deck.

QUARTER-DECK. See *Deck* and *Poop.*

QUARTER-FAST. See *Fast.*

QUARTER-GALLERIES. See *Gallery.*

QUARTER-GUNNER, in a ship of war, an able seaman, generally one of the gunner's crew, appointed to act as his assistant under the gunner's mates. Quarter gunners do not appear now to be noticed in the Queen's regulations.

QUARTER-MASTERS, in a ship of war, or steam ship, &c., attend to the steerage of the ship under the direction of the officer of the watch: they have also to attend to the stowing of the hold, the hoisting of signals, &c.

QUARTER-MEN. Foremen, that is men employed under the

master shipwrights, in the royal dockyards, to superintend, each, a certain number of workmen.

QUARTER-PIECES. Pieces of timber, one of which is bolted on the after-end of each of a vessel's quarters: they are

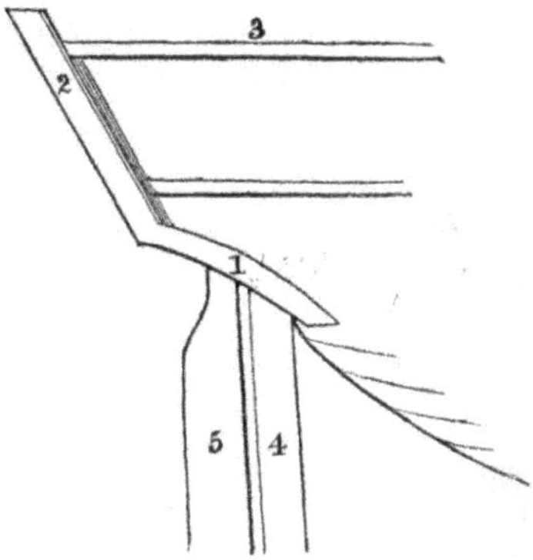


1. Quarter piece.
2. Side counter timber.
3. Rail.
4. Stern post.
5. Rudder.

intended principally to cover in the after butts of the planking in the quarter. If there be a quarter-gallery, the quarter-piece forms its after end.

QUARTER-STANCHIONS. Strong stanchions in the quarters of a square-sterned vessel, one of which forms the outmost boundary of the stern on either side: it connects the main rail with the taffrail; the aftermost planks of the topsides and the planks of the stern are bolted to it, and in addition to other fastenings, its tail is secured by knees and bolts to the wing-transom. (Plate II. fig. 5, and IV. 28.)

QUARTER-TIMBERS. The framing timbers in a vessel's quarters.

QUARTER-WIND. A wind blowing upon a vessel's quarter. It is then said to be *quartering.*

QUAY (*Fr.* Quai). A convenient erection for vessels lying alongside in order to discharge and take in cargoes.

QUICK-WORK. The same as SPIRKETTING. Also a term for the planking between the quarter-deck ports in a ship of war.

QUOIN, or COIN (*Fr.* Coin). A sort of wedge placed on the bed of a gun-carriage for the breech of the gun to rest upon. See also *Beds.*

RABBET (*Fr.* Râblure), in Shipbuilding, an angular groove made in one piece of wood to receive the edge or end of another piece: as in the keel for the edge of the garboard-strake, or in the stem and stern-post for the hooding-ends.

RACK. To seize two ropes together with cross turns.

*To rack a tackle*, is to seize the two opposite parts of the fall together, in order to prevent it from rendering through the blocks. This is illustrated in *Seamanship* by Lieutenant Nares, figs. 82, 83, and 199*b*.

*A rack*, is a name for a board with holes in it, seized to the standing rigging below a vessel's top as a fair-leader for running rigging. Also a piece of wood having holes to serve as fair-

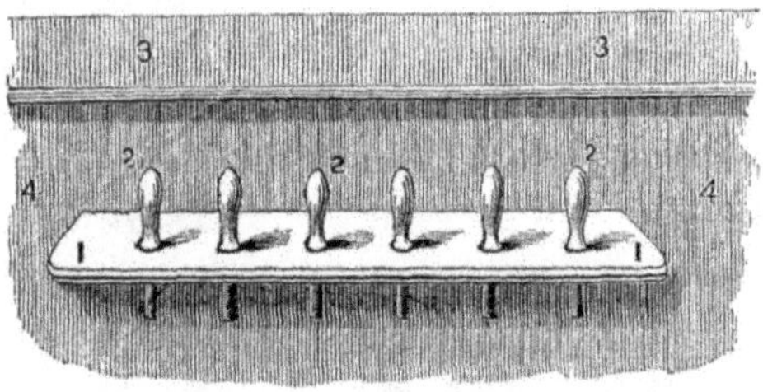

RACK WITH BELAYING PINS.

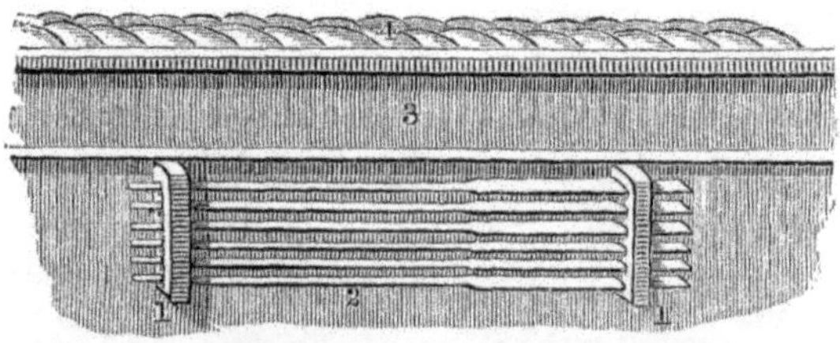

RACK FOR OARS — OAR RACK.

leaders, and tackspins in it for belaying ropes to, made fast across the shrouds inside near the rail. Beneath it there is a cleat fixed in one of the stanchions to take the rope round before belaying it, after it has been brought through the fair-leader. See *Rack-block.*

RACK-BAR. A billet of wood used for twisting the bight of a swifter round, in order to bind a raft firmly together.

RACK-BLOCK, or RACK. A course of blocks made in one piece of wood to act as fair-leaders.

RACKING. Spunyarn or other stuff used to rack two parts of a rope together.

RADIUS BAR OF PARALLEL MOTION. See description of *Steam Engine*, Sect. 21.

RAFIAU. A small boat of the Mediteranneau, worked with sails and oars. Its breadth is about equal to half its length. It rigs a lateen sail and a jib. (*Dict. de Marine à voiles.*)

RAFTS (*Fr.* Radeaux), are generally formed of one tier of logs, or of several tiers laid across each other, bound round by swifters, and also secured by means of raft-dogs, with chains rove through them. See *Rack-bar*, *Catamaran*, and *Fire-ship*.

RAFT-DOG, or RAFTING-DOG. A broad flat piece of iron having a sharp point, and at its other end an eye formed through which the raft-chains are rove.

RAFT-PORTS. Square holes cut in the bow or stern of a merchant ship for taking in and discharging timber cargoes. See *Ports*.

RAIL, or ROUGH-TREE RAIL. The moulded planks which are mortised into the heads of the stanchions, and in some cases, into the timber-heads, forming the upper fence of a vessel's bulwarks. (Plate IV. 25.)

There are also rails of this kind at other parts of the ship, as follows:—

FORECASTLE-RAIL. The rail extended on stanchions across the after part of the forecastle-deck. In like manner that across the fore part of the poop or quarter-deck is termed the *poop-rail.*

TAFFRAIL, or *Tafferel-rail.* The rail over the heads of the stern-timbers, extending across the stern from one quarter-stanchion to the other.

TOP-RAIL. A rail extended on stanchions across the after part of each of a vessel's tops. See *Counter-rail*, *Fife-rail*, *Head-rails*, *Sheer-rails*, *Stern-rails*, and also *Nettings* (*Hammock*).

RAISE. *To raise a sunken ship*, means to buoy her up in the water by some means or other. *To raise the tacks*, or *the sheets*, of square sails, implies to slack them off. *A vessel is said to be raised upon* when heightened in her upper works.

RAKE (*Fr.* Quête). Rake of the Sternpost, in Shipbuilding, 'the overhanging of a vessel's stem or stern beyond a perpendicular with the keel, or of any part or thing that forms an obtuse angle with the horizon.' This term is applied to *masts* when they are placed in the vessel with an inclination forward or aft, instead of being upright.

*To rake a ship*, is to fire into her in the direction of her length.

RAM, or BATTERING RAM. A long piece of hard wood hooped with iron or armed with iron caps at each end, and having an iron rod attached on each side, or rather edge, running nearly the whole length of the ram to serve as handles for a number of men; used in shipbuilding for driving out blocks from beneath a vessel's keel, and for driving planks an-end, when wedged to the ship's side before being fastened, &c. See *Steam Ram.*

RAM-LINE, in Shipbuilding, a small rope or line used for setting the frames fair, and also for forming the sheer of the ship: when used for the latter purpose it is adjusted on the ship's side by means of a long thin plank, called the *sheer-mould*, which has one of its edges curved to the extent of sheer intended to be given.

RAMED. A new vessel is said to be *ramed* when all the frames are set upon the keel, the stem and sternpost put up, and the frames properly adjusted with the aid of the ram-line.

RAM and RAMMER. See *Sponge of a Gun.*

RANGE, in Gunnery, the path or line described by shot from the mouth of the gun whence it is fired to the point where it first grazes or lodges. See *Point-blank.*

RANGE OF CABLE. A portion of a vessel's cable slackened round the windlass or bitts, and the bight of it laid abaft the same in the form of a French fake, of sufficient length to allow the anchor to sink to the bottom without check. *To range the cable*, means to lay it in the manner here described.

RANGE-HEADS. A name sometimes given to the windlass-bitts.

RANSOM (*Fr.* Rançon), in War, a price paid for the liberty of a prisoner, or for the restoration of a captured vessel, or of other property taken by an enemy. Also the act of redeeming from imprisonment or capture. The ransoming of a British ship is illegal.

RASING. Marking with a knife the form of a mould on a piece of timber; or making any mark with a *Rasing-knife*, which is a particular kind of knife hooked at its point.

RASING-IRON. A species of caulking-iron having its end

bevelled with a sharp point, for clearing the pitch and oakum out of a vessel's seams when required, in order to be caulked afresh.

RASING-KNIFE. See *Rasing.*

RATE. See *Chronometer.*

RATES *of Ships of War.* See *Navy (Royal).*

RATLINES, or RATLINGS (*Fr.* Enfléchures). The lines stretched horizontally from shroud to shroud, used to step upon in going aloft, or in coming down from the mast-heads.

RATTLE DOWN THE SHROUDS. To fix ratlines upon them.

RAVE-HOOK. An iron instrument used by caulkers to get the oakum thoroughly out of a vessel's seams when a rasing-iron would not penetrate deep enough.

RAZEE (*Fr.* Vaisseau rasé). A vessel cut down from a larger to a smaller size. In such a case the ship is said to be *razeed.* See *Frigate* and *Decker.*

REACH *of a winding river,* means any part of it which runs in a straight course. The reach of it which stretches out to seaward is termed the *sea-reach*; that which leads direct to any harbour is termed the *harbour-reach.*

In Seamanship, the term *reaching* is used in the same sense as *standing* off and on; a vessel also is said *to be on a reach,* when she is sailing by the wind upon any tack.

READY ABOUT. An order to the crew that all hands be at their stations, ready for tacking or putting the ship about.

REAMING. See *Reeming.*

REAR. 'The last division of a squadron of ships of war; or the last squadron of a fleet.' The foremost is called the *van.*

REAR-ADMIRAL (*Fr.* Contre-amiral). See *Admiral.*

REBATE. See *Rabbet.*

RECEIVERS OF DROITS OF ADMIRALTY and RECEIVERS OF WRECK. See *Admiralty (Droits of).*

RECEIVING SHIP. A vessel employed at any port to receive supernumeraries, or pressed or entered men for the Royal Navy; the port admiral's ship is generally selected for this purpose.

RECKONING (*Fr.* Estime). The estimation of a vessel's position by the courses steered and the distance run. When this is made merely by means of the log and compass it is termed *dead reckoning,* which requires to be corrected as soon as an observation of the sun or of other heavenly bodies is practicable.

A vessel is said to be *ahead of her reckoning*, when she is found, either by observations taken, or by making the land sooner than was expected, to be farther on in her intended course than the previous reckoning led them to anticipate. If the reverse be the case, she is *astern of her reckoning.*

RECOIL (*Fr.* Recul) in Naval Gunnery, the distance that a gun runs in upon deck after being fired; it more strictly implies the act of its running in.

RECONCILE, in Shipbuilding, to make one line join fair with another, or one piece of work answer fair with the moulding or shape of another piece. This term is especially applied to the reversion of curves.

RED-HOT SHOT. 'Balls made red hot in a furnace and in that state thrown out of guns against an enemy's ships or magazines.'

REEF. To reduce a sail by taking in upon its head, if a square sail; upon its foot if a fore-and-aft sail. Cunningham's Patent *self-reefing topsail* can be reefed and unreefed from the deck without sending any men aloft. This invention is applicable also to topgallant and other sails. *Howe's Patent Rig* for close-reefing topsails differs from the common rig by having double topsail yards. (*Kipping's Elementary Treatise on Sails and Sailmaking, Appendix.*)

*A reef* is that part of a sail which is comprehended between the head or foot of the sail and the first reef-band, or between any two reef-bands.

*A balance reef* is a fourth reef, used for the trysail when lying to.

REEF-BAND. A band of stout canvass sewed on in the way of the eylet-holes, in order to strengthen a sail at that part.

REEF-CRINGLES. See *Cringles.*

REEF-EARINGS. See *Earings.*

REEF-HOLES. The same as *Eyelet-holes.*

REEF-KNOT. See *Knot.*

REEF-PENDANT. A rope going through a cringle in the after leach of a boom mainsail, and through a sheave-hole in the boom, with a *tackle* attached to its end to rouse the after leach down to the boom while reefing. 'In large ships of war reef-pendants are used for all the courses; and in line-of-battle ships they are used also for the topsails, to rouse the leaches up to the yard when reefing.'

REEF-POINTS. Small pieces of line (commonly *white line*) made fast at their middle in the eyelet-holes for tying a sail up to the yard in the act of reefing it.

REEF-TACKLE. A tackle attached to each of the topsails of a square-rigged vessel for the purpose of tracing or lightening up the leach in the act of reefing. See also *Reef-pendant.* (Plate IV. 116, 125.)

REELS. Of these well-known machines for winding lines upon, the kinds used by seamen are for the *deep-sea-line* and *log-line.* See *Lead* and *Log-line.*

REEMING, in Shipbuilding, opening the seams of the planks with iron wedges, called *reeming-irons*, in order that the oakum used in caulking may be more readily admitted: the mallet commonly used for driving them is called a *Beetle.*

REEVE. To pass the end of a rope through a block or any aperture. *To unreeve* is the opposite term.

REFIT. To repair damages and put a vessel in proper condition for proceeding to sea. The term is also applied to putting the rigging in proper condition and setting it up again, which operation is termed *refitting the rigging.*

REFRACTION (*Fr.* Réfraction). An inflexion of the rays of light which proceed from any object, caused by its passing from a rarer into a denser medium. Thus the rays proceeding from a celes-

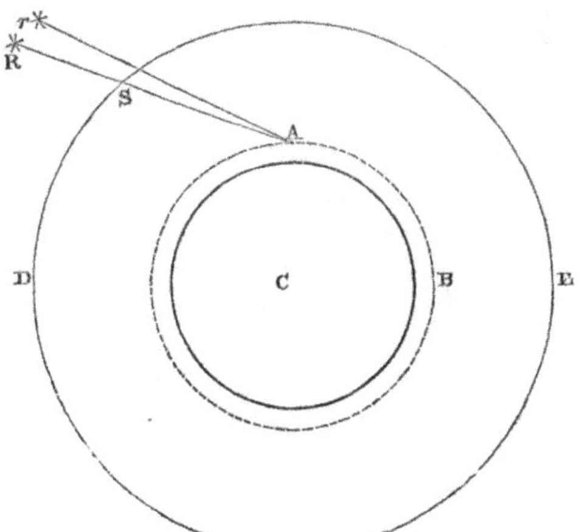


tial body, when they enter the atmosphere in an oblique direction, are turned out of their straight course, and incline more and more

towards the centre of the earth as they pass deeper into the atmosphere; they consequently strike the eye of an observer in a different direction from that of the object, and make it appear higher than its real place. For example, 'let A B represent the earth, and the space between it and D S E the surrounding atmosphere; R the point in which a star would be seen by an observer at A, if the intervening space were a void. Let the ray R S emitted by the star fall on the surface of the atmosphere at S. This ray, instead of proceeding in a rectilineal direction, will be refracted in the direction of the curve S A. The star R, instead of appearing to the observer at A, at its true place R, will be seen by him at r, in the direction A r.' This refraction or difference has therefore to be deducted from the apparent altitude of any object. 'An object at the zenith is not subject to refraction; and its effects increase proportionally as the body is nearer the horizon, where the refraction is greatest.' Refraction is influenced by the changes in the density of the atmosphere; and other physical causes, such as heat and humidity, also make it vary in different climates.

REGATTA. The name which was given to the races with boats on the grand canal of Venice; now applied to similar marine fêtes in this country, whether boats or yachts be the competitors.

REGISTER (LLOYD'S), AMERICAN LLOYD'S REGISTER, and FRENCH REGISTRE MARITIME, or VERITAS. See *Lloyd's Register.*

REGISTRY OF SEAMEN. A general register and record office of seamen in the mercantile marine, under the direction of a registrar-general, is appointed by the Merchant Shipping Act, the register being compiled from the agreements with seamen, &c., transmitted to the Registrar-General under the provisions of that statute, and from any other available resources. The registry tickets which for some time were given to seamen are now abolished.

REGISTRY OF SHIPS. See *Lloyd's Register.*

REGULATING CAPTAIN, in the Navy, 'the officer appointed to superintend the raising of seamen, and who examines them on their entry.'

REINSURANCE. See *Insurance.*

RELIEVER, in Gunnery, 'the training tackle at the hinder part of a gun-carriage.'

RELIEVING-TACKLES (*Fr.* Retenues). Tackles hooked to the tiller in a gale of wind to steer by, when any accident happens to the wheel or tiller ropes. Also a name for tackles passed under a vessel's bottom during the process of heaving down, in order to prevent her being canted over too much.

RENDER. A rope is said to render if it passes freely when hauled upon. A tackle in like manner renders when it is overhauled freely.

RENDEZVOUS (*Fr.* Rendezvous). The place appointed for a fleet of merchantmen to join convoy, or where the ships of any fleet are to rejoin in case of separation.

A name for any house on shore, used in entering men for the Royal Navy, or by a press-gang for securing men who are impressed.

RENTS, or SHAKES. Openings or cracks which take place in timber or planks when much exposed to the heat of the sun. Original defects of this kind in wood are called *shakes.*

REPEATERS, or REPEATING SHIPS (*Fr.* Répétiteurs). Vessels of war appointed by the admiral to repeat his signals throughout a fleet.

REPRISE. 'A vessel which having been captured by the enemy, is retaken before getting into port.'

RESERVE (NAVAL). See *Royal Naval Reserve.*

RESHIP. To put anything again on board of a vessel after it has been discharged. The operation is termed *reshipment.*

RETIRED LIST, in Marine Affairs, a list on which superannuated officers, or deserving officers whose health or age, or other circumstances, justify their retirement from active service in the Royal Navy, are placed.

RHUMBS, or RHOMBS (*Fr.* Airs de vent). Lines by which the card or fly of the compass is divided, representing the divisions of the horizon. See *Compass.*

RIBBANDS, or RIBANDS (*Fr.* Lisses), in Shipbuilding, pieces of wood temporarily nailed on the frames lengthways, in order to keep the body of the ship together and in its proper shape till the planking is brought on. The shores are set up beneath them. (Plate II. fig. 7.)

*The floor-ribband* runs round a little below the floor-heads, for the support of the floors. *The floor-guide* is a ribband which is placed between the floor-ribband and the keel.

RIBBAND-LINES, in Shipbuilding, diagonal lines laid down

on the body-plan: by means of these are marked off upon the moulds the points, called *surmarks,* where the respective bevellings are to be applied to the timbers. After the frames are put up, the ribbands are run over these points, or nearly so. In order to get the true bevellings of the different timbers, the ribband-lines are taken from the body-plan and laid down horizontally on the floor-plan; the bevellings are then taken at the above-mentioned points where the lines representing the frames intersect the ribband-lines so laid down.

RIBBAND-NAILS, are nails having large round heads; used chiefly for fastening ribbands. See *Nails (Ribband).*

RIBS. A figurative expression occasionally used for the frame timbers of a vessel. In iron ships the angle-iron frames *commonly* get the name of ribs.

RICKERS. Small spars from twenty to thirty feet long. They are cut up in short lengths to be used on board ships, especially for the purpose of stanchioning off the hold-beams in the way of the screws which are used in stowing flax cargoes, &c., and thereby preventing the pressure of the screws from springing any of these beams.

RICOCHET-FIRING, in Gunnery, is the method of firing a gun pointed below the horizontal elevation, whereby the shot rolls and bounds along.

RIDE AT ANCHOR. To lie at anchor, that is, to be anchored.

*To ride athwart* means to ride with the ship's side to the sea or current. *To ride between wind and tide* is to ride athwart by means of the opposite influences of the wind and tide. When there is a heavy sea running in a different direction from the tide, then by the opposite influences of the wind and tide, the ship may ride *athwart the sea,* or, by those of the wind and sea, *athwart the tide.*

Again, a vessel is said *to ride easy,* when she bears little strain on the cable, and does not pitch or roll severely. *To ride hard* is the reverse term.

RIDE DOWN any thing, to bend or bear it down by main strength and weight.

A rope, &c., also, is said *to ride,* when one turn gets over another so as to jam it in heaving on a capstan or winch.

RIDERS, in Shipbuilding, pieces of wood or iron fayed to the inside of a vessel at any part longitudinally, diagonally, or vertically, to bind her and give additional strength. See the articles *Braces*, *Keelson*, and *Trussing* (*Diagonal*).

When a rider is lengthened by means of several pieces butted or scarphed to it and each other, the first piece is termed the *first futtock-rider*, the next the *second futtock-rider*, and so on.

RIDERS (*Fr.* Porques). A term also applied to any tiers of casks stowed above the ground-tier or above any other tier in a vessel's hold.

RIDGE. A lengthened stretch of rocks, sand, or shingle.

RIDGE-ROPES, or MAN-ROPES, also termed the *Bowsprit-horses*. Two ropes fastened to iron stanchions on the top of the knight-heads, and running out one on each side of a vessel's bowsprit, above it, to the heart, for the men to hold on by when going out on the bowsprit. The bowsprit-netting for stowing the fore-topmast staysail in, is lashed between them about the bowsprit end. (Plate III.)

RIDING BITTS, or CABLE BITTS. Pieces of timber bolted securely to the beams, to which when at anchor the cable is made fast in a vessel that weighs its anchor by a capstan. See *Bitts*.

RIDING SCOPE *of a vessel's cable*, is the quantity by which she rides at anchor.

RIFLED GUN. 'A gun having spiral grooves cut inside the bore to give the shot a rotatory motion when fired, thereby making it take a much more correct line to the object.' See *Gun*.

RIG (*Fr.* Gréer). To fit the standing and running-rigging to a vessel's masts, &c. The term *rig* is also used in designating the particular mode in which a vessel is fitted with masts, sails, and rigging; thus she is said to rig such and such sails — to be schooner-rigged, barque-rigged, ship-rigged, &c.

RIG THE CAPSTAN. To fix the bars in the capstan-holes, in order to prepare for heaving.

RIG OUT *a boom*. To run it out from a yard, in order to extend a sail upon the boom.

RIGGERS. Men employed to rig and unrig, or to dismantle ships.

RIGGING (*Fr.* Gréement). A general name given to all the ropes or chains about the masts, yards, and other spars of a vessel.

The shrouds with their ratlines also are distinguished into

*main-rigging, fore-rigging, mizen-rigging, maintopmast-rigging,* &c., according to the masts with which they are connected.

*Running rigging* implies the ropes or chains that are used for hoisting the sails, bracing the yards, and for similar purposes.

*Standing rigging* is that which is set up for the support of the masts, as the shrouds and stays. The rigging of merchant shipping and yachts is treated of and illustrated in *Biddlecombe's Art of Rigging,* that of ships of war in *Nares on Seamanship.* It is said to be proposed to mast and rig the Shield or Cupola ships after Lieutenant Shuldham's patent plan of rigging in a triangular or tripod fashion. See *Shield-ships.*

RIGHT. A vessel is said *to right,* or *to righten,* when she resumes her vertical position in the water after having been listed over by the force of the wind or otherwise.

*To right the ship* is to cause her by any means to resume her vertical position.

RIGHT THE HELM. To put it amidships, that is, in a line with the keel.

RING BOLTS are bolts having an iron ring passing through an eye in one end of the bolt; they are used in shipbuilding with the wrain-staff in the ring, for setting to the planks. Ring-bolts are also fixed in a merchant vessel's deck for lashing the boats, &c. See *Bolts* (*Ring*).

RING-DOGS. See *Dog.*

RING-STOPPER. The same as *Cat-stopper.*

RING-TAIL. A small sail shaped like a jib, set occasionally in light winds; it is hoisted on the outer end of the main or spanker gaff, and extended on a boom called the 'ring-tail' *boom,* which is rigged out for this purpose on the main or spanker-boom. The main-topmast studding sail is sometimes used in this way.

RIPPING-IRON. A tool used in stripping copper or thin wood-sheathing off a vessel's bottom.

RISING-FLOORS (*Fr.* Acculement), imply those floor-timbers which rise gradually from the plane of the midship-floor, so as to sharpen the form of the vessel towards the bow and the stern.

RISING-LINE, in Shipbuilding, an elliptical line drawn on the plan of elevation to determine the sweep of the floor-heads throughout the ship's length. See *Shipbuilding.*

ROACH. An upward curve in the foot of a square sail.

ROAD, or ROADSTEAD. 'A place where there is anchorage and a certain degree of shelter for shipping.'

ROBANDS. See *Rope-bands*.

ROCKET. This well-known kind of firework is used in the naval service for signals.

*Congreve-rockets*, so named after the inventor, are destructive missiles, peculiarly serviceable for naval bombardment.

*Rockets* are also applied to the very important purpose of throwing a line over any stranded vessel in order to establish a communication between it and the shore, and so to land and save the lives of those on board. 'Manby's apparatus' is adapted for effecting this by means of a shot or a grapnel, &c., fired from a particular kind of mortar.

*Dennett's Rockets* are said to have been found to be a very successful contrivance for this purpose; but it would be still more available in many cases were vessels, according to Mr. Trengrouse's recommendation, furnished with such rockets for throwing lines on shore, which may require to be done in places where neither mortars nor rockets are at the time to be had; while, if, as usually happens, the vessel has been cast on a lee shore, the rocket would probably have the wind to aid its flight. The importance of supplying every vessel with such rockets and lines (whale-lines) has been repeatedly urged upon the notice of the public in the *Shipping and Mercantile Gazette.*

Some successful experiments have been made with an anchor apparatus invented by Mr. E. Frost, engineer, fired from the shore by one of Captain Manby's mortars. This 'anchor apparatus' is described as consisting of an anchor of iron 40 lbs. weight, formed by a shank about 2½ feet long, and 1½ inches broad, with a 2½-inch rope attached to the end of the shank which terminates in a ring. The shank at the other end is finished by a cup, or, as it might be called, half of a hollow shot, the conical end of which is next the charge when fired: into this hollow shot two moveable flukes are fixed, tied round the stock by a few pieces of cord to prevent the great strain which would otherwise be caused from the concussion ensuing when discharged from the mortar, and which causes them to fly open with great force.

The following are *Instructions to the Crews of Stranded Vessels in the use of Captain Manby's Apparatus for saving Lives from Shipwreck*, by Captain Pulling, R.N. :—

'In the first place, on a line being thrown on board by a rocket or mortar, haul upon it till you receive a tail-block with a whip rove through it.

'Secondly.—Make this tail-block fast to the masthead or some part of the hull, as most convenient, and when it is fast the ship is to make signal No. 1.

'Thirdly.—The party on shore will then haul off a hawser, the end of which is to be made fast above the tail-block; when it is fast the ship is to repeat signal No. 1.

'Fourthly.—Upon this warp, or hawser, will be a traveller, with a seat attached to it; in this one of the crew is to secure himself, and when he is ready the signal No. 1 is to be again repeated.

'Fifthly.—If the vessel is beyond the range of either rocket or mortar, a buoy (the larger the better) is to be bent on to a deep-sea line, or some other small rope, and thrown overboard clear of the wreck, over which a grapnel-shot will be thrown from the shore, and a communication thereby obtained. You are then to act as already pointed out in first, second, third, and fourth remarks.

'Sixthly.—When *tallies* are sent off with any part of the gear, the directions contained *thereon must be strictly attended to.*

'Seventhly.—All vessels should be provided with a flash-pan, musket, or pistol, with a flask of gunpowder, in order to make or answer night signals.

'The signals which will be used on the shore to communicate with the vessel are as follows:—

'No. 1, by day, a pennant, signifies, have you got hold of the line? No. 1, by night, one flash.

'No. 2, by day, a flag, signifies, are you ready? No. 2, by night, one blue-light.

'No. 3, by day, a pennant over a flag, signifies haul the line on board. No. 3, by night, two blue-lights.

'The signals to be used by the vessel, as directed in the foregoing instructions, are these:—

'Signal 1, by day, a man in some conspicuous part of the vessel waving his hat, denotes yes, or ready. Signal 1, by night, two flashes, to denote yes, or ready.

'Signal 2, by day, a man waving a handkerchief, or flag, denotes no, or not ready. Signal 2, by night, one flash, to denote no, or not ready.' See *Loaded Shell*, under which title the *Life-kite*, invented by Lieutenant Nares, R.N., is noticed.

RODGER'S ANCHORS. See *Anchor*, 3.

ROGUE'S YARN. A thread of worsted in the strands of

rope manufactured for the Royal Navy, introduced for the purpose of detecting theft or embezzlement: a different coloured worsted being used in each dockyard, it serves also to trace any bad rope to the precise yard where it was made.

ROLLER. The same as *Friction Roller*.

ROLLING. That motion by which a vessel vibrates from side to side. On this subject there occur in the *Shipwright's Vade Mecum* some valuable remarks which point out the importance of regulating the stowage of ballast and cargo, so that the centre of gravity may not be *too much* lowered. See *Laboursome* and *Stowage*.

ROLLING-CHOCK, or ROLLING-CLEAT. A piece of wood fastened to the middle of an upper yard, with a piece cut out of its centre so that it may half encircle the mast, to which it is secured by an iron parrel enclosing the other half of the mast. The purpose of this is for steadying the yard.

ROLLING-HITCH. See *Hitch*.

ROLLING-TACKLES, or YARD-TACKLES. Tackles attached to a lower yard when occasion requires, to steady it in a heavy sea. They are not required with iron trusses, by which in merchant vessels the yard is securely fixed to the parrel. 'In ships of war, a strop round the lower mast with a thimble in each quarter, is always fitted and kept on, to which, when required, at anchor, or under weigh, these yard-tackles are hooked.' Rolling-tackles are likewise used for topsail-yards when lowered down in order to reef, &c., if there be no rolling-chocks; but this is rare.

ROMBOWLINE, or RHUMBOWLINE. 'Condemned canvass, or rope, soft rope for nippers,' &c.

ROOM AND SPACE, or ROOM AND TIMBER, in Shipbuilding, the distance from the moulding-edge of one timber to the moulding-edge of the timber next to it; in simple words, the distance at which the frames are apart. See *Peake's Rudimentary Treatise on the Practice of Shipbuilding*, p. 18.

ROPE (*Fr.* Cordage, Aussière), is composed of hemp or other stuff, spun into large threads, which are called *rope-yarns*. A number of these yarns twisted together form a *strand*, and three or more strands twisted together form the rope. If composed of four strands (or, to use the technical term, 'four cant'), the strands are twisted round a small strand, which gets the name of a *heart*.

The smaller rope used on board a vessel, such as the cordage for running-rigging, &c., is made of three strands. This is termed hawser-laid rope. *Cable-laid* or *Water-laid rope* is formed by three of these smaller ropes laid up into one. It is used for rope-cables, hawsers, towlines, warps, &c. The first is termed *right-hand rope*, being laid up and coiled with the sun. Water-laid rope is coiled in the contrary direction, that is, to the *left hand*. *Shroud rope*, or *Shroud-laid rope*, is a finer quality of

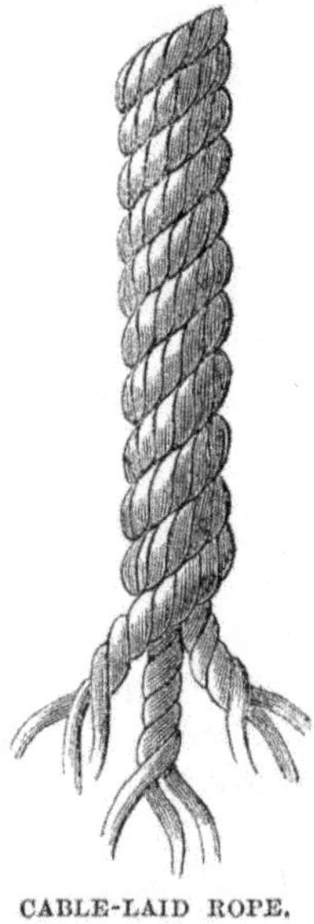

CABLE-LAID ROPE.

HAWSER-LAID ROPE.

SHROUD-LAID ROPE.

rope used for standing-rigging. *Twice-laid rope* means rope the strands of which have been taken down, and the best yarns selected and laid up again.

*White-rope* (*Fr.* Franc-filin), means rope not saturated with tar, that is, not tarred rope. See *Cordage* and *Wire-rope*.

*To rope a sail*, is to sew the bolt-rope round its edges.

Bolt-ropes. See the title *Bolt-ropes*.

Foot-ropes. Ropes stretching from the middle of a yard to each of its extremities, for men to stand on when reefing, furling, &c. See the title *Foot-ropes*.

Man-ropes. Ropes suspended from ornamental stanchions on each side of the gangway, to hold on by in going up or down a ship's side.

MAST-ROPES, or TOP-ROPES. Ropes used for sending a topmast or topgallant-mast up or down. See the title *Mast-ropes.*

TILLER-ROPES. Ropes attached to the extremity of the tiller, when there is no steering-wheel.

ROPE-BANDS, or ROBANDS. Small pieces of two-yarn foxes plaited, or of sennit or spunyarn, sometimes used to confine the head of a sail to its yard or gaff. They are not used with *jackstays*; a number of turns of a single rope-yarn being sufficient to secure the head of a sail to the jackstay. The upper corners of the sail are secured to its yard or gaff by earings.

ROPE-YARN (*Fr.* Fil de caret). See description of *Rope.*

ROSE, or STRAINER. A plate of copper or lead perforated with small holes, sometimes placed upon the heel of a pump to prevent anything being sucked in which might choke the pump. Roses are also nailed, for the like purpose, upon the holes which are made in the bottom of a steam ship to admit water for the boilers and condensers.

ROTHER. See *Rudder.*

ROUGH-TREE. An unfinished spar.

ROUGH-TREE RAIL. See *Rail.*

ROUND. To round a point, is to steer clear of, and go round it.

ROUND-AFT, in Shipbuilding, the outward curve or convex form of the stern from the wing-transom upwards.

ROUND-HOUSE. An erection at the middle of a vessel's deck, generally abaft the mainmast, for the accommodation of the officers. In some vessels a round-house is fitted up for the use of the crew. In ships of war this name is given to the poop; and hence the beams on which the poop rests are called the *round-house beams.*

ROUND IN. To haul in on a rope; especially on a weather-brace.

*To round in a tackle,* means to haul in the slack of it in a horizontal direction; the term *round up* is applied in a similar manner when the tackle is in a vertical or sloping direction. The reverse of these is *to overhaul the tackle.*

ROUND TO. When a vessel is sailing large or before the wind, to *round to* implies by means of the helm to bring her head round to the wind so close as to shiver the sails and thereby deaden her way. If the sails are then trimmed in such a way as to counteract each other, the vessel is *hove to.*

ROUND TURN. *To take a round turn of a rope*, means to pass it completely round anything in order to hold on. See also *Hawse*.

ROUND-UP *of the Transoms*; the segment of a circle to which they are sided: *of beams*, that to which they are moulded. (*Shipwright's Vade Mecum*.) See also *Round in*.

ROUNDING. A service of rope wound round a spar, or round a larger rope to prevent chafing. The operation itself is called *rounding*.

ROUNDLY. Quickly.

ROUSE, or ROWSE (*Fr.* Sailler). The same as to haul.

ROVER. A pirate.

ROVING COMMISSION. An authority granted by the Admiralty to the officer in command of a vessel to cruise where-ever he may see fit.

ROW (*Fr.* Ramer, Nager). To move a boat or vessel by pulling the oars or sweeps. The persons employed at this are called *Rowers*, or *Oarsmen* (Canotiers).

ROWLOCKS. Spaces cut in the gunwale of a boat for the oars to rest in while pulling. In some boats the rowlock is formed merely by two pins, called *thole-pins*, inserted into the gunwale, between which pins the oar works.

ROW-PORTS. Ports cut through the sides of any small vessel that may have occasion to use sweeps during calm weather.

ROWSE. See *Rouse*.

ROYAL (*Fr.* Cacatois). The small square sail set, in light winds, on the royal-mast and royal-yard (main, fore, or mizen). See *Mast*.

ROYAL NAVAL RESERVE. An establishment of volunteers, consisting of able merchant seamen who go through a course of drill and agree to serve on board of ships of war in case of need. They receive a fixed rate of compensation, and become entitled to a pension along with other privileges.

ROYAL NAVY. See *Navy*.

RUDDER (Gouvernail), that part of the helm which is hung to the after-part of a vessel's stern-post, and which is turned by the tiller so as to expose either side of it to the resistance of the water, in order to govern the direction of the ship's motion. (Plate IV. 6.)

1. There are two kinds of *patent rudders*, which it may be well

to notice, constructed so as to prevent water from getting into the rudder-case when the ship happens to fetch sternway. One of these is formed with an elbow, or bend inwards, beginning at the lower part of the rudder-case, whereby the centre of the upper part of the rudder-stock, which is rounded and fitted with great nicety, is brought to work in a line with the pintles: the other has the fore part of the main-piece (or 'rudder-stock')

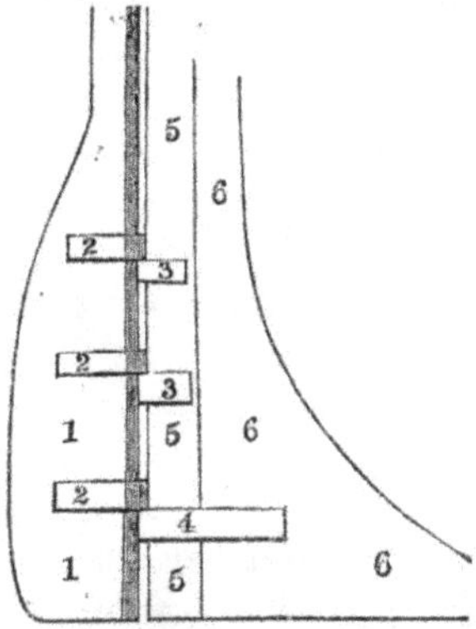


RUDDER OF A SHIP OF WAR.

1. Rudder.
2, 3, and 4. Rudder irons.
2. Pintles.
3. Braces.
4. Lower brace.
5. Stern-post.
6. Deadwood.

rounded so that it may fit into a hollow made in the stern-post to receive it, and the irons (or hinges) of the rudder so constructed that the rudder may turn upon a true axis at the centre of the stock.

2. HOLMAN'S PATENT RUDDER. In this new description of rudder the plan of hanging the helm on rudder-irons is superseded, and the notching made in the post, whereby it is weakened, is avoided.

3. MULLEY'S AUXILIARY RUDDER. The AUXILIARY AND RESERVE RUDDER, invented by Mr. W. R. Mulley, Plymouth, is about half the superficial area of the main-rudder, oblong shaped, and formed of separate bars of copper or iron, according as it is used in wood or iron ships, 'in such manner as will allow it to twist (its action resembling that of the fin of a fish) in and out of the quarter where it is hung at an optional depth below the water-line, and when not in use recessed so as to

take the shape of the bottom, leaving no projection whatever. The auxiliary rudders are worked each by a common steering-wheel, placed on either side, near that of the main-rudder, and are operated upon simultaneously with it under the same orders, having in case of sudden change of helm the advantage of being brought to act at once, while the main one has first to pass its neutral point. The apparatus is of the most simple kind, and requires but a small space in the hold. It consists merely of a vertical and a horizontal shaft, with a pair of wheels and pinions to move the segment shafts passing through the ship's side, and connected to the after end of the rudder. The required mechanical power for steering is of course much lessened by being applied so directly to that part. An indicator will mark the angle of the rudder. When not in use the steering-wheels and shafts are unshipped and the deck left clear.'

4. False Rudder. A framing of boards made to ship on to the back of the rudder in order to increase its breadth, and thereby augment the power of the helm. This is used chiefly in narrow rivers wherein the current is strong, and in canals. In vessels not provided with a false rudder, boards called *rudder-boards* are, when needful, nailed on each side of the rudder for the like purpose.

RUDDER-BANDS, or RUDDER-IRONS. The iron or composition hinges on which a rudder turns. That part of the rudder-band which is bolted to the sternpost, and into which the pintle goes down, is called the *brace, gudgeon* or *chalder.* (Plate IV. 7.)

*A Dumb-cleat,* or *Dumb-chalder,* is a sort of cleat (iron or composition) bolted to the back of the stern-post, for one of the pintles to rest upon, in order to keep the strain off the necks of the other rudder-irons generally, and so lessen the friction.

*The Rudder-pintles, or Rudder-pipes,* are the projecting prongs of the rudder-irons bolted to the rudder, and made to fit into a hole in the *rudder-braces,* or *chalders,* through which they pass down, and thus form hinges for the rudder to traverse upon.

RUDDER-BRACES. See *Rudder-bands.*

RUDDER-CASE, or RUDDER-TRUNK. A casing of wood fitted firmly into a hole, called the *helm-port,* in a vessel's counter: through it the rudder-stock is inserted.

RUDDER-CHAINS. The same as *Rudder-pendants.*

RUDDER-CHOCKS. Pieces of fir made to fit the excavation on each side of the rudder-stock, in case of the tiller being broken, and its being necessary to steady the helm amidships, while shipping a new tiller; they are in some cases also used when a vessel is at anchor.

RUDDER-COAT. See *Coat.*

RUDDER GUDGEON. See *Rudder-bands.*

RUDDER-HEAD. See *Rudder-stock.*

RUDDER-HOUSE, or WHEEL HOUSE. A kind of sentry-box or round-house, built over the steering-wheel in large ships for the shelter of the helmsman. See *Wheel-house.*

RUDDER-IRONS. The same as *Rudder-bands.*

RUDDER-NAILS, are similar to clamp nails, but used mostly for fastening the pintles and braces of the rudder. See *Nails.*

RUDDER-PENDANTS (*Fr.* Sauvegardes). Two ropes or chains attached to the back of a rudder, or hooked to a kind of iron crutch termed the *horns*, bolted to the back of the rudder; they have a ring at the loose end, to which tackles, called the *rudder-tackles*, are made fast, in order to steer the ship in case of the main piece (or 'stock') being broken about its upper end, or the tiller or any part of the steering apparatus being broken or rendered unserviceable. They also serve to save the rudder from being lost, should it by any accident be unshipped. The rudder-tackles are carried to each quarter and made fast on deck. These are used mostly in large ships.

RUDDER-PINTLES, or RUDDER-PIPES. See *Rudder-bands.*

RUDDER-STOCK. A name for the main piece of the rudder, which is connected by the rudder-bands to the stern-post. Its upper end, passing up through the helm-port in the vessel's counter to the deck, and into which the tiller is fitted, is called the *Rudder-head.* (Plate IV. 8.)

RUDDER-TACKLES. See *Rudder-pendants.*

RUDDER-TRUNK. The same as *Rudder-case.*

RULES OF THE SEA, or RULE OF THE ROAD. Certain regulations as to porting helm, &c., which have been generally recognised by seafaring men for the avoidance of collisions between ships at sea. The rule of the road is treated of in *Seamanship*, by Lieut. Nares, p. 83. There is an excellent treatise on the subject by Mr. Rothery, the registrar of the Admiralty court. The rules of the sea now enforced by law are those established by the Merchant Shipping Act, and the Merchant Shipping Amendment Act, followed by the English and French Regulations for preventing collisions at sea, which latter regulations came into force on 1st of June last, and are, by permission of the Admiralty, appended to this Dictionary.

RULE-STAFF. A lath about four inches in breadth; used, in Shipbuilding, for measuring the curve of a plank's edge in order to fay another plank to it. See *Spilings.*

RUMMAGE. A term employed to signify Custom-house officers searching a ship for smuggled goods. When rummaging a ship, they have a long steel spear to pierce any soft articles which may be suspected to conceal such contraband goods.

RUN. That part of a vessel's bottom abaft, which rises from the keel and bilge, and narrows towards the stern-post.

With reference to the ship's progress, also, we say she has *run* so many knots in an hour and so forth.

*Seamen* are said to be *engaged by the run*, when they ship with the intention of leaving the vessel at a certain port of destination.

*To let go by the run*, means to let go anything altogether, instead of merely slacking off the rope or tackle by which it is held fast.

*To run foul of* (*Fr.* Aborder), is to come in contact, while under weigh, with another vessel or any object. *To run down* a vessel, is to sink her by so coming into collision.

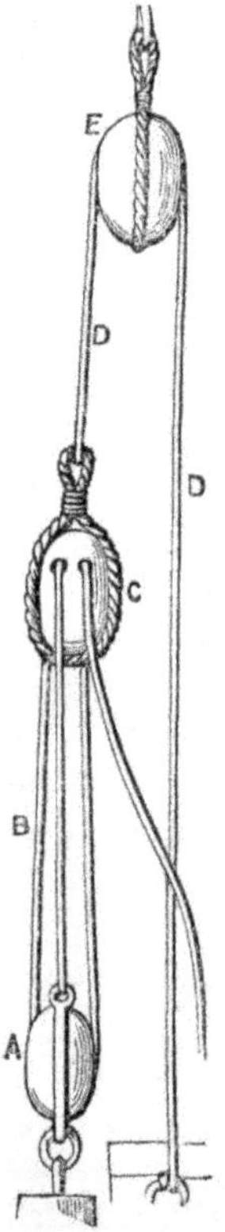


RUNNER AND TACKLE.

A. Single block.
B. Tackle.
C. Double block.
D D. Runners.
E. Runner block.

RUNG-HEADS, in Shipbuilding, a name formerly given to the *floor-heads.*

RUNNER-AND-TACKLE. A particular kind of purchase, resembling a burton, used chiefly in sloops. (See annexed sketch, and also Plate IV.)

RUNNING BOWSPRIT, is one that can be eased in like a jib-boom. See *Bowsprit.*

RUNNING DOWN CLAUSE, or COLLISION CLAUSE. A special clause very generally introduced into policies of marine insurance on ships, to include the risk of loss or damage for which the shipowner may become liable in consequence of the ship insured negligently coming into collision with other ships.

RUNNING FIGHT, at sea, a fight in which the enemy continues to be chased.

RUNNING RIGGING, implies the ropes or chains that are used for hoisting the sails, &c. See *Rigging*.

SACOLÈVE. A vessel of the Levant, having great sheer and the stern somewhat elevated. They generally have three pole-masts or two pole-masts and a jigger mast. (*Dict. de Marine à voiles.*)

SADDLE. A piece of wood fitted on a mast to bear up the inner end of a boom. In some parts of England this gets the name of a mast-rim. See also *Gun* (*Armstrong*).

SAFETY-KEEL. See *Keel*.

SAFETY-VALVES (*Fr.* Soupapes de sûreté). See description of *Steam Engine*, Sects. 41, 36, and 44.

SAG, when applied to the *hull of a vessel*, is the reverse of hogging. In seamanship, to *sag to leeward*, is the same as to fall to leeward when sailing close-hauled.

SAIK. 'A Levantine coasting vessel with a very large sail.'

SAILS (*Fr.* Voiles) are of two descriptions: *Square sails*, which hang from yards athwartships, as the courses, topsails, &c. of a square-rigged vessel; and *fore-and-aft sails*, which are set upon gaffs, booms, or stays, lengthways of the vessel. (Plates III. and IV.)

The edge of a sail at either side is called the *leach*, its lower end the *foot*, and its upper edge the *head* of the sail. See *Bolt-ropes*.

1. The most recent work on *sail-making*, including sails both for ships and boats is *Kipping's Elements of Sailmaking* (1862), *being a complete treatise on cutting out sails, according to the most approved methods in the merchant service*.

2. Mr. Orr's valuable invention of 'angulated' sails, especially applied to jibs, consists in making the foot of the sail form an obtuse angle with the after leech. See pages 90 and 92 of *Kipping's Elementary Treatise*.

3. *Trail's Patent Bands*, or *Protection to half-worn sails*, is another valuable invention. These bands, one inch in breadth, manufactured expressly for the purpose, are sewed in angular directions across the fore part of the sail, reversed on the opposite

side. By this simple contrivance the sail is very greatly strengthened. 'Should a sail of this construction at any time be split, the rent cannot extend beyond the limit of the diamond formed by the bands (three feet); and even in ordinary wear and tear, the bands will cause a sail to last much longer, as they relieve the canvass of all strain and of a great amount of friction.'

SAIL, is also a general name for any ship or ships when under canvass at sea. Thus, we speak of so many *sail*, that is, so many vessels being in sight. In like manner, a *strange sail* means a vessel of which we do not happen to know the name, or the place that she hails from. The term sail is also used to denote generally the sails or quantity of sails carried on a ship or boat.

To SAIL (*Fr.* Courir), is to move through the water by means of sails.

CROWD SAIL, or PRESS SAIL. To carry a 'press,' or great quantity of sail on a vessel.

MAKE SAIL. To increase the quantity of sail set on a vessel. It is sometimes incorrectly used in the same sense as to set sail.

SET SAIL. To spread a vessel's sails to the wind in order to get under weigh.

SHORTEN SAIL. To take in part of the sails that are set, either by reefing or furling, or by both of these operations.

SAIL-CLOTH (*Fr.* Toile). The same as *Canvass.*

SAIL-HOOK. A small hook used for holding the seams of a sail square in the act of sewing.

SAILING. The mode of navigating a vessel by applying the rules of plane trigonometry to ascertain her place at any time. The following are the different modes of navigating vessels; which can be properly understood only by consulting the scientific explanations which are given in treatises on navigation.

'1. CURRENT-SAILING. In places where there is a constant current or setting of the sea in a particular direction, allowance must be made for the change of the ship's place arising therefrom. The method of resolving those problems in sailing in which the effect of a current or of the heave of the sea, or of both, is to be taken into consideration, is termed *Current-sailing.*

'The best mode of trying the velocity of a current at sea, is by paying out a hundred fathoms of the deep-sea-line from a boat with a 56 lb. weight attached to its end, and the other end of the line made fast to the boat's bow; she will immediately swing to the tide, and ride as if by an anchor on the ground; the log may then be hove to ascertain the rate of the current.'

2. GREAT CIRCLE SAILING. This will be explained generally by the following remarks of Mr. Towson of Devonport, who has prepared and published tables for great circle sailing. 'It is known to all scientific seamen that the rhomb-line or the apparent course upon the chart drawn from one place to another is not the shortest in reality, but that the shortest line that could be drawn between any two points on the surface of the globe is an arc of the great circle that passes through them both. The rhomb-line could never coincide with the great circle unless both of the points through which it passed lay on the equator or on a common meridian. If we compare any number of arcs, segments of various radii all having the same chord, it will be found that the segment of the greatest circle would be the shortest line.'

In producing these tables Mr. Towson has rendered a most important service to navigation. See *Circles*.

'3. MERCATOR'S SAILING, consists in finding the difference of longitude by considering the meridians as parallel lines, and, of course, every parallel of latitude as equal to the equator. For this purpose, a table of meridianal parts (from which Mercator's chart is constructed) is employed.

'4. MIDDLE LATITUDE SAILING. In this, the departure computed by plane sailing is considered as a meridian distance, and the difference of longitude, on that supposition, is computed as in parallel sailing.

'5. OBLIQUE SAILING, consists in the application of oblique angled triangles to various cases at sea, as in coasting, surveying, &c.

'6. PARALLEL SAILING, consists in finding the difference of longitude from the departure made good, that is to say, from the distance sailed due east or west.

'7. PLANE SAILING, is founded on principles deduced from the supposition of the earth being an extended plane.

'8. TRAVERSE SAILING. When the ship is obliged to sail on different courses, the crooked line or track which she describes is called a *Traverse*, and the method of finding a single course and distance which would have brought her to the same place, is termed *resolving a Traverse*.'

SAILING DIRECTIONS. There are numerous works each

containing sailing and piloting directions for some of the principal places in the world.

SAILING MASTER. The same as *Master* of a ship of war.

SAILMAKING. See *Sails.*

SAILOR (*Fr.* Matelot). The same as *Seaman,* whether an ordinary or able seaman.

SAILOR'S HOMES, are places built by public subscription to give comfortable accommodation, &c., to sailors at moderate charges.

SALAMANDER. A piece of metal with a handle attached, which is heated for the purpose of firing guns. This is used in saluting, to enable the men to fire with the greater regularity.

SALA-SALA. A name given by the Malayans to the boats of India, called also *gourabes.* (*Dict. de Marine à voiles.*)

SALINOMETER (*Fr.* Salinomètre). A name given to a particular sort of *brine-gauge,* or apparatus (contrived by Mr. J. Scott Russell, civil engineer), for the purpose of indicating the density of brine in the boilers of marine steam engines, so as to show when it is necessary to cleanse the engine by blowing off, or by means of a brine-pump, of the deposit which salt water leaves in the boilers, and which tends to injure them, as well as to diminish the evaporative power. (*Practical Mechanic and Engineer's Magazine.*)

MATHER'S SALINOMETER AND AUTOMATIC MARINE BLOW-OFF APPARATUS, is a valuable apparatus which not only affords 'a constant accurate indication of the density of the water in the boiler, but is itself the means of discharging the dense stratum without any assistance from the engineer.'

SALLY-PORT. A place exclusively set apart for men landing from the boats of ships of war.

SALOON. A name for the main cabin of a steamer or of a packet ship.

SALUTE (*Fr.* Salut). A mark of deference or homage accorded on various occasions, generally by firing a ship's guns, striking any of her upper sails, or lowering a flag. A royal salute, that is to say, the salute given to Her Majesty, or any of the Royal Family, or to any foreign Sovereign, consists in firing twenty-one guns. As to saluting officers, &c., see chapter iii. of the *Queen's Regulations.*

SALVAGE (*Fr.* Sauvetage). The allowance or compensation made to any person or persons by whose assistance a ship and cargo or any part thereof have been 'saved from impending peril or recovered after actual loss.' The property to which such assistance has been rendered is said to be *salved*, and the persons rendering it are called *salvors*. Salvage is now regulated by the Merchant Shipping Act. The law of salvage is ably treated in *Maclachlan on the Law of Merchant Shipping*. A digested index to the valuable reports of Dr. Lushington's decisions of salvage cases in the *Shipping Gazette* is appended to the periodical series of *Maritime Law Cases*, reprinted from the *Law Times Reports*. All officers in command of Her Majesty's ships are 'to afford every possible aid to vessels in danger, distress, or in want of casual assistance,' subject to the rules in chapter xxiv. of *Queen's Regulations*. See *Salvage Loss*.

SALVAGE LOSS, in Marine Insurance; when a loss of ship or cargo happens, and the underwriters become liable to pay the amount insured on the property lost, taking credit for the net proceeds of what is saved, this is termed a total loss with salvage, or a salvage loss.

SAMPANE. 'A small hatch-boat of the Chinese ports and rivers.'

SAMSON'S POST. A large piece of timber with notches made in it, used in a vessel's hold for various purposes, particularly for fixing screws upon when stowing bale goods. In a ship of war, Samson's posts are put up diagonally between decks for getting a purchase upon.

SAND-STRAKE, in Shipbuilding, a name sometimes given to the garboard-strake. See *Strake*.

SAVE-ALL. A small sail occasionally set under a main, spanker, or swinging-boom. See *Water-sail*.

SCANT, expressed of the wind, implies that it is somewhat contrary to a vessel's course.

SCANTLINGS, in Shipbuilding, implies the relative breadth and thickness of the timbers, planks, &c. For tables of scantlings reference may be made to *Lloyd's Register of British and Foreign Shipping*, and to the valuable old work, *Hedderwick on Shipbuilding*. The former contains also tables of the dimensions of frames, plating, &c., of iron ships. The scheme or scantlings of the principal portions of ships of war may be seen in *Peake's Rudimentary Treatise on the Practice of Shipbuilding*, p. 108.

SCARPH (*Fr.* Écarver). To lap the tapered ends of two

pieces of timber over each other, and join them firmly together, so that they may form an even surface. The joining is called *a scarph* (*Fr.* Écart). Scarphs are often secured by means of dowelling, tabling, or boxing. See *Hook-scarph* and *Shifting*.

SCEND. See *Send*.

SCHOONER (*Fr.* Goëlette). A small vessel with two masts, and no tops, the mainsail and foresail being each set on a gaff and boom. *A fore-and-aft schooner* has a cross-jackyard, on which a square sail is set when occasion requires; all her other sails are fore-and-aft sails. *A topsail schooner* (which is the most common rig for schooners) carries a square fore topsail, and frequently also a square topgallant sail and royal. There are some schooners with *three masts*; they likewise have no tops. A *three-masted schooner* has its mizenmast rigged like the mainmast of an ordinary schooner; she carries also a main-topmast staysail.

SCHOONER-RIGGED BOAT. A boat with two polemasts and a bowsprit, having its foresail and mainsail suspended by gaffs instead of sprits. These sails in a Bermuda schooner-rigged boat are 'sometimes called *Bermuda sails*, from their being narrow at the head, broad at the foot, with great hoist and considerably more rake than common schooners.' *Kipping's Elementary Treatise on Sails and Sailmaking*, p. 125.

SCOOP. A name given to a piece of wood somewhat like a ballast-shovel, used in trimming grain. See also *Sheet*.

SCOPE. The *riding-scope* of a vessel's cable, is the quantity by which she rides at anchor.

SCORE. A groove in a block, or in a dead eye.

SCOUR *the Coast*. To send detached parties of seamen ashore from a ship of war, at different points along a coast, in order to fire quick and heavy discharges of guns or musketry, for the purpose of dislodging an enemy.

SCRAPER (*Fr.* Gratte). A small triangular iron instrument, having all its edges sharp, and a handle fitted to its centre; used to scrape off the dirty surface of the planks of a vessel's bottom, sides, decks, &c.

SCRAPE-STRAKES, or more properly *Topside-plank*, or *Topsides*, are the outside strakes of plank in a ship's side, between the sheer-strake and upper black-strake. (Plate IV. 31.)

SCREEN-BULKHEADS, are partitions of thick woollen cloth, put up in the cabins of a ship of war when cleared for action, the wooden bulkheads being removed.

Hatchway-screens, or Fire-screens, are pieces of thick woollen cloth put round the hatchways of a ship of war in time of an engagement.

SCREW-COLLIER. See *Collier.*

SCREW-DOCK. See *Caisson.*

SCREW GAMMONING. A chain or plate fastened by means of a screw, used to secure a vessel's bowsprit down to the stem-head. See *Gammoning.*

SCREW-PILE LIGHTHOUSE. See *Lighthouse.*

SCREW PROPELLER, or SHIP PROPELLER. A contrivance for superseding the use of paddle-wheels as a motive power for steam vessels. The idea of such a mode of propulsion

FIG. 1.

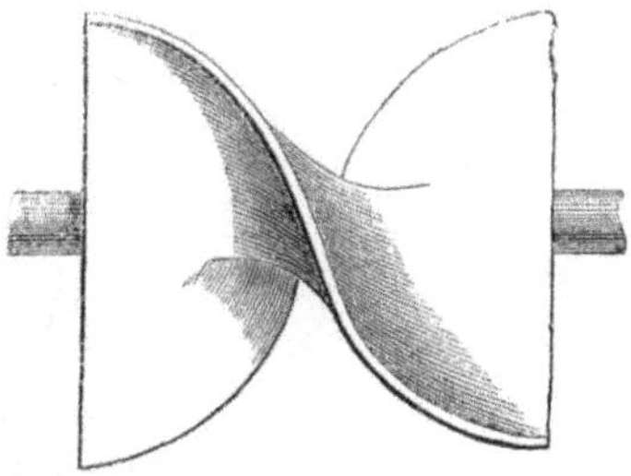

FIG. 2.

seems to have been entertained by Watt, although not carried out by him practically. In *Murray's Rudimentary Treatise on the Marine Engine*, p. 147, it is mentioned that 'Dr. Shorter, a practical mechanic of this country, succeeded in propelling a vessel by a screw in 1802;' various patents were afterwards taken out, but 'it was not till Captain Ericcson and Mr. F. P. Smith brought out their experimental vessels in 1837, that the screw came into use as a propelling power.' The screw propeller patented by Mr. F. P. Smith, originally received the name of the *Archimedean screw*, and was first introduced in a vessel of about 150 tons burden, called the 'Archimedes.' A double-threaded screw of the description shown in figs. 1 and 2 was applied to this vessel; but its length being found to occupy too much of the dead wood, the screw was gradually reduced in length by Mr. Smith in the course of a series of experiments until it assumed the form of a two-bladed screw as shown in fig. 3, which was adopted by him for the screw of H. M. steam ship

FIG. 3.

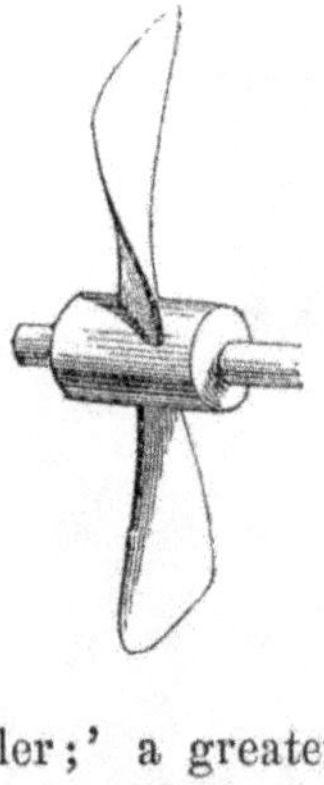

FIG. 4.

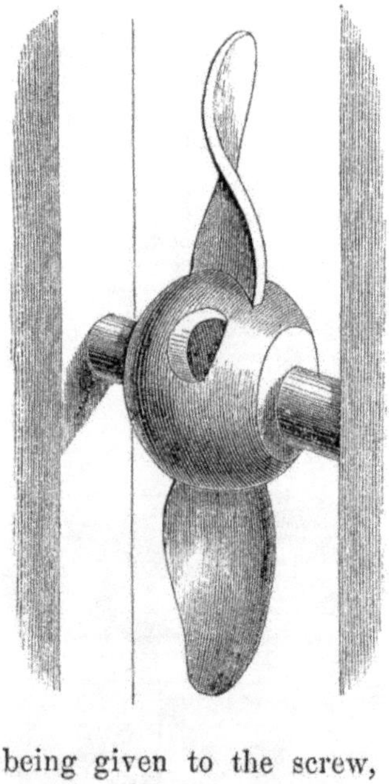

'Rattler;' a greater surface being given to the screw, when intended specially for the purpose of towing.

Fig. 4 is a sketch of Griffith's Screw Propeller.

The following remarks on the subject were offered in the first edition of this Dictionary:—

'The difference between the movement, situation, and speed of the screw propeller, and those of the paddle-wheel, necessarily causes a difference in the arrangement and application of the machinery by which they are respectively driven.

'1. The circular movement of the paddle-wheels is in the same direction as the line of the keel, but that of the screw is at right angles to it; and therefore the direction of the moving power of the screw, instead of being fore-and-aft, must be across the ship.

'2. In a vessel propelled by paddles, the centre line of the paddle-shaft requires to be considerably above the water-line, and lies athwartships; whereas the screw is inserted in a hole made in the dead wood near the stern-post, with its centre so far below the water-line as to keep the whole of the screw completely submerged; hence, the shaft whereon the screw revolves must be placed below the water-line more than half the length of the diameter of the screw, and the shafting of the engine, instead of being nearly as high as the deck, must be proportionally lowered.

'For these changes the side-lever engine is not at all adapted; but the common land-beam engine, slightly modified, and placed across the vessel, makes a good driving power for the screw; as well as the direct action engine, in which the motion is at once communicated from the piston-rod to the crank by means of the connecting-rod alone.

'3. When the amount of propelling surface is properly proportioned to the power of the engines and size of the ship (putting all other circumstances out of consideration), the vessel's speed depends on the quantity of space travelled over by the paddle-floats in a given time, which is equal to the number of feet in the circumference of the paddle-wheel multiplied by the number of revolutions it makes in that time—or, to the space gone through by the screw in a given time, which is equal to the number of feet in the "*pitch*" (that is, in the distance one turn of the thread of the screw is from another) multiplied by the number of revolutions of the screw in that time. Now, to go through the same quantity of space as the paddles do in the same time, the screw requires to make a greater number of revolutions; for, the length of the pitch of a screw is not nearly equal to the circumference of a paddle-wheel in two vessels of the same size.

'In order to transfer the power from the crank-shaft of the engine to the screw-shaft in such a manner as to give it the increased number of revolutions thus required, there have been as yet only two methods adopted; one by means of spur-wheels and pinions, the other by belts and pulleys: but there are great objections to both of those methods on board a ship. Where the spur-gearing is used, the engine is placed nearly at the same part of a vessel as it is in a ship propelled by paddles, and the screw-shaft is extended in length along the vessel sufficiently far to bring the end of it immediately under the end of the crank-shaft: the latter, which is parallel with the shaft of the screw, has a large spur-wheel fixed upon its end, the teeth of which catch those of a pinion fixed upon the screw-shaft; there are as many times more teeth in the wheel than in the pinion, as the number of revolutions of the screw-shaft must exceed those of the crank-shaft; and thus the required increase of velocity is communicated to the screw. Where belts are used, drum-pulleys with belts placed round them are fixed upon the shafts, and the large wheel or drum-pulley, which is fixed on the crank-shaft, is as many times greater in circumference than the small one, which is fixed upon the screw-shaft, as will give to the latter the increased number of revolutions that are required.

'The screw propeller may be considered as yet in its infancy, and there is no doubt that the plans for driving it must undergo great changes before it is brought to perfection.'

Since the above was written the screw propeller has come into general use in the ships of the Royal Navy and merchant steamers.

The progress of the invention is comprehensively treated of in *Murray's Rudimentary Treatise on the Marine Engine*, and in *The Marine Steam Engine*, by T. J. Maine and Thomas Brown.

Among the several varieties of the screw described in these works, such as those of Mr. Lowe, Mr. Sunderland, Mr. Steinman, and of M. Carlsund and M. Sorensen of the Swedish Navy, the following have distinguishing names:—

Maudslay's Feathering Screw.
Hodgson's Parabolic Propeller.
Macintosh's Elastic Propeller.
Woodcroft's Increasing Pitch Screw.

The Maugin screw used in ships of the French Imperial Navy requires a very small aperture for the well in the ship's stern to enable it to be used as a *lifting-screw*, that is, to enable the screw to be disconnected and lifted out of the water when required.

SCREW-SHIP. A ship in which the screw propeller is used as a motive power.

SCREW STEAM GUN BOATS. See *Gun Boat.*

SCREW WELL. An aperture or hollow trunk constructed over the screw in any steam ship for the purpose of allowing the screw propeller to be disconnected and lifted out of the wat‑ when required.

SCROLE-HEAD. See *Head.*

SCUD. To run right before the wind in a storm. The most approved sail for scudding with is a reefed foresail: if the sea be high, a close reefed maintopsail is a valuable auxiliary to it. The gale may be so violent as to render it dangerous to carry any sail at all, in which case the vessel is made to scud under bare poles. See *Dana's Seaman's Manual.*

There is this advantage in scudding with a reefed foresail and close reefed maintopsail, if the ship will bear it, that when there arises any apparent danger of the vessel being pooped, the foresail may be brailed up and the vessel laid to.

A veteran naval officer who has assisted in the compilation of some portion of this Dictionary, recommends scudding under a foretopsail. Every seaman knowing the sailing qualities of his own ship ought to judge accordingly.

*Scud,* is also a name given by seamen to the lowest clouds, when, in squally or tempestuous weather, they are driven through the atmosphere with greater rapidity than the clouds which float above them.

SCULL (*Fr.* Godille). A short oar. *To Scull,* means to impel a boat by putting out an oar in the row-lock which is generally cut in the top of the stern, and forcing it alternately from side to side, reversing the blade each time, so as to give it a motion like that of a fish's tail. A person who is impelling a boat in this manner is called a *Sculler.*

SCUPPER (*Fr.* Dalot). A leaden pipe let into a vessel's water-ways and through her side, to carry off any water from the decks.

ANNULAR SCUPPER. A particular kind of scupper, invented by Captain Henry Downes ; 'its peculiarity consists in having a broad copper ring fixed over the pipe flap, and a moveable concentric ring inserted,' by which the scupper hole can be enlarged from two inches to three and a half inches diameter. (*United Service Magazine,* 1842.)

SCUPPER NAILS. Short nails with very broad flat heads,

used for nailing down pieces of leather under the scuppers to carry off water and for other purposes. See *Nails*.

SCUTTLE (*Fr.* Ecoutillon). A square opening cut through a vessel's deck or through any of her hatches; it is furnished with a hatch called a *Scuttle hatch*, for covering it when required.

AIR-SCUTTLES, or AIR-PORTS (*Fr.* Ventouses). Square holes cut in the sides, &c., of a vessel for the admission of air. See *Ports*.

*To scuttle a vessel*, means to cut or bore holes in any part, in order to make her sink.

SCUTTLED-BUTT (*Fr.* Charnier), or (as it is generally abbreviated) SCUTTLE-BUTT. A cask with a square hole cut in its bilge, kept on deck to hold water for ready use. In ships of war this is now little used. In merchant ships an iron tank is sometimes employed instead of it.

SEA (*Fr.* Mer). A general term for the whole body of salt water on the terraqueous globe. The term *sea* is also applied to a smaller collection of the waters of the ocean, such as the Mediterranean Sea, or Black Sea: and to a single wave or a succession of them, as when we speak of *high* and *heavy seas*. So a heavy sea is said to be rolling in any particular direction. See *Ocean*, and *Head Sea*.

*A cross sea* implies the meeting of adverse waves obliquely or otherwise; the state of the sea when it is rolling heavily in one direction, and the shifting of the wind raises another succession of waves in a different direction. Such a sea is very dangerous for deeply-laden ships or for open boats.

A vessel is said *to be struck by a sea*, or *to ship a sea*, when a high rolling wave breaks on board of her.

The following eloquent remarks, quoted from *Malte Brun's Physical Geography*, are extremely interesting:—'The *colour of the sea* varies very much in appearance, but it is generally of a deep blueish green, which becomes clearer towards the coasts. This apparent colour of the sea seems to arise entirely from the same causes which impart a blue shade to distant mountains, and which give the atmosphere its azure hue. The other shades in the colour of sea-waters depend on causes which are local, and sometimes illusory. It is said that the Mediterranean Sea, in its upper part, has sometimes a purple tint. In the Gulf of Guinea the Atlantic has a whiteish appearance; and in the Indian Ocean around the Maldive Islands the sea is black. It is yellowish between China and Japan, and greenish to the west of the Canaries and Azores. The Vermeille, or Vermillion Sea, near California, has received its name from the red colour which it often assumes. The same phenomenon was observed at the mouth of the Rio de là Plata by Magellan, and also in other places.'

'The *light*, or *sparkling of the sea*, is a magnificent and imposing spectacle, which exhibits the greatest brilliancy between the tropics. Sometimes the vessel, while ploughing her way through the billows, appears to mark out a furrow of fire ; each stroke of the oar gives rise to sparks of light, sometimes brilliant and dazzling, at other times tranquil and pearly. These moveable lights are grouped in endless varieties. Here thousands of luminous points, like little stars, appear floating on the surface, and then, multiplying together, form one vast sheet of light. There the scene becomes more tumultuous, the refulgent waves heave up, roll, and break in shining foam. At other times we see large sparkling bodies, resembling the forms of fishes, pursuing each other, disappearing, and bursting forth anew.'

*Maury's Physical Geography of the Sea* is a repertory of valuable information regarding the currents, its tides and meteorology, &c. See also the title *Currents.*

Some observations as to the temperature of the sea will be found under the title *Thermometer.*

*A* SEA BOAT, or *a good sea boat,* implies any vessel that falls easily in the rolling and pitching motions, so as not to strain herself and endanger the masts and rigging.

SEA COAST. The same as *Coast.*

SEACRAFTS, in Shipbuilding, the uppermost strake of ceiling, which, like the bilge plank, is thicker than the rest of the ceiling. See *Clamps.*

The *seacraft of a boat* is the narrow board running fore and aft, nailed to the timbers for the thwarts to rest upon. It is also called the *thwart-clamp.*

SEAFARING MAN (*Fr.* Homme de mer). The same as a sailor or seaman.

SEAMAN (*Fr.* Marin). An individual practically occupied in the navigating of ships.

An *able*, or *able-bodied* seaman (distinguished by the initials A. B.) is one who understands and can assist in working the ship, or (as seamen themselves express it) who can 'hand, reef, and steer,' and who is also a good workman upon rigging, &c.; inferior hands go under the rating of *ordinary* seamen. Each man contracts, and is rated for the wages and duty of an able, or of an ordinary seaman, when he ships.

In the *Law relating to Merchant Seamen,* Mr. Symons, quoting from *Serjeant Shee's edition of Lord Tenterden's Treatise on the Law of Merchant Ships and Seamen,* observes that in case of disobedience, or disorderly conduct, on the part of a seaman during the course of a voyage, it is lawful for the master to correct him in a reasonable manner, but that it behoves the master to be very careful in the exercise of this power, and not to make it a pretext for cruelty and oppression. 'Except in cases requiring his immediate interposition, he should take the advice of the persons next below him in authority, as well to prevent the operation of passion in his own breast, as to secure witnesses to the propriety of his conduct,' and *to the moderation of the punishment inflicted.*

'A hasty or intemperate blow given by the master cannot be justified.' 'The law is too watchful over the safety of all to allow the slightest violence to be done to the person of any, except in self-defence, or for the maintenance of discipline, to ensure the safety of the persons on board.'

'The mate or other officer in charge of the ship, in the absence of the master, may exercise the power of restraining any offender, but he should reserve the question of punishment for the judgment of the master, who is to act in concert with his officers.' The 2nd chapter of Mr. Symons' Treatise ought to be well considered by every shipmaster.

On the subject of mutiny or piratical revolt, the charge of Mr. Justice Williams to the jury in the trial of the crew of the 'James Campbell' at the Western Circuit Court, Exeter, on July 26, 1847, gives a lucid exposition of the law and may be very suitably quoted here. He said that the indictment proceeded on an Act of Parliament passed in the reign of King William III., by which it is provided that 'if any seaman should confine his master, or make a revolt in his ship he should be deemed a pirate, and be liable to transportation or imprisonment; that the law would not suffer the seaman to make a revolt and confine the master because he issued unjust orders, or because his conduct was harsh, unreasonable, or vexatious, otherwise there would be an end of maritime discipline ; but that the only instance in which seamen could be justified in imprisoning the master and depriving him of his command is where his conduct is proved to have been such as to give reasonable grounds of apprehension that unless the crew confined him they were in danger of their lives or of suffering some grievous bodily harm.'

SEAMANSHIP. The art of working a ship or performing her various evolutions at sea. On this subject a variety of useful information is presented throughout this Dictionary ; and attention may be directed to the valuable old work, still a standard book on seamanship, entitled *Darcy Lever's Young Sea Officer's Sheet Anchor*, and the following more recent publications: *Glascock's Naval Service or Officer's Manual, Martello's Naval Officer's Guide, Seamanship both in Theory and Practice, Dana's Seaman's Manual* (1859), *Tinmouth's Inquiry into various important points of Seamanship, Boyd's Naval Cadet's Manual*, and *Seamanship, Illustrated, by Lieut. George S. Nares, R.N.*

SEA-MARK (*Fr.* Balise, Amer). See *Leading-Marks.*

SEAMS. The joinings of the edges of planks in a ship or boat. See *Caulk* and *Pay.*

SEA-PORT. The same as *Port.*

SEARCHER. An officer of customs who is employed in taking an account of goods to be exported to foreign parts.

SEARCHER, or GUN-SEARCHER. An iron instrument with several sharp-pointed prongs and a wooden handle: this is used for working up and down in the bore of a gun to discover if it be honeycombed, a little wax being for such purpose put on each prong.

SEA-REACH. The reach of a winding river which stretches out to seaward. See *Reach.*

SEASONING, in Shipbuilding, a term applied to the keeping a vessel standing a certain time, after she is completely framed and dubbed out for planking, which, says the author of the *Shipwright's Vade Mecum*, should never be less than six months when circumstances will permit. Mr. Blackburn, in his *Treatise on Shipbuilding*, suggests that where the ship in frame would be exposed to the effects of every kind of weather, it would be better to put the timbers, beams, &c., when worked to their proper dimensions, under a shed in a suitable situation. All ships of war are built under cover. It is, however, deserving of consideration, whether rain or even frost be not a useful agent in assisting to clear away the natural sap from the wood, especially at least if it be hard wood.

*Seasoned plank*, or *timber*, is 'such as has been cut down and sawn out one season at least, particularly when thoroughly dry and not liable to shrink.' (*Shipwright's Vade Mecum.*)

Saturation with oil is found to be a good preservative for wood. See *Kiln* and *Dry-rot.*

On the subject of the preservation of wood reference may be made to the *American Journal of Science,* vol. xxxv. p. 267.

SEATING, in Shipbuilding, that part *of the floor* which fays on the dead-wood, or on the keel; that part *of a transom* which fays against the stern-post.

SEAWAY. A vessel is said to be in a seaway when under weigh or at anchor in an open place where the sea is rolling heavily.

SEAWORTHY. A term implying that a vessel is in every respect fit for her intended voyage, not only that the hull and furniture of the ship are in a sufficient condition, but that the master and crew are competent, that the lading is not greater than what is proper for her to carry on the voyage, and that, in fine, the ship is provided with all which is required for the purpose of a safe and careful navigation. A vessel may be seaworthy for lying in a port, yet not in a fit condition to proceed to sea, that is unseaworthy for the voyage on which she is bound.

SECTION, in Shipbuilding, a representation or draught of a portion of the ship cut by a plane in any particular direction. If it cut the vessel lengthwise, it is called a *Longitudinal Section*; if at right angles to the keel, a *Transverse Section. A Midship Section,* implies a transverse section in the middle of the vessel. *A Load-water Section* is a horizontal section at the load-water line.

SEIZE. To fasten ropes, or different parts of one rope, together by turns of small stuff: for example, the fastening of the ends of shrouds after being turned in round the dead-eyes.

The small line, spunyarn, or marline, used for such purposes is called *Seizing.* The mode of making a *round-seizing* and a *throat-seizing* on the bight of a rope is explained and illustrated in *Boyd's Naval Cadet's Manual.*

Other kinds of seizings, as a flat-seizing, a racking-seizing, are illustrated in *Seamanship, by Lieutenant Nares,* p. 21.

ROUND SEIZING.
(After Darcy Lever.)

THROAT SEIZING.
(After Darcy Lever.)

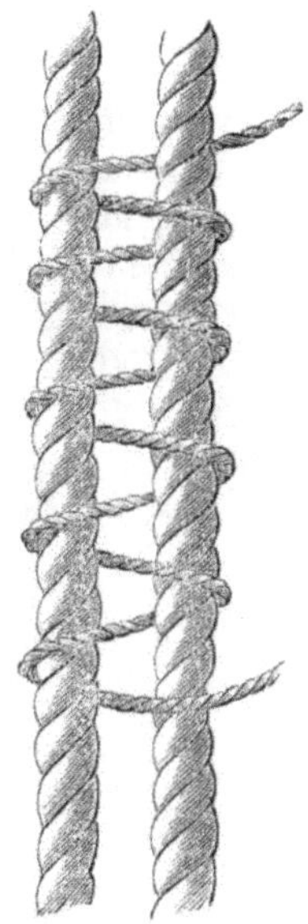

RACKING SEIZING.
(After Lieut. Nares, R.N.)

SELF-REEFING TOPSAILS (CUNNINGHAM'S PATENT). See *Reef.*

SELVAGEE, or SELVAGEE STROP. A skein of ropeyarns or spunyarn marled together; used in hoisting anything. See also *Collar.*

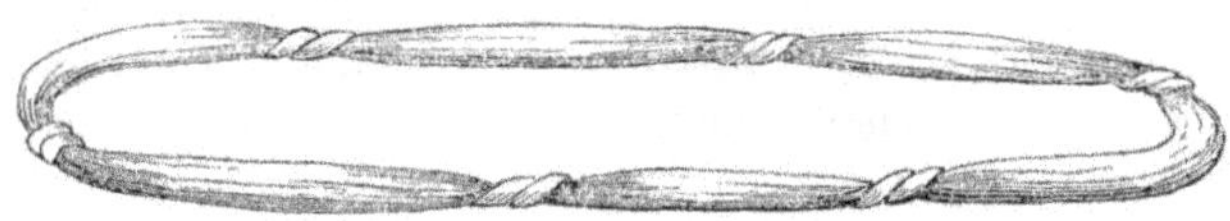

SELVAGEE. (After Darcy Lever.)

SEMAPHORE. A mast or post set up on the coast for the purpose of making telegraphic signals to ships, &c. The use of semaphores as a means of conveying communications from one place to another is now superseded by the electric telegraph. See *Telegraph.*

SEMIDIAMETER (ALLOWANCE FOR). See *Altitude.*

SEND, or 'SCEND. A vessel is said to *send*, when she pitches her head into the trough of the sea.

SENNIT, or SINNET. 'A braid formed by plaiting rope-yarns, or spunyarn together.'

SERVE. *To serve a rope*, is to wind small stuff, as ropeyarn, spunyarn, or the like, round it to keep it from being chafed. The stuff so wound is called *Service*. It is put on against the lay of the rope, and is hove taut by means of a *serving-board* or a *serving-mallet*. See *Serving Mallet*.

SERVICE (*Fr.* Fourrure). See *Serve*.

SERVING BOARD. See *Serving Mallet*.

SERVING MALLET. A cylindrical piece of wood, having on one side a groove to fit the convexity of the rope which is to be served, and in the middle of the opposite side a handle. This is used to turn the service round, and heave it tight round the rope. See *Serve*.

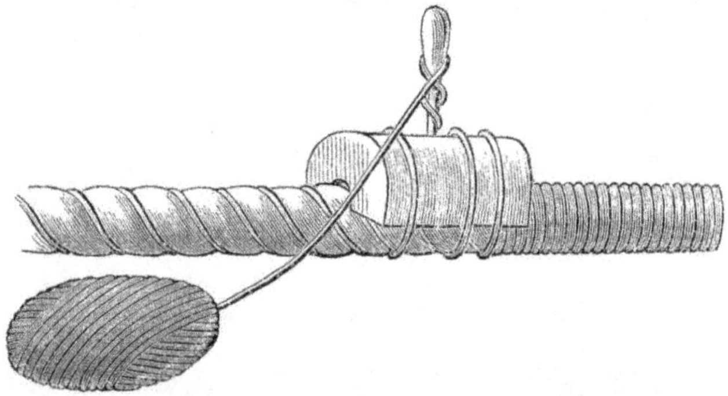

SERVING MALLET. (After Darcy Lever.)

*A Serving Board* is a flat piece of wood of oval form, with a groove in it, and tapering to one end as a handle. The *serving-board* is used for small ropes, and the *serving-mallet* for large ropes. See *Darcy Lever's Young Sea Officer's Sheet Anchor*.

SET. *The set of a current* means its direction. A current also is said *to set*, that is, to run in any particular direction. *To set up rigging* (*Fr.* Rider) is to increase its tension by means of tackles. *Set to sail* is to spread a vessel's sails to the wind in order to get under weigh.

SET-BOLT. See preceding article.

SET ON! The order to set the engine going, on board of a steamer.

SETTEE. A two-masted vessel, peculiar to the Mediterranean.

SETTEE SAIL. A quadrilateral sail, in a boat having its head bent to a lateen yard, hanging obliquely to the mast (*Kipping's Elementary Treatise on Sails and Sailmaking*, p. 127).

SETTING, in Shipbuilding, implies the operation of making the planks of a vessel fay close *to the timbers* and also *to each other*: the former is generally done by driving wedges between the planks and a *wrain-staff*, inserted through a ring-bolt; the latter, by driving wedges between the planks and a bolt called a *Set-bolt*, driven into an auger-hole made in the timber.

SETTLE. To lower, or to be depressed. Thus a vessel is said to *settle* when she sinks deeper in the water after springing a leak.

SEW (pronounced sue). A vessel aground is said to have *sewed* so many feet or inches, when the ebbing tide has fallen so many from the height to which the water first reached when she was driven ashore or laid on the ground.

SEXTANT (*Fr.* Sextant). Hadley's sextant is 'an instrument constructed on the same principles as the quadrant; but, as it is used chiefly to measure the *angular* distance' between the moon and the sun or a star, in order to determine the longitude, its arc is 'extended to 120° for the purpose of measuring their distance when greater than 90°; it is also provided with some appendages not commonly annexed to a quadrant,' to enable the observation to be taken with greater accuracy; the frame is generally made of brass or other hard metal. (*Norie's Epitome.*)

The quadrant reads off miles; but the sextant is subdivided more minutely so as to read off parts of a mile.

SHACKLE. An open link of iron, or species of clamp, with a bolt for securing it. Shackles are used (among other similar purposes) for coupling the parts of a chain-cable at various lengths, in order that they may be readily disconnected when required: pins of hard wood are preferable to iron for forelocking shackle-bolts, because iron pins are apt to get fixed in with rust, and in the event of having to slip from an anchor, may on this account cause the loss of the whole cable. These are termed *chain-shackles*, or *chain-cable-shackles*. The *Anchor-shackle* is that which connects the chain with the anchor. See *Span-shackle*.

SHACKLE-CROW. A bar of iron with a shackle at the bent end; it is used for drawing bolts. See *Crow.*

SHAKE. *To shake a vessel in the wind,* means to bring her head so near the wind, when close-hauled, as to shiver the sails.

SHAKEN, or SHAKEY. The condition of plank or timber which has shakes or rents in it, and will not bear fastening or caulking.

SHAKES. The staves of large casks taken asunder and bound up closely together; which is sometimes done (particularly with casks for the use of whale-fishing vessels) in order to save stowage room. See also *Rents.*

SHAKINGS. A name given to 'small fragments of ropeyarn or of cordage, bits of oakum, old lanyards, &c., in short, to any kind of refuse arising out of the wear and tear of ropes.'

SHALLOP. 'A name applied to a small vessel having two masts; and also to fishing and other boats.'

SHALLOW. Not deep; a piece of water which has little depth at any time.

SHANK OF AN ANCHOR (*Fr.* Verge d'une ancre). See *Anchor*, 1.

SHANK-PAINTER (*Fr.* Serre-Bosse). A short piece of rope or chain, or both, used to secure the shank of an anchor to the ship's bow after being fished, and to ease it down again before dropping anchor. If, after the buoy is streamed, the cat-stopper and shank-painter be let go at the same moment, and the anchorage consists of hard ground, there is a risk of breaking one of the arms or even the stock of the anchor by its striking the bottom with one of these parts instead of with the crown of the anchor.

SHARP. See *Bluff*, *Brace*, and *Trim.*

SHEATHING (*Fr.* Doublage). Thin boards, or sheets of copper, yellow-metal, zinc, or galvanized iron, nailed over the bottom of a vessel. Wood-sheathing is used most generally for covering a vessel's bottom that has been partially wormed. See *Copper* and *Doubling.*

SHEAVE (*Fr.* Réa). A wheel (or, as it is called in mechanics, a pulley) either of wood or metal, inserted into a hole called the *sheave-hole,* either in a block, or in a yard-arm, mast, or boom, &c.

SHEEPSHANK. A kind of knot, or hitch, or bend, used to shorten a rope temporarily. When top-gallant masts are struck, their backstays are *sheepshanked*, so as to shorten them for being set taut.

SHEEPSHANK. (After Darcy Lever.)

*To* SHEER ALONGSIDE, means to steer a vessel so as to bring her gently alongside of another or of any object. *To sheer off*, is to steer her so as to keep clear of or move off from it. See the articles *Anchor*, 20, and *Break-sheer.*

SHEER. The longitudinal curve downwards of a vessel's topsides or upper works. It is sometimes called a *Spring*. See *Ram-line.*

SHEERS (*Fr.* Bigues). Two rough masts or spars set up like two legs of a triangle, and lashed together at their upper end, from which tackles are suspended: guys are also attached to it, in order to keep the sheers upright, and to steady them. They are used, in Shipbuilding, for hoisting the stem, stern-post, frames, &c.; or, generally, for the purpose of taking out and putting in the lower masts of any vessel.

SHEER-DRAUGHT, SHEER-DRAWING, or SHEER-PLAN. The same as *elevation*. See *Shipbuilding*, 1.

SHEER-HULK. An old worn-out ship, fitted with sheers, used for lifting and putting in the lower masts of large ships. See *Hulk.*

SHEER-MOULD, in Shipbuilding, a long thin plank having one of its edges curved, used for adjusting the ram-line on the ship's side. See *Ram-line.*

SHEER-PLAN. See the title *Sheer-Draught.*

SHEER-POLE, or STRETCHER. An iron rod stretched along the shrouds and seized firmly to each of them at the top of their dead-eyes, serving to prevent the shrouds from twisting at that part. It has often an eye in the end for making fast a rope or hooking on a tackle to.

SHEER-RAILS. A name for the mouldings round a vessel's topsides.

SHEER-STRAKE, or PAINT-STRAKE, in a ship or in a boat, the uppermost strake of outside planking. See *Strake.*

SHEET (*Fr.* Écoute) *of a course.* The rope or chain by which its clue is hauled aft; in vessels of burden, the standing part of the sheet is hooked to an eye-bolt in the ship's side, and the sheet is rove through a block at the clue of the sail: there is a tack and a sheet to each clue of a course. The sheets of any *upper square sail* are in like manner made fast to the clues, and they are rove through a sheave-hole or block at each of the yard-arms, in order to extend the sail to the yard. The sheet of a *fore-and-aft mainsail*, or of a *spanker*, *trysail*, or *spencer*, is attached to the boom. That of a *storm trysail*, or of any *fore-and-aft head sail* is made fast to the after lower corner of the sail. (Plates III. IV. and V.) See *Flowing-sheet.*

*To sheet home*, means to haul home a sheet. See the article *Home.*

SHEET-ANCHOR. See *Anchor*, 5.

SHEET-BEND. See *Bend.*

SHEET-COPPER. See *Copper.*

SHELF-PIECES, or SHELVES. Strakes of plank worked round the interior of a vessel edgeways to the ship's sides, for the purpose of receiving and securing the ends of the beams, as the 'upper-deck shelf' the 'gun-deck shelf,' &c. They are also called *stringers*, under which head a more full description is given. (Plate II. fig. 6.)

SHELL (*Fr.* Bombe). The name now given to a bomb or bomb-shell. See *Bomb*, and *Bomb Vessel.*

SHELL (SHRAPNELL). See *Shot.*

SHELVES. Any shoals or rocks lying immediately beneath the surface of the water.

SHIELD SHIP or Cupola Ship. A ship of war or floating battery, covered with iron plates outside, sloping over the deck,

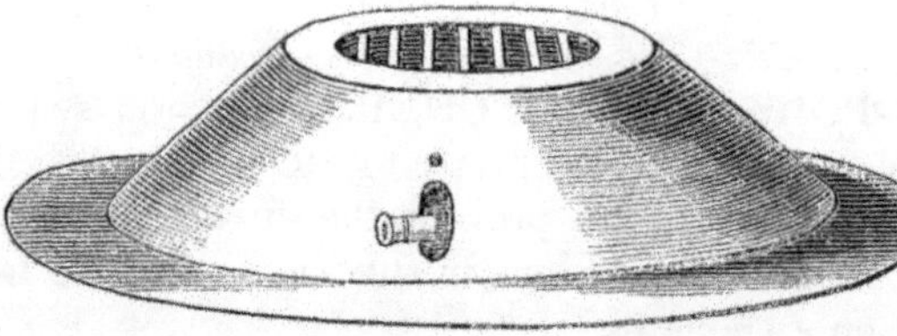

fitted with one or more *shields* or *cupolas* of the kind here illustrated; each of these shields carries one or more heavy guns, fixed in slides in the interior of the shield, which is moved round, when occasion requires, on a central pivot, by the ship's steam machinery; the men working the guns are thus turned in it entirely under cover, and the ship has no gun-ports in her sides. The shields, invented by Captain Cowper Coles, R.N., are of various forms. He has also contrived similar revolving *turrets* for forts or shore defences. An account of the Shield Ship, and of his triangular or tripod method of rigging it, has been published by Captain Coles. See *Cupola Ship* and *Floating Battery* (*Ericcson's*).

SHIFT. See *Shifting*.

SHIFT *the helm*. To put it from starboard to port, or the reverse. SHIFT *the sails*. To trim them to the wind when it changes or when the ship or boat alters her course.

SHIFT OF WIND (*Fr*. Saute de Vent). A change in the direction of the wind; it is then said to shift.

SHIFTING, or SHIFT, in Shipbuilding, the overlaunching of one plank or piece of timber upon another, so that the butts or scarphs of each may be sufficiently far apart to afford strength and stability to the vessel. When this is properly attended to in the general construction of the vessel, she is said to be well *shifted*. The keelson is said to 'afford shifts to the scarphs of the keel:' for example, the scarph of the keel may be amidships, and then care will be taken to have the scarph of the keelson either before or abaft it. The proper regulation of the shiftings is laid down with great accuracy in *Lloyd's Register of British and Foreign Shipping*.

SHIFTING-BOARDS. One or more wooden partitions put up fore-and-aft in a vessel's hold, and firmly supported on each side by pillars, or 'stanchions' of wood, for the purpose of preventing the shifting of a cargo, such as grain, when stowed in bulk.

SHIFTING CENTRE. See *Meta-Centre*.

SHIFTING STAGES. Any platforms or scaffoldings on which shipwrights perform their work. See *Stages*.

SHINGLE. Small round stones or gravel gathered from the sea-beach, used for dunnage or ballast.

*To* SHIP (*Fr*. Embarquer), means to put anything on board, or to enter on board of a vessel: also, to insert anything in its proper place, as to ship the rudder; in this last sense, *to unship* is the opposite term. See *Oar*.

A vessel is said to *ship a sea*, when a wave breaks over her deck.

SHIP (*Fr*. Bâtiment, Vaisseau, Navire). A name applied in common language to any vessel intended for the purposes of navigation, such as a merchant ship, or a ship of war; it is especially applied to vessels of considerable burden. In a more confined sense, it denotes a vessel having three masts with tops and yards to each. See *Hospital Ship*, *Neutral Ship*, *Receiving Ship*, *Steam Ship*, *Transport Service*, *and Vessel.*

SHIP OF THE LINE (*Fr.* Un bâtiment de haut bord) is a ship of war of sufficient force to have a station in the line of battle. See *Line.*

Sketches of such ships carrying guns on two decks, and on three decks in addition to the guns on the quarter deck, waist, and forecastle are given under the title *Decker.*

SHIP-BREAKER. A person whose occupation is to take vessels to pieces, in other words to break up ships.

SHIP-BROKERS are persons who undertake the management of business matters between shipowners and merchants in the way of procuring cargoes and charters for vessels, &c. They generally act also as insurance brokers. See *Brokers.*

SHIP-BUILDING (*Fr.* Construction). The art of constructing vessels for navigation. An individual so employed is called a *Shipbuilder*, or *Shipwright* (*Fr.* Constructeur).

1. The principal PLANS used in shipbuilding are:—1. *The Sheer-Draught*, *Sheer-Drawing*, *Sheer-Plan*, or *Elevation*, which is a vertical and longitudinal view of the ship, representing her outboard works from the wales upwards, and also the keel, stem, and stern-post, with a sectional view of the centres of the frames, laid off at their proper distances upon the keel, and marked from the dead-flat, in numerical figures towards the stern-post, and in letters of the alphabet towards the stem. 2. *The Half-breadth Plans*, or *Floor-Plans*, which are sections upon a longitudinal plane, whereon are represented the water-lines and the ribband-lines. 3. *The Body Plan*, which is a representation of vertical transverse sections, before, at, and abaft the dead-flat.

2. Of the MODELS used in shipbuilding, we may notice the following:—*A bulkshead model*, is one formed by vertical pieces of board representing half frames, which are fastened to a board corresponding with the centre line of the vessel. *A Key Model*, or *Water-line Model*, is formed by pieces of board laid on each other horizontally: these boards, being all shaped from the lines on the paper, when put together and fairly adjusted, present the true form of the ship.

3. The LINES employed in shipbuilding are as follows: — *The Bearding Line*, which is described under the article *bearding.*

*Buttock-Lines*, and *Bow-Lines*, longitudinal curves at the buttock and bow representing the ship's body cut in vertical section. *The Cutting-down Line*, a curve in the sheer-draught corresponding to the upper surface of the throats of the floors amidships, and to the under side of the keelson. *Diagonal Lines*, or *Ribband Lines*, cutting the body-plan diagonally from the timbers to the middle line; they regulate the position of the ribbands, and when laid down on the floor-plan, give points (called *surmarks*) at their intersection of the frames for the bevellings of the timbers. *The Level-Line*, a horizontal line struck between the surmarks of a floor-timber, upon which line a large square is placed, with a plummet, in order to set the floor-timber, when laid upon the keel, to a proper level. *The Middle-Line*, or *Centre-Line*, a line run from the stem to the stern-post, dividing the ship into two equal parts. *The Rising-Line*, an elliptical line drawn on the plan of elevation to determine the sweep of the floor-heads throughout the ship's length, and thus ascertain the shape of the bottom as to its being full or sharp. *The Top-timber Line*, or *Top-breadth Line*, a curve describing the height of the top-timbers, which gives the sheer of the vessel. See also the article *Water-Lines*.

4. SWEEPS, are the arcs of circles used in the body-plan to describe the form of the timbers.

5. The figure of the ship abstractedly considered is divided into two principal parts. The FORE-BODY, or that part before the midship-frame, as seen from ahead; and the AFTER-BODY, or that part abaft the midship-frame, as seen from astern. *The Fore* and *the After Cant-bodies*, are those parts inclined towards the stem and towards the stern-post,, which form the shape forward and aft. THE SQUARE-BODY, or MIDSHIP-BODY, is that part between the cant-bodies, in other words *amidships*, where the timbers are perpendicular to the keel. Plates of the fore-body and after-body of an *iron* ship are given in *Grantham on Iron Shipbuilding*, pp. 61 and 64.

6. The breadth of a vessel is usually distinguished into EXTREME BREADTH, measured at the midship frame from the outside of the wales on each side: MAIN BREADTH, measured from the outside of the black strakes: and TOP-TIMBER BREADTH or TOP-BREADTH, from the outside of the plank-sheer. *The upper Height of Breadth* is marked by a line where the topsides begin to incline inwards: *the lower Height of breadth* by a line

where the bottom begins to arch inwards. See *Straight of Breadth.* (*Hedderwick on Shipbuilding. Creuze's Treatise on Naval Architecture.*)

7. Mr. Blackburn, in his *Treatise on the Science of Shipbuilding,* very properly notices, that, in constructing ships, care ought to be taken not to place together those kinds of timber which are known to disagree in their nature, and to destroy each other: he further remarks, that the oak of Northern Europe and that of North America prove extremely pernicious to our native oak, and that a decayed piece of timber placed in contact with a sound piece will hasten the destruction of the latter. When it happens to be indispensably necessary to place any such kinds of timber together, a piece of hair-felt may be introduced between them, in order to prevent these injurious effects. Zinc preserves iron, but iron destroys zinc; and copper or lead, especially the former, destroys iron. The modern system of Shipbuilding as applied to ships of war is occasionally compared with the mode adopted for merchant vessels in *Peake's Rudiments of Naval Architecture*, an elementary work fully illustrated.

Captain Boyd in his *Naval Cadet's Manual* gives a few extracts on this subject from *Fincham's Outlines of Naval Architecture.*

SHIPCHANDLER. A person who sells all kinds of miscellaneous articles required in the outfit of ships. A *Dealer in Marine Stores* is a sort of shipchandler, selling old and second-hand stores.

SHIPMASTER. A common name for the captain or commander of a merchant vessel.

*The Mercantile and Maritime Guide, by Graham Willmore and Edwin Beedell*, has now taken the place of *Steel's Shipmaster's Assistant* as a valuable repertory of information for master mariners.

SHIPMENT. The act of shipping goods or any other thing on board of a vessel. Also, any one of the several individual parcels of goods shipped.

SHIP-OWNER. A person who has the right of property in a ship or vessel, or any share therein. Persons who have each a certain number of shares are called severally *part-owners.*

SHIP PROPELLER. See *Screw Propeller.*

SHIPPER. An individual who sends goods on board of a vessel, to be forwarded by her.

SHIPPING. Ships in general: a number of vessels.

SHIPPING MANIFEST. See *Manifest.*

SHIPPING MASTERS. Officials appointed under legislative enactment to attend to the shipping or engaging, and the discharging of seamen, &c.

SHIP-SHAPE. A cant phrase used to imply *according to the fashion of a ship*, or *in a seaman-like manner.*

SHIP'S HUSBAND. An agent for the owners of a vessel, employed to take a general management thereof, and render an account to his employers. See *Husband* (*Ship's*).

SHIP'S LOG. See *Log-line*, 3.

SHIP'S PAPERS. Certain writings or documents descriptive of a vessel, her owners, cargo, &c., as the certificate of registry, manifest, agreement with seamen, muster-roll, bills of lading, and so on. Also, those documents required to be on board a neutral ship in order to vindicate her title to that character. (*Maunder's Scientific and Literary Treasury.*) See *Marshall on Insurance.*

SHIPWRECK (*Fr.* Naufrage). The destruction of a vessel by being cast ashore, or driven upon rocks, &c. In such a case, also, both the vessel and the mariners are said to be *shipwrecked* (*Fr.* dégradé).

SHIPWRIGHT (*Fr.* Constructeur). A shipbuilder: a person occupied in the building and repairing of vessels. The workmen so employed under a master-shipbuilder are called either *shipwrights* or *carpenters.* The individual who has the chief superintendence in the building and repairing of Her Majesty's ships, at any of the royal dockyards, is styled the *master-shipwright.*

SHIVER *a sail.* To shake the wind out of it and thus make it collapse, either by hauling on the braces, or by bringing the vessel's head up to the wind.

SHOAL. The same as shallow, but more particularly applicable to a sand-bank which dries at low water. *A vessel is said to shoal her water*, when she comes from a greater to a lesser depth of water.

SHOD. The anchor is said to be *shod* when, in breaking out of the ground, a quantity of firm soil adheres to it, so as to prevent it from again taking hold. See *Anchor*, 21.

SHOE (*Fr.* Semelle) *of the Anchor.* A flat piece of hard wood, hollowed out on one side, suspended by a lanyard, with the hand, in order to prevent the pea of the anchor from ripping the bows, while hoisting the anchor after being catted or while lowering it down.

SHOE *of the Forefoot*, in Shipbuilding, an iron plate fixed on the lower part of the gripe and the fore end of the keel, outside, to strengthen them and prevent chafing.

SHOE PIECE. A piece of wood with a hollow in it for the lower end of any spar such as a derrick, or an anchor-davit, or sheers resting in.

SHOLES (in some places pronounced *showles*). Pieces of plank placed under the soles of standards, or under the heels of shores, in docks or on slips where there are no groundways, in order to enable them to sustain the weight required, without sinking. (*Shipwright's Vade Mecum.*)

SHOLES, or SHOLE PIECES, are also pieces of plank fixed under anything by way of protection, such as a piece put on the lower end of a rudder, that in the event of the ship's striking the ground, it may be knocked off without injury to the rudder.

SHORE, or SEA-SHORE (*Fr.* Côte, Rivage). The land along the sea-side. See *Bold.*

SHORE (TO) (*Fr.* Accorer). See *Shores.*

SHORE-DUES. The same as *Harbour-dues.*

SHORES (*Fr.* Accores). Pieces of timber used, in Shipbuilding, as temporary supports and for other purposes. Hence, *to shore* (*Fr.* accorer) means to prop up with shores.

Dog-shores, are shores used to prevent a vessel from starting while the keel-blocks are in the act of being taken out, preparatory to launching.

Skeg-shores. Pieces of plank put up endways under the skeg of a heavy ship, to steady her afterpart a little at the moment of launching. See *Skeg.*

Spur-shores, or Spurs. A name for shores placed in a horizontal position, or set up diagonally. Spur-shores, placed diagonally, are used for setting straight any piece of timber, such as a keel-piece, which happens to have a crook upon it; one end of the shore being fixed in the ground, with a piece of plank (sometimes called a *slip*) at its butt for wedging upon, and the other end set up against the article that is intended to be straightened. Shores of this description are set in the same way against a plank which is bolted and forms a flange to the groundways, for better security in launching a vessel.

SHORT LINK CHAIN. See *Chain.*

SHOT (*Fr.* Boulet). A general name for all sorts of balls or bullets used for fire-arms. The cast-iron balls fitted to the size of the bore of a heavy gun or cannon are termed *Round-shot.* Two of these connected together by a chain form what is called *Chain-shot. Grape-shot,* consists of a number of balls placed in the form of a bunch of grapes round an upright piece of iron fixed in the middle of an iron plate fitting the bore of a gun, the shot being marled strongly over with canvass. *Case-shot,* or *Canister-shot,* consists of smaller balls in a cylindrical case or canister; it is used when fighting at close quarters.

*The Shrapnell Shell,* or *Spherical-case Shot* (invented by General Shrapnell), consists of a light cast-iron hollow ball, filled with musket shot, and sufficiently thin to allow of its bursting with a small quantity of powder, which is shaken into the interstices; it has a fuse hole, into which a fusee is inserted to explode the shell during its flight, and after the shell thus bursts, the balls retain nearly the same direction (merely diverging laterally), which would not be the case if burst with much powder. 'This kind of shot is more effective at a greater range than grape or canister shot.'

*Red-hot Shot* are 'balls made red-hot in a furnace, and in that state thrown out of guns against an enemy's ship or magazine.'

SHOT-RACKS. Wooden frames fixed at convenient places in a ship of war to contain shot. Iron rods, hollowed out so as to hold the shot, are now very generally used instead of these shot-racks.

SHOULDER BLOCKS. See *Block,* 12 a.

SHOULDER-OF-MUTTON SAIL. A kind of triangular sail, so called from its peculiarity of form, and used chiefly to set on a boat's mast. The sail is commonly bent to a yard which hoists perpendicularly to the mast, and is attached to it by two crances: it is hauled up and down on the mast by means of halyards. The upper corner of the shoulder-of-mutton sail is sometimes converted into a gaff-topsail, which can be lowered snugly behind the other part of the sail when required, to diminish the quantity of sail aloft.

SHOVE OFF! An order to the bowman of a boat to push her off with a boat-hook or otherwise, in order to leave the ship, or jetty, &c., which she happens to be alongside of.

SHOVEL *for a gun.* See *Worm.*

SHROUDS (*Fr.* Haubans). A set of ropes reaching from the

mast-heads to a vessel's channels, set up for the support of the masts. They are distinguished into main, fore, and mizen-shrouds, maintopmast shrouds, maintopgallant shrouds, main royal shrouds, &c., according to the masts which they support. See *Ratlines* and *Rigging*. See also *Bowsprit-shrouds*, and *Futtock-shrouds.*

SHROUD-BLOCKS. See *Dead-eyes.*

SHROUD-STOPPER. A piece of rope made fast above and below the damaged part of a shroud which has been injured by shot or otherwise, in order to secure it.

SHROUD-TRUCKS. Small pieces of wood with holes in them, but no sheaves, seized on the shrouds as fairleaders for the running-rigging.

SHUT IN. The land which a vessel has left is said to be *shut in,* when a point of land intercepts the view of it. The reverse of *opened out.*

SHY. The wind is said to be shy, when it will barely allow a vessel to sail directly for her point of destination, to sail directly on her proper course. See *Course.*

SICK-BAY. A place set apart in a ship for invalids or wounded men.

SICK-BERTH ATTENDANT, formerly termed *Loblolly Boy*; in a ship of war, a person who attends the surgeon and his assistants.

SIDE-BOYS, in a ship of war, are boys employed to take charge of the man-ropes, and attend on any officers or other individuals coming on board from or going off in a boat.

SIDE-KEELSONS. See *Keelsons* (*Sister*).

SIDE-LEVERS (*Fr.* Balanciers). See description of *Steam Engine,* Sect. 21.

SIDE-RODS. See description of *Steam Engine,* Sects. 23, 24, and 25.

SIDEREAL DAY. The interval between the departure and return of a meridian to a star.

SIDING DIMENSION, in Shipbuilding, implies the breadth of a piece of timber; *Moulding dimension,* is depth or thickness. The timber is said to be *sided* or *moulded* so many inches.

SIGHTS, are of various descriptions; they are used for giving a just direction to the line of vision, as in pointing a gun, &c. See *Dispart.*

SIGHT-VANES. See *Quadrant.*

SIGNALS (*Fr.* Signaux) *at sea*, are signs made for the purpose chiefly of exchanging communications between ships at a distance from each other, or between a ship and the land. This may be done by hoisting flags, by signal lights, or firing guns, &c. With regard to the first of these methods, the code of signals which has been in most common use is that of Captain Marryat. There is likewise a code of signals by Mr. Watson for the use of ships at sea or when arriving off stations on the coast.

*The Commercial Code of Signals for the Use of all Nations*, with the *British Vocabulary*, compiled by J. T. Forster, Master R.N., edited by W. F. Larkins, of the Board of Trade, and published by authority of that Board at the office of *The Shipping and Mercantile Gazette*, contains general and international signals, to enable ships when at sea to communicate with each other, or with people on the shore; also Admiralty notices as to lights and fog signals, &c. Intimation is given therein that 'should any foreign country adopt flags different from those in the *Commercial Code*, plates corresponding with these will be published for insertion in signal books as soon as communicated.' The new edition of the *Commercial Code of Signals* contains the Mercantile Navy List.

*The Companion to the Commercial Code of Signals* (published by C. Wilson, late J. W. Norie and Wilson) makes the flags used in that Code 'available for interchanging the latitude or longitude, and contains other analogous information, with tables of longitude assimilated to the meridians of Amsterdam, Cadiz, Greenwich, and Paris, rendering the indications of a ship's reckoning instantly available for navigators of all nations.'

Captain Colomb's *Patent Flashing Night Signals* are made by the flashing of one white light, with intervals of darkness; his system is said to be closely assimilated with that of signals by flags now in use.

A signal of *distress* is made with the union down, in the topmast-rigging of a vessel's after-mast.

SIGNS OF THE ZODIAC. Equal parts into which it is divided by astronomers, each containing thirty degrees. See *Zodiac*.

SILL, or CILL, OF A DOCK. The piece of timber against which the gates shut.

SILLS, or CILLS, OF PORTS, in Shipbuilding, pieces of

timber put in horizontally between the framing to form the top and bottom of a port.

SILT UP. Any part of a river, or of a harbour in connection with it is said to silt up, when the *Silt*, that is, the deposit carried down by the river fills it up partially or wholly.

SINGLE ACTION ENGINE. See *Atmospheric Engine.*

SINNET. See *Sennit.*

SIRMARKS. See *Surmarks* and *Ribband-lines.*

SISTER BLOCKS. Blocks or bull's-eyes seized between the topmast shrouds, for the topsail lifts and reef tackles to lead through. See *Blocks.*

SISTER-KEELSONS. See *Keelson* (*Sister* and *Bilge*).

SKEEDS. See *Skids.*

SKEET. A piece of wood or iron with a groove in it, used for throwing water over the planks of a ship's sides. This is done in warm climates in order to prevent their being rent by the heat of the sun.

SKEG. A name given to the after part of a vessel's keel.

SKEG-SHORES. Pieces of plank put up endways under the skeg of a heavy ship, to steady her after-part a little at the moment of launching. They are made to turn on a hinge, and fixed so as to fall readily when the ship starts.

SKIDS, or SKEEDS. Pieces of plank formed to fit a vessel's topside, and extending from the wales to the top of the side. They are used to preserve the side from being injured by weighty bodies when hoisted into or lowered out of the ship. Some old ships, such as whalers, &c., have them *fixed* to the sides.

BOAT-SKIDS are similar portable pieces used in like manner to prevent chafing, &c., when a boat is hoisted or lowered.

SKIDS. A name also given to pieces of plank put under a vessel's bottom for the purpose of launching her off when she has been driven ashore.

SKID-BEAMS. See *Spar-deck* and *Gallows.*

SKIFF. A popular name for any small boat. See also the article *Boat,* 2.

SKIN. That part of a sail which is outside and covers the rest of the sail when it is furled. Also, familiarly, the sides of a vessel's hold; thus, an article is said to be 'stowed next the skin.' (*Dana's Seaman's Manual.*)

SKINNING. A term used for *planking* a vessel.

SKIPPER. A familiar name for the master of a merchant vessel.

SKYLIGHT. The window by which a vessel's cabin receives light from above the deck.

SKYSAIL. A light sail, in a square-rigged vessel, next above the royal. It is set either on the pole of the royal mast, or (when this mast has no pole) on a spar, called a *sliding-gunter-mast*, which rests upon the topgallant-masthead, and extends upwards, forming a pole above the royal mast. Either of these poles gets the name of the *skysail pole*.

SKY-SCRAPER (*Fr.* Aile de pigeon). A name sometimes given to a skysail when it is triangular.

SLAB-LINE. A rope used to haul up the slack of a course, in order to prevent it from shaking, or being split, in the act of hauling up the sail. Or, a rope occasionally made fast to the foot of a course, or of a topsail, to keep it from chafing on the stay in calm weather, &c.

SLACK (*Fr.* Balant) *of a rope*; any part of it which hangs down loose.

SLACK IN STAYS. If a vessel work slowly in tacking, she is said to be *slack in stays*.

SLACK WATER. The interval between every flood-tide and ebb-tide, during which there is little or no change in the height of the tide. See *Tides*, 2.

SLATCH. A term which has been used to denote the duration of a passing breeze.

SLAVER (*Fr.* Négrier). A ship employed in the inhuman traffic termed the *Slave Trade.*

SLEEPERS, or ENGINE-BEARERS, in Shipbuilding, pieces of timber placed between the keelson or keelson-riders in a steam ship, and the boilers of the steam engine, to form a proper seat for the boilers and machinery.

SLEEPERS. A term also sometimes applied to knees at the ends of the wing transom for strengthening the connection between the stern-frame and the after body of a vessel. See *Pointers.* Also, 'two cross pieces over a ship's top, to secure the top down to the cross-trees and trestle-trees.'

SLICES. *Wooden slices* are large wedges of hard wood used for raising a ship when on a slip or in a dock where there are no screws for the purpose. They are driven in beneath her with a ram.

*Iron Slices* are iron wedges for splitting out the keel-blocks before a ship is launched, or for splitting a keel or keelson out in short pieces, in order to put in a new one. *A slice*, or *slice-bar*, also means a bar of iron with a sharp end, used to strip off sheathing, ceiling, &c.

SLIDE-VALVES, with their appendages. See description of *Steam Engine*, Sects. 3, 4, 5, and 31.

SLIDE-VALVE CASING. See description of *Steam Engine*, Sect. 2.

SLIDING-BAULKS. See *Launching Ways*.

SLIDING-GUNTER MAST. See *Skysail*.

SLIDING-KEELS, in Shipbuilding, pieces of wood or iron made to lower down through the main keel so as to protrude below it when required. These are serviceable in diminishing the tendency of any vessel to roll; and they serve to prevent a sailing vessel from falling to leeward when close-hauled. If a vessel be fitted with three sliding keels, the fore keel will serve to bring her about when the after keel is hove up, and the after keel will make her wear quickly when the fore keel is up. See *Charnock's History of Marine Architecture*.

SLIDING PLANKS. See *Launching Ways*.

SLING. To sling a cask, or boat, or any other thing, is to place and secure it in slings for the purpose of hoisting or lowering it.

SLINGS. The name given to a large rope or chain, fitted so

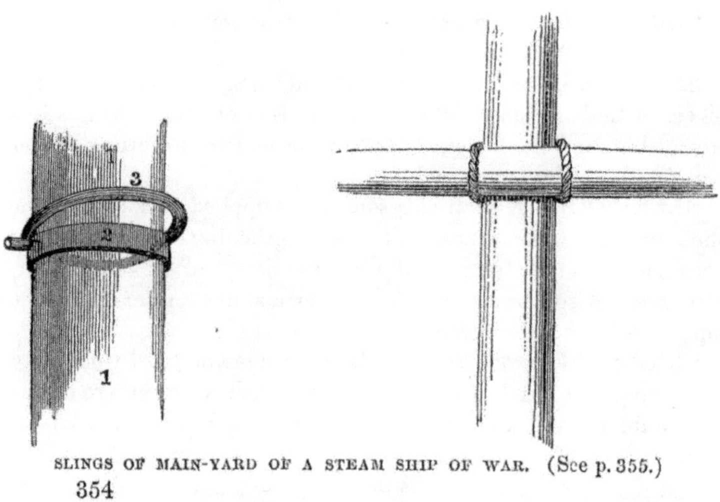


SLINGS OF MAIN-YARD OF A STEAM SHIP OF WAR. (See p. 355.)

as to go round, or furnished with hooks to attach to any article which is to be hoisted or lowered; as *cask-slings*, or *butt-slings*, *bale-slings*, *boat-slings*, *can-hook-slings*, &c. A variety of such slings are illustrated in *Seamanship*, by Lieutenant Nares, p. 13, and at page 39 of *Biddlecombe's Art of Rigging*.

SLINGS OF A YARD, that part of it encircled by the *Sling-hoop*, which suspends it from the mast, or by which it is hoisted and lowered. A lower yard is hung by chains called *chain-slings*, attached to the sling-hoop and mast-head. An upper yard is hoisted and lowered by its *tye*, which passes through a block attached to the sling-hoop. (Plate IV.) See p. 354.

SLING-DOGS. See *Dog*.

SLING-HOOP. See *Slings of a yard*.

SLIP. The sloping foundation laid for the purpose of building a ship upon and launching her. See also *Shores* (*Spur*).

There are also slips on which vessels may be drawn up for receiving repairs. The most important of these is Mr. Morton's *Patent Slip*: it consists of a frame having a centre-piece for the ship's keel to rest upon, and two side pieces apart from the centre; the whole connected together near the lower end by cross beams with knees. There are also arms at regular distances from each other, to each of which is attached a sliding block of wood for hauling in beneath the ship's bottom, in order to steady her when she is properly grounded on the centre-piece; this framework gets the name of the *cradle*: it moves upon truck wheels with flanges to guide them, and is drawn up and let down upon a cast-iron railway, by means of a chain, or a succession of iron bars, connecting it with a steam engine, or with any purchase. Without entering into a more minute description of Mr. Morton's invention, we shall notice merely that, on the very superior patent slip erected by him at Dundee, whereon ships of 1,000 tons burden can be hauled up, Mr. Brisbane when superintendent of it introduced a method of steadying vessels properly upon the cradle, which has been attended with much advantage: four large iron bars, the lower ends whereof traverse upon an iron bolt, which serves as a pivot, and passes through an iron clamp fixed, where it may be required, to the cradle, and with ropes attached to their upper ends, are placed, two a little abaft the ship's forefoot, and two a little before her heel, lying lengthways on the top of the frame till she is hauled to a proper berth, in which they serve to keep her. They are then raised one after another by means of the ropes till their heads appear above water, the two after ones on each side of the stern-post, and the two fore ones on each side of the stem; there are also ropes crossing the bows, attached to the fore arms of the cradle, and two other ropes crossing the stern, attached to two arms opposite to the ship's quarters. These ropes may be led to a windlass, or winch, in order to be hove taut. When the whole is fairly adjusted, the other ropes usually attached to dolphins, or to the shore (excepting one head-rope made fast to the bars), are cast off, and the cradle and ship are drawn up.

A Patent Hydraulic Purchase Machine has been invented by Mr. Miller, of the firm of Messrs. Bell and Miller, dock engineers, Glasgow, for drawing up vessels on 'Morton's Slip.'

SLIP THE CABLE. To let it all run out, instead of weighing the anchor. See the article *Chain.*

When it is impossible or might be attended with danger to weigh the anchor, and it is therefore determined to slip from it, then, if consistent with safety, as much of the chain as can be done is hove in, and a buoy with a buoy-rope bent to the chain outside the hawse-hole before unshackling it. By this means as much of the chain as possible is retained on board.

If the pin with which the shackle-bolt is forelocked has got fixed in with rust, which is apt to happen when the pin is of iron instead of hard wood, and the shackle consequently cannot be cast off, it may be necessary to let the whole chain run out. The shackle-bolts themselves are also apt to get fixed in with rust, and they should therefore be from time to time taken out for the purpose of being cleaned and greased, in order that they may be in proper condition for unshackling when required.

SLIP HOOK, or LIFE HOOK (CAPTAIN KYNASTON'S PATENT). 'An invention not only to provide a hook of great strength and compactness of design which may with ease and certainty be released from any body to which it is attached, while a pressure is exerted on it, but by the addition of the circular plates or guard pieces (as shown in the figure) so effectually to shield the points of the hooks, while supporting a strain, that they cannot by any possibility become accidentally released.' This kind of hook is 'especially useful on shipboard in securing and slipping towing cables, or tow ropes, in ships or boats—for letting go a spring—for temporarily securing a vessel alongside a wharf or hulk—for hanging on to a buoy—and such like operations, and for the still more important purpose of suspending and disengaging a ship's boats at sea. When used for this latter purpose two hooks of the kind, inverted, as shown in the wood-cut, are shackled by their loops to the rings of the usual chain slings, at either end of the boat, while the points of the hooks are received by rings or shackles on the lower blocks of the usual tackles: then by means of a connecting span or pendant, with a block at each end, the relieving lines shown in the wood-cut are rove, and thereby made to act simultaneously; and when it is required to attach or disengage the hooks, the use of a single rope is found to accomplish the operation with the greatest ease and security.'

The hooks are tested to lift a weight *three* times greater than that to which they are applied, and they are marked accordingly.

SLIP ROPE. A rope bent to anything in such a manner that it may be slipped when required.

SLIP WAY, in Shipbuilding, the same as *Slip*.

SLIPPERY HITCH. A hitch made so unskilfully that it will not hold.

SLIVER, in Shipbuilding, any thin piece of wood used as a filling.

SLOOP (*Fr.* Sloup). A vessel with one mast, commonly rigged wholly with fore-and-aft sails; namely, a boom mainsail,

A SLOOP RIGGED LIKE A CUTTER.

1. Jib. 2. Foresail. 3. Mainsail. 4. Gaff topsail.

foresail, gaff-topsail, jib, and jib-topsail. Some sloops have no gaff-topsail, but a square topsail, and topgallant sail.

Sloops are also furnished with a square sail to set on a yard, called the *cross-jack-yard*, or *square-sail-yard*, when going free, or running before the wind.

SLOOP OF WAR. Any ship of war commanded by a Commander in the Royal Navy. If a steam vessel it is termed a *steam sloop of war*.

SLOPS. A name for clothes and other furnishings for the outfit of seamen. In a ship of war, these are supplied by the purser, and deductions made on such account from the men's wages.

SLUDGE. 'A stratum of detached ice crystals, or of snow, or of the smaller fragments of brush ice floating on the surface of the sea.' See *Ice-berg*, 16.

SLUDGE-HOLES. See description of *Steam-Engine*, Sect. 40.

SLUE. To turn anything round or over.

SMACK (*Fr.* Semaque). A large kind of sloop having a gaff-topsail and a running bowsprit. The smacks originally built as packets to ply between London and Leith and other ports were formed with a clean bottom with a view to good sailing qualities, carrying very heavy sails, and therefore requiring a large complement of men: most of these have now been converted into schooners, which can be worked with fewer hands. See *Fishing Smacks*.

SMALL ARMS. A general term for weapons of offence and defence carried in the hand, such as muskets, pistols, tomahawks, and boarding pikes.

SMALL ROUND. That end of the shank of an anchor which is next the stock. See *Anchor*, 1.

SMART TICKET. A certificate granted by the surgeon, and passed by the commanding officer of a ship of war in favour of any person who has been wounded or hurt in the service, in order that he may receive a single gratuity, or a pension from Greenwich Hospital.

SMOKE SAIL. A small sail put up for the purpose of preventing the smoke of the galley from going aft to the quarter-deck when the ship is riding head-to-wind.

SMUGGLING, with reference to sea affairs, means defrauding the public revenue by importing or exporting goods without paying the customs duties exigible upon them; an offence to which heavy penalties or fines, and other punishments are attached.

A vessel or an individual employed in such illegal traffic is called a *Smuggler* (*Fr.* Smogleur, Contrebandier). See *Contraband Goods.*

SNAKE (*Fr.* Serpenter). To pass small stuff across a seizing at the outer turns by way of finish. To attach lengths of rope between two stays or backstays.

SNAPE, or FLINCH, in Shipbuilding, to bevel the end of anything so as to fay upon an inclined surface.

SNATCH-BLOCK. A single block with a notch cut in one cheek, to receive the *bight* of a rope or fall, so as to save the trouble of reeving and unreeving the whole. See *Block*, 10.

SNIFTING-VALVE, or TAIL-VALVE (*Fr.* Soupape reniflante). See description of *Steam Engine*, Sect. 13.

SNOTTER. A rope going over a yard-arm with an eye forming a becket to bend a tripping-line to in sending down top-gallant and royal yards: mostly used in ships of war. Also, a piece of rope fitted round a boat's mast, having an eye in it to receive the lower end of a sprit.

SNOW (*Fr.* Sénau). See *Brig.*

SNUBBING. Checking or easing off a little of a ship's cable or hawser, in order to prevent a sudden jerk when bringing the vessel up, or on other occasions.

SNY. In Shipbuilding, a plank is said to have *sny*, when its edge has no upward curve. *Hang*, is a term applied in the same way when it has a downward curve.

SOLSTICE. See *Ecliptic.*

SOLSTITIAL POINTS. See *Ecliptic.*

SOUND (*Fr.* Sonder). To ascertain the depth of water by a lead and line, or otherwise. By putting a little grease on the lead the nature of the bottom is ascertained. See *Lead*, and *Well.*

The depths of water so ascertained at sea or in a river are termed *soundings*. *To strike soundings*, is to find bottom with the deep-sea-lead on coming in from sea. A vessel is then *in soundings.*

*Massey's Patent Sounding Machine*, is an instrument which ascertains the depth of water, and registers it by means of an index connected with a fly or rotator in the centre of the instrument. It is explained and illustrated in *Seamanship*, by Lieut. Nares, p. 15, fig. 52.

*Walker's Protected Sounding Machine* is a more recent contrivance of this kind.

*Ericcson's Lead*, or *Patent Sounding Instrument*, is adapted for the same purpose: a description of it may be seen in the *Nautical Magazine*, vol. 5.

Sounding-Rod (*Fr.* Sonde). A slight bar of iron marked with a scale of feet and inches, used to ascertain the depth of water that may happen to be in a vessel's hold.

SOUND. 'A strait or inlet of the sea between two capes or headlands.' See the following article.

SOUND-DUES. A toll or tribute formerly levied by the King of Denmark on all merchant vessels passing the strait called the *Sound*, which connects the North Sea with the Baltic. There were not only duties on the cargoes of such ships, but also light dues and other exactions levied: and all vessels passing the Sound, whether laden or in ballast, were required on this account to come to anchor at Elsineur for clearance.

SOUTHING (*Fr.* Chemin au sud). The distance sailed southwards. See *Northing*.

SPALING, or BAULKING, in Shipbuilding, means keeping the frames to their proper breaths by *cross-spales*, or *baulks*, which should so remain till some of the deck beam knees are bolted.

SPAN. A rope or chain made fast at its ends, for a purchase to be hooked to its bight: such as that used on a gaff for the peak purchase to hook on to.

Also, a double rope with thimbles seized betwixt the two parts, stretched across the rigging as a fair leader for ropes.

*A span of rigging* implies the length of shrouds from a dead-eye on either side round the mast-head, and down to a dead-eye on the same side of the ship.

SPAN-SHACKLE, or SPAN-SHACKLE BOLT. A large bolt with a triangular ring attached to it for lashing anchors, boats, or spars thereto.

SPANISH BURTON. See *Burton*.

SPANISH WINDLASS. A wooden roller having a rope wound round it, through the bight of which rope an iron bolt called a *woolder* is inserted as a lever for heaving it round.

This is used in setting up rigging, and for similar purposes. (Illustrated in *Seamanship* by Lieut. Nares, fig. 90.)

The long-boat of a large ship is often fitted with a Spanish windlass amidships when required to lift an anchor.

SPANKER, or DRIVER (*Fr.* Brigantine). The aftermost sail of a ship or barque. It is a fore-and-aft sail setting on the mizen mast with a boom and gaff. It is often called the *Mizen.* See the article *Trysail.*

SPANNER (or LEVER) OF PARALLEL MOTION. See description of *Steam Engine*, Sect. 21.

SPARS (*Fr.* Espars). The general name for all masts, yards, booms, gaffs, &c.

*Rough spars*, are trees in their unfinished state when cut down, suitable for making masts, yards, &c.

SPAR-DECK, properly signifies a temporary deck laid on any part of a vessel ; and the beams whereon it rests get the name of *skid beams.* 'Thus, a spar deck may be laid in the hold just above the keelson, when endeavouring to float a stranded ship. The term *spar-deck* is now also applied to a ship's upper deck—that is, to the quarter-deck, gangways, and forecastle of a deep-waisted vessel.'

SPEARS. See descriptions of *Jack-Screw*, and *Pump.*

SPECK-BLOCKS. See the article *Flensing.*

SPECK-FALLS. See the article *Flensing.*

SPECKSIONEER. See the article *Flensing.*

SPEED INDICATOR. See *Log-Line.*

SPELL. 'The common term for a portion of time given to any work. *To spell*, is to relieve another person at his work.' (*Dana's Seaman's Manual.*)

SPENCER. A fore-and-aft sail set with a gaff, and sometimes also with a boom, hoisting from a small mast called a *spencer-mast*, just abaft the fore or main mast of a ship or barque. Brigs and schooners have often a spencer abaft the foremast.

A description of a contrivance to serve the purpose of a cork jacket, called after the name of its inventor *a spencer*, is given by Dr. Burney in his edition of *Falconer's Marine Dictionary.*

SPERONARE. A Maltese boat of ancient construction, very remarkable for its speed. It is flat-bottomed and has a mast at the bow rigged with a sprit-sail. (*Dict. de Marine à voiles.*)

SPHEREOMETER. A contrivance 'for facilitating great circle sailing by obviating abstruse calculations.'

SPIDER. 'An iron outrigger to keep a block clear of the ship's side.' (*Seamanship*, by Lieut. Nares, fig. 10.)

SPIDER-HOOP. The hoop going round a mast to secure the shackles to which the futtock-shrouds are attached.

The iron trusses of lower yards are often connected to these spider-hoops.

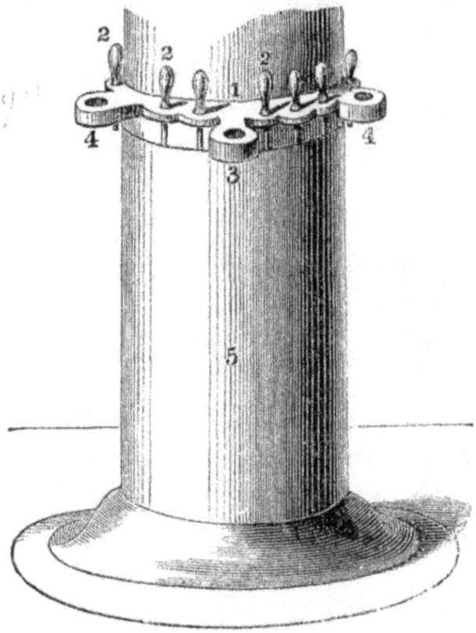


SPIDER HOOP (in a ship of war).

1. Spider-hoop.
2. Belaying pins.
3. Socket for main boom.
4. Socket for swinging boom.
5. Mast.

The name of *spider hoop* is also given to a hoop of iron with belaying pins attached to it, or an iron hoop encircling a wooden rim, into which such pins are inserted for belaying brails or braces to. These are fitted round the masts within a few feet from the deck.

SPIKE *a gun*. To choke up the vent, so as to render the gun unserviceable.

SPIKES, or SPIKE-NAILS. A name for nails of four inches and upwards in length, used for ceiling, &c. See *Nails*.

SPILES. Small wooden pins used as plugs for nail holes; for instance, where sheathing has been taken off a ship's bottom.

SPILINGS, in Shipbuilding, the dimensions of the curve or

sny of a plank's edge. They are commonly measured by means of a rule-staff fastened for this purpose on the ship's timbers.

SPILL *a Sail*: to take the action of the wind off it, either for safety or facility of management.

SPILLING-LINES. Ropes used in bad weather to spill a sail, in order that it may be furled with safety. They are used principally for the lower sails.

SPINDLE. A pin or bar, on which anything revolves; as the iron pin whereon a vane or a capstan turns.

SPIRKETTING, in a ship of war, the strakes of ceiling-plank which work up to the sills of the ports of the several decks; as the *gun-deck spirketting*, the *upper-deck spirketting*, and so on.

In merchant vessels, when there is a strake of ceiling wrought between the upper-deck and the plank-sheer, it is called the *spirketting*, or *quickwork*.

SPIT. A projecting point of a sand-bank.

SPLICE. To join two ropes together, by opening and interweaving their strands: or, to interweave the strands of the end of a rope between those of the bight. The joining so effected is termed *a splice* (Épissure). Explanations of various kinds of splices, with illustrative sketches, are given in *Dana's Seaman's Manual*; also in *Seamanship*, by Lieutenant Nares, figs. 56 to 64, 93, 95, and 97.

SPLIT. A sail is split, when rent by the violence of the wind.

SPLITTING OUT BLOCKS. A process sometimes resorted to when it is necessary to remove the blocks on which a vessel rests on a slip or in a dock, from beneath any part of her keel or bottom, and the pressure is so great *that they cannot be driven out without being split.*

SPONGE *for a gun.* A cylindrical piece of wood covered with lambskin or coarse wool, used for cleaning out, or (as it is termed) 'sponging' the gun after it has been fired. The sponge for a carronade is screwed on the top of a staff, to the other end of which there is generally fixed a wooden *rammer*, for *ramming* or *driving* the charge home when loading the piece: for a long gun the sponge and rammer are fixed each on a separate staff.

SPONSINGS, or SPONCINGS, in a steam ship, the curve of the timbers and planking towards the outer part of the wing before and abaft each of the paddle-boxes. See the article *Wing*.

SPOON-DRIFT. A sort of 'showery sprinkling' of the sea-water swept from the tops of the waves by the violence of the wind, and driven along before it over the surface of the sea.

SPRAY (*Fr.* Écume). 'An occasional sprinkling dashed from the top of a wave by the wind or by its striking an object.'

SPRING. A rope put out at either side of a vessel (generally abaft) and made fast to her cable, while at anchor, for the purpose of changing her position, or of steadying, or casting her, as may be required. Springs are used on other occasions; for example, in mooring a vessel at a quay, &c.

*A spar is said to be sprung* when it is cracked or split without the part being altogether broken off; and the crack is called *a spring*.

SPRING *a leak*. To begin to leak.

SPRING *the Luff*, is to bring a vessel's head closer to the wind. See *Luff*.

SPRING-STAY. A smaller stay before the regular one to assist it in a fore-and-aft-rigged vessel.

SPRING-TIDE (*Fr.* Vif de l'eau, Maline). See *Tide*, 4, 5.

SPRIT, or SPUR, in a sheer-hulk, a spar for keeping the sheers out to the required distance in order to preserve the head of them plumb with the centre of the ship when taking out or putting in masts.

SPRIT. A pole used for spreading the sails of some boats. Its lower end rests in a becket or snotter, which encircles the lower part of the mast, and the other end spreads and raises the outer upper corner of the sail diagonally. A sail so rigged is called a *spritsail*.

SPRITSAIL. A boat's spritsail is a quadri-lateral sail, having its fore leech attached to the mast by lacings. It is elevated and extended by a small pole called a sprit, crossing the sail diagonally, and its lower end resting in a wreath or collar of rope called a *snotter*. (*Kipping's Elementary Treatise on Sails and Sailmaking*, p. 121. See also *Spritsail-yard*.)

SPRITSAIL-YARD. A yard slung with a parrel across the bowsprit, or secured in this position to the knight-heads. It is used to spread the guys of the jib-boom and flying jib-boom. There was formerly a sail bent to it, called the *spritsail*. See *Whiskers*.

SPUE THE OAKUM (*Fr.* Vomir). A vessel is said to spue the oakum when her straining and labouring at sea forces the oakum out of the seams of her planks.

SPUNYARN. A cord formed by twisting two or more rope-yarns together.

SPUNYARN WINCH (*Fr.* Moulinet à bitord). See *Winch.*

SPURS. See *Shores* and *Sprit.*

SPUR-SHORES. See *Shores* and *Sprit.*

SPURLING LINE. A line extended athwartships between the two foremast shrouds of a vessel, with thimbles spliced into it to serve as fairleaders for the running-rigging.

Also a name for the line which communicates the movements of the steering-wheel to the pointer of a tell-tale.

SPY-GLASS. The same as *Telescope.*

SQUALL (*Fr.* Bourrasque, Grain). A violent gust of wind. The following description of squalls is extracted from the introduction to *Horsburgh's India Directory*: —

THE ARCHED SQUALL, is one which is frequently experienced: it is 'usually distinguished by the arched form of the clouds near the horizon; but sometimes it assumes the appearance of a dense black cloud, particularly when highly charged with rain or with electric matter.' From the time of its being seen above the horizon, its motion is sometimes so rapid as scarcely to allow a ship to reduce the necessary sail before the wind reaches her, which happens when the cloud has approached the zenith. As a general rule, it may be observed that these squalls are seldom so furious when they are followed, as when they are preceded by rain.

THE DESCENDING SQUALL, issues from clouds which are formed in the lower parts of the atmosphere near the observer; hence it is not so easily anticipated as the former, because clouds thus formed generally produce showers and successive squalls.

THE WHITE SQUALL, 'is not often experienced, but it sometimes happens near, or within the tropics, especially in the vicinity of mountainous land. This squall generally blows with great violence for a short time; and as it is liable to happen when the weather is clear, without any appearance in the atmosphere to indicate its approach, it is consequently very dangerous. The only mark that accompanies it is the white broken water on the surface of the sea which is torn up by the force of the wind.'

Some further interesting particulars are noticed by Captain Horsburgh on this subject.

SQUARE. *To square a vessel's yards*, is to lay them at right angles to her keel by trimming with the braces, at the same time bringing them horizontal by means of the lifts.

*A vessel is said to have square yards* when they are unusually long. *A sail is said to be very square in the head* when it is broad at the head.

SQUARE-FRAMES, in Shipbuilding, are those frames which are square with the line of the keel, having no bevelling upon them.

SQUARE KNOT. See *Knot*.

SQUARE-RIGGED. Having square sails.

SQUARE-SAIL. A quadrilateral, that is, a four-cornered sail, set across a vessel, having its head extended by a yard.

SQUARE SAIL BOOM. A boom hooked on to an eye-bolt in the fore part of the foremast in any fore-and-aft-rigged vessel, for the purpose of booming out the square-sail, and setting the lower studding-sail.

SQUARE SAIL YARD. See *Cross-jack-yard*.

SQUARE TUCK. When the after part of a ship terminates in a straight plane which is nearly vertical, instead of the plank running up to the counter, she is said to have a *square tuck*.

SQUARING OFF, in Shipbuilding, signifies plugging off and otherwise tightening the treenails, and chinsing all rents and shakes in the planks, after the seams have been caulked.

STAGES, or STAGING (*Fr.* Échafauds). Any platforms or scaffolding on which shipwrights perform their work, whether in building or repairing vessels: they are also termed *Shifting-Stages*. The stages erected to convey timber, &c., on board, are called *Stage-gangways* or *Brows*.

*Floating-stages*, used in like manner for shipwright's performing their work, are a kind of raft in form somewhat resembling a small punt.

STANCHIONS, or ROUGH-TREE TIMBERS (*Fr.* Étançons). Upright pieces of timber placed at intervals along the side of a vessel to support the bulwarks and rail. (Plates II. fig. 6, and IV. 26.) There are, in like manner, *Stanchions* to support the gallows and fife-rail. The stanchions for the hammock-nettings, awning, &c., are made of iron. See also *Quarter-stanchions*. *Stanchions*, or (perhaps more properly) *Pillars*, also mean the square or turned pieces of timber, &c., erected perpendicularly under the middle of the beams as supports. Those which are under the hold-beams of a merchant vessel, and rest on the top of the keelson or keelson rider, are called *Hold-stanchions* (*Fr.* Épontilles): those which are immediately above these and between the hold-beams and upper-deck beams are called the *'tween deck stanchions.* They are sometimes made of iron. In iron ships these stanchions consist of simple round bars of iron, and are generally applied to the alternate deck beams. See *Grantham on Iron Shipbuilding*, p. 33.

STANDARDS. Upright posts erected round a shipbuilding or repairing slip for the purpose of supporting stages, &c., on which to perform the work. The most efficient kind of standard is that which is split with a saw right down the middle, wooden nuts being bolted between the halves to keep them asunder; bolts are driven through the standard at convenient heights to support the ends of the *Bearers*; that is, the pieces of plank placed on edge for the stages to rest upon.

STANDARD-KNEES, or DECK-STANDARD KNEES, in Shipbuilding, iron knees having two tails, the one tail going on the bottom of a deck-beam, the other on the top of a hold-beam, while the middle part is bolted to the ship's side. (Plate II. fig. 6.) These, as well as double-tailed fore-and-aft knees, are also called *Staple-knees*, or *Staple-lodging knees.*

A knee fayed vertically beneath a *hold-beam*, with one arm bolted on the lower side of the beam, is termed a *hanging-standard knee.*

STAND BY! An order to be prepared.

STAND OFF AND ON. To stand alternately on different tacks from and towards the shore; in other words, alternately to recede from and approach the land while sailing by the wind.

A vessel is said to be *standing* on a certain tack or in a certain direction to windward when she is sailing on that tack or in that direction.

STANDING BACKSTAYS. Ropes extended from the topmast, topgallant mast, and royal mast heads, to the afterpart of each channel for the support of these masts. (Plates III. and IV.) See *Backstays.*

STANDING-JIB. The same as *Jib*; a large sail extended on the *jib-stay* to the extremity of the *jib-boom* which runs out from a vessel's bowsprit. The flying jib sets outside of it on the flying jib-boom.

STANDING-LIFTS. Ropes which come from the mast-heads to the ends of the upper yards to keep them steady when the sail is not set. See *Lifts.*

STANDING-RIGGING, implies the ropes or chains that are used for the support of the masts. See *Rigging.*

STANDING PART (*Fr.* Dormant) *of a Rope.* That part which is made fast to the strop of one of the blocks of a tackle.

The standing part *of a hook,* is that part which is attached to a block, chain, or anything which is to heave the hook up with a weight suspended to it.

STANTIONS. See *Stanchions.*

STAPLES. Crooked pieces of iron with their points made sharp so that they may be driven into anything; they are used for various purposes, as for securing a vessel's false keel to the main-keel; when applied to this purpose in a coppered vessel, they are made either of mixed metal or of copper.

STAPLE-KNEES, or STAPLE-LODGING KNEES. See *Standard-knees.*

STARBOARD, or STARBOARD-SIDE (*Fr.* Tribord). The right hand side of a vessel, looking forward.

STARBOARD THE HELM. To put the tiller to the starboard side of the ship. See *Helm.*

STARBOWLINES. A cant name used by sailors for the men in the starboard watch. *Larbowlines* is in like manner applied to those in the larboard, or (as it is now called) the port watch.

STARS. See *Constellations.*

START *an Anchor.* To make it lose its hold of the ground. *Start a cask,* to open it. *Start a tack,* or *a sheet,* to slack it off a little. See also *Butt* and *Harpoon.*

STATION-BILL. A list of the appointed stations of a ship's company when working her.

STAY. To tack a vessel: to go about: or to bring the ship's head up to the wind in order to put her about.

A vessel in the act of tacking is said to be *in stays,* or to be *hove in stays*: if she work slowly in tacking, she is said *to be slack in stays*: and if her head will not come round, she is said *to miss stays.*

STAY (*Fr.* Étai). A large rope used to support a mast, and leading from its head down to some other mast or spar, or to some part of the ship. Those which lead forward are called *fore-and aft stays*, and those which lead down to the vessel's sides *backstays*. (Plates III. IV. and V.)

In large vessels there are *two* fore-and-aft stays to the main-mast, and often also to the fore and mizen masts. On the aftermost of the two, which used to be the smaller, and was termed a *spring-stay*, a staysail is in some ships hoisted.

A mast is said to be *stayed forward* when an additional strain is put on its stay or stays, in order to make it incline a little forward.

FUNNEL-STAYS. Chains or ropes, leading from eye-plates near the top of the funnel to the ship's sides, used to secure the funnel of a steam ship.

STAY-BARS, or STAY-RODS, for framing of marine engine. See description of *Steam Engine*, Sect. 34.

STAY-PEAK. See *A-stay*.

STAYSAIL. A triangular sail which hoists upon a stay: as the *main, fore*, or *mizen staysail, topmast staysail*, and *topgallant staysail*. The *royal staysail*, used chiefly in ships of war, is extended on the main-royal stay.

Spencers are now commonly used instead of *lower* staysails.

STAYSAIL-NETTING. The netting above a vessel's bow-sprit, for stowing away the fore-topmast staysail.

STAY-TACKLE. A tackle suspended (generally by a pendant) from a vessel's fore or main stay, for hoisting in and out boats, or moving other heavy bodies.

STEADY! An order to the steersman, while under way, to keep the ship's head as it is at the moment. In a ship of war, when close-hauled, '*thus!*' is the order given.

STEALER, STEALING-STRAKE, or, perhaps more properly, STOWING-STRAKE, in Shipbuilding, a name given to the fore-most or aftermost plank in a strake which is not run all the way to the stem or stern, but is tapered off, and butts against a notch or *joggle* in another plank. This method of working the plank, when the end next the stem or stern has to be wrought very narrow, is adopted for the purpose of avoiding the sny occasioned by a full bow or quarter. See *Jugle*.

STEAM-BOAT (*Fr.* Bateau à vapeur, confined in its sense in France to a steamer under sixty horse-power). The same as *Steam-Ship*: more properly applied to the smaller class of steamers.

STEAM CHEST (*Fr.* Réservoir pour la vapeur). See description of *Steam Engine*, Sect. 37.

STEAM CRANE. See *Crane*.

STEAM CYLINDER, with appendages. See description of *Steam Engine*, Sects. 1, 22, and 23.

STEAM ENGINE (MARINE), or THE MARINE ENGINE. The name given to steam engines which are used to propel vessels, whether on the ocean or on rivers. Steam vessels, in this country, generally use *condensing* engines; and, although there are various plans of constructing these, yet the principle of the engine is the same in all; they have all the same main acting parts, though not put together or worked in the selfsame manner.

The kind of engine formerly in most general use for the purposes of navigation was the *Side-lever Engine*, in which the motion is communicated by the intervention of side-levers.

The different kinds of steam engines now in use are noticed at the end of this article. For the purpose of definition, the following description of the *Side-lever Condensing Engine* with short D slide-valves is here given just as it was prepared for the first edition of this Dictionary.

In Plate I., fig. 3 shows the engine erected in its place in the ship; fig. 1 is a plan of the engine, and fig. 2 a longitudinal section; all of them showing the engine at half-stroke, that is, with its side-levers level.

### STEAM CYLINDER.

1. *The Cylinder* (C, Plates I. and II.), being the chief part of the engine (for it is within this that the power of the steam is applied to give motion to the machinery), ranks first in describing the parts. It is simply a cylindrical tube of metal bored to the diameter required. The relative power of the engine is proportionate to the size of this diameter.

The cylinder is steam-tight at the foot, and firmly bolted to the engine bottom, and closed above by the *cylinder-cover*, which is a lid of metal with a hole in the centre for the piston-rod working through; this hole is kept steam-tight by a 'stuffing-box,' on the top of the cylinder-cover, filled with hemp kept well soaked with tallow, and the cover of this box, being screwed firmly on the hemp, presses it together and against the piston-rod, and thus prevents steam from passing through.

2. *Slide-valve Casing* (B, Plates I. and II.). On one side of the cylinder is this casing which covers the *nosles* (or *steam*

*ports*), and confines the *slide-valves.* The steam which is to be introduced into the cylinder enters the casing from the boiler by the steam pipe *p.* Within the casing, at the top and bottom of the cylinder, are the two *nosle-faces,* which are square plates of brass raised upon the cylinder, one round each of the steam ports, for the valve-plates to slide upon. These *steam ports* (the upper port marked *o*, and the lower port *u*, in fig. 2) are oblong passages leading from the nosle-faces to the inside of the cylinder: by them the steam enters and returns above and below the piston.

3. *Slide-valves* (D, sections in Plates I. and II.). The use of these is to change the admission of the steam into and its eduction from the cylinder by the upper and lower steam ports alternately. The valves shown here are what are called the short D slide-valves, each resembling a half cylinder with a plate across its diameter, which thus gives it the form of the letter D, whence they derive their name. They slide with the flat part or diameter of the D upon the nosle-faces.

Directly facing the steam ports there are recesses in the casing, called packing-boxes, filled with hemp-packing and tallow, which are pressed against the back or cylindrical part of the slide-valves by means of screws, and as there is no passage through the valves, these packings form steam-tight partitions separating the top and bottom of the casing from the middle part; they also serve to press the valves against the nosle-faces.

The steam pipe *p* from the boiler enters the casing at the middle part, and the eduction of the steam takes place from the top and bottom of the casing by passages leading directly into the condenser. With reference to the following explanation, *it must be particularly kept in mind, that in the engine which is here shown, the middle of the casing alone communicates with the boiler, and its two ends both communicate with the condenser.*

When the valves are at the centre of their stroke, the valve-faces, which are somewhat broader than the steam ports, completely cover these ports. The distance between the valve-faces is such that, when the valves are at the top of their stroke, the top valve-face must have passed above its port *o*, leaving it open to the centre of the casing, and thus letting steam in to the top of the cylinder; and the under valve-face must also have passed above its port *u*, leaving it open to the foot of the casing, and thus letting the steam from the bottom of the cylinder into the condenser. Figs. 1 and 2 in Plate II. show the valve-faces at their two extreme positions: fig. 1 shows the lower port open to the steam and the upper one to the condenser; and fig. 2 shows the bottom open to the condenser and the top to the steam.

See Section 31 of this description.

4. *Slide-valve Rod* (*f*, sections in Plates I. and II.). The slide-valves are connected by this rod, jointed to both, and passing out through the casing-cover, the opening in which is kept steam-tight, in the same manner as that in the cylinder-cover for the piston-rod, by a stuffing-box.

5. The weight of the slide-valves is balanced by the *counter-balance weight* (*i* in figs. 1 and 2, Plate I.), which is suspended from the end of a *lever j*; fixed upon the *weigh-shaft* or *wiper-shaft g*, on that side which is opposite to the valves. This forms an equipoise to the valves, and takes their weight off the work of the engine. The journals or bearings on the ends of the wiper-shaft lie in bushes, which are fixed upon the frame of the engine.

6. *Cylinder Escape-valves* (*a* in figs. 1 and 2, Plate I.). At each end of the cylinder is a small conical valve, called an *escape-valve*, for the purpose of letting off any *water* that may collect above or below the piston, and which, owing to the very incompressible nature of water, would do serious injury unless allowed an outlet. Each of these valves is kept on its seat by a spring of a pressure exceeding that of the steam, but not sufficient to resist the water when forced by the piston.

7. *Throttle-valve* (not seen in the Plates). This is a valve in the steam pipe, used for the purpose of shutting off and letting on the steam, and for regulating the quantity; it is moved by a small lever at the side of the steam pipe.

8. *The Piston* (P in fig. 2, Plate I.) is a body of metal fitting the bore of the cylinder, and made to slide easily upwards and downwards within it, in order by its reciprocating movement to communicate motion to the engine. Steam is kept from passing between the circumferences of the piston and cylinder by means of cast-iron rings encircling the circumference of the piston; the rings are cut into several portions and pressed against the cylinder by springs placed behind each of the parts; there are generally two or more rings, the cutting of one coming under a solid part of another. They form an excellent packing, which improves after being in use for a short time.

9. *The Piston-rod* (R in fig. 2, Plate I.) is firmly fixed in the piston by a key driven through both. This rod passes through the

cylinder-cover, as already noticed, and is connected to the side-levers by the cross-head T and side-rods *l*, Plate I.

10. Having described the different parts in connection with the cylinder, let us now see how they act. Suppose the throttle-valve to be opened, for admission of steam to the cylinder, the piston to be at the top of the cylinder, and the slide-valve at the top of the casing; both valve-faces being above their ports, the upper port (*o* in fig. 2, Plate II.) is open to the steam in the middle of the casing, while the lower port *u* is open to the foot of the casing, and consequently communicates with the condenser; the steam then rushing in from above presses down the piston. When the piston reaches the bottom of the cylinder, the slide-valves are lowered to the position shown in fig. 1, Plate II., and both valve-faces being now below their ports, the lower port *u* is in its turn open to the steam in the body of the casing, while the upper port *o* is open to the top of the casing, and thus communicates with the condenser; consequently, the steam from the body of the casing is admitted below the piston and raises it again, the steam that is above passing at the same time to the condenser. When the piston reaches the top, the valves are again reversed, and so on, alternately lowering and raising the piston.

### CONDENSER.

11. *The Condenser* is a very important part of the low-pressure engine, as it is within it that the steam, after having done its duty in raising or depressing the piston, is instantly reduced to water of about a seventeen-thousandth part of its bulk, thus leaving the rest of the space void.

In the marine engine it is a large chamber (V in Plate I.) standing close to the cylinder, and about the centre of the engine. A pipe *z'* called the *injection pipe*, with a cock fitted thereto, is fixed in its interior, and communicates with the water on the outside of the ship; from this pipe a shower of water constantly plays into the condenser while the engine is working; the water is injected in such a manner that the steam entering from the cylinder must mix with it, and is thereby instantly condensed, by which means a vacuum is made in that end of the cylinder which is for the time in communication with the condenser, thus taking away all obstruction from one side of the piston, and giving no hindrance to the pressure of steam upon the other side.

Numerous plans have been tried to condense by surface cooling instead of by injection. This is a desirable improvement for several reasons: it would require a smaller air-pump, and would give a considerable saving in the wear of boilers, besides allowing them to generate steam more speedily, for the same water could be returned to the boiler, and the only additional water required would be a supply to make up for leakage. Among the many plans which have been tried for condensation by surface cooling, *Hall's Condenser* is especially to be noticed. It is composed of a number of tubes of a very small bore, which are immersed in flowing water, and are thus kept always cool; hence the steam on entering them is condensed on the cold sides. This has been found to answer very well, but is not equal to condensation by jet.

The condenser is generally cast in a piece with the *engine-bottom* K, so as to make a firm substantial body, and the main centre gudgeon for the side-levers working upon is fixed through the condenser at the centre of the engines.

12. *Blow-through Valve* (not shown in Plates). This valve is for the purpose of admitting steam into the condenser, in order to clear it of air and water before starting the engine. It accordingly opens a communication between the middle part of the slide-valve casing and the condenser, both the steam ports *o* and *u* being at the same time shut.

13. *Tail-valve* (*k* in fig. 2, Plate I.). The *tail-valve,* or *snifting-valve,* is at the opposite side of the air-pump from the condenser, and is connected with the latter by a pipe under the air-pump; it opens when pressed by steam entering the condenser by the blow-through valve, but the weight of the atmosphere is sufficient to keep it shut so long as there is a vacuum in the condenser.

When the blow-through valve is opened, the steam from the casing (the throttle-valve being at the same time open, and the injection-cock shut) rushes in and fills the condenser, and by its elastic force drives out through the tail-valve any gases and water which may have accumulated in the condenser.

### AIR-PUMP.

The use of this pump is to remove the water and gases accumulating in the condenser while the engine is at work.

14. *The Air-pump* (A in Plate I.) consists of a metal *barrel* or cylinder, wherein a *bucket* or open piston Z is worked from top to bottom by means of the *pump-rod* G with its *cross-head* Q, by

which the rod is moved up and down. It is provided with certain valves which we shall describe in succession.

15. *The Foot-valve* S is a flat plate of metal filling up the passage between the air-pump and condenser. It turns upon a hinge at the top, and when pressed from the condenser opens towards the air-pump, so as to allow water to flow through, but, when pressed from the pump, falls shut and prevents all passage.

16. *The Bucket-valve* W is a round valve which opens upwards when pressed by water in the air-pump beneath it, but when such pressure is withdrawn, falls shut by its own weight, so that no water can return which has once passed through.

17. *The Discharge-valve* E′ is of the same construction as the bucket-valve, and opens in the same way; it covers the top of the barrel, opening when pressed from below, and when not so pressed falling shut, and thus preventing all passage of water back again.

18. Now suppose the bucket Z to be at the foot of the air-pump: when the engine begins to move it upwards by means of the pump-rod G, if there be any water above the bucket-valve W it will be lifted along with the valve, and this water pressing against the discharge-valve E will raise it, and entering the hot-well H flow through the discharge-pipe *g* into the sea. When the bucket rises, it will leave behind it a vacuum, causing the water and gases accumulated in the condenser to press open the foot-valve S, and to enter at the foot of the air-pump till the balance of pressure is restored, when the foot-valve will close from its own weight. When the bucket again begins to descend from the top of the barrel, the upward pressure on the discharge-valve E′ will cease, and the valve will therefore fall by its own weight, and by that of the water and atmosphere above it; as the bucket descends it therefore leaves a void behind it, and the pressure of the bucket upon the water and gases below it will cause them to raise the valve W and pass above the bucket till it reaches the foot of the air-pump, when the ascent will commence as before. By this means the air and water are drawn out of the condenser, and discharged at the top of the air-pump.

The air-pump is closed at the top by a cover of much the same form as the cylinder-cover, and is bolted on to the engine-bottom by a flange near the foot of the pump. The air-pump is either made of brass, or lined with that metal, to prevent corrosion from the salt water, which has a very injurious effect on cast iron.

All the valves exposed to the action of salt water are for the same reason also made of brass.

The cylinder stands at one end of the side-levers, and the air-pump near the other end, between the condenser and connecting-rod N, so that when the piston is at the top of its stroke, the air-pump bucket is at the bottom of its stroke, and so on alternately.

19. *Hot-well* (H in fig. 2, Plate I.). As already adverted to, this forms part of the discharge passage from the air-pump into the sea, and it is intended as a reservoir whence to feed the boiler with the warm water received out of the condenser, part of which is for that purpose drawn off from the hot-well by means of the *Feed-pump r*, worked by two side-rods attached to one of the side-levers. When there is a sufficiency of water in the boiler the feed-pump is still kept working, but the water is returned by another pipe into the discharge passage.

The gases which enter the hot-well from the air-pump ascend into the *Air-cone a c*, and escape through a pipe at the top of it.

20. For the purpose of saving fuel, especially in long voyages, the steam is made to work expansively. To effect this, the steam is, by means of the *Expansion-valve* (not shown in the Plates), shut off in its passage to the slide-valves, when the piston has travelled a certain distance in the cylinder, which is regulated by the engineer adjusting that valve so as to shut off the steam at any part of the stroke that his experience finds to be suitable. When the steam is thus cut off, the quantity which has already entered the cylinder sends the piston the remaining distance by its inherent expansive force, whereby a great part of the elasticity of the steam is made use of that would otherwise be lost.

The parts which have been described are those which have to do with the immediate action of the steam. We shall now explain the mechanical arrangements for transmitting the reciprocating movement of the piston to the rotative motion of the paddle-shaft, and the method in which the valves and pumps, &c., are worked.

21. *Side-Levers* (L in Plate I.). Of these there are two, one on each side of the cylinder, alongside the engine, resembling the beam of the ordinary land engine. They work upon a centre gudgeon, which is a large rod of malleable iron fixed through the condenser in the very centre of the engine. A pin or centre is

fixed at each end of both levers, one at the cylinder end, to which the side-rods *l* are connected, and one at the crank end, to which the connecting-rod N is strapped. Both ends of the levers are forked, and the straps of the side-rods and the cross-tail X are connected to the pins between the branches. There are also several studs along the centre line of the levers to which the pump-rods and the *parallel-bar* (*d* in fig. 2) are connected.

In order to reconcile the curved sweep which the ends of the side-levers describe with the perpendicular movement of the piston-rod by means of which they are driven, a *parallel motion* is formed between the rods *d* and *l* and the side-levers and the rod *c*, which, by the intervention of a lever *e*, causes the *radius bar of parallel motion c* (in fig. 2) to guide the side-rods *l* in such a manner that their upper points may move in connection with the cross-head T in a direct line up and down. The lever *e* is called the *Spanner* or *Lever of Parallel Motion*: *b* is the *Parallel Motion Shaft*.

22. *Cylinder Cross-Head* (T in Plate I.). On the top of the piston-rod is the cross-head, stretching out athwart the cylinder. The bearings on the end of it, from which the cylinder side-rods hang, are directly over the bearings on the ends of the side-levers.

23. *Cylinder Side-Rods* (*l*, figs. 1 and 3, Plate I.). These rods hang from each end of the cross-head, one on each side of the cylinder, and they are connected to the pins of the side-levers below; thus forming links between the cross-head and side-levers, and causing the whole to move simultaneously.

24. *The Air-Pump* has a *cross-head* (Q in figs. 1 and 2, Plate I.) and *side-rods* (*m* in fig. 1), similar to those of the cylinder, and connected to the side-levers in the same manner. Its cross-head is kept moving in a direct line by two *guide-rods* (4 in fig. 2).

25. *The Feed-Pump* (*r* in Plate I.) is also worked by *side-rods*, but connected only to one of the side-levers, the side-rods hanging one on each side of it.

26. *The Bilge-Pumps* (*s* in figs. 1 and 3, Plate I.), which are pumps so placed as to clear the ship of bilge-water, are each worked by a single link off one of the levers. Each engine has two bilge-pumps: in iron vessels the pipes connected with these pumps are laid through the water-tight bulk-heads, right fore-and-aft, so that they may clear the whole ship.

27. *Connecting-Rod* (N in fig. 2, Plate I.). This rod serves to

connect the side-levers and crank together. The foot of it is fixed into the cross-tail X, and the other end is strapped on to the crank-pin.

28. *Cross-Tail* (X in figs. 2 and 3, Plate I.). The cross-tail is of the same form as the cylinder cross-head: it has iron straps catching the pins in the ends of the side-levers.

29. *Crank* (U, figs. 1 and 2, Plate I.) and *Crank-Shaft* Y. When there are two engines, as is generally the case in sea-going vessels, the crank-shaft is in three pieces; the *intermediate shaft* (Y 2 in fig. 1), common to both engines; and the two *Paddle-Shafts* Y, one to each engine, on which the paddles are fixed: when the crank-pins are in their places, all these move as firmly as if they were one piece.

*The Crank* is a bend or knee on the shafting, which, being pushed up on one side and pulled down on the other, moves the shafts round with a circular motion. It is composed of two pieces, being two arms or slabs of iron, one on each shaft.

*The Crank-Pin* (*x* in fig. 1, Plate I.) goes through both arms of the crank at their extremities: to this pin the connecting-rod is attached.

30. In the manner now described, all the working parts are connected together. When the piston-rod moves up, the side-rods must accordingly go up along with it, as well as those ends of the side-levers to which they are attached: this will depress the other ends of the side-levers to which the connecting-rod is attached, and the connecting-rod will bring down the crank till the piston arrives at the top of the cylinder, at which time, the steam being reversed, the piston begins to descend; consequently, the side-rods and the cylinder ends of the side-levers must descend along with it, and the other ends of the side-levers with the connecting-rod will rise, taking the crank up on the opposite side from that on which it went down, till the piston arrives at the foot of the cylinder, when, the steam being again reversed, the crank is carried round again.

The air-pump being towards that end of the side-lever which is farthest from the cylinder, its bucket takes an opposite movement from that of the piston; so when the steam piston is moving up the air-pump bucket is going down.

31. The slide-valves are moved by the *Eccentric*, which is shown in fig. 3, Plate II. E is a side view of the eccentric, and S shows the hoop within which it plays.

The eccentric, as is shown here, is a wheel placed upon the crank-shaft with its centre not at the same point, but to one side of the axis of the shaft, 1 being the axis of the shaft, and 2 the centre of the eccentric; so that when the shaft revolves upon its centre 1, the centre 2 of the eccentric describes a circle round 1. If the distance that 2 is placed from 1 be half the length which the slide-valves are required to travel, then the diameter of the circle round 1 will be the whole length of travel. See explanatory diagram, fig. 4.

In order, then, to communicate motion to the slide-valves, the hoop s in figs. 1, 2, and 3, Plate II., with a rod *v* branching off one side of it, is placed on the circumference of the eccentric, within which hoop the eccentric is allowed to turn smoothly; the other end of the rod *v* catches the end of the gab-lever *m*, which is fixed on the weigh-shaft, and moves simultaneously with it, as does also the slide-valve lever *h*, which is fixed on the same shaft; this lever *h* is connected with the valve-rod *f* by a jointed strap which prevents the upper end of the rod from being moved out of the direct line in the short distance it has to travel up and down. In the diagram (fig. 4) the same letters are used to indicate the levers and rods as in the figs. 1 and 2. The full lines show the eccentric at its extreme outward position, the eccentric rod *v* catching the gab-lever *m* at the point *a*. When the paddle shaft makes half a revolution, it will carry the centre of the eccentric from 2 to 3, and put the eccentric into the position shown by the dotted circle; the rod *v* being thus pushed out will move the lever *m* from *a* to *a′*, consequently the lever *h* will be carried from *b* to *b′*, and the extremity of the valve-rod *f* moved from *c* to *c′*, which (if these two levers be of equal length) will be the same distance as the centre of the eccentric moved from 2 to 3. If the paddle-shaft complete the full revolution, the eccentric, with the rod and levers, will be carried from the position indicated by the dotted lines back to their original position. Figs. 1 and 2, Plate II., show the eccentric connected with the slide-valves at their two extreme positions. Fig. 1 shows the valves full down, and fig. 2 shows them full up: U points out the positions of the crank at the same times.

32. The eccentric has a notch, or *gab* as it is called, fitting a pin in the *gab-lever m*. By lifting the end of the eccentric rod off this pin in the gab-lever, the connection between the engine and slide-valves is broken, and the valves can then be worked by

hand, by means of a series of levers fitted to them for this purpose.

The valves open the ports, both for the admission and eduction of steam a little before the end of the stroke of the piston, and thus the steam, entering just before the piston comes to the end of its stroke, serves as a cushion, and gives the piston an easy turn on its next stroke. To effect this, the eccentric is set so as to give its strokes a little before the crank.

The eccentric is loose on the crank-shaft, and has a catch or projection upon it, with a corresponding projection on the shaft; the catch has two faces, one suiting the direction of the valves when the engine is going forward, and the other when it is backing, so that the same eccentric serves to drive the engine either way.

33. The most critical position of the crank is when it is either at the top or bottom of its stroke, for there the pressure of the steam has no effect in turning the crank, which must trust to the impetus it has already received. This, in a single engine, gives a very unequal motion to the paddles, making them go quick at one point and slow at another: but when there are two engines, this effect is counteracted by the cranks being set at right angles to one another; thus, when the starboard crank is at its top or bottom point, where the steam has no effect upon it, the larboard crank is horizontal, and exerting all its force, and helps to carry the starboard one over its centre, by which means an equal motion is given to the engine at all its different points.

34. The paddle-shafts and intermediate shaft rest on the top of a strong *frame* (1 in fig. 2, Plate I.), supported on columns and bolted firmly to the engine bottom; and the diagonal part of this framing extends down to the cylinder, to which it is securely fixed. Each engine has two of these frames, the whole supported by strong malleable iron *stay-bars* or *stay-rods* (*i* in figs. 1 and 2). Each engine also has supports catching the beams of the vessel above the engine. The framing shown here is of cast iron, but a malleable iron framing is coming into use, which is much lighter, and at the same time very elegant. The side-levers, we may notice, are also sometimes made of malleable iron, which is a great saving of weight.

35. *The Paddle-Wheels*, or *Paddles*, by the action of which upon the water the ship is impelled, revolve within a strong framing of wood standing out on each side of the vessel; the

principal part of this framing consists of the projecting ends of the *paddle-beams* with a fore-and-aft beam of wood fitted between them, called a *spring beam,* which supports the outer end of the *paddle-shaft,* the iron axis whereon the paddle-wheels revolve. A semicircular casing called the *paddle-box,* mounted on this frame, covers in the upper half of each wheel. The propelling boards fixed on the radiating arms of the wheel near their extremities are termed *floats*: the arms are bound together by strong iron rings. Farther explanations are given under the article *Paddle-Wheel.* See also the article *Screw-Propeller.*

36. Before starting the engines, the throttle-valve (Sect. 7 of this description) is opened, and the body of the slide-valve casing is thus filled with steam. The blow-through-valve (Sect. 12) is next opened, through which the steam rushes and fills the condenser. The steam being of a higher pressure than the atmosphere, drives out through the snifting-valve *k* (Sect. 13) any water and air that may have gathered in the condenser. The blow-through-valve is then shut, and the steam which remains in the condenser takes the form of water, and leaves a vacuum in its place. The engine is hereupon ready for starting.

The injection-cock is now opened, and a shower of water plays into the condenser. The slide-valves are either raised or lowered by hand as may be required to suit the position which the crank occupies at the time. In the position shown in Plate I., the piston requires to move up in order to urge the vessel forwards; consequently the valves must be lowered by hand, when the steam will rush in below, and there being a vacuum above, the piston will rise, taking along with it the side-rods and cylinder end of the side-levers, and sending down the connecting-rod and crank, which brings round the paddle-wheels and urges the vessel onwards. When the piston has nearly arrived at the top of the cylinder, the slide-valves must be raised by hand in time to give the piston the turn. The steam now rushes in above the piston, while the steam below passes into the condenser, and is instantly reduced to water; this creates a vacuum below the piston; the steam then forces down the piston, sending down the side-rods and cylinder ends of the side-levers, and raising the connecting-rod, and also the crank on the opposite side from that on which it went down, and thus the paddles are kept turning in the same direction. After a few turns by hand, the gab of the eccentric-rod (Sect. 28) is allowed to fall upon its stud on the gab-lever (which is termed *putting the engine in gear*); the slide-valves are then worked by the engine itself, which is by this time set in active motion.

When required to stop slowly, the engineer diminishes the supply of steam by means of the throttle-valve (*at the same time easing the safety-valve*), and the motion of the engine is thereby retarded; he then disconnects the eccentric-rod, or, as it is termed, *throws the engine out of gear*, and puts the slide-valves at half-stroke by hand, which causes both valve-faces to cover their ports, and, the steam being thus completely cut off from the cylinder, the engine soon stops. If required to stop instantaneously, heave the engine out of gear, shut the throttle-valve, at the same time easing the safety-valve, cut off the injection-water from entering the condenser, and raise or depress the slide-valve according as may be required, in order to reverse the steam, by which means the impetus of the piston is thus overcome. In order to reverse or 'back' the engine, taking it in the position shown in Plate I., the slide-valve requires to be *raised* by hand, so that the steam entering above may depress the piston, lower the side-rods and cylinder ends of the side-levers, raise the connecting-rod and crank, send the paddles round in the backward direction, and thus urge the vessel astern.

The eccentric being loose and having two ways of catching, adapts itself to either way the engine goes.

### THE BOILERS.

37. *The Boiler* (N in Plate I. fig. 3) is an apparatus which, being partly filled with water, and fire applied to the outside, generates steam to supply the engine.

*Boilers are made either of malleable iron plates or of copper—the latter makes a much superior boiler, as it does not corrode like iron, and though much more expensive in the first cost, copper boilers will last out two or three sets of iron boilers. Copper boilers are therefore generally used by vessels on distant stations, to avoid the necessity of frequent renewal. The shape of the boilers for marine engines is of little consequence, as the furnaces and flues are in the interior; their shape is therefore adapted to economise room, and the spaces between them and the ship's sides are used as coal boxes.*

The boiler is usually in two or more pieces, and the steam from the boilers of both engines is collected in a *steam chest* (o in fig. 3) placed on the top of them. The pipe which leads the steam to the engines proceeds from this chest.

The best kind of boiler is the *Tubular Boiler*, the furnace mouths for which enter from before or abaft, and the flame and smoke pass through tubes running right through the boiler, surrounded by the water. But, in general, boilers are made simply with *flues* or passages from the furnaces taking as many turns as possible through the water. In fig. 3, *t* is the neck of the flues.

38. *The Funnel* (N in Plate I. fig. 3) is fastened on the top of the steam chest where the flues for both boilers meet.

Water is supplied to the boilers (while the engines are at work) by means of the feed-pumps, which draw it from the hot-wells. But before the fires are on, the boilers first get water by opening the blow-off pipes to the sea, which fills them up to the water-line: the additional water still required is then forced in by the *deck-pumps.* These are pumps at the side of the vessel worked with a lever by manual power, for the purpose of washing the decks, &c.: when the engine is going, they can be connected to it for the use of the ship.

40. Each boiler has a *man-hole,* secured by a door, for convenience of getting in to clean them; this operation requires to be done frequently, as the salt and other matter contained in the water, if allowed to remain long, forms on the inside of the boiler a crust which, being a bad conductor of heat, both wastes fuel and leaves the shell of the boiler exposed to the fury of the fire. There are also *sludge-holes* at the ends of the water passages between the flues, by which the deposit can be raked out.

41. *The Safety-valve* (*a* in Plate I. fig. 3) is a conical valve communicating with the boiler and opening outwardly; it is so loaded that when the steam in the boiler exceeds its proper pressure, it raises the valve and escapes by a pipe called the *waste-steam pipe* (*b* in fig. 3).

The safety-valves are generally situated on the top of the steam chest, at the foot of the funnel.

The best plan of loading a safety-valve is by means of an upright rod, which a number of weights are bored to fit so as to be easily slipped off and on—with a lever to lift them off on emergencies. This is better than a valve with a loaded lever, for, in a heavy sea, the jerking of the lever must be continually changing the pressure.

See Sect. 36 of this description.

42. *Gauge-Cocks.* For ascertaining the height of the water in the boiler, three or more pipes are used, having a cock (called a *gauge-cock*) to each. The lowest pipe is fixed in the side of the boiler, at a depth below which the water should never be allowed to pass, and the highest a little above the proper height of the water. When the cocks are opened and water comes from the lowest pipe and steam from the highest, there is a proper supply of water in the boiler; but if both send out steam, there is too little water, and if both emit water there is too much.

A neater apparatus than the above is a glass tube fixed on the front of the boiler, furnished with a cock at top and bottom—the lower cock at such a depth as always to communicate with the water, and the upper one communicating with the steam: when both cocks are opened together, the water will rise in the tube to the exact height that it is in the boiler, and thus show what quantity is within.

43. *Mercurial Gauge.* To show the pressure of the steam more accurately than can be done by the safety-valve, this gauge is used, consisting of a curved tube, partly filled with mercury; one branch of the tube is open to the steam in the boiler, and the other to the atmosphere; the tube has a scale attached to it, divided into pounds, and this indicates exactly how much either the steam or the atmosphere preponderates the one over the other.

44. Each boiler ought also to have an *internal safety-valve*, opening from the outside, in order to allow air to enter the boiler when the pressure becomes too weak within; because, after blowing-off the boilers, and when the steam within them has cooled down, they would be left in a state of vacuity, and exposed to the external pressure of the atmosphere: such a valve counteracts this, and allows the air to enter when the pressure within becomes weakened.

45. *Blowing-off.* At the foot of each boiler there is a pipe called the *blow-off pipe*, communicating with the sea, and furnished with a *cock* to open or shut it. At the end of every voyage, the blow-off cocks being opened, the steam forces out the water and leaves the boilers empty: the operation is termed *blowing-off.* These cocks are opened also at intervals in the

course of the voyage, to allow the brine which collects at the bottom of the boilers to be blown off; care being taken not to keep them too long open, and so endanger the boilers by letting the water get too low. In some vessels *Brine-pumps* are used for clearing the boiler of this deposit. See *Salinometer.*

The most important and comprehensive work on the subject of the Steam Engine, Steam Navigation, and Steam Naval Architecture, is Mr. Tredgold's valuable Treatise.

Instead of the side lever engines above described, *direct acting engines* are now generally used, in which 'the connecting rod is led at once from the head of the piston-rod to the crank without the intervention of side-levers.'

The varieties of the direct acting engine, including the annular engine, atmospheric engine, double cylinder engine, Fairbairn's engine, Gorgon engines, Humphrey's engine for screw ships, Maudslay and Field's engines, Miller & Ravenhill's engines, the oscillating engine, oscillating horizontal engine, steeple engine, and trunk engine, may be found described and mostly illustrated in *Murray's Rudimentary Treatise on the Marine Engine*, and in *The Marine Steam Engine, by T. J. Maine and Thos. Brown, for the use of Officers in the Navy.*

The general adoption of the screw instead of paddle-wheels as a means of propulsion has also brought into use other modifications of the marine engine in order to suit the horizontal position of the screw shaft, and, in case of ships of war, to obtain protection to the machinery from an enemy's shot. 'With this view the cylinders of *screw engines*' (that is, of engines on board a vessel using a screw propeller) 'are often placed either horizontally or diagonally in the ship.'

STEAM FRIGATE. A large armed steam ship with a battery on a flush upper deck, and a tier of guns on the main deck. See *Frigate.*

STEAM HOIST. See *Hoist.*

STEAM NAVIGATION. The navigating of steam vessels.

STEAM PACKET. A steam vessel employed in trading regularly between two places with goods and passengers. See *Packet.*

STEAM PIPE. See description of *Steam Engine*, Sect. 2: *Waste-Steam-Pipe*, Sect. 41.

STEAM RAM. A vessel propelled by steam to run end on against an 'enemy's ship and crush it in,' the projecting stem or prow being formed of solid iron, forged and fitted as a means of offence for that purpose. Mr. James Nasmyth states that one of the iron steam rams projected by him, of 2,000 tons, would crush in the side of any armour-plated ship.

STEAM SHIP (*Fr.* Bâtiment à vapeur, applied by the French to a steamer above 60 horse-power), STEAM VESSEL, STEAM BOAT, or STEAMER. A vessel propelled by means of steam power, whether through the intervention of paddle-wheels or of a screw-propeller. Steamers are generally built long, narrow, and low, and often flat-floored. See *Filling-Timbers.*

The term *Steam Boat* is evidently more especially applicable to a vessel of little power and burden : *Steam Ship* to greater vessels.

The orders given to direct the engineer in regulating the movements of a steamer by the action of the marine-engine, may be here noticed. *Go a-head!* (or *Go on!*) *Turn a-head! Half-turn a-head! Full speed! Half speed! Stop her!* all of which are self-explanatory phrases. *Ease her!* or *Slow her!* means to reduce the speed of the engine somewhat. *Go slow!* is the order to cut off as much of the steam as is practicable, still keeping the engine in play. *Back her!* is to reverse the movements of the cranks so that the paddles may move round in a backward direction tending to urge the vessel astern. See description of *Steam Engine*, Sect. 36, and *Engine Room Telegraph.*

A PADDLE STEAMER is a steam ship propelled by paddle-wheels: A SCREW STEAMER, one in which the motive power is a screw propeller.

The 'Great Eastern,' of 13,343 tons register, and 18,915 tons burden, the largest steam ship which has been built, is fitted both with screw engines and paddle engines. Authentic plates of this vast iron steam ship are given in *Grantham on Iron Shipbuilding,* but the description of it there given is subject to correction in some of its details.

STEAM SLOOP OF WAR. Any steam vessel of war commanded by a commander in the Royal Navy.

STEAM TUG, or TUG. A steam vessel employed for towing. See *Towing-Bridle.*

STEAM VESSEL (*Fr.* Bâtiment à vapeur). The same as *Steam-Ship.*

STEAM WINCH *with deck pumps.* A machine invented by Messrs. Taylor & Co. to draw water from the fore or after hold of a ship in case of springing a leak, or from the sea in case of fire.

STEAM YACHT. A vessel of pleasure or state propelled by steam-power.

STEAMER. See *Steam Ship*, and *Kiln*.

STEAMING PLANKS. See *Kiln*.

STEEP-TO. A shore or bank is said to be *steep-to*, if it deepens very rapidly in the water.

STEELER. See *Stealer*.

STEER (*Fr.* Gouverner). To guide a ship or boat by the management of the helm. The person who steers is called the *Helmsman*, or *Steersman*.

*To steer small*, means to steer steadily, without putting the helm too much to either side. *To steer large*, is the reverse.

STEERAGE. That part of the 'twixt decks which is immediately before a vessel's cabin, and separated from it by a bulkhead. In merchant ships this space is sometimes fitted up with berths for the petty officers and sailors; but the latter more commonly occupy the forecastle.

In a vessel carrying passengers, those who do not occupy the main cabin and quarter-deck are termed *Steerage passengers*.

STEERAGE, also implies the act of steering: hence, a vessel is said to have *steerage-way* when she has sufficient way to give the helm effect.

STEERING-SAILS. See *Studding Sails*.

STEERING-WHEEL. A wheel erected on a frame either before or over a vessel's tiller, having a horizontal shaft or axle to which a barrel is fixed for winding the wheel-chains around, in order to give greater power and facility in steering.

The wheels in ships of war are double, that is to say, there are two wheels on one shaft or axle, with the barrel abaft them. There is also a tell-tale in front, attached to the aftermost of the two standards on which the axle rests. See *Wheel-ropes*.

*A Steering Apparatus*, contrived by Messrs. Clarke & Pirnie, of Newburgh in Fife, consists of an endless screw revolving between two metal blocks fixed in the deck at one side of the shaft of the steering wheel, and parallel to it: abaft the rudder head there is a sproket wheel on the shaft of the steering wheel, and another sproket wheel of the same diameter immediately opposite to it on the shaft of the screw, with a pitch chain over them for driving the screw. The latter acts upon the segment of a toothed wheel (serving the purpose of a tiller) fixed on the side of the rudder-head. Between each end of the screw shaft and an abutment on the metal block a piece of cork or (which would be preferable) a steel spring is introduced for the purpose of giving the rudder a little play in a heavy sea.

STEERSMAN. See *Steer.*

STEEVE. A bowsprit *steeves* more or less according as it is elevated more or less from the horizontal. *The Steeve* is the angle which it makes with the horizon. (*Dana's Seaman's Manual.*)

STEM (*Fr.* Étrave). The principal timber at the foremost extremity of a vessel, into a rabbet in which the ends of the bow-plank on each side are fixed. Its lower end is scarphed to the keel, and the bowsprit rests on its upper end. It gets the name

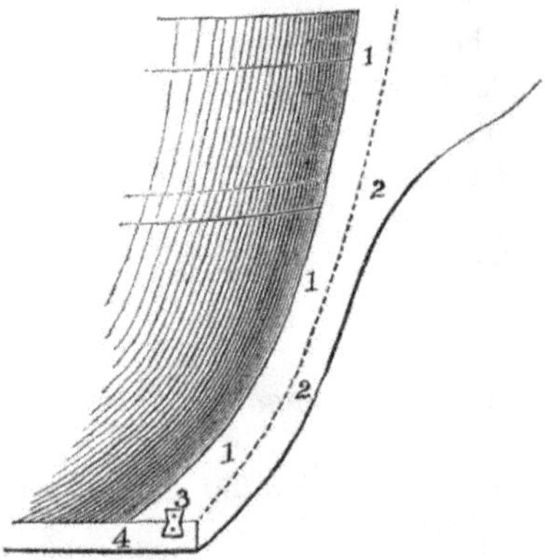


1. Stem or main stem.
2. Cutwater or false stem.
3. Dovetail plate.
4. Keel.

of the *main stem,* to distinguish it from the *cutwater* or *false stem,* which is a piece fayed to the fore part thereof. See *Cutwater.* The main stem, when made of two or more pieces, is usually hook-scarphed. (Plate II. fig. 7: Plate IV. 14, 15.)

STEM-KNEES. Crooked pieces of timber, the bolting of which connects the keel with the stem. See *Deadwood.*

STEMSON. A piece of compass timber wrought on the after part of the apron, to afford additional strength in ships of great burden. Its lower end scarphs on to the keelson, and it should be continued upwards beyond the scarphs of the apron sufficiently far to give a good shifting.

STEP *of a lower Mast.* A clamp of wood bolted on the top

of the keelson, having a mortise into which the tenon on the heel of the mast is inserted. In ships employed in the timber trade, the step of the mizen-mast is, for convenience of stowage, fixed between two of the 'twixt deck beams.

*To step a mast*, is to put it into its step. See also *Boxing.*

STEPPING-LINE. See *Bearding.*

STERN (*Fr.* Poupe). The aftermost part of a vessel above the wing-transom. (Plate II. fig. 5.)

BY THE STERN. If a vessel's stern be lower in the water than her head, she is *by the stern.*

STERN-BOARD. In beating to windward if a vessel fetches sternway on either tack instead of gaining ground she is said *to make a stern-board.* See *Board.*

STERN-BOAT. A name commonly given to the jolly boat, if hung to davits over the ship's stern.

STERN-DAVITS. Pieces of iron or timber projecting from a vessel's stern to hoist boats up to. See *Davits.* (Plate IV. 39.)

STERN-FAST. A rope or chain by which the stern of a vessel is secured to a wharf or quay.

STERN-FRAME (*Fr.* Arcasse). See *Transoms.*

STERN-KNEE. See *Sternson.*

STERN-MOST. The reverse of *Head-most.*

STERN-POST (*Fr.* Étambot). The principal piece of timber in a vessel's stern-frame; to it the rudder is hung and the transoms are bolted. Its lower end is tenoned into the keel. The after ends of the outside planking butt against the stern-post. (Plate II. fig. 5: Plate IV. 5.) The stem and stern-post are the two extremes of a vessel's frame.

THE FALSE STERN-POST is a piece tabled on to the after edge of the main stern-post for the purpose of increasing the action of the rudder, and thereby improving the steering. (Plate IV. 4.)

THE INNER STERN-POST is fayed to the fore edge of the main stern-post, which it serves to strengthen; and its upper end forms a seat for the wing-transom. It also affords a sort of deadwood, on the fore part of which the other transoms are bolted, whereby their lengths are preserved—an object of great importance for the security of the ship, in binding her sides properly together at that part.

They are often named, shortly, the *Main-post, False-post,* and *Inner-post.*

STERN-RAILS, or RAILS OF THE STERN. Narrow

pieces of projecting plank on which mouldings are raised, arranged on a vessel's stern and counter in various forms, according to the fancy of the builder. Of these, there are in very large ships three kinds: the *Knuckle-rails* (at the knuckles of the stern-timbers), the *Counter-rails,* and the *Foot-rails.* See *Counter-rails.*

STERN-SHEETS. The after part of a boat abaft the rowers, furnished with seats for passengers.

STERN-TIMBERS. A general name given to all the timbers in the stern-frame. See *Timbers.*

STERN-WAY. A vessel has stern-way when moving astern. *To fetch stern-way* (*Fr.* Culer), is to acquire motion astern.

STERNSON, or STERN-KNEE. A piece of compass timber forming a continuation of a vessel's keelson, and extending over the deadwood to the stern-post, which is secured to it by bolts.

STEVEDORE. See *Stivadore.*

STEWARD. The person who attends in the cabin and serves out provisions to passengers in a merchant vessel, packet, or steamer. See also *Purser.*

STIFF, expresses the quality of a vessel which is able to carry a great deal of sail without lying over much on her side—the reverse of *Crank.* (*Dana's Seaman's Manual.*)

STIFF BREEZE, implies a wind somewhat stronger than a fresh breeze but not so violent as a gale.

STIRRUPS. Short pieces of rope, each having a thimble spliced into its lower end, through which the foot rope is rove. See *Foot-ropes.*

STIVADORE, or STEVEDORE. A man whose occupation is to stow cargoes on board of ships. Mr. Maclachlan, in his *Treatise on the Law of Merchant Shipping,* observes that 'familiar mention of such a person with the same functions exactly is made in the *Consolato del Mare,* where his name in the original Catalan of that celebrated collection of sea laws is *stibador,* the original, no doubt, of the word now in use.'

STOCK *of an Anchor.* A beam of wood or a bar of iron secured to the upper end of the shank, at right angles with the arms. An iron stock is usually fixed with a lock, and unships, for convenience in stowing it on deck.

RUDDER-STOCK, or MAIN PIECE OF RUDDER. A name for the piece which is connected by the rudder-bands to the stern-post.

STOCKS. The blocks and shores upon which a vessel is

built. Hence, a ship or boat, in the course of building is said to be *on the stocks.*

STOMACH-PIECE. The same as *Apron.*

STOKE-HOLE. A scuttle in a steamer's deck, to admit fuel for the engine. It is also applied to a space for the men standing in to feed and trim the fires.

STOKER, or FIREMAN (*Fr.* Chauffeur). A person employed to feed and trim the fires for the boilers of marine steam-engines. Those who stow and trim the fuel are termed *Coal-Trimmers.*

STOOL. The lowest transom of a vessel's stern-frame, or, more correctly, a chock introduced beneath the lowest transom: to it the lower ends of the fashion pieces are secured.

BACKSTAY-STOOLS. Small channels worked in abaft the principal channels, in some ships, for the chains and dead-eyes of the backstays in order to spread the backstays.

STOP. A temporary fastening for a rope; generally of rope-yarn. The operation is called *Stopping.* A *Stop* also means a projection for anything to rest or bear upon.

*To stop a leak* (*Fr.* Boucher). To close or secure any occasional aperture by which a vessel or boat is making water.

STOP THE VENT, means to thrust a plug into the vent of a muzzle-loading gun while sponging the piece and ramming home the charge, so that any spark or fire in the gun may be extinguished. See *Vent-Plug.*

STOP-WATER-BORES, in Shipbuilding, auger holes made, one through the keel and the after corner of the stem-foot, another through the keel and the fore corner of the stern-post, at their joining with the keel; a treenail (called the *stop-water*) being driven through each, to prevent the admission of water into the ship, at these joints.

STOPPAGE *in transitu.* The exercise of that right which the law gives to the consignor (or the shipper) of goods to stop them *in transitu*, that is, *on their passage* to the consignee (or the buyer) when the latter has become bankrupt or insolvent, and 'before or at their arrival at the place of destination to cause them to be delivered to the consignor himself or to some other person for his use.'

STOPPER (*Fr.* Bosse). A stout rope with a knot at one end, and sometimes a hook at the other, used for various purposes about a vessel's deck; as for checking and holding fast (or *stoppering*) a rope cable when it is veered out, for which purpose the hook is attached to a ring-bolt on deck, the knot having a lanyard made fast to it. For chain cables there are stoppers of various kinds adopted, such as *an iron clamp with a lever*, or a *double claw of iron with a rope attached to it*, and so on.

The following is a sketch of a chain-cable-stopper used in ships of war.

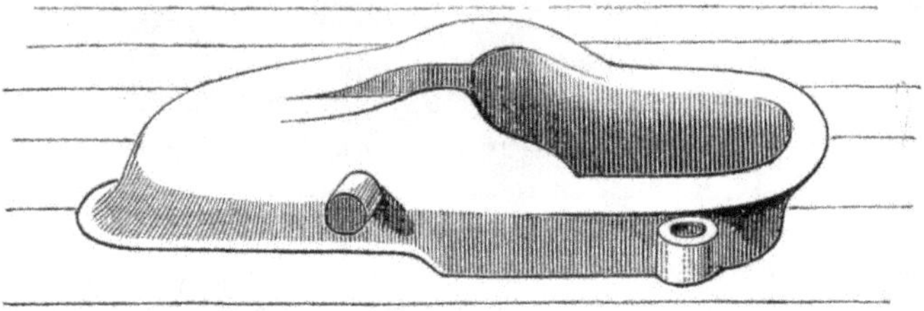

COMPRESSORS, COMPRESSOR-STOPPERS, or COMPRESSOR CHAIN CABLE-STOPPERS, which are of various forms, are made on the principle of holding the chain by compression. In the annexed sketch of *Wardill's Stopper*, by turning the screw *s* with the

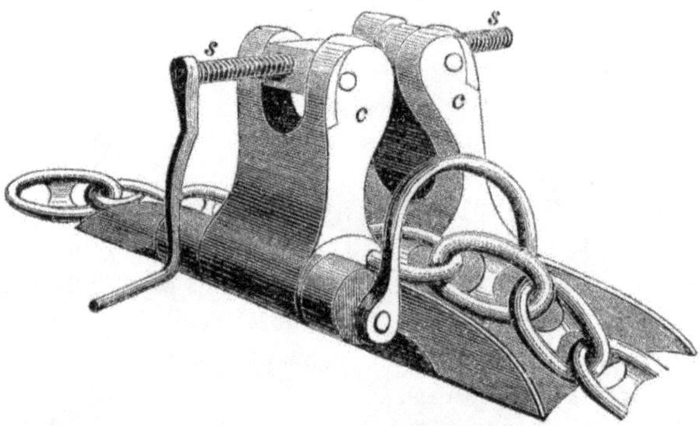


hand, the parts *c* are instantly brought together to hold the chain, or separated to let it run.

CATHEAD-STOPPER, or CAT-STOPPER. A piece of chain rove through the ring of an anchor for hanging it by when catted, or previously to bending the cable. See *Cathead-stopper*.

COMPRESSOR-STOPPER. See *Stopper*.

PREVENTER-STOPPERS. Short pieces of rope, knotted at one end, used for securing the clues of sails in a ship of war during action, and also for assisting the tacks of courses when much strained.

Rigging-stoppers, are for setting up and securing any shroud that happens to be shot away in time of action.

Shroud-stopper. A piece of rope made fast above and below the damaged part of a shroud which has been injured by shot or otherwise, in order to secure it.

STORES OF A VESSEL, SHIP'S STORES, or MARINE STORES. The ropes, sails, provisions, and other outfit with which she is supplied. These are included in the insurable value of the ship.

The term *Ship's stores* is often peculiarly applied to the provisions and other articles of refreshment shipped for the use of the master and crew. Those for the use of passengers are termed *passenger stores.*

STORE-ROOMS. See *Cockpit.*

STORE-SHIP. A ship for carrying stores to ships of war, whether on our own coasts or on distant stations.

STORMS (*Fr.* Orages). Various kinds of storms or tempests may be found noticed under the heads *Ecliptic, Gale, Hurricanes, Monsoon, Squall, Typhoon,* &c. The subject is treated of in *Reid's Law of Storms,* and in *Maury's Physical Geography of the Sea and its Meteorology. The Storm Compass* by Captain A. B. Becher, R. N., is a familiar explanation of the great principles of the hurricane, illustrated with diagrams.

STORM-SAIL. Any sail made of very stout canvas, of smaller dimensions than a sail in ordinary use, to be employed instead of it in heavy weather.

STORM WARNING SIGNALS (REAR-ADMIRAL FITZ-ROY'S). See *Barometer.*

STOVE. See *Bilge,* and *Kiln.*

STOW-WOOD (*Fr.* Bois d'arrimage). Billets of wood used as chocks for steadying casks in a vessel's hold.

STOWAGE (*Fr.* Arrimage). The disposition of a vessel's ballast, stores, and cargo. This term is likewise used to denote space for *stowing* goods, &c., in other words, *Stowage-room.*

1. The stowage of a vessel's cargo ought to be conducted under the special superintendence of the master, who is responsible along with the shipowner for any injury arising to the goods from improper stowage.

2. The cargo ought to be defended from contact with the ship's sides and bottom, more particularly from the latter by sufficient dunnage; and the pumps should be carefully sounded and

attended to, during the process of loading, as well as during the course of the voyage. If a vessel have a lower deck, and it be caulked, this ought also to be dunnaged.

3. In Mr. Lorimer's *Letters to a Young Master Mariner*, valuable suggestions are presented as to the care which should be taken that one description of goods be not exposed to receive damage from another, for example, packages of silk by being stowed under casks of oil, sugar, or other commodities liable to damage from leakage, by being placed under casks containing any liquid, or crates, by being placed in contact with each other. It is also noticed therein, that salt should be separated from other goods by bulkheads: that grain and seed, when stowed in bulk, ought to be secured by planks (*shifting-boards*), so as to prevent their shifting when the vessel lies over; and further important remarks occur in regard to the stowing of casks and of goods in bags.

4. Captain Horsburgh, in the introduction to his *India Directory*, very properly recommends that all the light goods should be stowed along the ship's sides and at the extremities, and the heavy articles in a longitudinal section over and each side of the keel from the fore to the after hatchways, as circumstances may require; adding, that the dead weight may be carried in this manner up to the deck, or to any height consistent with the stability of the ship. He mentions that this plan was adopted in the case of a vessel whose cargo consisted chiefly of iron, and that she was very easy during her passage from London to Bombay.

5. We may add that if a vessel be loaded too much by the stern, this will make her not hold a good wind, or, in other words, make her have a tendency to fall off with her head from the wind when closehauled, in consequence of her fore part not presenting a sufficient resistance to the fluid. On the other hand, if loaded too much by the head, she becomes too ardent.

6. In timber-laden ships it is of great importance that the ground-tier of the cargo be laid with due care, so that it may sustain an equal pressure of the rest of the cargo at every part; and that the corners of the foremost and aftermost ends of a few of the tiers above it be kept several inches clear of the ceiling, so as to prevent the possibility of their resting on the inward curve of the bow or stern. See also *Boyd's Naval Cadet's Manual*, p. 77, and *Instructions for the Stowage of Mixed Cargoes*, prepared by

H. C. Chapman & Co., Liverpool, and published under the direction of Lloyd's Committee.

STOWAGE GOODS. Those which usually pay freight according to their bulk. See *Dead-weight.*

STOWAGE-ROOM. See *Stowage.*

STOWER. See *Wrain-staff.*

STRAGGLING MONEY, in the Royal Navy, 'the money given to those who apprehend deserters, or people who have overstaid their leave of absence, or straggled.'

STRAIGHT OF BREADTH, in Shipbuilding, the space before, at, and abaft the dead-flat, in which the ship is of the same uniform breadth. (*Shipwright's Vade Mecum.*)

STRAINER. See *Rose.*

STRAIT (*Fr.* Étroit). A narrow passage or channel connecting a gulf with the sea, or any part of the sea with another.

STRAKE (*Fr.* Virure). A single range of planks abutting against each other, wrought from one end of a ship or boat to the other, whether externally or internally.

*The internal planking* of the ship is called *Ceiling.* See that article, and also *Clamps, Limber-strake,* and *Spirketting.* (Plate II. fig. 6.)

Of the *outside planking* we shall here notice the following, with special reference to the articles *Plank-sheer* and *Wales.* (Plate II. fig. 6.) *The Garboard strake* is the first strake next the keel: its edge is let down into a groove or channel in the side of the keel, called the rabbent of the keel. The plank between the garboard-strake and lower backstrake is called generally *the bottom plank*: that on the *bilge* of the ship is thicker than the rest of the bottom plank. *The Black-strakes* are the strakes, one or more, immediately above and below the wales, thinner than these, but thicker than the rest of the planking: the black-strakes below the wales get the name of diminishing strakes. (Plate IV. 32, 34.) *The Scrape-strakes,* or more properly *Topside-plank* or *Topsides,* are the strakes between the sheer-strake and upper black-strake. (Plate IV. 31.) *The Sheer-strake,* or *Paint-strake* is the uppermost strake of plank immediately below the plank-sheer: it generally has a moulding corresponding with that on the edge of the plank-sheer. (Plates II. fig. 6 and IV. 30.) See also *Binding-strake, Landing-strake,* and *Sand-strake.*

STRAND (*Fr.* Toron). A number of rope-yarns twisted together. Three or more strands twisted together form a rope.

STRAND, also denotes a sea beach.

STRANDED. A rope is said to be stranded when one of its strands is broken. See also *Stranding.*

STRANDING (*Fr.* Échouage, applied to any grounding), in Marine Insurance, implies generally the act of a vessel being driven ashore, taking the ground not in the ordinary course of the navigation, but by reason of some unforeseen accident, and remaining stationary for some time. If a mere instantaneous stoppage takes place (as for a minute and a half) the ship is not considered to be stranded within the meaning of the memorandum at the foot of a policy of insurance.

STRANGE SAIL, means a vessel of which we do not happen to know the name, or the place that she sails from.

STRAP. See *Strop.*

STRAY-LINE. See *Log-line*, 3, and *Harpoon.*

STREAK. See *Strake.*

STREAM. A vessel in a river is said to be *in the stream*, when she is lying off from the shore so that they have to communicate with her by means of boats. See also *Iceberg*, 17.

*To stream a buoy*, means to let it drop into the water previously to casting anchor.

STREAM-ANCHOR, is of a size between the small bower anchor and the kedge, and is used for warping and like purposes. See *Anchor*, 8.

STREAM-CABLE. A hawser or rope used to moor the vessel to the shore. It is the largest of the water-laid ropes of a vessel. See *Cable.*

STRESS OF WEATHER. When a vessel has, in consequence of the severity of a storm, or in consequence of encountering a heavy gale of contrary wind, to run for a place of safety, or to put back to the port which she sailed from, she is said to do so *through stress of weather.*

STRETCH. To sail by the wind under a crowd of canvas.

STRETCH OUT! An order to a boat's crew to pull strong.

STRETCHERS. Pieces of wood placed across a boat's bottom, inside, for the oarsmen to set their feet against in rowing. Also cross pieces of wood put between a boat's sides to keep them apart when hoisted up on a vessel's deck and griped. (*Dana's Seaman's Manual.*) See also *Sheer-pole.*

STRIKE (*Fr.* Amener). A term applied to the lowering of sails, or hauling down of colours, as a token of surrender or salute; and also to the lowering an upper mast and securing it by lashing its heel to the mast below. See also the article *Sound.*

STRINGERS. Strakes of plank wrought round the inside of a vessel close to the under sides of the beams. They are bolted to the clamps and timbers, and are scarphed to each other. As they are put on edgeways to the ship's sides or to the clamps, and serve as a shelf to rest the beams upon, they are generally called *Shelf-pieces*, or *shelves.* (Plate II. fig. 6.)

If shelf-pieces have not been introduced at the first, it is often found necessary to resort to them, as an assistance to the other fastenings, when the ship is found to be working about the water-ways; and they afford a very substantial binding, both in the athwartship and fore-and-aft directions.

STRIP THE MASTS (*Fr.* Dégarnir). To dismantle a ship; that is, to clear the masts of their rigging and other furniture.

STROKE. A single pull of a rower upon his oar.

STROKE OF THE SEA. The shock occasioned to a vessel by the sea striking her.

STROKE-OAR. The aftermost oar of a boat.

STROKESMAN. The man who pulls the stroke-oar.

STRONG-BACK, *for the Chain Cable*, a piece of wood laid over the cross piece of the windlass bitts, one end of it having a rope attached to it, and made fast to an eye-bolt in the ship's deck, and at the other end a rope to lift all the turns of the chain clear of the windlass and make them fast to the strong-back when heaving at the windlass for any purpose where the chain is not used.

STROP (*Fr.* Estrope), or STRAP. A piece of rope spliced and put round a block to keep its parts well together, and by which it is suspended: it sometimes also encircles a thimble with a hook attached to it. *Blocks* have now generally iron strops, which are found to be more snug as well as durable. Strops for *dead-eyes* in like manner are of iron. Those for *buoys* are often made of rope; iron buoys have a ring at each end, by either of which they may be suspended.

The fittings of block-strops are illustrated in *Seamanship* by Lieutenant Nares, p. 26.

Any short piece of rope, with its ends spliced together, gets the name of a *strop*. Such strops are used for various purposes, as for hoisting a tackle to.

STUD-CHAIN, is chain made with a cast-iron stud introduced into the middle of each link crossways, dividing the link into two equal parts, thereby strengthening each, and keeping the links endways to each other. See *Chain*, 2.

STUDDING-SAIL (*Fr.* Bonnet), pronounced by seamen Stunsail. A light quadrilateral sail set outside of any square sail, on a boom, called the *studding-sail boom*, rigged out for that purpose from the yard arm; its head is extended by a *studding-sail yard*, which is hoisted by a whip purchase called the *studding-sail halyards*. They sometimes improperly get the name of

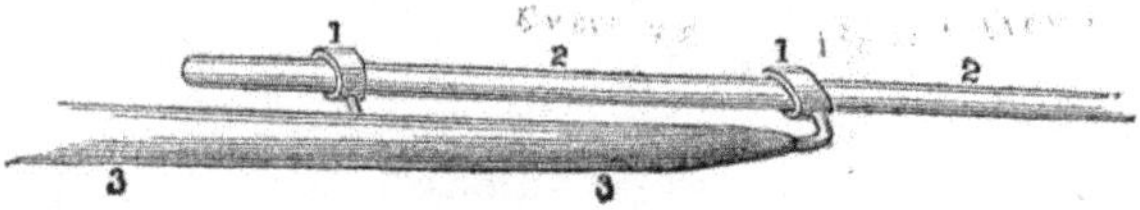


*steering-sails*. Studding-sails are carried only with a fair wind, and in moderate weather. They are named according to their respective positions, the *lower*, *topmast*, *topgallant*, and *royal* studding-sails.

SUB-LIEUTENANT. See *Lieutenant*.

SUBMARINE TELEGRAPH. See *Telegraph*.

SUBMARINE THERMOMETER. An instrument invented by M. Clement reaching below the surface of the water, and which shows by means of a graduated scale in the between decks any change in the temperature of the sea. See *Thermometer*.

SUBSTITUTE-RUDDER. The same as *Jury-rudder*.

SUCK. A pump is said to suck when the water has been pumped out until it is so low at the pump foot as to admit air.

SUFFERANCE. See *Transire*.

SUIT OF SAILS (*Fr.* Voilure). The whole sails required to be bent for a vessel.

SUPERANNUATED, in reference to the Royal Navy, is a term applied to any officer who has by permission left the service on retiring pay, on account of old age or infirmity.

SUPERCARGO (*Fr.* Subrécargue). A person employed to go out in a merchant vessel bound for foreign ports, in order to take charge of her cargo, and dispose of it there to the best advantage.

SUPERHEATED STEAM, is steam the heat of which has

been raised by a certain process after being generated. See *Superheater.*

SUPERHEATER. A contrivance for increasing 'the temperature of the steam to the extent it would lose in its way from the boiler until exhausted from the cylinder.' When the temperature is so increased, it is called *superheated* steam. 'Thus, if the temperature of the ordinary steam in the boiler is 276°, and the temperature of the steam when in the cylinder (before expansion takes place) is only 252°, there is a serious loss of pressure entirely due to loss of temperature. To obviate this the steam is passed through the superheater and increased in temperature about 50°; this keeps the steam in the cylinder at the temperature due to its pressures before and after expansion. Many boilers give out what is termed "wet steam;" but if it be passed through a superheater it is converted into dry steam of the proper pressure. This not only increases the supply of steam, but eases the air-pump, as it does not require so much cold water to condense it. Several patents have been taken out for this purpose, and have been successfully applied.' The system seems to have been introduced by Mr. Wethered, whose patent apparatus is fully noticed in *Murray's Rudimentary Treatise on the Marine Engine*, p. 110. 'In "*Beardmore's*" patent the steam is made to travel (through a number of small tubes) several times across the uptake or foot of the chimney before it enters the steam pipe. "*Partridge's*" patent is very similar, the difference being that he places the tubes vertically instead of horizontally.'

SUPERNUMERARIES, as relative to maritime affairs, imply men over and above the established complement of a vessel.

SUPPLEMENT *of Longitude.* The term commonly applied to its complement, or what it wants of 180°.

SUPPORTERS, in Shipbuilding, cleats or knees, one of which is fitted to each cathead in large ships.

SURF. The foam occasioned by the breaking of the sea upon the shore.

SURGE. A large swelling wave.

SURGE. *To surge a rope* or *cable*, is to slack it up suddenly when it renders round a pin, or round a winch, windlass, or capstan. See *Capstan.*

A ship is said *to surge* on a reef when she rises and falls with the heave of the sea, so as to strike heavily on the reef.

SURGEON (*Fr.* Chirurgien). This name is given to the person engaged to act in a medical capacity on board of any merchant ship, whether he may have been authorised by law to practise in this kingdom as a physician, surgeon, or apothecary.

In the medical department of the Royal Navy there are a director-general, inspectors general and deputy, inspectors general of hospitals and fleets, staff surgeons, surgeons, and assistant surgeons. See chap. 52 of *The Queen's Regulations.*

SURMARKS, or SIRMARKS. See *Ribband-lines.*

SURVEY (*Fr.* Visite). An inspection by practical men of a vessel or her stores, or of goods laden on board. It is usual and proper to employ at least two *surveyors* (*Fr.* experts) to report in any case of damage to ship or cargo: when goods have been sea-damaged, the master of the vessel, also, ought to be called to attend the survey upon them, and to certify the nature of the damage. See the title *Hydrography*, also chap. 38 of *The Queen's Regulations for the Government of Her Majesty's Naval Service.*

SURVEYOR OF THE NAVY. The duties of this official are in general to take the superintendence of the 'matériel' of the Royal Navy, to submit to the Board of Admiralty the programme of works for the year, and to fix the dockyards where they can best be executed, to report as to changes advisable in the number of workmen at the dockyards, to report those who from age or infirmity are not properly capable of doing duty, to examine all surveys on Her Majesty's ships, to report what ships are worn out, or what ships building are so deteriorated as to render it advisable to bring any of them to sale, or to take the ship to pieces, to be prepared with any information that may be required as to the selection and preparation of ships for commission, &c.

SWAB. A mop made of ropeyarns and having a rope handle; used for cleaning and drying decks.

FIRE-SWAB. See *Tompion.*

SWAGGING OFF. See *Swig.*

SWAY UP (*Fr.* Guinder). To throw a strain on a mast-rope, and start the mast upwards, so that the fid may be taken out previously to lowering the mast. To raise a yard-arm in the act of sending down the yard.

SWEEP. To *drag* the bottom of the water for an anchor or any bulky object. It is performed thus: two boats each take an end of a hawser, its bight having weight sufficient to sink it to the bottom, on its reaching which the boats pull away abreast of each other, at a certain distance apart, until they find an obstruction to the rope; they then keep crossing each other until the bight of it is twisted round the obstructing object, which may be the thing sought for, and bring both ends of the hawser round the stem or stern-roller of a launch, they heave the object up with a tackle made fast on board the launch.

SWEEPS, signify large oars used in small sailing vessels. See also *Shipbuilding*, 4.

SWEETENING COCK. See *Bilge-water.*

SWELL (*Fr.* Houle). The heavy rolling of the sea after a storm. That which is occasioned along the shore by a distant storm is called a *ground-swell.*

Malte-Brun says, 'a strong, constant, and equal wind produces a *swell*, or long ridgy waves which all rise as it were with the same front, push forward with uniform velocity, and precipitate themselves in regular succession on the shore.'

SWIFT. To bring two shrouds or backstays together in order to stretch them for getting the rigging properly set up. It is done by a tackle, called the *swifter-tackle*, made fast from shroud to shroud, with the falls leading down to the deck. It may also be used to tighten any rope in a similar way. *To swift in the bars of the capstan*, is to secure them in their places in the capstan by means of the swifter.

SWIFTER. The forward shroud of a lower mast. Swifters also mean ropes used to confine the *capstan-bars* to their places when shipped. Swifter is also a name given to a rope or chain used to secure a raft: for this purpose chain is best adapted.

*To swifter the bars of the capstan* is to connect their outer ends together with a rope.

SWIFTER TACKLE. See *Swift.*

SWIG, or SWIG OFF. A term applied by sailors to the act of hauling off upon the bight of a rope, when its lower end is held fast, in order to get greater purchase than by hauling directly. This is often resorted to in taking the anchor aboard by means of the fish-tackle, after being catted, in hauling on the braces, &c.

SWIM. To move along the surface of the water by means of the simultaneous movement of the hands and feet, if the back be uppermost; or of the feet alone, if the breast be uppermost. If a man remain quiet in the water, by gently treading in it with his feet downwards, he will float upright with his head sufficiently above water to give perfect freedom of breathing even in a heavy sea. If he lay himself quietly on his back he will float, and can then swim, as already noticed, by striking out his feet and drawing them back again alternately.

SWINGING-BOOM. A name for the boom which stretches the foot of a lower studding-sail: the lower studding-sail yard stretches the head of the sail, which is hoisted up to the lower studding-sail boom.

SWIVEL. A species of large link of iron in a chain cable, made so as to revolve upon an axis in order to keep turns out of the chain. It is introduced at that part of the chain which is below water when the ship is at anchor. Being apt to get fixed or injured by rust, it is now rarely used. See *Swivel Stock.*

SWIVEL STOCK. An upright piece of wood which is made to step, or is fixed in the bows of a boat, for the purpose of shipping into it a small gun, which gets the name of a *swivel*; working on a pivot so as to turn in any direction.

SWORD MAT. A mat woven by means of a piece of wood resembling a sword.

SYMPIESOMETER, or NEW AIR BAROMETER. An instrument invented for measuring the weight of the atmosphere by the compression of a gaseous column. It is said to be sooner sensible of the changes of the atmosphere than the common marine barometer, and not to be affected by the motion of a ship at sea.

The following account of this instrument is given by its inventor, Mr. Alexander Adie, of Edinburgh, who, among other improvements that he has made upon it since it was first introduced, mentions in particular 'more perfect methods of fixing the scales, and the use of acid in place of oil to contain the enclosed gas, the advantage wherefore is that it does not change with climate, which the oil was subject to.' He also states, that a great number of sympiesometers are now made in London without proper attention to the scales, which has tended much to injure the high character which the instrument at first bore.

'The principle of the sympiesometer consists in employing an elastic fluid or gas, different from air, and any liquid excepting quicksilver, which neither acts upon the gas which it confines nor is perceptibly acted upon by the air, to the contact of which it is in some measure exposed. Hydrogen gas, azotic gas, or any of the gases not liable to be absorbed by the enclosing fluid, may be used; but I prefer hydrogen gas as superior to any other that I have tried.

'The enclosed gas with which the bulb and part of the tube is filled, changes its bulk, or occupies more or less space, according to the pressure of the atmosphere upon the surface of the fluid. The scale for measuring the change in the bulk of the gas, occasioned by a change of pressure, is formed experimentally.

'As the bulk of the gas is altered by any change that takes place in the temperature of the atmosphere, it is necessary to apply a correction on this account. For this purpose, the principal or barometric scale is made to slide upon another scale, placed either below it or on one side of it, which is divided into degrees and tenth parts, so as to represent the change of bulk in the gas produced by a change of temperature under the same pressure, and corresponding to the degrees of a common thermometer attached to the instrument, the scale of which is also divided into degrees and tenth parts of a degree.

'When the sympiesometer is hung up for observation, the cistern must be opened by pushing up the small slider at its mouth, having previously unturned the nut at the bottom, which is placed there to keep it down in carriage, and prevent the escape of the fluid from the cistern. If any of the fluid at the top of the column should be separated, which sometimes happens in carriage, hang it up for a few minutes to drain, then turn it into a horizontal position, so that the fluid may run quickly up, until the separated portion of it disappear, when it must be turned slowly upright. This operation may be repeated, if found to be necessary, till the column of fluid be joined.

'In cases where the fluid has been very much separated, from bad usage in carriage, or from placing the box with the top of the sympiesometer down, it is to be corrected by holding the sympiesometer with the top up, and having the stopper of the cistern close; shake the instrument by jerking it downwards, then hang it up to drain, when the column of fluid will be got to join.

### MANNER OF USING THE INSTRUMENT.

'Observe the temperature by the thermometer, and set the pointer above the top of the sliding-scale opposite to the degree of temperature upon the fixed scale; and then the height of the fluid, as indicated on the sliding scale, will be the pressure of the air required.

'Suppose the temperature observed by the mercurial thermometer to be 52° 4′, then slide the sympiesometer scale until the pointer is at 52° 4′ on the fixed scale, at the right hand side under the sliding scale; it is to be observed that the numbers on this scale, and also on the thermometer, read downwards, and the top of the column of red fluid stands opposite to the second division above the third-tenth higher than the number 30. The height of the barometer is then 30 inches $\frac{3}{10}$ and $\frac{4}{100}$ of an inch, or 30·34 inches. The tenths are easily distinguished from the hundredth parts, by the lines being drawn longer. As it is convenient to know what change has taken place since the last observation, the circular register at the bottom of the frame should be set, by turning the division on it corresponding to that indicated by the sympiesometer to the fleur-de-luce or index. When the column of fluid descends, bad weather may be expected, and when it rises the weather will in general be fine.'

A veteran naval officer, who has supplied much useful information for the present edition of this Dictionary, states that he worked one of the first sympiesometers which Mr. Adie made, and saved himself from many a gale by following its indications; and he considers that no ship ought to be without one. Many seamen think that this instrument is too sensitive, and sometimes alarms the mariner unnecessarily. In France, M. Gaudin has endeavoured to render it still more sensitive in its action.

SYPHERED, implies a mode in which two planks are joined together with bevelled ends. The same as *Mitred*.

T-PLATES, in Shipbuilding, are plates of iron in the form of the letter T they are used for various purposes.

TABLE LAND. Flat country. A long tract of land, flat on the top.

TABLE MONEY. An allowance to flag officers, &c., in addition to their pay, to meet the necessary expenses of their mess-tables.

TABLING, in Shipbuilding, letting one piece of timber into another by alternate recesses and projections on each, to prevent the pieces from drawing asunder or slipping upon one another. See also *Dowells*.

TACK (*Fr.* Virer de bord). To put a vessel about; that is, to change her course from one board to another by bringing her head up to the wind, putting the helm a-lee till the wind bear upon the sails on the opposite side of the ship, so that the side which before was the lee side now becomes the weather side.

See *Stay and Wear*, and the following article *Tack*.

The term *Tacking* is likewise applied generally to the act of *Beating to Windward.*

TACK (*Fr.* Amure). The rope or chain by which the weather clew of a course is hauled forward and down to the chestree or bumpkin. See *Sheet.*

*The tack of a fore and aft sail*, is the rope which keeps down its lower forward clue ; and *of a studding sail*, that which keeps down its lower outer clue. The tack of a lower studding sail is called the *Out-Haul.*

'When a vessel is close-hauled, the tacks are hauled forward on the weather side, in which case those tacks are said to be *aboard.* When close-hauled, with the wind on the right hand, she has her *starboard tacks aboard*, and is said to sail *on the starboard tack* ; if the wind be on the left hand, she has her *port tacks aboard*, and is said to sail *on the port tack.*' (*Norie's Epitome of Navigation.*)

TACK also signifies that part of a sail to which the tack is attached. See *Sheet.*

TACKLE (*Fr.* Agrès et apparaux, Tackle and apparel). Under the words *tackle, apparel, and other furniture*, often used with reference to questions of marine insurance, are comprehended the rigging, sails, spars, anchors, cables, boats, guns, cooking utensils and other ship-chandlery wares ; in short, every article with which the ship is fitted out. All these, along with the provisions for the use of the master and crew, are included in the term outfit or stores.

TACKLE (*Fr.* Palan). A purchase formed by a rope rove through two or more blocks. That part of the rope which is made fast to the strop of one of the blocks is called the *standing part* ; the part hauled upon is termed the *fall* ; and the rest are called *running* or *leading* parts. The block or blocks made fast to the running part of the tackle are called *running blocks.*

FISH-TACKLE. The tackle used to hoist the anchor up to the gunwale after it has been catted. See *Fish the Anchor.*

GUN-TACKLE PURCHASE. This is formed by a rope rove through two single blocks, the standing part being made fast to the strop of the fixed block. (See *Nares on Seamanship*, Plate 185, and illustration p. 406 hereof.)

LUFF-TACKLE PURCHASE. A tackle composed of a single and a double block, the standing part of the rope being made fast to the strop of the single block. See *Luff-Tackle.*

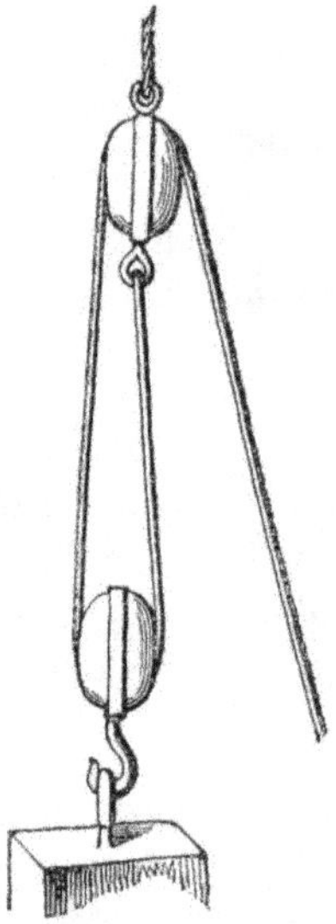

GUN-TACKLE PURCHASE.

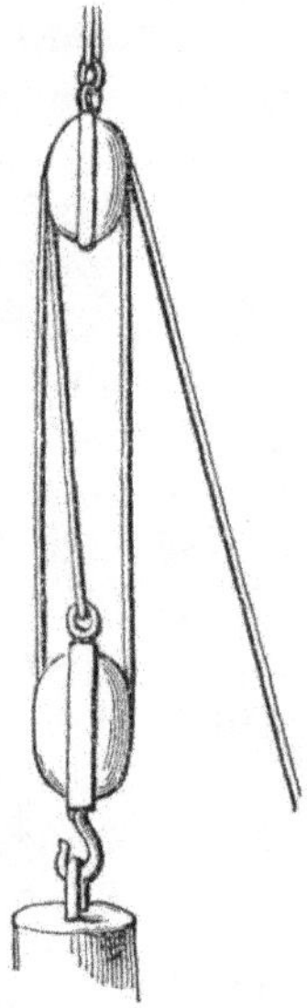

LUFF-TACKLE PURCHASE.

REEF-TACKLE. A tackle attached to each of the topsails of a square-rigged vessel for the purpose of tracing or lightening up the leech in the act of reefing.

STAY-TACKLE. A tackle suspended (generally by a pendant) from a vessel's fore or main stay for hoisting in and out boats, or moving other heavy bodies.

TOP BURTON TACKLE. A small tackle formed by several blocks till the rope becomes three or four fold ; used for setting up topmast shrouds. See *Burton.*

TRAIN-TACKLES. Luff-tackles, the double block being hooked to an eye-bolt, and the single block to a ring-bolt in the deck, used on board a vessel for running guns in and out. See *Train-Tackles.*

WATCH-TACKLE, HALF-WATCH TACKLE, or TAIL-TACKLE. A luff-tackle purchase with a hook in the end of the single block, and a tail to the upper end of the double block. One of these purchases, with a short fall, is kept on deck at hand, in order to clap upon standing or running rigging when required, to get a strain on ropes, such as the topsail sheets and halyards, &c.

For further information on this subject, see *Boyd's Naval Cadets' Manual*, p.107; *Seamanship*, by Lieut. Nares, p. 48, where the relative degrees of power obtained by different kinds of tackles are explained; also the titles *Burton*, and *Runner and Tackle.*

TACKLE-FALL. See explanation of *Tackle.*

TACKSPINS, or BELAYING-PINS, are pins inserted into holes in the fife-rail and other parts of the vessel when required, for belaying running gear to.

TACTICS (NAVAL). The art of arranging and conducting the warlike operations of fleets.

TAFFRAIL, or TAFFEREL-RAIL. The rail over the heads of the stern-timbers, extending across the stern from one quarter stanchion to the other.

TAIL. A rope spliced into the end of a block, used for making it fast to rigging, spars, &c. Such a block is called a *Tail-Block.*

A ship is said to *tail up* or *down the stream*, when at anchor in a river, according as her stern swings up or down the river by the influence of the tide. (*Dana's Seaman's Manual.*)

TAIL ON! or TALLY ON! An order to take hold of a rope and to pull. (*Dana.*)

TAIL-TACKLE, or WATCH-TACKLE. See *Tackle* (*Watch*).

TAIL-VALVE, or SNIFTING-VALVE. See description of *Steam Engine*, Sect. 13.

TAKE OFF. The wind is said to *take off* when it becomes less violent, or subsides into a calm.

TAKE TO. When hauling in upon a rope with the hand, 'take to!' is an order to secure the part hauled in round a tackspin, bitt-head, &c., or to lead it to a capstan, winch, or other purchase.

TALLY ON. See *Tail on.*

TANKS, or WATER-TANKS. Cisterns made of malleable iron plates, for keeping a stock of water; they are formed of such shapes as to fit into those parts of the ship where they are to be placed without occupying much space.

'When the water is kept in large tanks, they ought to be sounded morning and evening, and the result marked in the log-book, in case of leakage.'

TAPPET. See *Gun (Armstrong).*

TAR (*Fr.* Goudron). A liquid gum taken from pine or fir trees, and prepared by boiling. With this the ropes whereof a vessel's rigging is composed are saturated; and it is used for various other purposes. A coating of tar is always laid on under wood or copper sheathing: if the vessel be not sheathed, *coal-tar* is usually employed for paying her bottom, because it dries sooner and makes a smoother surface; but vegetable tar is better calculated for preserving the timber.

This operation is called *tarring* the ship's bottom. The rope so saturated is likewise called *tarred rope.*

TARPAULING, or TARPAULIN (*Fr.* Prélart). A piece of canvass daubed with tar or painted; used to cover the hatches of a vessel at sea, in order to prevent water from getting in at the seams, and for other purposes.

TARTAN (*Fr.* Tartane). A small vessel of the Mediterranean, having a main mast and jigger mast, the former rigged with a lateen sail and yard. There are some tartans of larger dimensions. (*Dict. de Marine à voiles.*)

TAUGHT, or TAUT. A term generally used for tight, when applied to a rope or chain. *To taughten,* is to haul taut (*Fr.* Embraquer).

TAUNT. High or tall: commonly applied to masts.

*All-a-taunto,* is a phrase denoting that a vessel is fully rigged out, with all her upper masts and yards aloft.

TAUT. See *Taught.*

TCHIKIRNE. A Turkish barge of about 200 burdens. It has a pole-mast. (*Dict. de Marine à voiles.*)

TEAMING-PUNCH. An iron instrument used for driving out bolts.

TELEGRAPH. A machine or contrivance for communicating intelligence at a distance by means of signals agreed on to represent certain letters, words, or ideas.

The electric or magnetic telegraph so long used on railways is now made use of instead of the *semaphores,* or telegraph signals used for conveying shipping intelligence on land.

The submarine electric telegraph is known to every one as now uniting continents together by a chain of communication for the interchange of thought. It is composed of twisted copper wire, insulated by means of gutta percha, or some other suitable covering. See *Engine Room, Telegraph,* and *Signals.*

TELESCOPE (*Fr.* Lunette). A well-known optical instrument for observing distant objects: there are two kinds, the reflecting and the refracting telescopes, the latter of which is best suited for observing the heavenly bodies. (*Squire's Grammar of Astronomy.*)

TELL-TALE (*Fr.* Axiomètre). A pointer connected with the steering apparatus for the purpose of indicating the position of the helm at any time.

Also, a name given to a *Hanging-Compass.*

TEND. 'To watch a vessel at anchor, at the turn of tides, and cast her by the helm, and some sail if necessary, so as to keep turns out of her cable.'

The term *tending* also implies the movement itself by which a vessel swings round her anchors in a tideway at the turn of the tide.

TENDER. The same as *Crank.*

TENDER. A small vessel employed in the service of Government to attend on ships of war, and on squadrons of them, in order to carry orders or intelligence from one place to another, to convey volunteers and impressed men, &c.

TENON (*Fr.* Tenon). The end of one piece of timber diminished and made square so as to fit into a corresponding hole, called the *Mortice,* in another piece, for the purpose of joining the two pieces together. The pieces are said to be *tenoned* into each other: thus, the stern post is tenoned into the keel.

A tenon is made on the heel of a lower mast to fit into the step.

TESTING *a chain cable.* Trying its strength by a machine which strains it with a force greater than the absolute strength of the rope cable it is intended to supersede. This is usually done in the workshop by means of a hydraulic machine.

THAUGHTS. See *Thwarts.*

THERMOMETER. A well-known instrument for measuring the temperature of the air, or of any matter, formed on the principle that the expansion and contraction of certain substances (such as mercury) are proportional to the increase and diminution of heat. This instrument is of much use at sea as indicating, by the diminution of the ocean's temperature, the near approach to land, shoals, icebergs, &c.

M. Clement of Rochefort has invented an instrument of this kind, called a *Marine,* or *Sub-Marine, Thermometer,* which is peculiarly suitable for the last-mentioned purpose: it is formed of platina and silver, and reaching below the surface of the water, it shows with great delicacy, by means of a graduated scale in the between decks, any change in the temperature of the sea.

At a distance from land 'the mean temperature of the waters of the ocean at their surface is higher than that of the atmosphere with which they are in contact,' and 'a diminution of their temperature becomes very obvious as we approach the land.' Malte-Brun further observes, referring to the authority of Humboldt (*Voyage aux Régions équinoxiales*), that the water over a sand-bank is colder than the deep ocean around it, an effect which Sir H. Davy attributes to radiation and evaporation; and that this difference increases the nearer the bank is to the surface of the water. 'The more extensive a sandbank is, so much the colder is the water which covers it. We must of course except those banks which are situated between two adjoining capes, and those which are exposed to regular currents.'

THICKSTUFF. A name for plank when above four inches in thickness.

THIMBLE. An iron ring having its ring concave on the outside for a rope, or the strop of a block, or the cringle of a sail to fit snugly round, and prevent a hook from chafing it. Thimbles are also used for other similar purposes.

THOLE-PINS, or THOLES. Two pins inserted into the gunwale of some boats, between which the oar works. See *Row-locks.*

THORO' PUT. This term is generally used to imply the parts of a fall not leading fair, but crossing each other; a turn of one of the blocks in the proper direction *takes out the thoro' put.*

THREE MASTED SCHOONER. See *Schooner.*

THROAT. *The inner end of a gaff*, where it widens and hollows in to fit the mast. *The central part of the hollow of a Breast-hook, Transom, or piece of knee-timber*: we may notice that, in shipbuilding, the bolt through the throat of a breast-hook, or of a transom, is always driven from the inside. See also description of *Anchor.*

THROAT-BOLTS. Bolts fixed in the lower part of the main-top and the end of the gaff, for hooking the throat halyards to. In sloops and schooners, the throat-bolts are fastened through the mast above the cross-trees, and each bolt has a spur on its lower part to prevent the neck being broken by the up and down strain.

THROAT-BRAILS, are those for brailing up a sail to the throat of a gaff.

THROAT-HALYARDS. Those attached to the inner peak of a gaff. See *Halyards* and *Throat-bolts.*

THROTTLE-VALVE. See description of *Steam Engine*, Sect. 7.

THROUGH. In Shipbuilding, *through-bolts*, or *through fastenings*, imply bolts or fastenings which go quite through the timbers and plank of a vessel, in contradistinction to *dump bolts*, or short bolts. See *Bolts*, 8. Treenails are through fastenings.

THRUM. To stick short strands of yarn through a mat or piece of canvass in order to make a rough surface: this forms what is called a *thrummed mat*, which is used about a vessel's rigging at any part to prevent chafing.

THUS! An order to the steersman in a ship of war, when closehauled, to keep the ship's head as it is at the moment. See *Steady.*

THWARTS. The seats across a boat upon which the oarsmen sit: they are secured to the boat's sides by means of small knees of wood or iron, in order to bind her together.

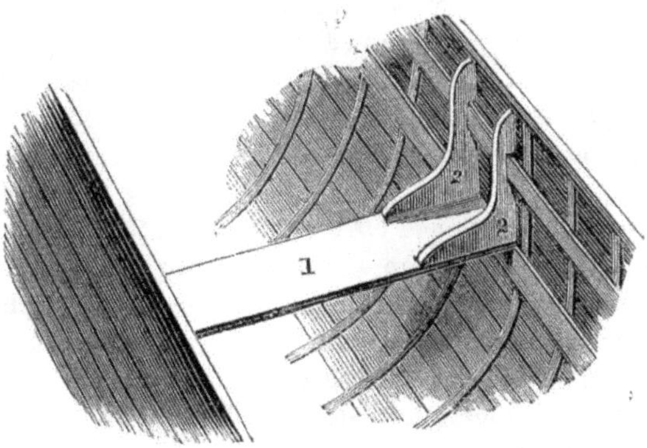


1. THWART. 2. KNEES.

In a publication of very old date (*The Military and Sea Dictionary*, London 1708), this word is spelt *thaught*, which is in keeping with a very common pronunciation of it at the present day.

THWART-CLAMP, or SEA-CRAFT. The narrow board

running fore and aft in a boat, nailed to the timbers for the thwarts to rest upon.

THWARTSHIPS. See *Athwartships.*

TIDES (*Fr.* Marées). The regular periodical oscillations or alternate rising and falling which take place in the waters of the sea, generally twice in the course of a lunar day—that is, in twenty-four hours nine minutes of mean solar time, throughout the greater part of the ocean, and of the gulfs, bays, friths, and rivers which communicate freely with it.

1. These rising and falling tides form what are called a *flood* and an *ebb*, a *high* and *low water*: the whole interval between high and low water is called a *tide.* The water is said to *flow* and *ebb*: and the rising tide is called the *flood-tide* (*Fr.* flot), and the falling the *ebb-tide* (*Fr.* jusant, baisse, èbe).

2. The interval between every flood-tide and ebb-tide, or rather about every high and low water, during which there is little or no change in the height of the tide, is termed *slack water.*

3. The line made by the tide upon the shore when at its greatest height is termed *high water mark,* or *flood-mark.*

4. The cause of tides is the attraction of the sun and moon, chiefly that of the latter object: they differ at different places, and are subject to periodical variations everywhere; these varying heights of tide succeed each other in a regular series, alternately diminishing and increasing; the greatest is termed a *spring-tide* (*Fr.* vif de l'eau) and the least, a *neap-tide* (*Fr.* amortissement) each series is completed in somewhere about fifteen days.

5. These last-mentioned effects are regulated by the varying relative positions of the sun and moon. At new moon, when it is in conjunction with the sun, the tides are raised by their joint attraction, which occasions the highest *spring-tides.* When they are in opposition, each raises the tides opposite to it, and this, in like manner, occasions spring-tides. But at the quarters, the sun tends to raise the tides where the moon would depress them, and to depress them where they would be raised by the moon, which produces *neap-tides.* When the moon is in *perigee*—that is, at her nearest distance from the earth, she raises the tides most: the contrary happens when she is in *apogee.*

The tides in high latitudes generally rise and fall more than those in low latitudes.

Although in most places the tide flows twice every twenty-four hours, Mr. Horsburgh remarks that this is not universally the case, for amongst several of the eastern islands within the tropics, it flows only once in twenty-four hours; the passage of the moon over the meridian of any place commonly makes high water there, but in some places the tide is highest when the moon is in or near the horizon; in many places, also, beyond the tropics the tide flows only once in twenty-four hours, particularly on the southern coast of Van Diemen's Land, while at Port Dalrymple, on the north coast of that island, the tide flows twice in twenty-four hours.

Valuable information regarding the tides and currents of the ocean is contained in *Maury's Physical Geography of the Sea and its Meteorology*; and *The Admiralty Manual of Scientific Enquiry.*

LEE TIDE. A tide running in the same direction with the wind. The reverse is a WEATHER TIDE, that is, a tide running to windward. *See the Admiralty Manual of Scientific Enquiry.*

TIDE-BALL. A ball hoisted to different heights from time to time along an upright pole, to indicate the heights of tide at different hours.

TIDE-GATE. See *Tide-way.*

TIDE-HARBOUR, or TIDAL-HARBOUR. A harbour wherein the tide ebbs and flows: in contradistinction from a wet dock.

TIDE-RODE. The situation of a vessel at anchor when she is swung round by the force of the tide, and rides with her head to it: if swung by the force of the wind, she is said to be *wind-rode.*

TIDE-SURVEYOR. The officer of customs who superintends the tide-waiters, &c., and admeasures vessels for registry. See *Customs.*

TIDE-WAITERS, formerly called also TIDESMEN, are boarded on vessels from foreign parts to prevent frauds on the revenue. See *Customs.*

TIDESMAN. A man employed at tide's work. See also *Tide-waiters.*

TIDE-WAY, or TIDE-GATE. A channel wherein the tide runs strong.

TIDE'S WORK. A period of labour during the ebbing, slack water, and flowing of a tide at low or at high water. Thus, assistance may be engaged so long as the state of the tide will allow it to float a vessel off the strand at each interval given by the flood-tide, or to stop her leaks &c. at each interval given by the ebb-tide ; either of which duties will constitute a *tide's work.* When assistance is engaged at so much per tide, it is evidently to be understood in a similar sense, according to the nature of the duties to be performed. *To work double tides* means to perform two tide's work in the twenty-four hours.

TIE. See *Tye.*

TIER (*Fr.* Rang). A row of any thing, as of shores, of ships, of guns, &c.: a range of casks. Also, 'the range of the fakes of a cable or hawser.' See *Ground-tier. The Cable-tier,* is the place in the ship's hold, or between decks, where the cables are stowed. (*Dana's Seaman's Manual.*)

TIGHT, or WATER-TIGHT (*Fr.* Etanche). A ship or boat is said to be tight, when so compact in every respect as to prevent the admission of water: the reverse of *leaky.*

TILLER (*Fr.* Barre de gouvernail Timon). A bar of wood or iron fitted into the head of a rudder, as a lever to turn the rudder in steering.

The extremity of it, to which the tiller-rope or chain is attached is called the *tiller-head.*

TILLER-ROPE. The rope attached to the extremity of the tiller, when there is no steering-wheel.

TILT. A name which has been given to an awning extended over the stern-sheets of a boat.

TIMBER. Under this title special reference is to be made to articles *Seasoning* and *Dry-rot.*

1. Timber used for shipbuilding and similar purposes is classed into *straight* timber, *compass* timber, and *knees.* The first serves for keel pieces, beams, &c., and also to be cut up into planking and boards. Knees are used to connect the beams with the framing, and to connect other parts together.

2. In order to entitle a merchant vessel to the highest class in *Lloyd's Register of Shipping,* the principal kinds of timber allowed to be made use of in the construction of the ship's hull are English, African, and live oak, and East India teak.

3. Cedar is a very good wood for shipbuilding. Honduras mahogany is now in frequent use for wales, topside-planking, top-timbers, stanchions, &c.: it is a hard wood, light, and little subject to decay, whether covered in or exposed to the weather.

4. It is said that the oak surpasses all other trees in strength; those of temperate climates being the best; and that trees

which, like it, grow slowly, have the greater proportional strength.

5. It would be too extensive a subject here to enter upon a full account of the purposes to which different kinds of timber are thus applied; we shall notice only the following:—Pine and fir trees give excellent mast-pieces. American yellow pine is used for moulds. For the pumps, larch (or metal) is now commonly used; elm for shells of blocks and bull's-eyes; *lignum vitæ* for sheaves and friction rollers; ash or American hiccory for hand-spikes; ash and fir for oars. Beech is ill-suited for oars, as it soon becomes very brittle, and is also subject to get twisted. See *Treenails* and *Mane*.

6. The following note of the specific gravity of different kinds of timber, &c., is obtained from *Grier's Mechanics' Calculator* and *Roberts's Mechanics' Assistant*.

| | Weight of a cubic foot in ounces | | Weight of a cubic foot in ounces |
|---|---|---|---|
| Distilled water | 1000 | Lignum vitæ | 1333 |
| Sea water | 1028 | Mahogany (Honduras) | 560 |
| Ash | 760 | Mahogany (Spanish) | 852 |
| Beech | 696 | Oak (Danzig) | 760 |
| Cedar | 596 | Oak (American) | 872 |
| Cork | 246 | Oak (English) | 970 |
| Elder | 695 | Pitch pine | 560 |
| Elm | 556 | Teak | 745 |
| Fir (forest) | 694 | Walnut | 671 |
| Fir (Riga) | 750 | Willow | 585 |
| Larch | 544 | | |

TIMBERS (*Fr.* Couples). A general name for the pieces of timber which compose the frame of a vessel. See *Floor-timbers, Frames,* and *Futtocks.*

Bow-timbers. The timbers that form the bow of the ship. (Plate II. fig. 7).

Counter-timbers. The timbers wrought into a vessel's counter, consisting of the short stern-timbers, and the lower parts of the long stern-timbers.

Cross-timbers, or Cross-pieces. Short timbers laid across the keel of a heavy ship of war, and scarphed to the lower ends of the first futtocks, whereby a greater degree of strength is obtained: they are not common in ships built for the merchant service.

FASHION-TIMBERS. Two timbers in the run of a vessel united one to each end of the transoms, to form the shape of the stern-frame. See *Fashion-pieces.*

FILLING-IN-TIMBERS. Those timbers which are introduced in some vessels between the frames, for the purpose of making a solid framing. See *Frames.*

FLOOR-TIMBERS. Large and strong pieces of timber placed across a vessel's keel at right angles to it, forming the lower structure of the frame. (Plate II. 6.) See *Floor.*

HALF-TIMBERS. The short timbers (or futtocks) in the cant bodies: they are placed so as to give good shiftings.

HAWSE-TIMBERS. The upright timbers in the bow in which the hawse-holes are cut See *Hawse.*

QUARTER-TIMBERS. The framing timbers in a vessel's quarters.

ROUGH-TREE-TIMBERS. See *Stanchions.*

STERN-TIMBERS. A general name given to all the timbers in the stern-frame. *The long stern-timbers* extend from the wing-transom up to the taffrail: *the short stern-timbers* from the wing-transom to the arch-board or to the name-board. (Plate II. fig. 5.)

TOP-TIMBERS. See *Futtocks.*

TIMBER-CONVERTER. The person who at a dockyard has the charge of converting timber for its different shipbuilding purposes. See *Converting.*

TIMBER-HEADS. The ends of the timbers which come above the decks: they are used for belaying ropes to. (Plate IV. 27 and 22.)

TIMBER-HITCH. See *Hitch (Timber).*

TIMBER AND ROOM, ROOM AND TIMBER, ROOM AND SPACE, or BERTH AND SPACE, in Shipbuilding, the distance from the moulding-edge of one timber to the moulding-edge of the timber next to it.

TIMENOGUY, in a ship of war, a rope rove through a thimble on the clue of the mainsail or foresail, and carried fore-and-aft outside of the rigging, as a guy to clear the clues from the rigging; or seized for the like purpose to a cleat attached to the foremost swifter or shroud on each side, to keep the tacks and sheets up, in working the ship; or made fast to the stock of the waist-anchor to keep the tacks and sheets from fouling on the stock. It is rarely if ever required.

TIMONEER. A name given to the helmsman.

TOGGLE. A pin used for inserting through the bight or eye of a rope, or the strop of a purchase-block, or through the eye of a bolt to which some leading block is secured, in order to fix it in its place, or through the eyes of two ropes to connect them together. Toggles are also used for making fast the small chain which connects the jib-sheet, or the foresail-sheet, with the corner of the sail in small craft, and pins of a similar description are generally welded by the middle to the end of raft-chains.

TOMAHAWK, or POLE-AXE. A weapon somewhat resembling an axe, carried by boarders in a ship of war. There is a piece of rope attached as a becket for the hand to go through. It is also used in merchant vessels for cutting away the wreck of masts and rigging &c. when an accident occurs.

TOMPION. A piece of wood put into the muzzle of a gun to prevent the admission of water. A lanyard is attached to it, and to a wad which is driven firmly into the piece before putting in the tompion. A 'fire-swab,' also, which is made of rope-yarns, is commonly secured to the tompion, and is saturated with water to wet the gun, in order to cool it, and clear away any particles of powder &c.

TONGUE. A long tapered end of one piece of timber fitted like a tenon into the end of another piece, which is forked to receive it. The pieces are secured by bolts and hoops binding them together. The operation, which forms a kind of scarph, is called *tonguing*; its most common application is for the purpose of lengthening masts, and, along with fishes, for repairing yards when sprung at the slings.

See also *Iceberg*, 18.

TONNAGE (*Fr.* Tonnage, Jaugeage, Capacité). The cubical contents of a ship or vessel reduced into tons. The *register* (or *registered*) *tonnage* of a ship is the tonnage of a ship ascertained according to certain rules prescribed by the legislature, and accordingly registered as the tonnage on which the public burdens on shipping are exigible. Mr. Peake, in his *Rudimentary Treatise on the Practice of Shipbuilding*, p. 73, explains the mode of ascertaining the tonnage of a ship by the old measurement, termed the *Builders' Tonnage*: the general terms of which are 'The burden in tons = length of keel for tonnage × breadth for tonnage × half breadth for tonnage, divided by 94.' The new tonnage is regulated by the Merchant Shipping Act. See the article *Burden*.

New vessels are commonly understood to be sold according to the old measurement of tonnage, unless otherwise stipulated.

TOP (*Fr.* Hune). A platform placed over the head of a lower mast in a square-rigged vessel, resting on the trestle-trees, to spread the rigging, and for the convenience of men aloft. The tops are named after the respective masts to which they belong, *main, fore,* and *mizen tops.* (Plates III. and IV.) See *Top-Armour*, *Top-Lining*, and *Top-Rim.*

To Top Up *a yard* or *a boom*, &c., means to raise one end of it by hoisting on the lift. See *Topping-Lift.*

TOP AND BUTT, in Shipbuilding, a method of working planks cut out of long tapering trees by laying their broad and narrow ends alternately fore and aft, lining a piece off every broad end the whole length of the shifting. By this method every other seam produces a fair edge: it is adopted principally for ceiling. See *Butt*, and *Touch.*

TOP-ARMOUR. An ornamented board fitted to the after part of a vessel's top, covering in the ends of the trestle-trees, the top-rim, &c.

TOP-BLOCK. A block hooked to the lower part of the cap through which the top-rope for sending a topmast up and down is rove. See *Mast-Rope.*

TOP-BURTON TACKLE. See *Burton.*

TOPGALLANT BULWARKS. The same as *Quarter-Boards.*

TOPGALLANT FORECASTLE. A sort of cabin formed by a short deck raised above the forecastle deck.

TOPGALLANT MASTS and SAILS (*Fr.* Mât de perroquet, *Topgallant Mast*; Perroquet, *Topgallant Sail*). See *Mast.*

TOPGALLANT QUARTER-BOARDS. The same as *Quarter-Boards.*

TOP-HAMPER. Any unnecessary weight, either aloft or about the topsides or upper decks.

TOP-LIGHT. A signal lantern carried in a vessel's top.

TOP-LINING. A platform of thin board nailed upon the upper part of the cross-trees on a vessel's top. See also *Lining.*

TOPMAST (*Fr.* Mât de hune). The second mast above the deck next above the lower mast, main, fore, or mizen.

TOP-MAUL. A maul used for driving out and in the fid of any topmast when required.

TOP-MEN. The gangs of able seamen who, among other

duties, are employed in a vessel's tops and about the upper masts and rigging (main, fore, or mizen), are designated respectively *main, fore*, or *mizen* topmen. See *Captain*.

TOPPING-LIFT. A rope used for topping up the end of a main, spanker, or swinging boom. (Plate III. No. 5.)

DAVIT TOPPING-LIFT. A rope secured to the outer end of a davit, and rove through a block made fast to a vessel's mast aloft, with a tackle attached. Such lifts are generally employed for the davits of anchors, to assist in keeping the anchor clear of the rail when bringing it in-board to be stowed on deck.

TOP-RIM. A thin piece of board bent round a vessel's top, giving it a finish, and covering in the ends of the cross-trees and trestle-trees, so as to prevent the topsail from being chafed.

TOP-ROPE. The same as *Mast-Rope*.

TOPSAIL (*Fr.* Hunier). The second sail above the deck on any mast (main, fore, or mizen). See *Gaff-Topsail.*

TOPSAIL HAUL! The order given to haul the after yards round when the ship is head to wind in tacking.

TOPSAIL SHEET BITTS are pieces of timber used for belaying the topsail sheets to. Those for the *fore-topsail sheets*

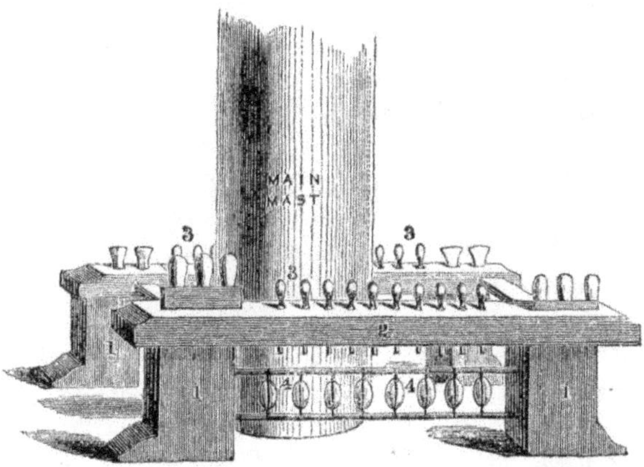


MAIN-TOPSAIL SHEET BITTS OF THE 'NORTHUMBERLAND' STEAM SHIP OF WAR NOW BUILDING. (Drawn, by permission, from model.)

1. Topsail sheet bitts.
2. Cross pieces.
3. Belaying pins.
4. Rails for topsail sheet blocks.

are let down into the deck before the foremast. In merchant vessels the gallows-stanchions, or sometimes the fife-rail stanchions, serve as bitts for the *main-topsail sheets.* The *mizen-topsail sheets* are belayed to a cleat on the mast: this is likewise the case in most small vessels, with the fore-topsail sheets, which pass through the eye of an iron hook fixed through the deck. See also *Partners.*

TOP-SIDES. That part of a vessel's sides which is above the wales. See *Strake.*

TOP-TIMBER LINE. A curve describing the height of the top-timbers, which gives the sheer of the vessel. See *Ship-building.*

TOP-TIMBERS. See *Futtocks.*

TORMENTOR. The *Cook's tormentor* is a name given to a large iron fork used on board of a vessel for lifting out beef while cooking.

TORNADO (*Fr.* Tornade). A Spanish word adopted into our language denoting 'a sudden and violent storm at sea,' or 'a violent squall rising suddenly from the shore and veering round all points of the compass. It is especially applied to a hurricane of this kind on the coasts of Senegal during summer, indicated by a squall from the south-east; a heavy increasing cloud approaches, and the moment when the wind comes to blow with impetuosity is preceded by a calm with thunder and lightning. In the vicinity of Natchez such storms occasionally come on from the south-west.'

TOSS *an oar.* 'To throw it out of the rowlock, raise it perpendicularly on its end, and lay it down in the boat with its blade forward.' (*Dana's Seaman's Manual.*)

TOT. A name for a small measure, made of wood or bone, used in some ships for serving out the seamen's grog.

TOUCANG. A fishing boat of the Straits of Malacca resembling a French lugger. (*Dict. de Marine à voiles.*)

TOUCH, in Shipbuilding, the broadest part of a plank, worked either top-and-butt or anchor-stock.

*A sail is said to touch* when the wind strikes the leach so as to shake it a little. Hence *Luff and Touch her!* is an order to bring the ship's head up to the wind until the sails shake: this is done either to give facility when lowering sails in order to reef &c., or for the purpose of stopping the ship's way.

*A vessel is said to touch at any port or place* when she stops or anchors at it in the course of a voyage.

TOUCH-HOLE. See *Vent of a Gun.*

TOW (*Fr.* Remorquer, Touer). To draw a vessel along by means of a rope attached to another ship or boat. See *Towing-Bridle.*

TOWAGE (*Fr.* Touage). The act of towing.

TOWING-BRIDLE. A piece of stout chain with a hook at each end for hooking to an eye-bolt on each side of a steamer's deck, and having in the centre of its bight a large hook, called a *Towing-hook,* fitted for the purpose of making fast a tow-rope when required.

A TOWING-TIMBER or TOWING-POST is a substantial piece of timber inserted through the deck of a steamer for the like purpose.

TOWING-HOOK. See *Towing Bridle.*

TOWING-POST. See *Towing Bridle.*

TOWING-TIMBER. See *Towing Bridle.*

TOW-LINE (*Fr.* Touée). A water-laid rope of a size between the hawser and the largest warp: it is used in cases where the latter may be of insufficient strength.

TOW-ROPE (*Fr.* Touée). Any rope used for towing.

TRABAC, or TRABACOLO. A merchant vessel of the Adriatic somewhat resembling a French lugger. (*Dict. de Marine à voiles.*)

TRACE UP, or TRICE UP. To haul up anything and make it fast as a temporary security.

TRACING-LINE, or FANCY-LINE. A line attached to the topmast and topgallant backstays, and made fast to the mast a little below the top, in order to keep these backstays steady when the ship heels over with the wind.

TRACK. To haul a vessel along, more particularly in a narrow river or canal, by means of a rope carried on shore. A vessel adapted for being transported solely in this way gets the name of a *Track-boat.*

The line of a ship's course in the water is called her *Track.*

TRACK-BOAT. See *Track.*

TRADER. A vessel employed regularly in any particular trade, whether foreign or coasting.

TRADE-WINDS (*Fr.* Alizés). A name given to certain regular winds which blow within or near the tropics, more especially in the open parts of the Pacific and Atlantic Oceans.

Although the chief region of these winds is between $23\frac{1}{2}°$ north and $23\frac{1}{2}°$ south latitude, yet 'in some parts of the world they extend to latitude 28° both N. and S. of the equator, while at other places well within the tropics, and even close to the line, totally different winds prevail.'

The trade-winds are distinguished into the NE. trade-wind, which blows on the north side of the equator, and the SE. trade-wind, which blows on the south side of the equator. 'In point of fact, however, they seldom blow directly from NE. and SE.: the only general assertion with respect to them which can safely be made is, that they blow more or less from the eastern towards the western half of the compass,' and they vary in their direction and strength at different seasons. The southern margin of the NE. trade-wind varies considerably with the season of the year; from December to May inclusive it frequently reaches so far as the 3rd degree of north latitude, though it ranges about 5° and 6° north; from June to November it is shifted back as far sometimes as 13° north, and seldom extends as far south as 8° north latitude.' From January to May, the northern limit of the SE. trade-wind is about 1° or 2° north latitude; in summer and autumn it is a degree or two still further to the northward of the line.

At the tropical borders of both trades, they are found to blow very nearly from the E. point. At their equatorial limits—that is to say, at the southern margin of the NE. trade-wind and the northern margin of the SE. trade-wind—they blow directly from the N. and S. respectively: the meeting of the two opposite currents here produces the intermediate space called the *calms* or *variables.* It varies in width from 150 to more than 500 miles, being widest in September, and narrowest in December or January: in this region, calms, southerly and south-westerly breezes, or, according to Horsburgh's account, winds from the westward, and sometimes violent squalls, are met with, the laws of which are not so readily understood as those of the trade-winds, and are consequently not so easily allowed for in the practice of navigation.

The above account is extracted from the second series of *Fragments of Voyages and Travels by Captain Basil Hall*, who therein refers to *Horsburgh's India Directory* and *Professor Daniell's Meteorological Essays* as the best authorities on such subjects.

In the *Dictionnaire de Marine à voiles et à vapeur* it is stated that westerly winds are sometimes met with near the equator in the Pacific Ocean a great way to the westward of New Guinea, and also in the Atlantic Ocean westerly winds at times occur near or a little to the northward of the equator, forming a counter current to the regular north-east and south-east trade-winds which prevail on each side of it.

In the Introduction to his *India Directory*, Captain Horsburgh mentions that trade-winds are constant only in the ocean at a considerable distance from land.

The most valuable recent accession of information on this subject is contained in *Lieut. Maury's Investigations of the Winds and Currents of the Sea*, which first appeared in the Appendix to the *Washington Astronomical Observations for* 1846, and was reprinted at Washington, U.S., in 1851. Lieut. Maury has also published *Wind and Current Charts*.

The subject is treated of likewise in *Maury's Physical Geography of the Sea*.

TRAILBOARDS. Ornamented boards between the cheek-knees. (Plate IV. 7.)

TRAINING SHIPS. Ships on board of which youths are educated and trained to seamanship before entering into active service in the Royal Navy; as the Britannia at Portland, the Boscawen at Southampton Water, the Implacable at Devonport. There are also training ships or 'school ships' for the merchant service, first introduced in Liverpool, and now extended to London and elsewhere.

TRAIN-TACKLES. The tackles used on board a vessel for running guns in and out: for this purpose luff-tackles are used, one on each side of the gun, the double block being hooked to an eye-bolt in the rear of the gun-carriage, and the single block to a ring-bolt in the deck; by 'choking the luff' they also serve to prevent the gun from running out and jamming the men while loading it.

TRANKEY. A particular kind of boat running between Muscat and Bussora in the Persian Gulf.

TRANSHIP. See *Transship*.

TRANSIRE. A document passed through the custom-house specifying the goods shipped by a coasting vessel for any particular voyage. On the back of this a *sufferance*, that is, an order, or a written permission for their discharge, is granted by the custom-house at the port of destination.

TRANSOM-KNEES. Knees which have one arm applied to

either end of a transom, and the other running diagonally along, and bolted to the ship's side. They serve as an important binding. In order to take up less space in the cabin, they are often made of iron. (Plate II. fig. 5.)

TRANSOMS, in Shipbuilding, beams of wood fitted horizontally between the fashion-pieces, and bolted to the fore part of the stern-post. The uppermost of them, which is the longest, is termed the *main-transom* or *wing-transom*. The whole of these connected together compose what is called the stern-frame of the ship. (Plate II. fig. 5.) See *Stern-post* (*Inner*), and *Stool*.

It is important to notice that the efficiency of transoms in binding the ship's sides together depends much upon their length: a vessel with short transoms in her stern-frame would, therefore, require to be the more carefully strengthened inside by pointers and crutches.

TRANSPORT (pronounced transpórt). To move a vessel along from one place to another, either by warping or by towing. See *Chock* (*Transporting*).

TRANSPORTS (*Fr.* Transports), pronounced tránsports, are Merchantmen hired, or ships of war employed by the Admiralty for the conveyance of troops, naval stores, ammunition, &c.

Of the various denominations of ships in the tránsport service *Cartel-ships* are such as are employed for conveying and exchanging prisoners; they are generally old ships of war: *Convict-ships*, are those employed for carrying convicts; *Naval Store ships* are for the conveyance of stores and ordnance to the dockyards and arsenals at different stations abroad, for which purpose ships of war are exclusively employed; *Troop-ships* are intended chiefly for conveying cavalry and their horses.

TRANSSHIP (often or commonly spelt *tranship*). To remove a cargo from one ship to another.

TRANSVERSE SECTION, is a section cutting the vessel at right angles with the keel. See *Section*.

TRAVELLER. An iron ring fitted to run out and in on a boom or gaff, for the purpose of extending and taking in the outer corner of the sail. See *Out-hauler*.

THE FORE-SHEET TRAVELLER is a ring of the same description, which traverses on the fore-sheet horse of a fore-and-aft rigged vessel. See *Horse* (*Fore-sheet*).

THE JIB-TRAVELLER of a sloop traverses on the bowsprit; that of a fore-and-aft schooner, or of a square-rigged vessel (both of which have standing bowsprits), traverses on the jib-boom. When taking in the jib, it is important to ease it in by means of the traveller, so that it may be stowed with greater facility than on the boom end, as the stowing of this sail may be otherwise attended with danger unless it is furnished with brails. Ships of war have generally also a spare jib-traveller on the jib-boom.

TRAVERSE. The crooked line or track described by a vessel when she is obliged to sail on different courses. See *Sailing* (*Traverse*).

TRAVERSE-HORSES. A name formerly given to jackstays sometimes used for fore-and-aft sails to traverse upon. See *Jackstays.*

TRAVERSE-SAILING. See *Sailing* (*Traverse*).

TRAWLING. The operation of fishing with a trawl-net. See *Drag-net.*

TREBISOND. A Turkish boat or small vessel having a long mast placed at about two-thirds of her length from the bow, on which mast a square sail is set. It has great sheer, sharp bows, and a round stern. (*Dict. de Marine à voiles.*)

TREENAIL-PLUG and TREENAIL-WEDGE. See *Treenails.*

TREENAILS (*Fr.* Gournables). Cylindrical pins (generally made of oak or Dantzic fir) driven through the sides and bottom of a vessel in order to secure and bind her planking and timbers together; to assist in preventing the treenail from starting either way, a four-cornered pin of hard wood with a sharp point (called a *treenail-plug*) is then driven into its outer end, and a wooden *wedge* of hard wood into its inner end. Iron bolts are sometimes used in preference to treenails for the topsides and wales, because the planks are apt to rot should any bad treenails happen to be employed. In the parts below water good treenails are preferable, on account of the tendency of iron to corrode. By a recent regulation of *Lloyd's Register of British and Foreign Shipping*, every vessel which would rank ten years A 1 or upwards is entitled to an extension of two years on that class, if fastened with copper or yellow metal bolts, to the exclusion of treenails. A species of hard timber called locust makes excellent treenails: it does not appear to be subject to infection; at all events, treenails of it, in the heart of decayed English oak timber. have been found not in the least touched with rot. See *Through.*

TREND. See *Anchor*, 1.

TRESTLE-TREES (*Fr.* Elongis), or TRUSSEL-TREES. 'Two strong pieces of timber placed horizontally and fore-and-aft on opposite sides of a mast-head, to support the cross-trees and top, and also for the fid of the mast above to rest upon.'

TRICE. See *Trace.*

TRICK. The time allotted to a man to stand at the helm, which is commonly two hours.

TRIGGER, in Shipbuilding, a kind of iron dog fastened to the bilgeways and sliding-planks as a holdfast. After the dog-shores have been knocked off, it is driven out, to allow the vessel to descend.

TRIM *of a vessel or of a boat* (*Fr.* Balancer). The proper disposition of the weight which she carries. When there is only ballast on board, she is said to be in *ballast-trim.*

A vessel is said *to be trimmed* 'by the head,' when the weight is so disposed as to make her draw more water towards the head than towards the stern, and 'by the stern' when the reverse is the case.

To TRIM (*Fr.* Orienter) also signifies to arrange the sails by the braces &c. with reference to the wind; and the sails are said to be trimmed to the course which is to be shaped. *To trim sharp upon a wind,* is to adjust the sails so that the ship may keep as close to the wind as possible.

TRINCADOUR. A kind of launch or long boat of the Spanish coasts, strongly built, but finely moulded, and a good sea-boat. (*Dict. de Marine à voiles.*)

TRINITY HOUSE COMPANY. A kind of guildry corporation, 'founded in 1815 in the parish of Deptford Stroud, in the county of Kent.' It is composed of seamen of experience and acknowledged skill. Among other privileges, this corporation have authority to license pilots within certain limits. And officers desiring to be qualified to take charge as pilots of any of Her Majesty's vessels are examined in pilotage by the Trinity Board.

TRIP *an Anchor*, to raise it clear of the bottom: the anchor is then said to be a-trip.

TRIPPING-LINE, is a line used for tripping an upper-mast, that is, for starting it from the fid in order that it may be lowered by means of the mast-rope.

There are also *tripping-lines* used on board ships of war, for hauling the lifts and braces off the yard-arms preparatory to sending down a top-gallant or royal yard.

TROOP-SHIP. Any ship of war employed, when occasion requires, in the conveyance of troops. See Chapter XXI. of *The Queen's Regulations.*

TROPICS (*Fr.* Tropiques). Two lesser circles of the sphere parallel to the equinoctial, and 23° 28′ distant from it, being the limits of the sun's greatest declination north and south. That in the northern hemisphere is called the tropic of *Cancer*, and that in the southern hemisphere the tropic of *Capricorn*; so termed because they touch the ecliptic at the beginning of these constellations or signs of the zodiac. (*Squire's Grammar of Astronomy; Norie's Epitome.*) See *Astronomy*, 5, 6.

TROUGH *of the sea*. The hollow formed between two waves. A vessel when lying *in the trough of the sea* (*Fr.* entre deux des lames) is in the greatest danger of being struck by a wave. When lying to she is often exposed to being brought into this position by some sudden shift; it then becomes necessary to embrace the first opportunity of wearing the ship round in order to bring her on the other tack.

TROW. A flat-bottomed vessel peculiar to the Severn, drawing little water. It has a mast, on which usually a square sail is set.

TRUCK. A circular piece of wood fixed on the head of each of a ship's highest masts, with small holes or sheaves in it for signal halyards to be rove through. Also, the wheel of a gun-carriage. (*Dana's Seaman's Manual.*)

SHROUD-TRUCKS. Small pieces of wood with holes in them, but no sheaves, seized on the shrouds as fairleaders for the running-rigging.

TRUNDLE-HEAD. In the case of a double capstan, the drum-head of the lower capstan is called a *Trundle-head.* See *Drum-head.*

TRUNK-ENGINE. A direct acting steam engine in which the end of the connecting-rod is attached to the bottom of a hollow trunk passing steam-tight through the cylinder cover. 'The cylinder is horizontal and connected at once with the screw-shaft.' (*Murray's Treatise on the Marine Engine*, p. 14; *Boyd's Naval Cadet's Manual*, p. 486; *Maine and Brown's Treatise on the Marine Engine.*)

TRUNNIONS. The two knobs or arms which project from

the opposite sides of a gun, serving to support it on the cheeks of the carriage, and on which, as an axis, it is elevated or depressed. See *Gun*.

The *trunnion-piece* of an Armstrong gun is 'a ring or belt with two projecting trunnions forming pivots for the gun when on its carriage.'

The TRUNNIONS of oscillating cylinders are 'the hollow axes upon which they vibrate and through which the steam passes into the belt leading round the exterior of the cylinder to the valve-casing.' (*Murray's Treatise on the Marine Engine.*)

TRUSS. The rope by which the centre of a lower yard is kept in towards the mast; there are small tackles attached, so that it may be slacked off or hauled taut at pleasure. In most merchant vessels *iron* trusses are now used, having a joint which allows the yard to move in any direction.

TRUSS also signifies an ornamental bracket fixed on the stern of some vessels to support the carved work on the stern windows.

This term is also applied to the *Truss-pieces* used in the system of diagonal trussing.

To TRUSS UP A SAIL, is a term sometimes applied to brailing it up.

TRUSSEL-TREES. See *Trestle-Trees.*

TRUSS-HOOPS. The hoops round a yard, and also round the mast, to which an iron truss is fixed.

TRUSSING (DIAGONAL), in Shipbuilding, a particular method of binding and strengthening a vessel internally: the system introduced by Sir Robert Seppings, of which a full description is quoted in *Mr. Creuze's Treatise on Naval Architecture*, consisted of a series of timbers, called *riders,* laid diagonally on the framing from one end of the ship to the other, along with pieces of timber placed in a fore-and-aft direction over the joints of the frame-timbers at the floor-heads and first futtock-heads, having their ends coaked or dowelled to the edges of the diagonal riders, while into each compartment formed by this frame-work in the hold a piece of wood, called a *truss-piece* or *truss,* was introduced, with an inclination opposite to that of the riders, thereby dividing it into two parts. Mr. Creuze describes a modification of the system of diagonal trussing which is now adopted for Her Majesty's ships, consisting of two ranges of iron riders or braces bolted securely through the ship's bottom; the lower range is brought upon the inside of the frame, and the ceiling worked and scored over them, the upper ends of this range extending forward in the fore body and aft in the after body of the vessel, and the direction of the upper range, which is fayed to the ceiling, crossing that of the lower range at right angles. This latter method seems applicable to merchantmen, whether sailing vessels or steamers, wherein space can ill be afforded. Planks bolted in a similar manner diagonally over the ceiling form an efficient binding, well suited for merchant vessels.

TRUSS-PARREL. That part of a rope-truss which goes round the yard.

TRUSS-PENDANTS. Those parts of a rope-truss to which the truss-tackles are hooked. See *Naval Line.*

TRUSS-PIECE, or TRUSS. See *Trussing* (*Diagonal*).

TRYING A VESSEL WITH WATER, means filling her with water in order to ascertain whether she is perfectly tight or not. In quiet weather this may be ascertained by means of smoke; which is done by placing two or three kettles on the top of the ballast or dunnage, with a little heated coal-tar and sulphur in each. A few bundles of straw are put over each kettle, and set fire to. The hatches and all other openings on deck are then closed, and the smoke soon extinguishes the fire. At the same time this process kills all vermin in the ship.

TRYSAIL. A fore-and-aft sail, with a boom and gaff, and hoisting on a lower mast, or on a small mast, called the *trysail mast*, close abaft that mast. This name is generally confined to the sail so carried at the main-mast of a full rigged brig or snow (Plate IV. 106, 41, 42); that which is carried at the fore-mast or main-mast of a ship or barque, or at the fore-mast of a brig or schooner, being called a *spencer*, and that which is set on the mizen-mast of a ship or barque, a *spanker* or *driver*. See *Brig.*

TRYSAIL is also the name given to a sail set on a fore-and-aft rigged vessel (on the main-mast if a two-masted vessel) hoisted by a gaff, but having no boom at its lower edge; this is used only in bad weather as a *storm-trysail.* A piece of rope or iron going across the stern is used in some vessels for the storm-trysail sheet-block traversing upon, and gets the name of the *trysail-sheet horse.*

The *mizen-trysail* is a sail 'occasionally used in ships of the Royal Navy instead of the spanker in stormy weather.'

TUBULAR BOILER. See description of *Steam Engine,* Sect. 37.

TUBULAR BOAT-BUOYS. See *Life-Boat.*

TUCK, in Shipbuilding, the after part of the ship where the ends of the planks of the bottom are terminated by a moulding wrought across the counter, termed the *counter-rail, tuck-rail,* or *tuck-moulding.*

When the after part of the ship terminates in a straight plane which is nearly vertical, instead of the plank running up to the counter, she is said to have a *square tuck.*

TUG. A steam-vessel employed for towing.

TUMBLE-HOME, TUMBLING-HOME, TUMBLING-IN. The inward curve on a vessel's topsides. The opposite of *flaring out.*

TURK'S-HEAD KNOT. A certain species of ornamental knot: it is sometimes wrought on man-ropes. See *Knot.*

TURN. *To take a turn of a rope* means to fasten it by passing it round anything. See *Round-turn*, and *Hawse.*

TURN IN. The ends of a vessel's shrouds carried round the dead-eyes, and laid back in order to be fastened by seizings, are said to be *turned in.*

We also use the terms *turn in* and *turn out* with reference to men going to rest in and quitting a berth or hammock.

TURNING TO WINDWARD. The same as *Beating to Windward.*

TURN UP! The order given to send the men up from between decks.

TURRET. The same as shield. See *Cupola Ship, Shield Ship.*

The name turret seems to have been first applied to that kind of shield used in the floating batteries recently constructed in the Federal States of America.

TWIDDLING-LINE. A piece of small rope, sometimes secured to an eye-bolt on deck and brought round one of the spokes on each side of the steering-wheel, in order to steady it when required.

TWO-BLOCKS. See *Chock-a-block.*

TYE, or TIE. A rope or chain attached at one end to the middle of an upper yard, going through a sheave-hole or hanging-block at the top of the mast, and having a fly-block made fast to its outer end for the halyards to be rove through: or rather the tye, as now commonly fitted, is of chain, one end of which is hooked to the lower part of the cap; it passes through an iron block, called the *tye-block*, attached to the sling-hoop at the middle of the yard and through a sheave-hole or hanging-block at the head of the mast, the other end being hooked to the fly-block through which the halyards are rove. This is used for hoisting and lowering any upper yard. See *Slings.*

JIB-TYE. A tye rove through a sheave or block on the fore-topmast head, for hoisting the jib.

PEAK-TYE. A tye used in some ships for hoisting the peak of a heavy gaff.

TYE-BLOCK. See *Tye.*

TYPHOONS (*Fr.* Typhons), or, more properly, TY-FOONGS. Dangerous tempests which are liable to happen in the Chinese Seas. They blow with greatest fury near land, and seldom reach farther south than 14° north latitude. They frequently commence without giving much indication of their proximity, and a series of fine weather and calms is apt to be succeeded by a Tyfoong. Marine barometers or sympiesometers seem to afford the best means of anticipating these tempests. From December to May tyfoongs seldom or never occur. The remainder of the year is subject to them; and the most violent of these seem, of late years, to have been experienced in the months of June and July, and about the equinox in September. (*Horsburgh's India Directory.*)

UMYAK. In Greenland, the *umyak* is the boat worked exclusively by the women, as the *kayak* is by the men. Both of them serve for fishing, and for transporting families from place to place. The umyaks are made of a wooden frame covered with seal skins. (*Dict. de Marine à voiles.*)

UNBALLAST (*Fr.* Délester). To take the ballast out of a ship.

UNBEND. To cast off or untie. Thus to unbend (*Fr.* Déverguer) the sails is to loose and cast them off from the yards, booms, or stays.

UNDER-BEVEL. See *Bevelled.*

UNDER FOOT. When an anchor is dropped from a vessel which has headway, the anchor is said to be *let go under foot.*

UNDER-RUN *a warp.* To run a boat along underneath it, in order to clear it if any part of it below water be foul, &c. See 'weigh' under the article *Anchor.*

UNDER SAIL, or UNDER CANVASS, implies that a vessel is in motion with her sails set.

UNDER WAY. This expression, often used instead of *under*

*weigh*, seems to be a convenient one for denoting that a ship or boat is making progress through the water, whether by sails or other motive power. See *Under Weigh.*

UNDER WEIGH, often written UNDER WAY (as in Falconer's *Dictionary of the Marine*). A vessel is *under weigh* when she weighs her anchor or quits her moorings. See *Under Way.*

UNDERWRITER. See *Insurance (Marine)*, 1, 2.

UNFURL (*Fr.* Déferler). The reverse of *Furl.*

UNION. The upper inner corner of a British ensign. The rest of the flag is called *the fly.*

UNION DOWN. 'The situation of a flag hoisted upside down, bringing the union down instead of up. Used as a signal of distress.' (*Dana's Seaman's Manual.*)

UNION-JACK. A small union flag formed by the intersection of the red and white crosses. See *Jack.*

UNMOOR (*Fr.* Démarrer). The reverse of *Moor.*

UNREEVE. The reverse of *Reeve.*

UNRIG (*Fr.* Dégarnir). The reverse of *Rig.*

UNSEAWORTHINESS (*Fr.* Innavigabilité). The reverse of *Seaworthiness.*

UNSHIP. See *Ship.*

UPHROE. See *Awning.*

UPMAKING, in Shipbuilding, pieces of plank or timber piled on each other as a filling up; more especially those placed between the bilge-coads and the ship's bottom, preparatory to launching.

UPPER DECK. See *Deck.*

UPPER MASTS, SAILS, and YARDS. See *Masts.*

UPPER WORKS (*Fr.* Hauts, Œuvres mortes). That part of a vessel's hull which is above the wales.

UP WITH THE HELM, means to put it a-weather.

UVRON, or EUPHROE. See description of *Awning.*

VACA. A large canoe with a single outrigger, of Tongatabou. It has a platform amidships, on which is raised a seat for the native chiefs. (*Dict. de Marine à voiles.*)

VALVES (*Fr.* Soupapes, Valvules). See alphabetical index to description of *Steam Engine*, Plate I.

VAN. 'The foremost division of a squadron of ships of war.' See *Rear.*

VANE (*Fr.* Girouette). A small kind of flag traversing on a spindle, worn at a mast-head to show the direction of the wind.

DOG-VANE. A small vane made of feathers, or of buntine, placed for the above purpose in a position near the deck, so as to be conveniently seen by the quartermaster of a ship of war when conning during the night, or by the helmsman, or the officer on watch in a merchant vessel.

VANG. A rope leading from the peak of the gaff of a fore-and-aft sail to the rail on each side of the vessel; used for steadying the gaff. (*Dana's Seaman's Manual.*) See Plates III. and IV.

VANGEE. See description of *Pump.*

VARIABLES. See *Trade-winds.*

VARIATION (*Fr.* Variation). See *Compass*, and *Magnetic.*

VEER (*Fr.* Filer). To let out. As 'veer away the cable,' that is, slack it and let it run out.

*To veer a buoy in a ship's wake,* means to slack out a rope to which the buoy has been attached, in order to let it go astern, for the purpose of bringing up a boat that has fallen astern, or of picking up a person who has fallen overboard.

*The wind is said to veer,* when it shifts or changes. It is said to *veer aft* when it comes to blow more from astern, and to *haul forward* if the reverse. See also *Wear.*

VEER AND HAUL. To slack out and haul in a rope alternately.

VENT (*Fr.* Lumière) *of a gun.* The touch-hole or aperture through which the fire is communicated to the charge.

VENT-BIT. A species of gimlet used for clearing the vent of a gun when choked.

VENT-FIELD. A rectangular piece of the metal raised a little upon a gun; through it the vent is bored.

VENT-PIECE. See *Gun* (*Armstrong*).

VENT-PLUG. A tight plug made of leather, plaited rope-yarn, or oakum, which one of the men thrusts into the vent of a muzzle-loading gun, pressing upon it with his thumb in order to *stop the vent,* while sponging the piece and ramming home the charge, so that any spark or fire in the gun may be extinguished. In the practice of Gunnery, it is of the utmost importance that this operation be carefully attended to. In a breech-loading gun, such as the Armstrong gun, it is avoided.

VENTILATOR. The same as *Wind-sail.* There are other

ventilators now used for the like purpose of supplying fresh air below deck by means of air pipes or tubes. See also *Blast Engine.*

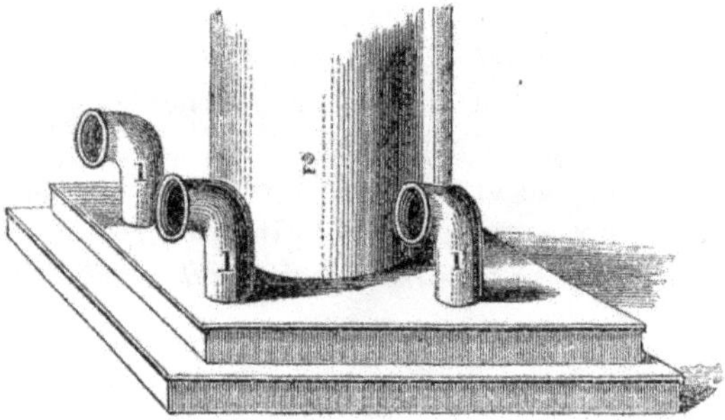


VENTILATOR OF THE 'NORTHUMBERLAND' STEAM SHIP OF WAR NOW BUILDING.
(Drawn from model.)

1. Ventilators. 2. Steam funnel.

VERTICAL CIRCLES (*Fr.* Verticaux). Great circles of the celestial sphere passing through the zenith and nadir and intersecting the horizon at right angles. See *Azimuth Circles.*

VESSEL (*Fr.* Bâtiment, Navire, Vaisseau) may be defined in the words of Dr. Johnson as 'any vehicle in which men or goods are carried on water.' It perhaps more properly applies to any kind of small ship; but throughout the present Dictionary, whenever ships in general are spoken of the term *vessel* is used instead of *ship* in any case where it is thought that doubt might arise as to the intended meaning, *ship* being, in nautical language, more peculiarly applicable to a vessel with three masts, having tops and yards to each.

VICTUALLING-BILL. A custom-house warrant for putting on board a ship's stores.

VICTUALLING-YARDS. Places where provisions and similar stores for the Royal Navy are deposited. See *Dockyards.*

VOLUNTEERS. See *Royal Naval Reserve.*

VOYAGE. A journey by sea: more especially the passage of a ship to distant parts.

WADS (*Fr.* Valets) are made of junk or rope-yarns, twisted together in a cylindrical shape, or formed like a grommet; they are used to keep the shot home to the cartridge in the breech of a gun. When loaded for immediate firing, there is no wad *between* the shot and the cartridge; but if loaded merely to be ready for sea service, a wad is also attached to the cartridge in order to let it be drawn without injury, if required.

WAFT, properly *Weft.*

WAIF. The same as *Weft.*

WAIST. That part of a vessel which is contained between the elevation of the quarter-deck and forecastle, having the upper-deck for its base or platform.

When the quarter-deck and forecastle are elevated considerably above the upper-deck, the ship is said to be *deep-waisted.*

WAIST-ANCHOR. A spare bower anchor in a ship of war.

WAIST-BOARDS. The bulwarks made to fit into a vessel's gangway on either side.

WAISTERS. 'Green hands, or broken-down seamen,' who used to be placed in the waist of a ship-of-war, to do duty not requiring a knowledge of seamanship.

WAIST-TREE, or ROUGH-TREE. A spare spar placed along the side of a ship's waist where there happens to be no bulwark, in order to protect persons from falling overboard.

WAKE. The transient impress left in the water by a vessel passing through it. A vessel is said to *sail in the wake of another* when she follows at a little distance in the same track, and *to cross in the wake of another* when she crosses the track over which the other has passed.

WALES, or BENDS (*Fr.* Préccintes). The thickest strakes of plank put round the outside of a vessel between the black-strakes. In merchantmen, the wales are always opposite to the lower hold-beams, at which part it is considered that the ship most requires a defence from external injuries above water; they form very important binding strakes, the fastenings of the hold-beams going through them. (Plate II. fig. 6.; Plate IV. 33.)

In a three-decked ship of war, the strakes between the several ranges of ports, commencing from beneath the upper-deck ports, are called the *channel-wale*, the *middle-wale*, and the *main-wale*; the strake immediately above the main-wale is called the black-strake, and the uppermost strakes of plank are called the sheer-strakes. See *Strake.*

WALL-KNOTS. See *Knot.*

WALL-SIDED. A term applied to a vessel's topsides 'when the main breadth is continued very low down and very high up so that they appear straight and upright like a wall.' (*Shipwright's Vade Mecum.*)

WANE. An imperfection in timber or plank implying a want of squareness at one or more of its corners; when it has such a deficiency it gets the name of *Wane-wood.*

WARDEN *of a Dockyard.* The officer in charge of the ingress and egress at the dockyard.

WARD-ROOM, in a ship-of-war, the mess-room for the lieutenants and other officers. Its position depends on the size and rating of the ship. In frigates and sloops-of-war the gun-room serves for the ward-room.

WARE. See *Wear.*

WAREHOUSING (or BONDING) SYSTEM. The establishment of warehouses, under the charge of officers of the customs, in which goods may be deposited, without any duty upon them being exacted, until they be cleared for home use or for exportation.

WARP (*Fr.* Grelin). A water-laid rope of smaller diameter than a hawser, used for transporting vessels in harbour and for other purposes. A vessel is supplied with warps of various sizes.

When a kedge is put out from the ship with a warp, and she is moved along by heaving on the capstan, windlass, or winch, this operation is termed *kedging* or *warping* the ship. When moved along in a similar manner by means of a warp made fast to a dolphin, or to any object on shore, this is termed *warping* her.

WARRANT OFFICERS. A distinguishing title for those officers in the Royal Navy, such as the *gunner, boatswain,* and *carpenter,* whose warrant of office gives them the charge of certain of the ship's stores. These officers rank and command in the order here named, and are each divided into first, second, and third classes. A gunner of the first class ranks and commands next below a second master, who is a commissioned officer. *Subordinate officers* are midshipmen, masters' assistants, and naval cadets, who likewise rank and command in the order here named, a midshipman being next below a carpenter. See *Commission.*

WARRANTY, in the contract of marine insurance, a condition or engagement expressed in writing on the face or margin of the policy that a certain thing has happened or is to happen. In the law maritime, 'A mere representation may be equitably and substantially answered, but a warranty must be strictly complied with.'

WASH-BOARDS (*Fr.* Fargues). A shifting strake of boards along the topsides of any small vessel which has no bulwarks, used occasionally to keep out the spray. Also a light strake of board above the gunwale of a boat, either fixed or shifting.

WASTE-STEAM PIPE. See description of *Steam Engine*, Sect. 41.

WATCH (*Fr.* Quart). The crew of every vessel while at sea is divided generally into *two* portions, called *watches*; one, the *starboard-watch*, which in the merchant service is the captain's watch, and is often commanded by the second mate; the other, the *port-watch*, which in the merchant service is commanded by the chief mate. In the Royal Navy, these watches are commanded by the lieutenants successively.

The periods of time occupied by each part of the crew alternately while thus on duty are also termed *watches*.

The following is the succession of these watches, commencing at noon. (The time is in most vessels marked by *bells*, which are struck every half hour.)

| | | Bells |
|---|---|---|
| P.M.—12— 4 | (the afternoon watch) | 8 |
| 4— 6 | (the first dog-watch) | 4 |
| 6— 8 | (the second dog-watch) | 4 (counted 5 to 8) |
| 8—12 | (the first night watch) | 8 |
| A.M.—12— 4 | (the middle watch) | 8 |
| 4— 8 | (the morning watch) | 8 |
| 8—12 | (the forenoon watch) | 8 |

The purpose of dividing the time from 4 to 8 P.M. into two half watches of two hours each (called *dog-watches*) is to make an uneven number, seven instead of six, throughout the twenty-four hours, and so to alter the watches kept from day to day by each portion of the crew; otherwise the same watch would stand during the same hours for the whole voyage.

When this alternation of watches is kept up throughout the twenty-four hours, it is termed having *watch-and-watch*—in distinction from keeping all hands at work during one or more watches. (See *Dana's Seaman's Manual.*)

ANCHOR-WATCH. A small watch consisting of one or two men, appointed to look after the ship while at anchor or in port. 'As the starboard and port watches in the Royal Navy have each a first and second part, they form four watches when required, one of which in turn is always the anchor-watch.'

WATER. When a vessel ships a sea or seas, she is said to 'take water on board.' A ship or boat admitting water is said to be leaky, or to *make water.*

HIGH-WATER, and LOW-WATER. The alternate rising and falling of the waters of the sea form what are called *high* and *low* water. See *Tides.*

WATERAGE. The charge for the use of a boat in conveying anything.

WATER BALLAST PLATFORM. A platform forming the upper part of a compartment for containing water to be used as ballast in a steamer. The water is admitted by a hole below, which is plugged securely after the necessary quantity enters the compartment.

WATER-BORNE. Goods carried by sea or on a river are said to be *water-borne.*

WATER-CASKS (*Fr.* Pièces à eau). See *Tanks.*

WATER-GUARD. The customs officers employed in preventing any fraud being practised on the revenue in the case of vessels arriving at or departing from a port.

WATER-LAID ROPE. See *Rope.*

WATER-LINES, in Shipbuilding, 'those horizontal lines supposed to be described by the surface of the water on the bottom of the ship, and which are exhibited at certain depths upon the sheer draught.' (*Shipwright's Vade Mecum.*) The most particular of these are: *the light water-line,* which shows the depression of the ship's body in the water when she is light or unladen; and the *load water-line,* which exhibits her depression in the water when laden.

The light water-*line,* or *mark,* indicates the depth of the ship's immersion without any ballast or other weight in her; the *ballast-mark,* the depth to which she is immersed with her usual weight of ballast on board.

WATER-LOGGED. The state of a vessel whose hull is sunk deep, in consequence of an extraordinary weight of water received into her by a leak or otherwise. In this condition she is nearly or altogether unmanageable, and would sink, unless by means of exertion at the pumps, or owing to their being a light floating cargo, such as timber, on board.

WATER-SAIL, or SAVE-ALL. A small sail occasionally

set under a main, spanker, or swinging boom. It is seldom used, and only in fine weather.

WATER-SPOUT (*Fr.* Trombe). A remarkable species of whirlwind which is sometimes met with at sea, mostly during the day, and in warm climates. When it is forming at a small distance, 'a portion of a dense cloud is observed to descend and stretch itself towards the sea in a conical shape;' at the same time the surface of the sea under it ascends a little way in the form of vapour, 'from the centre of which a small cone proceeding upwards unites with that projected from the cloud.' Captain Horsburgh (in the introduction to his *India Directory*, from which these particulars are extracted) mentions that water-spouts sometimes disperse suddenly without being completely formed; 'at other times they move rapidly along the surface of the sea, and continue a quarter of an hour or more before they disappear.' He remarks that small vessels are in danger of being capsized when they have much sail set, and that large vessels, if their topsails be not clued up, and the yards secured, 'may have them carried up to the mast-heads by the force of the whirlwind, and thereby lose their masts,' and 'that in the vicinity of a water-spout the wind is subject to fly all round in sudden gusts, rendering it prudent for ships to take in their square sails.'

WATER-TANKS. Cisterns made of malleable iron plates, for keeping a stock of water. See *Tanks.*

WATER-TIGHT. The reverse of leaky. See *Tight.*

WATER-WAYS (*Fr.* Gouttières), in Shipbuilding, the thick planks at the outside of the deck, wrought over the ends of the beams, and fitting against the inside of the top-timbers, to which, as well as to the ends of the beams, they are bolted, and thus form an important binding. Their inner edge is chimed to form a channel for water to run off the deck. (Plate II. fig. 6.) See *Peake's Rudimentary Treatise on the Practice of Shipbuilding,* p. 51.

WAY *of a vessel* (*Fr.* Air). Her progress or motion through the water.

See *Fresh-way,* and *Under-weigh.*

WAYS. See *Bilge-ways, Ground-ways,* and *Launching-ways.*

WEAR, or VEER. To bring a vessel upon the other tack by turning her head round away from the wind. Wearing causes the ship to lose ground, and is consequently never practised except when she will not *stay*, or where staying might be attended with danger.

WEAR AND TEAR, when expressed of a vessel, may be defined as its ordinary decay and deterioration arising in the prosecution of a voyage or voyages. This phrase is also made to comprehend those damages and losses, such as the splitting of sails under ordinary circumstances, &c., which the shipowner has to bear, in distinction from those damages and losses arising from perils of the sea for which the insurers are liable.

WEATHER, in sea phrase, is used to distinguish the side from which the wind blows, *lee* being the opposite term. Thus we speak of the *weather-side* of the ship, her *weather-quarter*, the *weather-braces*, &c. In like manner, *a weather-shore* means a shore lying to windward. *A weather-tide* is a tide running to windward; a *lee-tide*, one running in the same direction with the wind.

*To weather any object*, means to succeed in sailing to windward of it.

WEATHER-BITT. To take a turn with the bight of a cable round the windlass end, in order to prevent it from slipping round the windlass when the ship is at anchor; this is done sometimes to save the trouble of stoppering, or in vessels which have no stoppers.

WEATHER-GAUGE. When one vessel is to windward of another, she is said to have the weather-gauge of such ship.

WEATHER-HELM. A vessel is said to carry *a weather-helm* when, owing to her having a tendency to gripe, the helm requires to be kept a little to windward (or, as it is called, *a-weather*) in order to prevent her head from coming up in the wind while sailing close-hauled. She carries *a lee-helm* if it is necessary to keep the helm a little *a-lee*, in order to prevent her head from falling off. Owing to the action of the water upon the rudder, a lee-helm is more apt than a weather-helm to make a ship leewardly. A slight alteration of the position of the masts, in many cases, remedies such defects.

WEATHERLY. A ship is said to be *weatherly* when she holds a good wind, that is, when, owing to her trim, to the shape of her bottom, or to the depth of her keel, she presents so great a lateral resistance to the water while sailing close-hauled that she makes very little lee-way. *A leewardly ship* is the reverse.

WEATHER-ROLLS. The rolls which a vessel makes *to windward* in a heavy sea upon the beam. Weather-rolling is attended with danger, as it exposes the deck to the coming wave, and care should be taken to prevent it by keeping sufficient sail aloft.

The sudden rolls which a vessel makes *to leeward* are termed *lee-lurches.*

WEATHER-TIDE. A tide which will carry a vessel in the direction from which the wind blows. *A lee-tide* is one which will carry her away from the direction from which the wind is blowing.

WEDGE. A tapered piece of wood forming a well-known mechanical power. Such wedges are much used in the building and repairing of ships, and they get the name of *sett wedges.*

*Iron wedges* are used for splitting out blocks and for similar purposes.

TREENAIL WEDGE. A wooden wedge driven into the inner end of the treenail to prevent it from starting. See *Treenails.*

WEFT, WAIF, or WHIFT. A signal (most frequently for a boat) made by hoisting a flag rolled up lengthways and bound together with a few stops.

WEIGH. See the articles *Anchor*, 24; and *Underweigh.*

*To weigh a sunken ship* means to lift or raise her.

WEIGH-SHAFT, or WIPER-SHAFT. See description of *Steam Engine*, Sects. 5 and 31.

WELD. To join two pieces of iron together, by slightly fusing their surfaces, placing them in contact, and then hammering them.

WELL, or PUMP-WELL (*Fr.* Archipompe). A compartment formed by bulkheads round a vessel's pumps to keep them clear of obstructions, to protect them from injury, and also to give ready admittance for examining the state of the pumps. The pump is *sounded* by dropping a measured iron rod (called a *pump-rod*) down into it by a long line; hence the increase or diminution of leaks is readily ascertained.

*The well of a fishing-smack* is a compartment formed by bulkheads properly strengthened and tightened off, the bottom plank in the way of it being perforated with holes to give free admission to the water, so that the fish which are caught may be kept alive therein.

WESTING (*Fr.* Chemin à l'ouest). The distance sailed westwards. See *Northing.*

WET-DOCK. An artificial receptacle in which a uniform level of water is maintained to keep ships afloat while discharging and loading. See *Dock.*

WHALE-BOATS (*Fr.* Baleinières). See *Whale Fisheries.*

WHALE FISHERIES. On this subject various information is presented under the heads, *Flensing, Fortifying, Harpoon, Ice-berg,* &c.

It may here be noticed that, according to Captain Scoresby's opinion, a ship intended for the Greenland or Davis's Straits' fishing should be of from 300 to 400 tons admeasurement, very substantially built, doubled and fortified; should have six or seven feet perpendicular space between decks; should be furnished with a description of sails which are easily worked; and should possess the property of fast sailing.

The *Whale-boats* (Baleinières) being liable to receive damage both from whales and ice, are always carvel-built, a structure which is easily repaired. These boats are rounded at both ends, and clean both forward and aft, being formed somewhat like a gig, but with greater sheer and more strongly built. They are steered by means of an oar put out at the stern. In pulling, the oars are inserted each through a grommet attached to a single thole-pin: this avoids the noise which would be occasioned by unshipping the oars when they get near the fish. See *Billet-head.*

A great amount of valuable and interesting matter in regard to this subject generally may be found in *Captain Scoresby's Account of the Arctic Regions and Northern Whale Fishery,* which treats shortly also of the South Sea whale fisheries.

WHALER (*Fr.* Baleinier). A name for any whale-fishing vessel.

WHARF (*Fr.* Quai). An erection fitted for the convenience of loading and discharging vessels, and for receiving their cargoes into safe custody. The individual who has charge of it is called a *Wharfinger.* The dues for landing or shipping goods at a wharf get the name of *Wharfage.*

GUN-WHARF. A place prepared for landing and shipping ordnance for naval and military service.

WHARFAGE. See *Wharf.*

WHARFINGER. See *Wharf.*

WHEEL. The same as *Steering-wheel.*

WHEEL-HOUSE, or RUDDER-HOUSE. A kind of sentry-box, or round-house, built over the steering-wheel in large ships for the shelter of the helmsman. Sometimes the *hurricane-house* and *wheel-house* are in one.

WHEEL-ROPES (*Fr.* Drosses). Ropes rove through a

block on each side of the deck, and led round the barrel of the steering-wheel. *Chains* are now much more commonly used for this purpose than ropes; and ropes made of strips of raw hide are also frequently employed for wheel-ropes. When there is no steering-wheel, the rope is attached to the extremity of the tiller, and gets the name of the *Tiller-rope.*

WHELPS. Pieces of wood or iron bolted *on the main-piece of a windlass*, or *on a winch*, to save it from being chafed by the chain or rope, and also to make the chain hold more firmly on the windlass. *The whelps of a capstan* (see *Capstan*, woodcut No. 4) are pieces of wood bolted at certain distances round the barrel to save it from being chafed, &c.; they are thicker at their lower end so as to form an upward taper, in order to cause any warp that is hove upon to *fly up* when surging the capstan. Among the advantages afforded by *Gryll's Patent Whelps*, it is said that surging on capstans, windlasses, windlass-ends, and winches, is rendered unnecessary, as the chain fleets itself upon them, whereby a considerable saving of time arises in the process of heaving.

WHERRY. A very light-built sharp boat, pulled by oars, and seated for the accommodation of passengers.

WHIFT. See *Weft.*

WHIP. A purchase formed by a rope rove through a single

WHIP.

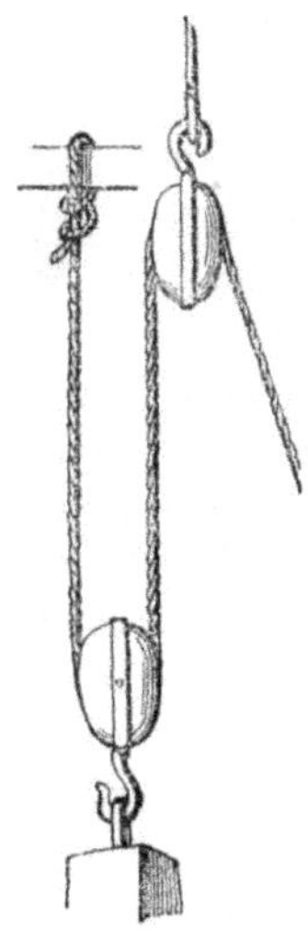

DOUBLE WHIP.

block. See *Dana's Seaman's Manual, Boyd's Naval Cadet's Manual, Nares on Seamanship.*

To WHIP, means to hoist by a whip. Also, to secure the end of a rope from fagging by means of a seizing of twine.

WHIP-UPON-WHIP, or A DOUBLE-WHIP, is one whip applied

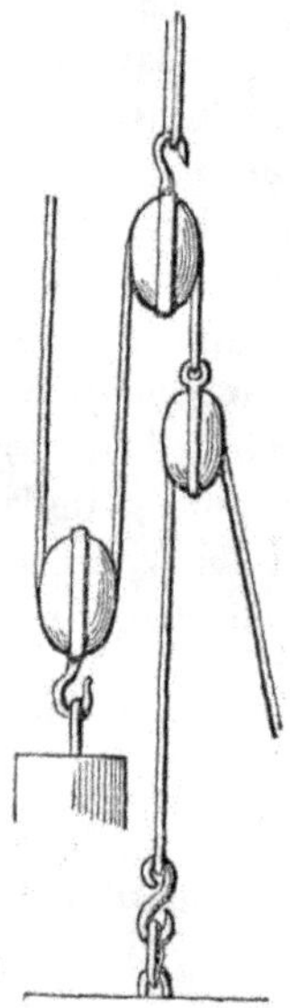

to the fall of another. See *Dana's Seaman's Manual, Boyd's Naval Cadet's Manual, Nares on Seamanship.*

WHIRLWIND (*Fr.* Tourbillon). A sudden and impetuous wind, having a spiral or whirling motion. Whirlwinds are sometimes occasioned by high uneven land when the wind is blowing strong. Gusts of this description from mountains descend sometimes on the surface of the contiguous sea. (*Horsburgh's India Directory.*) See *Water-spout.*

WHISKERS. Two booms rigged out one on each side before the knightheads, steadied at their inner ends by a gooseneck, which hooks into an eye-bolt fixed either in the hawse-wood or in each side of the bowsprit: they have sheaves or iron cleats near their outer ends, and are used instead of a spritsail-yard to spread the jib-boom guys, for the better security of this boom when the jib is set. Each whisker ships into and is confined by a clamp or crance at the outer end of the cathead. In ships of war they are commonly made of strong bars of iron fixed to and projecting from the catheads.

WHITE ROPE (*Fr.* Blanc cordage) means rope not saturated with tar, that is, not 'tarred rope.'

WHITE SQUALL. See *Squall.*

WHITWORTH GUN. See *Gun* (*Armstrong*).

WINCH. A species of small windlass or crab, turned round by crank-handles. *The double winch* is formed with two barrels, the one fitted with a spur-wheel and the other with a pinion, which give increased power. On board of a vessel it is commonly mounted upon the gallows-stanchions, and it is found particularly useful for merchantmen; in these, indeed, it has in a great measure superseded the use of the capstan. See *Whelps.*

A small winch with a fly-wheel is used in making rope or spunyarn: it gets the name of a *spunyarn-winch.*

WIND. Under this head reference may be made to the articles *Breeze*, *Gale*, *Hurricane*, *Monsoons*, *Squall*, *Trade-winds*, *Typhoon*, *Whirlwind*, &c. See also *Dove's Law of Storms.*

A vessel is said to be *all in the wind* when her head is too close to the wind, so that the sails are shivering.

A ship is *in the wind's eye* when, in sailing, her head comes so close to the wind as to cause the sails to lift at the weather leaches.

BETWIXT WIND AND WATER, is a phrase applied to that part of a vessel which is at the surface of the water.

HOLD A GOOD WIND. See *Weatherly.* ON A WIND. See *Close.* See also *Full and By*, *Ride*, *Shake*, and *Wind-rode.*

TO WIND *a ship* or *boat.* To bring her round till her head occupies the place where the stern was.

WINDAGE *of a gun* (*Fr.* Vent d'un boulet). The difference between the diameter of its bore and that of the shot.

WIND-BOUND. A vessel is *wind-bound* when detained in a harbour or roadstead by a contrary wind.

WINDING, expressed of a plank or piece of timber, implies that it is twisted or has an uneven surface: if quite fair, it is said to be *out of winding.*

WINDLASS (*Fr.* Guindeau). A machine which is erected on the fore part of a vessel's deck, for weighing the anchor, or obtaining a purchase on other occasions. It consists of a strong horizontal beam of wood called the *main-piece*, suspended at its ends by iron spindles working in collars or bushes inserted in the *windlass-bitts* and the *windlass-ends*, which are two horizontal pieces forming a continuation of the windlass outside these bitts, and connected with the main-piece by means of the spindles going through them. The main-piece has holes in it for inserting handspikes into, in order to heave it round when required. It has generally pieces of hard wood, called the *windlass-lining*, fitted and bolted round it to preserve it from being chafed, and also similar pieces of wood or iron projecting above the lining to make the cable hold on more firmly. These latter get the name of *whelps*, which are specially noticed under that head.

The different kinds of gearing invented for increasing the power and sureness of the windlass, the most important of which are those patented by Messrs. Tysack, Dobinson, and Co. and by Messrs. Pow and Fawcus (both of North Shields), have been long in general use. In employing these, handspikes are not required, although holes are nevertheless cut through the windlass to enable handspikes to be used in case of accident to the gearing. We have also further to notice Caldwall's Self-fleeting Windlass and Purchase, and Emerson and Walker's Windlass, which last is illustrated by the annexed figure. The windlass is turned by means of the capstan C fixed over it, and the chain is controlled at will in running out by means of the friction-bands F. See also *Spanish Windlass.*

WINDLASS-BITTS, RANGE-HEADS, or (as they are more commonly termed in England) CARRICK-BITTS. Upright pieces of timber bolted to a vessel's beams to support the windlass near its end. See *Bitts.*

WINDLASS-CHOCKS. Fore-and-aft pieces of oak fitted on the deck and bolted to the beams immediately before the windlass, their after ends coming partly under it, and the other ends being formed with a shoulder, between which shoulders and the windlass, when the ship is riding at anchor, wedge pieces are driven in to afford an additional support to the windlass.

WINDLASS-LINING. See description of *Windlass.*

WIND-RODE. The situation of a vessel at anchor when she is swung round by the force of the wind. See *Tide-rode.*

WIND-SAIL, or VENTILATOR (*Fr.* Ventilateur). A sort of long canvass bag turned bottom upwards, let down a vessel's hatchway for circulating air below; it is suspended by a whip and stretched out with hoops and guys, and has near its upper end an opening at the side, which is kept to windward by means of the guys.

WINDWARD (TO) (*Fr.* Au vent). See the articles *Lee*, and *Beating to Windward.*

WING, in Shipbuilding, that part of the hold or between decks which is next the ship's side, more particularly at the quarter. The term *wing* is also applied to the projecting part of a steam vessel's deck before and abaft each of the paddle-boxes; this is bounded by a thick plank called the *sponsing-rim* or *wing-wale*, which extends from the extremity of the paddle-beam to the ship's side.

WINGERS. A name for casks stowed in the wings of a vessel.

WING-TRANSOMS. See *Transoms.* (Plate II. fig. 5.)

WIPER-SHAFT, or WEIGH-SHAFT. See description of *Steam Engine*, Sects. 5 and 31.

WIRE-ROPE is usually made of iron wire in this country. For standing-rigging straight wires have been employed, parcelled and served with spunyarn, and saturated with some preservative from rust. Other wire-ropes are formed much in the same manner as ropes of hemp, the wires taking the place of rope-yarns, and being twisted into strands. The wire-ropes patented by Messrs. Robert S. Newall & Co. are made by machinery so contrived that 'to each wire a motion is given which prevents its being warped; the wires, generally six in number, are laid symmetrically round a core of hemp to form the strand, and the strands (also generally six) are in like manner laid round a core to form the rope, so that the strands are all at an equal distance from the centre of the rope; all the wires, therefore, are of the same length, and are subjected to an equal strain. They are only one-half the weight and one-sixth the bulk of hemp ropes of equal strength, besides being cheaper and more durable, and are well adapted for standing-rigging, particularly for that of steam vessels; for running-rigging they are not sufficiently flexible. Wire-rope is found to be an admirable lightning conductor.' Wire-rope seems to have been long in use in France and Saxony, and that invented by M. Albert in Hanover, before its introduction into this country, where patents for improvements in the manufacture of wire-ropes were successively taken out by Mr. Andrew Smith in 1839 and Messrs. R. S. Newall & Co. in 1840 and 1843.

A table showing the comparative weight and strength of wire and hemp-ropes is presented in the *United Service Magazine* for the year 1842.

The use of wire-rope instead of hempen-rope for the standing-rigging of merchant ships has of late become extensive.

WOODEN-BUOY. See *Buoy*, 9.

WOODLOCK, or KEY *of rudder*. A piece of hard wood put in immediately beneath one of the pintles of a rudder, with a bolt going through it and forelocked, to prevent the rudder from unshipping.

WOOD'S-ENDS, or WOOD-ENDS, or HOODING-ENDS, &c. See *Hoods*.

WOOD-SHEATHING is used most generally for covering a vessel's bottom that has been partially wormed. See *Sheathing*.

WOOLD, or WOULD. To bind with ropes; for example, where a spar that has been wounded or sprung has one or more pieces of wood bound to it in this way as a temporary fish.

WOOLDER. See *Spanish Windlass*.

WORK *a ship.* To direct her movements by the management of the sails and rudder. This phrase is especially applicable to the shifting of the sails and rudder at the proper time in the process of tacking.

*A ship is said to work* (*Fr.* fatiguer) when her fastenings at any part have become slack, and in consequence thereof she strains and yields in the pitching and rolling motions. See *Day's Work,* and *Observation.*

WORM *a rope* (*Fr.* Congréer un cordage). To fill up the spiral divisions between the strands by passing spunyarn or other small stuff along them in order to render the surface smooth for parcelling and serving. Stuff so wound round is called *worming.*

WORM, in Gunnery, an instrument resembling a double cork-screw, fixed upon a staff; it is used chiefly for drawing the remains of cartridges from a muzzle-loading gun; this operation is termed *worming the gun,* and requires to be done at least after every third discharge. For the operation of unloading a gun, a copper *shovel* is used, if practicable, instead of the worm, in order to remove the cartridge without rendering it useless.

WORMED (*Fr.* Piqué). The state of timber or plank when a number of internal cavities are made in it by a particular kind of worm, called the *Teredo navalis,* that abounds chiefly in tropical climates. Various preventives against this have been used for paying ships' bottoms with, as sulphur, or coal-tar and arsenic mixed, and that with a good degree of success, especially in ships going to the Mediterranean; but while these methods have the recommendation of cheapness, the coating of such material, by forming an uneven surface on the bottom, tends to deaden the ship's way. The only advantageous protection, therefore, seems to be a sheathing of copper or yellow metal.

WOULD. See *Woold.*

WRAIN-BOLT. A ring-bolt used in shipbuilding for *setting-to* the planks.

WRAIN-STAFF, WRUNG-STAFF, or 'DWANG-STAFF,' also called a STOWER, or TWISTING-STAFF. A sort of stout billet of tough wood tapered at the ends so as to go into the rings of the wrain-bolts for the purpose of setting-to the planks. See the title *Setting.*

WRECK (*Fr.* Naufrage, Bris). The same as *Shipwreck.* It

also implies the thing wrecked, whether the ship or goods or any part of them be spoken of.

WRECK INTELLIGENCER, or SMITH'S PATENT BUOY. A contrivance the object of which is to preserve ships' papers in case of shipwreck, &c. 'It consists of a hollow copper sphere, the buoyancy of which is further increased by cork floats; the upper part is closed by a lid fixed with screws and made water-tight by an india-rubber washer. It is weighted at bottom, so that it floats always mouth uppermost. To attract attention and be visible at a great distance, the lid is surmounted by a rod carrying a sphere of glass silvered in its interior, or by a piece of glass cut into a series of planes, and the upper part of the buoy is painted in stripes of variously-contrasted colours.'

WRECKERS. A term reproachfully applied to men who feloniously seek to enrich themselves with plunder from wrecks. It is sometimes also applied to salvors.

WRING *a mast.* To bend it by putting an undue strain upon the shrouds.

WRIST *of an anchor.* The continuation of the arm in a square or rounded form towards the *palm* or *fluke.* See description of *Anchor*, 1.

WRUNG-STAFF. A name commonly given to the *Wrain-staff.*

XEBEC (*Fr.* Chebec). A small vessel of the Mediterranean, very sharp built, having a great projection of bow and stern. It is navigated with sails and oars. Some of them are rigged with square sails set on pole-masts; others carry lateen sails. The foremast is usually stayed forward. (*Dict. de marine à voiles.*)

YACHT. A vessel of pleasure or state, whether propelled by sails or by steam power. In the latter case it is termed a *steam yacht.*

*Hunt's Yachting Magazine* contains a description of the building, masting, rigging, sailing, and general management of yachts.

YARD. A long cylindrical piece of timber having a rounded taper towards each end, slung by its centre to a mast. The yards are used for spreading square sails upon; they have sheave-holes near their extremities for the sheets reeving through. (Plates III. IV. and V.)

Either end of a yard, or rather that part of it which is outside the sheave-hole, is termed the *yard-arm*: the *quarter* of a yard is about half way between the sheave-hole and the slings. See *Parrel*, *Slings*, and *Truss*; and also the articles *Cross-Jack Yard*, *Lateen-Sail*, *Lug-Sail*, *Masts*, and *Square*.

The yard-arms in merchant vessels are commonly square-butted, in order that a sheave-hole may be cut through without weakening the yard. The yard has a small plate of iron on its lower part, close to each sheave-hole, to keep the topsail sheets, which are of chain, from chafing the yard. The sheave-holes are also shod with iron.

In ships of war, the yard-arms are generally round, with a cheek-block bolted and hooked on to each, for the topsail sheets, which are of rope, to be rove through.

YARD-ARM. See *Yard*.

YARD-ARM AND YARD-ARM, implies the situation of two vessels lying alongside of each other so near that their yard-arms cross or touch.

YARD-HORSES. Ropes attached to a vessel's yards for the men to stand on while reefing or furling. See *Horses*.

YARD-ROPES. Ropes rove through a sheave-hole at each yard-arm, and through blocks at the head of the lower mast of a sloop or schooner (whose lower square sail is not bent to the yard) for the purpose of hoisting and lowering down that sail.

YARD-TACKLES. Tackles used to steady a yard in the act of reefing the sail. These are not now used in the merchant service, the iron trusses rendering them unnecessary.

YAW. A term to imply that a vessel moves off the direct line of her course in steering.

YAWL. A name given to the smallest boat used by fishermen. See also the title *Boat*, 1, 2.

YELLOW METAL (MUNTZ'S PATENT). See *Copper*.

YEOMAN. A person appointed to assist in attending to the stores of the gunner, the boatswain, or the carpenter, in a large ship of war.

*The Yeoman of the Signals* is a person who has charge of the signals.

YOKE. A piece of board or metal made to ship on the head of a boat's rudder, with a line called the *yoke-rope* attached to each end, by which the boat is steered.

Also, 'a cross piece of timber or metal fitted on the rudder-head of a ship when a tiller cannot be used.' (*Seamanship, by Lieut. Nares*, fig. 1.)

YOU-YOU. A small Chinese boat impelled with the scull, used on rivers and in well-protected harbours and roadsteads. The Chinese are a people who make the most especial use of the scull in rowing, sometimes eight or ten men working at one scull. (*Dict. de Marine à voiles.*)

ZENITH. In Astronomy, the *zenith of any place on the globe* is 'that point in the heavens immediately above the place, and *the nadir* is that point immediately under it. Hence the zenith and nadir are the poles of the rational horizon,' from which at every point they are distant 90°. See *Circles.*

THE ZENITH DISTANCE of a celestial object is an arc of a vertical circle contained between the centre of the object and the zenith: if the object be on the meridian, it is termed *meridian zenith distance.* (*Norie's Epitome; Raper's Practice of Navigation and Nautical Astronomy.*)

ZODIAC, in Astronomy, a space including about $8\frac{1}{2}°$ on each side of the ecliptic, within which the motions of all the planets are performed. (*Baharie's Marine Board Examination.*)

The ecliptic or zodiac is divided by astronomers into twelve equal parts, called *signs of the zodiac*, each containing 30°. They are thus named:—

| 1 | 2 | 3 | 4 | 5 | 6 |
|---|---|---|---|---|---|
| ♈ | ♉ | ♊ | ♋ | ♌ | ♍ |
| **7** | **8** | **9** | **10** | **11** | **12** |
| ♎ | ♏ | ♐ | ♑ | ♒ | ♓ |

1. Aries (the Ram).
2. Taurus (the Bull).
3. Gemini (the Twins).
4. Cancer (the Crab).
5. Leo (the Lion).
6. Virgo (the Virgin).
7. Libra (the Balance).
8. Scorpio (the Scorpion).
9. Sagittarius (the Arrow-bearer or Archer).
10. Capricornus (the He-goat).
11. Aquarius (the Water-bearer).
12. Pisces (the Fishes).

The first six signs, being on the north side of the equinoctial, are termed *northern signs*; the last six, being on the south side of it, *southern signs.*

ZONES. In Geography, the earth is divided by certain imaginary circles parallel to the equator into portions called *zones*, which are distinguished according to their comparative degrees of heat and cold as follows: —

THE FRIGID ZONES, are 'those regions about the poles where the sun at certain seasons does not rise or set for some days; they extend round the poles as far as 23° 28′. The imaginary circle which bounds this limit in our northern hemisphere is called the *arctic polar circle*, and that portion of the globe included within it, the *north frigid zone.*' The circle and zone around the south pole are termed the *antarctic polar circle* and the *south frigid zone*. (*Norie's Epitome of Navigation and Nautical Astronomy.*)

THE TEMPERATE ZONES are comprehended between the polar circles and the tropics: the *north temperate zone*, between the arctic circle and the tropic of Cancer, and the *south temperate zone*, between the antarctic circle and the tropic of Capricorn.

THE TORRID ZONE, is the space included between the two tropics, over every part of which space in succession the sun is vertical at some time of the year.

# APPENDIX.

## REGULATIONS FOR PREVENTING COLLISIONS AT SEA,

ISSUED IN PURSUANCE OF

THE MERCHANT SHIPPING ACT AMENDMENT ACT, 1862,

AND OF AN

ORDER IN COUNCIL, DATED 9TH JANUARY 1863.

(*By Authority.*)

# NOTICE.

1. By virtue of the 'Merchant Shipping Act Amendment Act, 1862,' and of an Order in Council dated January 9, 1863, the following regulations, containing certain verbal Amendments, are substituted for the Regulations contained in the Schedule to the Act.

2. The following Regulations come into operation on June 1, 1863.

3. The following Regulations apply to all Ships, whatever their Nationality, within the limits of British Jurisdiction, and to British and French Ships, whether within British Jurisdiction or not.

4. The Order in Council containing these Regulations is published in the 'London Gazette' of January 13, 1863.

5. The French Copy of the Regulations in the following pages is reprinted from the French Version, as published in France under the Authority of the French Government.

T. H. FARRER,
*Assistant Secretary, Marine Department.*

BOARD OF TRADE:
*January* 1863

# REGULATIONS FOR PREVENTING COLLISIONS AT SEA.

APPENDED TO THE ORDER IN COUNCIL DATED JANUARY 9, 1863.

---

THESE REGULATIONS CAME INTO OPERATION ON JUNE 1, 1863.

---

CONTENTS.

# REGULATIONS FOR PREVENTING COLLISIONS AT SEA, &c.

*Preliminary.*

Art. 1. In the following Rules every Steam Ship which is under Sail and not under Steam is to be considered a Sailing Ship; and every Steam Ship which is under Steam, whether under Sail or not, is to be considered a Ship under Steam.

*Rules concerning Lights.*

Lights.

Art. 2. The Lights mentioned in the following Articles, numbered 3, 4, 5, 6, 7, 8, and 9, and no others, shall be carried in all Weathers, from Sunset to Sunrise.

Lights for Steam Ships.

Art. 3. Seagoing Steam Ships when under weigh shall carry:

(*a*) *At the Foremast Head*, a bright White Light, so fixed as to show an uniform and unbroken Light over an Arc of the Horizon of 20 points of the Compass; so fixed as to throw the Light 10 Points on each Side of the Ship, viz. from right ahead to 2 Points abaft the Beam on either Side; and of such a Character as to be visible on a dark Night, with a clear Atmosphere, at a Distance of at least Five Miles:

(*b*) *On the Starboard Side*, a Green Light, so constructed as to throw an uniform and unbroken Light over an Arc of the Horizon of 10 Points of the Compass; so fixed as to throw the Light from right ahead to 2 Points abaft the Beam on the Starboard Side; and of such a Character as to be visible on a dark Night, with a clear Atmosphere, at a Distance of at least Two Miles:

(*c*) *On the Port Side*, a Red Light, so constructed as to show an uniform and unbroken Light over an Arc of the Horizon of 10 Points of the Compass; so fixed as to throw the Light from right ahead to 2 Points abaft the Beam on the Port Side; and of such a Character, as to be visible on a dark Night, with a clear Atmosphere, at a distance of at least Two Miles:

(*d*) The said Green and Red Side Lights shall be fitted with inboard Screens, projecting at least Three Feet forward from the Light, so as to prevent these Lights from being seen across the Bow.

# RÈGLES À SUIVRE POUR PRÉVENIR LES ABORDAGES EN MER.

*Préliminaire.*

Art. 1. Dans les règles qui suivent, tout navire à vapeur qui ne marche qu'à l'aide de ses voiles est considéré comme navire à voiles ; et tout navire dont la machine est en action, quelle que soit sa voilure, est considéré comme navire à vapeur.

*Règles relatives aux feux et aux signaux en temps de brume.*

Art. 2. Des feux mentionnés aux articles suivants doivent être portés, à l'exclusion de tous autres, par tous le temps, entre le coucher et le lever du soleil.

Art. 3. Les navires à vapeur, lorsqu'ils sont en marche, portent les feux ci-après :

(*a*) *En tête du mât de misaine*, un feu blanc placé de manière à fournir un rayonnement uniforme et non interrompu dans tout le parcours d'un arc horizontal de 20 quarts du compas, qui se compte depuis l'avant jusqu'à 2 quarts en arrière du travers de chaque bord et d'une portée telle qu'il puisse être visible à 5 milles au moins de distance, par une nuit sombre, mais sans brume :

(*b*) *A tribord*, un feu vert établi de façon à projeter une lumière uniforme et non interrompue sur un arc horizontal de 10 quarts du compas, qui est compris entre l'avant du navire, et 2 quarts sur l'arrière du travers à tribord, et d'une portée telle qu'il puisse être visible à 2 milles au moins de distance, par une nuit sombre, mais sans brume :

(*c*) *A bâbord*, un feu rouge construit de façon à projeter une lumière uniforme et non interrompue sur un arc horizontal de 10 quarts du compas, qui est compris entre l'avant du navire, et 2 quarts sur l'arrière du travers à bâbord, et d'une portée telle qu'il puisse être visible à 2 milles au moins de distance, par une nuit sombre, mais sans brume :

(*d*) Ces feux de côté sont pourvus, en dedans du bord, d'écrans dirigés de l'arrière à l'avant, et s'étendent à $0^m.90$ en avant de la lumière, afin que le feu vert ne puisse pas être aperçu de bâbord avant, et le feu rouge de tribord avant.

Lights for Steam Tugs.

Art. 4. Steam Ships, when towing other Ships, shall carry Two bright White Mast-head Lights vertically, in addition to their Side Lights, so as to distinguish them from other Steam Ships. Each of these Mast-head Lights shall be of the same Construction and Character as the Mast-head Lights which other Steam Ships are required to carry.

Lights for Sailing Ships.

Art. 5. Sailing Ships under weigh, or being towed, shall carry the same Lights as Steam Ships under weigh, with the Exception of the White Mast-head Lights, which they shall never carry.

Exceptional Lights for small Sailing Vessels.

Art. 6. Whenever, as in the Case of small Vessels during bad Weather, the Green and Red Lights cannot be fixed, these Lights shall be kept on Deck, on their respective Sides of the Vessel, ready for instant Exhibition; and shall, on the Approach of or to other Vessels, be exhibited on their respective Sides in sufficient Time to prevent Collision, in such manner as to make them most visible, and so that the Green Light shall not be seen on the Port Side, nor the Red Light on the Starboard Side.

To make the Use of these portable Lights more certain and easy, the Lanterns containing them shall each be painted Outside with the Colour of the Light they respectively contain, and shall be provided with suitable Screens.

Lights for Ships at Anchor.

Art. 7. Ships, whether Steam Ships or Sailing Ships, when at Anchor in Roadsteads or Fairways, shall exhibit, where it can best be seen, but at a Height not exceeding Twenty Feet above the Hull, a White Light, in a globular Lantern of Eight Inches in Diameter, and so constructed as to show a clear uniform and unbroken Light visible all round the Horizon, and at a Distance of at least One Mile.

Lights for Pilot Vessels.

Art. 8. Sailing Pilot Vessels shall not carry the Lights required for other Sailing Vessels, but shall carry a White Light at the Mast-head, visible all round the Horizon; and shall also exhibit a Flare-up Light every Fifteen Minutes.

Lights for Fishing Vessels and Boats.

Art. 9. Open Fishing Boats and other open Boats shall not be required to carry the Side Lights required for other Vessels; but shall, if they do not carry such Lights, carry a Lantern having a Green Slide on the One Side, and a Red Slide on the other Side; and on the Approach of or to other Vessels, such Lantern shall be exhibited in sufficient Time to prevent Collision, so that the Green Light shall not be seen on the Port Side, nor the Red Light on the Starboard Side.

Fishing Vessels and open Boats when at Anchor, or attached to their Nets and stationary, shall exhibit a bright White Light.

Fishing Vessels and open Boats shall, however, not be prevented from using a Flare-up in addition, if considered expedient.

Art. 4. Les navires à vapeur, quand ils remorquent, doivent, indépendamment de leurs feux de côté, porter deux feux blancs verticaux en tête de mât, qui servent à les distinguer des autres navires à vapeur. Ces feux sont semblables au feu unique de tête de mât que portent les navires à vapeur ordinaires.

Art. 5. Les bâtiments à voiles, lorsqu'ils font route à la voile ou en remorque, portent les mêmes feux que les bâtiments à vapeur en marche, à l'exception du feu blanc du mât de misaine, dont ils ne doivent jamais faire usage.

Art. 6. Lorsque des bâtiments à voiles sont d'assez faible dimension pour que leurs feux verts et rouges ne puissent pas être fixés d'une manière permanente, ces feux sont néanmoins tenus allumés sur le pont à leurs bords respectifs, prêts à être montrés instantanément à tout navire dont on constaterait l'approche, et assez à temps pour prévenir l'abordage.

Ces fanaux portatifs pendant cette exhibition sont tenus autant en vue que possible, et présentés de telle sorte que le feu vert ne puisse être aperçu de bâbord avant, et le feu rouge de tribord avant.

Pour rendre ces prescriptions d'une application plus certaine et plus facile, les fanaux sont peints extérieurement de la couleur du feu qu'ils contiennent, et doivent être pourvus d'écrans convenables.

Art. 7. Les bâtiments, tant à voiles qu'à vapeur, mouillés sur une rade, dans un chenal ou sur une ligne fréquentée, portent, depuis le coucher jusqu'au lever du soleil, un feu blanc placé à une hauteur qui n'excède pas 6 mètres au-dessus du plat-bord et projetant une lumière uniforme et non interrompue tout autour de l'horizon à la distance d'au moins un mille.

Art. 8. Les bateaux-pilotes à voiles ne sont pas assujettis à porter les mêmes feux que ceux exigés pour les autres navires à voiles; mais ils doivent avoir en tête de mât un feu blanc visible de tous les points de l'horizon, et de plus montrer un feu de quart d'heure en quart d'heure.

Art. 9. Les bateaux de pêche non pontés et tous les autres bateaux également non pontés ne sont pas tenus de porter les feux de côté exigés pour les autres navires; mais ils doivent, s'ils ne sont pas pourvus de semblables feux, se servir d'un fanal muni sur l'un de ses côtés d'une glissoire verte, et sur l'autre d'une glissoire rouge, de façon qu'à l'approche d'un navire ils puissent montrer ce fanal en temps opportun pour prévenir l'abordage, en ayant soin que le feu vert ne puisse être aperçu de bâbord, et le feu rouge de tribord.

Les navires de pêche et les bateaux non pontés qui sont à l'ancre, ou qui ayant leurs filets dehors sont stationnaires, doivent montrer un feu blanc.

Ces mêmes navires et bateaux peuvent, en outre, faire usage d'un feu visible à de courts intervalles, s'ils le jugent convenable.

*Rules concerning Fog Signals.*

Fog Signals. Art. 10. Whenever there is Fog, whether by Day or Night, the Fog Signals described below shall be carried and used, and shall be sounded at least every Five Minutes; viz.:—

(*a*) Steam Ships under weigh shall use a Steam Whistle placed before the funnel, not less than Eight Feet from the Deck:

(*b*) Sailing Ships under weigh shall use a Fog Horn:

(*c*) Steam Ships and Sailing Ships when not under weigh shall use a Bell.

*Steering and Sailing Rules.*

Two Sailing Ships meeting. Art. 11. If Two Sailing Ships are meeting End on or nearly End on so as to involve Risk of Collision, the Helms of both shall be put to Port, so that each may pass on the Port Side of the other.

Two Sailing Ships crossing. Art. 12. When Two Sailing Ships are crossing so as to involve Risk of Collision, then, if they have the Wind on different Sides, the Ship with the Wind on the Port Side shall keep out of the Way of the Ship with the Wind on the Starboard Side; except in the Case in which the Ship with the Wind on the Port Side is close-hauled and the other Ship free; in which case the latter Ship shall keep out of the Way: but if they have the Wind on the same Side, or if one of them has the Wind aft, the Ship which is to windward shall keep out of the Way of the Ship which is to leeward.

Two Ships under Steam meeting. Art. 13. If Two Ships under Steam are meeting End on or nearly End on so as to involve Risk of Collision, the Helms of both shall be put to Port, so that each may pass on the Port Side of the other.

Two Ships under Steam crossing. Art. 14. If two Ships under Steam are crossing so as to involve Risk of Collision, the Ship which has the other on her own Starboard Side shall keep out of the Way of the other.

Sailing Ship and Ship under Steam. Art. 15. If Two Ships, one of which is a Sailing Ship, and the other a Steam Ship, are proceeding in such Directions as to involve Risk of Collision, the Steam Ship shall keep out of the Way of the Sailing Ship.

Ships under Steam to slacken Speed. Art. 16. Every Steam Ship, when approaching another Ship so as to involve Risk of Collision, shall slacken her Speed, or, if necessary, stop and reverse; and every Steam Ship shall, when in a Fog, go at a moderate speed.

Vessels overtaking other Vessels. Art. 17. Every Vessel overtaking any other Vessel shall keep out of the Way of the said last-mentioned Vessel.

Construction of Articles 12, 14, 15, and 17. Art. 18. Where by the above Rules One of Two Ships is to keep out of the Way, the other shall keep her Course, subject to the Qualifications contained in the following Article.

*Signaux en temps de brume.*

Art. 10. En temps de brume, de jour comme de nuit, les navires font entendre les signaux suivants toutes les cinq minutes au moins, savoir:

(*a*) Les navires à vapeur en marche, le son du sifflet à vapeur qui est placé en avant de la cheminée à une hauteur de $2^m.40$ au-dessus du pont des gaillards :

(*b*) Les bâtiments à voiles, lorsqu'ils sont en marche, font usage d'un cornet :

(*c*) Les bâtiments à vapeur et à voiles, lorsqu'ils ne sont pas en marche, font usage d'une cloche.

*Règles relatives à la route.*

Art. 11. Si deux navires à voiles se rencontrent courant l'un sur l'autre, directement ou à-peu-près, et qu'il y ait risque d'abordage, tous deux viennent sur tribord, pour passer à bâbord l'un de l'autre.

Art. 12. Lorsque deux navires à voiles font des routes qui se croisent et les exposent à un abordage, s'ils ont des amures différentes, le navire qui a les amures à bâbord manœuvre de manière à ne pas gêner la route de celui qui a le vent de tribord; toutefois, dans le cas où le bâtiment qui a les amures à bâbord est au plus près, tandis que l'autre a du largue, celui-ci doit manœuvrer de manière à ne pas gêner le bâtiment qui est au plus près. Mais, si l'un des deux est vent arrière ou s'ils ont le vent du même bord, le navire qui est vent arrière ou qui aperçoit l'autre sous le vent manœuvre pour ne pas gêner la route de ce dernier navire.

Art. 13. Si deux navires sous vapeur se rencontrent courant l'un sur l'autre, directement ou à-peu-près, et qu'il y ait risque d'abordage, tous deux viennent sur tribord, pour passer à bâbord l'un de l'autre.

Art. 14. Si deux navires sous vapeur font des routes qui se croisent et les exposent à s'aborder, celui qui voit l'autre par tribord manœvre de manière à ne pas gêner la route de ce navire.

Art. 15. Si deux navires, l'un à voiles, l'autre sous vapeur, font des routes qui les exposent à s'aborder, le navire sous vapeur manœuvre de manière à ne pas gêner la route du navire à voiles.

Art. 16. Tout navire sous vapeur, qui approche un autre navire de manière qu'il y ait risque d'abordage, doit diminuer sa vitesse ou stopper et marcher en arrière, s'il est nécessaire. Tout navire sous vapeur doit, en temps de brume, avoir une vitesse modérée.

Art. 17. Tout navire qui en dépasse un autre gouverne de manière à ne pas gêner la route de ce navire.

Art. 18. Lorsque, par suite des règles qui précèdent, l'un des deux bâtiments doit manœuvrer de manière à ne pas gêner l'autre, celui-ci doit néanmoins subordonner sa manœuvre aux règles énoncées à l'article suivant.

Proviso to save special Cases.

Art. 19. In obeying and construing these Rules, due regard must be had to all Dangers of Navigation; and due regard must also be had to any special Circumstances which may exist in any particular Case rendering a Departure from the above Rules necessary in order to avoid immediate Danger.

No Ship under any Circumstances to neglect proper Precautions.

Art. 20. Nothing in these Rules shall exonerate any Ship, or the Owner, or Master, or Crew thereof, from the Consequences of any Neglect to carry Lights or Signals, or of any neglect to keep a proper Look-out, or of the Neglect of any Precaution which may be required by the ordinary Practice of Seamen, or by the special Circumstances of the Case.

Art. 19. En se conformant aux règles qui précèdent, les navires doivent tenir compte de tous les dangers de la navigation. Ils auront égard aux circonstances particulières qui peuvent rendre nécessaire une dérogation à ces règles, afin de parer à un péril immédiat.

Art. 20. Rien dans les règles ci-dessus ne saurait affranchir un navire, quel qu'il soit, ses armateurs, son capitaine ou son équipage, des conséquences d'une omission de porter des feux ou signaux, d'un défaut de surveillance convenable, ou, enfin, d'une négligence quelconque des précautions commandées par la pratique ordinaire de la navigation ou par les circonstances particulières de la situation.

# DIAGRAMS

## TO ILLUSTRATE THE USE OF THE LIGHTS CARRIED BY VESSELS AT SEA

AND THE MANNER IN WHICH THEY INDICATE TO THE VESSEL WHICH SEES THEM THE POSITION AND DESCRIPTION OF THE VESSEL THAT CARRIES THEM.

*When both Red and Green Lights are seen.*

A sees a Red and Green Light ahead ;—A knows that a vessel is approaching her on a course directly opposite to her own, as B ;

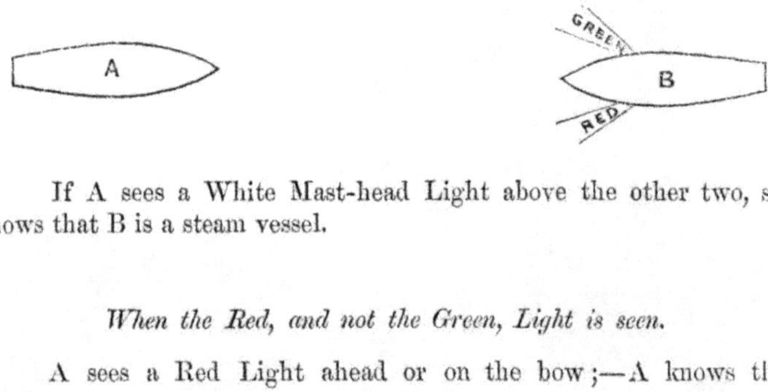


If A sees a White Mast-head Light above the other two, she knows that B is a steam vessel.

*When the Red, and not the Green, Light is seen.*

A sees a Red Light ahead or on the bow ;—A knows that either,

1, a vessel is approaching her on her port bow, as B ;

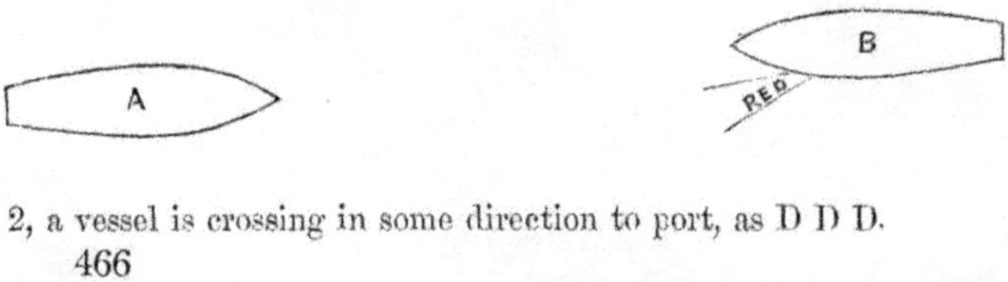


or, 2, a vessel is crossing in some direction to port, as D D D.

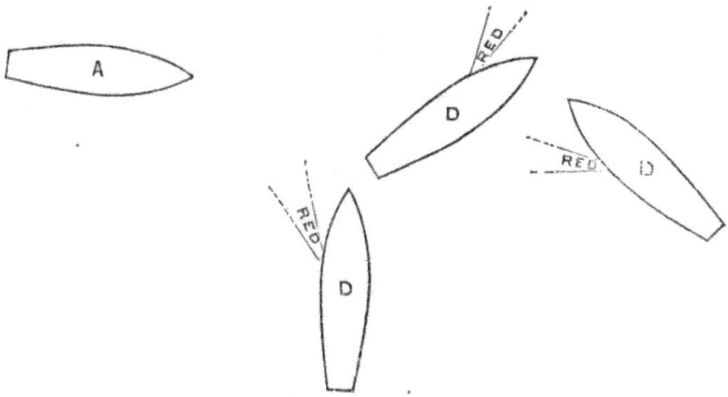


If A sees a White Mast-head Light above the Red Light, A knows that the vessel is a steam vessel, and is either approaching her in the same direction as B, or is crossing to port in some direction, as D D D.

*When the Green, and not the Red, Light is seen.*

A sees a Green Light ahead or on the bow;—A knows that either,

1, a vessel is approaching her on her starboard bow, as B,

or, 2, a vessel is crossing in some direction to starboard, as D D D.

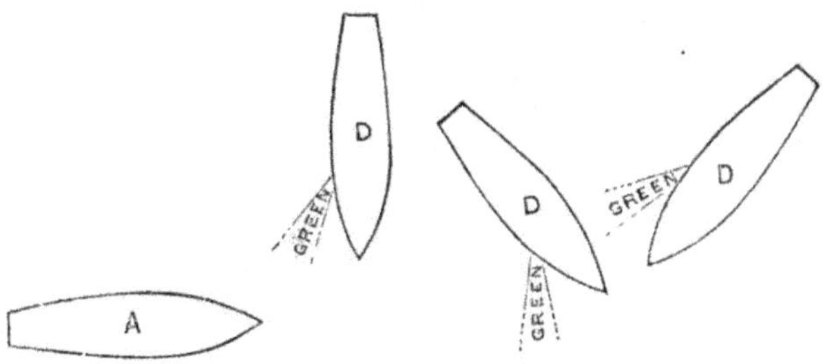


If A sees a White Mast-head Light above the Green Light, A knows that the vessel is a steam vessel, and is either approaching her in the same direction as B, or is crossing to starboard in some direction, as D D D.

# VOCABULARY

OF

## FRENCH NAUTICAL TERMS DEFINED IN THE FOREGOING DICTIONARY.



Abaca, *abaca*
Abandon, Abandonnement, *abandonment of a ship by her crew in case of extreme peril, or of a ship to her insurers*
Abattage, *heaving down*
Abattre, *to cast (in getting under weigh)*
Abattre en carène, *to heave down*
Abordage, *collision; running foul; boarding*
Aborder un bâtiment, *to run foul of a ship*
Aborder à le navire, *to go on board of the ship*
Aboutement, *butt of two planks*
Abri, *a small creek; a shelter*
Abrier, *to becalm*
Accore, *shore in shipbuilding*
Accorer, *to shore*
Acculement, *rising of the floor timbers; rising floors*
Acon, *barge*
Action, *action*
Adents, *dowells*
Affourcher, *to moor*
Affranchir, *to free*
Affréter, *to freight*
Affréteur, *freighter*
A-flot, *afloat; floating*
Agréer, *to rig*
Agréner, *to bale*
Agrès et apparaux, *tackle and apparel (of a ship)*
Aide, *mate; assistant (as carpenter's mate, surgeon's assistant, &c.)*
Aiguille aimantée, *magnetic needle*
Aiguillette, *lashing, seizing*
Aile de dérive, *leeboard*
Aile de pigeon, *sky scraper*
Air de vent, *rhomb line*
Alestir, *to lighten a ship*
Alizés, *trade winds*
Allége, *lighter; craft*
Alléger un navire, *to lighten a ship by the discharge of part of her lading*
Allumer, *to fetch the pump*
Almadie, *almady*
Alonges, *futtocks*
Alonges d'écubier, *hawse timbers*
Altitude, *altitude*
Amarrage, *lashing; seizing*
Amarrer, *to make fast; to belay; to seize*
Amener, *to lower; to haul down; to strike*
Amer, *sea mark*
Amiral, *admiral*
Amirauté, *admiralty*
Amorcer, *to prime*
Amorti, *neaped*
Amortissement, *neap tides*
Amure, *tack of a sail*
Ancrage, *anchorage*
Ancre, *anchor*
Ancre de cape, *floating anchor*
Ancrer, *to anchor*
Anémomètre, *anemometer*
Anges, *grape shot*

Angle horaire, *horary angle*
Anguillers, *limbers*
Annuaire de la marine, *navy list*
Anspect, *handspike*
Antenne, *lateen yard*
Apique, *apeak*
Apiquer, *to peak*
Appareiller, *to get under weigh*
Apprenti marin, *apprentice to the sea*
Approvisionnement, *naval stores*
Araignée, *crow-foot*
Arborer, *to hoist a flag or signal*
Arcasse, *stern frame*
Archipel, *archipelago*
Archipompe, *pump-well*
Architecture navale, *naval architecture*
Ardent, *ardent*
Armateur, *ship-owner*
Armée navale, *fleet*
Armer, *to fit out a ship*
Arrière, *after part (of a ship)*. à l'arrière, *aft*
Arrière-garde, *guard-ship*
Arrimage, *stowage*
Arrimer, *to stow*
Arriver, *to bear away*
Arsenal, *dockyard*
Artillerie, *artillery*
Artillerie de la flotte, *ordnance*
Artimon, *mizen*
Artimon (Mât d'), *mizen mast*
Aspirant de marine, *midshipman*
Assurance, *insurance*
Astronomie nautique, *naval astronomy*
Attraction locale, *local attraction*
Au plus près! *keep her close!* (*An order to keep the ship close to the wind*)
Augmenter de voiles, *to make sail*
Aussière, *rope, cordage*
Avances, *advances (to seamen)*
Avant, *fore part (of a ship); ahead*
Avarie, *average*
Aveugler, *to stop a leak, so that very little water is made*
Aviron, *oar*
Axiomètre, *tell-tale of the tiller*
Azimut, *azimuth*
Azimutal (Compas), *azimuth compass*

Bâbord, *port; larboard*
Bague, *hank*
Baie, *bay*
Baille de combat, *match-tub*
Baisse, *ebbing of the tide*
Balancelle, *balancelle*
Balancer, *to trim.* (*Applied to the proper disposition of weight in a ship or boat*)
Balanciers, *gimbals.* (*It also signifies side levers in a marine engine*)
Balancine, *lift*
Balant, *slack of a rope*
Baleinier, *whale-fishing ship*
Baleinière, *whale boat*
Balise, *beacon, sea mark*
Banc, *bank*
Banquier, *banker*
Barachois, *natural harbour*
Baraterie, *barratry*
Baromètre, *barometer*
Barque, *barque*
Barre au vent! *put the helm a-weather! up with the helm!*
Barre du gouvernail, *tiller*
Barrer, *to steer large*
Bassin, *basin; dock*
Bastet, *futtock staff*
Bateau, *boat, small craft*
Bateau à vapeur, *steam-boat; steamer*
Bateau de loch, *log ship*
Bateau pilote, *pilot boat*
Batelier, *waterman*
Bâtiment, *vessel; ship*
Bâtiment à vapeur, *steam ship*
Bau, *beam*
Bauquières, *clamps*
Beaupré, *bowsprit*
Bélandre, *bilander*
Ber, Berceau, *cradle*
Bernache, *barnacle*
Bigues, *sheers*
Bitord, *spunyarn*
Bitter, *to bitt*
Bittes, *bitts*
Bitture, *range of cable*
Blanc cordage, *white rope*
Blocus, *blockade*
Bois d'arrimage, *stow wood*
Bombarde, *bomb vessel*
Bombarder, *to bombard*
Bombe, *shell*
Bome, *boom*
Bomerie, *bottomry*
Bonnette, *studding-sail*
Bordage, *plank*
Bordée, *board (made by a ship on one tack)*
Bordier, *lap-sided ship*

Bosse, *stopper*
Bosse d'embarcation, *painter*
Bossoirs d'embarcation, *boat's davits*
Boucanier, *bucaneer*
Boucher, *to stop a leak*
Bouée, *buoy*
Boulet, *shot*
Bouline, *bowline*
Bouline (Nœud de), *bowline knot*
Boulons, *bolts*
Bourcet, *lug sail*
Bourrasque, *squall*
Boussole, *compass*
Boussole d'inclinaison, *dipping needle*
Bout, *head*
Bout-dehors de beaupré, *jib boom*
Bout-dehors de clin foc, *flying jib boom*
Brai, *pitch*
Branle, *hammock*
Brasse, *fathom*
Brasser, *to brace*
Brayer, *to pay with pitch*
Brig, *brig*
Brigantine, *spanker ; driver*
Brig goëlette, *hermaphrodite brig*
Bris, *wreck*
Brisants, *breakers*
Brise, *breeze*
Brûlot, *fire-ship*
Brûlot à vapeur, *steam fire-ship*
Brume, *fog*
But-en-blanc, *point blank*

Cabane, *berth*
Cabestan, *capstan*
Câble, *cable*
Câble-chaîne, *chain*
Cabotage, *coasting trade*
Caboteur, *large coasting vessel*
Cabotier, *small coasting vessel*
Cacatois, *royal.* (*A sail*)
Cacher, *to becalm*
Cadre, *frame of marine engine*
Cage à poules, *hen coop*
Cale, *hold*
Calfater, *to caulk*
Calie, *kalia*
Calme, *calm*
Calme plat, *dead calm*
Calmer, *to fall calm*
Canon, *gun ; cannon*
Canonnage, *gunnery*
Canonnier, *gunner*
Canonnière, *gun boat*
Canon-obusier, *howitzer*
Canot, *boat*
Canotier, *rower*
Cap, *head*
Capacité, *burden ; tonnage*
Cap de mouton, *dead eye*
Cape (A la), *lying to*
Capitaine, *captain ; commander*
Capteur, *captor*
Carénage, *careening place*
Caréner, *to careen*
Caret (Fil de), *rope-yarn*
Cargaison, *cargo*
Cargues, *brails*
Carguer, *to brail up*
Carie, *dry rot*
Carlingue, *keelson*
Caronade, *carronade*
Carte marine, *sea chart*
Carte réduite, *Mercator's chart*
Cartouche, *cartridge*
Casernet, *log book*
Cassé, *broken backed*
Catimaron, *catamaran*
Caye, *key*
Ceintrer, *to frap*
Cercles, *hoops*
Chaloupe, *long boat*
Chambre, *cabin*
Chantiers d'embarcation, *boat's chocks*
Chanvre, *hemp*
Chapelet (Pompe à), *chain pump*
Charbonnier, *collier*
Charger, *to load*
Charger la pompe, *to fetch the pump*
Charnier, *scuttle butt*
Charte-partie, *charter-party*
Châssis, *frame of marine engine*
Chauffeur, *fireman ; stoker*
Chavirer, *to capsize*
Chebec, *xebec*
Chemin, *way*
Chemin au nord, au sud, à l'est, à l'ouest, *northing, southing, easting, westing.* (*The distance sailed in any of these directions respectively*)
Chenal, *channel; fairway*
Chenaler, *to sail through a channel*
Cheviller, *to bolt*
Chevilles, *bolts*
Chicaner, *to lay too near the wind ; to hug the wind too close*
Chirurgien, *surgeon*
Chopine, *lower pump-box*
Chouquet, *cap*

Chute, *drop* or *depth of a lower square-sail*
Cigale, *anchor ring*
Citerne, *hotwell*
Civadière, *spritsail.* (Obsolete)
Clapet de fond, *foot valve*
Clavette, *forelock*
Clin, *clincher work*
Clin foc, *flying jib*
Cloison, *bulkhead*
Cobourgeois, *part-owner of a ship*
Coche (En), *atrip.* (*Said of topsails*)
Coiffer une voile, *to back a sail*
Coiffé, *laid aback; taken aback*
Coiffer les voiles, *to back the sails*
Coin, *quoin*
Colle marine, *marine glue*
Collet, *collar*
Collet d'un couple, *throat of a knee*
Collet d'une ancre, *crown of an anchor*
Collier d'étai, *collar of a stay*
Coltis, *cant timbers*
Commandant, Commodore, *commodore*
Compas, *compass*
Congréer un cordage, *to worm a rope*
Connaissance des temps, *nautical almanack*
Connaissement, *bill of lading*
Consignataire, *consignee*
Consignation, *consignment*
Constructeur, *shipbuilder*
Construction, *shipbuilding*
Consul, *consul*
Contrat à la grosse, *bottomry bond*
Contre-amiral, *rear admiral*
Contrebande, *smuggling*
Contrebandier, *a smuggler; an individual engaged in smuggling. See* Smogleur
Contrebordée, *opposite tack*
Contribution, *contribution*
Convoi, *convoy*
Coque, *hull*
Cordage, *rope; cordage*
Cordier, *ropemaker*
Corne, *gaff*
Cornière, *angle iron*
Corps, *hull*
Corsaire, *privateer*
Côte, *sea shore; coast*
Côté d'un vaisseau, *side of a ship*
Cotre, *cutter*
Couler, *to leak*

Couples, *timbers; frames*
Courant, *current*
Courbes, *knees*
Courir, *to sail*
Course, *cruise*
Courtier, Courtier maritime, *broker*
Coutures des bordages, *seams of the planks*
Creux, *depth of hold*
Crique, *cove; creek*
Croisière, *cruise*
Cuiller à brai, *pitch ladle*
Cuisine, *cook house; galley*
Cuivre, *copper*
Culasse, *breech* (*of a gun*)
Culer, *to make* or *fetch sternway*
Cure-molle, *dredging machine*

Dale de pompe, *pumpdale*
Dalot, *scupper*
Danger, *a bank, rock, or shoal, dangerous to navigation*
Débarquer, *to land; to discharge; to disembark*
Débris, *pieces of a wreck*
Décharger, *to discharge*
Déchouer, *to get a stranded ship afloat*
Déclinaison, *declination*
Défendre, *to fend; to fend off*
Défense, *fender*
Déferler, *to unfurl*
Dégager, *to clear*
Dégarnir, *to strip; to unrig*
Dégradé, *shipwrecked*
Degré, *degree*
Délester, *to unballast*
Démarrer, *to unmoor*
Démâté, *dismasted*
Départ, *departure*
Dépasser, *to outsail*
Déplacement, *displacement*
Dépression, *dip of the horizon*
Dérader, *to be driven from one's anchors*
Dérive, *leeway*
Dériver, *to make leeway*
Derrière, *stern*
Désarrimer, *to break bulk*
Détalinguer une ancre, Détalinguer un câble, *to unbend a cable*
Détresse, *distress*
Détroit, *strait*
Devant, *head* or *bow of a ship*
Déventer, *to take the wind out of a sail*

Déverguer, *to unbend a sail*
Déviation, *deviation*
Dingui, *dingy*
Dispacheur, *average adjuster*
Distance, *distance*
Distillatoire (Appareil), *distilling apparatus (for converting salt water into fresh)*
Dormant, *standing part of a rope*
Doublage, *doubling; sheathing*
Doubler, *to sheath*
Doublez! *pull away!*
Drague, *drag net*
Dresser la barre, *to put the helm amidships*
Drisses, *halyards*
Drosse, *tiller-rope; wheel-rope*
Dunette, *poop*
Dynamomètre, *dynamometer*

Eau de mer, *seawater*
Eau morte, *dead water*
Èbe, *ebb tide; ebb*
Écart, *scarph*
Écarver, *to scarph*
Eccentrique, *eccentric*
Échafauds, *stages*
Échelle, *ladder*
Échouer, *to ground; to run aground*
Éclipse, *eclipse*
Écliptique, *ecliptic*
Écoute, *sheet*
Écoutille, *hatchway*
Écoutillon, *scuttle*
Écouvillon, *sponge*
Écubier, *hawse-hole*
Écume, *spray*
Écurie, *transport ship for horses*
Élève, *apprentice*
Élongis, *trestle trees*
Embarcation, *boat*
Embarder, *to yaw; to break sheer*
Embargo, *embargo*
Embarquer, *to embark; to ship*
Embossure, *spring*
Embraquer, *to haul taut*
Empanner, *to bring by the lee*
Encâblure, *cable's length*
Encapé, *embayed*
Enfléchures, *ratlines*
Enfoncement, *a bight of a bay*
Ensabler, *to beach*
Entre deux des lames, *in the trough of the sea*
Entrepont, *between decks*
Enverguer une voile, *to bend a sail to its yard*
Envoyez! *put the helm a-lee!*
Éperon, *head; the upper part of the cutwater*
Épi de vent, *wind's eye*
Épissoire, *marling-spike*
Épissure, *splice*
Épontille, *stanchion; shore*
Épontilles de la cale, *hold stanchions*
Épontiller, *to shore*
Équateur, *equator*
Équipage, *ship's company; crew*
Équiper, *to fit out*
Escadre, *squadron of ships of war*
Escouade, *gang*
Escorte, *convoy*
Espars, Esparre, *spar*
Essieu de poulie, *pin of a block*
Est, *east*
Estime, *dead reckoning*
Estrope, *strop*
Étai, *stay*
Étale, *slack water.* (La mer est dite être étale)
Étalinguer un câble, Étalinguer une ancre, *to bend a cable to the anchor-ring*
Étalingure, *clinch*
Étambot, *stern posts*
Étambrai, *partners*
Étanche, *tight*
Étançon, *stanchion*
Étance, *shore, in shipbuilding*
Étoupe, *oakum*
Étrangloir à lunette, *compressor-stopper*
Étrave, *stem*
Étroit, *strait*
Éventer, *to heave a ship's bottom out of the water on either side; to fill a sail*
Éviter, *to swing*
Expert, *surveyor, &c.*

Faible, *crank*
Fardage, *dunnage*
Fargues, *wash-boards*

Fatiguer, *to work; to labour*
Fausse quille, *false keel*
Faux bras, *preventer braces*
Faux haubans, *preventer shrouds*
Felouque, *felucca*
Fer, *iron*
Ferler, *to furl; to hand*
Feutre, *felt*
Figure, *figure; figure-head*
Filer d'un câble, *to veer away a cable*
Filin, *line*
Filtre, *filter*
Flèche en culé, *gafftopsail*
Flot, *flood tide*
Flot (à-), *afloat*
Flotille, *flotilla*
Flotte, *fleet; navy*
Flotter, *to float*
Foc, *jib*
Fond, *bottom*
Forban, *pirate*
Force navale, *fleet*
Forcer de voiles, *to carry a press of sail*
Forme flottante, *floating dock*
Fortune (Mât de), *jury mast*
Fougue (Mât de perroquet de), *mizen topgallant mast*
Fougue (Perroquet de), Voile de fougue, *mizen topgallant sail*
Fourrure, *service*
Fraîchir, *to freshen.* (*Said of the wind when it increases*)
Frais, *fresh*
Franc filin, *white rope*
Franc tillac, *upper deck*
Frégate, *frigate*
Fret, *freight*
Fréter, *to charter; to freight*
Fumigation, *fumigation*

Gabare, *barge; lighter*
Gabarier, *lighterman*
Gaffe, *boat-hook*
Gaillard d'avant, *forecastle*
Galeasse, *galeass*
Galère, *galley*
Galerie, *gallery*
Galhaubans, *backstays*
Galion, *galleon*
Galiote, *galliot*
Gambes, *futtock shrouds*
Garant, *fall*
Garcettes, *gaskets*
Garde-corps, *man rope*
Gargousse, *cartridge*
Gargoussier, *match tub*
Gatte, *manger*
Girouette, *vane*
Glu marin, *marine glue*
Godille, *skull*
Goëlette, *schooner*
Golfe, *gulf*
Gondole, *gondola*
Gondolier, *gondolier*
Goudron, *tar*
Goupille, *forelock*
Gournable, *treenail*
Gouttières, *waterways*
Gouvernail, *rudder*
Gouverner, *to steer*
Grain, *squall; gust of wind*
Grand, *main.* (*Applied especially to whatever is connected with the mainmast*)
Grand mât, *mainmast*
Grand panneau, *main hatch*
Grande vergue, *main yard*
Grande voile, *mainsail; the principal sail set on the mainmast*
Grande voile d'étai, *mainstaysail*
Grappin, *grapnel*
Gratte, *scraper*
Gratter, *to scrape*
Gréer, *to rig*
Grelin, *warp*
Grément, *rigging*
Grenade, *grenade*
Gros de l'eau, *spring tide*
Grosse (A la), *on bottomry*
Guetteur, *look-out man*
Gueuse, *pig of iron for ballast*
Guibre, *cutwater*
Guigue, *gig*
Guindeau, *windlass*
Guinder, *to sway up*
Guinderesse, *mast rope*
Guipon, *mop*
Guirlandes, *breast-hooks*
Guitran, *pitch*

Habitacle, *binnacle*
Hâler, *to haul*
Hamac, *hammock*
Hanche, *quarter of a ship*
Harpon, *harpoon*
Harponner, *to harpoon*
Harponneur, *harpooner*

Haubans, *shrouds*
Haut, *deep waisted*
Haut-bord, *ship of the line*
Hauteur, *altitude*
Hauts, *upper works*
Havre, *harbour; haven*
Herminette, *adze*
Hisser, *to hoist*
Homme de mer, *seafaring man*
Hôpital (Vaisseau), *hospital ship*
Horizon, *horizon*
Horizon artificiel, *artificial horizon*
Houle, *swell of the sea*
Hune, *top*
Hune (Mât de), *topmast*
Hunier, *topsail*
Hydrographie, *hydrography*
Hydrographique, *hydrographical*

Île, *island*
Inclinaison de l'aiguille aimantée, *dip of the magnetic needle*
Inclinaison (Boussole d'), *dipping needle*
Innavigabilité, *unseaworthiness*
Inventaire, *inventory (of a ship's stores, &c.)*
Isthme, *isthmus*

Jaloux, *crank*
Jaugeage, *tonnage*
Jaumière, *helm port*
Jepan, *jepan*
Jet, *jettison*
Jeter, *to heave*
Jonque, *Chinese junk*
Journal, *log book; journal*
Jumelle, *fish*
Jusant, *ebb; ebb tide*

Kayak, *kayack*
Ketch, *ketch*
Kiosque, *kiosk*
Klipper, *clipper*
Koff, *koff*

Lame, *wave*
Lancer, *to launch*
Lantéas, *lanteas*
Large, *offing*
Largeur, *extreme breadth of ship*
Larguer, *to let go a rope, &c.; to bear away; to bear up*
Larguer un ris, *to let out a reef*
Latin, *lateen*
Latitude, *latitude*
Lazaret, *lazaretto*
Lége, *light*
Legislation maritime, *maritime law*
Lest, *ballast*
Lester, *to ballast*
Lesteur, Ballast lesteur, *ballast lighter*
Lettres de marque, *letters of marque*
Lever l'ancre, *to weigh the anchor*
Lieue, *league*
Lieutenant, *lieutenant*
Ligne, *line*
Lisses, *ribbands*
Livre de loch, *log book*
Loch, *log*
Lof! *order to luff*
Loffer, *to touch the wind*
Longitude, *longitude*
Longueur, *length*
Louvoyer, *to ply to windward; to beat to windward*
Lumière, *vent of a gun*
Lunette, *telescope*
Lusin, *houseline*

Machine alimentaire, *donkey engine*
Machine à action directe, *ou* à simple effet, *direct acting engine*
Machine aux cylindres oscillantes, *oscillating engine*
Machine à double action, *ou* à double effet, *double-acting engine*
Machine à vapeur, *steam engine*
Magnétique, *magnetical.* Le pôle magnétique, *the magnetic pole*
Maître (Quartier), *quarter gunner*
Maîtresse-ancre, Ancre de miséricorde, *sheet anchor*
Mal de mer, *sea sickness*
Mal de terre, *scurvy*
Maline, *spring tide*
Manche, *channel*
Manomètre de verre mercurial, *mercurial gauge*
Manquer à virer *to miss stays*
Marche, *headway; or rather, the rate of a ship's sailing. A sail is said to be* la marche du navire *if the ship sails with the greatest speed when that sail is set.* En marche, *under weigh*

Marcher, *to sail (with reference to the ship's speed)*
Marée, *tide*
Marées de quadrature, *neap tide.* See Vif de l'eau
Marie-Salope, *mud lighter*
Marin, *seaman*
Marine, *marine*
Maritime, *maritime*
Marque, *seamark*
Mât, *mast.* Grand mât, *mainmast*
Mât d'artimon, *mizenmast*
Mât de cacatois, *royal mast*
Mât de cacatois de perruche, *mizen royal mast*
Mât de grand cacatois, *main royal mast*
Mât de grand perroquet, *main top-gallant mast*
Mât de hune, *topmast*
Mât de misaine, *foremast*
Mât de perroquet, *topgallant mast*
Mât de perroquet de fougue, *mizen topgallant mast*
Mât de perruche, Mât de perroquet d'artimon, *mizen topgallant mast*
Mât de petit cacatois, *fore royal mast*
Mât de petit hunier, *or rather*, Petit mât de hune, *fore-topmast*
Mât de petit perroquet, *fore top-gallant mast*
Mâtelot, *sailor*
Mâter, *to mast*
Membrures, *frames of a ship*
Mer, *sea*
Méridien, *meridian*
Merlin, *marline*
Métacentre, *metacentre*
Mirage, *looming; illusion of sight at sea*
Misaine, *foresail*
Misaine (Mât de), *foremast*
Mole, *mole*
Mollir, *to fall calm; to ease off or slacken a rope*
Montre marine, *chronometer*
Moque, *dead eye*
Mortaise, *mortise*
Mortier, *mortar*
Mouillage, *anchorage*
Mouiller, *to anchor*
Moulinet à bitord, *spunyarn winch*
Mousson, *monsoon*

Nadir, *nadir*
Nager, *to row*
Naufrage, *shipwreck*
Nautique, *nautical*
Naval, *naval*
Navigable, *navigable*
Navigateur, *navigator*
Navigation, *navigation*
Naviguer, *to navigate*
Navire, *ship*
Négrier, *slaver*
Neutre, *neutral vessel*
Nolis, *freight*
Noliser, *to freight*
Nord, *north.* Un navire gouverne au nord, *a ship sails northwards*
Novice, *the same as* apprenti marin

Observation, *observation*
Obusier, *howitzer*
Occultation, *occultation*
Océan, *ocean*
Octant, *quadrant*
Œil, *œillet; eye*
Œuvres mortes, *the upper works of a ship*
Œuvres vives, *the parts of a ship which are under water*
Officier de la marine, *naval officer*
Orage, *storm*
Organeau, *anchor ring*
Orienter, *to trim a sail to the wind*
Orifice de nettoiement, *mud hole*
Ouest, *west*
Ouragan, *hurricane*

Pagaye, *paddle of a canoe*
Paillet, *mat*
Palan, *tackle*
Panne (Mettre en), *to heave to*
Pantoir, *pendant*
Paquebot, *packet ship; packet boat*
Paraglaces, *ice fenders*
Parallèle de latitude, *parallel of latitude*
Paratonnerre, *lightning conductor*
Parcloses, *limber boards*
Parfumer, *to fumigate*
Parlémentaire, *cartel ship*
Partance, *departure*
Passager, *passenger*
Passe-avant, *gangway*
Passeport, *passport*
Patamar, *patamar*

Pataras, *preventer shroud*
Patron, *master of a coasting vessel; coxswain of a boat*
Pavillon, *flag*
Pavois, *bulwarks*
Perroquet, *topgallant sail*
Petit, *fore*
Phare, *lighthouse*
Piahiap, *piahiap*
Pic, *peak*
Pièces à eau, *water casks*
Pilotage, *pilotage*
Pilote, *pilot*
Pilote-bot, *pilot boat*
Pincer, *to hug the wind*
Pinjadjap, *pinjadjap*
Pinnasse, *pinnace*
Pinque, *pink*
Piqué, *wormed*
Pirate, *pirate*
Piraterie, *piracy*
Piston, *upper pump box*
Plaisance (Bâteau de), *pleasure boat*
Plan, *draught or plan of a ship*
Plancher, *platform*
Polacre, *polacre*
Pompe, *pump*
Pompe à air, *air pump*
Pompe à chapelet, *chain pump*
Pompes d'épuisement de cale, *bilge pumps*
Pompes de saumure, *brine pumps*
Pont, *deck*
Ponton, *pontoon. A large flat-bottomed decked lighter, fitted with capstans and purchases for heaving down ships, &c.*
Porque, *rider*
Port, *harbour; port*
Porte-haubans, *channels*
Porter, *to stand.* Porter de la toile, *to carry a press of sail.* Faire porter, *or* Laisser porter, *to bear away*
Pot à brai, *pitch-kettle*
Poulie, *block*
Poulieur, *blockmaker*
Poupe, *stern*
Pourriture sèche, *dry rot*
Poutres de fondement, '*engine bearers*'
Prame, *praam*
Pratique, *pratique*
Préceintes, *wales; bends*
Prélart, *tarpauling*
Prendre, *to capture*
Preneur, *captor*
Presser, *to impress*
Prime d'assurance, *premium of insurance*
Prise, *prize*
Pros, *proa*
Proue, *prow*

Quadrature (Marées de), *neap tides*
Quai, *quay; wharf*
Quart, *watch.* Faire bon quart, *to keep a good look-out*
Quart de nonante, Quartier anglais, *quadrant*
Quête, *rake of the sternpost*
Quille, *keel*

Raban, *rope band*
Râblure, *rabbet*
Racage, *parrel*
Rade, *roadstead*
Radeau, *raft*
Radouber, *to repair*
Rafraîchir, *to freshen*
Raidir, *to haul taut*
Ralingue, *bolt rope*
Rame, *oar*
Ramer, *to row*
Rançon, *ransom*
Rançonner, *to ransom*
Rang, *tier*
Ras, *floating stage*
Rasé, *razee*
Ration, *allowance of provisions per day for each man on board*
Réa, *sheave*
Rechange, *spare*
Recul, *recoil*
Réfraction, *refraction*
Régulateur, *governor*
Relâcher, *to put into a port*
Rembarquer, *to reembark; also to go direct from one ship to another*
Remorquer, *to tow*
Rendezvous, *rendezvous*
Répétiteur, *repeating ship*
Représailles, *reprisals*
Réservoir à eau chaude, *hot well*
Réservoir pour la vapeur, *steam chest*
Retenue, *relieving tackle*
Revirer, *to go about; to put about*
Ride, *lanyard*
Rider, *to set up rigging*

Ris, *reef*
Risée, *gust; squall*
Rivage, *shore*
Robinets d'épreuve, *gauge cocks*
Rose des vents, *card* or *fly of the compass*
Roues à aubes, *paddle wheels*
Route, *course*
Routier, *book of charts and sailing directions*
Rumb, Rumb de vent, *rhumb line*

Sabord, *port; gun port*
Safran, *the after-piece of the rudder*
Sailler, *to rouse*
Saisines, *gripes; lashings*
Saisir, *to lash*, or *fasten securely with a lashing*
Salinomètre, *salinometer*
Salut, *salute*
Sangle, *mat*
Sancir, *to founder*
Santé, *lazaretto*
Santé (Officiers de), *health officers*
Saumon, *kentledge*
Saute de vent, *shift of wind*
Sauter, *to shift*
Sauve-gardes, *rudder-pendants*
Sauvetage, *salvage*
Scorbut, *scurvy*
Seau, *bucket*
Semelle, *shoe of an anchor*
Seneau, *snow*
Serpenter, *to snake*
Serre-bosse, *shank painter*
Serrer, *to furl; to hand*
Sextant, *sextant*
Signal, *signal*
Sillage, *way* or *wake of a ship*
Sloup, Sloop, *sloop*
Smack, *smack*
Smegleur, *smuggler; that is, a vessel engaged in smuggling. See* Contrebandier
Sonde, *sounding lead*
Sonder, *to sound; to heave the lead*
Soupape, *valve*
Soupape à purger d'air, *blow-through-valve*
Soupape reniflante, *snifting valve*
Soupape de sûreté, *safety valve*
Soupapes d'échappement, *escape valves*
Souquer, *to haul taut a rope made fast round anything*
Sous-barbe, *bob-stay*
Subjaler, *to foul*
Subrécargue, *supercargo*
Surventer, *to overblow; to blow hard*

Tactique navale, *naval tactics*
Tambours, *paddle-wheels*
Tampon, *hawse plug*
Taquet, *cleat*
Tartanne, *tartan*
Télégraphe marin, *marine telegraph*
Tenon, *tenon*
Tente, *awning*
Terre neuvier, *banker*
Tête, *head (of a mast, &c.)*
Tête croissée, *crosshead in a side-lever engine*
Têtière, *head (of a squaresail)*
Tillac, *deck*
Timon, *tiller*
Timonier, *helmsman*
Tirant d'eau, *draught of water*
Tirer, *to draw (speaking of a ship's draught of water); to fire a gun*
Toile, *sail-cloth; canvass*
Tonnage, *tonnage*
Tornade, *tornado*
Toron, *strand of a rope*
Torpédo, *torpedo*
Touage, *towage*
Touée, *towline; tow-rope*
Touer, *to tow; to warp*
Tourbillon, *whirlwind; tornado*
Tournevire, *messenger*
Trait, *sail.* Un trait carré, *a square-rigged ship; that is, one carrying squaresails*
Transport, *transport ship*
Travailler, *to labour*
Traverse, Tête croissée, *crosshead in a side-lever engine*
Traverser une ancre, *to fish an anchor.*
Trelingages, *catharpins*
Tribord, *starboard*
Trombe, *waterspout*
Tropiques, *tropics*
Trou d'homme, *man-hole*
Typhon, *typhoon*

Va-et-vient, *pass rope*
Vaigre, *ceiling*

Vaisseau, *ship; vessel*
Vaisseau hôpital, *hospital ship*
Vaisseau rasé, *razee*
Valet, *wad*
Valvule, *valve*
Varangue, *floor timber*
Variation, *variation*
Vent, *wind*
Vent (Au), *to windward*
Vent (Sous le), *to leeward*
Vent d'un boulet, *windage of a gun*
Ventilateur, *wind sail; ventilator*
Ventouse, *air scuttle*
Verge d'une ancre, *shank of an anchor*
Verge d'une pompe, *pump spear*
Vergue, *yard*
Verguez ! *man the yards !*
Vertical, *vertical*
Vice-amiral, *vice-admiral*
Vif de l'eau, Maline, *spring tide*
Vigie, *looko ut man*
Violons, *bowsprit bees*
Virer, *to haul upon*
Virer au cabestan, *to heave at the capstan*
Virer de bord, *to tack*
Virure, *strake*
Visite, *survey*
Visiter, *to survey*
Vivres, *provisions*
Vivrier, *victualling ship*
Voie d'eau, *leak*
Voile, *sail*
Voiler, *to set sails*
Voilerie, *sail loft*
Voilier, *sailmaker*
Volontaire, *volunteer*
Voilure, *suit of sails*
Vomir, *to spue (said of the oakum when it is forced out of a ship's seams)*
Voûte, *counter (of a ship)*
Voyage, *voyage*

Yacht, *yacht*
Yole, *yawl*

Zénit, *zenith*
Zodiaque, *zodiac*
Zone, *zone*

**PLATE I.**

## STEAM SHIP & STEAM ENGINE.

Fig 1. Plan.

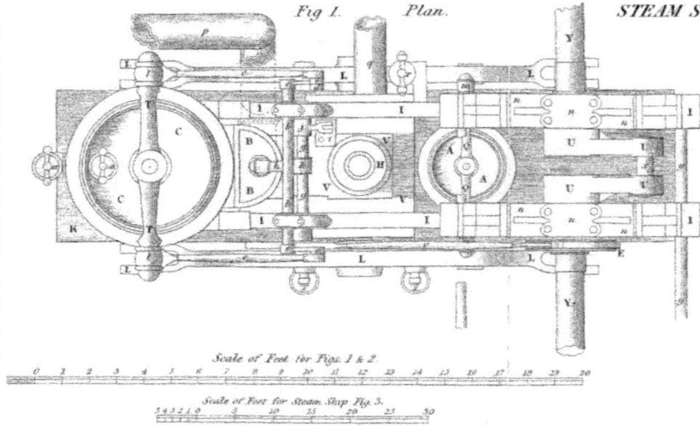


Fig. 2. Longitudinal Section.

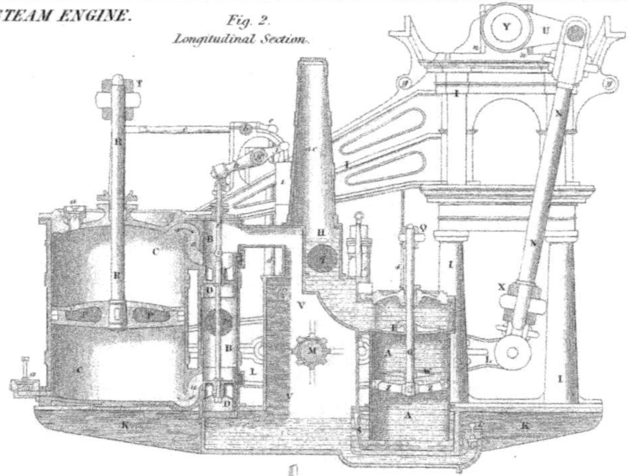

Fig. 3. Elevation of Steam Ship with Engine and Boilers.

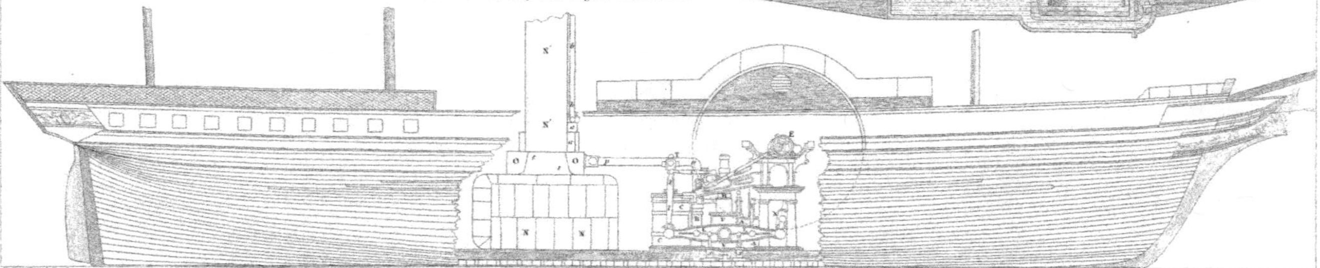

## ALPHABETICAL INDEX TO DESCRIPTION AND PLATES OF MARINE STEAM ENGINE.

## INDEX TO DESCRIPTION AND PLATES OF

# SECTIONAL SKETCHES OF MERCHANT VESSELS.

## INDEX TO FIG. 5.

### STERN FRAME.

1 Stern post
2 Transoms
3 Main transom, or wing transom
4 Transom knees
5 Quarter stanchions
6 Long stern timbers
7 Short stern timbers
8 Arch board
9 Fashion timbers

## INDEX TO FIG. 6.

### MIDSHIP SECTION.

1 Keel
2 Keelson
3 Keelson rider
4 Middle line, or *centre line*
5 Floor timber
6 Chocks for fillings to the timbers
7 Second futtocks
8 Short top timbers
9 Stanchions, or *rough tree timbers*
10 Rails, or *rough tree rails*
11 Upper-deck beam
12 Hold beam
13 Standard knees, or *deck standard knees*
14 Waterways
15 Planksheer
16 Sheer strake
17 Wales
18 Bilge planks (inside and outside)
19 Futtock planks
20 Limber boards
21 Clamps, or *sea crafts*
22 Shelf pieces, or *stringers*

## INDEX TO FIG. 7.

### FRONT ELEVATION OF BOWS IN FRAME.

1 Stem
2 Bow ribbands
3 Bow timbers
4 Knight heads
5 Hawse timbers

PLATE II.

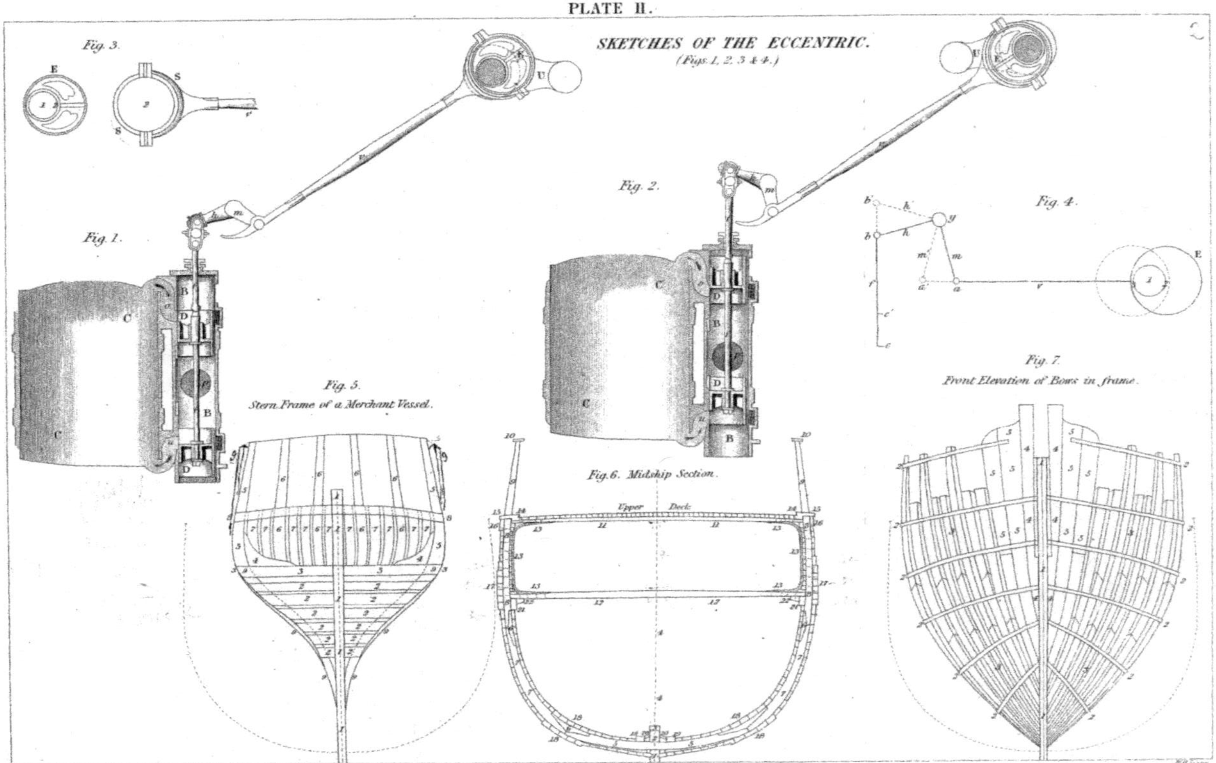
SKETCHES OF THE ECCENTRIC.
(Figs. 1, 2, 3 & 4.)
Fig. 1.
Fig. 2.
Fig. 3.
Fig. 4.
Fig. 5.
Stern Frame of a Merchant Vessel.
Fig. 6. Midship Section.
Upper Deck
Fig. 7.
Front Elevation of Bows in frame.

PLATE III.

*BARQUE.*

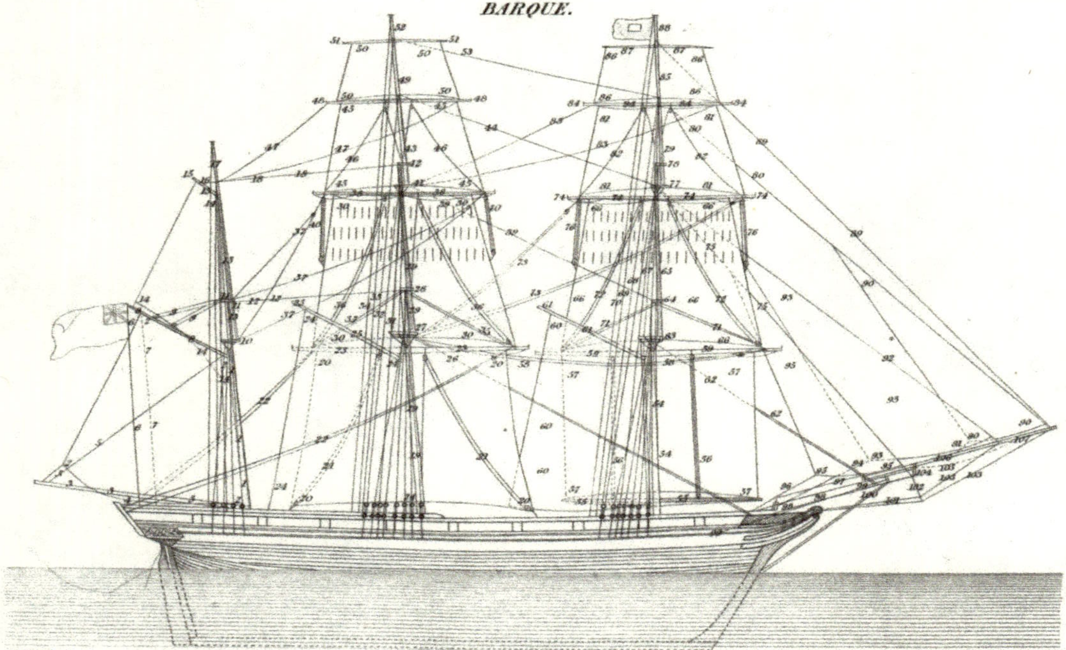

J. Brisbane

W. H. Lizars

## NUMERICAL INDEX TO PLATE OF BARQUE.

1 MIZENMAST
2 Spanker
3 Spanker boom
4 Spanker sheet and block
5 Spanker boom topping-lift
6 Signal halyards
7 Spanker vangs
(There are also vangs for the main and fore spencers, not laid down in plate)
8 Spanker gaff
9 Peak halyards
10 Mizen cross-trees
11 Mizen cap
12 Mizen stay
13 *Mizen topmast*
14 Gaff topsail
15 Gaff topsail gaff
16 Gaff topsail halyards
17 Mizen topmast pole
18 Mizen topmast stay
19 MAINMAST
20 Mainsail
21 Main clue garnets
22 Main braces
23 Main yard
24 Main spencer
25 Main spencer gaff
26 Main stay
27 Main top
28 Main cap
29 *Main topmast*
30 Main topsail
31 Maintopmast backstays
32 Maintopgallant backstay
33 Mainroyal backstay
34 Signal halyards
35 Main lifts
36 Maintopsail clue lines
37 Maintopsail braces
38 Maintopsail yard
39 Maintopmast stay
40 Maintopsail reef-tackles
41 Maintopmast cross-trees
42 Maintopmast cap
43 Maintopgallant mast
44 Maintopgallant stay
45 Maintopgallant sail
46 Maintopgallant clue lines
47 Maintopgallant braces
48 Maintopgallant yard
49 Mainroyal mast
50 Mainroyal
51 Mainroyal yard
52 Mainroyal pole
53 Mainroyal stay
54 FOREMAST
55 Bentick boom
56 Fore Bentick clue garnets
57 Foresail
58 Fore braces
59 Fore yard
60 Fore spencer
61 Fore spencer gaff
62 Fore stay
63 Fore top
64 Fore cap
65 *Fore topmast*
66 Fore topsail
67 Foretopmast backstays
68 Foretopgallant backstay
69 Foreroyal backstay
70 Signal halyards
71 Fore lifts
72 Foretopsail clue lines
73 Foretopsail braces
74 Foretopsail yard
75 Foretopmast stay
76 Foretopsail reef-tackles
77 Foretopmast cross-trees
78 Foretopmast cap
79 Foretopgallant mast
80 Foretopgallant stay
81 Foretopgallant sail
82 Foretopgallant clue lines
83 Foretopgallant braces
84 Foretopgallant yard
85 Foreroyal mast
86 Foreroyal
87 Foreroyal yard
88 Foreroyal pole
89 Foreroyal stay
90 Flying jib
91 Flying jib sheet
92 Jib stay
93 Jib
94 Jib sheet
95 Foretopmast staysail
96 Foretopmast staysail sheet
97 Ridge ropes
98 Bowsprit
99 Bowsprit shrouds
100 Bobstay
101 Martingale back-ropes
102 Dolphin striker, or Martingale
103 Martingale stays
104 Bowsprit cap
105 Footrope of jib-boom
106 Jib-boom
107 Flying jib-boom

NOTE.—The fore, main, and mizen masts of a SHIP are rigged in the same way as the fore and main masts of a *barque*, but on a *ship's* crossjack-yard, which is the lowest yard on the mizen mast, no lower square sail is generally set. The difference between a barque and a ship may therefore be simply stated thus: that a ship has a square topsail, topgallant sail, and royal, and mizen topmast staysail on the mizen mast instead of a gaff topsail. But in many large ships there is a gaff topsail carried on each mast in addition to the square topsail, in which case no main or mizen topmast staysails are required.

# ALPHABETICAL INDEX TO PLATE OF BARQUE.

PLATE IV.

*A BRIG,*

*or rather, A Snow.*

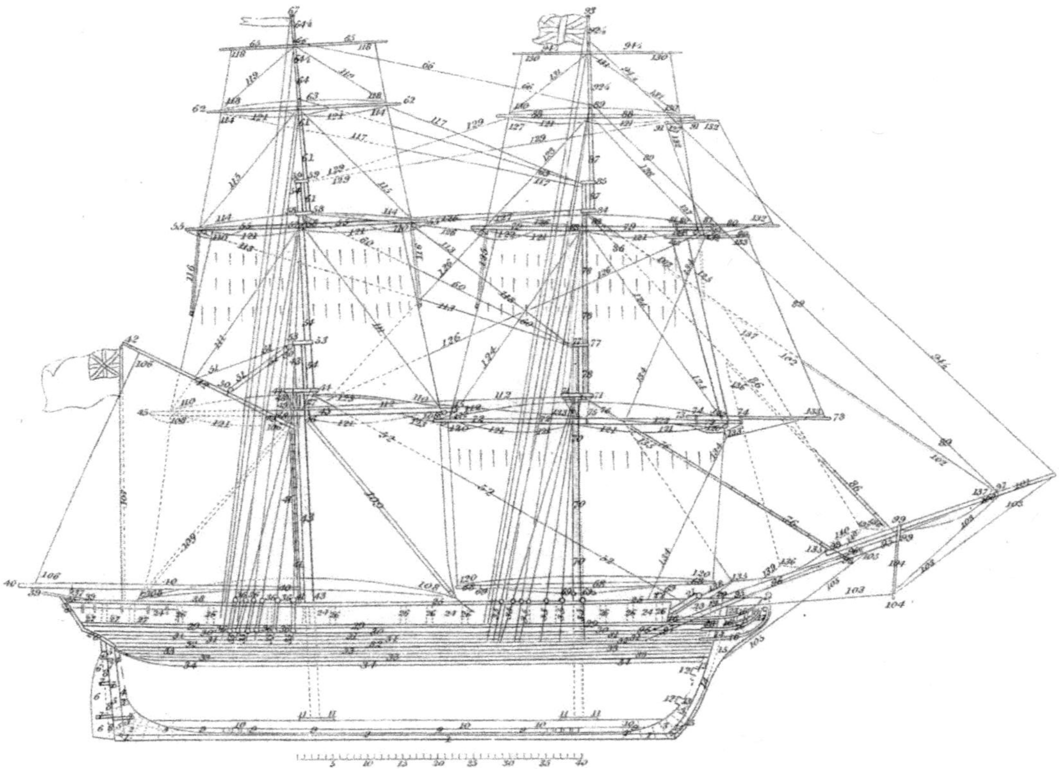

J. Brisbane del.t

H. Adlard sc.

## NUMERICAL INDEX TO PLATE OF BRIG.

1 Keel
2 Deadwood
3 Deadwood knees
4 False stern post
5 Stern post
6 Rudder
7 Rudder irons, or bands
8 Rudder stock
9 Timber spaces, with end section of a few of the timbers
10 Keelson, or kelson
11 Mast steps (When a large rider is put on the kelson, the step is sometimes dispensed with, the masts fitting into the keel with mortise and tenon)
12 End section of breast hooks
13 Apron, or stomach piece
14 Main stem
15 False stem, or cutwater
16 Head rails
17 Trail boards
18 The hawse hole. (The *hawse pipe* is a round piece of iron fitted into it.)
19 Hawse timbers
20 Knight heads
21 Cat head
22 Fore stanchion timber head
23 Head boards
24 Bulwarks
25 Rails
26 Stanchions
27 Timber heads
28 Quarter stanchions, on the outside of which the quarter pieces (or quarter monkeys) are bolted
29 Gunwale, or covering board
30 Paintstrake
31 Scrapestrakes
32 Upper blackstrake
33 Bends, or wales
34 Lower blackstrake
35 Chain plates—those for the fore-rigging being on the new plan
36 Dead eyes
37 Main sheet and main-sheet block
38 Topgallant bulwark and rail
39 Stern davits
40 Main or trysail boom (called the trysail boom on board of brigs or ships)
41 Trysail mast
42 Trysail gaff (see 50)
43 Mainmast
44 Maintop
45 Main yard
46 Sling hoop } of main yard
47 Slings } of main yard
48 Throat halyard blocks
49 Throat halyards
50 Gaff halyard blocks
51 Gaff halyards
52 Main stay (fastened to a breast hook about a foot above the deck)
53 Main cap
54 Maintopmast
55 Maintopsail yard
56 Slings, &c., of ditto (see 46, 47)
57 Parrel of ditto
58 Maintopmast cross-trees
59 Maintopmast cap
60 Maintopmast stay
61 Maintopgallant mast
62 Maintopgallant yard
63 Maintopgallant stay
64 Mainroyal mast with 'pole' above the yard
65 Mainroyal yard
66 Mainroyal stay
67 Truck of mainroyal mast
68 Bentick boom
69 Bentick boom slings or bridle
70 Foremast
71 Foretop
72 Foreyard
73 Foretopmast studding sail boom (see 90)
74 Boom irons of ditto
75 Sling hoop and slings of foreyard
76 Fore stay
77 Fore cap
78 Foretopmast
79 Foretopsail yard (see 82, 83)
80 Foretop*gallant* studding sail boom (see 91)
81 Boom irons of ditto
82 Slings of foretopsail yard
83 Parrel of ditto
84 Foretopmast cross-trees
85 Foretopmast cap
86 Foretopmast stay
87 Foretopgallant mast (see 80, 81)
88 Foretopgallant yard
89 Foretopgallant stay
90 Foretopmast studding sail yar
91 Foretopgallant ditto
92 Foreroyal mast with pole
93 Truck of foreroyal mast
94 Foreroyal yard
*94 Foreroyal stay
95 Bowsprit
96 Bowsprit shrouds
97 Jib-boom guys
98 Bowsprit heart
99 Bowsprit cap
100 Jib-boom
101 Flying jib-boom
102 Jib stay
103 Martingale stays
104 Dolphin striker, or Martingale
105 Bobstay (with connecting hoop at top)
106 Trysail
107 Signal halyards
108 Mainsail (see FOOT-ROPES, 121)
109 Clue garnets
110 Maintopsail
111 Maintopsail clue lines
112 Main braces
113 Maintopsail braces (see 116)

ALPHABETICAL INDEX TO PLATE OF BRIG.

114 Maintopgallant sail
115 Maintopgallant clue lines
116 Maintopsail reef tackles
117 Maintopgallant braces
118 Mainroyal
119 Mainroyal clue lines
120 Foresail
121 Foot-ropes
122 Foretopsail
123 Fore braces
124 Foretopsail clue lines
125 Foretopsail reef tackles
126 Foretopsail braces
127 Foretopgallant sail
128 Foretopgallant clue lines
129 Foretopgallant braces
130 Foreroyal
131 Foreroyal clue lines
132 Foretopgallant studding sail
133 Foretopmast studding sail
134 Studding sail sheets
135 Fore staysail
The main staysail (used in few vessels) runs on the *main*stay in a similar manner
136 Foretopmast staysail
137 Jib
138 Fore staysail sheets
139 Foretopmast staysail sheets
140 Jib sheets

---

ALPHABETICAL INDEX TO PLATE OF BRIG.

13 APRON, or STOMACH PIECE

33 BENDS, or WALES

BLACKSTRAKES:
32 Upper blackstrake
34 Lower ditto

105 BOBSTAY

BLOCKS:
37 Main sheet block
48 Throat halyard blocks
50 Gaff halyard blocks

BOOMS:
40 Main or trysail boom
68 Bentick boom
73 Foretopmast studding sail boom
80 Foretopgallant studding sail boom
101 Flying jib-boom
100 Jib-boom

BOOM IRONS:
74 Of foretopmast studding sail boom
81 Of foretopgallant studding sail boom

95 BOWSPRIT

96 BOWSPRIT SHROUDS

98 BOWSPRIT HEART

99 BOWSPRIT CAP

BRACES:
112 Main braces
113 Maintopsail braces
117 Maintopgallant braces
123 Fore braces
126 Foretopsail braces
129 Foretopgallant braces

12 BREASTHOOKS

24 BULWARKS
35 Topgallant bulwark

CAPS:
53 Main cap
59 Maintopmast cap
77 Fore cap
85 Foretopmast cap. See also BOWSPRIT CAP

21 CATHEAD

35 CHAIN PLATES

29 COVERING BOARD, GUNWALE, or PLANKSHEER

109 CLUE GARNETS

CLUE LINES:
111 Maintopsail clue lines
115 Maintopgallant clue lines
119 Mainroyal clue lines
124 Foretopsail clue lines
128 Foretopgallant clue lines
131 Foreroyal clue lines

CROSS-TREES:
58 Maintopmast cross-trees
84 Foretopmast cross-trees

15 CUTWATER

36 DEAD EYES

2 DEADWOOD

3 DEADWOOD KNEES

104 DOLPHIN STRIKER, or MARTINGALE

4 FALSE STERN POST

15 FALSE STEM, or CUTWATER

22 FORE STANCHION TIMBER HEAD

71 FORETOP

77 FORE CAP

84 FORETOPMAST CROSS-TREES

85 FORETOPMAST CAP

121 FOOT-ROPES

29 GUNWALE, or PLANKSHEER

18 HAWSE HOLE. See preceding index.

19 HAWSE TIMBERS

HALYARDS:
49 Throat halyards
51 Gaff halyards
107 Signal halyards

23 HEAD BOARDS

16 HEAD RAILS

## ALPHABETICAL INDEX TO PLATE OF BRIG.

# PLATE V.

*SCHOONER.*

J. Brisbane — W. H. Lizars

## NUMERICAL INDEX TO PLATE OF SCHOONER.

1 MAINMAST
2 Main sail
3 Main boom
4 Main sheet, and main sheet block
5 Main boom topping-lift
6 Vangs of main gaff
7 Signal halyards
8 Runner and tackle
9 Main gaff
10 Main peak halyards
11 Main throat halyards
12 Main cross-trees
13 Main cap
14 Mainstay
15 *Maintopmast*
16 Maintopmast backstays
17 Gaff topsail
18 Gaff topsail gaff
19 Gaff topsail halyards
20 Pole of maintopmast
21 Maintopmast stay
22 FORE MAST
23 Fore spencer
24 Fore spencer boom
25 Fore spencer vangs
26 Fore spencer gaff
27 Fore peak halyards (connected to gaff by the *bridle*)
28 Fore yard
29 Fore braces
30 Foresail and forestay
31 Fore staysail (and halyards)
32 Fore cross-trees
33 Fore cap
34 *Foretopmast*
35 Foretopmast backstays
36 Foretopgallant backstays
37 Foreroyal backstay
38 Signal halyards
39 Foretopsail braces
40 Foretopsail
41 Foretopsail yard
42 Foretopmast stay
43 Foretopmast cross-trees
44 Foretopmast cap
45 Foretopgallant mast
46 Foretopgallant braces
47 Foretopgallant sail
48 Foretopgallant yard
49 Foretopgallant stay
50 *Foreroyal mast* and *pole*
51 Foreroyal
52 Foreroyal yard
53 Foreroyal stay
54 Foretopgallant studding sail and yard
55 Foretopgallant studding sail boom
56 Foretopmast studding sail yard
57 Foretopmast studding sail
58 Foretopmast studding sail boom
59 Jib and jib stay
60 Jib sheet
61 Bowsprit
62 Bowsprit shrouds
63 Bowsprit heart
64 Bowsprit cap
65 Jib-boom
66 Martingale stay
67 Dolphin striker, or Martingale
68 Martingale back-ropes
69 Bobstay

---

## ALPHABETICAL INDEX TO PLATE OF SCHOONER.

BACKSTAYS:
16 Maintopmast backstays
35 Foretopmast backstay
36 Foretopgallant backstays
37 Foreroyal backstays

69 BOBSTAY

BOOMS:
3 Main boom
24 Fore spencer boom
55 Foretopgallant studding sail boom
58 Foretopmast studding sail boom
65 Jib boom

61 BOWSPRIT

64 BOWSPRIT CAP

63 BOWSPRIT HEART

62 BOWSPRIT SHROUDS

BRACES:
29 Fore braces
39 Foretopsail braces
46 Foretopgallant braces

CAPS:
13 Main cap
33 Fore cap
44 Foretopmast cap

CROSS-TREES:
12 Main cross-trees
32 Fore cross-trees
43 Foretopmast cross-trees

67 DOLPHIN STRIKER, or MARTINGALE

GAFFS:
9 Main gaff
18 Gaff topsail gaff
26 Fore spencer gaff

## ALPHABETICAL INDEX TO PLATE OF SCHOONER.

CPSIA information can be obtained
at www.ICGtesting.com
Printed in the USA
LVHW040356110522
718423LV00001B/164

9 783375 001322